Evelyn Hood, was born and raised in Paisley and currently lives on the Clyde coast with her husband. An ex-journalist, she has been a full-time writer for several years, turning her talents to plays, short stories, children's books and the novels that have earned her widespread acclaim and an ever-increasing readership.

Praise for Evelyn Hood

'Immaculate in her historical detail'
The Herald

'Quite simply, I couldn't put it down. A rich and rewarding read'
Emma Blair

'Evelyn Hood has been called Scotland's Catherine Cookson. Unfair. She has her own distinctive voice'
Scots Magazine

'An intriguing plot and a range of complex characters and lives . . . offers an extraordinary woman's perspective on history in a plain, satisfactory style'
Scottish Field

'Highly entertaining'
Manchester Evening News

'Bold and compassionate'
Liverpool Daily Post

D1329040

EVELYN HOOD OMNIBUS

A Certain Freedom

A Sparkle of Salt

sphere

SPHERE

This omnibus edition first published in Great Britain by
Sphere in 2009
Evelyn Hood Omnibus copyright © Evelyn Hood 2009

Previously published separately:
A Certain Freedom first published in Great Britain in 2005
by Time Warner Books
This paperback edition published in 2006 by Time Warner Books
Copyright © Evelyn Hood 2005

A Sparkle of Salt first published in Great Britain in 2003
by Time Warner Books
Published in 2004 by Time Warner Paperbacks
Reprinted by Sphere in 2007
Copyright © Evelyn Hood 2003

The moral right of the author has been asserted

A CIP catalogue record for this book is available from the British Library.

ISBN 978-0-7515-4150-2

Printed and bound in Great Britain by
Clays Ltd, St Ives plc

Sphere
An imprint of
Little, Brown Book Group
100 Victoria Embankment
London EC4Y 0DY

An Hachette UK Company
www.hachette.co.uk

www.littlebrown.co.uk

A Certain Freedom

To my husband, Jim, who deserves
a gold medal but will have to settle
for this book instead.

Acknowledgements

The fictitious summer camp at Portencross referred to in the book is based on a very successful summer camp held during the 1930s at Lunderston Bay, Gourock.

The suffragette quilt referred to in this book was made in Paisley, not Saltcoats, and is now on display in the Sma' Shot Cottages – the weavers' cottages owned by the Old Paisley Society.

I am indebted to the staff of Ardrossan and Saltcoats Libraries for their help in researching material for this book.

My thanks to Kathleen Degnan, the brains behind the title of this book. Bless you, Kathleen!

'Parenthood,' Hamilton Forsyth announced, 'is the necessary evil of a marriage.'

He stood in his favourite pose before the fireplace in his well-appointed drawing room, hands behind his back, sturdy body blocking out most of the heat from the room, and continued as three shocked faces turned towards him, 'And since my marriage has now ended with your dear mother's demise and you are now old enough to look out for yourselves, I consider that any obligation I have had towards you has also ended.'

'Father?' Belle quavered uncertainly, while her brother Walter said at the same time, 'Really, Papa, I hardly think it seemly to speak like that to us only hours after laying Mother in her grave!'

'You never were able to come up with the right comment for the occasion, were you, Walter? This is the perfect time. Another ten minutes and it will be too late.'

'What do you mean, Papa?'

Hamilton's face softened and he smiled at the youngest of his three children. Morna had always been his favourite, while Walter had been his wife's. Belle, the firstborn and plainest of the three, had never been anyone's favourite. 'I mean, Morna, my dear, that in ten minutes . . . nine and a half,' he corrected himself, consulting the fob watch he had just taken from its pocket in his black silk waistcoat, 'the cart will be arriving to take my belongings to the station.'

A murmur of consternation swept through the room. Walter, Belle and Morna glanced uneasily at each other, then Belle ventured, 'You are going away on business, Papa? At a time like this?'

'Not on business, my dear. I am leaving.'

'Leaving Saltcoats? Leaving home?'

'Saltcoats, Walter, is your home, not mine. It was never my home. This . . .' Hamilton swept out a hand to indicate the comfortable parlour, '. . . is no longer my home. It is the house I came to when I married your mother, and now that she has gone and I am no longer tied to the vows we made to each other, it is time for me to begin a new life.'

'Elsewhere in Ayrshire?' Belle struggled to make sense of what her father was saying.

'Certainly not in Ayrshire. Possibly Glasgow or Edinburgh or London or Paris.' Hamilton rubbed his hands together and smiled at his offspring, clearly relishing the prospect of his new life. 'This fine twentieth century we now live in is a mere nine years old. It's time the four of us seized its new prospects and carved out our own destinies.'

'But . . . but what about us?' Walter asked feebly.

His father's dark, well-shaped eyebrows lifted slightly. 'Why ask me? You're all adults now; you no longer need me. As I said earlier, you were the necessary result of our marriage. You gave great pleasure to your mother when you were small, and I will admit,' Hamilton said, his eyes resting for a moment on Morna's flower-like face, 'that there were times when I myself enjoyed your company. But now I must see to my own life and leave you to yours.'

'When will you return?' Belle asked, and her father gave the slightest of exasperated sighs before saying patiently, 'My dear, I do not expect to return, ever. That is what I am trying to explain to you. Frances is dead, you are all grown, and so our relationship is at an end. You have the house, which belonged to your mother and is now yours by right, not mine. You have the business that your grandfather started, which is also rightfully yours. And you have your mother's money. All I have taken for myself is the payment I earned by running the shop.'

'But . . . but . . .' Walter began to stammer, while Belle protested, 'You can't desert us – what will people say?'

'I don't care what people say. I won't be here to listen to them tittle-tattle. God knows I got enough of that in the shop during all the years of my marriage. It will be a relief to be free of it. Walter, you can run the business now, with Belle's help, of course. And if you decide against that, as you have never seemed all that interested in earning your own living,' Hamilton said with a sudden cold edge to his voice, 'it must be a comfort to you to know that since you are already promised to marry Clarissa Pinkerton you will be able to live in comfort on her father's money. It was a great relief to your mother when you and Clarissa became engaged. It was what she had wanted since you were toddlers together. Belle, you can no doubt continue to see to the bookkeeping in the shop, which you have done with great efficiency in the past. And as you also took over the running of this house after my poor dear Frances was forced to take to her bed, you will probably continue to do that as well. Who knows, perhaps one day you will find a man will . . . worthy,' Hamilton corrected himself swiftly, 'to offer you his hand and his home. As for you, Morna . . .' Again, his face softened. With her slender but rounded figure, her thick fair hair and her wide hazel eyes, Morna most resembled her mother. 'You,' Hamilton finished briskly, 'will have no bother in finding a suitable husband, although I would counsel you against Arthur MacAdam, since I have never considered him to be good enough for you. I trust that your brother will advise you when it comes to making your choice.'

'Father . . . !' Walter bleated, but was ignored as Hamilton consulted his watch again.

'No more time for discussion, Walter, and in any case, I have said all that I have to say and now I must be off.'

'But surely . . . a forwarding address . . . ?'

'Anything I leave behind can be disposed of, Belle, for I have no more need of it.' Hamilton pulled on the bell rope to summon the live-in maidservant. 'The cart will be here at any minute to collect my luggage. I shall walk to the station; the exercise will be good for me. I have always found funerals to be claustrophobic. Ah, Sarah,' he went on as the door opened, 'a cart will be calling in five minutes to collect the trunk from the front bedroom. Please ensure that the man handles it carefully. My hat and stick, if you will be so kind. Goodbye,' he said with one final glance at his family, then walked from the room, leaving them gaping at each other in silence.

'There now, that's them all done at last.' Annie McCall put away the last plate and shook out the dishcloth before hanging it in front of the fire to dry. 'What else needs seein' to before I leave?'

'Nothing else.' Sarah Neilson finished stacking the uneaten sandwiches. 'They'll likely not want much tonight. Folk never have an appetite after a funeral. I've got cold meat left, and pickle, and there's always cheese. You get on home.'

'If you're sure. He'll be in from the dockyard and our Maisie's such a dreamer, I can't trust her to have his dinner ready. She'll have the potatoes burned and the fish dried to leather if I know her.'

'Here . . .' Sarah reached up to the high mantelshelf, where Miss Belle had left the money to pay the heavy-work woman. 'Thank you for obligin' us today, Mrs McCall.'

'Och, you'd never have managed everythin' on your own, hen, not with it bein' such a big funeral.' The woman counted the money with a swift sweep of her eyes before stowing it carefully into the deep pocket of her apron. She took her shabby coat from the hook on the back door and began to struggle into it. 'Mrs Forsyth was well liked.'

'She was a good employer,' Sarah agreed bleakly. 'It'll not be the same without her.'

'You're no' worried about yer position, are ye? You'll be all right, lassie, they'd not be able tae manage without ye. I can't see that Miss Belle dirtyin' her hands in the kitchen, or the younger lassie either. They werenae raised tae it.' Annie's broad hands, the skin red and cracked from continual immersion in hot water, were clumsy as she buttoned her coat. Some of the buttons were missing, making the coat gape open in places.

'We never know what the future might bring,' Sarah said, and suddenly realised that she had laid one hand over her belly. She turned back to the table hurriedly, before the washerwoman's sharp eyes noticed, and began to wrap a generous handful of sandwiches in newspaper. 'Here, take these home with you.'

'Are ye sure?' Annie asked, her hand already reaching out for the packet. 'Ye'll no' get intae trouble for givin' them to me?'

'Nob'dy'll notice. Anyway, they'll probably not want tae eat leftovers from the funeral.'

'Rich folk can afford tae be fussy, but the likes of *us* can't. Thanks, pet,' Annie nodded and turned to the back door. 'I'll be in on Monday tae help with the washin' same as usual.'

Sarah wasn't alone for long. Five minutes after the washerwoman had gone she heard three quiet taps on the outer door. Her heart leaped with joy as she ran to open it.

Samuel Gilmartin slid into the kitchen and made straight for the fire, spreading his hands out to its warmth. 'I'm frozen . . . and starved intae the bargain. Is there anythin' tae eat?' He pulled his cap off. 'There's surely somethin' left over from the buryin'.'

Sarah cast an anxious look at the door leading to the rest of the house. 'Hush, Samuel, you don't want them tae hear ye.'

'Och, they're too busy with their own lives tae bother about what happens in the kitchen.' He pulled her into his arms and kissed her, then released her with a hearty slap on the backside. 'Go on now, girl, and get me some food. And a cup of tea wouldnae go amiss – unless,' he added hopefully, 'there's anythin' stronger left over from the funeral?'

'They'd never store strong drink down here, but I've got some sandwiches.' She had hoped that he would look in this evening, as he often did. Samuel worked as a delivery man for the greengrocer who supplied the Forsyth household, and the very first time she saw him Sarah had been bowled over by his wavy auburn hair, sparkling brown eyes, and ready, charming smile, not to mention his lovely Irish accent. She laid a plate of sandwiches on the table and watched him bite hungrily into the bread and meat. 'You're eatin' that as if you've not had food all day.'

'It's little enough I get. The mistress's carthorse eats better than I do. So,' he said through a mouthful of food, 'how did it go?'

'The funeral? The house was filled all afternoon. The last of the mourners went away not much more than an hour ago. Annie McCall came tae give me a hand. She's not long away.'

'I know that.' Samuel picked up another sandwich. 'I saw the two of ye through the window, chatterin' away like a pair of old biddies. I had to wait out in the cold until she'd gone.' He rose from his chair and rounded the table swiftly, reaching out for her and pulling her roughly into his arms. His lips gleamed greasily and she could taste roast beef when he kissed her.

'Mmm,' he said against her throat, 'you feel soft and warm. Like a loaf fresh from the oven. My bonny wee cottage loaf . . .'

She struggled to release herself. 'Samuel, supposing Miss Belle comes in and finds you?'

'Let her.' He captured her wrist and sat down, drawing her on to his lap, his free hand roaming over the soft outline of her rounded bosom. 'The way I feel tonight I can manage the two o' ye. It'd do her good – I'll wager she's not had a man yet, that one.'

'Samuel!'

'I'm only speakin' the truth. Mrs Smith sent me into Forsyth's the other week tae buy something for her, and Miss Belle was sittin' behind that wee window of hers at the back of the shop, handin' out change to the customers with a mouth on her as if she'd just caught the smell of a bad egg. Plain as a pikestaff, too. No wonder she's never found a man of her . . .'

Sarah squealed and shot off his knee as one of the bells on the wall jangled. 'That's the parlour – I'll have to go through.' Her frantic fingers buttoned the blouse that Samuel had begun to unfasten. 'And you shouldnae stay here. Someone might come in and find you!'

He settled himself more comfortably into the chair, grinning lazily up at her. 'Sure, who's goin' tae come in here when they can ring the bell every time they want you tae do their biddin'? Off with ye, woman, and see what yer masters desire. I'll just wait here for ye in the warmth.'

'Samuel,' she pleaded, and then, realising that he would not be moved, she fled through to the main part of the house, tweaking her apron bib into place as she went, then patting her hair to make sure it was still neat.

He was half-asleep in the warmth from the range when she returned ten minutes later. 'So what did they want this time?' he yawned, stretching his arms above his head.

'It's the master, Samuel. He's gone.'

'Gone where?'

'To the station, and it looks as if he's goin' tae be away for a good while. The carter came, and him and his lad had tae haul the big trunk that's only used for holidays all the way down the stairs. It was awful heavy – full tae the lid if you ask me.'

'So that's what the noise was.' Samuel scratched at his stomach with both hands. 'He'll be off somewhere on business, mebbe. How about another cup of tea before I get back to the lodging house?'

'D'you not think it's unusual tae be goin' away on business the very day he buries his wife?'

'Who knows the way the gentry think? And who cares?'

'He was still in his mournin' clothes.'

8

'Well, he would be, since he's just been widowed. Tea,' he reminded her.

'The rest of them looked ever so upset.' The big tin teapot was empty and Sarah's work-reddened fingers automatically went about the business of measuring out tea leaves from the caddy, her mind full of the scene she had witnessed upstairs. 'After I'd fetched his things and helped him on with his coat and brushed it down the way I always do, they all came out into the hall as he left, and then Mr Walter followed him out to the gate. It looked tae me as if they were arguin', and Miss Belle and Miss Morna were standin' at the door, watchin' them. Then Mr Forsyth started walkin' towards the station and Miss Belle told me to get back to the kitchen at once. Very snappy, she was.'

'These folk are as different from us as chalk from cheese. Change the subject, for any favour,' Samuel said, bored.

Sarah bit her lip and then, putting the battered tin teapot on the range to simmer, she sat down at the table and carefully folded her hands in her lap to stop their sudden shaking. Her heart began to beat harder and faster.

'Samuel, I've not been feelin' right these past few weeks.'

'It's probably to do with your mistress fallin' sick and dyin'. Funerals can upset women. You should hear the way the womenfolk weep and wail at funerals back home.'

'It's not that – at least, I don't think so. I think . . .' Sarah said, and then swallowed hard to control the sudden nausea rising in her throat. Now her heart was banging around beneath her clean apron bib like a small bird caught in a greenhouse. 'Samuel,' she said, her voice little more than a whisper, 'I think I might be expectin'.'

'Expectin' what?' He had settled down in the chair again, his long legs stretched across the rag rug and his hands linked comfortably over his belly.

'A b-bairn.'

'What?' He jerked upright, staring across at her. 'A bairn? You? How did ye manage that, ye daft girl?'

'You should surely know how.'

'Are you sayin' it's mine?'

'It can't be anyone else's.'

'Oh no!' Samuel scrambled to his feet, staring down at her. 'Ye'll not blame this on me, my girl.'

'But you're the only . . .'

'And how do I know that?'

'Because I'm tellin' you, that's how,' she began, and then, hearing a sound from beyond the inner door, 'Someone's comin'. Hide, quick!'

As he threw himself across the kitchen and into the tiny room where she slept, Sarah sped round the kitchen, lifting his plate and mug from the table and putting them on the draining board.

'Sarah? Oh, there you are,' Walter Forsyth said, from the doorway.

'Yes, Mr Walter. Do you want something?' Please God, Sarah thought, don't let him be wanting *that* – not tonight, not when Samuel was hidden in her cupboard of a room, listening to every word.

But for once, Walter had no thought of personal pleasures. 'Go upstairs immediately and strip the bed in the big front bedroom,' he ordered coldly.

'The master's room?'

'And when you've done that, clear everything of my – of Mr Forsyth's from the wardrobe and the chest of drawers. Everything,' Walter said tightly. 'You can pile it all on the bed for the moment. I'll arrange for boxes to be delivered from the shop tomorrow. You may leave my mother's clothes and possessions where they are for the time being.'

'But what'll the master say when he comes back from . . . ?'

10

'Just do as you're told, girl!' Walter almost shouted. 'And do it now, do you understand?'

'But it's nearly time to get your supper ready.'

'We'll not be taking supper tonight. For goodness' sake, Sarah, can you not just do as you're told?'

'Yes, Mr Walter. At once, Mr Walter.'

'That's better,' he snapped.

As the door closed behind him, Samuel emerged from the little bedroom.

'He's in a right pet, is he no'?'

'I told you that somethin' had happened. I'd best do as he says, Samuel. He'll only come back if I don't get upstairs right now.'

'And I suppose I'd best be off myself.' He gave a longing look at the teapot, now puffing steam into the air, then made for the back door.

She ran after him, catching at his arm. 'Samuel, about what I just told you . . .'

He disentangled her fingers from the sleeve of his jacket. 'And I told you, Sarah, it's nothin' tae do with me,' he said, and then, as she began to protest, 'I'm not ready tae settle down, and anyway, how could I house and feed a brat on the pittance Mrs Smith pays me, let alone you as well? I live in a lodgin' house as it is, and there's no room there for you. I'll have tae do better in life before I can even think about marriage and fatherhood.'

'But what am I tae do, Samuel?'

'There's ways and means, and women know about them. That sort of thing's no' a man's business.' He took her hands in his. 'Get rid of it, sweetheart, an' let's get back tae the way we were.'

'Samuel . . .' she began to beg, then stopped as the back door closed quietly but decisively behind him.

11

2

'I'm going to the shop tomorrow,' Walter announced as he and his sisters prepared to retire to their rooms. 'I see no sense in sitting around here.'

'What will folk think of us, going out in public so soon after laying Mother in her grave?'

'My dear Belle, what will folk think of us when they find out that Papa's gone? How can we mourn properly now? We have too much to do.'

'Perhaps he'll come back tomorrow,' Morna ventured, and her brother gave her a withering look.

'You saw the luggage he took with him. There can scarcely be anything of his left.'

'You must go to the bank tomorrow, Walter, to find out how much money we have,' Belle said suddenly.

'You're right . . . what if he's taken it all?' The colour ebbed from her brother's face and one hand flew up to stroke his silky moustache, as always happened when he was worried or upset. 'What if he's left us with nothing?'

'Didn't he say that he had taken nothing but the money due to him for running the shop?' Morna ventured.

'And how much would that be? For all we know he

might have decided that he was entitled to every penny we have!' Walter began to pace the comfortable parlour. 'I must call on Mr Pinkerton at once!'

'Tonight? But he won't be in the bank at this hour, he'll be at home, and how would he be able to tell you what's in our account?' Morna wanted to know.

'She's right, Walter. In any case, if you call on Mr Pinkerton you'll have to tell him about Father. Best to leave it for now,' Belle said anxiously. 'As Morna says, he might come back. And if he doesn't, we need to have time to decide what we're going to tell people. We must put on a united front, whatever happens. We're all we have in the world now.'

'Except Aunt Beatrice,' Morna suddenly remembered, and they looked at each other, horrified.

'I had forgotten about Aunt Beatrice,' Belle confessed. 'We have to tell her what's happened before she hears it from someone else.'

'This is our business, not hers. We will deal with it.'

'Walter, you know that anything that happens within this family is Aunt Beatrice's business. We must tell her – tomorrow,' Belle rushed on as her brother tried to object. 'We must! There's no other way. Sarah can take a note round to her house first thing. I'll see to it now.'

'I'll do it. You two go to bed, it's been a distressing day,' Walter ordered, making for the writing bureau. 'And while I'm at it, I'll tell Sarah to keep quiet about Papa leaving.'

It was just as well that the floor of the short, enclosed passageway between the hall and the kitchen had been left as unadorned wooden planks, because it meant that Sarah could tell when someone was approaching. She dashed the tears from her eyes as she recognised Walter's heavy tread, and was busy polishing silver when he came in.

'Ah, Sarah.'

'Yes, Mr Walter?' She stopped the work she had just started, and scrambled to her feet. 'Would you like some supper now? There's cold meat, and I can heat some soup.'

He tossed the offer away with a wave of his hand. 'We don't want anything to eat. We're all going to bed, and I suggest that you do the same.'

'Yes, Mr Walter.'

'Here.' He held out a sealed envelope. 'I want you to take this round to Mrs McCallum's house tomorrow morning, as soon as you have served breakfast.'

'Yes, Mr Walter.'

'You've cleared my father's room, I hope?'

'Yes, Mr Walter, I stripped the bed and then put everything of Mr Forsyth's on it, as you said. There wasn't much,' she ventured.

'I'll arrange for the shop boy to bring some boxes on the delivery cart tomorrow. You can pack everything into them. And you can serve breakfast at the usual time, since I will be going to the shop.'

Her eyebrows shot up in surprise, but her voice, when she said, 'Yes, Mr Walter,' was expressionless.

He studied her in silence for a moment, and she was readying herself for his usual suggestion when he said instead, 'By the way, Sarah, you know when to hold your tongue, don't you?'

'Oh yes, Mr Walter.' She folded her hands behind her back and stared fixedly at a point just below his chin. If there was one thing she knew, it was how and when to keep her own counsel.

'So you will not mention my father's departure to anyone, will you? Not to a single soul. Do you understand?'

14

'Yes, Mr Walter.'

'Good,' he said, and then, coming round the edge of the table and putting a hand beneath her chin, tipping her face up towards his own, 'You're a good girl, Sarah.'

'Thank you, Mr Walter.'

'Mmm.' He stared down into her brown eyes, and wondered how it could be that a mere servant could have such perfect skin. Then he leaned forward and brushed her lips lightly with his own before releasing her chin. 'A very good girl,' he said as his hand moved down to shape itself over the delightful swell of her bosom beneath her apron bib. For a moment he hesitated, his fingers tightening and the tip of his tongue slipping out to moisten his lower lip; then he reminded himself that this, after all, was the day of his mother's funeral, and turned away.

At the door, he paused. 'Sarah . . .'

'Yes, Mr Walter?'

'From now on,' Walter said, 'I am the master of this house. You must address me as "sir".'

'Yes, Mr . . . sir.' She bobbed a quick curtsey. He nodded, pleased, and went out.

Sarah heaved a sigh of relief. She was too worried about Samuel's visit, and his rejection of the news she had blurted out, to be bothered with Mr Walter's soft wet kisses and his clumsy fumblings tonight.

She turned the envelope over in her hands and then laid it on the table and picked up the heavy silver tablespoon she had been polishing. Her rounded face and smooth brown hair, parted in the middle and then drawn back behind her ears, were reflected in a strange, bulgy way on the back of the spoon. She stared at it, wondering what she was going to do.

The very thought of doing as Samuel wanted and

15

visiting one of the local women known to help single lassies who had fallen into trouble made her shiver with fear. Sarah was an orphan, raised by an aunt and uncle. Her closest friend had gone to one of those women, and had died a long and agonising death as a result. Sarah had been with her in those final, terrible hours, and the memory of it – the sounds, the smell of blood, the sight of the girl's pretty, laughing face distorted by pain and fear into an inhuman mask – was enough to make her gorge rise.

She dropped the spoon and fled to the sink, where she retched helplessly for several long minutes. Finally, the paroxysm over, she straightened and spat before fetching a cup and filling it from the single cold-water tap.

No, she couldn't bring herself to do as Samuel wanted. But what if he refused to do as she wanted? What if he refused to recognise the child she carried as his own, and to make an honest woman of her? She knew that she couldn't go back to the relatives who had raised her; they would only throw her out into the gutter and tell her that that was where she belonged. And she would lose her job for certain.

She paced the kitchen, her fingers laced together across her belly so tightly that the knuckles were bone white.

What was she going to do?

Belle moved quietly along the passageway from her own room to her parents' bedroom. The varnished door swung open under faint pressure from her hand, and she stepped inside. The room smelled mainly of the pomade her father used on his hair, with a familiar, underlying scent of her mother's lily of the valley toilet water

She closed her eyes, inhaling deeply and willing

16

herself back to the safe days of her early childhood, when this room had been a magic, warm place. She could recall her father, not dressed in mourning black as she had last seen him, but relaxed and smiling in his shirtsleeves and waistcoat, fondly watching her mother as she sat at the dressing table, brushing her long fair hair until it crackled.

Her eyes still closed, she turned towards the large bed with its ornate carved headboard, seeing in her mind's eye, her mother propped against a mound of pillows, her hair tied back with a ribbon, a frilled bed jacket around her shoulders. A shawled bundle was cradled in the crook of one arm while her free hand reached out to Belle.

'Come and see your new brother, my darling,' her mother had said, and eighteen-month-old Belle toddled across the floor. Her father's strong hands swept her up and placed her on the bed, where she snuggled into her mother's shoulder and gazed down at the tiny face floating in a snowy sea of silk and wool.

The second time it happened, she had been four years old and able to clamber on to the bed by herself. This time, the baby had been Morna, pretty as a doll.

'A little sister,' Frances had said, and then putting her free arm around Belle, 'my two beautiful little daughters!'

Belle opened her eyes and returned to the present to find that she was facing the long mirror her mother had loved so much. For a precious moment the glass showed her Frances's slender, graceful figure and delicate, pretty face; then the image broke up and re-formed to reflect Belle herself, with her father's heavier build and a combination of both parents' colouring. As a result, her hair was an indeterminate mousy brown, always worn in a 'cottage loaf' style, knotted at the top of the head. Her

17

heavy-lidded eyes were brown and her mouth small and anxious.

'My two beautiful little daughters,' Frances had said, but if there had been any fairy godmothers at the Forsyth christenings, they had given Morna all the beauty while Belle's gift had been a strong sense of duty.

It had stood her in good stead. After his marriage, Hamilton Forsyth had started to work in his father-in-law's ironmongery, and had proved to be more than worthy of his employer's trust. When Frances inherited the shop and Hamilton took sole charge, the business prospered even further under his shrewd management. He had eventually bought an adjoining shop and persuaded Frances to change the name above the door of the now impressive emporium from 'McCallum' to 'Forsyth'. He had taken his son and his elder daughter into the family business as soon as they left school; Walter to learn how to run the shop and manage the half-dozen employees, while Belle tussled with the bookkeeping.

She enjoyed the work and her natural skill with figures had, for the first time in her life, won her father's warm approval. It had given her secret pleasure to see that Walter, who was of a lazy disposition, was less successful as a pupil, and scarcely a day went by without him getting into trouble with his father.

She had been content with her lot, but now, she felt a sudden stab of resentment. Walter, being a man, was now the natural head of both household and business, when she herself would have been the better choice by far to run the business. Why should men automatically take charge of everything, even when they were less able than women?

'What are you doing?' Walter asked just then from

the doorway. Belle spun round as though caught in wrongdoing and then gestured to the bed, stripped to its mattress, which held the few possessions her father had left behind.

'I was just looking. You were right, he took almost all his own things.'

'I've told Sarah to pack everything away tomorrow. I will dispose of them. You'll have to see to the shop for me, Belle, while I do that and go to the bank. I must speak with Mr Pinkerton as soon as possible.'

'What about Mother's things?'

'You and Morna can attend to them. Keep what you want, and find someone who can make good use of what you don't.' He strode to the dressing table and removed the black velvet case that held their mother's jewellery. 'She would have wished you and Morna to have something to remember her by, but first I will select a few pieces for Clarissa. I'm sure Mother would have wanted my future wife to have her jewellery. I've written a letter to Aunt Beatrice and told Sarah to deliver it as soon as she's served breakfast. I said in it that Papa had to go away on business and that we had a matter that we wanted to discuss with her. I asked her to let me know when it would be possible for me to call on her during the day.'

'You think she'll wait for you to call?'

'I made it clear that I would prefer to speak to her in her own home. In the meantime . . .' Walter returned to the open doorway and stood there, waiting in unspoken invitation until Belle, with a last look around the room, passed him and went into the hallway.

'Will you move into that room?' she asked as he closed the door.

'Of course, but first it will be repapered and painted

19

according to Clarissa's wishes, since it will be her room, too, once we are married. Goodnight, Belle,' her brother said.

'So – this is a pretty kettle of fish.' Beatrice McCallum swept into the room where the three Forsyths had just started eating breakfast, unclipped the leads on the two King Charles spaniels she had brought with her, and ordered, 'Romeo, Juliet – sit!' As the dogs obeyed she added to Sarah, 'Bring another cup, lassie, and some toast. Hot, golden brown and with the crusts cut off.'

'Yes, ma'am,' Sarah gasped, and retired as Walter stumbled to his feet, almost knocking his chair over in his haste to draw out a seat for their visitor.

'Aunt Beatrice, I said in my letter that I would call on you later today.'

'I know that. I *can* read! And I can smell a scandal when it's right under m'nose. D'you think I'd just sit around and wait for you to call?' The chair gave a faint, protesting squeak as Beatrice settled her ample body on to it. She drew her gloves off and smoothed them before handing them to Walter. 'Put them on the sideboard, neatly. Now then, what's this nonsense about your father going out of town right after buryin' his wife? It must be very important business to take him away at a time like this. Is the shop in trouble – is that it?'

'The shop's fine, as far as we know. Belle's going in this morning while I go to the bank.'

'So it *is* trouble. I knew that Frances was too trusting, but there was no reasonin' with her. What did we know of Hamilton Forsyth?' Beatrice swept on in her booming voice, more used to calling dogs to heel than to drawing-room conversation. 'He wasn't a Saltcoats man – he didn't

20

even come from Ayrshire. Frances and her father were daft, lettin' a complete stranger take over the runnin' of that shop as if it were his own.'

'It's nothing to do with the shop,' Morna piped up. 'It's Papa himself. He's left Saltcoats and he says he's never coming back.'

'Never? What d'you mean, never? What's upset the man? Stop scratching, Romeo!'

'Nothing's upset him, as far as we know.' Belle toyed nervously with the cooling slice of toast on her plate. 'He just said that now Mother's gone he has no reason to stay here. He's starting a new life.'

'At his age? Stuff and nonsense!' Beatrice snapped. 'He has a good business and a comfortable home here. What more could any man want?'

'He said,' Morna's pretty face crumpled, 'that we are the necessary evil of marriage, and now that the marriage is over he's washed his hands of us.'

'Well, now, I can't argue with that,' Beatrice mused. 'It's the one blessin' of my own union with your uncle – that we were never landed with children. Dogs are more intelligent. But even so, most folk stand by their obligations.' Then she asked sharply, 'So what's he taken with him?'

'Very little, as far as we can see,' Walter took the floor, 'apart from his own clothes and possessions. He said that he was taking the money due to him for running the shop, but no more than that. That's why I must see Mr Pinkerton this morning, to find out how things stand with us, and Belle will go to the shop to see if everything's in order there.' He stopped abruptly as Sarah tapped at the door.

'I made fresh tea, Mrs McCallum, as well as the toast.' She set a tray down before Beatrice, who examined it minutely, laying the back of one hand against a slice of toast.

'Nice and hot,' she commented. 'You even remembered to bring a clean cup. More intelligent than the usual serving lassie. You may go,' she snapped, and Sarah fled. 'Morna, a little milk and one spoonful of sugar in that cup, if you please. If what you say is true,' the old lady went on, helping herself to a slice of toast, 'there's going to be a right scandal in the town. Behave yourself, Juliet, you know that you never get fed from the table. Belle, you can pour a cup of tea for me. You know what this town's like – pick a feather up from the pavement, and before you get home it's all round the place that you've stolen a chicken.'

'We can weather a scandal if we have to,' Walter said as his aunt spread butter liberally over her toast, 'as long as the shop and the bank account are safe.'

'Talkin' of the bank, what about your intended? How's Allan Pinkerton going to feel about his daughter marrying into a family abandoned by its father?'

Walter's cheeks reddened and one hand began to move towards his moustache before he caught himself in the act and forced it to join its companion behind his back. 'I must trust that Mr Pinkerton and Clarissa do not believe in visiting the sins of the father on the children,' he said, and his aunt gave a sudden bark of amusement. The two spaniels, sitting obediently on the carpet, lifted their heads swiftly and then lowered them again.

'It's to be hoped that you're right. Your mother had her heart set on that marriage, Walter, and so has Mrs Pinkerton. They'd the two of you promised to each other before you even went to dame school. And the marriage won't do the business any harm, either. But best prepare yourself for a disappointment.'

'I – all three of us – may have to prepare ourselves for more than one disappointment.'

'That's true. D'you want me to go to the bank with you?'

'I'll go on my own, Aunt Beatrice,' Walter said firmly. 'Now that Papa has gone, I'm head of this family.'

'I suppose you are. Well, it's one way of making you grow up,' Beatrice said, and bit fiercely into the slice of toast. 'I'll be keeping an eye on things, of course, for the sake of your poor mother, should you need me.'

3

'Life,' Walter announced after his aunt had left them to finish breakfast, 'is about to change for all of us.' He sliced the top off the boiled egg that Sarah had just delivered and salted it liberally.

'I don't see why.' Morna was toying sulkily with a piece of toast. 'We've still got this house to live in, haven't we? And the shop.'

'But we don't have Mother to run the house, and Papa no longer runs the shop,' her brother pointed out, digging his spoon into the soft egg yolk. 'We are orphans now, the three of us.'

'But Papa is still . . .'

'Orphans, Belle,' Walter interrupted firmly. 'As far as I am concerned — as far as this *household* is concerned — Hamilton Forsyth is as good as dead and buried. Our father no longer exists. You heard him wash his hands of us; now we must formally wash our hands of him. We must all be agreed on that.'

'It seems so final, though,' Belle protested. 'What if he were to take ill and come back to Saltcoats in need of our help? After all, we're his flesh and blood, you can't deny that.'

'For my part, he would be shown the door and reminded that he wanted to live his life in his own way,' Walter snapped. 'And there's no need to look shocked,' he added, glaring at his sisters, 'for we're our mother's flesh and blood too, and what d'you think she would make of the way he's treated us? To say nothing of the way he's treated her memory.'

'Walter's right,' Morna chimed in. 'Papa doesn't deserve any kindness from us. I vote that we attend to our own lives and leave him to his, whatever it may be.'

'I'm glad you said that, Morna, because I was about to raise the question of your own situation.'

'What do you mean, my situation?' Morna began to feel slightly uneasy. With both Walter and Belle established in the shop there had been no need for Morna to follow suit. Instead, she had stayed at home to keep her mother company and, as a hobby, attended weekly drawing and china painting classes at Miss Nairn's establishment for young women in Caledonia Road. She had a fairly busy social life, playing tennis, attending soirées and sometimes whirling around the roller skating rink in Glencairn Street in the company of Arthur MacAdam, one of her more regular suitors. Although at times she felt quite bored, she enjoyed her life of leisure and she didn't relish the prospect of change.

'If the money's still in the bank, and the shop is still ours,' she suggested hopefully, 'then nothing needs to alter, surely? We can go on as before, only without Father.'

'I doubt that,' Walter said ominously. 'Whether we like it or not, we're all going to have to make changes. You've been staying at home because Mother needed a companion. But there's no point now in you sitting around the house all day.'

'Sitting around?' Morna's voice began to rise. 'Do you really think that that's all I do?'

'It is, as far as I can tell, and that was all very well when Mother and Papa were here, but I think that Belle will agree with me that you can't expect us to keep you in comfort.'

Tears rose to Morna's thick-lashed hazel eyes. 'If Mother could hear you say such harsh things to me she would be most upset!'

'Mother is not here, and as I said, our lives have changed. It's time for reality to sink in, Morna — time for you to start contributing to the household expenses.'

'Belle, are you going to sit there and let him speak to me like that?'

Belle had carried on with her breakfast, quietly enjoying the discussion between her brother and sister. Since the day of Morna's birth she had lived in her young sister's shadow. While Morna was given piano and art lessons, her father had taught Belle arithmetic and bookkeeping in preparation for her duties in the shop; he had always made it clear that although he had no doubt that with her looks, Morna would have her pick of eligible male suitors, Belle would almost certainly have to learn to support herself.

'Belle!' Morna said sharply.

'I'm afraid that I agree with Walter. We must all earn our way. Remember that once Walter marries Clarissa you and I will have to become more independent.'

Morna put down her uneaten toast and looked from her sister to her brother in disbelief. 'You seriously think that I should go out and work?'

'Belle and I find employment pleasant enough.'

26

'But you're both needed in the shop. There's nothing for me to do there, is there?'

'Not unless you're willing to become a salesgirl, though I'm sure you could find something more agreeable than that.'

'Helping Aunt Beatrice to care for her beloved smelly dogs? Taking up nursing, or going on the stage?' Morna suggested sarcastically.

'I doubt if you're qualified for the stage, and nursing is a vocation. Teaching, perhaps?'

'I have no desire to teach. In any case, teaching is a vocation too.'

'I'm sure that many teachers take the work on as a means of feeding, clothing and housing themselves, rather than for the love of it,' Walter said dryly. 'There's a certain pleasure in knowing that you are earning your own way in the world, Morna.' He dabbed his mouth with his napkin, consulted his pocket watch and rose to his feet. 'You may even learn to enjoy the experience.'

The small town of Saltcoats in North Ayrshire, which began as a cluster of sixteenth-century cottages huddled on the shores of the Firth of Clyde, took its name from the local 'salt cottars' who harvested sea salt to cure fish caught by the local fishermen.

As time went on coal mining came to the area, and by the late nineteenth century the growing town, built on a large curving bay and with the majestic island of Arran not far offshore, became a popular holiday resort for folk desperate to exchange the smoke and grime of the inland towns and cities for the sweeping, sandy bays and invigorating sea air of the Firth of Clyde.

They flocked to the coast in their thousands every year by bus and rail, and during July and August many of the local families living in two crowded rooms somehow managed to cram themselves into just one room in order to let out the other to holidaymakers arriving for a week, or two weeks if they could afford it.

The oldest dwellings, little more than slums by 1909, were all close to the sea that in earlier days had provided the local people with their livelihoods, while the well-to-do built fine houses on the outskirts of the town. It was in one of those handsome grey stone homes in Argyle Road that the Forsyths lived. It was an area where the genteel inhabitants liked to keep themselves to themselves. Gossip, in their view, was for the lower orders and those who lived in the poorer area, where rumours spread as fast as head lice and outbreaks of scarlet fever.

Even so, news of Hamilton Forsyth's sudden departure from Saltcoats was known up and down the length of Argyle Road and even further afield by the end of the morning.

Walter returned to the shop in Dockhead Street just before noon. Belle had been waiting for him with growing impatience in the tiny office where she sat taking in money and doling out change. Normally it suited her to be stationed there, where she could keep an eye on the shop through the glass window, but today far too many of the customers seemed over-interested in staring in at her as though she were some strange specimen in a zoo. She emerged now and again to hurry to the door so that she could peer up the street in the hope of seeing her brother's sturdy figure striding in her direction, but when he finally arrived she was at her desk, dealing with a customer paying his monthly account.

The man, a regular client, took his money with a brusque nod before turning away to find himself face to face with Walter.

'Good morning, Mr McCormack, I trust you are well?'

The man gave a loud harrumphing cough and looked Walter up and down as though unsure as to just who he was, then muttered something and brushed past.

'It's been like that all morning,' Belle hissed through the slot left at the base of the window to allow money to pass between herself and the customers. 'Folk giving me strange looks, and some even behaving as if they don't know me! I thought you were never going to get here. Walter, what's . . . ?'

'Not here.' Her brother cast a swift look around the premises. 'Come into my office.' He snapped his fingers. 'Mr Stoddart, kindly take charge of the shop for a few minutes. Miss Campbell, to the cash desk, if you please.'

'Walter, I have had a dreadful morning!' Belle burst out as soon as she and her brother were in the back office with the door closed against any would-be listeners. 'People have been behaving so strangely. Some have wandered round the shop, peering at me when they thought I wasn't looking and then going out without buying anything. Those who did come in to buy have either cut me off as if I were a total stranger or asked after me with such sympathy that you would think that I'm the one who was ill, and not Mother. Even the staff are behaving strangely.'

'That's because everyone knows.' Walter threw himself into the swivel chair before his desk.

'About Father?'

'Of course about Papa, who else? I've had to put up with stares and smirks everywhere I went, even in the bank while I was waiting to see Mr Pinkerton. I've seen people whispering in the streets behind their hands, and watching me. God knows how they know, but they do! Even Mr Pinkerton knew why I wanted to see him.'

'The money . . .' Belle suddenly remembered.

'It's all there, just as Papa said. He must have been taking a wage from the place and investing it somewhere else all these years. But at least he's not left us destitute. Mr Pinkerton was sympathetic, I'll say that for him. He's as dumbfounded as we are over what has happened.'

'Did Father say nothing to him about his plans?'

'Not a word, as far as I can make out. But good riddance to him!' Walter spat the words out savagely. 'He's gone from our lives, Belle, and we must forget him.'

'How can we forget our own father?'

'From what he said last night, he has forgotten us already. What's good for the goose is good for the gander.'

'Did Mr Pinkerton mention Clarissa? Does she know?'

'Not as yet, he says. But fortunately he does not blame me, or any of us, for our father's sins. He still gives his blessing to our marriage.'

'Well, that's something,' Belle said with relief. Clarissa Pinkerton was her best friend, and both families had looked on her engagement to Walter six months earlier as an ideal match. For her part, Belle felt that Clarissa would be more of a sister to her than Morna had ever been.

'He's coming to the house this evening to go over some business with me and he will bring Clarissa with him. He says she is eager to spend some time with you and Morna. At least we have his support,' Walter said. 'As to the rest of the town, we must just ride out the storm.'

'You don't think it could have been Sarah, do you? Could she have realised what was going on and mentioned it to . . . no, of course not,' Belle corrected herself at once, 'she's only a servant, without the wit to work such things out. But she might have overheard us talking. If she's gossiped to any of the other servants in the

30

road I shall have her out of the house, bag and baggage, before the day is over!'

'It's not Sarah,' Walter said swiftly. 'I spoke to her last night, quite severely, and made her promise that she would not utter a word of what had happened.'

'You think that a servant girl can keep promises?'

'She would not dare to disobey a direct order from me, Belle, I can assure you of that. In any case, the damage is done and can't be undone. It's up to us now. If we can behave calmly and with dignity, folk will get tired of tittle-tattling soon enough. But for the moment,' Walter sighed heavily and got to his feet, 'we must go out into the shop and face them all.'

'It came as a terrible shock when Father broke the news to us, but after some consideration, all of us agreed that we stand united in our support for you poor souls. The wicked thing that your father has just done should not reflect upon you, my dearest friends.' Clarissa Pinkerton's voice was firm, and her large dark eyes were steady as she surveyed Belle and Morna. Everything about Clarissa was firm, even to her sturdy body, encased in a well-boned corset. 'Naturally, as soon as I heard the dreadful news I resolved to stand by Walter. We are pledged to each other for the rest of our lives and beyond, and so my place must always be by his side!' She paused to draw breath, patting her bodice lightly and beaming at her audience. 'My goodness, I feel almost like the heroine in one of those delightful romantic novels! Now you must not concern yourselves, my dears, for together we shall win through this adversity.'

'It's easy for you, Clarissa,' Belle said miserably. 'You didn't have to sit in the shop and watch people staring and whispering and . . . thinking things about you.'

'Oh, fiddle! No doubt there are those who will say that

31

I should turn my back on my poor innocent Walter in his hour of need, but I do not intend to pay any heed to them, and neither should you. Sticks and stones may break our bones, but whispers and stares can never hurt us or turn us from doing our duty. Hold your head high and pull your shoulders back,' Clarissa said briskly, following her own advice. She and the Forsyth sisters had known each other all their lives; even although Clarissa was six months younger than Walter, and therefore two and a half years younger than Belle, the three Forsyths had always been in the habit, during childhood, of deferring to her in the choice of games and activities. When she decided, in her mid-teens, to fall in love with Walter, their engagement had become inevitable, partly because Clarissa wanted Walter as a husband, and partly because they were eminently suited and both sets of parents desired the union as much as she did.

As she stood before them with her chin up, shoulders squared and head thrown back defiantly, she looked, Belle thought, like the pictures she had seen of a female singer dressed as Britannia. If Clarissa had suddenly seized the brass toasting fork from its place on the hearth and burst into 'Land of Hope and Glory' she would not have been in the least bit surprised.

Morna, for her part, glanced down at her own small, softly rounded chest and wished that her bosom was as magnificent as Clarissa's.

'Walter says that folk will soon get tired of talking about us.' Belle said.

'Of course they will! And we'll always stand by you.' Clarissa sat on the sofa beside her, taking Belle's hand in both of hers. 'Father has already said so, and Mama agrees. She would have come with us this evening if the shock of what has happened hadn't brought on one of

32

her headaches. As for me,' she added, her voice deepening and ringing out as though proclaiming an oath in public, 'I would marry Walter tomorrow if I could. I said as much to Papa on our way here, but he says we must observe a proper period of mourning for dear Aunt Frances.'

'What she would say about all this, I don't know,' Belle wailed.

'If she was still here it wouldn't have happened,' Morna pointed out. 'You heard Papa say that once the marriage was over there was no reason for him to stay.'

'I suppose,' Clarissa's voice was thoughtful, 'that when we marry, we will live here, since the house will now be Walter's.'

'Oh yes. He said to me only last night that he intends to have the main bedroom redecorated to your taste.'

'Really? I must have a good look at it . . . in a month or so, I mean,' Clarissa added swiftly. 'Or perhaps a week or so. In the meantime, I suppose the three of you will go on living here as before?'

'I'll certainly continue to run the household as I have done since Mother fell ill,' Belle agreed. 'And work in the shop. But once you and Walter marry . . .' her voice trailed away.

'You must both continue to look on this house as your own home, even after I become its mistress,' Clarissa said kindly. 'After all, we're more like sisters than friends and I would never seek to turn either of you out.'

'I may well have a home of my own by then,' Morna said swiftly.

'Indeed?' Clarissa's eyes widened and she gave an arch little giggle. 'Are you thinking by any chance of a certain Mr MacAdam?'

'Arthur would make a suitable husband,' Morna

acknowledged coyly, 'and I have good reason to believe that he is more than ready to settle down.'

'But that's grand news,' Clarissa gushed, smiling warmly at the younger girl. She had no objection to sharing her marital home with Belle, who would be more than willing to act as housekeeper as well as being very useful to Walter in the shop, but the prospect of sheltering *two* unmarried sisters-in-law under her roof was not attractive. 'You'll make an enchanting hostess in the home of the right man, Morna, and just think what fun you and I will have, setting up our new lives together!'

'I had no idea that Arthur MacAdam was on the verge of proposing marriage, Morna,' Belle said after the Pinkertons had gone home.

'What's that?' Walter asked.

'Morna has just told me and Clarissa that she is about to become engaged to Arthur MacAdam.'

'Indeed? That *is* good news, Morna. He's a fine young man.'

'Father seemed unsure of his suitability,' Belle pointed out, and her brother shrugged.

'I scarcely think that Father is a fit judge. For my own part, I have always liked Arthur.'

'But isn't it rather soon for Morna to be speaking of an engagement?'

'In view of Mother's passing, Belle,' Morna protested, 'we will of course wait a respectable length of time before making anything official.'

'No, I meant that you and he have only been walking out together for a few weeks at the most. He hasn't even come to tea yet. I had no idea that his feelings for you were so strong.'

'How often did Mother tell us that she fell passionately

in love with Papa from almost the first moment she laid eyes on him?' Morna asked irritably.

'I know, but I always thought she was romanticising. Do people really fall in love at first sight?' Belle wondered. 'Did you, Walter, with Clarissa?'

'What a thing to ask! And considering that I've known Clarissa almost all my life, what a daft idea! Children don't fall in love. Should I perhaps have a word with Arthur?' Walter asked his sister, suddenly reminded of his new role as head of the household.

'Certainly not. D'you want to frighten the man away? Let him declare himself to me first.'

'*If* he does. It still seems to me to be too early for you to be so certain of his feelings, let alone yours.'

'I have no doubt as to his feelings, *or* mine,' Morna snapped at her sister. She was already upset over Walter's suggestion that she should start thinking of ways to earn her keep, and Clarissa's reminder that once she married Walter she would be mistress of the house, and her somewhat condescending, 'I would never seek to turn either of you out,' had chilled Morna to the marrow. The prospect of being little more than an unwanted lodger in the house that had always been her home was frightening. Until that day she had had no desire to rush into marriage, but now, it seemed, she must give the idea serious thought. It would certainly be a much more attractive alternative to earning her own living.

Later, in her bedroom, she sat down by her dressing table to think the matter over carefully. Arthur MacAdam came from a respectable Saltcoats family. He was pleasing enough to look at, and he had always been both courteous and attentive towards her. In fact, now that she came to think of it, he had been most attentive at her mother's funeral, taking her arm as they walked from the cemetery, and proffering a snowy white handkerchief during the reception afterwards, when solicitous murmurings from the mourners had caused her cheeks to dampen with tears. She still had the handkerchief, washed and ironed by Sarah and put away carefully in one of the dressing-table drawers.

She took it out now and unfolded it carefully. It was made of stiff linen, and had his initials, A. MacA, in one corner. Morna ran a fingertip over the letters. Morna MacAdam. It had a certain ring to it. 'Mrs Morna MacAdam,' she said aloud, to her reflection, and then tried, 'Mrs MacAdam.' And then, extending a gracious hand towards the glass, 'How do you do? I am Mrs Arthur MacAdam.'

She tipped her head to one side and smiled prettily, pleased with the good solid sound of the name. No doubt, if she worked hard at it, she could come to love and respect Arthur. And she would far rather be mistress of her own house than become a poor relation in her brother's.

She and Arthur had arranged to go together to a musical concert in Saltcoats Town Hall at the end of the month; because she was in mourning she would not, of course, be able to go. She would send Sarah to his home in the morning to deliver the handkerchief, together with a nicely written note regretting that she must miss the concert, but suggesting that he might care to call at the house one day soon to take tea with her.

She folded the handkerchief carefully along the creases that had been ironed into it, and put it aside. She would write the note in the morning. And on second thoughts, she would not mention the handkerchief in her letter, but would keep it and give it to him in person.

She smiled again at her reflection, and decided that marriage might, after all, be quite pleasant.

4

The corset sprang joyously open as soon as the laces were loosened, and Sarah sucked air into her starving lungs in a great gusty sigh of relief. Glancing down, she saw that her white skin was covered with crimson weals where the corset, drawn as tight as she could manage, had bitten into tender flesh. She ran a hand over her belly, which had never been flat but had at least been soft. Now it was hard to the touch, a sure sign that the child within was growing. As she began to clamber into the washtub she had filled laboriously from water brought to boil in pots on the range she wondered how much longer she could manage to hide her condition from her employers.

It was almost midnight and the three Forsyths, who usually went to bed at around ten o'clock, were all sound asleep in their comfortable bedrooms two floors above the kitchen. Sarah had allowed plenty of time in order to be sure of that, and to be sure, too, that Mr Walter didn't take it into his head to come creeping down the stairs in search of her. Not that he had done so since the death of his mother.

The washtub was high sided and difficult to get into,

but Sarah was desperate and, after a struggle, she managed to lower her bare backside into the water, which was hot enough to make her moan softly, bite her bottom lip and squeeze her eyelids tightly shut. Even so, the pain was enough to force a few tears into her eyes. The tub was not meant to be used as a bath and she was wedged into it uncomfortably, her white thighs pressed against her belly and breasts, her knees almost beneath her chin. She had poured too much water into it, and some of it slopped over the sides. It was just as well that she had thought to spread newspapers over the kitchen floor.

The stinging sensation eased as her skin got used to the heat, and, reaching out to the bottle on the nearby stool, she uncorked it and took a sip. Liquid fire raced down her throat, burning everything in its path, and Sarah choked, a hand flying to her mouth as her stomach heaved and threatened to empty itself into the steaming water. How could anyone want to drink such stuff for pleasure? She had only been able to afford the cheapest gin; perhaps that was why it tasted so vile. She nerved herself to take another mouthful and then decided, as the neat alcohol threatened once again to come spouting back out of her, that perhaps it might be easier to have the baby.

But that was out of the question, so gin it had to be. She forced down some more and this time, thank the Lord, it seemed to go down more easily.

'Out of the question,' she whispered to herself, for soon, before the child she carried grew much larger, she would have to leave this house, the only home she knew. If Samuel refused to marry her and accept responsibility for the baby he had fathered on her, where could she go? She had nobody in the world but Samuel.

She said his name aloud, and the mere sound of it

gave her the courage to take another gulp of gin. She admired Samuel not only for his looks but also for his intelligence. He could talk about any subject under the sun. He was well read and subscribed to the local library. *And* he was ambitious.

'I'll not always be a delivery boy,' he often said, sitting at the kitchen table enjoying a cup of strong tea, a home-baked scone and Sarah's adoration. 'One day I'll find a way to rise in the world, you wait and see if I don't.'

It had been a dream come true when he started court-ing her, taking her out walking on her evenings off and teaching her something of the town she lived in, but seldom saw, since the Forsyth house was where she spent almost all her time. The first time he kissed her, his warm tongue slipping beguilingly into her mouth, his breath mingling with hers and his strong young body crushing her breasts against his chest, she had floated on air for the next three days. There had been more kisses, and then came the soft summer evening when they had become lovers. Sarah's body tingled even now, thinking of that first time below a hedge in a field near the town – the springy grass prickling against her naked back, the deli-cious warm weight of Samuel's body on top of her, the silkiness of his skin against hers, the strength of his arms and the sweet strong curve of his backside beneath her eager fingers.

There had been other times too, some of them right here in the Forsyth house, when the two of them wres-tled passionately in her narrow little bed, mouths locked together to prevent them from giving voice to their plea-sure lest they got carried away and were heard by the Forsyths who slumbered above them, safe in the knowl-edge that their servant, a good, well-behaved lassie, was snoring demurely in her chaste cot.

The thought of those night-time adventures set Sarah to giggling, and again she pressed a hand against her mouth, peeping up at the cracked, smoke-grimed ceiling.

Suddenly remembering that she was still wedged in the tub, she peered down into the water, not quite sure of what she might see. She had heard the other servant lassies talk of gin and a hot bath as a good way of getting rid of an unwanted pregnancy, but she was unsure as to what actually happened, and she had not dared to ask anyone for fear of her secret being found out.

The water was cooling and the gin almost finished. With a struggle and much slopping of water over the side of the tub, she managed to wriggle out, staggering slightly as she straightened her cramped body. After drying herself and pulling her nightgown on, she used a pail to empty the tub before mopping it and putting it away in its cupboard. Lastly, she gathered up the soggy newspapers and took them out into the back yard.

Back in the warmth of the kitchen she yawned and scratched her head, feeling pleasantly relaxed and sleepy. For some strange reason she felt as though the kitchen was circling slowly around her. She reeled into the room that was only large enough to hold her bed and a three-drawer dresser and blew out the candle before crawling beneath the blanket and folding her hands together under her chin, as her aunt had taught her.

'Dear God . . .' she mumbled, 'please . . .'

And then she fell asleep.

Morna spent most of the next day planning the scene that would greet Arthur MacAdam when he arrived to take tea with her. She would be in full mourning, of course, but the black clothing would contrast well with her fair hair and ashen cheeks.

Glancing into her dressing-table mirror she was annoyed to see that her cheeks were in fact flushed with excitement at the thought of the forthcoming meeting and the outcome she had planned for it. It was true that she looked very pretty, but ashen was the effect she needed. She would have to use face powder every day, just in case he arrived unannounced. She would be in the parlour, playing something sad on the piano – or perhaps she should be caught at her easel. She decided to start work right away on a likeness of her mother, painted from the family portrait on the parlour mantelpiece. She hurried downstairs and was annoyed, when she went into the room, to see that it was no longer in its usual place.

Sarah, working at the sink, jumped as Morna burst into the kitchen. 'Where have you put the family likeness that should be on the mantelshelf in the parlour?'

Sarah whipped round, wiping the back of her hand across her mouth. 'I didn't touch it, Miss Morna. It hasn't been there since the mornin' after the master . . . the mornin' after the mistress's funeral.'

'If you didn't move it, then who did?'

'I don't know, miss.'

'Oh, for goodness' sake!' Morna turned to flounce out, then turned back. 'Did you deliver that letter to Mr MacAdam's house?'

'Yes, Miss Morna.'

'Into his hands, as I said?'

'The maid took it from me. She said that Mr Arthur MacAdam was out, but she would see that he got it.'

'Oh. Very well. I'll have a cup of tea, Sarah, in the parlour.' Morna returned to the front room and stared at the various surfaces, wondering where the photograph could be. Walter must have put it away after their father's sudden departure. She started to search, and had just found it face down in a drawer in the writing table when Sarah brought a tray in.

'Put it down there,' Morna ordered, and then, as Sarah bent to obey and a shaft of sunlight fell on her unusually pale face, 'You're not ill, are you?'

'No miss, I'm fine.' Sarah's head felt woolly and her stomach was uneasy, but that was all. She was beginning to suspect that the scalding bath and the gin she had forced down had not had the desired effect after all.

'You can go now,' Morna said sharply as the maid stood before her, her brown eyes vacant. Honestly, she thought crossly when she was alone, there was no reason for Sarah to look so wan, and to have those shadows beneath her eyes. It wasn't as though it was *her* mother who had just died!

She looked into the mirror on the wall and ran a hand over her own cheeks, as though trying to smooth the colour out of them, then turned her attention back to the portrait. Perhaps it would be best not to attempt a painting of Mother, since faces were not her strong point.

Pouring tea, she decided that she would paint a nice vase of flowers instead. She would bring her easel down to the parlour and when Arthur arrived he would find her working on a pretty floral picture, her face suitably pale, with perhaps just a suggestion of delicate but becoming shadows beneath her eyes.

She smiled, thinking of his reaction. If their meeting went as she hoped, she and Clarissa might well have a double wedding once the period of mourning for her mother had ended. And there was no doubt that she would be the more beautiful bride.

'Two letters, both delivered by hand, sir,' Sarah said. 'One for you and one for Miss Morna.'

'To me, Sarah,' Walter said as Morna held out her hand. He took the envelopes from the little silver tray. 'Thank you, Sarah. That will be all.'

'I believe that one has my name on it,' Morna reminded him, stretching an arm across the breakfast table. Her brother leaned back in his chair so that the envelope was out of her reach.

'All in good time.'

'You're enjoying this, aren't you? You're enjoying being the head of the family, master of the house.'

'It has its rewards,' he acknowledged with a barely concealed smirk.

'My letter, if you please!'

'Walter . . .' Belle interceded. 'Give it to her. I don't want to start a headache before I've even reached the shop.'

'Oh, very well.' He handed the envelope over and Morna tore it open eagerly. Belle took the last piece of toast from the rack as the other two read their letters.

Walter finished first, groaning. 'I've been summoned to Aunt Beatrice's house to tell her what's happening with the shop.'

'When?'

'This morning, she says. As if I've not got enough to do!'

'I'll be in the shop, and Mr Stoddart is reliable,' Belle said calmly, spreading marmalade thickly on her toast. 'We'll see that everything runs smoothly.'

'But it's none of her business! When did she ever take an interest in the shop?'

'I expect she just feels that since Papa has gone, she is the senior member of the family . . .'

'She is the oldest by far, but not the head of this family,' Walter said haughtily. 'I am perfectly capable of seeing to the shop and to our financial affairs, and the sooner she understands that, the better.'

'Are you going to tell her so?' Belle's eyes were bright with interest and amusement.

'Of course!'

'I wish I could go there with you.' There was just a touch of malice in Belle's calm voice, and a smile tugged at the corners of her mouth. 'I doubt if anyone has defied Aunt Beatrice since Uncle Hector died. Perhaps not even before that.'

'Are you saying that I'm afraid to stand up to an interfering old woman?'

'I believe I am. What do you think, Morna?'

'What?' Morna dragged her eyes from the note in her hand.

'Don't you think that it's time Walter stood up to Aunt Beatrice? After all, it's not as if we're asking her to support us. We're not poor little orphans,' Belle said. Then, as Morna's gaze returned again to her letter, 'What's wrong? Is it bad news?'

'It's not from Papa, is it?' Walter chimed in. 'He's not thinking of coming back, is he? Because if he is, I shall forbid it.'

Morna pushed her chair back and got up. 'It's from Arthur MacAdam, saying how sorry he is that I won't be able to attend the concert with him next week. But he hopes to call on me soon.'

'That's good, isn't it?' Walter said encouragingly.

'Yes, it is. If you'll excuse me . . .' Morna made for the door.

'You haven't finished your breakfast.'

'I've had sufficient,' Morna said over her shoulder as she fled from the room.

'Do you think she's pining for Mother?' Walter wondered.

'More likely to be pining for Arthur MacAdam and the social life she's going to have to give up for the time being. I must get to the shop,' Belle said briskly, 'and you must call on Aunt Beatrice.'

'I hope she doesn't expect to be consulted on every aspect of our lives from now on. I have no desire to be ordered about as if I was one of her precious dogs.'

'They live more comfortable lives than a lot of humans,' Belle reminded him.

In the privacy of the small bedroom she had opted to move into a year earlier rather than continue sharing with Belle, Morna read Arthur's brief note for the tenth time. 'While I too regret that you will not be able to accompany me to next week's concert, and I thank you for your kind invitation to tea, I feel that it would be best that you and your family have ample time to mourn your recent bereavement before entertaining again. In the meantime, Miss Forsyth, may I wish you continued good health. Yours sincerely, Arthur MacAdam.'

Tears stung her eyes and blurred the handwriting before her. He had referred to her as Miss Forsyth, and signed the letter – if such a brief epistle could be graced with the word – with his full name, as though they were nothing more to each other than acquaintances. When she thought of all the times they had stepped around a dance floor together, the tennis games they had played, the solicitous way he had taken her arm when they spun together around the roller skating rink, the conversations they had had . . .

She crushed the note up and threw it into the wastebasket. How dare he treat her so coldly? How dare he desert her like this, and leave her to the tender mercies of her brother and, eventually, his new wife? She would not tolerate such behaviour!

45

As soon as she heard the front door close behind Belle and Walter she flounced downstairs to the parlour, where she opened the roll-top writing desk and found a sheet of notepaper and a pen.

'Dear Mr MacAdam,' she wrote. Let him see how hurtful it was to be addressed so formally by one thought to be a close and dear friend. 'While I appreciate your consideration, let me assure you that your friendship and your company at this sad time would be of consolation to me, and not a burden in any way. Indeed, it would be such a pleasure to be able to talk to someone as understanding as yourself, and . . .'

She stopped, read over the words she had just written, and decided that she sounded too desperate. She tore the page in half and started again, just as the door opened.

'Yes, Sarah, what is it?'

'I was going to start doing this room, miss.'

'Can't you see that I'm busy?' Morna snapped. 'Find something else to do. I'm sure there's plenty.' As the door closed she started on another letter, then stopped again, feeling that this time she was being too cold. It might be best to wait until she felt calmer. She picked up the two letters and carried them into the kitchen, where she threw them on the range and watched as they burst into flames and then became ash. After that, deciding that a cup of tea might calm her nerves, she went in search of Sarah.

'Tomorrow, Sarah, you must start to clean the house from top to bottom.'

'You mean like spring-cleaning, Miss Belle? But we've only just come into October.'

'I'm well aware of that, but since the big front bedroom's been stripped, you might as well start there and then do the rest of the house. You may tell Annie McCall to help with the heavier work,' Belle added.

The few possessions left behind by Hamilton Forsyth had been removed — Belle had no idea where they had gone and no intention of asking Walter what he had done with them. The feeling that with so many drastic changes in their lives, the house itself must be thoroughly cleared, cleaned and reclaimed had seized her.

'And be thorough, mind,' she added. The girl needn't think that she could slack just because her mistress had died.

Life had to go on, but sometimes, Belle thought as she took off the blouse and skirt she had worn to the shop and sluiced her face, arms and throat with cool water, going on was quite a struggle. The shop had been hot and busy, and she felt tired and dispirited. She longed for the days when her mother ran the house and she herself had only the shop to think of. When her mother fell ill Belle had been more than willing to take over the domestic duties, and she would have gone on working between house and shop for her father, but now everything had changed. If the clock could just be turned back — but it never could. No doubt they would all settle down again and get used to being three where there had always been five, but by that time Walter would be preparing for marriage, and Clarissa's arrival would cause yet another upheaval. Although she and Clarissa were fond of each other, Belle was not altogether sure that she would enjoy seeing someone else in charge of the family home.

Perhaps it was time she considered taking up some new interests and meeting different people; possibly even some presentable young man intelligent enough to value strength of character and a good mind over a pretty face and slim waist.

She smiled tentatively at her reflection in the dressing-table mirror. She had good teeth and her skin was as soft as the skin described in the romantic novels she and Clarissa had often giggled over together. She was not so very unattractive.

The small bronze gong in the hall sounded, summoning her to dinner. As she went downstairs Belle wished, not for the first time in her life, that she had been born as pretty as Morna.

Lucky, lucky Morna!

5

Morna only picked at her food that evening, pushing the rest around her plate until Walter snapped at her to eat it or stop tormenting it.

She pushed the plate away. 'I don't like mackerel!'

'You always have before,' Belle said reasonably.

'Then I don't like it now!'

'You're not sickening for something, are you?' The doctor had said that their mother had a weak heart; what if it were hereditary, Belle wondered in sudden panic. What if Morna had it, too?

'I'm in mourning, that's all. Grief causes some of us to lose our appetites,' Morna said, eyeing Walter's clean plate in a pointed manner. 'You've almost taken the pattern off that – nobody would know *you're* in mourning.'

'Sarah's a good cook, and in any case, I work hard and I need nourishment.' He leaned back in his seat, pushing the plate away. 'Something substantial for pudding, I hope, Belle?'

'Jam roly-poly.'

'Good,' he said with relish, and then, as an afterthought, 'I saw Arthur MacAdam heading for the tennis courts on my way home, talking with a pretty little thing – not someone I've seen before. They were both carrying rackets.'

'Arthur MacAdam? With a young lady?' Belle's eyes were bright with curiosity. 'But I thought that . . .'

'If you don't mind,' Morna said, 'I'm going to my room. I have a headache.'

'I'll tell Sarah to take your pudding up, shall I?'

'I don't want any pudding, Belle. I don't want anything, except to be left in peace.'

'Perhaps you should go after her,' Walter suggested as the door closed behind their younger sister.

'Best to leave her in peace, as she asks. If you want my opinion,' Belle said, 'poor Arthur MacAdam has no idea that he and Morna are more or less betrothed. I don't even know if she likes him very much. She only came out with the story when Clarissa told us that we were both welcome to stay on in this house once you and she were married.'

'Did she, indeed?'

'Indeed. And Morna promptly said that she would probably have her own home by then, with Arthur. I believe that she just wanted to be upsides with Clarissa. To think that just a few weeks ago everything was normal, apart from poor Mother's health. Now I'm wondering when this household will ever feel normal again. Surely nothing else can happen to upset us?'

'An upset is to be expected, after Mother's death.'

'And Papa's desertion.'

'That hasn't helped.' A steely note crept into Walter's voice and he reached across the table to pat her hand. 'We're going through a very difficult time, but together we shall overcome it, Belle, have no fear of that.'

'To be honest, that's of little comfort right now.' She drew her hand from beneath his and put it to her forehead. 'I do believe that I also feel a headache coming on.

I'd best go to my room and lie down. Ring for Sarah, will you, and tell her that Morna and I don't feel like eating any pudding tonight.'

Alone in the room, Walter Forsyth went towards the tasselled bell pull hanging by the fireplace, then changed his mind and went into the hall and along to the kitchen.

'I was just about to bring them through, sir,' Sarah said hurriedly, nodding at the table, where three portions of jam sponge sat on a tray.

'Then let me save you the walk.' Walter closed the door quietly and came towards her. 'My sisters both have headaches, and no appetite. I shall have my pudding in here, Sarah, and you shall have some with me.'

'Oh no, sir, I couldn't.'

'Indeed you could.' He pulled out two chairs as he spoke, setting a plate before each place. 'Sit down, Sarah, and eat with me.'

'But Miss Belle . . .'

'Is upstairs in her bedroom with the door shut. In any case, I am the master of the house now, and if I say that we eat pudding together, then you must do as I say, mustn't you?' He playfully caught her hand and pulled her towards one of the chairs. 'Won't you sit down, milady?'

He ushered her into the seat as though she were royalty, and when she would have drawn her hand from his, he retained it, kissing her fingers one by one. 'What pretty hands you have, Sarah.'

'They're all rough with work, sir,' she protested, her cheeks as red as her fingers.

'True, but they are pretty nonetheless.' He released her hand, only to move behind her seat so that he could bend to nuzzle at the curve of her neck. Sarah closed her eyes, knowing what would come next. And sure enough, within a few seconds Walter was smothering her ears with tickly, annoying kisses.

'So pretty,' he whispered. 'Delicate little shells. You have the ears of a lady, Sarah Neilson.'

'Do I, sir?' She set her teeth and stared with a nauseous fascination at the creamy yellow sponge and bright red jam on the plate before her, while Walter nibbled and kissed. The hot bath and the gin had done nothing for her; she was still with child, and feeling tired and nauseous all the time.

Finally, tiring of her ears for the time being, Walter asked, 'Where are the spoons, Sarah? No, don't get up, let me serve you for once.'

'Left-hand drawer of that dresser, sir.' She watched as he rummaged in the drawer, wondering if Samuel might look in this evening and hoping that if so, Mr Walter might be back in his own part of the house by then. The thought of the two of them coming face to face made her feel sick again. She pressed her hands against her rib cage and took a deep breath as Walter seated himself by her side and put the spoons down on the table.

Sarah watched as he dug deep into the pale yellow sponge, scooping up a great mound. He lifted the laden spoon to his mouth and a red cavity opened beneath his dark moustache to receive it.

'Mmmm, it's good. My sisters don't know what they're missing.' He scooped up another spoonful and began to chew it with relish, his eyes twinkling at her while the lower half of his face worked busily. He looked, Sarah thought, the nausea threatening to go out of control, like an oversized, moustached child devouring a hitherto forbidden treat.

'Go on, eat up,' he urged through the third mouthful.

'I don't like to, sir, not with you sitting here in the kitchen. It doesn't seem right . . .'

'Nonsense!' Walter sprayed crumbs over the table. 'It feels very right to me.'

'What would Miss Belle say, sir? And Miss Morna?'

'Don't you bother your pretty little head over what they might say.' He filled his spoon again. 'I'm the master in this house, and if I choose to eat my pudding in your company then that is my business and nobody else's. And I do choose.' He swallowed before continuing. 'I like being with you, Sarah. You're real, and decent, and warm and comforting. Here . . .'

He used his own spoon to dig a scoop of sponge and jam from the untouched plate before her. 'Open up,' he demanded, almost coyly, and she had no option but to obey. The spoon was immediately thrust between her parted lips, scraping against her lower teeth in a way that made her flesh crawl, then it withdrew, leaving what seemed like a great mass of soft, raspberry-tasting stuff in her mouth. She jerked away without thinking, and the bowl of the spoon trailed over her lower lip and chin, leaving them sticky.

'Good, eh?'

She mumbled through the food, nodding her head and praying that when she swallowed, it would stay down.

Walter was scraping his plate now. 'You make an excellent jam roly-poly, Sarah,' he was saying when the front doorbell jangled. Sarah jumped to her feet.

'I'll have to answer the door, sir,' she gabbled, and fled through the hall, her hands automatically straightening her apron and then her hair. She remembered, just before opening the door, to rub hard at her lips and chin with one fist.

Mr Pinkerton stood on the step, a bulky envelope beneath his arm. 'Is Mr Forsyth at home?'

Sarah almost said that Mr Forsyth had gone away, before remembering that the bank manager must be referring to the son and not the father.

'Yes, sir, he is. Come in please, sir.' She closed the door behind him and took his hat and stick, then showed him into the front parlour before hurrying to the kitchen, where Walter scowled when he heard about his visitor.

'Why did he have to come pushing in at this time of night?' he said crossly, straightening his cuffs. 'Follow me, Sarah, he may well want some tea.'

But Allan Pinkerton was in the mood for something stronger than tea.

'I'm here on business, with a pile of papers for you to sign, Walter, but since it's after business hours and we've both had our dinners, a drop of that fine port that your father always kept in there would not be out of place,' he said, nodding at the handsomely carved corner cupboard.

'Of course. Sarah, you can go now.'

'Yes, sir.' She closed the door and went swiftly through the kitchen and out to the water closet in the back yard, where she emptied her stomach of the unwanted jam roly-poly and her entire evening meal.

Samuel didn't come tapping at the door that night, which was just as well, since Walter's visitor stayed until late. Sarah, mindful of the spring-cleaning on the following morning, was almost dropping with tiredness when the parlour bell finally summoned her to fetch Mr Pinkerton's hat and stick and open the door for him.

As soon as it closed behind the banker's broad, straight back, Walter let out his breath in a great sigh of irritation. 'Damn the man, why did he have to choose tonight to see to business that could have easily been dealt with in his bank by day?' he grumbled, taking a step towards Sarah.

One hand was reaching out for her when Belle enquired from the stair landing, 'Who on earth was that, Walter?'

'Only Clarissa's father with papers for me to sign.'

'Do you know what time it is?'

'Yes, but he got well settled with Papa's best port and I thought he was going to stay for the night and take his breakfast with us in the morning. Go back to bed, Belle.'

'I won't settle for ages now,' she complained, coming down a step or two, her dressing gown pulled tightly around her uncorseted body. 'Sarah, bring me a cup of hot chocolate, will you? And Walter, get to your bed or you'll be fit for nothing tomorrow.'

'Just coming,' he called back, then muttered a curse beneath his breath. As Sarah went to make his sister's drink he followed her and managed a quick, clumsy fumble by the kitchen door before turning reluctantly towards the stairs.

Morna decided on the following morning to forgo her plan to write again to Arthur. Instead, she would take the handkerchief to his home that afternoon and hand it over to his mother. Mrs MacAdam had always been very kind to her, and would clearly look on her as a suitable daughter-in-law. She would be sure to be understanding, especially if Morna looked pale and wan and quite overcome by the distress of her mother's death and her father's cruel desertion.

Although she was quite hungry when she woke, she forced herself to pick at her breakfast, scarcely eating a morsel. Unfortunately Belle was too busy organising the spring-cleaning that Sarah was to start on that day and

Walter too lost in his own thoughts to notice their sister's lack of appetite.

She kept to her room all morning and punished herself further by refusing to eat any lunch. At two o'clock she dressed in the clothes she had bought for her mother's funeral before surveying herself critically in the full-length mirror in one corner of the room. It was most fortunate that black made the most of her fair looks, she thought, and a lavish application of face powder had worked well, making her look suitably pale; while the slightest touch of blue eye-shadow smoothed into the skin beneath each eye added to the delicate look. She smiled at her reflection as she arranged her fair hair so that a few curls were allowed to peep prettily from beneath her hat. Mrs MacAdam would be sure to take pity on her now, and even Arthur's heart, should he chance to come home while she was still there, sipping at a cup of weak tea and refusing as much as a biscuit, would melt at the sight of her.

'I'm going out for a while, Sarah,' she said, running the maidservant to ground in the room that had belonged to her parents. The curtains had been taken down and Annie McCall had carried the rugs down to the back garden, where she was beating dust out of them. The room, with its stripped bed, bare floor and air of desertion, was no longer her parents' domain. 'I should be home by five o'clock.'

'Yes, miss.' Sarah was on her hands and knees, scrubbing the skirting board.

The Three Towns, as they were known locally, consisted of Ardrossan, Saltcoats and Stevenson, strung along the coast and more or less blending with each other. The MacAdams lived in Caledonia Road, an extension of Argyle Road, leading almost to the border with Ardrossan.

The heels of Morna's black shiny boots tapped briskly along the pavement. It was grand to be out of the house and walking in the fresh air — so grand that she had to keep reminding herself that she was in mourning and must keep her head lowered and her eyes on the ground. It would never do to seem happy at such a time.

She resorted to the childhood game of counting the cracks between the flagstones, allowing herself to glance up only when she happened to be passing someone. She met several neighbours on her way to the MacAdams' house, greeting them with a subdued smile and a quiet voice. Much to her surprise, she was mainly greeted in return with inquisitive stares. Some wished her good day, but in the briefest of words, and one or two hurried past with eyes averted, pretending that they had not recognised her.

Unlike her brother and sister, Morna had not as yet experienced the local reaction to her father's sudden disappearance. She had heard Walter and Belle talking about the way people in the streets and customers in the shop were behaving, but it had never occurred to her that she, too, might be cold-shouldered by people she had known all her life. Morna was the most sociable member of her family, and was used to being liked and admired by everyone.

She had almost reached the house where Arthur MacAdam lived with his two younger sisters and his parents when the door opened and Mrs MacAdam, dressed to go out, paused on the top step to survey the blue sky, and then to glance first up the road, and then down, in Morna's direction. Just as Morna hastened her steps the woman turned swiftly and disappeared back into the house as though she had forgotten something. When Morna arrived at the door, it was shut.

A maidservant wearing a snowy white apron answered her knock. 'I'm sorry, Miss Forsyth,' she said when Morna asked for Mrs MacAdam, 'the mistress is not at home.'

'But I just saw her on the doorstep, turning back into the house. Of course she's at home!'

'I'm sorry, miss,' the woman repeated, for all the world as though she was a wind-up toy, 'the mistress is not at home.' Her small dark eyes were fixed on a spot just above and beyond Morna's right shoulder, and one big-knuckled, work-reddened hand smoothed her skirt over and over again in a nervous gesture.

'Is Mr Arthur at home?'

'None of the family is in, miss.'

'But . . .' Morna began, and then as the woman took a tiny step back from the door, gazing at her imploringly, clearly desperate for her to leave, she squared her shoulders and said in a clear, ringing voice, 'I see. Please tell Mrs MacAdam and her son that Miss Morna Forsyth called.'

It seemed to her that as she spoke her name, the girl's mouth twitched in the beginnings of a sardonic smile, and a gleam came into her sharp little eyes. Morna stood her ground, giving the servant her very best stony glare, and the smirk vanished as swiftly as it had arrived.

'Yes, miss – Miss Forsyth,' the maidservant said, and Morna, satisfied that she had put the impertinent minx in her place, turned and walked away, wincing as she heard the door close before she had taken the few steps to the garden gate.

She kept her head high as she walked along the pavement, biting her lip hard and resisting the desire to turn around to see if anyone was watching her retreat from the lace-curtained windows. She reached a corner, rounded it into a side street, and slowed to a standstill, remembering that Mrs MacAdam had been on the point of going out when she'd arrived.

She strolled on for a few yards before turning and sauntering back, trying to look as though she was merely taking the air and perhaps waiting for a friend. When she reached the corner she peered carefully round it, just in time to see Arthur's mother reappear on the top step. The older woman's glance swept down to the far corner, giving Morna time to duck back out of sight before Mrs MacAdam turned to look in her direction. She giggled, reminded of childhood games with her brother and sister and Clarissa Pinkerton and Arthur himself. If only, she thought, she could return to those happy, carefree days! Then as she heard approaching footsteps she ran a few swift steps on tiptoe before turning, drawing a deep breath, and strolling back to the corner just in time to step out in front of Arthur's mother. The woman came to a sudden stop, biting her lower lip.

'Mrs MacAdam!' Morna said sweetly, 'How fortunate! I was on my way to call on you.'

She watched a series of expressions flit over the older woman's face as she recognised the blatant untruth, realised that she could say nothing without admitting that she had made her servant lie on her behalf, then decided to go along with Morna's story.

'Indeed?' she said at last, fidgeting with the basket looped over her arm. Then, rallying a little, 'I'm surprised, my dear, to see you calling on people so soon after your poor mother's funeral and . . .' she paused, then said carefully, '. . . and everything.'

'To tell the truth, Mrs MacAdam, my brother and sister have had to see to the shop, and staying at home with reminders of poor Mother everywhere I looked was breaking my heart.' Morna had put a small lacy handkerchief into her pocket before leaving the house; now she took it out and put it to her lips. 'I had to get into the fresh air, and as I had a handkerchief of Arthur's to return, I thought that . . .'

'Arthur is away on business, but I can give it to him.' Mrs MacAdam, a small cold smile pinned to her lips, held out one gloved hand. 'I will see that he gets it.'

'Are you going to the shops? If so, we could walk together. There are a few items I need.'

'I am calling on a friend who lives nearby. We have arranged to go in to the town together,' Mrs MacAdam said.

'Oh. Then perhaps I might call on you tomorrow instead. The thing is,' Morna coaxed a tremor into her voice and applied her handkerchief to the corner of an eye, 'I miss Mother so very much, Mrs MacAdam, and with Belle and Walter out of the house most of the time I feel very alone. I would so appreciate the friendship and guidance of another woman, and since you and Mother were friends, I . . .'

'Miss Forsyth.' There was no warmth in Mrs MacAdam's voice, nor, when Morna ventured to look up, in her expression, 'You may well feel alone and even ostracised, but that has nothing to do with your poor mother's death. It is due to your father's disgraceful behaviour in deserting his family, friends and duties in such a cavalier way. I can only say that those of us who cared for Frances Forsyth are grateful that she, at least, has been spared the humiliation felt by the rest of us.'

'But you can't blame me for what Papa has done!'

'I don't blame you, I pity you,' Arthur's mother said flatly. 'But even so, you and your brother and sister must realise that in a small and close community such as Saltcoats you will find few doors open to you for some time.'

'But Arthur and I . . . !'

'Were childhood friends,' Mrs MacAdam said firmly, 'and nothing more than that. There is no point in trying to gain his sympathy, Miss Forsyth; I am confident that if you persist in your rather foolish endeavours you will quickly find that he is in complete agreement with his father and myself on this matter. You mentioned a handkerchief? I will return it to him.' She held her hand out again, and Morna had no option but to take the wrapped handkerchief from her bag and hand it over.

Mrs MacAdam acknowledged receipt with a faint nod of the head, then with a curt, 'Good day, Miss Forsyth,' she stepped around Morna and continued on her way.

Suddenly the street seemed to dissolve in a shimmer of tears, and Morna had to lean against some house railings while she dabbed at her eyes with the little handkerchief. When she could see again, she realised that a maidservant sweeping the steps of a house across the road was watching her. Morna tried to retaliate with her haughty stare, but just then an errand boy came along the pavement, a laden basket over his arm. As the girl put her brush aside and accepted a wrapped bundle from the basket she said something and the boy turned and gaped at Morna. She walked briskly around the corner, out of their sight. By the time she was halfway along the next road, she had begun to walk faster, and then to run.

All she wanted to do now was to get home and stay there for ever, and never have to see anyone else again in her entire life.

6

As soon as the front door closed behind Morna, Sarah clambered painfully to her feet and went to the window to watch the girl's slender, black-clad figure go down the garden path. As Morna turned to latch the gate, Sarah pulled back, in case she happened to glance up at the window. When she looked out again, Morna was walking briskly along the pavement.

Sarah rubbed both hands over her stomach and tried in vain to draw a decent breath. In an attempt to hide her swelling waistline she was lacing her corset so tightly these days that she could scarcely breathe even when upright. Bending down, or kneeling, made her feel as though a very strong man had wrapped his arms around her from behind, and was squeezing and crushing the life out of her.

She went into the bathroom and splashed cold water on her flushed face, then drank some from her cupped hands before returning, reluctantly, to the skirting board. When it was finished the pictures had to be taken down from the walls and dusted, then the wallpaper wiped before they were put back on their hooks. The tops of the wardrobes would have to be cleaned, the grate polished, and every curve and angle of the ornate metal bed frame gone over with a duster. No doubt Miss Belle would check everything when she got home.

When the room was finally finished and she and Annie had carried the heavy rugs back upstairs and laid them on the polished floor, Sarah straightened her aching back and ran a forearm over her sweating face.

'That'll do for today. We'll do the master's room tomorrow, and Miss Belle's too, if we can manage it. You can get off home now, Annie.'

'Are you sure? I can stay a bit longer if you need me. You look awful tired.' The woman's eyes were sharp, and without thinking Sarah folded her arms in an automatic attempt to hide her growing bulk from the other's gimlet gaze.

'Of course I'm tired, and who wouldn't be, with the funeral and all, then having to do the spring-cleaning out of season as well.'

'They never stop tae think of the folk that have tae do all the work, do they?' Annie said sympathetically.

Back in the kitchen, Sarah paid the woman, then once Annie had gone she sank into a chair by the kitchen and laid her head on her folded arms for a few precious minutes. It would have been so easy to close her eyes and drift into sleep, she realised, and dragged herself to her feet, terrified in case she did just that.

Instead, she stepped outside the back door in search of some fresh cool air, but her corset, biting into her cruelly now, made it impossible to catch a decent breath. If she didn't get some ease from the discomfort, she thought miserably, she would go mad. Returning to the kitchen, she glanced at the clock. Miss Belle would not be due home for an hour, at least.

Swiftly, Sarah shed her blouse and skirt and petticoats, then unfastened the corset and pulled it off. The relief, as the laces loosened and she was finally free of the instrument of torture, was indescribable. She sucked in a great lungful of air, and let it out again in a sigh of sheer animal pleasure, her nails scratching busily at her hot, itchy torso.

Belle hated quiet days in the shop because the minutes dragged by when there was nothing to do. The few customers who came in bought little, and as Walter said, it was depressing to think of wages being paid to the employees who, with nobody to attend to, were standing around doing nothing.

'All I can think of,' Belle told her brother, 'is the spring-cleaning at home. I could just as well be there, making sure it's done properly and giving Sarah a hand, than sitting here.'

She had to say it twice more before Walter agreed to release her. She almost skipped out of the shop and set off at a brisk pace for the house, free at last to get on with some worthwhile work.

She used her door key rather than ring the bell and take Sarah away from whatever work she was doing, but as soon as she stepped into the hall she realised that the place was unnaturally silent, with none of the bustle to be associated with spring-cleaning – no footsteps, voices, or sounds of furniture being moved. She stood for a moment, head cocked to one side, frowning, and then without stopping to take off her hat or coat, she went straight to the kitchen and threw open the door.

Sarah, luxuriating in the relief of being free of the corset, stretched her arms high above her head, fingers spread as far as they could go, and took in great deep breaths, letting them out again very slowly. With each breath, a little of the hot tiredness that had plagued her all day eased away. When the kitchen door opened she spun round, startled, trying at the same time to cover herself with her arms.

'Sarah?' Belle Forsyth said. 'Sarah, what do you think you are doing?' And then, as the maidservant swung round to face her, and she took in the heaviness of the girl's normally trimly corseted body, and the full curves of her white-skinned, blue-veined breasts and belly, Belle's eyes widened in sudden, shocked realisation.

'Sarah Neilson!' she said. 'You wicked, wicked girl!'

Belle's furious tirade finally ended with, 'You may prepare the dinner, but I will serve it. I will not have you coming into the dining room, do you understand?'

'Yes, ma'am.' Sarah's voice was a whisper, her eyes lowered. All Belle could see were the reddened, puffy lids.

'And you will leave at the end of the week, do you understand *that*?'

'Leave? But where will I go, miss?'

'That,' Belle said icily, 'is not my concern.' And then, giving in to a hint of natural curiosity, 'What about the – the man? I take it that you know who's responsible for – for this?' She indicated Sarah's thickened body with a wave of one hand and a disgusted curl of her lip.

'I can't . . . he doesn't . . .' Sarah said, and began to weep again.

'He's married?' Belle asked, horrified. 'You wicked girl, have you destroyed the sanctity of some poor woman's marriage with your loose morals?'

'Oh no, Miss Belle, I would never do that!'

'Then he is surely free to marry you. You must make certain that he does his duty by you, Sarah.'

65

'He can't marry me!' Sarah sobbed.

'Why not?'

'He just can't, miss. I know he can't.'

'Then you should have thought of that sooner, you foolish girl. You had a good home here, didn't you? We've been kind to you, and paid you well enough, haven't we? My mother spent many an hour teaching you how to be a good maidservant, and what thanks do we get? I will give you until Saturday night,' Belle said magnanimously, 'so that you can finish the spring-cleaning. After that, you're out of here. In the meantime, I don't want you to step beyond that door while my brother and sister are in the house, do you understand? You can do the housework and complete the spring-cleaning when we are all out. For the moment, since we are alone, you may make tea and serve it to me in the parlour.'

Her final salvo as she marched off to the parlour to start writing an advertisement for the *Ardrossan & Saltcoats Herald*, was, 'And for goodness' sake get dressed. There's no need to look like the slut you are!'

Sarah, still weeping, did as she was told, squeezing herself back into the corset and buttoning her blouse up to the throat. She made the tea and took it into the parlour, where Belle greeted her with a stony stare. Sarah slunk back to the kitchen, where tears splashed on to the potatoes as she began to peel them.

Her mind raced around as frantically as a rat she had once seen trapped in a metal cage. The Forsyths' house was the only home she had. Where was she to go? Perhaps she *should* find some woman who could get rid of the bairn in her belly. Plenty used their special skills, and not all died from the experience.

But that would cost money, and she only just had enough saved from her meagre wages to pay for a bed for a few nights while she looked for work. If she spent what little she had on an abortion she would have to sleep out on the streets. But on the other hand, if she allowed the child to be born there would be little chance of finding work then. She and her bairn, always assuming that the little mite was born alive, would both starve in the gutter.

She sobbed aloud as the thoughts, like the trapped rat, banged frantically against the bony, constricting walls of her skull.

In the parlour Belle was near to tears herself. Didn't she have enough to worry about with Mother dying and Papa deserting them and half the town, the half that mattered, at least, pointing and whispering and sniggering, without having to start interviewing applicants for the post of servant? How could Sarah do this to her?

She rubbed at her forehead and then pressed the palms of her hands tightly against her closed eyes, but the headache refused to go away. She longed to lie down in her darkened room with a cloth soaked in cool water on her forehead, but now that she was, to all intents and purposes, mistress of the house, she could not afford such luxuries. Life was so unkind!

She drained her cup and had only just started work on the advertisement when Morna came home, slamming the front door behind her and sweeping into the room like a sudden thunderstorm.

'I hate this town!' she announced, pulling her hat off and throwing it across the room. It landed on the arm of a chair and bounced off again, on to the floor. 'I hate everyone in it. And I hate Mother for dying, and Papa for leaving us just when we needed him most!' First one glove, and then the other, was removed and hurled to the carpet.

Belle paused, pen in hand, and gave her sister a look of pure loathing. 'Please be good enough to hate everyone and everything in the privacy of your own room, Morna. I am very busy at the moment.'

'Mrs MacAdam had the impudence to tell me that she doesn't want Arthur to have any more to do with me – with us!' Morna kicked her hat across the room and threw herself into a chair. 'And all because of Papa! He's ruined my life! How could he do this to me? What harm have I ever done to him – or to Mrs MacAdam, for that matter?'

'Morna, go to your room and lie down for half an hour. You need to compose yourself.'

'How can I compose myself when I've just been insulted by one of Mother's closest friends?'

'If you had to work in the shop as Walter and I do, you would have become accustomed to such treatment. It will pass; people will soon forget.'

'I won't. I won't ever forget! That – that woman,' Morna said scathingly, 'will live to regret the day she slighted me. She'll soon be begging me to marry her precious son, and then see how *I* treat *her*!' Then, as her sister merely looked at her before returning to her writing, she got up again and announced with dignity, 'I am going to lie down. I need to rest.'

'Pick up your hat and gloves and take them with you,' Belle said without turning round.

'Sarah can do it. That's what we pay her for, isn't it?'

'Sarah is . . . busy with the spring-cleaning at the moment. Take them upstairs,' Belle repeated with a note of steel in her voice. Morna hesitated, and almost defied her sister, but after a glance at Belle's set mouth and determined eyes, she did as she was told before flouncing out of the room.

★ ★ ★

The three Forsyths ate a cold supper, helping themselves from serving dishes laid out on the dining-room sideboard to sliced beef and salad and cold boiled potatoes, followed by the rest of the previous day's jam sponge, also cold and with no custard. When Walter complained that this was scarcely a meal fit for a man who had been working all day, Belle informed him that Sarah had enough to do with the spring-cleaning. Each word was posted through set lips and, like his younger sister, Walter decided against an argument.

Instead, he swallowed a mouthful of roast beef and nodded at Morna's plate, where the food was being cut into very small pieces and then pushed around with a fork. 'That food costs money – my money. If you're going to waste it you might at least leave it in a fit state to be returned to the kitchen.'

'I'm not hungry.'

'No need to take it out on the beef. I doubt if Arthur MacAdam will be pleased once it's his food you're spoiling,' Walter said, and then, as his sister dropped her fork and burst into tears, 'What's the matter now?'

'Could you not have just kept your mouth shut?' Belle hissed at him.

'I only said that I was concerned for Arthur's house-keeping money if she's going to play around with good food like that once they're married.'

'We're not getting married,' Morna sobbed.

'Not right away, of course. You'll have to wait for a suitable period of mourning, like Clarissa and me, but . . .'

'Don't you ever listen to a word I say? We are not – getting – *married*!' Morna spaced the words out, throwing each one across the table at him. 'Not after a suitable period of mourning, not ever, because Arthur's family disapproves of the way Papa has abandoned us.' She dabbed at her face with her linen napkin. 'We've done nothing wrong – nothing, and yet we're all three of us being treated as outcasts because of that man!'

'You mean the engagement's been called off? When did this happen? Nobody's spoken to me about it. Am I or am I not,' Walter demanded, laying down his own knife and fork, 'the head of this house? Here I am, waiting for Arthur to come and ask me for your hand in marriage, and the next thing I hear is that this engagement of yours is off before it was on! Who decided that?'

'Mrs MacAdam,' Morna sniffled. 'I went calling on her this afternoon, and the maidservant said that she wasn't in, though I knew that she was, for I had seen her about to go out . . .'

'You went calling less than a week after Mother's funeral? For goodness' sake, Morna, have you no grasp of simple etiquette?'

'I was returning a handkerchief Arthur had loaned me. And I was in need of company. It's been very lonely here, without Mother.'

'You could have called on Aunt Beatrice. It's acceptable to call on relations.'

'I wanted comfort, not ordering about and dog-talk,' Morna snapped. 'But it seems that Mrs MacAdam was not at home to me.'

'The weather was pleasant,' Walter pointed out. 'She may well have been taking the air, or visiting a friend.'

'I saw her! She came out on to the top step as I was walking towards the house, and then rushed inside when she saw me. When I asked for her the maid said that she wasn't in, although I knew full well that she was. So then I waited around the corner until Mrs MacAdam came out again . . .'

'And accosted her in the street?' Belle said, shocked.

'I only wanted to explain how lonely I was and how much I would appreciate her company to help me through this very difficult time.'

'Yes, yes, but what did she say?' Walter was growing impatient. It was difficult enough to make out what his sister was saying because of her sniffling, without having to listen to more than was necessary.

'She made it clear to me that she and her family no longer cared to have any social connection with us, because of what P–Papa had done. And when I sent a friendly note inviting Arthur to tea, he wrote back to say that it was best to leave things for now.'

'What were you doing, inviting a young man to tea so soon after Mother's funeral?' Belle wanted to know.

'It's acceptable, I suppose, since Morna and Arthur have an understanding,' Walter pointed out.

'So Morna has said,' Belle said, adding sweetly, 'but perhaps Arthur was not of the same mind as she was.'

'Are you saying that I made it up?' her sister demanded hotly.

'No, but you might have been a little – presumptuous?'

'How dare you! I've been jilted, and I can't bear it!' Morna wailed, and fled from the room, sobbing.

'That girl,' Walter observed when he and Belle were alone, 'seems to have forgotten how to leave a room with dignity.'

'She's very upset, with all that's happened.'

'Belle, we are all very upset, but all of us, Morna included, have to make the best of our unfortunate situation.' Walter sighed and pushed his plate away. 'I myself feel as though I have aged several years in the past few days.'

'You haven't finished your beef. I thought you were very fond of cold beef.'

'On occasion, perhaps, but cold food lies heavily on my stomach at the end of a busy day.'

'The weather's mild enough – very mild for October. Cold meat can be quite refreshing on a mild day.'

'Possibly, but not today.' Walter glanced at the bell pull and pushed his chair back. 'I think I would like some tea. I'll ring for Sarah.'

'I'll make it,' Belle said swiftly. 'I've set Sarah to polishing the silver and it will keep her busy for the rest of the evening.' She began to gather the plates and stack them on a tray. 'I'll just take these things to the kitchen while I'm at it.'

7

Morna did not reappear, and her brother and sister, after working on the shop accounts for an hour, both decided that they, too, were ready for an early night.

'Not that I'm likely to sleep,' Belle said as they parted in the upstairs hall. 'Between the heat and everything else, I've scarcely slept these past few nights. I waken at every creak the house makes.'

Walter had planned to creep downstairs to visit Sarah once the house had quietened down for the night, but after his sister's parting remark he decided that he dare not risk it. Instead, he tossed and turned in his comfortable bed, his mind dwelling longingly on Sarah's narrow cot with its thin, lumpy mattress, rough sheets and threadbare blankets. None of those discomforts meant anything to him because they were well compensated for by Sarah's presence. The fact that she smelled of grease and harsh soap bothered him not a bit. Her hands might be work-roughened, but the creamy-skinned body hidden by day beneath drab clothing was soft and warm and her hair, when he loosened it and let it tumble across his face and throat, felt like a silken curtain. As for her small, neat ears . . .

Walter groaned and turned over for the twentieth time in a vain search for peace and rest. It was those pretty ears, peeping demurely from beneath the two smooth, neat wings of her chestnut brown hair, which had caught his attention when Sarah first came to work for his mother. Walter, who had never noticed anyone's ears before, loved to stroke them and kiss them and feel them against his face. Clarissa's ears were larger and quite ordinary, and on the only occasion he had tried to fondle them he had been rebuked so severely that anyone would have thought he had attempted to unfasten her blouse.

He would miss being able to spend time with Sarah once Clarissa became his wife and mistress of the house; but on the other hand, he thought, brightening, he could probably persuade Clarissa to continue to employ the young servant rather than find a replacement of her own choosing.

Walter's last thought, as sleep finally reached out to draw him into its soft, warm embrace, was that he must make quite sure that Sarah did everything she could to impress Clarissa on her visits to the house.

While Morna dreamed of meeting and marrying a rich man, becoming a respected and sought-after local hostess and snubbing Arthur MacAdam and his mother at every opportunity, Walter yearned to be in Sarah's bed rather than his own and Belle's mind was full of worries about how she could best cope with the shop, the house and her younger sister's turbulent romantic life, Sarah was weeping softly in the kitchen.

'Ah, now, why d'ye want to go on like that?' Samuel Gilmartin protested. 'Most girls would be happy to get rid of an unwanted bairn, so's they could get on with their own lives.'

'But I'd have to pay one of those women that help girls out and I don't have enough money, not now that Miss Belle's goin' to turn me out with nowhere to live!'

'She'll not do that if ye get rid of it.'

'She will.' Sarah cringed at the memory of the things Belle had said to her. 'She'll say that she can never trust me again. Can we not find a room to rent, Samuel? That's all we need,' she begged, 'a tiny little room that doesn't cost much. We could pay the rent from our wages.'

'How can you pay rent if you've no work and a bairn on the way?'

'I can find somethin' to do — I could be like Annie, doin' washin' and heavy work. I don't need tae be a housemaid.'

'You'd have tae stop work when the bairn arrived.'

'Only for a little while, and when I start again I could wrap it in a shawl and take it with me. Plenty of women do that. I'd not let you down, Samuel, honest!'

He glowered at her, chewing his lower lip. He had arrived late, his breath heavy with cheap beer and his body eager for hers. Heedless of her worries about one of the family finding them together, he had taken her to bed at once. Now he was drinking tea, since she had nothing stronger to offer him, before returning to his lodgings.

'How do I know that?' he asked sulkily. 'How do I know ye haven't already let me down?'

'What d'you mean?' She scrubbed the back of her hand across her face, smearing the tears she was trying to mop up.

'How do I know it's mine, that's what I mean. I don't want tae spend the rest of my life raisin' another man's bastard, do I?'

'Of course it's yours! How could you say such a thing?'

He had the grace to look a little ashamed of himself.

'I've known plenty of men who've been tricked intae marriage,' he muttered, 'and then found themselves raisin' bairns that look nothin' like them.'

'This one'll look like you, you needn't worry about that.' For a fleeting moment, Walter Forsyth swam into Sarah's mind, but she dismissed him at once. Samuel was a strong and exciting lover, while Walter's attentions – and that was all they were – were quite pathetic. Sarah only put up with them because her job depended on keeping him happy; besides, for some reason she felt sorry for him.

There was no possibility that Walter could have fathered the child she carried, she thought, and leaned forwards, holding Samuel's gaze with her own. 'It's yours,' she said, 'yours and nob'dy else's, you can take my word on that.'

He finished off the last of his tea and got to his feet. 'I'm goin' now.'

'Samuel, please.' She flew round the table to clutch at his arm. 'What am I to do? I have to leave here at the end of the week!'

'Ye know what ye have tae do, lassie, for I've told ye often enough. Get rid of it and get yerself another position, then ye can let me know where tae find you.'

'Samuel . . . !'

'There's no sense in any more talkin',' he said roughly, pushing her away and making for the back door. 'I've had enough of it.'

Then he had gone and she was left alone in the kitchen. Not quite alone, though, for there was still the baby. Sarah clutched at her belly, frantic with worry.

'Now that Morna's marriage plans have come to nothing, Belle, we must find some other occupation for her. A live-in companion perhaps – she has some experience of that, since she kept Mother company.'

'I doubt if she would be in favour of that suggestion.'

'I doubt if she would be in favour of any suggestion,' Walter sighed. Now that it was near to closing time the steady flow of customers had eased, leaving the two of them free to count the day's takings in the office behind the shop. 'But I will not support her as Papa did! I shall tell her that if she refuses to find a position for herself, she must come in to the shop with us.'

'D'you really see Morna as a shop assistant?' Belle asked nervously. The thought of her younger sister flouncing around the shop with her airs and graces and no doubt finding ways to insult or upset the handpicked, carefully trained staff, was unnerving.

'Not for a minute. She would look on it as lowering herself.' Her brother stacked a pile of coins neatly and started counting out more. 'She's not daft — she'll find her own salvation rather than work for us. She has no choice. You and I have earned our way since we left school — why shouldn't she?'

'She wasn't brought up to it, while we were.' Now that the threat of having to work with Morna was abating, Belle found herself pitying her younger sister. 'It's not her fault, Walter. Mother greatly appreciated her company, while Papa was quite content to support her.'

'*He* may have been content, but *I* most certainly am not going to follow his example. Morna would be well advised to seek a position as companion to some elderly person; she plays the piano and has a pleasing voice, should anyone need to be read to.' Walter counted the piles of coins, noted the sum on a sheet of paper, and began to stow the money away in canvas bags. 'We'll give her two weeks,' he decided, 'and then she will have to accept whatever we find for her, like it or not.'

A thought struck Belle. 'If she's really determined to

continue living at home, perhaps we can ease the burden on me by suggesting that she take over the running of the house?'

'There's no need for that.' Walter had been flipping swiftly through the notes taken from the till. Now, scribbling down another figure, he murmured absently, 'Sarah's perfectly capable of working on her own, and she can be trusted. She doesn't need supervision.'

'I mean when Sarah's gone – we could suggest to Morna that she should take on the duty of interviewing for a new servant and then supervise the girl until she learns to do things properly. That would keep her busy and . . .'

'What do you mean, when Sarah's gone?' Walter asked sharply. 'She's not found another position, has she?'

'Not as far as I know – nor will she find a position with a respectable family in her condition.' Disgust thickened Belle's voice.

'Condition? What condition?'

'Really, Walter, do I have to say it? Surely you must know what I mean.'

'Yes, you do have to say it.'

Belle coloured, looking away from him, fiddling with the ledger lying on the sloping desk. 'She's – going to have a child.'

'What?'

'No need to sound so surprised. It happens quite frequently to women of Sarah's class – though I thought that she would have shown more sense.'

'Are you sure of this, Belle?'

'Of course I'm sure. I went home early yesterday and found her – well, I realised as soon as I set eyes on her. I can't think why I didn't notice it earlier, but with all that's been going on, that's understandable. Poor Mother would turn in her grave if she knew about it,' Belle swept on, not even noticing that the colour was draining from her brother's face. 'To think of the years she spent training that girl, and this is the way she rewards us – just when we most need her!'

'What about the – the father?'

'What indeed? I asked, of course, but I got nothing out of her, except that they can't marry. It sounds to me as though the man is already married, but she claims that he is not. You would think, if that is true, that there can be nothing in the way of him making an honest woman of her and accepting responsibility for his own child. Not that it's any concern of ours,' Belle finished briskly, 'so don't fret about it, Walter. I've already put a notice in the *Ardrossan & Saltcoats Herald*. I wonder if Aunt Beatrice would be willing to send her housemaid round to us for part of each day until we're settled again? I shall ask her.'

'Sarah . . .'

'She will be out of the house at the end of the week – once the spring-cleaning is finished. It would be useful, of course, to keep her on until I find someone else, but best to get rid of her as soon as possible. Now then, how much are you taking to the bank?'

She opened the ledger and dipped her pen into the inkwell, waiting. Then, as no reply came, she turned to look at her brother. 'Walter?'

'What?'

'I asked you how much you're taking to the bank. Are you all right?' Belle asked with sudden concern. 'You look quite pale.'

'I just . . . I felt a sudden twinge of indigestion,' Walter said, and forced his mind back to business.

It seemed to Walter that the evening dragged on forever. He and his sisters had been invited to the Pinkertons' home for supper, and he had been looking forward to a hot, cooked meal instead of the cold food they were getting at home because of the spring-cleaning. But when it came to it, the excellent supper prepared by Mrs Pinkerton's efficient cook/housekeeper seemed to have no taste to it. Nor did the glass of port or the cigars that he and Mr Pinkerton shared in the older man's comfortable study after the meal. Walter, who had never taken to cigars, sucked hard at his and then blew the smoke out at once, surrounding himself with a thick blue-grey cloud.

Afterwards, the two men joined the ladies for an evening of card games and music, with Morna playing the piano and Clarissa singing. Then finally he and his sisters were free to walk back home through the cool night air.

'Tea, I think,' he said as they were taking their coats off in the long narrow hallway. 'I'll go and tell Sarah.'

He turned eagerly towards the kitchen, but Belle put a restraining hand on his arm. 'I told her to go to bed early in order to make an early start tomorrow morning – there's a lot to be done by the end of the week. I'll make the tea,' she said, and brushed past him.

Sarah was down on her knees, clearing the night's ashes out of the kitchen range, when Walter came downstairs in the morning. The noise made by the poker as she wielded it fiercely between the bars drowned out the sounds of the door opening and his slippered feet crossing the linoleum. When he put a hand on her shoulder she jumped and squealed, dropping the poker.

'It's all right, it's only me.'

She gaped up at him, struggling to collect her wits. 'What are you doing up at this hour, sir? Are you ill?'

'Not a bit of it.'

'You want your shaving water; I can have it ready in no time at all, sir.'

'You'll not bother yourself, Sarah. Here . . .' He drew her to her feet, regardless of the fact that her hands were filthy with coal dust and ashes, and led her to the table. 'Sit here,' he said, drawing out a chair. 'I want to talk to you.'

'But the range . . . !'

'The range can wait.'

'It can't, sir. If it's not riddled out first thing in the morning it gets choked up and then it won't heat the water, and then I'll be in trouble,' she protested as he pushed her down on to the chair.

'Just you sit where you are and let me see to the range.' His eyes still on Sarah, he picked up the poker by the wrong end and then yelped and dropped it. It clattered back on to the hearth while Sarah jumped up from the chair.

'Oh, sir, you've burned yourself! Here.' She caught his hand and examined it, then pulled him across to the sink and turned the tap on. 'Hold your hand beneath the cold water to soothe it,' she instructed, then flew to fetch the tub of bicarbonate of soda and a clean cloth.

'There,' she said when the hand had been patted dry and the burned fingers liberally scattered with soda before being carefully wrapped up. 'Does that feel better?'

'Much better. Sarah . . .' he began, but she was already back at the range, grasping the poker by the handle instead of the poking end, as Walter had done, and rattling it between the bars.

'I must just do this first, sir,' she said breathlessly as she worked. 'Then I'll build the fire up again before fetching your shaving water to your room.'

She had hoped that he would go back upstairs and leave her in peace to get on with her work, but when

81

she had finished with the range and got to her feet, rubbing her hands together to remove the worst of the coal dust, he was still sitting at the table, staring at her.

'Sarah, your eyes are all red.'

'It's the heat from the range.' She rubbed at her eyes, not realising that she was only transferring what was left of the coal dust to her face.

'Why didn't you tell me?'

'Tell you what, sir?'

'About the child you're carrying. How long have you known about it?'

Sarah's heart, already low, dropped into her shabby, much-mended boots. 'Only a few weeks, sir,' she mumbled, staring down at her hands as they plucked nervously at her apron.

'Why didn't you tell me?'

Astonishment brought Sarah's eyes up to meet his. She had expected him to be as outraged as his sister, but instead he was looking at her kindly.

'Tell you about something like that? I couldn't, sir! I'm going at the end of the week,' she added hurriedly. 'Miss Belle said I could stay until I'd finished the spring-cleaning, if that's all right with you, sir.'

'It most certainly is not all right with me,' he said firmly, and her aching heart gave an added twinge. She had counted on a few more days under the Forsyths' roof – a little extra time in which she might come up with a solution to her problem.

'You want me to go now, sir?'

'Of course I don't want you to go now, or at the end of the week, or at any time. Do you really think so little of me, Sarah?'

'Sir?'

'Do you think,' Walter said, 'that I would treat the mother of my unborn child so harshly?'

Sarah fumbled blindly for a chair and sank into it. She knew that it was wrong of her to sit in the presence of one of her employers, but between worry, lack of sleep and shock at what he had just said, her knees suddenly felt so weak that her only alternative was to fall to the floor at his feet. 'Your child?' she whispered.

'You're staying here, Sarah. You and I will be married as soon as it can be arranged. A quiet affair, of course, given my mother's recent passing, but essential under the circumstances.'

'But you're already promised to Miss Pinkerton . . .'

'How in the name of honour can I go through with that arrangement while you're carrying my child, Sarah? I may have behaved badly towards both of you, but at least I know now where my duty lies. We shall be married,' Walter said firmly, 'as soon as possible.'

'Sir, I cannae marry you!'

'Why not?'

'Because it's not your . . .'

Walter reached out and took one of Sarah's work-roughened, ash-streaked hands in his. 'Not my responsibility? I think it is, Sarah. I'm not one of those men who look on girls of your position as mere vessels on which to slake their desires. You know that I've always cared for you, and I want to do right by you and acknowledge our child as mine. Sarah Neilson . . .' He dropped to one knee, still clutching her hand in his. 'Will you do me the honour of consenting to become my wife?'

8

Sarah's head teemed with more thoughts than it could safely hold as she gazed down at Walter Forsyth's uplifted face, suddenly realising that if he wanted to do right by the child he believed that he had fathered on her, the bleak future stretching before her might be turned around.

But the flash of hope was fleeting. She knew in her blood and her bones and in the very womb where the foetus nestled, that the child was Samuel's. Walter's fumbling, clumsy lovemaking could surely never result in the creation of another human being. Only Samuel's lusty coupling could have brought about this burden she carried within her, and she could not deny it, even to save herself and the unborn infant.

'You cannae marry me!' She jumped from the chair and fled across the kitchen towards the back door. It was still bolted and Walter caught up with her as she fumbled desperately to open it.

'Why not?'

'It wouldnae be right – I'm a servant lassie, and you're . . .'

'Sarah, I'm a man and you're a woman, and in there . . .'

his free hand touched the soft roundness of her belly as he turned her to face him, '. . . is our child. My child. I have a right to claim my own child, surely?'

'But what'll the townsfolk say? What'll Miss Belle say, and Miss Pinkerton?'

'I don't care what any of them have to say. Be damned to the lot of them,' Walter said passionately. 'This is our concern, Sarah, and nobody else's. Say you'll marry me and the whole world can go to hell as far as . . .'

'What's going on?' Belle said from the kitchen doorway. She was still wearing her nightclothes, and her brown hair, normally knotted on top of her head, hung over one shoulder in a thick plait. 'What's all the noise about?' Then, as she saw the two of them together, her brother's hand gripping the maidservant's arm, her puzzled expression turned to anger. 'What has the slut been up to now? She's not trying to steal from us, is she? Sarah Neilson, you wicked girl – you can just leave today, and never mind waiting until the end of the week!'

'That's enough, Belle. Sarah's done nothing wrong.'

'Nothing wrong? What about the child she's carrying, and her not married?'

'That's why I'm here – to make amends for my wrongdoing.'

'What wrongdoing? You're not making any sense, Walter,' his sister said impatiently. 'For goodness' sake, man, get out of the kitchen and let the girl get on with her work. Sarah, the range must be choked, for there's no hot water upstairs. You'll have to boil kettles and bring them up to the bedrooms. And hurry!'

'Sarah,' Walter said, 'will do nothing of the sort. You and Morna can wash in cold water for once, or see to your own kettles. Sarah's not in a fit condition to fetch and carry for you.'

'That is not my concern. While she's under our roof she'll . . .'

'It may not be your concern, Belle, but it's mine. You might as well know that I have just asked Sarah to marry me.'

'Mar . . .' Belle swayed slightly, then leaned against the door frame, one hand clutching at her throat. 'You? Marry with her? Have you gone clean out of your senses?'

'On the contrary, Belle, I think I've just found them.'

For a moment Belle's mouth worked soundlessly, and then, as she looked from the maidservant's flushed, tearful face to Walter's smug smile, understanding dawned. 'You mean that you're . . . ?'

'I am the father of Sarah's child,' Walter confirmed proudly. 'And you, my dear Belle, are soon to become an aunt.'

Morna, awakened from sleep by the noise, arrived in the kitchen to find Belle standing in the middle of the room, both arms flailing about and scream after scream pouring from her throat. Walter was trying to wrestle her into a chair while Sarah filled a cup with water from the tap.

'What's happened? Has she had a seizure?'

Walter yelped as one of Belle's flailing hands caught him on the nose. With difficulty, he captured both wrists and managed to force her down on to the chair. 'She's just being daft,' he said breathlessly. 'Sarah, where's that water?'

'Here, sir.'

The maidservant arrived by his side with the cup just as Belle, with a roar of 'Don't you touch me!' ducked her head and sank her teeth into one of the hands imprisoning her. Walter yelped again and released her at once. She bounced to her feet just as he snatched the cup from

Sarah, and instead of holding it to his sister's lips as he had first intended, he dashed its contents into her face.

The screams stopped at once, to be replaced by strangled gasps as the shock of the cold water took what little breath was left in Belle's lungs. She sank back down on to the chair, wiping her incredulous eyes.

'I'm wet!' she said, stunned.

'Well, at least you're quiet, too.' Walter examined his bitten hand, rubbing at the marks her teeth had left on the skin. 'It's a wonder you didn't draw blood!'

'It's a pity I didn't!' Belle snapped back at him, while Morna asked, bewildered, 'What's going on here?' She, too, was still dressed for sleep, her soft fair hair caught back by a narrow ribbon.

'Ask him,' Belle snarled, and then, with a glare at her brother, 'Murderer!'

'Walter? Who's he murdered?'

'Nobody, she's havering. I'm no murderer – I'm bringing new life into the world, and what's wrong with that?'

'What's wrong with it?' Belle's voice began to rise again. 'What's wrong with getting the servant lassie with child and then announcing that you're going to marry her? What's Clarissa going to say about that? What'll her father say, and Aunt Beatrice, and all the folk that come into the shop?'

'Sarah's having a baby?' Morna asked. And then, as neither her brother nor her sister seemed interested in replying, 'Is this true, Sarah? Are you having a child?'

Sarah had been trying to bury herself in a corner; now, addressed directly, she hung her head and whispered, 'Yes, miss.'

'And it's yours, Walter? But how can it be yours when you're promised to Clarissa?'

'Don't be so childish, Morna,' her brother snapped. 'This is 1909, not the nineteenth century. I'm sure that all those novelettes you've been reading must have taught you something of the facts of life.'

'And you're going to marry Sarah, and not Clarissa?' Morna went on, and Belle let out a pathetic bleat reminiscent of a lost lamb searching the fields for its mother.

'I am going to marry the mother of my child, yes. Would you expect your brother to do otherwise under the circumstances?'

'I think that Clarissa might expect you to do otherwise,' Morna said. 'Does she know yet?'

Which was enough to send her sister into another fit of hysteria.

'Ye've lost the few wits God gave ye, Walter Forsyth,' Beatrice McCallum said flatly. 'And betrayed poor Clarissa Pinkerton intae the bargain.'

'On the contrary, Aunt Beatrice, I have found my wits. Surely you can see that as a man of honour I have no choice but to marry Sarah Neilson and acknowledge her child as my own.' Walter's eyes were bright, his voice exultant. After years of living in his father's shadow, constantly assessed and found wanting, he felt that he had at last come into his manhood. He had behaved stupidly but he was going to accept full responsibility for his own actions. He was going to become a father, master of his own fate at last.

'Of course ye've got another choice, man! Find somewhere for the lassie to stay and settle some money on her – Meggie Chapman that used tae be your nurse has a lodgin' house down by the water, has she no'? I'm sure she would offer Sarah and the bairn room and board in return for help in the house.'

'But I care for Sarah.'

'Care for her? She's a servant, Walter. If I'd a sovereign for every servant my Hector bedded – though mostly in his mind, I'll tell ye, for I saw tae it that he got little chance tae do it in the flesh – I'd be a wealthy woman,' said Beatrice, ignoring the fact that thanks to Hector's prudent thriftiness and knack for investment, she was already a wealthy woman.

'I've already asked Sarah to become my wife.'

'And look what's come of it,' the old woman shot back at him. 'She's cryin' in the kitchen, your poor sister's havin' the vapours up in her bedroom and the shop's bein' left tae run itself. Romeo here's got more sense than you have.'

The dog she had brought with her today was stretched out on the parlour rug in a patch of sunlight. Now he lifted his head at the sound of his name, licked his owner's boot, and settled back down again with a contented sigh as Beatrice went on, 'You've caused more confusion in this household than your father did. And what about Mr Pinkerton? D'you think he's goin' tae stand idly by and watch his daughter bein' jilted? She could take ye tae court for breach of promise, d'ye realise that?'

'I suppose I should go and see her today.' Walter ran a hand over his chin and added, 'After I've shaved, that is. And broken my fast.'

'And who's tae make your breakfast and take up your shaving water?'

'Why, Sar . . .' Walter began, and then, as his aunt gave him a grim nod, he amended it to, 'I shall see to it myself.'

'I can't stay here,' Belle wailed, scrubbing at her eyes with a damp wad of handkerchief.

'Of course you can.' Beatrice told her, having left Walter to feed himself. 'Who's goin' tae run the house if you don't?'

'And who's going to interview the applicants for the post of serving lassie?' Morna broke in. 'I don't know how to do that sort of thing, Belle.'

'I don't care if the house goes to rack and ruin and falls down around Walter's stupid ears! Why should I look after things for him, when he's let us down so badly? I wish Mother were still here. I wish Papa hadn't gone away!'

'If you ask me, your father would have been no help at all, and your poor mother's been spared a terrible shame.' Beatrice glanced again at her elder niece's distraught, tear-stained face and began to soften a little. 'If you're so determined not to stay in this house you'd best come to me for a day or two, until you feel better. Morna, help your sister to get ready. I'm goin' downstairs to have another word with Walter before he goes runnin' off to Mr Pinkerton and makes things even worse than they are already.'

'Poor, poor Clarissa, what's she to do now? She might never speak to me again!'

'And her father might refuse to go on handlin' your accounts,' Beatrice said on her way out. 'That would be even worse.'

'You'll not be gone for long, will you?' Morna begged as she packed some clothes for her sister. 'You'll be back tomorrow?'

'How can I ever return to this house if Walter persists in this daft ploy of his?'

'But you must,' Morna protested, appalled. 'What's going to happen to me if you don't?'

'You can come to Aunt Beatrice's with me.'

'And live with those horrible little dogs?'

'Then stay here and take my place. It's time you learned to do something useful.'

Morna's lovely eyes filled with tears. 'Belle, how can you speak to me like that? I'm your sister – Mother always told you to look out for me.'

'She didn't mean all your life,' Belle said, almost out of her mind with misery. 'She didn't mean once you were old enough to look after yourself! Oh, Morna, I wish she were still here. None of this would have happened if she had still been here!'

'If Sarah's really carrying Walter's child then it surely must have happened before Mother died,' Morna pointed out, and then sighed as her sister burst into fresh tears.

After lecturing Walter on the need for approaching Mr Pinkerton with an air of humility and bitter regret, Beatrice McCallum went to the kitchen, where Sarah was polishing the silver as though her life depended on it.

'Well now, this is a pretty kettle of fish,' the older woman said, and then, as Sarah jumped to her feet, 'sit down, lassie, and get on with what you're doin'. Romeo, behave yourself,' she added sharply to the dog, which was nosing around. Romeo obediently flattened himself against the floor while his mistress hauled a chair out from under the table and sat down.

'It seems that my nephew's determined tae marry you, for all that I've tried tae explain tae him that he's bein' a fool.'

'It wasnae my doing, Mrs McCallum. I told him that we couldnae marry, what with him bein' who he is and me bein' who I am. But he'll no' listen.'

'He's got a bee in his bonnet about doin' the right thing by you, though if you ask me, he should have thought of that a good sight sooner than this. If he had, my niece wouldnae be havin' hysterics upstairs and poor Clarissa Pinkerton would still have a weddin' to look forward to.'

'She still can as far as I'm concerned,' Sarah said at once.

'No, she can't, for he's just gone off to speak to her father.'

'Already?' Sarah jumped up as though to run after him, then sank back into her chair when the older woman said, 'He'll be well along the road by now. You'll never catch him up.'

'I wish he hadn't done that!'

'What will you do if the Pinkertons talk him out of marryin' you?'

'I'll . . .' Sarah hesitated, then said lamely, 'I'll manage.'

'D'ye have any fam'ly to go to?'

'Not now.'

'Friends?' Beatrice probed, and then, as Sarah shook her head, 'So what are you plannin' to do? Birth your bairn in a ditch? You think that the two of you can live on grass like the cows in the fields?'

Sarah's eyes filled with ready tears. 'That might be better than marryin' Mr Walter and settin' the family against each other.'

'Lassie, this fam'ly began to fall apart the day Walter's father left. D'you care for him?' Beatrice asked, adding when the girl stared at her in bewilderment, 'Walter, I'm talkin' about, no' his father.'

'I like him well enough,' Sarah said evasively.

'Enough to let him get you intae the fam'ly way.'

'It was . . .' Sarah hesitated, then mumbled, '. . . he was always lonely, Mr Walter. I felt sorry for him. And he was kind to me.'

'Not many folk take the time tae be kind tae servant lassies,' Beatrice agreed. 'But when all's said and done he's a grown man with a mind of his own, and if he's willin' tae marry with ye and you're willin' tae pledge yerself tae him, then I suppose that that's goin' tae be the way of it.'

'You mean you'd give your blessing?' Sheer shock brought a squeak to Sarah's voice on the final word.

'It's no' for me to say aye or nay if ye're both set on it.'

'But you're his aunt!'

'No' by blood, though. Did ye not know that?' Beatrice asked. 'Then again, why should ye? McCallum's your late mistress's own name. Hector McCallum's wife died in childbirth, and the poor wee bairn with her, and he took me on as his housekeeper. I looked after him for years, then finally, since he was gettin' older and he'd never met anyone else he wanted tae marry, he settled on me.'

'You married your employer?' Sarah had forgotten her polishing and was leaning across the table.

'I did – though not for the same reason as you and Walter,' Beatrice added firmly. 'It caused a right stooshie in the town at the time, I can tell you, but folk got over it, just as they'll get over Walter marryin' you, given time.'

'Miss Pinkerton won't get over it.'

'She's no' daft, and I'm sure she'll realise soon enough that there's better fish in the sea and Walter wasnae the right one for her. Those two were thrown together by their parents when they were just bairns; they never had the chance to make their own minds up. You might even be doin' them both a blessin'. Now then, lassie,' Beatrice McCallum went on briskly, 'I know that your late mistress, rest her soul, thought well of ye, and from what I've seen and heard I think ye're a sensible enough girl, so I'm willin' tae teach ye the things ye need tae know if ye're tae be mistress of this house instead of just the servant lassie. First of all, there's another servant tae hire in your place. Belle's already put an advertisement in the newspaper, but she's comin' tae stay with me for a few days, just till she gets used tae the idea of what's happened, so I'll do the interviewin' along with ye. Then there's . . .'

She began to tick each item off on her large-knuckled fingers as she talked, and Sarah watched and listened, caught up in a situation that was carrying her helplessly along with it.

Between them, Walter and his aunt were offering her salvation. She still felt that she should refuse it and be honest with them both, but nobody was giving her the opportunity. At least Walter wanted her and her baby, which was more than could be said for Samuel. Despite the need to be honest with him, and with Mrs McCallum, she was beginning to think that it might be best for her and her unborn child if she just held her tongue and went along with what was being arranged for her.

9

Beatrice McCallum was a natural-born meddler, and it had been a while since she had enjoyed herself so much. Fortunately for Sarah, the woman considered her a decent, honest and hard-working lassie, and she secretly believed that with some careful tutoring from a mentor such as herself, the maidservant might even make a better wife for Walter than Clarissa.

Hector McCallum, Beatrice's husband, should by rights have inherited the ironmongery business set up by his father, but Hector's interests and ambitions had been with bricks and mortar, and dogs. His first wife had had money of her own, and Hector had put it to work, buying up old properties that could be renovated and rented out. Because he and his wife were both thrifty and had little interest in luxuries, and because he invested his profits sensibly, Hector soon became quite a wealthy man.

His private passion was breeding King Charles spaniels, and again, he did well financially selling the puppies. While he was alive the back garden of the Caledonia Road house was filled with kennels and runs.

As a result of his investments and his lucrative pastime,

Beatrice found herself comfortably off when she was widowed. Since she had never shared her husband's business interests she promptly sold all of his properties, and with Allan Pinkerton as her adviser she invested the proceeds wisely. Most of the dogs were also sold, though she kept Romeo and Juliet, personal gifts from her husband.

Her first step in sorting out the pickle Walter had got himself into was to visit the banker and issue a carefully worded and most regretful reminder that if her nephew and nieces were forced to find another bank, then as their only blood relation she herself would have no option but to follow suit. Her wealth by then was sufficient to persuade the banker that it would be in his best interests to retain the Forsyth account and to forget about encouraging his daughter to sue Walter for breach of promise.

Beatrice then called on the Pinkerton household, where she commiserated warmly with Clarissa and her mother.

'I cannot understand what has got into that nephew of mine,' she said, sipping tea and accepting a sugar biscuit. 'I've tried to get him to see sense, but it's no use. To think that he's thrown away the chance of marryin' into this family – what his poor dear mother would say, I don't know.'

'I can only think,' Mrs Pinkerton said coldly, 'that Walter has taken after his father.'

Beatrice nodded sagely. 'Breedin' will tell,' she pronounced. 'Hamilton never would talk much about his background, and given the way he suddenly upped and left, without as much as an explanation, there was probably bad blood in his background. Gypsy blood, for all we know.'

'Gypsy blood?' Clarissa asked, horrified, while her mother shuddered visibly.

'Look at the way he just left, with no preparation and scarcely takin' anythin' with him,' Beatrice pointed out, breaking off a piece of biscuit and tossing it into the air. Juliet, the dog chosen to be her canine partner for the day, fielded it neatly before it could land on the thick carpet. 'Is that not the way of gypsies?'

'I'm beginning to think that Clarissa may have had a fortunate escape,' Mrs Pinkerton said faintly.

'Fortunate? I'm jilted in front of the whole town and you think that I'm fortunate?' Clarissa's voice began to tremble and she dabbed a small handkerchief at her eyes. 'I truly cared for Walter. I was looking forward to becoming his wife!'

Beatrice leaned over and patted her arm. 'I know how much you cared for him, my dear, and so did poor Frances. She went to her grave a happy woman, believin' that her beloved son's future lay with you. It's just a mercy that she didn't live to see where his foolishness has led him. But I've come here today to ask you to be compassionate, Clarissa. It's my belief that his father's cruel desertion, coming so soon after his mother's death, has confused poor Walter. He has sinned against you, of that there is no doubt, but he himself, poor youth, has been sinned against.'

'Not least of all by that hussy of a maidservant,' Mrs Pinkerton said heatedly. 'She ought to be whipped out of the town! How dare she aspire to marriage with someone of Walter's status!'

'My sentiments exactly,' Beatrice agreed. 'But the important thing now is to protect Clarissa's good name, is it not?'

'There's nothing wrong with Clarissa's good name. It's your nephew's name that'll be dragged through the mud!'

'That it will, and there's little that I can do about it,'

Beatrice said sorrowfully, 'for he's brought it upon himself. But just think how folk will admire you and look up to you, Clarissa, once they see that you have the nobleness of spirit to rise above pettiness and thoughts of revenge. To forgive is divine, is it not?'

'I suppose it is,' Clarissa said slowly.

'It's what sets the naturally noble folk apart from the others. There is nothing more admirable than a woman who can forgive those daft enough to sin against her,' Beatrice said. 'And I'll tell you another thing, my lass. What's meant for you won't go past you. It seems clear to me that this engagement between you and Walter has come to an end because you're meant for someone better than him.'

'That's certainly true,' Clarissa's mother snapped. 'I'm grateful to you, Mrs McCallum, for your understanding. You're quite right, of course; Clarissa must remain aloof, and distance herself from Walter and his strange goings on. That way, folk will realise that this disgraceful episode has nothing to do with her. More tea?'

'Thank you, but I must go. I have so many things to attend to.'

Beatrice rose, and was about to take her leave when Mrs Pinkerton said, 'Was there not a similar sort of scandal a good while ago within Walter's family? Some other relation who married his servant girl?'

'You'll be thinkin' of Frances's older brother Hector, a widower who married his housekeeper. I was the housekeeper,' Beatrice said sweetly. 'Good day to you.'

As she made her way to the hardware shop, Beatrice McCallum marvelled over how swiftly scandal died and folk forgot. Little more than a dozen years earlier she had been called an upstart to her face while walking along a street in Saltcoats, and her employer-turned-husband had been treated as a renegade for marrying his housekeeper. A more timid couple might have moved to start a new life elsewhere, and goodness knows there had been no shortage of people willing and ready to suggest it to them, some in anonymous letters, but they had both been made of sterner stuff. They knew that people forgot easily, and as time passed they began to be accepted back into society. Beatrice had no doubt that with careful planning the same thing would happen to Walter and Sarah.

On reaching the shop she marched straight through to the office, where Walter was trying to make sense of the books.

'You can stop worrying about being taken to court by Clarissa, for I've talked her out of it.'

'Her father almost threw me out of the bank,' he said glumly. He had never been good at figures, and his head was aching.

'Can you blame the man? But fortunately they've had the sense to realise that they'll only bring unwanted attention down on themselves if they pursue you over the way you've treated Clarissa. And Allan Pinkerton's agreed to keep you on as a client, though I think you should deal carefully with the man for a good long while. Be respectful when you speak to him.'

'How did you manage to get the Pinkertons to agree to all that?' Walter asked, astonished.

'I've got my ways,' Beatrice said with an enigmatic smile.

'You couldn't get Belle to come back to the shop, could you? I can't make head nor tail of all this bookwork. I've got enough to do trying to run the shop without having to see to this as well.'

'She'll be back on Monday, but you'd be advised to

be on your best behaviour with her as well. You've upset a lot of folk round here, Walter.'

'I know, but I've got to do the right thing. Surely you see that, Aunt Beatrice?'

'I suppose I do. But remember this – once you've made your bed, you have to lie in it.'

'I'll do that with pleasure, Aunt Beatrice. I've spoken to the minister; he's agreed to marry Sarah and me a week next Tuesday morning, in the vestry. A very quiet wedding.'

'It'll have to be. I suppose you'll want me to sort out a new serving lassie for you?'

'If you would. There are some letters for Belle – I think they might be from women seeking the post,' Walter said vaguely.

'I'll go to the house now and have a look at them. Sarah can sit with me when I interview the women, for she needs to learn how to do that sort of thing. And she'll have to be taught how to run a house as its mistress instead of the servant. I'll see what I can do with her. Juliet, you naughty dog! Why couldn't you have waited until we got outside? Better get one of the shop lassies to bring a mop and bucket, Walter,' Beatrice said, and went on her way, leaving her nephew to contemplate the pool on his office floor.

'Is it true what I'm hearin'? Are you goin' tae marry Walter Forsyth?'

'Oh, Samuel, you've come at last!' Sarah pulled Samuel from the dark night and into the lamp-lit kitchen. 'I've been out of my mind with worry – desperate tae see you!'

'Not desperate enough tae come to the shop and ask for me.' His usual smile had been replaced by a scowl, and his eyes were hard and narrowed.

'You've no notion of what it's been like here, Samuel. Miss Belle's gone to stay with Mrs McCallum and Miss Morna's in a right sulk about it all. What with one thing and another I've scarcely had a minute to . . .'

'Ye've not answered my question,' he interrupted. 'Is it true that ye're goin' tae marry Walter Forsyth?'

'No!'

'Ye're lyin', Sarah.' He took her wrist in a painful grip. 'It's all round the town. They're sayin' that he's determined tae marry ye – and that you've accepted him.'

'It's true that he's asked me,' she admitted, and then, hurriedly, 'but I've not said yes to him. It's no' him I want, Samuel. You know that!'

He released his hold on her. 'What I want to know is, why should a man like Mr Walter Forsyth – a man with a fine house and plenty of money and a woman already promised to him – suddenly propose marriage tae his servant girl?'

Sarah swallowed hard, rubbing at her arm, and then as he loomed over her, waiting for a reply, she mumbled, 'It's – he's got some sort of daft notion in his head.'

'What sort of daft notion?' he asked, his voice suddenly quiet. She looked up to see that he was staring at her hands, which, without her realising it, had automatically moved to cover her stomach.

'Have you been lettin' Mr Walter Forsyth tumble ye, Sarah?' Samuel persisted. 'Have you been pleasurin' him as well as me?'

'No – it wasn't the way it was with you . . .'

'Was it no'?'

'It was just a few kisses. You know what masters can be like with their servants,' she gabbled. 'He meant no harm, Samuel.'

'It must have been more than a few kisses, since it

101

seems tae me that he thinks ye're carryin' his babby. And you swearin' tae me that there was nob'dy else. I was right tae doubt ye, was I no'?'

'Samuel, it's yours, I swear it!' She ran after him as he made for the door, catching again at the sleeve of his shabby jacket. 'Samuel, please!'

'I tell ye what,' he said, shrugging her off as though she were no more than a troublesome fly, 'if it's mine then you'll do as I say and get rid of it so's we can go back to the way we were, with the cups of tea and the kisses and cuddles, and mebbe a wee tumble now and again for friendship's sake. But if it's his then ye can keep it an' marry the man, and the two of youse'll be welcome tae each other as far as I'm concerned. But I'll tell ye one thing – Samuel Gilmartin won't share a woman with any man.'

The door closed behind him, and by the time Sarah had torn it open again he was gone. She was taking her jacket from the nail where it hung, determined to follow Samuel and beg him, on her knees if need be, not to desert her, when Walter came into the kitchen.

'Sarah? Where are you going at this time of night?'

'For a walk,' she said swiftly. 'I thought I'd clear my head.'

'It's too cold for that. You could catch a chill, and that would be bad for you and the child.' He took the jacket from her and hung it up again, then led her to the fire-side chair and tenderly settled her into it. 'My poor little love, it's been a bad time for you, hasn't it, with Belle being so silly about everything. But you mustn't worry your pretty little head about it. She'll come to love you just as I do, and so will Morna. And soon you'll take your rightful place upstairs as my wife and mistress of the house. I've already spoken to the minister, and it's to be in the vestry next Tuesday morning,' he added cheerfully, and when Sarah burst into tears of misery and despair he knelt beside her, taking her into his arms and stroking her hair.

'There, there, my darling, there's nothing to worry about. I'll look after you from now on. You and our child,' he promised, 'for the rest of our lives.'

Sarah, utterly wretched, wept all the more.

'Here, lassie, this is your wedding gift from me.' Beatrice thumped the heavy volume on to the kitchen. 'You can read, I suppose?'

'Of course I can read!' During the night Sarah had cried until she could cry no more, and had then begun to face facts. She was pregnant with Samuel Gilmartin's child, but Samuel refused to accept responsibility whereas Walter Forsyth was not only willing but also eager to offer a home to both Sarah and the child. As the alternative was to starve in a ditch, she had come to realise in the cold, grey, morning light, that she had no option but to marry Walter.

Having accepted that, she had found an inner strength. Without Samuel she could never be truly happy again, but the next best thing was to make the most of being Walter's wife. Being condescended to by Mrs McCallum, who didn't even live in the house, was not part of being Walter's wife.

'Aye, I suppose you can, since you seem to be a sensible lassie,' the older woman conceded amiably. 'Well now, this book tells you all you need to know about how to run a house and how to treat servants, so keep it by you at all times and don't be shy about askin' me if there's anythin' frettin' you. I've arranged for some women to come here this afternoon to be interviewed for the post of servin' lassie . . . don't worry now,' Beatrice added swiftly as the girl shrank back and turned pale. 'I'll see to them, for I'm used to it. All you have to do is sit with me and watch and listen. And ask any questions that come to you. And you can sit with us too, Morna,' she added as her younger niece came into the kitchen.

'Sit with you?' Morna cast a disdainful look at the table. 'I've come to say I want a cup of tea. I'll drink it in the front parlour.'

'If you want it you'll drink it here, then help me and Sarah to find another maidservant.'

'Why do we need another? Isn't one enough?'

Beatrice suppressed an exasperated sigh. 'With your brother taking Sarah here for his wife next week, they need a new servant in her place. You can help us tae find someone suitable.'

'What would I know about suitable servants?'

'One day you'll be interviewin' for your own home, no doubt. There's no harm in finding out how it's done.'

'But . . .'

'Sit down, Morna,' Beatrice said firmly. 'I'll make the tea and we'll just about manage a cup before the first one arrives.'

The middle-aged woman was very capable and would make a suitable housekeeper, Beatrice thought during the interviews, but she had the look and manner of someone who might ride roughshod over a timid mistress, and Sarah would have enough to cope with as it was. Mentally she crossed the woman off her list, together with the next applicant, a superior being who was more of a lady's maid and would almost certainly sneer at a young woman who, lady of the house or not, had until recently been the servant. Beatrice, remembering her own early experiences, refused to put Sarah through the unnecessary humiliation that she herself had suffered.

'Well, what d'you think?' she asked when the last applicant had gone and the three of them – Beatrice, Sarah and Morna – were alone in the kitchen. 'I favoured the grey-haired one myself. She's gettin' on but she seems willin' enough, and she's got experience.'

'The fourth one,' Morna said decisively. 'She's been employed in some large houses and she has a good sense of etiquette.'

'Etiquette doesnae bring up a shine on a table or clean out a grate well,' Beatrice said dryly.

'She would be very helpful in other ways.'

'If you want a personal maid that badly, lassie, you'd best hire your own and find the money to pay her, for I don't see Walter putting his hand in his pocket on your behalf. Now then, Sarah, what did you think of them?'

'Me?' Sarah said, startled at being consulted. 'Whatever you think best, Mrs McCallum. Or whatever Miss Morna thinks.'

'So it's to be the one I like,' Morna said triumphantly, rising to her feet.

'Hold on a wee minute, now. As from next week Sarah's goin' tae be the mistress of this house. It'll be her job to train up the new servant, and so she must decide which one she wants to hire. Which is it to be, lass?' Beatrice asked her, ignoring Morna's flushed, angry face.

Sarah hesitated, then said shyly, 'I liked the young girl.'

'Her? She's not got any experience,' Morna sneered, 'and she's such a plain little creature. Did you not see the way she scuttled in and scuttled out again? It would be like having a mouse about the place. I'd be hard put to it not to set traps every time I saw her.'

Sarah almost caved in, but there was something about

105

the encouraging glint in Beatrice McCallum's eyes and the lift of her strongly marked brows that urged her on. 'She's eager to learn, and she comes from a large family, so she's used to takin' on her share of hard work,' she said doggedly. 'If I was to choose, I'd choose her.'

'Then that's settled. You and I will visit her home tomorrow morning and tell her that she's engaged. It'll give us a chance to have a look at her mother and find out if she's from a dirty house or a clean one. And then,' Beatrice went on, paying no heed to Morna's outraged gasp, 'we'll catch the train to Irvine to buy your wedding outfit, Sarah.'

10

Standing by Walter's side in the church vestry, dressed in the bottle-green flannel skirt and three-quarter-length jacket that Beatrice McCallum had bought for her, Sarah Neilson felt as though she were locked in a dream. Even as she obediently repeated the minister's words all she could think of was that she should be back at the house doing the ironing, or the baking, or turning out one of the bedrooms.

When the brief ceremony was over and they emerged from the side door of the church into the cold, dull November day, Walter shook hands with the minister and the church organist, who had agreed to be one of their witnesses. Money changed hands discreetly and then, leaving minister and organist behind, he and Sarah left the vestry with Beatrice, their other witness.

'I think that went very well,' Walter said cheerfully, taking Sarah's hand and drawing it through his arm. When she flinched back, startled, he tightened his arm against his side so that her hand was trapped. 'You're my wife now,' he reminded her with a smile. 'You're Mrs Walter Forsyth. From now on, my dear, we walk through life together.'

At his insistence they went from the church to a photographer's studio where, once again, Sarah numbly followed instructions. First of all she sat in a chair, hands clasped on her lap, while Walter stood behind her, handsome in his black frock coat and striped trousers, high-collared white shirt and dark-blue patterned waistcoat and tie. His bowler hat was held in the curve of one arm while his free hand rested lightly but possessively on his new wife's shoulder.

After they were pictured standing together, it was Walter's turn to take the high-backed chair while Sarah stood by his side, her gloved hand on his shoulder. Waiting for the photographer to prepare his camera, she looked down at her new husband's crisp dark hair and his hands, long fingered and with clean, oval nails, resting on his knee, and wondered when she was going to wake up from this strange dream and find herself in her little room by the kitchen, tumbling sleepily from her narrow cot to clean out the grate and set the fire.

'Ready?' the photographer asked, and she glanced up just in time to be blinded by the phosphorus flash.

Again, Walter drew his bride's hand through the crook of his elbow as they continued their walk to the house, pinning her as firmly into place by his side as her hatpins secured the cream straw hat, trimmed with a great mass of flowers, on her head.

As they progressed along the pavement with Beatrice McCallum walking just ahead of them, they met a few people going the other way. The passers-by acknowledged Beatrice with smiles and nods of the head, but in every case, once they recognised the couple walking arm in arm behind her, the smiles froze and eyes swivelled away. Unperturbed, Walter tipped his grey bowler hat to each and every one of them, calling out a cheery greeting.

'Don't let them trouble you, my dear,' he said as Sarah's hand trembled against his sleeve. 'They will come round in time.'

They had just turned the corner into Argyle Road when, to her horror, Sarah saw Samuel Gilmartin's delivery cart standing by the kerb outside a house. Her heart lurched and she tried to hurry her step in order to get past before Samuel himself appeared, but with a firm nudge of the elbow Walter kept her to his own even pace.

They had almost drawn level with the gate when Samuel came along the path, whistling cheerfully. He paused at the gate to let them past, glancing at them without great interest, and then looking again, swiftly.

Sarah, unable to meet his gaze, ducked her head and stared down at the pavement.

'Chin up, my dear,' Walter said in a quiet but clear voice. 'Don't forget that you're my wife now. You can carry yourself with pride in this town.' He patted the fingers trembling against the crook of his arm, and said again, firmly, 'Chin *up*.'

Sarah did as she was told, just in time to see Samuel whip his cap off and clutch it to his broad chest in a gesture of mocking servility. Then they had passed him by and she could feel his eyes boring into her back.

'That man,' Beatrice said, 'was being impertinent.'

'Nonsense, Aunt Beatrice, he was merely paying his respects to his betters. My dear, you're shivering,' Walter added solicitously to his bride. 'I should have insisted on you wearing warmer clothes. Finery's all very well, but we must consider the child's welfare. Never mind, we're almost home.'

When they reached the house he rang the bell and then, after waiting for a few seconds, rapped the handle of his walking stick against the door's stained-glass panel. There was a flurry and a scurry along the narrow hall and then the door flew open to reveal Nellie, the new servant, peering around its edge and bobbing a series of little curtsies as the three of them entered.

'A little faster from now on, if you please,' Walter said as he passed by the maid. 'People do not care to be kept waiting, especially on their own doorsteps.'

Sarah would have given much to be able to take refuge in the familiar kitchen, but instead she had to go into the front parlour, where the round table had been covered with the late Mrs Forsyth's best lace tablecloth and set with plates of sandwiches, cakes and biscuits.

'Tea, please, Nellie,' Walter ordered, adding, as the little maid ducked into another curtsey before scurrying to the door, 'and not too strong, mind. We're not navvies!'

'I could show her . . .' Sarah began, but he put a hand on her arm as she tried to follow the girl to the kitchen.

'She has to learn, my dear, and in any case, this is where you belong now.' He indicated the room, adding, 'But where's Morna? She should have been waiting to greet us.'

'I'll go to her room and . . .'

'Sit down, Sarah, I'll go.'

'Yes, do sit down, my dear,' Beatrice said kindly when they were alone. 'You must be feeling tired.'

'Oh no, Mrs McCallum.'

'Confused, then. It must have been quite a confusing day for you. I will go and see how the maid's getting on. After all, the girl's still new to this house.'

Left on her own, Sarah nervously jumped to her feet again and moved around the room, restless and ill at ease. Pausing before the mirror above the sideboard, she looked at her own reflection and was startled to see herself dressed in clothes other than her usual work dress and apron and cap, and with a beautiful three-strand pearl choker encircling her neck.

On the previous evening Walter had presented her with the black velvet case that had previously stood on his mother's dressing table. Sarah gasped as the jewels within sparkled up at her.

'This,' Walter announced pompously, 'was my mother's jewellery, and now, my dear Sarah, it is yours.'

'Mine? Oh no,' she said in sudden panic. 'No, I can't!'

'Of course you can. She was the last Mrs Forsyth and from tomorrow you will be the new Mrs Forsyth.'

'But Miss – your sisters should surely inherit all this.'

'They have each chosen some pieces, but it is only right that most of it should go to my wife. Now then . . .' He dipped his fingers into the case, and Sarah's eyes were dazzled by flashes of brilliant light as he stirred the contents around. There was the blue of sapphires, the green of emeralds, and the rich crimson glow of rubies; but above all, the clear vivid gleam of diamonds. There was gold and silver, tiny stud earrings and elegant drop earrings, as well as bracelets, rings and necklaces. It must, she thought, be worth hundreds if not thousands of pounds, all contained in one box.

'Ah.' Walter drew out a ring set with diamonds and rubies. 'You don't have an engagement ring – will this do?' He seized her left hand, but to his disappointment the ring would not go beyond the knuckle.

'It's the housework,' she said apologetically. 'It swells the joints.'

'Never mind, I'll have it enlarged for you.'

'No, don't spoil it!'

'Nonsense, it won't damage the ring, and you should be able to wear it since it's yours. No sense in letting it lie in a box where nobody can see it or admire it.' He set the ring aside and brought out a triple string of pearls. 'This, I think, for tomorrow. They will be perfect for your wedding day. Allow me.'

Before she could protest he had looped the strands around her throat and was fastening the diamond clasp at the nape of her neck. 'There – look at yourself, Sarah.'

The pearls were like a cold hand encircling her neck and when she reluctantly lifted her chin and looked at her reflection she saw that they looked ridiculous above her plain blouse.

'They don't look right . . .'

'Of course they don't suit the clothes you're wearing now, but tomorrow you will be in the wedding finery that Aunt Beatrice helped you to buy. The pearls will look splendid then. Turn around to face me,' he ordered, and when she obeyed, he clipped on the matching earrings before putting his hands on her shoulders and easing her back to face the mirror.

'There,' he said with satisfaction, standing close behind her, smiling at her reflected face. 'They suit you even better than they suited Mother. You have such beautiful little ears, Sarah. You have no idea how much I have wanted to decorate those perfect lobes with jewels – and now, my darling, the day has come!'

He bent and kissed one ear, then let his tongue trail around its outline, as he had done so often before. Sarah gave an involuntary shudder, and Walter, mistaking the tremor for a shiver of passion, murmured thickly, 'It won't be long, my dearest dear, before we are joined for ever as man and wife!'

Now, standing before the mirror on her wedding day, Sarah put a hand up to touch the pearl choker. It felt all wrong, wearing something that had once graced Frances Forsyth's elegant neck.

She wasn't used to wearing a hat for so long; it felt heavy, and her head itched. She reached up to scratch what she could reach of her scalp, and was drawing the first of the hatpins out when Beatrice returned.

'Tea will be brought in a moment. Keep your hat on, my dear,' she added swiftly. 'It's expected of a lady, though you may remove your gloves before eatin'.'

Sarah, crimson with embarrassment, immediately thrust the pin back in, wincing and biting her lip as it dug into her scalp. She blinked hard to hold back tears of pain as Walter ushered his younger sister into the room.

Morna's face was stiff with resentment and disapproval. 'Isn't the tea here yet?' she wanted to know.

'It's on its way. But before we have tea . . .' Walter went to stand by Sarah, putting an arm around her waist, '. . . I think you should congratulate us on our marriage, Morna, and welcome your new sister-in-law into the family.'

Morna looked for the first time at Sarah, and her beautiful hazel eyes widened as she recognised the pearls clasping Sarah's throat and on her ears. For a dreadful moment Sarah thought that the girl was going to make a scene, but just in time, Beatrice McCallum, who had been watching the three of them closely, said, 'Morna?' and after a swift glance at her aunt Morna forced a smile to her lips.

'Congratulations, Sarah, on making a very suitable marriage. And welcome to the family. Walter . . .' the smile began to slip as she looked up at her brother, '. . . I wish you whatever you may wish yourself.'

'In that case, my dear Morna, you have just wished me a very long and happy life with my dear wife and the family soon to be.'

'Not as graceful a speech as it might have been, Morna,' her aunt said dryly, 'but I suppose that it will suffice. Ah,' she went on as the door opened and Nellie appeared, carefully balancing the silver tray, 'here's tea. And very welcome it is too.'

There was an awkward moment when they took their seats at the table. Morna would have seated herself at the end, opposite her brother, but he firmly moved her aside and nodded Sarah towards the chair.

'Would you pour for us, my dear?'

'Let me,' Beatrice said swiftly. 'Let Sarah be a guest in her own home just this once, since this is her weddin' day.'

'Of course. Morna, you may pass the sandwiches,' Walter said smoothly and his sister, white with anger, did as she was told while Beatrice poured tea skilfully. Sarah watched her every move, knowing that from now on she herself would be expected to undertake that task.

Like most people of her class, Sarah Neilson had lived with hunger. She was fortunate in that, while growing up in her aunt's household, and then working for the Forsyths, she had had enough food to keep her strong and active, but the luxury of eating until she could eat no more was alien to her. She had always looked forward eagerly to the next meal, and as soon as it was over she began to look forward all over again to the next. But today, her marriage day, her appetite had entirely deserted her, and she could scarcely manage a small sandwich and a piece of shop-bought sponge cake that was so dry that every crumb threatened to stick in her throat.

Walter insisted on staying away from the shop for the rest of the week, and it was a relief to the other three inhabitants of the house when he finally returned to work. As she had always done, Sarah accompanied him to the front door, helping him on with his coat before fetching his hat and stick from the hatstand. She ran a brush over his coat and then opened the door for him, settling so well into the routine she had followed every morning when her mistress was alive that she was taken aback when he stooped to kiss her cheek.

'I shall be home for lunch at one o'clock, my dear. You should go out for a short walk this morning. The fresh air will do you good.' And then, peering up into the grey early-November sky, 'But be sure to put on warm clothing.'

As the door closed behind him Morna came into the hall.

'I've finished breakfast, Sarah. Now I have some letters to write and I do not want to be disturbed. I would like tea brought to my room at eleven o'clock.'

'Yes, Miss Morna,' Sarah said automatically, and then hurried to the kitchen, where Nellie was washing the breakfast dishes.

The girl spun round nervously when her mistress entered. 'I didn't hear the bell, missus. Mebbe it's broken . . .'

Sarah smiled at her. 'I didn't ring it, and you're best to call your mistress "ma'am", not missus.'

'Ma'am,' the girl repeated obediently, and then, realising that water was dripping from the ends of her fingers on to the floor, 'Oh, mis – I mean, ma'am!'

'It's all right, water's easily mopped up.' Sarah fetched a cloth and knelt down to mop the drips.

'You shouldnae be doin' that!' Nellie said, scandalised. 'That's my job!'

'You get on with the dishes and let me deal with this. Then,' Sarah said firmly, 'I'll show you how to make the beds and put the bedrooms to rights.'

★　★　★

The new little maid was eager to learn, and Sarah more than happy to teach her, for otherwise her days would have been long and lonely. Morna kept herself to herself, though Beatrice McCallum made a point of coming in every other day to have afternoon tea with Sarah. Under her kindly tutoring the girl learned to pour tea and pass the sandwiches that she and Nellie had made earlier, as well as the scones and cakes that she herself had baked, since Nellie had not yet mastered the art of managing the kitchen range. So far, her attempts at baking had resulted in items that were either pale or burned to a crisp.

'You're doing well,' Beatrice said, ten days after Sarah's marriage. 'You need have no concern if any of your neighbours should call on you.'

'They won't, Mrs McCallum. They pass me in the street with their noses in the air and look the other way when I go intae the shops. The assistants can scarce bring themselves tae serve me.' Sarah swallowed hard to deter the tears of self-pity threatening to thicken her voice. Even the other maidservants in the street, always ready with a friendly smile and wanting to chat, had taken to avoiding her when she went out. She was neither servant nor gentry now, and so both sections of the community had disowned her.

'Give them time and they'll come round.'

'Will they? Miss Belle hasnae called once, and this is her house.'

'My dear, you must remember that it's Walter's house now, and as his wife you have more right to be here than Belle.'

'But this is where she's always lived!'

'And where she can live again once she comes to acknowledge you as her sister-in-law and her equal.'

'That would be very hard for her, and for Miss Morna.'

'You really must stop thinking of them as Miss Belle and Miss Morna, Sarah. As for things being hard for *them*, I imagine,' Beatrice said shrewdly, 'that they have not been at all easy for you either, and yet you are doing your best and doing it well. My nieces could use some of your courage.'

Sarah smiled wanly, and Beatrice went on, 'I know that it can't be easy for you, Sarah. You look pale – are you getting enough fresh air?'

'Walter insists that I take a walk every morning, for the bairn's sake.'

'Then perhaps you need more rest. Are you sleeping well?'

'Well enough,' Sarah lied. To her great relief her new husband had announced on their wedding night that for the child's sake – his favourite phrase these days – he would not claim his conjugal rights until the baby had been safely delivered. But the nights were still a torment, for she was unable to get comfortable, being unused to sleeping in such a soft bed, never mind the fact that she, a mere servant, was in the bed that until fairly recently had been occupied by her master and mistress. The night hours dragged by slowly while she lay listening to Walter snoring and huffing and snuffling only inches away, and all she could think of was Samuel. The pain of missing him was so bad that almost every night her pillow was dampened with her tears, and in the mornings, when Walter bounded out of bed refreshed, Sarah was as tired as she had been the night before.

'Hmmm.' Beatrice leaned forwards, peering into her face, and Sarah recoiled slightly, certain that the older woman's sharp eyes would penetrate into her mind, see her utter wretchedness and somehow guess the cause of it. But instead Beatrice said, 'Then perhaps you need to lie down for a little while each afternoon to keep your strength up. And take a glass of tonic wine every day. I will have some delivered. Come along, Romeo . . .' she nudged the sleeping spaniel with the tip of her boot, '. . . we must leave young Mrs Forsyth to rest.'

Today was the day that Samuel delivered the groceries. As soon as the door had closed behind her visitor Sarah hurried to the kitchen, intending to send Nellie off to some other part of house while she herself remained in the kitchen until he arrived. But Nellie was busy in the pantry, sorting out a pile of fresh vegetables.

'Oh – has the greengrocer's delivery arrived already?'

'He's just this minute away, ma'am. Did you want to speak to him?' The little maid wiped her hands on her work apron, smearing it with earth from the leeks she had been putting away. 'I can run and fetch him, he can't have gone far.'

'No, it's all right. I just thought I might give him next week's order, but it can wait.' Sarah's voice shook with disappointment, and she put a hand to her mouth and coughed in an effort to hide her sudden weakness.

'Are you all right, ma'am? You look awful upset. Are you ill? D'ye want me tae run for the master, or fetch Miss Morna from her room?'

'No, I'm fine. There's nothing wrong with me that can't be cured by a cup of tea.'

'You've just had tea, ma'am,' Nellie said, perplexed.

'I know, but I fancy some more. And I'm sure you'd like some too.'

Nellie's eyes rounded. 'Me, Mrs Forsyth? In the middle of the afternoon?'

'Why not? I'll finish the vegetables and you fetch the tray from the parlour, then make tea for the two of us in the tin pot,' Sarah said briskly. When the little maid had scurried off to do her bidding, she took on the task of storing the vegetables, thinking as she handled them of Samuel's hands packing them into the box in readiness for the delivery. She found herself caressing the cool green leeks, the rounded firm globes of the onions, the carrots with their green feathery tops, in much the same way as he had once caressed her. Her longing to be with him again burned afresh, and if Nellie hadn't staggered back into the kitchen just then, her thin legs buckling under the weight of the silver tray, Sarah might well have ended up in tears.

11

A month after his marriage Walter Forsyth let himself into the house in the early afternoon and was puzzled to find the place silent and seemingly empty.

'Sarah?' he called, and then, since there was no reply, 'Nellie?'

Again he was greeted with silence. Becoming alarmed, he looked first into the parlour, then the small dining room, before hurrying upstairs to find the marital bedroom empty. He ran back downstairs, by now convinced that Sarah had been taken seriously ill and conveyed to the hospital, and went into the kitchen. It was also empty, but the back door stood slightly ajar, and he could hear voices and laughter in the yard behind the house.

He went outside to be greeted by the sight of his wife beating a large carpet slung from a stretch of clothes line, while their maidservant unpegged and folded dried clothing from the other two ropes.

'Sarah? Sarah, what do you think you're doing?'

She spun round guiltily, the smile fading from her flushed face. 'Walter, I didn't expect you home so early.'

'Obviously.' His voice was grim. 'And it's as well that I did come back early. Goodness knows what harm you might be doing to yourself and the child.'

'I'm only beating the dust from the carpet from Miss Belle's room. We thought we would clean the room thoroughly to make it ready for when she . . .'

He stepped forwards and took the carpet beater from her unresisting fingers, thrusting it at the frightened maid, who stood with a half-folded towel clutched to her flat little chest by both fists. Mutely, she unclenched one in order to take the beater from him.

'Perhaps,' Walter said icily, 'you would be good enough to see to the carpet when you have dealt with the laundry. After all, that's what I pay you to do.' And then, ignoring the girl's whispered, 'Yes, sir,' he escorted his wife into the house.

'What,' he asked again when they were in the parlour, 'do you think you were doing?'

'I was only helping Helen.' A few strands of hair had been loosened by Sarah's exertions; she tried to capture them and tuck them back into the soft roll of hair.

'Helen?'

'It's Nellie's real name, only everyone insists on calling her Nellie.'

'And in this household,' Walter said, 'we will continue to call her Nellie. Helen is too fine a name for a maid of all work. I don't know what her parents were thinking of, giving her such a name. And I don't know what you were thinking of either, Sarah. Quite apart from your delicate condition, it's unseemly for the mistress of the house to be beating carpets. That's what I pay the maid for.'

'I was only showing her how to do it properly.'

'It didn't look like that to me. What if someone had

come to call on you? What would they think of me if they found my wife covered in dust and with a carpet beater in her hand?'

'There's no danger of that, Walter,' Sarah protested. 'Nobody has called here since our marriage. The neighbours won't even acknowledge me in the street or the shops. Hel – Nellie's the only companion I have when you're at the shop.'

'There's Morna,' Walter was saying when the door opened and his sister hurried in, her arms full of clothing. As Walter's angry pacing had taken him to the bay window, Sarah was the first and only person she saw.

'There you are, Sarah. There's a nasty stain on one of my blouses, I think it might be ink from when I was writing a letter. See if you can remove it, and while you're at it, these other things need washing and ironing as soon as . . .'

'What do you think you're doing, Morna?' Walter interrupted, and his sister spun round to face him.

'Walter – what brings you home at this time of day?'

'Never mind me, what makes you think that Sarah – my wife – should wash and iron your clothes?'

'Because she's . . .' Morna stopped suddenly, biting her lip, then finished lamely, '. . . she's much better at these things than I am.'

'That's because she had to learn how to do them. Just as you will have to learn to do them for yourself.'

'Me? Why should I? I never had to do that sort of thing when Mother and Papa were here. Sarah always attended to my clothing – to all our laundry.'

'Because she was Mother's servant,' Walter acknowledged coldly, 'but now that she is the mistress of the house, how dare you presume to go on treating her like a servant?'

'I don't mind, Walter.' Sarah reached out to take the

bundle from Morna. 'To tell the truth, time passes slowly these days and I welcome something to do.'

Walter moved to one side, blocking her way and making it impossible for her to take the clothes from Morna. 'Morna will see to her own possessions.'

'The new maid . . .'

'If you want your laundry done and your every whim obliged, Morna, then I will expect you to contribute from now on towards the girl's wages.'

'What?' Morna's flushed face suddenly went white with anger. 'Where would I get the money from, when you've cut my allowance?'

'As I have already suggested, you could find work.'

'If Mother and Papa heard you speak to me like that . . .' Morna's lower lip began to tremble.

'If they were here we would not be having this conversation. I am the master of the house now, and by God,' Walter's voice was tight with exasperation, 'I intend to make sure that everyone under my ·roof knows it. Everyone! In future, Morna, you will obey my rules or you will find somewhere else to live.'

His sister hurled the clothes at his feet, where they lay in a colourful heap. 'So you're throwing me out of my own home now, just as you threw poor Belle out!'

'Belle knows full well that she is welcome to come back any time she wishes, and you are also welcome to stay, but only on the understanding that you both accept Sarah as my wife and your equal.'

Sarah watched, appalled, as brother and sister faced each other, Morna with her fists clenched and Walter cold and aloof.

'Then you leave me with no option,' Morna said through gritted teeth. 'I am leaving this house, Walter, and I doubt if I will ever come back to it again.'

'That, my dear, is up to you. No, Sarah,' Walter said, putting a hand on her arm as she started to protest, 'Morna is a grown woman and it's time she behaved like one, instead of a spoiled child.'

'Oh!' Morna's fists opened into claws and for a moment Sarah thought that the girl was going to fly at her brother and tear her fingernails down his face. She could tell, by the way Walter tensed, that he thought the same.

Then Morna said, 'I shall leave this house now!'

'No – please!'

'As I said, Sarah, it's up to Morna. If she no longer wants to live here, she is free to go.'

'But where to?'

'Anywhere, as long as it's not here,' Morna said, turning to the door.

'Before you go, Morna, pick up your clothes.'

She turned back again, glared at Walter, then with a sudden, furious movement bent and scooped the blouses and skirts into her arms.

'Walter . . .' Sarah said as the door closed.

'Let her go. I will not have her treating you as though you were still the servant. I suppose,' he said angrily, 'that this monstrous behaviour of hers has been going on behind my back ever since we married?'

'I didn't mind helping her.'

'But I mind. I will not have my wife treated like a skivvy.'

'They're your sisters, Walter. Your family!'

He put an arm around her shoulders. 'You're my family now, Sarah; you and the child. As long as we have each other we have no need of anyone else,' he said.

Fine words, as Beatrice McCallum was wont to often say, do not fill stomachs. As the door of the house where she had enjoyed a comfortable life closed behind Morna she suddenly realised the enormity of what she had just done. It was one thing to fly into a rage with Walter, but quite another to let her anger leave her homeless.

The weather that morning had been clear and sunny, but without Morna noticing it had become overcast, with heavy sullen clouds coming in over the Firth of Clyde. As she stood on the path, wondering what to do next, a stray snowflake drifted down, followed by another, and then another. It was as though they had chosen her exit from the house to remind her that it was now early December, a bad time to make oneself homeless.

She almost turned back to ring the bell and announce that she had decided to forgive her brother and remain beneath his roof, but was halted by the prospect of humiliating herself in such a manner, not only before Walter's amused eyes and sneering grin, but before Sarah, who until recently had made Morna's bed, darned and washed her clothes and obeyed her every command.

A tear began to well up in Morna's eye, and was firmly blinked back. She would not, *could* not, beg to be taken back. She picked up her two small cases and walked firmly down the path and along the road without bothering to close the wrought iron gate behind her. Let Walter close it, or Sarah, or the useless, tongue-tied fool of a girl they had seen fit to employ.

She pulled her shoulders back and lifted her head high on her slender, elegant neck until she was out of sight of anyone who might have been watching from the parlour's bay window. Then she had to stop, lower her cases to the ground, and lean against a wall for a moment because her knees had suddenly become quite weak. Where could she go? Dependent as she was on Walter for an allowance, she had very little money in her purse, certainly not enough to pay for a room. Her small share of the profits from the shop were locked away in a bank account and could not be touched until she was twenty-one years old, or until she married. The first event was still some two and a half years away, and the second – her eyes filled with tears of self-pity – would probably never happen now. In any case, women of her station couldn't stay on their own in hotels or boarding houses. But she had to find somewhere to sleep while she decided what to do next.

She would have liked to confide in Belle, but Belle would probably be in the shop, where the staff could, and no doubt would, spy and eavesdrop and store up even more gossip about the Forsyth family and their scandalous goings on. She could imagine the whispers already – 'Threw his sister out, him and that servant he's taken as his wife. Poor Miss Morna, what will become of her now? No skills at all, and who would want to marry her after all that's happened in that house?'

She could go to Aunt Beatrice's, where no doubt she could share Belle's room for the time being, but the thought of living under her aunt's roof made Morna shudder. And although she had never lacked for company among the town's young men and women, she realised now that the people she had been in the habit of referring to as 'friends' were in reality little more than acquaintances.

She flushed at the memory of Mrs MacAdam saying coldly, 'You will find few doors open to you until such time as your father's actions fade from people's minds.' No doubt most, if not all of the people she and her family had known and consorted with, would be of the same mind as Arthur's mother. And now, by marrying Sarah, Walter had made things much, much worse.

In that moment Morna hated her father and brother

with such passion that she kicked one of the suitcases, causing it to fall over right in the path of a little boy running along with his face tilted to the sky and his chubby hands outstretched to catch the fat snowflakes still drifting down. The child recoiled, his face beginning to crumple, and the plainly dressed young woman following close behind caught his arm and hustled him past, glaring at Morna as she skirted the suitcase.

'Naughty lady,' she heard the boy say as they hurried off, and the woman replied, 'Yes, a very rude lady!'

Morna glared at their retreating backs and then all at once the answer came to her. The child had been quite well dressed, and the woman was probably his nursemaid. Morna, Belle and Walter had had a nursemaid when they were children, a pleasant woman who had married and, with her husband, taken over a lodging house down by the shore. On several occasions Belle had taken Morna to visit Meggie who would surely be willing to offer her former charge a room for the night.

Morna smiled, picked up the suitcases, and set off with renewed confidence.

The lodging house owned by Billy and Meggie Chapman was down by the river, in Quay Street, largely inhabited by fisher folk and, in the nineteenth century, the legendary Betsy Miller, for many years captain of the brig *Clytus*. Once, Belle had insisted on reading a newspaper article about the redoubtable Betsy Miller to her disinterested brother and sister. It concerned an incident when the *Clytus*, caught in a storm, was in grave danger of being wrecked on the shore at the nearby town of Irvine. 'Lads,' said Betsy to her crew, 'I'll go below and put on a clean sark [chemise], for I wud like tae be flung up on the sands kind o' decent. Irvine folks are nasty, noticin' buddies.'

While the lady was changing her clothes, the *Clytus* had managed to struggle to deep water and safety. Betsy's crew claimed ever afterwards that her clean chemise had been the saving of them all.

'I'd like to grow up to be a strong, capable woman like that,' thirteen-year-old Belle had said, her eyes shining, while Morna wanted to know, 'Was it a pretty chemise, with blue ribbons?'

The memories fled as Morna stood looking down Quay Street. The buildings were old and the gutters choked; when it rained, as it did frequently, water tended to lie on the surface, where it became stagnant. The snow began falling faster. Soon it would cover the pavements, roofs and gardens in Argyle Road with a pretty white veil; but in Quay Street the delicate flakes seemed to melt as soon as they landed. If it snowed hard enough, and for long enough, the street would be covered with little more than a dirty grey slush.

Arriving at the door of the lodging house, Morna set her cases down with a sign of relief and, unable to find a bell pull, thumped on the scarred wooden panels with her fist.

The tenements on either side of the narrow lane were like cliffs dominating a dark ravine. A few people passed as she waited for someone to come to the door – pale-faced women in shabby clothes and one or two men, all hurrying to get into shelter and away from the thickening snowfall. The men eyed Morna in a way that made her shiver, and one, old and with a mop of grey hair matted with dirt, made a point of passing so close to her that she could smell his unwashed clothing and the nauseating reek of cheap whisky. He gave her an almost toothless grin, and she spun round and hammered with desperation at the door, which finally opened.

'Meggie?'

The large woman in the doorway peered blankly at her visitor for a moment before recognising her. 'Miss Morna, is it you?' One hand, red and shiny and steaming from recent immersion in hot water, automatically went up to tidy the wisps of hair straggling around her flushed face.

Morna noticed that the old man had paused only yards away and was eyeing her from top to toe in a most impertinent fashion. 'Of course it's me, Meggie, let me in!' She thrust one of her suitcases into Meggie Chapman's hand and moved forwards. Meggie retreated before her, and then, as Morna slammed the door, the older woman led the way down a dark passage and into the kitchen at the back of the house.

The room was filled with the aroma of the soup simmering gently on top of the kitchen range. Meggie poured two cups of black tea and added generous spoonfuls of condensed milk that made it taste unbearably sweet but did nothing to relieve the harsh flavour. Morna's thick cup was chipped almost all round the rim. She took a cautious sip and then set the cup down, trying to hide her disgust.

Meggie picked up a knife that was lying on the table beside a tin basin half filled with peeled potatoes, then took a potato from the sack on the floor and began to work on it. 'Ye don't mind me gettin' on while we talk, do ye, Miss Morna? The men need a good dinner when they come back from their work and there's so much tae do. It's a while since you've been here, eh? Miss Belle looks in now and again, but she's not been for a wee while. Not since . . .' She stopped abruptly, then said, 'I was awful sorry tae hear about yer ma. She was a good employer tae me.'

'And you'll no doubt have heard about my father leaving us, and about my brother marrying our servant. Of course you have – gossip travels fast in Saltcoats.'

'Aye, I've heard, and I'm sorry about the troubles you and Miss Belle have been goin' through. The mistress would be sore upset if she knew what had happened after her passin'.'

'Meggie, she must be turning in her grave right now. And I know she'd say that I'm doing the right thing by coming to you for help. As you said yourself, she was a good employer and she'd want you to do all you can for me. The thing is,' Morna swept on before Meggie had a chance to speak, 'I need a room.'

The potato Meggie had been peeling slipped from her hand and splashed into the basin. She stared at her visitor. 'A room? Here?'

'It's what you and your husband do, isn't it? You run a lodging house, and I'm in sore need of lodgings. D'you think I make a habit of carrying these around with me when I go calling on folk?' Morna indicated the suitcases by the door.

'But this is a lodgin' house for workmen. It's no' good enough for a lady like you, Miss Morna!'

'If I had the money I would, of course, go to a hotel. But for the moment beggars can't be choosers. Now then, do you have a room for me?'

'But . . . would ye not be better off stayin' in comfort in yer own home?'

'How can I possibly stay in a house where my brother's lost his wits and set up the servant girl in my mother's place? You've no idea what it's like, Meggie! Walter's quite beyond listening to reason, and now he's brought in a new servant who has no idea of what she's supposed to do.'

'What about Miss Belle? Is she managin'?'

'Obviously you haven't heard all the gossip. Belle's already left. She's living with our Aunt Beatrice.'

'There you are, then,' Meggie said, her face brightening. 'Mrs McCallum's got a fine big house; ye'd be more comfortable there with yer sister than in a place like this.'

'Mrs McCallum's got a fine big kennel,' Morna corrected the woman icily. 'It's overrun with dogs and she pays more attention to them than she does to people. I don't know how Belle can stomach it. I know that I couldn't. Do you have an empty room or don't you?'

'There's one – but it's not fit for the likes of you, Miss Morna,' Meggie repeated.

'Needs must.' Morna pushed the mug of tea away and got to her feet. 'Let me see it.'

12

Morna's heart plummeted when she saw the room. It was little more than a cupboard, with barely enough space for the single bed, a dresser with three drawers and an upright wooden chair. The narrow window looked out over a small dreary backyard festooned with lines of washing.

'You see?' Meggie was almost in tears with embarrassment. 'It does fine for a man who's out at work all day and just wants somewhere tae sleep at night, but it's not nearly good enough for a lady like yersel', Miss Morna.'

Morna, almost in tears herself, swallowed hard, then said with forced firmness, 'It'll do until I find somewhere more suitable. All it needs is a bit of a clean out.'

'I've got the men's dinner tae see tae . . .'

'Then we'll work on the room together,' Morna said generously. 'Do you have an apron I can borrow?'

There was little that could be done to make the dark narrow room more attractive, but with Meggie doing most of the work, they dusted the few pieces of furniture, washed the window and swept the floor. Meggie stripped the thin blankets and sagging, stained mattress from the iron bedstead and found a slightly better mattress as well as some bedding from her own store. She also found patterned curtains. 'There,' she said when they were in place, 'that makes the room look much better.'

Privately, Morna thought that the red and blue curtains only made the rest of the room look even more sad and dingy than it had before, but reminding herself that she had nowhere else to lay her head that night, she held her tongue.

The lodging house had room for ten tenants alto-gether, she was told as she sat in the kitchen watching Meggie make the dinner. The ground floor was taken up with the kitchen and adjoining washhouse, with a communal dining room and a parlour for the use of the lodgers at the front of the building.

'Most of the lodgers sleep up in the attic, and me and Billy have a room at the front of the house on the same floor as you,' Meggie explained as she chopped onions. 'There's another two wee rooms there for folk that like their privacy and are willin' tae pay a wee bit extra. One of them's the room you're takin'; the man that had it died just last week.'

'In that room?' Morna asked, horrified.

'No, he was killed in an accident on the railway, poor soul. Buried in a pauper's grave, for he'd nob'dy in the world tae give him a proper send-off.

'The top floor's just one big room with eight cots in it.' Meggie tossed several double handfuls of the onions into a huge pot simmering on the range, wiped her stinging eyes with the back of a plump forearm, and scrubbed her hands against the sacking apron she wore. She disappeared into the small pantry and returned with a stained paper parcel which she unwrapped on the table to reveal a large slab of dark red meat mottled with strings and clumps of grey-white fat. Morna recoiled from the sight and smell of it.

'What's that?' It looked to her like something Aunt Beatrice would feed to her yapping dogs.

'Tonight's stew.' Meggie clamped one hand on the revolting mess and used the other to saw at it with a large carving knife. 'The men like a plate of stew after their day's work.'

Morna moved to a chair at the far end of the table, trying hard not to look at the meat being dissected at the other end, but even if she managed to avoid looking at it, she could still smell it. The thought of actually eating it was repellent, though once it had joined the vegetables in the pot and the whole concoction had been simmering for a good while the smell began to seem more tempting. It had been a long day and she had eaten nothing since breakfast.

When the town's sirens began to signal the end of the working day Meggie carried cutlery and plates to the dingy room where her lodgers ate and then returned to the kitchen to cut a loaf into thick slices.

'Billy and me eat here, for there's not room for all of us in the other room when the house is full. You'll eat with us, of course,' she said, and then, as the front door opened and a man's voice called her name, she went on, 'That's Billy now; he's usually first in.'

There was something about the woman's voice, and the tension in her face as she watched for the kitchen door opening, that made Morna uneasy. She had never met Meggie's husband and had no idea what sort of man he was.

'He'll not mind me being here, will he?'

'No, no,' Meggie assured her without much conviction as the door swung open and Billy Chapman walked in.

For some reason, possibly because Meggie was quite tall for a woman and well-built into the bargain, Morna had expected her husband to be large, but the man who marched into the kitchen and tossed the canvas sack he carried into one corner was at least half a head smaller than Meggie and only about half her girth. His movements and his manner were those of a larger man and his voice, when he barked, 'Is the dinner ready?' was deep and powerful.

'Aye. I'll put yours out now, Billy.'

'Dae that. I'm bloody famished.' He grabbed the back of a wooden chair and hauled it out from the table. Meggie flinched at the obscenity and looked apologetically at Morna.

'Billy . . .' she began, but her husband had noticed their visitor.

'Who's this?' Instead of sitting down, he stayed where he was, his dirty hands gripping the chair back as though ready to use it as a weapon.

'It's Miss Morna, Billy.' Meggie was ladling soup into a bowl as she spoke. 'Ye've heard me speakin' about Miss Morna that I used tae look after afore we got married.' She set the bowl before her husband.

'Oh aye. Just visitin', are ye? Callin' on a faithful old servant?' A faint sneer underlined the last three words.

'Not exactly,' Morna began as the street door opened again. Deep voices could be heard in the hallway, together with the clatter of boots on the wooden flooring.

'We'll tell you later, Billy. Best get the men's dinners first,' Meggie said hurriedly. Using both hands she hefted the heavy soup pot from the range and glanced at Morna, nodding towards the bread slices which she had piled on to a tin tray. 'Bring them through for me, will ye?'

Morna was happy to oblige rather than be left alone with Billy Chapman.

The long table was crowded with men and the room rang with the sound of their loud rough voices, but when the two women entered the voices died away and Morna suddenly found herself the centre of interest.

'Who's this then, Meggie?' one of the men asked. 'Got yersel' a new servin' lassie, have ye?'

'Ye must be payin' her awful well, judgin' by her fine clothes,' someone else said, and Morna went crimson as a snigger ran all round the table.

'Now you behave yerselves, lads. This is Miss Morna Forsyth that I used tae look after when she was a bairn, and she's come tae call on me.' Meggie dumped the pot of soup down on the table. 'Put the bread down there, pet.'

Morna did as she was told and then stood close to Meggie as the woman ladled soup into the bowls stacked on the table. As each bowl was filled it was passed to the nearest man, who passed it on round the table. They were all dressed in heavy working clothes, and some still wore their cloth caps. Their clothes were shabby, and their hands, Morna noted with a shiver of disgust, were filthy, the nails black. She winced as she watched dirty fingers seizing slices of bread and cramming them into mouths.

'They haven't even washed,' she whispered as she and Meggie left the men to their meal and returned to the kitchen. 'You always made us wash our hands before we ate.'

'They're too hungry tae wash first. It'd be more than my life was worth tae tell that lot they werenae goin' tae be fed until they wash their hands.' Meggie's hearty laugh boomed out and her large bosom shook with mirth.

'But think of the filth they're putting into their mouths with the food! They'll make themselves ill!'

'Not them. They've eaten dirt all their lives and it's not done them any harm. It's the way they are,' Meggie said, and Morna shivered again.

'Come tae live with us?' Billy Chapman's mouth fell open in astonishment and Morna, catching a glimpse of half-chewed stew and potatoes behind a ragged wall of yellow teeth, looked away hastily. Despite her earlier misgivings the stew was edible, but now she suddenly realised that she had lost her appetite.

'Why wid gentry like her want tae live with us?'

'I told you, Billy, she doesn't get on with the lassie her brother's married tae, and she's got nowhere else tae stay.'

'What about yer friends? Surely a fine lady like yersel' has plenty o' them?'

'Not the sort of friends who would welcome me into their homes,' Morna said bleakly.

'And you thought *we* would? Well, I suppose this is a lodgin' house,' the man said, scraping up the last of the stew and mopping the gravy with a wedge of bread. 'But it's for workin' men. Women cause trouble.'

'I can assure you that I have no intention of "causing trouble", as you put it,' she snapped, deeply offended by the accusation. The man must be mad to think that she could be interested in any of the loud, dirty creatures who were wolfing their food down in the other room.

'Women always cause trouble.'

'Billy, it's not for long,' Meggie pleaded. 'Just until she finds somewhere else.'

'If she's lodgin' here then she'll have to pay for the room. Two shillin' a week.'

'Two shillings?' Morna asked incredulously, and only just managed to stop herself from going on with, 'For that nasty little cupboard?'

'It's an awful lot, Billy. More than we would charge a man.'

'A workin' man,' he pointed out. 'You and me know how much every penny matters tae folk that have tae slave till they drop for no more than a pittance. Wealthy folk can afford tae pay a bit more.'

'I can't. I've scarcely got any money at all.'

'So ye're expectin' me and my wife tae feed and house ye for nothin', are ye? Just because she was once your nursemaid?'

'No, but – you'll have to give me time. I'll find some sort of work.'

'Doin' what?' he asked derisively, and then, as she fell silent, he shrugged his muscular shoulders. 'All right, ye can stay, but until ye can pay yer way ye'll have tae work for yer keep. That means helpin' Meggie here tae see tae the house. And she'll have tae do her fair share, Meggie. You're not her servant any longer. Now that that's settled . . .' Billy Chapman pushed himself back from the table and began to unfasten the thick leather belt around his waist, '. . . I'll have a cup o' tea. And ye can let the lassie pour it, Meggie. She's had her dinner – she might as well start earnin' it.'

Only pride kept Morna from running back home or begging her Aunt Beatrice for help. While Billy Chapman sat by the range on that first evening reading his paper and smoking his foul-smelling pipe, she and Meggie cleared the table in the dining room and washed and dried the dishes. They brought in a great pile of washing from the back-yard and spent the rest of the evening ironing and folding, sewing on buttons and mending tears. Then, after Billy had gone to his bed, they steeped oatmeal for breakfast and set the long table in readiness for the next morning.

When she was finally free to escape to her narrow little room she stripped and washed herself as best she could in water so cold that it might have been lying out in the yard all day, drying herself with a threadbare towel that, as Aunt Beatrice might say, was worn enough to spit peas through. She was pulling her nightdress over her head when she heard a floorboard creak just outside the door.

'Meggie?' she asked tremulously. There was no reply, so she crept over to press her ear against the crack between the door and the frame. All was silent but she was certain that there was someone in the darkness outside; someone breathing and listening – and waiting.

'Go away!' Morna said fiercely. 'Go away or I'll scream for Mr Chapman!'

Again, there was no sound, but as she looked down she thought that she saw the door handle moving very slightly. There was no lock or bolt on the door, but she snatched up the little wooden chair and wedged its back firmly beneath the door handle. 'Go away!' she said again, and after a moment she heard another board creak, but further away this time, as though whoever had been hovering on the other side of the door panels had realised that he was not going to get into the room, and had retreated.

She stood listening for a long time, one hand pressed against her fast-beating heart, but all was quiet.

Before getting into the bed she hauled the blanket and sheet off and examined the mattress, but although Meggie Chapman's home might be shabby, it was clean, and there was no sign of bedbugs. Reassured, Morna blew out her candle.

The mattress was thin and lumpy and the blanket in-adequate on such a cold night. She curled into a tight ball, convinced that she would never manage to sleep, exhausted though she was, but even as the thought went through her mind her eyes closed. Before she knew she had slept, Meggie was tapping on the door and whispering to her that it was time to start making the men's breakfasts.

With no time to brush her hair out or pin it up properly, only a splash of icy water for her face and little more than a minute to pull her clothes on, Morna felt as though she had been dragged through a hedge backwards, but even so, the men eyed her appreciatively as they gathered to break their fasts. She looked back at each one of them stonily, trying to work out which of the noisy, grimy lot had been creeping around outside her door the night before.

It was clear from the way Meggie treated them and the way they behaved towards her, that the woman looked on her lodgers as the children she had never borne. She treated each one of them with the same cheerful affection she had shown to Morna, Walter and Belle years before. To Morna, it was like watching a lion tamer working confidently within a cage full of dangerous and unpredictable beasts.

One lodger stood out from the others; a younger man, less rough and rowdy than his companions. Once or twice Morna happened to catch his eye and each time he gave her a warm smile, but she looked away at once. She stayed close to Meggie at all times and every time the older woman left the room Morna followed close on her heels.

'Ye've no need tae worry about the men,' Meggie assured her when they were back in the kitchen. 'They're just a bunch of grown laddies – loud and daft, mebbe, but not a bad bone between them. We'd not let them stay here if they were out tae cause trouble.'

'Are you sure about that? Someone was outside my room last night.'

'Ach, he'd just be goin' tae the privy out in the back-yard. We don't let them use the one by the kitchen; Billy likes to keep it just for the two of us – and you, now.'

'Whoever it was tried the handle of my door.'

'Did he now?' Meggie said, a sudden glint in her eye.

'I had to push the back of the chair under the handle before I felt safe enough to go to bed.'

'We'll see about that,' Meggie said, and before Morna could utter another word the woman had stormed out of the kitchen and along the passageway to the front room. Morna, cowering at her back, heard a sudden babble of male voices as the door was thrown open; a babble that stopped as though cut by a knife when Meggie said in a bellow that seemed to fill the entire house, 'Which one of youse was sniffin' around outside that lassie's door last night?'

She waited and then, as nobody spoke, swept on with, 'Right. I'll just say that I know he's no' speakin' up because he knows as well as the rest of ye that he'd be put out right this minute tae sleep in the streets. But there'll be no more warnin's. Miss Morna Forsyth's a lady and she'll be treated as such while she's livin' under my roof. Is that understood?'

There was an immediate rumbling chorus of agreement. 'That's better,' Meggie roared. 'This is a lodgin' house, no' a madhouse, and I'll thank the lot o' ye tae remember that!'

She slammed the door and came back along the passage, sweeping Morna before her into the kitchen. 'That's them told. Lucky Billy's already gone off tae work, for he'd have made the man speak up all right, and then kicked him out intae the street. We'll say nothin' of this tae him.'

'Whoever it is'll be angry with me,' Morna whimpered. 'I wish I'd never said anything to you.'

'Away ye go, lassie, nob'dy's goin' tae bother ye, let alone be angry with ye, for they all want tae keep a roof over their heads and food in their bellies and they know well enough that I'll no' have any badness in this house. Now then,' Meggie said briskly, 'we can sit down and have our own breakfast while they finish theirs and get off tae work.'

Morna had thought, when she ventured from the kitchen to collect the breakfast dishes, that all the lodgers had gone out into the still-dark morning and the coast was clear, but when she went into the stuffy front room one man remained at the table, a newspaper held up before him.

'Oh . . . !' she said in dismay, and was backing out hurriedly when the newspaper was lowered and the young man she had noticed earlier said, 'Don't leave on my account, miss.'

'I thought everyone had gone.'

'I start work later than the others, for I work in a shop, not the dockyard or the railway,' he said in a soft, pleasing Irish accent. And then, nodding towards the newspaper, 'I like to take advantage of the peace once they've all gone. It's the only time I have for a quiet read.'

Morna moved back into the room. This one was safe enough; she was quite certain that he was not the man who had silently tried her door handle the previous night. 'Go on reading, I won't be a minute,' she said, but he had already put the newspaper aside and leaped to his feet.

'I've finished it. Let me help you.'

'You don't have to.'

'Sure, and it's no bother at all. I like to be useful.' He

smiled down at her, a dazzling smile that seemed to light up his entire face, and began to stack the plates and mugs, making good use of every inch of the tray.

'You're better at this than I am,' Morna said ruefully, watching his deft movements.

'That's because I'm probably more used to this sort of work than you are. My parents had a large family and we were all expected to turn our hands to whatever needed doin'. Now a lady like yourself would leave this sort of work to her servants, am I not right?'

'You are, but now I'm going to have to learn to do these things for myself.' She reached out to lift the full tray, but he had already picked it up as though it weighed next to nothing.

'I'll take it; it's too heavy for you,' he said, and then, with a mock bow, 'Lead on, my lady, and I shall follow, though it may be to the ends of the earth.'

'The kitchen will do,' Morna said primly, and was glad, as she went ahead of him, that he could not see the smile spreading across her face. It had been a long time since she had had cause to smile.

Meggie was up to her elbows in dishwater. 'Doin' your good deed for the day, Sam?' she asked as the two young people came into the kitchen.

'Aye, Meggie, I am, and it's a pleasure to help such a lovely young lady. Two lovely young ladies,' he added, setting the tray down.

'It's well seen that you've kissed the Blarney Stone,' the woman said amiably. 'Away tae yer work now and let us get on with ours.

'He's a nice lad, but ye have tae take everythin' he says with a pinch of salt,' she went on when the lodger had gone, with one final sparkling smile for Morna. 'Irishmen are given to flattery. It's nice, mind. Scotsmen can be awful slow with the compliments and a woman likes a wee bit of attention now and again.'

'He's cleaner than the rest; he said he doesn't work in the dockyard or on the railway.'

'Sam Gilmartin works for Mrs Smith that runs the greengrocer's in Hamilton Street. It's handy to have a lodger in that sort of work,' Meggie said as she plunged a pile of plates into the sink, splashing water everywhere, 'because some days Mrs Smith lets him bring back a box of greens that havenae sold. Use that cloth hangin' on the nail, Miss Morna, tae dry the dishes. Then we'll give the house a clean. We can leave the washin' till this afternoon.'

'But we ironed the laundry last night!'

'That was yesterday's washin'. The men pay a few pence extra every week tae get their clothes seen tae,' Meggie explained. 'And with so many of them in dirty work I have tae use the washtub every day. Ye'll find that there's never a spare minute in this place!' She gave a rusty chuckle, while Morna felt her heart sink.

13

By the time Meggie was satisfied with their labours that morning Morna was aching all over, and would have given the very clothes off her back for the chance to wash in hot water and then crawl into her narrow, lumpy bed to sleep for at least twelve hours. But there was still the shopping to do.

'Those men work hard and they need a lot of food to keep their strength up.' Meggie pushed her feet, lumpy with bunions, into shoes well worn down at the heel and wrapped a woollen shawl around her shoulders. 'And if we don't get to the shops in good time we'll have missed all the bargains. Here . . .' She thrust a huge shopping basket at Morna, '. . . you can carry that.'

'But people will see me!'

'Aye, lassie, they will, and they'll mebbe stare and whisper, but ye made yer choice when ye knocked on my door, and ye cannae hide away for the rest of yer life. Best tae face them all and get it over with.'

There were stares aplenty. Even folk who didn't know who Morna was gaped as the two of them went from shop to shop, for she and Meggie, one in clothes that had seen better days and the other smartly dressed, made an ill-assorted pair. But Meggie was right – she couldn't hide away in the lodging house for ever, so she lifted her chin high and stared past the curious faces instead of full at them. But when she realised that they were in Dockhead Street, and that Meggie was guiding her towards the entrance to Forsyth's shop, she faltered.

'I can't go in there!'

'I need gas mantles and that's where I always buy them.' The older woman gripped Morna's arm with a large firm hand and marched the girl into the shop. 'Besides, I think you owe it to yer brother and sister tae let them know ye're safe, and bidin' with me.'

As it happened, Belle had emerged from her small cubby-hole in order to show one of the assistants how to set up a display. When she saw the newcomers she immediately left the girl and came hurrying over. 'Morna, I've been so worried! Where have you been?'

'With me, Miss Belle, and she's quite safe.'

'Meggie?' Belle stared, then rallied. 'She's staying with you? But you run a lodging house, don't you – for work-men?' She said the final word with a faint shudder of distaste.

'Aye, Miss Belle, I do, and glad the poor souls are for somewhere tae lay their heads and fill their bellies after a hard day's work. Miss Morna's earnin' her keep by helpin' me until she can find somewhere more suited. I'll just go and see about they gas mantles,' Meggie said tactfully.

'You can't stay in that lodging house!' Belle said as soon as the sisters were alone.

'Why not?'

'Because it's completely unsuitable! Come with me,' Belle demanded when her sister pursed her lips and glared at her. She caught Morna's arm and dragged her into the

146

back office where Walter was working on a ledger. 'Walter, Morna's gone to stay with Meggie Chapman in that lodging house down by the shore. Tell her that she must go back home at once!'

'It seems to me, Belle, that nobody can tell Morna anything these days. But I am sure she knows that any time she cares to return to Argyle Road my wife and I will be pleased to see her.'

Every fibre of Morna's being longed to be back in her comfortable room with a servant down in the kitchen to minister to her needs, but her pride would not let her admit it. So she drew herself up, stiffening her spine until she could almost hear it creaking under the strain, and said coldly, 'I am very well suited where I am.'

'What's got into you, Morna? If Mother only knew the worry you've caused us!'

'The worry *I've* caused? What about—'

'That's enough, Morna,' Walter thundered, and then, at an agitated gesture from Belle, who could see through the observation window behind her brother that some of the people in the shop were turning to stare, he lowered his voice and went on, 'As I said, you are welcome to return to the house at any time. Your room is still there, waiting for you, but whether you like it or not, Morna, it is my house now, presided over by my wife, and you must accept that.'

'Accept that the house I was born in, the house I grew up in, is now the domain of our kitchen maid? How can you ask me to accept such a situation?'

Colour stained Walter's cheekbones. 'Sarah stopped being our kitchen maid the day she married me,' he said stiffly. 'Are you going to see reason and come back to Argyle Road or are you not?'

'I am not!'

'In that case I shall tell Sarah that she may look on your room as the new nursery,' he said, and left the office.

'Morna, see sense!' Belle begged, almost in tears. 'We can't let this business tear the family apart.'

'Walter seems to have done that already. I will not go back to that house under his terms.'

'Then come to Aunt Beatrice's. She has room for us both.'

'And let her start telling me what to do? She'd be just as bad as Walter. Belle, I left most of my clothes and all of my jewellery in my room. Could you arrange to have it packed up and taken to Aunt Beatrice's for safe keeping?'

'But you'll need your clothes, surely?'

Morna, thinking of the tiny cold room where she had spent the night, with its shaky dresser and the nail hammered into the door to act as a hanger, gave her sister a smile with more bitterness in it than amusement. 'I've got all I need for the moment. You'll make sure that the rest of my things are kept for me?'

'Of course, but Morna, you can't stay in a place like that. It's not seemly.'

'It will do for the moment.'

'And then where will you go? What will you do? How will you support yourself?'

'I'll think of something,' Morna said. But as she and Meggie left the shop she had to swallow hard to halt the tears pressing against the backs of her eyes. Only a month or two earlier her life had been comfortable and safe, but now the future, which had once consisted of marriage to some as yet unknown man who adored her and was willing to give her everything she might want, had become an unknown journey. And she had no way of knowing what might lie at the end of it.

★   ★   ★

'Perhaps,' Clarissa Pinkerton said thoughtfully, 'the maidservant will die in childbirth. Do you think that's likely?'

'I don't know,' Belle said, startled.

'It does happen, you know.' Clarissa paced around Beatrice's parlour, which, unlike most homes of the era, was quite sparsely furnished and allowed room for pacing. 'But then again, servants tend to be strong.'

'You surely don't want the girl to die, do you?'

'I was thinking that if she did die, Walter would be left a widower with a small child. He would require comforting and the child would need a mother.'

'You would consider marrying Walter after what he's done to you?'

'I'm a foolish girl, I know, but to tell you the truth, Belle, I have never in my life considered marriage to anyone but your brother. Even when we played together as children I always saw Walter as the father of my dolls.'

'Oh, Clarissa!'

'I know – it's a foolish weakness of mine, but I can't seem to shake it off.'

'You would even raise Sarah's baby as your own?'

'I admit that if the child also died during the birth that would make life easier. But if it were to survive I could perhaps come to look on it as my own and be a good mother to it. A better mother, I am sure, than that girl could ever be,' Clarissa said, wrinkling her nose. 'And it would be a very unselfish act, don't you think? Forgiving the man who had so grievously wronged me, in order to care for him and for his motherless child.' She paused in her pacing, thinking, and then added cheerfully, 'And of course, there are always nursemaids. We rarely saw my mama all through the years of our childhood. We were in the nursery with the nursemaids and she was busy with the house, and visiting friends and entertaining. That's as it should be. Yes, I am convinced that I would be willing to marry Walter if he were to become free of that dreadful girl. And just think . . .' she came to where Belle was sitting, taking both hands and pulling her friend to her feet, '. . . you and I would be sisters-in-law, just as we have always wanted. Now wouldn't that be a lovely, happy ending to all this unpleasantness?'

At that moment, if Clarissa had only known it, Sarah would almost have been willing to look favourably on the other girl's plans for her early demise. She was bent over a basin in the front bedroom, relieving her queasy stomach of the lunch that Walter had insisted on her eating, while Nellie stood by, wringing her hands.

When the paroxysm was over, Sarah wiped her mouth and smiled faintly at the little maid. 'There now, all over. No need to look so worried; women can have upset bellies when they're carrying bairns.'

'But not all the time, surely.'

'It's not all the time, Nellie, it's only now and again.' Sarah picked up the basin and carried it out of the bedroom and along the passage to the bathroom as the maid hurried after her.

'Let me do that for you, ma'am. You should be havin' a rest, like the master says ye have tae do every afternoon. You look so pale!'

'I don't want to lie down; I want a cup of tea to take the bad taste from my mouth. And I can manage the basin fine,' she added firmly as Nellie tried to take it. 'You go and make tea for the two of us and I'll be down in a minute.'

Alone in the bathroom she splashed cold water on to her face and then dried herself slowly, staring into the mirror. As Nellie had said, her normally pink cheeks were pale, and quite sunken, as though the child within her was drawing flesh from her face and using it to swell her belly. She emptied and rinsed the basin listlessly before taking it down to the kitchen.

The tea was welcome, but the smell of mutton boiling on the range for that evening's dinner made her stomach twinge uneasily again. She stepped out of the back door and took several deep breaths of air before returning to the kitchen table. 'While we're drinking our tea I'll show you how to polish Mrs Forsyth's silver,' she said briskly.

'You mean your silver, ma'am. You're Mrs Forsyth,' the maid said, perplexed.

'I was speaking of the master's mother. She was my mistress up until she died and Mr Forsyth went away and Mr Wal – my husband became the master,' Sarah was trying to explain when there was a swift, familiar rat-a-tat on the back door. Before Nellie could scramble to her feet it swung open and Samuel Gilmartin walked in, a basket over one arm.

'Delivery, Nellie,' he said cheerfully, then stopped as he saw Sarah.

'Mornin', madam.' He put a faint emphasis on the second word.

Sarah's heart, as always happened when she saw him, gave a jump and then began to beat faster.

'You're early on your rounds today.'

'Mrs Smith wants me back at the shop to help with shiftin' things around.' One hand swept aside the cutlery they had been about to clean, so that he could set the basket on the table. 'Hope that's not inconveniencin' you – madam.'

'Of course not. Nellie, put the vegetables away. Would you like a cup of tea, Mr Gilmartin?' Sarah jumped up and went to fetch another cup from the dresser.

'Are ye sure that's allowed, *madam*?' Again, he sneered out the final word with mock servility, and Sarah felt heat rise to colour her pale cheeks. When she turned, clutching the cup in both hands, she saw that he was standing by the table, chin jutting out, his gaze sweeping slowly down from her face to the firm swell of her stomach.

'It's allowed if I say it is,' she shot back at him and poured the tea with shaking hands while Nellie, quite unaware of the tension between her two companions, unpacked the basket, darting like a busy little field mouse between the table and the pantry until Samuel stopped her with a hand on her arm.

'Save yer legs, lass,' he said. 'Take the basket tae the shelves, like this.' He picked it up and went into the pantry, closely followed by Nellie.

Left alone in the kitchen, Sarah sat back down again and waited, listening to Samuel's musical voice rising and falling. The door was almost completely closed and she couldn't make out what he was saying, but judging by Nellie's frequent giggles and the occasional squeal of shocked amusement, he was charming her the way he had once charmed Sarah. The way, she thought, sick with longing for him, he probably charmed all the maidservants on his rounds.

It seemed to take a long time before the two of them emerged from the pantry, the basket empty, Nellie glowing, and Samuel smiling lazily at her as he slid on to a chair opposite Sarah and picked up the cup waiting for him. He took a deep drink and then gave a sigh of pleasure and ran a hand over his mouth. She watched, mesmerised.

'Well now, you make a lovely cup of tea, madam. Or is it you that makes it?' he added, turning to Nellie. When she nodded, beaming, he said in his soft, seductive Irish brogue, 'Perfect, it is. Hot and strong, just the way I like it.'

He emptied the cup with a second swallow, and when Nellie asked eagerly, 'Would you like some more?' said, 'Lass, I'd like fine tae stop and drink more tea with ye, but I've got the rest of my deliveries to make, and your mistress here'll be givin' the both of us the edge of her tongue if I keep ye from yer work any longer.' He stood up, grinning down at the little maid. 'But there'll be other days,' he added, then picked up his basket and turned to go.

'Wait . . .' Sarah said swiftly. 'I'll pay you the money owed.'

He raised his eyebrows at her. 'You can pay Mrs Smith at the end of the week. Is that not what the last mistress of this house always did?'

'The money's here, and I know how much is due. I might as well give it to you now.' She got up and went to the inner door. 'Follow me,' she said, and saw him wink at Nellie before doing as he was bid.

In the front parlour he stared at the pictures and the flock wallpaper, the ornaments, heavy window hangings and comfortable chairs, and then gave a long, low whistle. 'Well, Sarah, ye've landed on yer feet, have ye no'?'

'I'd as soon be livin' in one room with you.' The words were out before she could stop them. She put a hand on his arm, but he freed himself with a shrug.

'Then you're a fool.'

'No, I'm just a lassie who wants to be with the right man.'

'Is that me ye're talkin' about? Did I not tell ye that I'm no' the marryin' kind?' he said, then went over to the mantelshelf and picked up a china ornament, turning it over in his big hands. 'Though mebbe I should start thinkin' the way you did, for I'd not mind livin' in this sort of comfort for a change. Tell me,' he went on, putting the ornament back exactly where he had found it, 'who else lives in this house now, besides you and yer fine new husband and that bonny wee maidservant?'

Her heart twisted in her breast at his description of Nellie, who was quite plain, but who had looked almost pretty earlier as she glowed beneath Samuel's admiring attention. The girl was clearly smitten and would be a ripe plum for his plucking if he so minded.

'Only the three of us.'

'What happened tae the rest of the Forsyth fam'ly, then?'

'Miss Belle's stayin' with her aunt just now.'

'There's another one, is there not? A pretty lass with hair the colour of a cornfield under the summer sun, and bonny eyes that would charm the soul out of a man.'

Sarah's heart twisted again. 'Miss Morna? You've seen her?'

'Only comin' out of the front door now and again when I've been deliverin' vegetables round the back,' he said casually. 'So – is she not livin' at home any more?'

'She's . . .' Sarah didn't have the faintest idea where Morna had gone to; Walter, when asked, had merely snapped that his sister had made her bed and now she must lie in it as best she could. 'She's with friends,' she finished lamely.

'Is that right, now? With friends? Well, it's been nice seein' ye, Sarah, and seein' how well ye've done for yersel', but I'll have tae go on my way, so if ye want tae pay me for the vegetables ye'd best be getting' on with it.'

'Samuel . . .'

'I've got work tae do. Some of us still have tae earn our keep.'

Defeated, she went to the writing bureau where, she

knew, Walter kept some money. There was enough, and she carefully counted out the right number of coins and then handed them over to Samuel, who pocketed them before pulling his cap down over his head.

'Can you not stay and talk for a few minutes? I've missed you these past weeks.'

His eyes laughed at her, but not in a friendly way. 'And why would a fine lady like you want tae talk tae a message lad like me?'

'Samuel, please,' she begged, but he had already moved out into the hallway and was heading for the front door. Sarah caught up with him and put a restraining hand on his arm just as the door opened and Walter came in, halting at the sight of the two of them standing close together in the narrow hallway.

14

'What's this?'

Sarah stared at her husband in dumb dismay, and it was left to Samuel to say easily, 'I've just been deliverin' the vegetables, sir, and the mistress here was payin' me what's due.'

'Paying you? You gave this man money?' Walter turned to his wife.

'I – I thought it was the right thing to do . . .'

'My dear, we never give money to the delivery people. For all we know they might just run off with it.'

Sarah dared not look at Samuel, but she was keenly aware of the way his big body tensed with anger at the accusation.

'I'd never do that, *sir*,' he said with just enough emphasis on the final word to make it sound like an insult. 'Bein' poor doesnae mean that I'm dishonest as well.'

Walter ignored him. 'How much did you pay him?' he asked, and when Sarah named the sum, he swung round to Samuel, his hand outstretched. 'Give me the money.'

When it had been placed in his palm he counted it

out carefully, then nodded. 'It's the correct sum. Did you make him sign a receipt for it?'

'There was no need. I knew that . . .'

'Never pay money without getting a receipt. Wait here,' Walter ordered Samuel, then took Sarah's arm and drew her with him into the parlour, where he found a sheet of paper in the bureau. As he dipped a pen in the inkwell and wrote a few brief words, Sarah looked towards the open door. She could see Samuel in the hall, standing where he had been left, his back to her and his fists tightly clenched by his sides.

'You – fellow. Come in here,' Walter called when he had finished writing, and when Samuel appeared at the parlour door he said, 'Come over here and mark this paper with a cross.'

As Samuel passed Sarah, she could feel the waves of anger flowing from him, and was terrified in case his rage broke. There was no doubt at all that he was by far the stronger of the two men, and if provoked enough he could possibly kill Walter with one blow.

Dumbly, she watched as he picked the sheet of paper up, ran his eyes over it, then said, 'I don't need tae make a cross, Mr Forsyth. I can read and I can sign my name.'

'Oh? Then do so,' Walter said coldly, and when Samuel relinquished the pen and stepped back he lifted the paper and examined it closely. 'Hmmm. Very well, here's the money. Make sure that every penny of it is put into Mrs Smith's hand.'

'I'd as soon leave it with you, Mr Forsyth, so that Mrs Smith can send in her account and be paid in the usual way.'

Samuel's voice was soft, yet it held a note that brought colour to the other man's cheeks and a snap to his voice when he retorted, 'And so would I, but apparently my wife would prefer to trust you to deliver it yourself. So take it.'

Samuel hesitated, swinging his head round to look at Sarah with eyes that burned with such cold anger that she was convinced his temper was about to break. She took a step towards the door, ready to run to the kitchen and scream for Nellie's help, but he turned back to Walter and held out his hand for the money. Once it had been transferred, Walter led the way out into the hall, stepping back so that he stood between Samuel and the front door.

'The servants' entrance is at the back of the house. The front entrance is for the family and their friends.'

Samuel hesitated, then shrugged and tugged at the peak of his cap. 'Aye, sir. Thank you, sir,' he said, and then as he turned to walk past Sarah, 'and thank ye, ma'am, for the tea. It was very welcome.'

As she pressed herself against the wall to let him by, Sarah was briefly aware of the familiar smell of him – a blend of sweat and sheer masculinity. She stayed where she was as Walter passed her in turn, aware of his entirely different smell of hair oil and soap. When the door at the back of the hall closed behind the two men she sagged against the hatstand as her knees threatened to give way.

Samuel swaggered through the kitchen, picking up his empty basket and tossing a cheerful wink in Nellie's direction as he opened the back door. Even as he stepped into the backyard he heard the door slam violently behind him. The cocky grin immediately vanished, to be replaced with a snarl of rage and hatred. Turning, he lifted one hand in an obscene gesture in the direction of the closed door before walking around the side of the house.

The slam of the back door brought Sarah to her senses.

Realising that she couldn't afford to be found swooning in the hall, she hurried into the parlour, where Walter found her tidying her hair with trembling fingers before the mirror.

'Sarah, my dear,' he began, in the voice he used for gentle chastisement, 'you must remember in future that I pay the household bills at the end of each week. You do not give money to errand boys. These people can't be trusted – for all we know they could pocket it and take to their heels.'

'But Samuel Gilmartin has been making deliveries here ever since Mrs Forsyth first employed me. I know that he would never steal money.'

'That's because he hasn't been tempted – until now. Where did you get the money?' Walter wanted to know, and when Sarah's pale face turned crimson and her eyes flew to the bureau drawer, he pulled it open and looked inside. 'I hope he didn't see you take it from here? He did, didn't he?' he rushed on as she opened her mouth to deny the charge. 'For goodness' sake, Sarah, you must learn to be more cautious! That man is taking advantage of your new position within this household, and I will not have it! Is it true that you allowed him to drink tea in my house?'

'He called when Nellie and I were making tea in the kitchen . . .' Sarah faltered.

'If Belle had any sense of duty she would be here, teaching you how the mistress of the house behaves,' he fumed. 'Nellie should have been making the tea and you should have been waiting for it in here, not in the kitchen where that man could worm his way into your favour! I shall complain to Mrs Smith and tell her that he is not to call here again.'

'Walter, no! You could lose him his place!'

'I have no intention of demanding his dismissal – but if Mrs Smith sees fit to turn him off I would not argue with her. He has a bold and insolent way of looking at his betters. When I ordered him to leave by the back door he strutted out like the cock of the walk. He'd be better employed in the dockyard or on the railways. A bit of hard work would do him no harm at all,' Walter said grimly, and then, as his wife's eyes filled with agitated tears, he relented and went to her, taking her hands in his and kissing her forehead. 'There, there, my dear, you mustn't get yourself upset, it's bad for the child. Come along now, I'm going to take you upstairs so that you can rest for an hour. You see what that lout has done?' he continued as he eased her into the hallway. 'He's upset you with his insolence. I promise you, my dear, that you will never have to set eyes on him again.'

It was hard to believe, Morna thought, as she went out to the small, weed-choked backyard to hang out the last of the day's washing, that she had been living in the lodging house for three whole weeks. On her first night there, the night someone had tried to get into her room, she had not thought that she could stand another minute in the place, with its smells and damp walls and, above all, the big, dirty, frightening men who lodged there. But faced with the alternatives – either returning to Argyle Road to eat humble pie and become little more than the poor relation, subservient to the woman who had once fetched and carried for her, or going to live under Aunt Beatrice's thumb – she had gritted her teeth and stayed put.

It had not been easy. The house was bitterly cold, the food monotonous and the work hard. The men, with their loud deep voices and their hungry eyes and their big hands, still frightened her, but she had learned to pay them as little attention as possible, and never to look any of them in the eye. She still wedged the chair beneath her door handle every night, though as far as she knew there had been no further attempts to intrude on her privacy.

Meggie had a kind heart, and since she still saw Morna as one of her former little charges she had done her best, when the men were at work and the two of them were in the house on their own, to let Morna off her household duties. This suited Morna, but as soon as the bells and sirens around the town began to signal the end of the working day for the factories and the docks she had to rise from Billy Chapman's comfortable chair by the kitchen fire and busy herself at some task or other before the man came home. Billy believed firmly in the adage that a woman's work was never done – in his house, at least. Men were entitled to their time off because men did proper work, but women were different.

Today was Saturday, and on Saturday afternoons and Sundays, when Billy and the other men folk were around the house, Meggie and Morna worked without a pause. That afternoon the men were all out about their own business, most of them in the local public houses, but even so, the two women kept busy, never knowing when Billy might suddenly appear.

Morna had not yet decided what she should do next. She was beginning to think that she would have to settle for a position as companion to some elderly lady, if she were fortunate enough to find an elderly lady willing to take her on. And yet she still had the nagging sense that there was something better waiting for her. There *must* be something better waiting for her!

The tufts of grass staggling through cracks in the broken

flagstones were stiff with frost. The wet clothes heaped in the old tin basin at her feet would soon be frozen into boards, but they would have to stay out overnight because the kitchen was already filled with washing hung from the overhead lines and heaped on the big wooden clothes horse in front of the fire. Cold though the air was, Morna took a moment to stretch her aching back and then studied her hands, roughened by work and reddened by frequent immersion in water. The nails, once neatly shaped ovals, now tended to break and split. She gave a heavy, self-pitying sigh and began to peg the first item – a work shirt as big and thick as her winter coat – on the sagging rope. Once it was in place she bent to take the next garment from the basin, then as she straightened and found herself looking into a man's face, she jumped and gave a little meowing sound of fright and surprise. The rough wooden clothes pegs fell from her hands.

'Sorry, miss, did I startle ye?'

'Of course you startled me,' she snapped, her heart pounding. 'What are you doing out here?'

'Enjoyin' a bit o' peace and quiet, just.' Samuel Gilmartin held up his open book as proof. 'I cannae sit and read in the house, for there's always someone willin' tae make a fool o' me, and that just leads tae a fight, an' Meggie throwin' us out intae the street tae cool down. D'ye want some help with that?'

He picked up the pegs and reached out for the shirt she was holding, but Morna twitched it out of the way. 'I don't need help.' She knew that out of all the lodgers she could consider herself safest with him, for he had never shown her anything but courtesy, but even so she was still on her guard. 'The clothes pegs, if you please?' she said, holding out a hand. And then, as he put them into her palm, 'Please go on with your book.'

As she worked her way along the line she kept darting little glances at him to make sure that he wasn't ogling her. He sat in a corner, sheltered from the worst of the wind by the wall, his auburn head, bright as a polished chestnut in the one stray shaft of sunlight that had found the courage to venture into the dreary little yard, bent and his eyes intent on his book. It seemed to be quite a large volume and on several occasions she caught him in the act of turning a page.

Finally her curiosity got the better of her. 'What are you reading?'

He looked up, his wide brown eyes unfocused for a few seconds, as though he were still in the world of the book; then they cleared and he said, '*Nicholas Nickleby*, by Charles Dickens. Have you read it?'

'I know of Charles Dickens, of course,' said Morna, who had never actually read any of his books. Her taste ran more to light romantic stories.

'The man had a fine understandin' of what life was like in his day for ordinary folk. It's no' changed all that much,' Gilmartin said. 'I've learned a lot from him.'

'Where do you get the books from?' Morna folded another shirt and dropped it into the basket, then tucked the clothes pegs into the big pocket of her apron.

He grinned at her. 'Ye're thinkin' that a man like me could never have the money tae buy books like this. An' ye're mebbe wonderin' if they're stolen. I get them from the lib'ry – the library,' he corrected himself before she had a chance to pretend that she had been thinking nothing of the sort.

'Isn't there a subscription to pay?'

'Aye, it costs me two shillin' an' sixpence a month, but for that I get tae read all the books that I cannae afford tae buy. Though I sometimes buy a book from one of the second-hand shops or a pawnshop if it's one I'd want tae read again and again.'

Heavy clouds had begun to mass overhead and the bitter, salt-laden wind blowing in from the sea carried more than a threat of further snow on the way. Morna's nose began to run and she fumbled in her sleeve for a handkerchief. Her hands were turning numb, making it difficult to cope with the clothes pegs. 'It's not a day for sitting outside.'

Samuel shrugged his shoulders, clad in nothing more than a shirt and a thin jacket. 'Ach, I'm used tae the cold. And this corner's fairly sheltered.'

'You like reading?'

He nodded. 'My father was a great reader. We always had books in our house. He even had a fine set of encyclopedias that he'd saved for years tae buy when he was a young man, before he married my mother. Nearly everythin' I know I learned from his books. I brought them over from Ireland with me when I came here. He left them tae me when he died.' Then, with a faint shrug, 'Well, he didnae exactly leave them tae me because he died in an accident and he'd no way of knowin' his life was comin' tae a sudden end, God rest the man. But nob'dy else wanted them. If I'd not taken them they'd have been thrown out or sold for drink money. Here, let me.'

He put the book aside carefully and jumped up to help her as she struggled with a large bed sheet that was doing its best to entangle her in its chilly, wet, wind-blown folds. He liberated her deftly before subduing the sheet and pegging it securely to the rope, then he picked up the next item. When she tried to protest he said, 'Four hands can do the job in half the time.'

For a moment the two of them worked in silence, then

Morna stopped, her head cocked to one side. 'What's that sound? Church bells on a Saturday?' And then, as realisation dawned, 'It's the twenty-fifth, isn't it? It's Christmas Day!'

'Aye, that's right. Not that it means anythin' tae the likes o' us – the likes o' me,' he added swiftly. 'You'll no doubt be visitin' with yer own folk later, though.'

'Where did you learn to hang up washing so quickly?' she asked, in an attempt to change the subject rather than come up with an answer. The attractive grin lit up his face again.

'From my mother – she brought us all up tae help around the house, lads as well as lassies. She thought that readin' was nothin' more than a waste of time and a luxury for the rich.'

'Perhaps she was right.'

'Not at all.' Gilmartin picked up the final item just as her own fingers were reaching for it. 'The way I see it, God gave every one of us brains and he'd never have done that if we werenae meant tae use them. I like tae find out all about anythin' and everythin'. I've got what ye might call an enquirin' mind.'

'And do you put your knowledge to good use?'

'I will, one day. For now, I'm just a deliveryman,' he said, and then, the smile fading from his face and his voice, 'at least, I was. I've just been turned off. That's why I'm readin' in the yard on a Saturday instead o' bein' at work.'

'Why were you turned off?'

He shrugged. 'One of the customers said I was insolent.'

'Were you?'

'I didnae think so, but he's got money and a fine house while I've got nothin', so he won the argument, as ye might say.'

'What will you do now?'

'For one thing, I'll be sure tae get my own back on the man that got me turned off.'

The reply was so unexpected, and delivered in such a cold, malevolent voice, that Morna took an involuntary step back. All at once the usual carefree sparkle had left his eyes to be replaced by a cold, hard light. His eyelids had lowered until the eyes were little more than two glittering slits and his mouth hardened, pulling down at the corners, while the muscles stood out on his jawline and throat. Suddenly, she saw Samuel Gilmartin in a new light – a frightening light.

Then as swiftly as it had arrived the dark mood vanished and he was giving her an easy, rueful grin and a shrug of the shoulders. 'I'll be standin' at the dockyard gates on Monday with the other poor wretches desperate for work,' he said. 'All of us hopin' the foreman'll pick us out of the crowd.' And then, spreading his hands out and wriggling the fingers at her, 'So take a last look at my nice clean hands. After Monday I'll no' be able to get the dirt and grease out of them, no matter how hard I scrub. But I cannae live on fresh air and books, can I?'

'Can you not get another delivery job?'

'Not in this area. Who'd want tae hire a man that gives insolence tae the gentry?'

'But you said you weren't insolent.'

'I said it was my word against his. I'm poor and I'm nothin' and I'm Irish intae the bargain. Folk like me don't even need tae open our mouths tae be accused of impertinence tae our betters. "Dumb insolence" it's called when we keep our tongues still.' He leaned forward, holding her gaze with his. 'Tell me this – can you put yer hand on yer heart and say that ye've never accused a servant lassie or a shop assistant of givin' offence when mebbe

166

it's been you that's just been a wee bit quick tae take offence when none was intended?'

Morna drew herself up to her full height. 'How dare you question me like that? It's none of your business! You're being . . .'

She stopped short, flushing to the roots of her hair as he finished the sentence for her. 'I'm bein' insolent, am I no'? Now d'ye see how easy it is for the likes of you tae put the likes of me in the wrong? At least when I'm workin' in Ardrossan dockyard, Miss Morna Forsyth, I'll be with folk that don't take offence easily. Or if they do . . .' he curled one hand into a fist and chopped it sharply through the air '. . . they sort it out in their own way and then it's done with. Here, I'll carry that for ye.' He picked up the peg bag and the empty tin basin and went ahead of her into the house.

Morna lingered for a moment, listening to the faint sound of the church bells calling the faithful to Christmas worship. Most Scots celebrated Ne'erday – New Year's Day – rather than Christmas, but her mother had loved to decorate her home for Christmas. Now, shivering in the cold, shabby, overgrown, sunless backyard, Morna recalled Christmases when she and her brother and sister and parents had attended church in the morning before going home to unwrap their gifts from each other beside a tree hung with glittering baubles. Then – her mouth began to water – they would sit down to a huge Christmas dinner, followed by a lazy afternoon in front of the fire.

The longing for those lost days threatened to overwhelm her, but she managed, by biting her lower lip hard, to bring herself under control. She was about to follow Samuel Gilmartin into the house when she noticed that he had forgotten his book. Picking it up, she saw that the pages were covered by small, densely packed print, with not a single illustration to please the eye. What sort of working man would be interested in something that looked so dull?

She closed it and carried it indoors, puzzling over this ordinary man who enjoyed reading.

On the following Monday morning Samuel Gilmartin left the house early.

'So's I can be one of the first at the dockyard gates,' he explained briefly to Morna when they met in the dark narrow passageway. She, heavy-eyed and still half asleep, was on her way to the kitchen to help Meggie. 'I have tae make sure that I'm picked tae do a day's work, at least. I've got tae pay for my lodgin's.'

'Have you had something to eat?'

'Aye, and I've some bread and drippin' in my pocket.' He gave her a brief grin, and as they passed each other she was aware of the clean soapy smell she had begun to identify with Samuel.

15

Samuel Gilmartin was taken on at Ardrossan dockyard as a labourer, but Morna could see the heart going out of the man as he returned to the lodging house at the end of each day with so much grease and dirt on him that he was scarcely recognisable from the other men. He tried his best to clean himself up, washing in a small tin basin that he kept in the room he shared with several others and then changing into the worn but clean garments that were all he had other than his work clothes; but it was almost impossible to shift the grease from under his fingernails and between his fingers.

'It seems a shame that he's having to find work as a labourer when he already had a decent enough job with Mrs Smith,' Morna said as she and Meggie worked in the lean-to washhouse. Meggie was stirring the clothes around in the big copper boiler while Morna, her sleeves rolled up to above the elbows, struggled to turn the handle of the old mangle. The floor was puddled with water that had poured from the clothes as they were transferred from the washtub to the big basin where they awaited their turn in the mangle, and the small dark space where they worked was steamy and airless — but at least it was warm. Sweat ran down Morna's beet-red face and her hair, pinned back that morning, hung in damp wisps around her cheeks and neck.

'It's a shame right enough, but that's the way it is for the likes of us, and there's nothin' we can dae about it.' Meggie deftly twisted the pole she was using and then heaved it up, leaning back to take the strain. The end of the pole rose from the steamy water, a soggy mass of material entwined around it. With a swing of her strong arms the woman delivered the soaking bundle, raining water all the way, to the battered tin basin.

The washhouse, damp and humid, was a haven for wood lice, and as Morna bent to lift the next garment from the basin she suddenly noticed one particularly large creature marching towards her. She jumped back with a squeal of disgust.

'What is it?' Meggie asked, and then, as Morna, shuddering, pointed at the floor, 'A slater? Ach, they're no harm tae ye, lassie. They're more scared of you than you are of them.' She slammed her shoe down on the insect, squashing it flat, then returned to her work.

'But I d–don't *like* them!' Morna whimpered. The house, like all its neighbours, was overrun with slaters, and every night she took her bedding apart and checked it before settling down to sleep. Twice, she had found one of the creatures in the bed, waggling its antennae at her.

'Life's full o' things we don't like, but we just have tae thole them,' Meggie was saying. 'Just as Samuel Gilmartin has tae take whatever job he can find. It's that or starvin' in the gutter for folk like him and me and Billy and the other lads. That's another thing that folk like us just have tae thole. But it's different for you, lassie; you were meant for a better life than we have. Ye shouldnae be workin' here like a skivvy.'

'Try telling that to my brother!' A pair of trousers was going through the mangle and Morna had to struggle to turn the handle as the folds of thick material jammed between the rollers.

'I'm tellin' it tae you, hen, for you're the one that can dae somethin' about it.'

'Such as what?' Morna asked through gritted teeth. She gave one last determined heave, putting so much effort into it that for a moment she thought the buttons on her blouse were going to tear themselves from their buttonholes, then at last the big rollers submitted and the trousers were forced through, shooting a jet of water in their wake. It spattered over her arms and she paused to catch her breath, snatching up a thin towel and using it to mop herself. 'A job as a washerwoman? Or perhaps,' she said wryly, 'I should go and stand at the dockyard gates. I'm sure that this mangle's given me enough muscle to do a man's work.'

Meggie held her own brawny arms up. 'Housework does that, lassie, but I was born tae earn my own livin' while you were born tae be a lady. A right bonny wee thing ye were too,' she recalled fondly. 'Pretty as a picture, sittin' up in yer perambulator like a princess. Folk were always stoppin' me when I took ye out, just so's they could have a look at ye in the beautiful clothes yer mother made for ye. She was a lovely lady, yer mother!'

'Yes,' Morna agreed, then, as memories of her happy childhood brought longing to her heart and a lump to her throat, she swallowed hard and went on briskly, 'but she didn't raise me to earn my own keep.'

'You were so bonny from the start that she thought ye'd marry a man able tae take care of ye. And so did I.'

Morna thought of Arthur MacAdam and again, the

lump began to form. 'Who'd want to marry me now, looking the way I do?'

'That's what I mean. It frets me tae see ye workin' away like this, Miss Morna. Look at yer poor wee hands . . .' Meggie took one of them in her own hot, damp grip '. . . all roughened with the work. Ye'll be gettin' calluses next.'

Morna knew well enough that she would soon have to start thinking of her future, but hard though life was in the lodging house at least she had a roof over her head. Besides, she felt safe with Meggie. 'But what else can I do?' she said feebly. 'I've not been trained to any sort of work.'

'Could Mr Walter no' find a place for ye in the shop?'

'He's got Belle running things for him, and even if he did agree to employ me, I'd not want to work for him. And don't tell me that beggars can't be choosers, Meggie,' Morna added as the older woman began to speak. 'I'm fine where I am for the moment. Something's sure to turn up. Sure to,' she added, without much hope, and began to stuff a patched vest through the mangle.

Morna, who had never before cared about anyone but herself, became quite concerned over the change in Samuel Gilmartin within a week of him starting work at the docks. He became quiet and morose; when she tried to strike up a conversation his replies were brief and usually bitter. One day he sat down to dinner sporting a black eye and split lip.

'What happened?' Morna asked, horrified.

'He walked intae a wall,' one of the other men said, and a roar of laughter went round the table, ebbing and then swelling again when another man asked slyly, 'Goin' tae kiss it better, lassie?'

'If that's the case, me and big Jamie here'll just nip oot

the back an' gie each other a good punchin' so's ye can kiss us better an' all,' someone else leered.

'Mind yer manners!' Meggie rapped, catching the direction the talk was taking as she came through the door carrying a basin filled with boiled potatoes. Then, as Samuel looked up and her eyes fell on his bruised and battered face, 'Mercy me, laddie, ye've never been fightin', have ye?'

'Ach, it happens tae all of us when we start a new job,' one of the older men assured her. 'The lad had tae get blooded.' He snatched at Samuel's wrist and held his hand up to display skinned knuckles, 'An' he stood up for himsel' well. It was a bonny fight! Gonnae entertain us again tomorrow, Sammy?'

'Mind yer own business!' Samuel snarled, freeing himself and getting up from the table so swiftly that his chair toppled and crashed to the wooden floor.

'Here, what about yer dinner?' Meggie called after him as he slammed out the room.

'I'll have it,' half a dozen voices chorused.

'Ye will not. That lad's put in a hard day's work and he needs his meat. Here, Morna . . .' Meggie shovelled a generous helping of potatoes on to Samuel's discarded plate of stew '. . . you can take that up tae him.'

'And make sure that you're no' the puddin', lass,' one of the men added, then yelped as the back of Meggie's large hand flicked painfully across his ear.

Samuel was sitting on the edge of his cot in the dreary, low-ceilinged dormitory. 'I don't want it,' he said as soon as Morna put the plate down on the bed beside him.

'Eat it,' she insisted, and after a moment he picked the plate up. His first mouthful was slow and reluctant, but once he had tasted the food, hunger overcame him and he began to shovel up large mouthfuls.

'What happened?'

'Ach, there's always someone who wants tae prove that he's cock of the walk,' he said indistinctly. Fragments of food sprayed out and he rubbed the back of his forearm across his mouth before taking another forkful.

'Could you not have ignored him?'

His brown eyes no longer sparkled and the look he gave her made her feel small enough to walk under a closed door. 'And be bullied by him and his like for the rest of my life?'

'It's not fair,' Morna burst out. 'You deserve better than that.'

'I deserve nothin', have ye no' realised that yet? I'm just a labourer . . . a nob'dy with no rights.'

'You're an educated man.'

'I'm self-educated, an' that stands for nothin'. It's worse than nothin',' he added viciously, 'because it makes me different from the rest, an' that's the worst thing tae be when ye're with a gang of workin' men. Here,' he pushed the empty plate at her. 'Ye can take this back tae the kitchen.'

'Your face looks sore.'

'It'll mend. Then it'll get bust again.'

'Can I do something to help you? Iodine, or mebbe . . .'

'I'm goin' tae sleep,' he interrupted rudely, and turned over on his side, away from her.

Morna hesitated, then turned towards the door. She had reached it when he said, 'Mebbe there *is* somethin' ye can do for me.'

'What?'

He was sitting up again, the evening light from the small window she had cleaned only hours earlier making the bruising on his face stand out lividly.

'Ye could teach me figures.'

'Figures?'

'Aye, addin' and takin' away and the like. And workin' with money. I suppose you know about those things?'

'A little. Not enough to teach anyone.'

'All I'm askin' is for you tae show me what ye know. It's the only way I can get away from the docks and intae somethin' better.' She had moved back towards him, close enough for him to reach out and take her wrist in an urgent grip. 'Will ye dae it?'

She looked down at the hand on her arm, with its torn knuckles and the black rims beneath broken, once carefully trimmed nails. 'I'll try, but I might not be any good.'

'Ye'll be better than nothin', an' nothin's all I've got at the minute. I cannae pay ye more than a few pence a week.'

'I don't want your money,' she said hurriedly, and he glared with his one good eye while his grip tightened painfully on her arm.

'An' I don't want your charity. Thruppence a week, right?'

'Right,' Morna agreed against her better judgement. How could she teach anything to anyone?

Samuel Gilmartin proved to be a quick learner, and thanks to his thirst for knowledge teaching him arithmetic proved to be easier than Morna had first thought. In the evenings, when Billy and the other men tended to be in the nearby public house, Meggie allowed the two of them to use the kitchen table while she sat in her chair by the range, knitting and darning and, as often as not, snoring with her head tipped uncomfortably back and her mouth gaping like a cave while Samuel mastered the intricacies of addition, subtraction, multiplication and division by moving groups of dried peas around the table.

To her surprise, Morna began to look forward to their evening classes. Her pupil's triumphant pleasure at each step forward and his appreciation of her help gave her a much-needed sense of achievement. On the evening when he soared through the multiplication tables from one-times-one to twelve-times-twelve with scarcely a moment's pause for thought she felt as though they had climbed a mountain together and arrived at the top to see beautiful scenery spread out far below.

'Bravo!' She clapped her hands, but quietly, mindful of Meggie's slow, heavy breathing. 'You go to the top of the class!'

'Ach, it was nothin',' he said modestly, though his face, still carrying faint smudges of bruising, glowed.

'I can't believe how quickly you've learned it.'

He shrugged, and then allowed a delighted grin to slip through. 'You're a good teacher, and I was desperate tae learn, for I'll go mad if I have tae stay in that dockyard much longer.'

'You're going to look for other work? Where?'

He glanced over his shoulder, saw that Meggie was sound asleep, then leaned forward and said in a low voice, 'Forsyth's are lookin' for a shop assistant.'

'My brother?'

'Aye, yer brother. That's why I asked you tae help me with my sums – I'd seen the notice in their window.'

'They've surely filled the post by now.'

'Aye, they did, for the notice disappeared. But today it was back again. They cannae have been pleased with whoever got the place. But *I'd* find ways tae please them if I could just get the chance. D'ye think I know enough about figurin' tae be able tae work in a shop?'

'Maybe – if folk use dried peas instead of money.'

'I've thought about that.' He got up and dipped deep into his pockets, then laid a handful of silver and copper coins on the table. 'I've been savin' up for this. You're a customer and you want tae buy . . .' he looked around and then pointed at the battered tin teapot on the range, '. . . that bonny china vase. It costs ninepence, madam.'

Morna hesitated, and then, as he nodded encouragingly at her, she selected a florin and pushed it towards him. 'There you are, my good man.'

'Thank you, madam.' He studied the coin for a moment, reminding her of the days when she had watched her father playing chess with Mr Pinkerton, then selected several coins and slid them along the table. 'One shillin' and thruppence change. Am I right?'

'You are. And while I'm here, I'll just have that elegant figurine as well.' Morna indicated Meggie, sprawled in her chair with her nose pointed ceilingwards. 'How much is that?'

It turned into a game, with the two of them giggling behind their hands like conspirators while Meggie's heavy breathing developed into soft snores.

'So will I do?' Samuel asked when the clock on the mantelshelf showed that Billy and the other men would soon be back.

'As far as the money's concerned, you'll do. But . . .' She stopped, reluctant to dim the pleasure he was taking in his success.

'But what? Go on, now, ye have tae tell me,' he coaxed. 'You're my friend, and who else but a friend would tell a man the truth?'

'You have a bonny accent, Samuel, but . . .'

'Ach, is that all that's frettin' ye?' He rose with one easy movement, stepped back from the table, gave her a deep bow, and said, 'Cock a doodle doo, my dame has lost her shoe, my master's lost his fiddle-stick, and knows not what to do. Mary, Mary, quite contrary, how does your garden grow? With silver bells and cockle shells, and pretty maids all in a row. How many miles to Babylon . . .'

'Stop, stop!' Morna protested through giggles.

He bowed again, and then asked as he sat down, 'How many marks out o' ten? I cannae rid myself of my Irish accent, but I've tried tae tone it down a bit.'

'The accent is pretty to listen to and I think that the ladies who go into the shop will be quite charmed by it. How did you learn to speak like that?'

'By listenin' to you, of course. And the money I've saved is for some decent clothes, so that I can look my best. D'you think I could persuade your brother to give me the position?'

'It's more likely you'll have to please my sister. Walter has never been as interested in the shop's affairs as Belle.'

'D'ye tell me?' Samuel's eyes narrowed slightly. 'So it's the ladies of your fam'ly that have all the brains?'

'No, just Belle. She's very good at figuring, while Walter's more interested in his new wife.'

'New wife? So you've a sister-in-law as well as a sister?'

'I wouldn't say that.' She spoke without thinking and then, as he raised his eyebrows, 'Walter married our servant lassie. That's why I'm lodging here.'

'So you don't approve of what your brother's done? I quite agree,' Samuel said earnestly. 'Different classes don't mix well. I mind a neighbour of ours at home who did much the same thing. It was a poor sort of marriage, and the woman soon ran off with someone of her own sort and left him countin' the cost of his foolishness.' Then, casually he asked, 'Your sister, the one that sees to the shop – does she approve of the marriage?'

'Belle? She does not. She left home before I did. She's staying with our aunt, Mrs Beatrice McCallum.'

'Would that be Mrs McCallum in Caledonia Road? I

used tae deliver to her house when I worked for Mrs Smith,' Samuel said. 'I'm sorry there's trouble in yer family, Miss Morna, and I hope it will soon pass. Blood kin shouldnae fall out.' He reached over, and had taken possession of her hand and raised it to his lips before she knew what was happening. She let out a surprised squeak, which was answered by a sudden loud snore from Meggie.

On Meggie's advice, Samuel found a smart suit in a pawnshop. 'Some poor soul's misfortune has become my good luck,' he told Morna, adding blithely, 'Ach, but isn't that always the way of it?' And then, in a lower voice, 'There's just one last thing, Miss Morna, that ye could do for me, if only ye would.'

'What's that?'

'D'ye think ye could put in a good word for me with yer sister?'

'I don't know . . .' Morna faltered. 'I've scarcely spoken to her since I came here.'

'Then she must be missin' ye. You could do two kindnesses with one visit – make her happy, and help me intae the bargain. Would it be that hard?' he added as she hesitated. 'Ye never know, I might be the one that brings the two of yez together again. And that would make me feel as if I've gone some way to repayin' ye for all yer kindness tae me.'

When Samuel coaxed in his lovely Irish accent, he was hard to resist, Morna thought, little realising that only months earlier her sister-in-law, then the Forsyth housemaid, had fallen under the spell of the same caressing voice and beseeching eyes.

16

Rather than warn Belle of her coming, and perhaps having to face a snub, Morna called at her aunt's house unannounced. The maid who answered the door left her standing on the step while she went to fetch Belle, who came bustling along the hallway almost at once.

'Oh, Morna, I'm so pleased to see you! Come in out of the cold . . .' She ushered her sister into the parlour. 'Are you well? Are you going back to stay with Walter and . . . and Sarah?'

'This house,' Morna said, 'still smells of dog. How can you bear it?'

'One becomes used to it, and Aunt Bea has been very kind.'

'Where is she?' Morna looked around, half-expecting her aunt to bounce up from behind an overstuffed chair. One never knew with Aunt Beatrice.

'In the kitchen. She may come through later. It's Romeo,' Belle explained, her voice suddenly sombre. 'Aunt Bea's favourite dog. He's very ill, and not expected to last much longer.'

'Oh?' Morna was inspecting a chair for dog hairs before sitting down.

'She's very upset. She's had a bad chill lately, mainly brought about by walking the dogs in the rain for too long, and her own health is not so good. But tell me about you.' Belle's eyes skimmed over her sister, noting the pale face and the casual hairstyle – much less elaborate than Morna's usual. 'Where have you been living?'

'With Meggie and her husband.'

'Still? In their lodging house!'

'I have nowhere else to go,' Morna said coldly. 'Has the child arrived yet?'

'No, but it won't be long now. Walter's so taken with being a husband and a prospective father . . .' Belle stopped suddenly as the maid brought in a tea tray.

'Mrs McCallum says she'll join ye in a wee while, Miss Belle, as soon as Romeo settles,' she reported as she set the tray down.

'What were you saying about Walter?' Morna prompted as soon as the woman had gone.

Belle scowled as she picked up the silver teapot. 'He's scarcely ever in the shop these days. Too busy preparing for fatherhood and teaching that new little wife of his how to be mistress of her own home. You'd think nobody had ever become a parent before!'

'Perhaps he's determined to prove that he can be a better parent than Papa was to us.'

'Perhaps,' Belle said without conviction.

'So you're left to run the place on your own?'

'It's hard work, but Walter was always more of a hindrance than a help where the shop's concerned; Papa knew that.'

'He should have left the shop to you.'

'If you recall, he didn't leave it to any one person,

since it wasn't his to leave. It belongs to the three of us,' Belle said, and then, as Morna removed her gloves, revealing work-roughened hands, 'Don't tell me that Meggie has you doing menial work in that lodging house of hers?'

'I have to earn my keep.'

'Oh, Morna, what would Mother say?'

'If Mother were here to pass judgement on any of this, you and I would still be at home and Sarah would still be in the kitchen where she belongs. And tell me, pray, what work was I trained for? If I want to eat then I must help in the lodging house.' Morna went over to take her cup of tea, and then said as she returned to her chair, 'About the shop . . . if it was left to the three of us, then surely I must have some say in the running of it?'

Belle, about to take a sip of tea, lowered the cup back down to its saucer, eyeing her younger sister warily. 'You want to work there?'

'With you and Walter? I doubt if that would be a good idea for any of us. No, but I know of someone who would like to be interviewed for the post you're advertising. He stays in Meggie's lodging house . . .'

'Then he'd not be the right person for us,' Belle said immediately.

'You're wrong; he's ambitious and clever – he reads books, and he's good with figures and he's got a good brain.'

'What work does he do just now?'

'He's in Ardrossan dockyard – but only because he's not been able to find anything better. He hates being there, and I'm sure that he would be of great use to you. You might at least see him, Belle.'

'And if I don't consider him suitable?'

'Then he would accept your decision. He knows that

you and Walter wouldn't consider hiring anyone just to please me. Will you agree to see Samuel Gilmartin?'

'Is that his name? Oh, very well, tell him to call tomorrow morning. But I'll make no promises,' Belle added as the door opened and her aunt came in.

'My dear Morna, how good of you to call.' Beatrice came to a standstill in the middle of the room and waited, head slightly tilted to one side. Morna, taking the hint, set her cup aside and rose to kiss her aunt on the cheek.

'Tea, Aunt Beatrice?' Belle asked, and Beatrice nodded, moving to the chair Morna had just vacated, leaving the girl with no option but to collect her cup and saucer from the small side table and find somewhere else to sit.

'How is Romeo?' she asked, catching Belle's silent signals.

'Not at all well. The poor old fellow has come to the end of his time.' Beatrice's normally strong voice shook, and she bit her lip, then rallied and turned her attention to Morna. 'Where have you been staying these past weeks, my dear?'

'With Meggie Chapman – our former nursemaid. Meggie Butcher as was,' Morna explained as her aunt looked puzzled.

Beatrice's frown cleared. 'Ah yes, I remember Meggie Butcher. A very able young woman; your dear mother thought the world of her. What happened to her?'

'She married, Aunt Beatrice, and now she and her husband have a . . .'

'A small hotel near the shore,' Belle interrupted smoothly. 'Morna is helping Meggie to run the place, but only until she finds work more suited.'

'Good,' Beatrice said absently. She got to her feet and picked up her untouched cup and saucer. 'I think, my dears, that I will go back to the kitchen to sit with Romeo. We have so little time left together.'

'But she'd only just arrived!' Morna burst out as soon as the door had closed behind their aunt. 'Anyone would think that Romeo was her husband or her sweetheart to hear her talk, instead of just an old dog!'

'He was a gift from Uncle Hector. She can't imagine life without poor old Romeo.'

'She doesn't look well.'

'She's been staying up at nights with the dog, and as I told you, she recently suffered from a bad chill. She's not getting any younger.'

'I suppose not. Why didn't you let me tell Aunt Beatrice the truth about Meggie's lodging house?'

'I thought it would upset her to know that one of her nieces is living and working in a place like that.'

'I doubt if anything would upset Aunt Beatrice. I believe that you're ashamed of me, Belle,' Morna challenged, and her sister flushed.

'I'm not ashamed of you at all!'

'Good. I scarcely think,' Morna said with a return to her former haughtiness, 'that someone who works in trade has the right to look down on anyone else.'

'I may work in trade,' Belle pointed out, stung. 'But you do menial work. It must be quite a shock to your poor hands to have to wash and clean instead of holding a paintbrush or playing "The Blue Danube" on the piano. I take it that Meggie doesn't have a piano?'

It was Morna's turn to colour. Her mouth tightened and she was about to deliver another insult when she recalled that she had come to the house to ask Belle a favour. She picked up her gloves, and rose. 'I must go. Belle, you will give Samuel Gilmartin a fair hearing tomorrow, won't you?'

Belle, ashamed of her sudden anger, nodded. 'I said that I would.' At the door she added tentatively, 'Will you visit us again?'

'Perhaps,' Morna said, and walked swiftly down the path and out of the gate.

Beatrice, kneeling by the dog basket in the corner of the kitchen, looked up as Belle went in. 'Is Morna gone? She looks tired,' she went on when Belle nodded.

'I wish she would go back home,' Belle fretted. 'But she's stubborn. Even when she was tiny she was stubborn. If you told her not to fall over a cliff she'd do it rather than pay heed to you.'

'You have to admire her determination to stand on her own two feet, hard though it must be after a lifetime of being cosseted. And it won't do her any harm to find out how other folk have tae live.' Beatrice stroked the little dog's head and murmured to him before lifting him carefully into her arms. 'Help me up, Belle,' she instructed, struggling to her feet. When Belle had done as she was told, her aunt went on, 'Ena, come and help Miss Belle tae carry the basket intae the parlour. Romeo and I will be more comfortable there.'

She refused to go to her room that night, so Belle and the maidservant brought pillows and blankets downstairs, so that Beatrice could stay with her sick pet.

When Belle went downstairs for breakfast in the morning, the table in the small dining room was set for one.

'The mistress is having somethin' on a tray in the parlour,' Ena said. 'She looks worn out, Miss Belle, could ye no' persuade her tae go tae her room for a lie down after?'

'I'll try, but you know what she can be like.'

'Aye,' said Ena, who had started working in the house when Beatrice was housekeeper. 'A right thrawn old – lady. She says ye've tae break yer fast and then go through tae her. I'm bein' sent out tae do the shoppin'. She's given me a list as long as my arm – it'll take me all mornin' tae do it!'

Beatrice's eyes, as she looked up at her niece, were pools of exhaustion and sorrow. She was sitting on the floor by Romeo's basket and looked as though she had been there all night.

'Aunt Bea, don't you think you should rest?'

'There'll be plenty of time for that later.' She stroked the dog's head. 'I think it's time to put him out of his misery, poor old man.'

'You want me to send Ena to fetch the veterinary?'

'Tuts, lassie, there's no need for that. I used tae help Hector with his dogs, and I know what tae do. There now, my lad,' Beatrice said gently as Romeo struggled to get up. 'Just you lie easy, son. I've given Ena a shoppin' list that should keep her out of our way for a while, so first of all, Belle, I want you to make certain that she's gone, then you can go to my bedroom and fetch the tin box that's pushed right to the back of the wardrobe. There's also a small key on a key ring in my jewellery box on the dressing table. Bring them both down here tae me.'

When Ena had stamped off along the pavement with the big shopping basket over her arm, Belle brought the battered box and the key downstairs.

'Now go and heat some milk and put it into Romeo's bowl – warm but not too hot, just right for him to drink. And bring a teaspoon too,' Beatrice ordered before returning her attention to her dying pet.

When Belle did as she was told, her aunt unlocked the tin box and took out a brown glass medicine bottle. 'Ten drops should do it.' She added them to the milk with a steady hand and then she helped the old dog to sit up before feeding the milk to him spoonful by spoonful. He drank it trustingly, his eyes, no longer as bright as Juliet's, fixed on her face the whole time.

'There now – good lad,' Beatrice said when the bowl was empty. 'You can rest in your basket now. Belle, mind you wash the bowl out well, then you can fasten the bottle tightly and put it back in the box. Lock the box and put it and the key away where you found them. Then go and sit in the dinin' room until I call for you.'

'What was in the bottle?'

'Just somethin' that Hector used tae give his dogs when life got too much for them. It's a kind endin' with no pain. Romeo'll just go off tae sleep, but this time he'll not wake up,' Beatrice said with a tremor in her voice.

Banished to the dining room, Belle glanced anxiously at the clock. There was no knowing these days if Walter was going to grace the shop with his presence or not, and there were two people to interview that morning for the assistant's post – three, she suddenly remembered, including the man that Morna had come to see her about. She bit her lip and then decided that if Walter didn't turn up they would just have to wait until she arrived, for she could not leave her aunt in her time of need. Come to think of it, she would prefer to interview them herself, for she had a better idea of the sort of assistant they required.

Just then she heard Beatrice call and went into the parlour to find her aunt standing by the basket, damp-eyed but calm.

'It's over.'

'So soon?' Belle could scarcely believe it, and yet there was a strange stillness in the room; a sense of empty space, as though something that had been alive was no longer there. She glanced at the basket where Romeo looked as though he was in a peaceful sleep and might waken at any moment, eyes bright and tail wagging.

'Aye, he's gone to his Maker. I've got no truck,' Beatrice said with a flash of her usual spirit, 'with this nonsense about dogs not bein' allowed intae heaven. They were made the same way we were and by the same personage, and tae my mind what comes from the Creator returns tae the Creator. I've said that tae the minister time and again but the man'll just not listen tae me. Fetch the blanket I left ready in the kitchen and we'll take Romeo tae the garden shed. The gardener's comin' in later and he can lay him tae rest beneath the trees at the end of the garden.'

The thought of carrying the dead dog filled Belle with horror, but she had no option but to do as she was told. The neatly folded blanket waited on the kitchen table and she had just lifted it and was nerving herself to return to the parlour when she heard Juliet barking and someone knocked at the back door.

The gardener has come early, Belle thought with relief; but the young man standing on the doorstep, though strongly built and with the healthy complexion of someone used to being out of doors, was obviously wearing his best clothes.

'Yes?'

'Would you be Miss Forsyth?' He had a soft voice with a pleasing accent.

'I am.'

'Good mornin', ma'am, I've come about the position.'

'The position?' Belle echoed foolishly, her mind filled with the scene she had just left in the parlour.

'The position of shop assistant, ma'am. I believe your sister, Miss Morna Forsyth, mentioned my name to you.' He had taken his bowler hat off to reveal a head of auburn hair, well slicked down with hair cream. 'Samuel Gilmartin, at your service, ma'am.'

'Oh – you were supposed to call at the shop, not here.'

'At the shop, you say?' He took a step back. 'My apologies, ma'am, I must have misunderstood; I thought I was expected to call here. I'll go to the shop, then?'

'Yes you should, and wait there for me,' Belle said, and was about to close the door when Beatrice said from behind her, 'Who is it?'

'Nobody,' Belle said shortly, but Beatrice was already by her side.

'You – what is it you want?'

'It seems that I made a mistake, ma'am. I was told to attend Miss Belle Forsyth to be interviewed for the post of shop assistant, but I should have gone to the shop and not come here. I'm very sorry, ma'am,' he said humbly, and then, nodding towards the wire run, where Juliet was going hysterical at sight of her beloved mistress, 'I see that ye're a dog lover like myself, ma'am?'

'Quiet!' Beatrice roared, and Juliet paused and then sat down, whining. 'Come in, young man, I have some work for you.' She swept Belle aside and opened the door wide. 'My other dog has just died . . .' Her voice broke slightly, but she shook off the hand that Belle laid on her arm, drew herself to her full height, and went on, 'He's in the parlour. I wonder if you would mind carrying him to the garden shed for me? I can't let Juliet into the house until he's gone. My gardener will bury him this afternoon.'

'Of course I will. Anythin' I can do to help, ma'am,'

Samuel Gilmartin said eagerly, wiping his feet vigorously on the mat before venturing into the kitchen.

Once in the parlour, he dropped to his knees beside the basket, running a gentle hand over Romeo's still, small body. 'Ah, would ye look at the poor old soul, he's so peaceful. Here, give me the blanket . . .' He wrapped the dead dog as gently as a mother swaddling her firstborn, then straightened, Romeo cradled in his arms. 'There now,' he said, and smiled at Beatrice, who smiled back.

As the three of them went into the back garden Juliet burst into delighted barks at sight of her mistress.

'That wee one's wantin' fed by the sound of it,' Samuel Gilmartin said as he laid Romeo's body down in the shed. 'I tell you what, ma'am, why don't I dig a grave for this little fella while you see tae the other? Then you can have a decent wee burial whenever you're ready.'

'I couldn't ask you to do that. The gardener will be here later.'

'I'd count it as a privilege, ma'am. I love dogs myself, and I'd like to help you in your time of suffering,' he said earnestly.

'But you'll spoil your clothes,' Belle pointed out, and he turned his warm smile on her.

'I'll be careful.' He began to remove his jacket. 'You'll want him settled as soon as possible, ma'am. Just show me where you keep your spade and where you want me tae dig, and then you go off and see tae the other wee dog. It sounds upset, so it does,' he added as Juliet began to howl.

17

'That young man is both charming and understanding,' Beatrice said as she and her niece took Juliet into the house.

'Too charming, perhaps.'

'Nonsense. He's willing, and he likes dogs. What more can you ask for in a shop assistant?'

'Someone who's good with figures and able to deal with customers?'

'As to the customers, you need have no worries on that score. So that just leaves the ability to work with figures. Come along now, Juliet, your Auntie Belle shall help me to feed you and make a fuss of you. Did we leave you out in the garden all alone, then? Poor little lass.'

By the time Juliet had been fed and petted the grave was ready. Samuel laid Romeo within it and stood back, head bowed and hands clasped before him, while Beatrice said a swift prayer.

'A very moving service, ma'am, if I may say so,' he said, and then, picking up the spade, 'Now then, I'll just finish the job and be on my way.'

'You'll come into the house and have some breakfast,

young man. I owe you that, at least,' Beatrice said firmly when he tried to protest. 'Knock on the back door when you're done here.'

Ena was in the kitchen, unpacking her shopping basket with Juliet frisking around her ankles. 'Ena, make fresh tea,' her mistress instructed her, adding, 'there's a young man coming in soon to wash his hands, and he's going to be hungry. Make some breakfast for him and bring him through to the dining room when he's ready.'

'Yes, ma'am,' the maid said, used to her employer's whims.

'I should be getting off to the shop. I have folk to interview.'

'You can just stay here, Belle, and interview your first applicant while he's eating his breakfast,' Beatrice said, and went upstairs to brush her hair and wash her face and hands.

It was clear to see from Samuel Gilmartin's expression when the large, generously filled plate was set before him, that he was very hungry; Belle expected him to shovel the food into his mouth, but to her surprise he ate neatly, using his knife and fork to cut small portions and emptying his mouth before answering the questions Beatrice fired at him.

'So – where are you employed at the moment?'

'I've been workin' as a labourer at Ardrossan dockyard, ma'am, for the past week or so.'

'You're not of a mind to stay there?'

'I hate it,' the young man said flatly. 'It's not for me at all.'

'There's a big difference between labouring in the dockyard and serving customers in a shop,' Belle pointed out coolly, and his brown eyes caught and held hers.

'There is, Miss Forsyth, and I can understand you thinkin' that a man can't move easily from one tae – to

– the other. But I can, I promise you. All I need,' he added earnestly, his gaze moving back to Beatrice, 'is the chance to prove it.'

'Are you any good with figures? Sums of money?' Belle persisted.

He had finished eating and not a crumb was left on the plate. He pushed it away and sat back in his chair. 'I like figurin',' he said, and went on to give correct answers to the imaginary purchases she set him.

'Well now,' Beatrice interrupted after five minutes, 'I think we have a good idea of your abilities, Mr Gilmartin, and it's my belief that you would make an excellent shop assistant.'

'Thank you, ma'am!' His face lit up, while Belle glared at her aunt.

'I have other people to interview,' she said swiftly.

'I could look in this afternoon to see if you've made a decision,' he offered, getting to his feet. 'But for now, I've taken up enough of your time. Thank you, ladies, for your kindness and hospitality, and my condolences, ma'am,' he added to Beatrice, 'for your sad loss. Just remember that you gave your wee dog a very happy life, and for that he'll bless you through eternity.'

'So you believe that animals can aspire to heaven and eternity, young man?'

'Of course – don't they have souls like the rest of us?' said Samuel.

'A most agreeable young man,' Beatrice said when she and her niece were alone. 'You must employ him, Belle!'

'I'm not sure that someone used to working in the dockyard could settle in a shop.'

'You heard him say that he's longing to improve his lot. He deserves a chance, surely?'

'We'll see,' Belle said, and left for the shop, her mind in turmoil. Part of her felt that Samuel Gilmartin had been too glib and her aunt too easily won over, while another part was interested in finding out if a silk purse could really be made from a sow's ear.

The day had started well, with grey skies but visibility clear enough to give sight of Ailsa Craig, a rocky, conical-shaped islet known to the Ayrshire folk as Paddy's Milestone, since it stood halfway between Scotland and Northern Ireland. But by mid-morning the clouds had thickened and lowered and the white-flecked sea was driving hard on to the shore. Paddy's Milestone had disappeared completely, as had most of Arran. Sleet had begun to fall and by the time Morna struggled to the shops it had turned to icy, driving rain. The old umbrella she had found in the wash-house was torn and leaking, and it came as a great relief when she left the final shop and headed back to Quay Street to find that the rain had eased.

'Morna Forsyth? Is it really you?' The ringing tones caused several heads to turn, and Morna winced. The last thing she needed was to be recognised and sneered at. She turned reluctantly, weighed down by the heavy basket she carried, to find that the woman confronting her was smiling, pleased by the meeting.

'It is you – how lovely to meet up with you again.' Then, with a laugh, 'You don't remember me, do you? Ruth Durie – we were at school together.'

'Ruth, of course.' Now she was able to place the long thin face with its direct, deep blue eyes below strong black brows and thick black hair that used to escape with relentless regularity from its restraining ribbons but was now trapped beneath a straw hat.

'So, you're still living in Saltcoats. Come and have a

cup of tea,' Ruth suggested. 'We have so much to catch up on.'

'I can't. I have to get back.'

'Still at home, or married with a house and husband of your own? As you can see...' Ruth drew her left glove off and waggled her long ringless fingers, '... I have no husband, and little wonder. Who would put up with me? But you were made for marriage, weren't you?'

'I'm not married, nor am I living at home. I'm helping a friend to run her lodging house,' Morna said stiffly.

'Indeed? Here, let me help.' Before Morna could protest the other girl had caught at the handle of the basket and turned to walk alongside her, the basket swinging between them. 'I've just moved back from Glasgow. My parents have both died and the family house belongs to my brother and me now. I've set up a small school there.'

'You're a teacher?'

'Oh yes, it's what I've always wanted to do,' Ruth said enthusiastically, steeping out so quickly that Morna was in danger of being tugged along by the basket. 'You must come to tea and hear all about it. And I want to hear all about what has been happening to you too.'

They were nearing Quay Street and Morna, reluctant to let the other girl see the lodging house, took a firm grip on the basket and slowed down, forcing Ruth to do the same. 'I'm kept very busy, Ruth, I have little time to spend on visiting.'

'Oh, please! I seem to spend most of my time with the wee ones, and delightful though they are, I'm longing for some adult conversation. Say you'll come, even for a little while. Next Thursday afternoon. Will you be free next Thursday afternoon?'

The rain returned, even harder than before. Morna was

sure that she felt a dampness in her left shoe. 'I'm not sure – but I'll try,' she said, deciding that her best chance of escape was to agree to the meeting.

'Please do. You remember our house in Ardrossan Road? I'll expect you at three o'clock.'

'Goodbye, Ruth,' Morna said firmly, retrieving control of her basket. Why, she asked herself grumpily as she hauled the heavy basket the rest of the way on her own, had she agreed to see Ruth again? They may have been classmates several years before, but they had never been friends. Indeed, their interests had been very different; Morna preferring the company of the more frivolous girls in the class, while Ruth, in constant pursuit of knowledge and enlightenment, never seemed to lift her head from a book. Morna vaguely recalled her, tall and angular, leaning against a wall during the playtimes, reading while all the other children played at hopscotch or skipping games or, like Morna and her cronies, gossiped and giggled in a corner of the play-ground. What could she and Ruth possibly find to talk about now, when Ruth was a teacher and Morna was . . .

She groaned as she reached the Chapmans' door and set the basket down in order to lift the latch. What would Ruth make of her former classmate living in a shabby lodging house and earning her keep as a skivvy?

Meggie was pinning on her hat when Morna went into the kitchen. 'I have tae go out, pet. Wee Mrs McKay along the road's birthin' her bairn an' she needs me. Can you peel the potatoes for tonight's dinner? An' the soup'll need a stir now and then.'

'Will you be back to see to the meat?' Morna quavered. She could eat the stuff – though only because the hard work made her hungry – but the thought of handling the great slabs of raw fat-laced meat made her feel sick.

'Aye, I will, if you dae the carrots and onions beforehand. Now where's – here it is.' Meggie picked up a small coil of rope from the dresser, and Morna eyed it nervously.

'What do you need that for?' Her knowledge of childbirth was very sketchy, but she could not believe that ropes were necessary.

'Tae fasten tae the bedposts, of course, so's she's got somethin' tae pull on when the pain gets bad,' Meggie said briskly. 'There's a pile o' darnin' in that basket that could do with a good goin' over with a needle.' Then she was out of the door while Morna was still wrestling with the thought of the pain becoming so bad that the expectant mother was forced to pull on a length of rope. With just a few words, Meggie had turned childbirth into some sort of tug of war. Morna shuddered, then began to put the shopping into the cupboard.

She left the vegetables for as long as she could in the hope that Meggie would return and deal with them, but after almost an hour of sitting by the fire forcing a big darning needle through thick socks and yellowed vests she decided that peeling and dicing onions and carrots was preferable to feeling like Cinderella without any hope of a fairy godmother arriving to save her.

Ten minutes later, weeping over a pile of onions and wondering if she would have been better off with the darning, she heard the street door open. Her hope that Meggie had returned was dashed when the kitchen door was thrown open and Samuel Gilmartin swept in, grinning from ear to ear.

'I got the position,' he exulted. 'I start next Monday and it's all thanks tae – what's wrong? Has Meggie been shoutin' at ye?' Then, as Morna gave a huge sniff and shook her head, holding out a half-peeled onion, 'Och, is that all it is? Here . . .' He took the onion and the knife from her and laid them down, then led her over to the kitchen sink, where he turned on the single tap and then pushed her hands beneath the flow of cold water. 'Hold them there for a minute,' he instructed.

Almost at once the unbearable stinging in her eyes began to ease and after another minute she was able to shake the water from her hands and turn the tap off. Being old and very stiff, it continued to dribble water until Samuel reached over her shoulder and turned it off completely with a swift twist of his wrist. Then he spun her around to face him.

'D'ye have a handkerchief?' When she produced one from the pocket of her sacking apron he took it from her and mopped her eyes. 'There now, is that not better? Have ye never heard o' takin' the sting of the onions away by puttin' yer hands under cold runnin' water? Take a good blow, now,' he went on, clamping the handkerchief to her nose. Enraged, she snatched it from him and turned away. When she had managed to sort herself out she whirled around to face him again.

'Of course I know that cold running water takes the sting away, but Meggie's out with a rope, helping some neighbour to have a baby, and that beastly tap's too stiff for me and – and . . .' she blinked up at him with eyes that were still painful.

'Poor wee lass,' he commiserated, and then, the huge smile breaking over his face again, 'but did ye not hear what I said? I got the position!'

'At the shop?'

'Aye, at the shop. No more getting meself filthy dirty in that dockyard!' he crowed, and before she knew what was happening Morna was being whirled around the kitchen with her feet several inches off the ground.

'Put me down,' she squeaked, and when he finally did so, 'Who interviewed you for the position?'

'Your sister, like you said she would.'

'And she took you on, just like that?'

'Ah well, your aunt put in a good word for me.'

'My Aunt Beatrice McCallum? She was interviewing along with Belle?' Aunt Beatrice seemed to be poking her nose in everywhere.

'Not exactly. Y'see, I went tae your aunt's house by error, thinkin' that Miss Forsyth was to interview me there.'

'But I told you to go to the shop.'

'I must have been so excited at gettin' the chance of an interview that I got myself confused,' Samuel said glibly. 'And as it happens, one of your poor aunt's wee pet dogs had just died. So I helped her out by diggin' a grave and buryin' the poor wee thing, and she gave me breakfast in return.'

'I don't see how . . .'

'Never mind that; the thing is, I got the position on a month's trial. I'm on the first rung of the ladder and it's all thanks to you. I love you, Miss Morna Forsyth!' His arms were still linked loosely around her waist, and in order to look up at him she'd placed her hands lightly on his shoulders; with one of his sudden and unexpected moves Samuel ducked towards her and gave her a lusty kiss full on the lips.

'Samuel!' She pulled away, embarrassed and horrified.

'Sure and I just wanted to say thank you.'

'You could have found another way to say it.' Morna's face was hot and her hands fluttered like birds over her hair and clothing in an orgy of patting and tidying.

'What other way? You name it and I'll do it.'

'Finish off the onions and then do the carrots and the potatoes.'

'With pleasure,' he said, and whipped off his jacket before settling down to the task.

'Fraser Walter Forsyth,' Walter said in ringing tones.

'Where d'ye get the Fraser from?'

'Mother's mother was a Fraser, Aunt Beatrice. It's a proud name that should be kept in the family.'

'Hector's a proud name too. You could name him after yer uncle.'

'Hector doesn't have the same weight to it. No, it's to be Fraser Walter Forsyth.' Walter rolled the words around his tongue as though sucking a particularly pleasant-tasting sweet.

A shaft of weak February sunlight suddenly shone through the window on to the baby's face. His eyes immediately shut tightly and he gave a little snuffling sneeze. Walter turned so that his body was between the bright light and the baby, bouncing the shawled bundle lightly in his arms, 'Belle, first thing tomorrow you must arrange for a sign writer to paint the words "Forsyth and Son" over the shop front. Young Fraser here shall have a fresh new sign in his honour.'

'I doubt he'll be bothered,' Beatrice said dryly, easing a coin into the baby's tiny hand for luck. Then, as the perfect little fingers immediately curled around her offering, 'Would ye look at that, now? He knows the value of silver already, for all that his name's longer than he is.'

'He's only one day old; of course he's small,' Walter defended his firstborn, while Sarah's aching body felt as though it had given birth to a young bullock, hooves and all, rather than the little scrap that Walter was so proudly showing off to his sister and aunt.

'And how are you, Sarah?' Belatedly, Beatrice remembered that the new member of the Forsyth family had a mother.

'Tired, of course, but in good health, according to the doctor. She did very well, didn't you, Sarah?'

Beatrice surveyed the paper-white face on the pillow and said kindly, 'You look tired, my dear. We should leave her to rest, Walter. And the little one too.'

'Indeed.' Walter handed his son reluctantly to the nurse and ushered his sister and aunt from the room. 'Go to sleep, Sarah,' he ordered his wife as they went. 'I will be back later to see how you both are.'

Alone at last, Sarah held her arms out for the baby. 'Give him to me.'

The nurse frowned. 'He needs his rest as much as you do, Mrs Forsyth. Your husband has scarcely let the wee soul lie in his cradle since he was born.'

'Just for a moment,' Sarah begged, and the child, smelling sweetly of soap and powder, was placed carefully in the crook of her elbow.

'A moment only, while I get his cradle ready.'

Young Fraser Walter Forsyth was already half asleep, but as his mother peered at him, anxiously searching for signs of auburn hair, brown eyes, and neat handsome features, he opened his dark eyes wide and stared up at her. His hair was dark too, and the baby face, made for a snub button of a nose, bore instead an appendage that, like Walter's and his father's before him, was always going to be slightly too large for its surroundings. Without doubt this child was a Forsyth, not a Gilmartin.

The nurse finished fussing over the elaborate cradle that Walter had had made for his son and turned to the bed in time to see Sarah's eyes flood with weak tears. One of them splashed on to the baby's cheek, and he screwed up his own dark eyes and let out a mew of protest.

'There now, I knew that you were overtired,' the nurse scolded, hurrying to snatch her precious charge away from danger. 'You must think of the child's well-being, Mrs Forsyth. If you let yourself become fatigued then it will affect your milk and it's this poor wee thing who will suffer. Come along now, little man.' She gathered the baby into her capable arms and bore him off to his rest, while Sarah turned her face into the pillow and wept quietly for the child she had hoped to bear – Samuel's child.

18

'Poor wee mite,' Beatrice McCallum said as she and Belle walked away from the house an hour later. 'Imagine havin' Walter for a father.'

'I'm sure he'll be a very good father,' Belle said sharply. She herself had little love for her brother, but it offended her to hear someone else criticise him.

'Oh, there's no doubt o' that as far as the material things of life are concerned, but I'm talkin' about the adventurous side of growin' up. Hamilton was always pompous and Walter's taken after him – that's why he's the way he is. A boy needs a bit of adventure tae bring out the best in—' A bout of coughing cut her sentence short, and she stopped, fishing in her pocket for a handkerchief.

Belle supported her aunt until the paroxysm was over, then said, 'You shouldn't have come out of the house on a cold damp day like this – I told you that earlier.'

'Nonsense, I couldn't miss the chance to see Sarah and the wee laddie for myself. It was just a tickle in the throat – the remains of that cold I had last week.'

'Mebbe so, but you're going to have a hot poultice on your chest tonight, and a hot toddy to drink too.'

'Ach, you're nothin' but a fuss, Belle Forsyth,' the old woman grumbled, although secretly she quite enjoyed being fussed over from time to time, and also appreciated her niece's company in the house. 'It's just as well that the tickle waited until now,' she said as she and Belle started walking again. 'If it had happened in the house, Walter would no doubt have had the whole place fumigated in case his son caught the smit from me.

'How's that young man gettin' on?'

Belle, thinking her aunt was still referring to the new baby, was confused. 'What young man?'

'The one that came tae my house lookin' for work in the shop.'

'Oh, Samuel Gilmartin.' Without realising it Belle raised one hand to her hat, checking that it was neatly settled on her head. 'He's doing very well. In fact, he's quite an asset, now that Walter's more interested in his child than his work.'

'Why don't you invite him for his supper tomorrow night? And I'm talkin' about Mr Gilmartin, not your brother,' Beatrice added as her niece looked at her, startled. She knew, from months of sharing the same house with her niece, that Belle's mind could not leap from one subject to another as easily as her own.

'Invite him for supper? But Aunt Beatrice, he's one of our employees!'

'What difference does that make? He was very helpful when he was here last, buryin' poor wee Romeo and bein' so kind and understandin'. I was very taken with him and I'd like fine tae see him again. Ask him, Belle; and you can tell him that I'll not take no for an answer.'

There was something about Samuel Gilmartin that had caught Belle's attention from the moment he began working in the shop. Even when she was not looking at him, or looking *for* him, she could somehow tell just where he was; and on the many occasions she was unable to resist the temptation to check her instinct, it was always proved right.

Samuel also had a knack of always being where he was most needed – opening the door for important and valued customers, stacking a shelf that was beginning to empty, offering help to one of his colleagues or assistance to someone who was not quite certain as to what they wanted to buy. Whatever he was doing and whoever he was with, he was unfailingly cheerful, and he seemed to be able to sense the customer's wishes in an instant. He could switch with ease from being subservient to quietly sympathetic. The rest of the staff liked him and even Walter, after his initial reluctance to approve of someone hired by Belle rather than himself, had acknowledged that he was an admirable assistant. As for Belle herself, although he had only been working in the shop for a matter of weeks she found herself becoming more and more dependent on the young Irishman, for he was reliable and never had to be told anything twice. She now knew that the dockyard work he had hated so much was completely wrong for him.

Now, sitting at Beatrice McCallum's table, she was taken aback by the sheer power of Samuel's presence. All through supper Beatrice had been busy drawing him out, and he had responded with his usual cheerful honesty, talking easily and warmly of his family and his life in Ireland. Since there was no need for Belle to make conversation she was content to keep her eyes on her plate, letting his soft pleasant voice flow around her ears like music. An occasional surreptitious glance from beneath lowered eyelids made it possible for her to see his deft hands, the fingernails cut short and well scrubbed, and when he laughed, as he did easily and often, the sound rippled through her like skilled fingers caressing the strings of a harp.

On the few occasions when she looked at him properly his auburn hair lit the room like the autumn bonfires she, Morna and Walter used to dance around in the back garden as children, and his laughing eyes sparkled at her.

Although Beatrice, in her high-backed chair at the head of the table, ate very little, Belle was pleased to see that she looked better than she had done for weeks. Tonight there was colour in her face and her grey eyes, which had become as dull as stones since her favourite dog's death, sparkled just as much as Samuel's – so much so that Belle felt like a crow in the presence of two exotic, beautiful birds.

'Have ye done?' Ena asked from the door. 'Are ye finished yer puddin's?'

'Mr Gilmartin?'

'There's nothin' left but the pattern and even that looks delicious, so ye'd best take it away before I disgrace myself.' Samuel turned his warm smile on the servant. 'Are you the cook as well? That was the best meal I have ever eaten.'

Ena flushed with pleasure, but her voice was as dour as ever as she accused, 'You've been kissin' the Blarney Stone and no mistake.'

'I never have,' he protested. 'My mother, bless her, always insisted on her children showing their appreciation. "It's all very well thankin' the Lord before ye eat," she always said, "but don't forget the Lord's servant that saw tae the makin' of yer food. Thank Him afore ye settle tae eat, and thank her after ye're full." So . . .' He sprang up to open the door for her, 'I thank you, ma'am, from the bottom of my heart.'

'Are you sure about the Blarney Stone?' Ena asked dryly, but as she went out her smile deepened to a broad grin.

'And my thanks to you too, Mrs McCallum, and Miss Forsyth, for invitin' me into your lovely home and makin' me feel so welcome,' Samuel said earnestly as he closed the door and returned to the table. 'Ye've no idea what a pleasure it is tae eat a fine meal in such good company.'

'What are you used to, then?'

'Me? Oh, I live in a lodgin' house down by the shore. It's a good lodgin' house too, don't get me wrong, Mrs McCallum. The couple who own it are decent people, and the lodgers are all looked after as well as they can be.'

'It's owned by Meggie Butcher, Aunt Beatrice,' Belle explained. 'Her married name is Chapman.'

'Of course, I remember now. That's where Morna went when she left home.'

'That's right, Mrs McCallum. Fortunate for me that she did go there, for it's thanks to her that I ended up working where I am now. As I said, the lodgin' house is as good as any can be, but it's not like being in your own home. They feed us and house us, and we can expect no more. All the other lodgers work in the Ardrossan dockyard or on the railways.'

'Perhaps you should find somewhere more congenial now that you're working for the Forsyths,' Beatrice suggested.

'To tell ye the truth, I've been thinkin' that myself. I'd like fine tae have a wee room tae myself where I could keep my books and be able tae read without bein' laughed at. But . . .' he glanced quickly at Belle, '. . . I'm still workin' out my month's trial and I'd not want to make a move until I'm sure of the position.'

'You've been in the shop for the better part of a month,

have you not? And from what my niece tells me you've been giving satisfaction. Belle?'

Belle's face warmed under the expectant gaze of two pairs of eyes. Why, she asked herself, did Aunt Beatrice always have to be poking her nose into everything? Aloud, she said, 'My aunt is right, Mr Gilmartin. Your first month is almost over and I think I can speak for my brother and myself when I say that you have been most satisfactory.'

'God bless you, Miss Forsyth! You'll not regret puttin' your trust in me,' he said warmly. And then, with one of his infectious laughs, 'Now here's me been talkin' and talkin' about my past and my ambitions and never thinkin' how tired you must be with the sound of my voice.'

'Not at all,' Beatrice assured him firmly. 'I asked you to tell me all about yourself, and it has been a most interestin' story.'

'You're very kind, Mrs McCallum. Didn't I think, when I first started, that I had nothing much tae say? And now I find that I've talked all through our supper. In fact, I've taken up enough of your valuable time. I should be goin'.'

'It's early yet.' Beatrice put out a detaining hand as he began to get to his feet. 'Ena will be taking tea into the parlour and we can't let you go until you've had a cup. Can we, Belle?'

'That's very kind of you,' Samuel said, and then darted forwards as Beatrice put her hands on the arms of her chair and began to ease herself upright. 'Can I assist you, ma'am? Just lean on me, and let me know if I'm doing things the wrong way.'

'Tell me, Mr Gilmartin,' Belle heard her aunt say as she followed the couple, now arm in arm, across the hall to the parlour, 'do you play cribbage?'

'No, Mrs McCallum, but I'm a very quick learner.'

'Then I shall teach you, and then you can come and

play cribbage with me every week. You would be doing Belle a favour, for I enjoy my games of cribbage, but she finds them tedious.'

'I don't, Aunt Beatrice. It's just that I have the shop accounts books to keep in order, and they take up so much time in the evenings.'

'I would be charmed, Mrs McCallum,' said Samuel, and then, with a slight bow in Belle's direction, 'particularly if it gave me the opportunity to help you as well, Miss Forsyth.'

'A most remarkable young man,' Beatrice McCallum said when their visitor had gone. 'Quite impressive, wouldn't you say?'

'It's hard to believe that he came from such lowly beginnings,' Belle admitted.

'Tush – that has nothing to do with it. I came from lowly beginnings myself, and I've done quite well.' Beatrice looked around the comfortable, well-furnished parlour. 'It's all a matter of smeddum, Belle. Do you know that word?'

'I can't say that I do, Aunt.'

'I thought not. It means having strong spirit, determination and the will to get somewhere. I have it and so does Samuel Gilmartin. He will go far, mark my words,' Beatrice said, and then, giving her niece a mischievous sidelong glance, 'I never looked for another husband after your Uncle Hector died, for it seemed to me that one husband is enough for any woman, but if I were twenty years younger I do believe that that young man might just have been able to change my mind.'

'Aunt Beatrice, how can you say such a thing?'

Beatrice leaned over and patted her niece's hand. 'Perhaps, my dear, I enjoy teasing you now and again.

Pay no attention; it's just my way. But now I'm going to leave you in peace to work on your ledgers. Pleasant though this evening has been, I feel quite tired now. I do believe that I shall sleep well for a change.'

Meggie came back from the shops and hunted the house for Morna, finally running her to ground in the attic bedroom, where she was changing the grey sheets on one of the beds. 'I've just heard,' she said, still in her hat and coat.

'Heard what?' Morna stuffed a sheet into the basket, trying to touch it with her fingertips only, and turned the thin, stained mattress over. It was just as stained on the other side.

'Mr Walter's wife's had a wee laddie. Ye're an auntie, Miss Morna.' The woman's heavy face was beaming.

'Am I, indeed?' Morna shook out a fresh sheet – patched, and already patterned with its own stains – and began to smooth it over the mattress.

'Ye'll be goin' tae see the wee one?'

'I don't see why I should.'

'But he's yer own flesh an' blood!'

'So Walter says.'

'Miss Morna! That's a cruel thing tae say.'

'Even if the child had Clarissa Pinkerton as its mother I doubt if I would be rushing to see it,' Morna said. 'I don't care for children, I don't care for Walter, and I most certainly do not care for his maidservant wife.' There was another reason, but it was not one that she could admit to Meggie – she did not have the money to buy a gift for the child, and nobody visited a newborn child without some sort of gift.

'But the wee thing's innocent of any wrongdoing, and a bairn's a bairn. Ye should go and pay yer respects.'

'I most certainly will not.' Morna moved on to the next bed, while Meggie stared at her, baffled, then remembered something else.

'Is this not the day ye're supposed tae be visitin' with that friend ye met in the town last week?'

'Yes, but I'm not going there either.'

'Why not?'

'For goodness' sake, Meggie – it's not as if we were close at school. We barely exchanged half a dozen words, and no doubt she'll have heard by now all about the way my father walked out, and about Walter's behaviour. I have no doubt that once she finds out the truth about what has been happening she will be as reluctant to entertain me to tea as I am to go.' Morna still burned with shame at the memory of the way Mrs MacAdam, the woman who might so easily have been her mother-in-law, had looked at her and spoken to her on their last meeting; she had no wish to see that look on Ruth's face.

'But ye need tae be with yer own sort of folk again. If ye won't go tae see the newborn babbie, at least have tea with yer friend. Tae please me,' Meggie coaxed, and Morna, too tired to argue any further, gave in.

Ruth threw open the door before Morna had even had time to lift the heavy brass knocker. 'I was watching for you coming along the road. In you come – tea first, I think. This way.'

The entrance hall, Morna noticed as she followed her hostess, was wider than the Forsyths', and the stairway curving to the upper floor more grand. A telephone stood on a small ornate table, and there was even a brass gong on a stand. She had expected to be ushered into one of the two front rooms, but instead Ruth passed them and opened a door at the rear of the hall. They went through another short, narrower hall and arrived, to Morna's astonishment, in the large, cluttered kitchen.

'Sit down and we can talk while I make the tea.' Ruth swept a pile of books from a chair by the table, deposited them on the floor, and bustled over to the range, where a large kettle was simmering.

Morna took a seat, looking around the place. It was as though Ruth spent most of her time in the kitchen. Dishes were stacked on the draining board and a large cast-iron pot and a pile of vegetables stood at one end of the big, well-scrubbed kitchen table she had been seated at, but judging by the papers and books scattered over the rest of the table, it was also used as a desk.

'You live here on your own?' she asked, wondering why, in a house with several rooms, Ruth should choose to live in only one.

'Most of the time. My brother Tom is assistant minister at a church in Glasgow, but he comes here occasionally, and always in the summer, of course.'

'You don't have a servant to look after you?'

Ruth had measured tea into a china pot and added boiling water; as she set the kettle back on the hob she turned and gave Morna a wide smile, 'Good gracious no. Why would I want another woman to cook for me and clean up after me when I've got two perfectly good hands of my own? I wouldn't demean any woman in that way.' She delved into a cupboard and produced a biscuit barrel and a plate. 'There's Anna, of course – she lives down by the river and she has a sick husband and five children to care for. She brings her youngest to my little school every morning and stays to help with the children. She does some housework too, but that's because she needs the money badly. It's a fair exchange of skills, since she's much better at housework than I am, and in return I teach her little one and give Anna a small wage, which helps to feed and clothe her family.'

She laid the plate of biscuits on the tray, then went back to the cupboard and produced more plates. 'I made sandwiches for this afternoon, and Anna very kindly made a jam sponge for us. Unfortunately, I was never taught to bake and I can never make the time to learn. Do you know how to bake?'

'I've never had the need to bake,' Morna said, surprised by the question.

'I know what you mean,' Ruth agreed sympathetically. 'Our education was sadly lacking in practical matters, wasn't it? That's why I have to rely on Anna. Once a week she teaches the children something of cooking and baking. They love it, and I must say that it has helped me too.'

She fell silent, concentrating on cutting the sponge cake into delicate sections. Morna picked up a magazine that lay close to her hand and gave it a casual glance. Then she looked again.

'Are you interested in the suffragette movement?'

'Of course, aren't you?'

'I don't know anything about it,' Morna admitted.

'Really? You must borrow some of my literature; I'm sure you would find it interesting,' Ruth said, and then as Morna, raised to believe that the suffragette movement was unfeminine, disruptive and unnecessary, struggled to think of some way to reject the offer without giving offence, 'Tea's ready. I thought we would have it in the little front parlour.'

19

'My mother would be happy to know that her special little room is occasionally used for its proper purpose,' Ruth said as she set the tray down on a polished circular wood table with curved legs, 'I tend to spend all my time in the kitchen because it's warmer and everything I need is near to hand.'

'It's a beautiful room,' Morna said in delight. The room was restful, with its soft, comfortable chairs and flowered wallpaper in pastel shades. The polished floor was covered with rugs and pale green leaves were woven into the fawn curtains. A piano stood against one wall, and a small writing desk in the corner. There was also a lacquered wood chest of drawers inlaid with exquisite flower and leaf patterns.

Morna ran her fingertips over it lightly. 'I have never seen anything so perfect!'

'It was a gift from my father to my mother. He brought it home after a trip to Japan. I lit the fire especially for your visit,' Ruth went on, 'and what we need now are crumpets to toast at the flames. I do believe I have some.' As she went towards the door she added,

'Father brought the prints from Japan too. Mother loved them dearly.'

The prints were of mountains and deep blue lakes, delicate trees and flowers, and graceful Japanese ladies in rich robes taking tea, playing musical instruments and writing at low desks. Morna studied each of them closely before turning back to look around the lovely room. Its comfort provoked a sudden flood of longing for the home she had left; the home now presided over by Walter's wife. Tears sprang to her eyes, and she only just had time to blink them away before her hostess reappeared, a plate of crumpets in one hand and a butter dish and two toasting forks in the other. She speared a crumpet on one of the forks and offered it to Morna, then did one for herself. 'Come and kneel on the hearthrug.'

'The prints are beautiful. I used to go to painting classes,' Morna said wistfully as they settled on the rug together, 'but if I tried every day for the rest of my life I could never produce such perfect work.'

'At least you're artistic. Poor Mother, I must have been a sore disappointment to her. Instead of appreciating beautiful things as she did, I followed my father into the academic world. She would have loved to have a daughter like you, Morna. Oh, we adored each other, but I couldn't help being me.' She turned her crumpet so that it could toast on the other side. 'I used to envy you when we were at school together.'

'Envy me? Why would you do that?'

'Because you were so pretty – and now you're quite beautiful. And you laughed a lot and had fun. I knew even then that you were the sort of daughter my mother would have enjoyed. I heard, after we left school, that you stayed at home as your mother's companion. And I also heard of her recent death. I am so sorry, Morna.'

'No doubt you've heard of what happened after Mother died.' Morna heard a harsh note creep into her voice. 'About my father going off to goodness knows where and abandoning us? And about my brother Walter breaking off his most suitable engagement to Clarissa Pinkerton and choosing to marry our maidservant instead?'

'Yes, I did hear all that,' Ruth said calmly. 'One cannot help hearing gossip in a small place like Saltcoats.'

'And yet you invited me to your house for tea.'

'I think they're both ready now. Why shouldn't I invite you for tea?' Ruth went on as butter melted into the hot crumpets.

'Nobody else cares to know me now,' Morna said bitterly. 'I'm an outcast in my own home town.'

'Then the loss is theirs, for they must all be behaving very childishly. They'll forget about those small scandals in time.'

'I doubt if I ever will.'

'What is there to fret over? Your father did his duty by his wife and children, and once he was widowed and his family grown he decided to seek out a new life for himself – and to give you and your brother and sister the chance to find yourselves as adults. As for Walter – I admire him for realising that just because a woman is in service, she is no less important than her mistress. Just think,' Ruth swept on, oblivious of Morna's shock at such blasphemy from one who should know better, 'of all those poor souls who are only raised in order to look after their parents and then find themselves alone in middle age, with no lives of their own.'

'I can't say that I have found myself as an adult,' Morna protested angrily. 'I'm living in a lodging house run by my former nursemaid and her husband and I'm expected to earn my keep by working as a servant. That's not what I had wanted out of life!'

'Why are you in this lodging house? Did your brother put you out of your home?'

'I went of my own accord. How could I stay there and see our servant take my mother's place as mistress of the house?'

Ruth used her napkin to wipe melted butter from her chin and then glanced pointedly at Morna's reddened fingers. 'So, in protest, you chose to become a servant yourself.'

'You do your own housework.'

'From choice, and in my own home. It must be difficult, I know, to suddenly see the woman who used to be your servant girl become your sister-in-law,' Ruth said gently, 'but she was your brother's own choice and surely you would prefer to see him content in a marriage of his choosing than unhappy in one that was probably arranged for him and for his fiancée by their parents? Is she so terrible, this new wife of his?'

'Not terrible, just . . .' Morna struggled to find the right words.

'Just not of our class? My dear, in the path I've chosen I meet a lot of women, many of them "not of our class". And it has made me feel that we might all be better off blending our differing outlooks and talents. We can learn so much from each other. Talking of talent, I seem to recall that you were a proficient pianist. Do you remember that school concert when you were the star performer of the evening? You played a beautiful piece on the piano; my mother spoke of it for weeks afterwards.'

'To a Rose.' Morna recalled the concert as though it had been yesterday. 'It was one of my mother's favourite pieces.'

'Play it for me now,' Ruth said suddenly.

'I couldn't! I haven't played the piano for a long time and my fingers have become quite stiff and swollen.'

'Please try, Morna. Mother's piano has been neglected too, and I would so like to hear it being played again,' Ruth coaxed and Morna, who had been longing to go to the piano from the moment she had entered the room, needed no further encouragement.

It took several false starts before her fingers began to feel comfortable on the keys, but once that happened they began to work of their own accord and the music came, shakily at first and then confidently. She followed 'To a Rose' with 'The Blue Danube' waltz, and then stopped and turned on the piano stool. 'I'm very much out of practice.'

'And I am no judge. To me, it sounded delightful. Thank you. Now if you've finished your tea, you must come and see my classroom.'

They crossed the hall to a large, elegant room that must once have been a beautiful drawing room. Now it was furnished with three long low tables surrounded by small chairs. A desk stood in the corner and slates were laid out on the tables.

'This was our family drawing room, but as you can see, it makes a perfect classroom now. I had the carpets taken up as well and now the floor is well marked by the children's boots. I am leaving it as it is, for it's wrong to expect children to creep about like little mice.'

'Do you enjoy teaching?'

'I adore it,' Ruth said. 'Here, of course, my pupils are all very young. My aim is to start them off with a year's general tuition before they go to the public school. I always think of children's minds as hungry little mouths, open wide and desperate to be fed with information.'

'I don't remember feeling like that when I was at school.'

'Ah, but that was because our minds were force-fed with facts, and that,' Ruth said, her voice suddenly steely, 'is a terrible thing to do to any human being, especially a child. I can remember sitting in the classroom when I was only about seven years old, wondering if three and eight really did make eleven, or if the teacher was just teaching us a lot of lies to amuse herself. Children need to find things out by their own efforts. That's the way I teach, and it is so rewarding. I think that you would enjoy it, Morna.'

'Me? I couldn't teach! What do I know of academic things?'

'I wasn't thinking of reading and writing or grammar and arithmetic. I can deal with those subjects, but I know nothing of music and art. My little pupils would love to learn something of those subjects, and you could teach them, if you were willing to come and work with me.'

'I couldn't!' Morna said again.

'I think you could. Remember what I said earlier about those hungry little minds? I want my pupils to enjoy learning, and I'm sure that you could find a way of making your subjects palatable.'

'You are offering me a position in your school?'

'I wouldn't be able to pay you much. I draw my pupils from the tenement buildings down by the shore and their parents can't afford to pay more than a few pence a week.'

This was yet another shock. 'I thought you were teaching children of – of our own class,' Morna said awkwardly.

'Parents of "our own class", as you put it, can afford to send their children to music and painting classes, as your parents did. I teach children who would otherwise have no hope of learning such subjects. I want to show them that there's more to life than poverty and drudgery. You would be welcome to live here rent-free as part of your remuneration.'

'But how could you afford to pay me at all, since the parents can't pay you much?'

Ruth's shrug indicated that to her, money was of little importance. 'As you already know, Tom and I own this house, which means that I have no rent to pay. My parents left me a small allowance and I have few needs of my own. I earn a little by writing articles for various publications.'

'You're a writer? How wonderful to have such an ability.'

Ruth laughed. 'If you care enough about any subject under the sun, Morna, you will find that you have the fire and the ability to work at it. This is quite a large house with plenty of space; it would be such fun to have your company and I think you would enjoy the work. And if a little extra learning early in life, and an appreciation of beautiful things like music and art – if you agree to join me – could give even one of those little ones the chance to do something different with their lives, then it will all be worthwhile. You could use the little parlour as your classroom, since the piano is already in there. We can easily set up an easel there too. Please consider my offer, Morna. I would like to have a friend to share this big place with me. I enjoy what I am doing, and so, I hope, do my children. And so would you!'

'Do it,' Meggie begged when Morna told her of Ruth's offer.

'You think I could?' Morna longed to take the chance that her former classmate offered, but at the same time the challenge terrified her.

'I know ye could, Miss Morna. And ye cannae stay

here for ever; ye know that this house and this life's no' right for the likes of you.'

'I'll miss you, Meggie.' She reached across the table and took the woman's hands, still hot and damp from washing dishes in the sink, in her own. 'You've been so good to me, taking me in as you did when I had nowhere else to go.'

'And you've worked hard and never complained, though I know fine that it's not been easy. But at last ye've got somewhere else tae go, and I'm not far away,' Meggie coaxed. 'You'll still visit me, I hope, for I'll want tae know how ye're doin'.'

'Of course I'll visit you.'

'So ye're goin'?'

'I think I am,' Morna said slowly, and then, with dawning excitement, 'Oh, Meggie, I feel as if I'm setting out on such an adventure!'

During her stay in the lodging house Morna had often encountered local children running around the streets in gangs, so absorbed in their own noisy games that as often as not she had had to skip aside in order to avoid being mown down. Once, deep in thought and unaware of danger, she had been knocked off the pavement by a lad almost her own height, and had narrowly escaped falling headlong into a steaming pile of horse manure. The basket of messages had been sent spinning, with packages and paper bags streaming out of it.

'Out o' ma way,' the boy had roared at her, stopping only to stick his tongue out at her and then snatch up a dropped carrot before speeding off. Ever since, she had felt quite shaky each time she came across the street gangs, and her first sight of the half a dozen or so shabbily dressed children clattering into Ruth's house froze the blood in her veins. How she could possibly manage to control this lot of small savages, let alone teach them anything?

'I think you should assist me for the first week,' Ruth had said as she helped Morna to unpack her small suitcase in the comfortable bedroom that had been prepared for her, 'so that you and the children can get to know each other. And you can also observe my teaching methods.'

'What if I turn out to be hopeless?'

'Of course you won't be hopeless. If you know anything about music and drawing then you have knowledge that you can pass on to others. The important thing to remember is that the children want to learn, and that they want to enjoy learning. Just watch me.'

It was obvious from the first that the children, much younger than the youth who had frightened her, adored Ruth, who behaved towards them as though she were a mixture of older sister and mother. The schoolteacher element was there too, but in moderation; her rules, though firmly endorsed, were sensible rather than restrictive.

School, Morna thought, as she watched the first morning's class, had never been like this. By the time the children, all dressed in brightly coloured smocks that Ruth had had made for them, were sent scurrying along the hallway to the kitchen for their mid-morning break, Morna had begun to wish that her own schooldays had been half as interesting and rewarding.

In the kitchen, Anna, a thin, anxious-looking woman, was pouring milk into mugs from a huge jug while some of the children bustled importantly around, handing out biscuits from a box on the kitchen table. 'One each, mind,' one of them was saying sternly. 'Yous can all count tae one and that's the number of biscuits, mind!'

The three adults also had milk, though Morna would much rather have had a cup of tea. Afterwards, they all took part in an energetic ball game in the back garden for fifteen minutes before class began again.

'When it rains we do exercises in the classroom after milk and biscuits, because young children need to work off physical energy in order to get their minds to concentrate,' Ruth explained as they shepherded their young charges back to the house. 'But I like to get them outside as much as possible. We're going to do botany in the summer.'

'You know about botany?'

Ruth grinned. 'I know about gardening and I know that I haven't the time to keep this place as tidy as it was in my parents' day. I can't afford a gardener, so in the spring the children will learn how to plant flower seeds and grow vegetables, and how to weed. It will be good for them *and* for me. And if it works then they can take flowers and vegetables home to their mothers.' Then, as they waited for the little ones to settle themselves back into their small chairs, she said, 'I seem to remember that you were good at needlework too.'

'I know how to embroider,' Morna said cautiously.

'Admirable!'

'Do you mean that you want me to teach that as well?'

'What a good idea, if you can find the time – but let's not put too much on your shoulders at the start of your career. It was another project I had in mind. A group of friends meet here one evening a week to make a patch-work quilt. I would help them but unfortunately I'm no seamstress,' Ruth admitted ruefully. 'Put a threaded needle into my hands and I'm quite likely to prick my fingers on it and get blood all over the material. Perhaps you could help them instead?'

'A sort of sewing bee?'

Frances Forsyth and several of her friends, including Clarissa Pinkerton and her mother, had been members

223

of a sewing group, meeting in each other's houses and combining trite conversation with stitching. Morna had considered it boring, and had resisted her mother's attempts to get her to join in.

'I'm not sure they could be described as a sewing bee. We have some interesting meetings. They're coming on Wednesday evening and I know that they could do with some help. You wouldn't mind, would you?'

'Oh no,' said Morna, polite on the outside, but sighing inwardly.

20

Morna was dismayed when she received the invitation to Fraser Walter Forsyth's christening. She had been too busy settling into Ruth's home and way of life to give any thought to Walter and Sarah or their newborn child, and the invitation was a sudden, sharp reminder of their existence and her duty as the child's aunt.

It wasn't just a case of attending the ceremony – she would be expected to take a gift for the baby, and she was still as poor as a church mouse. The small monthly allowance she had received from her father, and then Walter, had ceased after she'd stormed out of the family home, and she had been too proud to ask her brother for money.

She was on the point of asking Ruth for a loan when she remembered the jewellery she and Belle had inherited from their mother.

'I took all of it, and your clothes, to Aunt Beatrice's,' Belle said when her younger sister called at the shop, 'not that there were many trinkets left once Walter had claimed the best of them for Sarah. You'll have received your invitation to wee Fraser's christening?'

'That's why I need my share of the jewellery,' Morna admitted. 'I'll have to buy him a christening gift, and I've not got much money.'

'I could lend—'

'No, Belle, I'll not be beholden to you. And I'd not want to wear Mother's jewellery either, so it won't be missed. When can I come to the house?'

'I'll tell you what – why don't I bring it to Ardrossan Road? Next Tuesday afternoon would suit me. It'll be no bother,' Belle rushed on before Morna could object. She was desperate to see what sort of place her sister was living in now, *and* keen to meet Ruth Durie.

A brisk March wind blew Belle up the path and in through the door as soon as Morna opened it.

'My goodness, what a day!' Belle puffed as she un-buttoned her coat. 'I took a wee walk down to the shore this morning to clear my head, and the sea's just covered with white horses as far as you can see. Spray's being thrown up the beach and halfway across the road. Oh, this is very nice,' she went on as Morna ushered her into the small parlour. 'A big difference from where you were stay-ing last. It's such a relief to know that you're living in a respectable house again. I was worried about you when you were sharing that house with all those rough men, and nobody to look out for you.'

'Meggie looked out for me very well and I'm grateful to her for all she did for me. I'll just fetch the tea – you'll be ready for it on a day like this.'

Morna returned to the parlour, teapot in hand, to find her sister studying the tray, with its two cups and saucers, 'Is your employer not joining us for tea?'

'She's had to go to Greenock to – see some folk.'

'That's a pity. I've been looking forward to meeting her.'

'Did you bring the jewellery?'

'Of course I did.' Belle produced a small box and as soon as she had served the tea, Morna began to sift through the meagre contents. 'This ring, for instance, with the emeralds. I would never wear it. And there's this brooch too.'

'It was one of Mother's favourites.'

'But never one of mine. I remember scratching my face on it once, when she picked me up. It goes too,' Morna said decisively. 'Do you think that these two pieces could raise enough money for a suitable gift?'

'More than enough. How are you going to sell them?'

'I'm taking them to McKellar's the auctioneers. I've already spoken to them and I think they'll be fair.'

'If that's what you want to do.'

'It is. How's Aunt Beatrice?' Morna remembered to ask.

'I'm concerned about her,' Belle said. 'It sounds daft, but ever since Romeo died she seems to have lost all interest in life – apart from visiting Walter's child. She and Sarah have become quite friendly.'

'Like calling to like,' Morna said dryly.

'Don't be a cat, Morna. Sarah seems to be a good mother and there's no doubt that Walter's happier than he has ever been. That's why he's never in the shop these days. I do the work while he takes the lion's share of the profits.'

'You know that Papa always looked on Walter as a liability rather than a help. You should get him to make you a partner since you're the one who's holding it all together for him.'

Belle's mouth tightened. 'We've only just paid to have "Forsyth and Son" repainted above the window, if you please. I doubt Walter would think that "Forsyth and Sister" had the same grand look to it. So you're settling in to this teaching then?'

'I like it well enough.' Morna was surprised at how much she was enjoying herself. With Ruth's help she had managed to work out a basic lesson programme, and the children's enthusiastic response had helped her to gain confidence.

'It's surprising to think of you teaching bairns when you've not had any training.'

'I only teach music and painting, as I know enough about those subjects to get by. Ruth sees to everything else.'

'She must be very clever.'

'She is. How is Samuel Gilmartin doing in the shop?' Morna asked, anxious to get the conversation away from Ruth and her little school. As yet, Belle had no idea that the pupils came from the poverty-stricken part of Saltcoats.

'He's doing very well. He has a very quick mind for a man of his background; he only has to be told a thing once and he's grasped it. He's even come up with some ideas of his own. He's very good with the customers too,' Belle went on. 'Especially with the ladies.' And then, as her sister raised an eyebrow, 'By that I mean he's patient with them, and good at advising them as to their purchases. Walter never had the patience for them.'

Belle glanced at her empty cup. 'I've got a real thirst this afternoon. Let's have a fresh pot of tea.'

Morna, who had been hoping to work on the following day's lessons once her sister had gone, suppressed a sigh. 'Of course. I'll not be a minute.'

'There's a bell pull by the fireplace.'

'There's little sense in pulling it since there's nobody in the kitchen to hear it.'

'Is it the maid's afternoon off?'

'Yes.' In an attempt to hide the fact that she and Ruth did their own housework, Morna had had the tea ready when Belle arrived. 'I won't be a moment,' she said.

'I'll come and help.'

'There's no need,' Morna protested, but her sister was determined and there was nothing Morna could do but lead the way to the kitchen, grateful that at least she had had the foresight to gather up all the suffragette literature and put it out of sight, just in case.

Belle's eyebrows rose as she looked around the kitchen. 'Your maidservant could do with a bit of training. This place looks as if a hurricane has blown through it.'

'That's because the children were in here this morning, taking their mid-morning milk.'

'They sit in the kitchen? And I thought you said that the maid was having her afternoon off – she could at least have put the place to rights before she went,' Belle was saying when the door opened and Ruth swept in, rosy-cheeked from the March winds.

'Tea, Morna, for the love of God. I'm parched. Oh, good afternoon.' She dumped a pile of papers on the table and beamed at Belle. 'I didn't realise that you were entertaining.'

'This is my sister, Belle. She brought some of my things, now that I have more room for them. Belle, this is Ruth Durie.'

'How do you do?' Ruth peeled a glove off and held out her hand. Belle shook it.

'How do you do?' she replied faintly, and then, 'Did you know that you appear to have hurt your hand? And that there's a rip in your sleeve?'

'Sorry about that.' Ruth sucked at her torn knuckles. 'I'll put something on them later, and perhaps you'd be kind enough to mend the jacket for me, Morna? Your sister is a much better seamstress than I could ever be,' she added to Belle, who sank on to a chair.

'Have you been in an accident?'

'More planned than accidental. A meeting in Greenock,' Ruth said blithely, 'and some uninvited, but not unexpected, arrivals. One of them tried to snatch at the placard I was carrying, and when I did my best to prevent him my hand was banged rather hard against a wall. Then in the general mêlée someone caught at my sleeve and almost took it off. But even so, it was a worthwhile meeting,' she added, while Belle, who had happened to sit down just where Ruth had tossed the papers, caught sight of one of the headlines, and froze.

'We were having tea in the little parlour,' Morna said swiftly, 'we came through to make a fresh pot.'

'Lucky that I came in just when you were making it. Let's go back to the parlour.' Ruth, ignoring the china cups and saucers on the dresser, picked up one of the children's mugs from the draining board and led the way, asking Belle over her shoulder, 'Has Morna shown you the classroom yet? You must come and see it. We're very proud of our pupils, aren't we, Morna? And you should be very proud of your sister, Miss Forsyth, for the little ones are enjoying their piano lessons, and their singing and painting. I'm so pleased that I met up with her again.'

'You didn't tell me,' Belle hissed when Morna accompanied her to the garden gate half an hour later, 'that your friend was one of those suffragettes!'

'Why should I?'

'For goodness' sake, Morna, did you not see the state of the woman? She looked as if she'd been brawling in the street like a common fishwife.'

'It's not her fault if other folk interrupt meetings.'

'She's not tried to get you to go to one of them, has she?'

'No, but I was wondering,' Morna said to irritate her sister, 'if I should go with her one of these days, to see what it's all about.'

'Oh, Morna, you wouldn't! Here was me thinking that you'd managed to land on your feet at last, and now I find you're mixing with women who make exhibitions of themselves in public, and teaching slum children.'

'Just because the children are poor it doesn't mean that they have no right to enjoy singing or playing the piano or drawing pictures. And Ruth and her friends are all respectable women.'

'You've met some other suffragettes?' Belle almost shrieked.

'They come to the house for meetings and I've joined one of their sewing bees.'

'You're not helping to sew those banners about votes for women, are you?'

'No, it's a quilt, and it's very well done. I find their conversation extremely interesting,' lied Morna, who found that most of it went over her head. But she enjoyed the sewing, and when they weren't harping on about the need for female emancipation, Ruth's friends could be witty and interesting. 'Thanks to Ruth I'm meeting a lot of people.'

'Yes – raggedy street children and militant women. What Mother would say . . .'

'The children – most of them, at any rate – are bright and eager to learn. And Ruth's friends come from all walks of life – there's a minister's wife, a singer, and folk from tenements as well as big houses. You'd be surprised, Belle.'

'Anyone we know?'

'They come from all over.' Belle had probably met some of the women socially, but Morna was not about to start gossiping.

'What if you end up in prison? It happens to these suffragettes, you know.'

'Then I shan't expect you to visit me,' Morna said, 'but I'm more likely to end up in bed with a chill if I stand out in this wind for much longer. Goodbye, Belle. You must come and visit me again soon.'

'You can be sure that I will, for someone has to keep an eye on you,' Belle said, and stamped off, her back rigid with outrage.

Ruth was writing at the kitchen table when Morna went back indoors. The wind had strengthened; it moaned around the corner of the house, and as Morna repaired Ruth's jacket she could see the bare branches of trees in the garden whipping around under its onslaught. Across the table Ruth's hand travelled over page after page, pausing only to dip her pen in the inkwell. The words seemed to pour from the nib of their own accord, though occasionally she tutted or gave an annoyed hiss and ran a thick black line through a word or phrase before rushing on again.

Finally she set the pen down and sat back with a sigh of pleasure. 'Finished. I shall read it over later and put it in the post tomorrow.'

'How can you work so fast?'

'It's easy when you care enough about your subject.' Ruth got up from the table and stretched. 'When you care, the words and thoughts are burning you up inside, and you have to let them out.' She put her hands on her hips and moved into a series of the bending exercises she gave the children when rain or cold trapped them indoors. 'I like your sister,' she said, twisting the top half of her body first to one side and then the other like a gymnast.

'Do you?' To Morna's mind Belle had been rather terse and unfriendly.

'She's very real, isn't she? Don't you hate those women who only say what they think they ought to say, or what they think you want to hear?'

'I thought that she was rather impolite. It's not like Belle, but she was annoyed with me.'

Ruth flopped forwards from the hips like a rag doll, fingertips brushing the floor, and then began to draw herself upright, straightening her spine bit by bit. 'She was annoyed with you because you left her to find out for herself that I support the suffragette movement, and that the children we teach come from the wrong part of town. It came as a shock to her, for she had assumed, as you did when you first came here, that because I was raised in a large house I would teach children from this area.' Ruth used both hands to push back the thick black hair that had become dislodged from its hairpins during her energetic exercising. 'I notice that my magazines have been tidied away, and I realise that I arrived home earlier than expected, thanks to the meeting being disrupted. Are you truly so ashamed of me and my beliefs, Morna?'

'No! It's just that – I knew that Belle would disapprove . . .'

'I think you should let your sister make her own mind up,' Ruth said mildly. 'And she can only do that if you tell her the truth instead of trying to hide things from her. I believe that that is the real reason why she was upset. Perhaps one day when we know each other better I might be able to explain my political beliefs to her, and tell her that working in Glasgow and seeing how women in large industrial communities tend to be treated as little more than child-bearing workhorses made me realise how much we females need to have the right to control our own bodies and our own lives. That means having some control over the way our country is run, and *that*, in turn, means having the right to vote. But . . .' she flung out her hands and smiled down at Morna, '. . . I made up my mind when I asked you to come here that I would not force my beliefs down your throat, so I think we should occupy our minds instead with the much more important matter of what we should have for our tea.'

The North Parish Church was cold on that chilly early-March day and Fraser Walter Forsyth, slumbering contentedly, woke with a shocked cry as water from the font was dripped on to his smooth forehead.

Mortified, Sarah noted some ladies in the congregation covering their ears with elegantly gloved hands. Fortunately, the short christening service was soon over and the wailing baby handed back to his mother. Recognising her arms he fell silent and started instead to butt his white-capped head impatiently against her new blue jacket in search of milk as Sarah and Walter began the long walk to the door.

Heedless of the silent criticism wafting like incense from the body of the kirk, Walter smiled to the left and right while Sarah was keenly aware that several members of the congregation made a deliberate point of ignoring the christening party.

Only two pairs of eyes bored into her so hard that they caught her attention. The first belonged to Clarissa Pinkerton who, when she caught Sarah's attention, stared coldly and deliberately for a long moment before tilting her chin and turning away her beautifully coiffed head, topped by a wide-brimmed hat smothered with artificial flowers.

Sarah, her face burning, looked swiftly to the other

side of the church and then gasped. That couldn't be Samuel Gilmartin sitting in the back row! To the best of her knowledge he was not a churchgoer, and even if he were, why would he be in that particular church on that particular day, the day of her child's christening? It must have been her imagination, she thought as she and Walter reached the door, with no opportunity for her to look back.

Once out in the churchyard she would have liked the chance to watch the other worshippers emerging, but Beatrice McCallum was saying, 'I think Sarah and the wee one should go on home with me and Belle and Morna. You can't keep the bairn outside on a cold day like this with just a christening shawl around him.'

Walter peered at his son, now wrinkling his face against the stiff sea breeze, and drew a corner of the shawl more closely over the bald little head. 'You're right, Aunt Beatrice. You go on up the road, Sarah, and I'll wait here and issue folk with invitations to the house.'

'D'you think anyone will accept an invitation to the house?' Sarah asked as she and Beatrice went along Manse Street with Belle and Morna walking behind them. Walter was determined to behave as though there had been no estrangement between himself and the townsfolk and she could not bear the thought of him standing in the chilly churchyard, being spurned by everyone.

'They might, even if it's only out of nosiness. Thank goodness that's over; I can't be doin' with all that formality. A lot of fuss that doesn't mean anythin'.' Beatrice, who used to stride briskly along the street, her dogs scurrying to keep up, now thumped a sturdy walking stick on the pavement with each step she took.

'Walter's heart's set on a proper christening with a party in the house afterwards for all his friends and neighbours.

He's desperate for folk to accept him again, and if that's what he wants then it's what I want too.'

'You're a good wee wife, Sarah Forsyth. If you ask me, he's better off with you than with that snooty Clarissa Pinkerton. But don't let him get away with too much,' Beatrice counselled as they left Manse Street behind and crossed over to Caledonia Road. 'The way to treat husbands is to let them win the wee battles while you win the big ones – but still lettin' them think they're the winners, of course.' She let out a yelp of laughter that turned swiftly into a bout of coughing so bad that she had to stop and lean against a wall.

Sarah, alarmed at the way the old lady's face was purpling, used her free hand to rub Beatrice's back while Belle, who had caught up with them, offered her handkerchief and Morna stood back, chewing at her lip.

When the attack finally ended and Beatrice had got her breath back, albeit wheezily, Morna said, 'Mebbe you should just go into your own house and have a rest, Aunt Beatrice. We're almost outside it now.'

'Not a bit of it, lassie! I've got through the worst part of today and I'm not goin' tae miss the best part. Belle, take the bairn so's I can hold Sarah's arm.'

'Me?' Belle asked, horrified.

'Aye, you. Ye can surely carry a wee thing like Fraser the rest of the way?'

'Could you not take my arm and leave him with his mother?'

'I'm in the middle of talkin' to Sarah,' her aunt said blandly, and Belle had no option but to do as she was told.

'Would you not like to hold him?' she asked her sister as they followed the others up the hill.

'You're his godmother,' Morna pointed out just as

Fraser realised that he had been given over to a stranger who was not used to holding babies. He peered up into his aunt's face for a long moment and then favoured her with a gummy smile.

'My goodness, Morna, would you look at that!'

Morna, craning to peer at the baby, was blessed not only with a smile, but a gurgle of approval.

'He's not too bad-looking when he smiles, is he?'

'He's Walter's double. Healthy-looking, though. She seems to be a good mother,' Belle said as they turned right into Argyle Road.

'Did you see Clarissa's face when we were walking out of the church? She looked as if she'd a strong lemon sweetie in her mouth.'

'Poor Clarissa, I'm going to have to call on her tomorrow. It must have been an ordeal for her, watching Walter's son being christened.'

Particularly, Belle thought as they followed their aunt and Sarah in to the Forsyth house, as poor Clarissa had pinned her hopes on Sarah dying in childbirth and leaving the way free for Clarissa to reclaim her husband.

Walter arrived five minutes later with the minister and Fraser's godfather, a town councillor and former school-friend of Walter's. 'Unfortunately the cold weather sent most of the congregation hurrying home before I had the opportunity to invite them to the house,' he said as he came in.

'There's far too much food then.' Beatrice, recovered from her coughing bout, peered at the loaded table. 'You seem tae have felt the need tae feed the entire town.'

'One must be prepared, Aunt Beatrice.'

'It's an awful waste of good food.'

'I'll take what's not wanted,' Morna said. 'The children that Ruth and I teach would enjoy a wee treat and I could hand some in to Meggie Chapman on my way home.'

Walter began to protest, but Beatrice said loudly, 'That's a very good idea, Morna. Good food is never wasted when someone can enjoy it. Now then . . .' she seized a glass of sherry from the tray on the table. 'A toast to Fraser Walter, and . . .' she paused, taking time to look at her young relations one by one, with a special, warm smile for Sarah, '. . . to the Forsyth family. Ye're all doin' very well, and I've no doubt that there are better times tae come.'

21

The nurse hired to look after the Forsyth baby was only in residence for four weeks before she and Walter quarrelled. He slammed the door behind her back.

'Good riddance to her. No woman is going to tell me when I am allowed to pick up my own child in my own house. I never cared for her in any case,' he said, regardless of the fact that he had chosen the woman personally and bragged constantly about her efficiency and excellent references.

As he went upstairs to the room that had once been Morna's, Sarah trailed along behind him, weak with relief. The nurse had more or less taken over the running of the entire household, completely intimidating her. 'Nellie and I can manage very well together,' she said as they reached the upper landing.

'Nonsense, my dear, you have more than enough to do looking after the house, and me, and entertaining.'

'The only people who visit are Belle and Mrs McCallum, and they don't come often.'

'But folk will soon start visiting again,' he assured her. Fraser, sound asleep in his bower of lace, muslin and ribbons, woke with a start as he was scooped up into his father's arms, and burst into panic-stricken wails.

'There, there, my little man.' Walter marched around the room, rocking his son. 'Did the nasty nurse frighten him, then? Never mind, we'll find a much nicer one for you, won't we, Mama?'

'I would really prefer to look after him myself, Walter . . .'

'Sarah, my dear, women of my station – our station in life do not look after their own children. My sisters and I always had nursemaids, and it did us no harm, did it? Besides,' he swept on while Sarah thought of the three Forsyths, now living in three different houses within the same small town, and having little to do with each other, 'I can't afford to be known as the man who couldn't even provide a proper nursemaid for his son. There, there,' he added to the baby, who was working himself into a frenzy.

'We must at least take the time to choose carefully,' Sarah said, raising her voice above Fraser's screams. 'We want to be sure that we get the right woman this time.'

'Indeed we do. Fraser, Fraser, this is not the way little men behave, is it?' Walter thrust his moustached face down towards the baby, and Fraser, who had paused to catch his breath, took one look and roared even louder.

'Could he be hungry?' Walter wondered.

'He was fed just before you came home.'

'But he's a growing boy. Go to your Mama, Fraser,' Walter said, and thrust the angry little bundle into his wife's arms before hurrying downstairs to read the evening paper.

The baby's face was dark red and his eyes scrunched up into a series of tight little lines, while screams poured from the perfect circle of his mouth. Sarah settled herself in the low nursing chair, rocking and crooning until the screaming finally subsided to sobs then hiccups. He stared up at her from drowned dark eyes and she covered his little wet face with kisses.

She fetched a clean cloth and dried his tears, but when she tried to put him back in his crib to continue his interrupted sleep he stiffened and began to fret. Sarah carried him back to the chair and unfastened her blouse. He wasn't hungry, but he fastened on her breast eagerly, in need of its comfort. After only a few sucks, he was asleep. She sat on, watching him. He might not be Samuel's, as she had hoped, but he was hers, and she loved him with all her heart.

'It's time,' Walter said on the following morning, 'that we showed Fraser the shop that he's going to inherit one day.'

'Isn't he a little young to appreciate that?'

'What I meant, my dear, is that I think it's time my employees met my son. We will walk down there together once he has been fed and bathed. The fresh air will do him good.'

'We could visit your aunt instead.'

Walter shook his head firmly. 'According to Belle, Aunt Beatrice has come down with another of her chills – I don't know what's wrong with her this year, she's been poorly ever since the turn of the year and it's almost the end of March now.'

'She's bound to feel better when the weather improves.' Sarah herself felt as though she were trapped in the house by the howling winds and sudden heavy showers, although on the few occasions when she had managed to go out she had enjoyed standing by the shore, watching the foam-capped waves race in as though frantically trying to escape the Irish gales driving them like cattle on the way to market. She particularly liked the way the larger waves offshore smashed themselves against the small tower at the end of Saltcoats harbour and then exploded upwards in a froth of snowy foam that rose into the grey sky and hung for a breathtaking moment before giving up and falling back into the sea to start all over again.

'I don't want Fraser anywhere near her until she has made a complete recovery,' Walter was fussing on, oblivious of his wife's thoughts.

'It might cheer her up to see him, and he's a very healthy baby.'

'Exactly, and I intend to make sure that he remains healthy. I'm surprised at you, Sarah; don't you know that when a small child falls ill he remains sickly for the rest of his life? My sisters and I,' Walter said proudly, 'were always healthy, and my dear mother put it down to her custom of swabbing out our throats regularly to avoid diphtheria and tonsillitis. You should do the same with Fraser.'

He insisted on Sarah dressing in her wedding outfit – her best clothes – and then the handsome perambulator had to be carefully prepared before Fraser was tucked in. They paraded slowly along the pavement, Sarah pushing the perambulator, while Walter walked by her side, one gloved hand resting proudly and possessively on the side of the handle. He tipped his bowler hat to everyone they met; some nodded and murmured a greeting, and some did not, but they all looked curiously at Sarah and the baby carriage before their eyes slid away.

'Shoulders back, my dear, and head high,' Walter said every now and again. 'Remember that you are my wife now, and the mother of my son.'

When they reached the shop he proudly pointed out

the new gilt lettering above the door.' "Forsyth and Son". That's me, Fraser, and you,' he told his heir, who was half asleep and sucking his fingers. Then he studied the two shop windows carefully before giving a quick, approving nod. 'Belle said that the new man she hired had dressed the windows – he seems to have done it quite well.' He stepped into the doorway, checking to make sure that it, and the stretch of pavement fronting the shop, had been well brushed, and waited there until someone inside the shop noticed him. There was a sudden flurry of activity before the door opened wide.

Walter stepped inside and then turned. 'Come along, my dear.'

'The perambulator . . .'

'Bring it in,' Walter commanded with just a shade of irritation creeping into his voice. 'The doorway is wide enough, and our visit today is to introduce the new arrival to the staff, after all.'

Carefully, unused to the high perambulator since the formidable nurse had never allowed her to take it out, Sarah managed to steer it into the shop, and immediately found herself the centre of attention. All pretence at normality had ceased and employees and customers alike stood gaping at her.

'Close the door, man, we're all safely inside now and the draught is not good for the child. A chair for Mrs Forsyth,' Walter went on crisply.

'Certainly, Mr Forsyth.' Sarah had been so busy manoeuvring the perambulator into the shop that she had taken no notice of the person holding the door open. Now, as he passed her on the way to the back office, she became aware of the way he walked, and the set of his head above broad shoulders.

Her heart began to flutter. She stared after the man,

scarcely aware of Walter easing her aside and taking charge of the baby carriage. He wheeled it into a corner, nodding to the staff to come forwards one by one to see the precious heir to the Forsyth emporium.

Samuel Gilmartin – for it was unmistakably Samuel Gilmartin, though his shabby working clothes had been replaced by a white shirt, pale blue cravat and dark blue jacket, waistcoat and trousers – reappeared, carrying a wooden chair. He glanced at the staff lining up to pay homage to the baby, and at Walter Forsyth, bending to ease the silk coverlet aside so that Fraser's tiny face could be seen more easily, and then set the chair down a little distance away. Removing a snowy handkerchief from the breast pocket of his jacket with a flourish, he made a great show of dusting the chair. 'Won't you sit down, Mrs Forsyth?'

'Samuel?'

'Samuel Gilmartin, at your service.' He gave her a brief bow, 'I don't believe we have met, ma'am.'

'You work here?'

'Did ye not know?' He moved between her and the others so that only she could see the mocking amusement in his eyes – eyes that still had the power to make her weak with longing. 'You're no' the only one who's managed tae come up in the world, Sarah. The difference is that I used my head and my wits, while you . . .' he took a moment to look her up and down with studied insolence, '. . . used yer body.'

She sat down, lacing her fingers tightly in her lap to prevent them from shaking – or, worse still, from reaching out to touch him. 'But how did you get him to hire you, after that time he found us together in the house?'

'I was a message lad then, and dressed like a message lad. He saw me that day, but he didnae *look* at me.' Samuel's top lip curled in a sneer. 'He's scarce looked at me or spoken tae me since I started workin' in here, for I'm still beneath his notice. In any case, it was Miss Belle who hired me, and I'd no trouble with her.' He leaned closer, his voice lowered to a murmur. 'So here I am with my feet under the Forsyths' table, just like you. I may not have your husband's money, and I may not have you, Sarah, but I still have a way with the ladies, and that's goin' tae take me further than you've got. Just you wait and see.'

'You're not goin' tae tell Walter about . . . ?' They had both reverted to their normal speech, Samuel because he wasn't trying to impress, Sarah because she was agitated.

'About us? There's more than one way tae skin a cat,' Samuel said, then, jerking his head at the others, 'Would ye look at them? They're like fairy godmothers at a christenin', fallin' over each other tae wish yer bairn well, in the hope that it'll keep them in *that* one's good books.' He indicated Walter, who was beaming smugly. 'It must make ye proud tae know ye've birthed such an important wean. And tae think . . .' he smiled down on her; a smile that curved his mouth without touching his eyes '. . . that I wanted ye tae get rid of it. Ye'd have lost more than an unwanted bairn, eh?'

'Ah, good morning, Sarah.' Belle Forsyth had come to investigate the cause of the commotion among her staff. 'You've brought the child, I see.'

'Walter wanted everyone t-to see him,' Sarah stammered.

'And now that they have I hope that they will return to their work with added enthusiasm.' Belle indicated the few customers who were watching with ill-disguised curiosity from a distance. 'Samuel, perhaps you could . . .'

'Of course, Miss Forsyth. I'll get them back to work before you can dot an "i" or cross a "t".'

'Thank you.' Belle touched his arm briefly and watched him go for a moment before turning back to Sarah, the smile she had produced for Samuel disappearing. 'So how are you keeping, Sarah?' she enquired politely.

'I'm – very well, thank you.'

'I'm glad to hear it.' Belle's attention was already back with Samuel, who was dropping a brief word in one ear and then another. In no time at all most of the staff had returned to their duties while he himself glanced over at Belle. Sarah, watching like a hawk, saw her sister-in-law incline her head just a fraction of an inch in the direction of a well-dressed woman examining an ornate teapot stand. Samuel responded with a similar imperceptible nod and went over to the woman. It was as though, Sarah thought with a stab of jealousy, he and Belle were equal partners rather than employee and employer.

'Belle,' Walter called out, 'come and see your nephew.'

'I have already seen him, Walter, several times.'

'But small babies change all the time. You haven't seen him today,' he insisted, and with a sigh so faint that Sarah only just heard it, his sister did as she was told. Rather than be left on her own, Sarah went with her.

'He looks well,' Belle said after a cursory glance into the perambulator, where Fraser was beginning to stir. 'Did you see the window dressing? What do you think of it?'

'It seems to be in order.'

'Mr Gilmartin is an asset, Walter, and a great help to me, with you being so preoccupied at home these days. You are not intending to return there at once, are you?' Belle swept on, 'There are several pressing matters that I must speak to you about.'

He frowned, then shrugged. 'Oh, very well. Sarah, can you manage to take the child home without my assistance?'

'Of course, Walter.'

'I will be home for lunch,' he assured her, and beck-oned to the nearest employee, who happened to be Samuel. 'The door, if you please,' he instructed, and followed Belle into the back office.

As Sarah struggled to turn the perambulator in the shop's confined space, Samuel sprang forward. 'Allow me, Mrs Forsyth.'

'Samuel . . .' she began as soon as they were out in the street and away from listening ears.

'I almost forgot – I haven't paid homage tae the young master.' He leaned forwards to look into the perambula-tor. Fraser's dark eyes – his father's eyes – returned the stare with interest. He gurgled and smiled up at Samuel, but the smile was not returned. Instead, Samuel straight-ened very slowly before turning to look down into Sarah's white face. 'Well now,' he said, his voice so low that she could scarcely make it out against the background of street noises, 'isn't that one just the spit of his father? You must be quite relieved about that, Sarah.' And then, his voice suddenly lashing out at her, 'Or did ye already know, when ye were pesterin' me tae marry ye, who the true father was?'

'I swear that I thought he was yours!'

'Did ye? Or did ye think that I'd be more easily snared intae marriage than him? Is that it? Aren't you the lucky one, now, with yer mistress dyin' and yer master goin' off just at the right time? If they'd both been in the house ye'd never have coaxed Mr Walter Forsyth intae marryin' ye when I refused.'

'I wanted him to be your child!'

Samuel's eyes were like chips of ice. 'You swore tae me that I was the only man in yer life, when all the time ye were beddin' the son of the house. Have we not both of us had a lucky escape? You've got what ye wanted – marriage with yer bairn's true father, and a rich man intae the bargain, and as for me — I've got what I want.' He jerked his head in the direction of the shop, 'And I'll have more besides. Oh, I can promise ye that, *Mrs* Sarah Forsyth.'

Sarah was trembling so badly on the walk back to the house that she could scarcely keep the perambulator on the pavement. Her heart was chilled by the look in Samuel's eyes at the sight of Walter's likeness stamped on her baby's features, and his final words rang through her head. She had no idea what he meant, but she was frightened.

Defying Walter's wishes, she went to Beatrice McCallum's house, where the old woman was resting on the sofa in her front parlour.

'Ye didnae bring the wee fellow with ye?' she asked, disappointed.

'He's in his perambulator at the back door. Walter says . . .' Sarah stopped, colouring.

'He's scared that his son'll catch whatever I've got?' Beatrice finished the sentence for her. 'Walter takes after his father — Hamilton always flew intae a right fret whenever one of his bairns fell ill, in case it was passed on tae him. You fetch the laddie in, m'dear — what I've got won't ail him for many a long year yet. If it makes you feel easier in your mind you neednae bring him too close. I just want tae see his bonny wee face.'

When Sarah carried the baby into the parlour and sat down, Juliet, who had been lying at Beatrice's feet, came over to investigate, tail wagging. The baby beamed and reached out a little starfish hand.

Beatrice's eyes locked on to his bright face. 'It does me good just tae look at him. He's at the beginnin' of his life and I'm at the end of mine.'

'You're nowhere near that!'

'Lassie, there comes a day when ye just know that it's time tae go home. It's as if ye're beginnin' tae outstay yer welcome.'

'What does the doctor say?'

'Och, him!' Beatrice gave a wave of the hand. 'They always have tae put names on everythin'. The truth of the matter, Sarah, is that once Romeo went I knew that my turn was on its way. He was the last gift I had from my husband and I suppose that in a way he took Hector's place. Losin' him was like bein' widowed all over again.'

'But what would I do without you?' Sarah burst out without thinking.

'You'll do very well, for you're a sensible lass, Sarah Forsyth, and you'll put more strength intae my nephew's spine than that young woman he nearly wed. All you need now is tae have more faith in yerself, and tae stand up tae Walter a bit more for he needs tae be led, not followed.'

Sarah sighed, reminded of her latest problem. 'The nurse has left. She and Walter didn't get on.'

'D'ye tell me?' Beatrice McCallum said with a touch of irony in her voice and just a hint of a smile on her lips. 'I suppose they had words over which of them knew best for the wee laddie there?' And then, as Sarah nodded, 'I was never blessed with bairns of my own, but I always thought that it's the mother who knows her own bairn best. If there's times when you and Walter don't agree on the way things are bein' done for yer son you'll have tae be ready tae speak up. Walter's soft – he'll give in once he sees that you're determined.'

'What do I know about nursery nurses?'

'I'm not so far gone that I cannae help ye there,' Beatrice said just as the door opened and Ena brought in the tea. 'The very person. Pour the tea, will ye, Ena? My hands are shaky today and Mrs Forsyth's busy with the bairn. And tell me if ye know of any good child nurses in the town that might be lookin' for work.'

'There's Leez Drummond that was married ontae my cousin's man's brother Jockie,' Ena said as she poured tea.

'Jockie that was a fisherman?'

'Aye, that's him. Drowned at sea less than a year after him and poor Leez wed. She was the eldest o' a big fam'ly,' Ena said, taking a cup of tea over to her mistress, 'so she grew up knowin' how tae look after bairns. She worked as a nursemaid afore she married Jockie and she went back tae the same work when she was widowed. I heard the other day that she wasnae very well pleased with where she is. She's been thinkin' of movin' out of Saltcoats tae some place where there's more folk with the money tae pay tae have their children cared for.'

'Ask her tae come here at ten o'clock tomorrow morning,' Beatrice said. 'You come along too, Sarah, and bring the wee one with you. We'll interview the woman together.'

'What should I tell Walter?'

'Tell him nothin' at all. If the woman doesnae suit us, or we don't suit her, there's no harm done.'

22

The postman brought a lot of letters for Ruth every morning. She usually glanced briefly at the envelopes during breakfast, then waited until after the morning class before settling down at the kitchen table to open them, but on this particular morning she pulled one out of the pile and slit it open with her butter knife. After scanning the contents swiftly she pushed her half-eaten breakfast away and jumped to her feet.

'I must go to Glasgow at once.'

'Glasgow? But it's a school day!'

'Nevertheless, I must go at once, if I want to catch the next train. A friend needs my help.' Ruth was already on her way to the hall, where Morna, hurriedly swallowing down a mouthful of toast, found her pushing her arms into her coat sleeves.

'But what . . .'

'Have I got enough money for the train?' Ruth delved into the large bag she took with her whenever she went out, and checked the contents of her shabby purse. 'Yes, I have.' She tugged her coat straight, buttoned it, and took her hat from its hook on the coat stand.

'Ruth, the children will be here soon.'

'You must see to them, Morna. I should be back by mid-afternoon.' Ruth fastened her hat to her head with long, sharp hatpins, thrusting each one in with the speed and skill of a magician pushing swords through a box containing his female assistant.

'But I can't teach them anything except painting and music!' Morna wailed, wringing her hands.

'Then let it be a painting and music day.' Ruth opened the door and glanced up at the sky. 'The weather seems to have taken a turn for the better. You can take them into the back garden,' she said, and as she hurried down the steps the next few sentences floated back over her shoulder. 'Anna will help you. You'll manage splendidly, I know. Back in the afternoon.'

Then she was gone, out of the gate and along the road, leaving Morna trembling on the top step.

To Sarah's horror, Walter had shillied and shallied about going to the shop. 'Now that you don't have a nursemaid, it might be best if I stayed here to help you with the child.'

'I can manage very well, Walter, truly I can,' Sarah protested, and he smiled at her, a kindly, patronising smile.

'But you're still very new to motherhood, my dear. Perhaps I should . . .' he began, and then as Fraser, lying in his mother's arms, turned a deep red colour, frowned massively, and held his breath, concentrating on something important that was going on out of sight of his parents, he asked, 'What's the matter with him? Is he ailing?'

'No, not at all,' Sarah said, and then, as her son gave a satisfied sigh and the deep flush began to ebb, 'but I think I must take him upstairs at once and change his napkin.'

Evidence of the soiled napkin was already beginning to taint the air in the parlour. Walter gave a grimace of distaste. 'On second thoughts, Sarah, I am needed in the shop today. Are you sure you can manage?'

'Quite sure.'

'Send the girl for me, if necessary.'

'I will, Walter,' she said, carrying her smelly bundle out of the door.

'They're in the front parlour, ma'am,' Ena said as she opened the door to Sarah.

'Thank you.' Sarah hesitated as she heard a burst of laughter from behind the varnished panels. She had assumed that by 'they' the maid meant that the woman to be interviewed for the post of nursemaid had already arrived, but mingled with Beatrice McCallum's familiar cackle was the deeper laughter of a man. She turned back to question Ena, but the maid had already bustled off to her kitchen, leaving Sarah with no option but to open the door.

'Ah, there you are, Sarah,' Beatrice greeted her. 'Do you know Mr Gilmartin, who works in Forsyth's shop?'

'We met yesterday, when Mr and Mrs Forsyth brought their son in,' Samuel said as he rose to his feet. 'The image of his father.'

'With good fortune he may grow out of that,' Beatrice said dryly, and then, to Sarah, 'Samuel brought me some items from the shop. I would ask you to join us, Samuel, but Mrs Forsyth and I have business to attend to.'

'I must be off in any case. Miss Belle will be wondering where I've got to.'

'Blame me for keeping you back, if you must. Oh – and it would be best if you didn't mention meeting Sarah here this morning.'

'My lips are sealed.' Samuel beamed down at Beatrice. 'Don't trouble your maidservant, Mrs McCallum, I should know my own way out by now. Good morning to you – and to you, Mrs Forsyth.'

'A most agreeable young man,' Beatrice said when they were alone.

'He comes here often?'

'Once a week, for supper. He plays cribbage very well and he has such a cheerful nature. He does me the world of good,' answered Beatrice, who did indeed look more like her former energetic self. 'Tae tell the truth, my dear – and you're the only one who'll understand what I'm sayin', he's a breath of fresh air after dealin' with Hamilton and Walter and Allan Pinkerton. They're all decent upstandin' men, but not one of them with an ounce of humour. Even my own Hector had tae have the stiffness teased out of his soul, bless him. But Samuel's got such an easy manner. Belle's become very dependent on him; she says that he's an efficient assistant.' And then, as the doorknocker was thumped and the little clock on the mantelshelf chimed the hour, 'Ah, that must be Mrs Drummond, exactly on time.'

Leez Drummond was a tall, slender woman, grey haired and neatly dressed.

'So, is this the wee one that's in need of a nursemaid?' she said as soon as she came into the room. 'Come to Leez, my mannie, and let's see what we think of each other.'

Fraser gave an astonished little gasp as the stranger plucked him from his mother's arms without so much as a by-your-leave. He was about to turn his still-bald head in search of Sarah when Leez made a strange clucking, crooning noise in the back of her throat. Curiosity overcoming panic, Fraser looked up at her and was met by a beaming smile. He smiled back and gave a little chuckle, nestling closer to her.

'Well then,' Leez sat herself down, 'that's us introduced and pleased with each other. Now I must meet your mother and find out what she thinks of me.' And giving Fraser a finger to clutch, she turned her warm smile on Sarah. 'Forgive me, Mrs Forsyth, but I've found that if the bairn doesnae care for me there's no sense in wasting the parents' time. You've got a fine wee lad here.'

'I've asked you tae my house, Leez,' Beatrice said, 'because wee Fraser's a firstborn, and Mr Forsyth's no' quite grasped what the bairn and his mother are lookin' for. He's no' very sure what he's looking for himsel', but he doesn't know that.'

'Men folk like tae think that they're in charge,' said Leez, rocking Fraser in the crook of her arm, 'that doesnae worry me.'

'I thought not. Do you have any questions, Sarah?'

'Why are you leaving the people you work for now, Mrs Drummond?'

'My present employer's youngest has just started school and I prefer tae care for younger bairns. They're more interestin'.'

Five minutes later Beatrice said, 'Well I think that's it settled, don't you, Sarah? We'll have a cup of tea to celebrate, if you'll be good enough to ring for Ena.'

'Walter . . .'

'Leave Walter to me,' Beatrice said blithely. 'I'll write to him this very mornin', tellin' him that I've arranged for a suitable nursemaid to call at the house tomorrow mornin'. Will eleven o'clock suit you, Leez? We'll let him think that he's the one who's hired you, so you and Sarah had best behave as if you've not set eyes on each other before.'

When Leez Drummond had gone Beatrice beamed at Sarah. 'That was a good mornin's work, was it not? You

255

couldnae find a better nurse, Sarah. Be sure to let me know what happens.'

'I will.' Sarah got up and went to lift Fraser, who had fallen asleep in a chair, packed in snugly with cushions. He was sleeping so soundly that he hung bonelessly in her arms, his mouth gaping open. He even slept the same way as Walter, she thought. Aloud, she said, 'I hope we haven't tired you out, Mrs McCallum.'

'On the contrary, you've done me good. Mebbe I should have more visitors,' Beatrice said.

'We'll just have to turn today intae a bit of a holiday,' Anna said once she'd been told that she and Morna were on their own.

'Send them all home, you mean?'

'No, no,' the woman said, and Morna's heart, which had begun to lift, sank again. 'They'll have tae stay here, but we'll no' be able tae teach the things Miss Durie teaches. Unless you. . . ?'

'I don't know about anything except music and painting.'

'Then we'll spend the first half of the mornin' playin' games in the garden – it's a cold day, but if we keep them runnin' about they'll stay warm enough. And one of the farmers delivered a sack of early Ayrshire potatoes here the other day – I'll boil up a big pot and the bairns can eat them nice and hot for the mornin' break, instead of milk and biscuits. Then before they go home they can all crowd intae your room for some singin'.'

'I don't think I know enough songs.' They were standing in the entrance hall, thigh-deep in a sea of small children, all talking at once; every now and again one of the more exuberant youngsters thumped against an adult leg, causing the owner to sway and stagger slightly.

'Nursery rhymes'll do, and there's always music hall songs. I like the music hall,' Anna said with enthusiasm. 'I can teach them the words if you can thump the tunes out on the piano. I think there's some music in the piano stool; you look while I get them intae the back garden. The games'll help tae wear them out.'

Personally, Morna doubted if anything could tire her small pupils out. She and Anna organised three-legged races, tying stick-thin little ankles together with the children's threadbare scarves and anything else they could find in the house. After that they brought chairs out and set up obstacle races, then played Blind Man's Buff. Then they all trooped into the kitchen, where each child was given a hot potato wrapped in newspaper.

'What can we do next?' Morna whispered to Anna as the children bit into the tasty potatoes.

'Egg and spoon race – there's plenty of spoons in the kitchen.'

'You can't use real eggs!'

'Golf balls,' said the inventive Anna. 'I mind Miss Ruth showin' me a whole drawer full of them and tellin' me that her father was a great golfer. You keep them happy while I fetch the balls and the spoons.'

Morna, digging back into her own childhood, introduced her small pupils to Statues, which they loved. They were all stealing up on her from behind, smothering excited giggles and ready to freeze the instant she turned to face them, when Anna appeared from the back door carrying a large tray laden with spoons of all shapes and sizes, together with a bowlful of golf balls.

'Right, then, the wee-est weans get the biggest spoons and the rest of ye get the small spoons. That'll make it more fair.'

After the race they went into the parlour where Anna led the singing, acting out each song to make the children laugh. Many of the songs were new to Morna, but she did her best to follow them on the piano – although the way the youngsters bawled them out in various keys while spluttering with laughter at Anna's antics, nobody would have noticed if Morna had been playing something entirely different.

'"Onward Christian Soldiers"!' Anna suddenly cried out, and while Morna was thinking how grateful she was to be given a song she could play, the older woman went on, 'Come on, everyone, follow me. You too, Miss Forsyth. The music hall always has a grand finale, and this is ours.'

Singing lustily, she led her little band out of the parlour, along the hall, and into the kitchen. Still singing, she managed to supply every child with a spoon and something to hit with it – pots, kettles, roasting trays, cake trays, pot lids and enamelled bowls – and then led them out to circle the garden like a conga line, bawling the hymn at the top of their voices and beating time on their improvised instruments. Following along, hitting a pot lid with a wooden ladle, Morna glanced up and saw one or two curtains twitching in the adjoining houses. The neighbours would not be best pleased at the din, she thought with a trace of guilt, but she was enjoying herself so much that she dismissed the thought almost at once.

Back in the main classroom the children, flushed with excitement, chattered like a flock of sparrows as Morna and Anna got them into their outdoor clothes. Anna was just saying, 'An orderly line, if you please, two by two,' when the sound of a motor car stopping outside the gate sent the little ones scurrying to the bay window.

Anna followed them, and her hand flew to her mouth. 'It's Miss Durie, and she's got someone with her.'

Morna reached the window in time to see Ruth alighting on to the pavement and then reaching back into the cab. Slowly, carefully, she eased the other passenger out, then as the cab drove off she helped the woman in through the gate.

'I'll put a hot-water bottle in the spare room bed,' Anna said. 'Thank goodness it's kept ready and aired. You go and help, Miss Morna, and you lot,' she added firmly to the children, 'stay in this room and wait for me. Sing "Old MacDonald Had a Farm" – and remember that I'll be listenin', so none of your nonsense.' Starting off the first line of the song as she went, she rushed to the kitchen while Morna went to the front door.

Ruth had managed to half-carry her companion halfway up the path by the time Morna reached them.

'Let me help. Anna's putting a hot-water bottle in the spare bed.'

The woman Ruth had brought back with her was thin, with bowed shoulders. Each step seemed to be too much for her, but with Ruth on one side and Morna on the other they were soon in the hall, which rang with 'Old MacDonald Had a Farm' sung in more keys than Morna had ever thought possible.

'How lovely,' the newcomer said in a thin, exhausted voice, 'to hear bairns sing again.'

'That's our pupils. Into the parlour, I think,' Ruth said. 'You can rest there, Christina, while we get your room ready and the bed warmed.'

'Thank you.' The woman sank gratefully into the depths of a comfortable armchair and smiled up at the two of them. While helping her into the house, Morna had got the impression that she was elderly, but the pale, drawn face looking up at her was quite young.

'Now just you sit there quietly,' Ruth instructed. 'Morna,

come and help me, if you will. How did you and Anna get on?' she asked as the two of them went to the kitchen.

'Very well. Anna was so good with them.'

'She always is, bless her. She's been a real tower of strength to me on several occasions. Brandy, I think, with an egg beaten into it, for the moment. Then,' she said over her shoulder as she fetched a glass and the brandy bottle, 'we'll get her upstairs and try her with some soup.'

There were quick heavy steps on the stairs and Anna appeared. 'The bottle's in the bed and I've put a match to the fire. The room should warm up quickly. If you don't need me for anything else, Miss Durie, I'll get that noisy lot home and leave you tae see tae your guest.'

'Thank you, Anna!' Ruth swept her into a warm hug. 'You're a wonder.'

'Och, away wi' ye,' Anna protested, blushing with embarrassment and pleasure. 'I'll see ye both tomorrow, eh?'

Walter insisted on taking time off from the shop to interview the applicant for the post of nursemaid. 'I don't doubt that you could manage very well on your own, my dear,' he said indulgently, 'but I have no wish to see a nursemaid like the last woman looking after our child. It's better that we interview her together.'

Sarah grew nervous as the time set for Leez Drummond's arrival came closer. She had set her heart on employing the woman – what if Walter took a dislike to her and the search had to go on?

She jumped when the doorbell jangled and made an instinctive move to answer the summons, but Walter held up an admonishing hand. 'It is no longer your job, Sarah. Let the girl do it, since that's what I pay her for.' And then, drawing his watch from its pocket in his waistcoat, 'She's very prompt – a good beginning.'

Today, Leez had an air of humility and deference. She sat on an upright chair, hands clasped in her lap, meekly answering the questions he fired at her.

'I had to ask our last nursemaid to leave because she insisted on deciding on the way my son was raised,' he said when he had run out of questions. 'I will not be dictated to in my own home with regard to my own child, Mrs Drummond.'

'Indeed, sir, I agreed wholeheartedly. With me, the child's well-being comes first, with the wishes of the parents following closely behind,' Leez said sweetly.

'Well said, Mrs Drummond. You mentioned references?'

'I have references from all my previous employers, including the lady I am working for at present.' Leez delved into her bag and produced some envelopes, tied with a ribbon. 'Not many, as you see, but I tend to stay in each place for a number of years. This creates a stable background for the little ones.' And then, as Walter reached out a hand for the references, 'I wonder – might I see your little boy?'

Sarah, glancing across at her husband and receiving a slight nod, jumped to her feet. 'I'll bring him down.'

When she returned with Fraser in her arms, Walter was still studying the written references, while Leez waited serenely. Her face lit up when the baby was carried into the room. 'May I, Mrs Forsyth?' She held out her arms, and Sarah put the child into them. As she had done before, Leez summoned the clucking, crooning noise from the back of her throat – almost like a contented hen, Sarah thought in wonderment – and as before, Fraser beamed and gave a little chuckle as he nestled against her.

'Now aren't you just the bonniest wee man?' Leez said, and as he cooed his complete agreement with the statement, 'And so like your Papa. You're going to grow up to be very handsome.'

Watching her husband's reaction to the woman's comments, Sarah thought for a moment that he too was going to break into chuckles and crooning, just like his son. But he managed to contain himself, saying only as he put the last of the references back into its envelope, 'You seem to have won his confidence already, Mrs Drummond.'

'He's a lovely little boy, sir, and I would consider it an honour to be entrusted with his care.'

'Then I think the matter is settled, since your references are all excellent. What do you think, my dear?' Walter turned to her wife, as though suddenly remembering her.

'I don't think that Fraser could be in better hands.'

'Then all we need to discuss,' Walter said briskly, 'are your wages and the date on which you can commence employment here, Mrs Drummond.'

'I believe that that woman will do very well as our nurse-maid,' he said when Leez had gone. 'She seems biddable and sensible, not like the last nurse at all. She impressed me greatly.'

'And me. Your aunt will be pleased to hear that you approve of her recommendation.' Sarah, who had been practising the long word, said it slowly and carefully.

'Oh, it has little to do with Aunt Beatrice's recommendation – I would certainly not entrust my son to anyone merely because my elderly aunt approves of her.'

'Of course not, Walter.' Sarah smiled down at Fraser, who was now slumbering in her arms and quite unaware of the careful deception that had been played out over his little head.

23

The brandy and raw egg revived Ruth's visitor and enabled her, with help, to go up to the bedroom prepared for her.

'She must have been very ill,' Morna said as she and Ruth went to the kitchen to heat up some soup. 'Has she been in hospital for long?'

'Not hospital, prison.' Ruth gave an amused snort. 'No need to look so shocked, my dear, we're not harbouring a vicious criminal, though most of the members of our learned and respected legal fraternity would have it so.' She began to ladle soup from the large pot into a smaller one, then said in a puzzled tone, 'This little pan has a dent that I haven't seen before.'

'One of the children must have hit it too hard. We were marching around the garden singing "Onward Christian Soldiers" and marking time with spoons and pots.'

'Ah, I see. Would you set that tray for me, please? I think there's a pretty little tray cloth in that drawer, and a napkin.' Ruth indicated the drawer with a jerk of her chin. 'Did the children enjoy themselves?'

'Very much.'

'Good,' Ruth said, stirring the soup.

'What did she – Christina – do?'

'Broke some windows, I think. And no doubt resisted arrest – and why not? Once sentenced and imprisoned in Duke Street she went on a hunger strike as part of her continuing protest, so they began to force-feed her.'

'How do they do that?'

'Several strong warders hold the woman immobile while a tube is forced down her throat and into her stomach. Then food is sent down the tube.'

Morna swallowed hard. 'I would be sick if that happened to me.'

'Being sick is not allowed. They merely pinch your nose and cover your mouth and . . .' Ruth glanced at her assistant's growing pallor and ended with, 'But enough of that. Our job is to help her to regain her health – beef tea and soups and coddled eggs and jellies. We're going to be busy over the next week or two.' She dipped a spoon into the now-simmering soup, blew lightly on its contents, and then tasted it. 'Ready. Why don't you tidy the classroom in readiness for tomorrow, while I take this up to Christina?'

And, Morna suddenly remembered with a rush of guilt, she must go out to the back garden and hunt for the golf balls that had belonged to Ruth's late father, and were now scattered all over the place.

A week later Christina Baird was well enough to come downstairs. Most of her time for the first few days was spent enjoying the April sun, but after that she began to help Ruth in the classroom. The children took to her at once, the girls describing her as a princess from a fairy story. Morna could understand why, for now that

Christina was eating properly and sleeping well, her sky-blue eyes took on a lively sparkle and her small, neat mouth was always ready to curve into an infectious smile. Her thick hair was almost golden and it was easy to believe that should she choose to release it from the hairpins it could tumble down in a shimmering ladder for a prince to climb in order to rescue her from the tower where she was held prisoner.

While she was there, women visited almost every afternoon to sit in the kitchen, discussing meetings past and planning meetings in the future. The entire house seemed to throb and crackle with their energy and enthusiasm, and Morna, awed into shyness by this strong sisterhood, tended to retire to the parlour. But whenever the patchwork quilt was brought out and spread over the table there was no question of her hiding away; for the first time in her life she was singled out for special praise because, the others insisted, she was undeniably the best needlewoman in the group.

It was when she was working with the other quilters that Morna felt that she was part of the sisterhood. The silk quilt, now nearing completion, was made up of squares, oblongs, triangles and diamonds, in all the colours of the rainbow. It seemed to Morna that all the seasons were represented, from autumn's soft browns, golds and beige, through winter's cool strong blues and crisp snowy white and into the greens, fresh blues, pinks, reds and orange of spring and summer, all radiating out from the centre towards the beautifully embroidered silver-beige of the broad border.

The centre itself fascinated her; it consisted of a large diamond bordered in grey and black, broken into four smaller diamonds, two green and two white. Each of the smaller diamonds contained a wheel sent against a violet background, and each wheel had a square centre and four triangular spokes, two wheels with green spokes and two with white.

'It's the symbol of the suffragette movement,' one of the needlewomen explained when Morna asked about the central emblem. 'The colours represent our purpose – the G of green also stands for the first letter of Give, the W of white stands for the first letter of Women, and the V of violet shares its first letter with Votes.'

'Some say,' said Christina, stitching a section of the border, 'that green represents hope, purple – rather than violet – represents dignity, and white stands, of course, for purity in both public and private life.' She smiled warmly at Morna. 'These virtues are what all women, including suffragettes, aim for. Why don't you come to Paisley with us at the end of the month to hear Mrs Pankhurst speak? It's going to be a wonderful event!'

And to her own surprise, Morna agreed.

The sun, just beginning to disappear over Arran, the largest of the offshore islands in the Firth of Clyde, was an iridescent orange ball. As it dipped further, the island's mountain range, known because of its shape as the Sleeping Warrior, was outlined against it in sharp black. The final rays painted the clouds above the island dusky pink and then all at once the sun was gone completely.

The placid stretch of sea between the island and the mainland lost the last of the sun's glittering reflections and adopted instead a mantle of soft grey, broken here and there by black streaks where islets, hidden at high tide, poked their inquisitive heads above the surface.

'This,' Christina said, 'must be one of the most beautiful places on God's earth.'

'Maybe, but if you turn around you'll see the oldest

buildings in the town. They should have been pulled down long ago.'

Christina held up an elegant hand in protest. 'My dear Morna, the houses are man's work. Look out over the water – see God's work and let your soul absorb the peace of it. A sight like this just confirms my earnest belief that folk should be like nature – free to grow as they will, and not constrained by man-made laws.'

'But surely we must have laws. Without them we would be little more than heathens.'

'Oh yes, we need some, but only the sensible laws that benefit folk, not those passed by shallow, greedy people who think to protect their own freedom by withholding it from everyone else.'

'I believe that I have as much freedom as I could wish,' Morna protested, and the older woman laughed, slipping a hand through her companion's arm.

'Then I am pleased for you – but there are so many different freedoms, and some folk who should have a fair slice of the cake are fortunate to be thrown a handful of crumbs now and again. Come on, Ruth will be wondering where we are, and it's turning cold now that the sun has gone.'

They were walking towards the Durie house when a man shouted, 'Miss Morna!' and she looked up to see Samuel Gilmartin running down Caledonia Road. The two women paused as he crossed over to where they stood, beaming.

'It's a while since we last met, miss. How are ye?'

'Very well, thank you, Samuel. You look extremely well yourself.'

'I am, thanks to you. Did ye know that I've moved tae new lodgings in Melbourne Terrace? Miss Morna taught me how to count money and give change so that I could obtain work in her family's shop,' he explained to Christina, who was studying him with interest. 'It's because of her that I've gone up in the world, and I'll never forget her for it.'

Morna, astonished at the change in him – the smart suit, the air of confidence where there had once been such despair and bitterness – suddenly remembered her manners. 'This is Samuel Gilmartin,' she told Christina. 'Samuel, this is Mrs Baird, who is staying with us at the moment.'

'How do you do, ma'am.' Samuel whipped off his bowler hat. 'I hope you're enjoyin' your stay in Saltcoats?'

'I am. We've just been down to the shore to watch the sun set,' Christina told him.

'I've been callin' on your aunt, Miss Morna. The two of us enjoy a game of cribbage once a week. I don't know if you've seen her recently?'

'Not recently.' Morna immediately felt guilty; she was so busy these days that she tended to forget that Aunt Beatrice's house was only a few minutes' walk from Ruth's.

'If I could be so bold as to suggest a wee visit . . .' Samuel's face and voice were solemn now. 'The lady's not been too well this winter and tonight she was coughin' and wheezin' so much that I didnae – didn't,' he corrected himself carefully, 'stay as long as usual. I think she'd a bit of a fever on her too.'

'A personable young man with his fair share of Irish charm,' Christina said when they had parted from Samuel and were continuing their walk to Ruth's house, 'and he's to be admired for making the effort to better himself. But at the same time, there's something about him . . .'

'What sort of something?'

'If I were you, my dear, I'd not put my full trust in him.'

'You think he might take money from the shop?'

'I doubt if he would be so foolish as to bite the hand that feeds him. When I warned you not to put too much trust in him I meant in other ways,' Christina said, and then, with a quick laugh, 'but perhaps I'm just suspicious of all men these days!'

Women were converging from all directions on Paisley's Clark Town Hall when Morna, Ruth and Christina arrived from the nearby railway station. A large number of women had got off their train when it reached Paisley, all bound for the same destination.

The hall was packed, and when Morna commented on the smattering of men among the ranked women, Ruth said, 'There are many men sympathetic to our cause and interested in attending meetings.' Then, with a slight hardening to her voice, 'But our gatherings also attract men opposed to us getting the vote for some reason they have yet to explain.'

'Perhaps that's because they can't. Come along . . .' Christina drew her companions over to one of the tables set to the side. They were stacked with literature as well as lapel badges, and judging from the queues at every table, they were doing brisk business.

'Don't you already have a badge?' Morna whispered to Ruth.

'Yes, but this one belongs to the night Mrs Pankhurst came to talk to us. In any case, the movement needs all the money it can get.'

'The badge is certainly pretty,' Morna conceded as she pinned hers to the lapel of her jacket. It was in the suffragette colours – green, white and violet – and she felt quite proud to be wearing it in the company of women from all walks of life. The entire hall, and the front of the stage, was draped with banners and ribbons in the same three colours.

Just as they took their seats four neatly dressed women walked on to the platform and a wave of applause from the front rows was quickly taken up by row after row until the entire hall was filled with it. One of them stepped up to the lectern and waited calmly for the applause to end.

'Is that Mrs Pankhurst?' Morna whispered to Ruth.

'No, it's Dr Katharine Chapman; she's in the chair for tonight.'

Dr Chapman opened the meeting. When she began to speak there was none of the shouting and lectern-thumping that Morna had expected; instead, her audience listened intently as, in a clear, carrying voice, she spoke of the aims of the Women's Social and Political Union, organisers of that evening's meeting. The next speaker was both witty and perceptive; Morna found herself following and agreeing with every word, and she joined in the delighted howl of laughter when, in answer to a male voice shouting from the back of the hall, 'What you women need's a man!' the speaker said sweetly, 'If you find one, sir, you might be gracious enough to introduce him to me.'

When she sat down there was a sudden, excited hush as the chairwoman stepped forward to introduce Mrs Emmeline Pankhurst on her first visit to Paisley. As the main speaker, a straight-backed woman with great elegance in the way she moved and spoke, took her place the applause rose to the very rafters.

When Mrs Pankhurst sat down after a rousing and impassioned speech Morna joined in the applause, clapping so hard that her hands glowed as though she had been nursing hot coals all evening. Even so, they could not match the glow in her heart and mind as she went from the hall to the street, determined to pick up the cause of the suffragette movement and make it her own. She vowed to read all the literature piled on Ruth's kitchen table, and to march proudly through the streets, proclaiming her belief in votes for women in ringing tones.

She also resolved to visit Aunt Beatrice the very next day to tell her all about the meeting. At last, she thought as she, Ruth and Christina were swept towards the railway station in a tide of excited, chattering women, Aunt Beatrice would be proud of her, instead of looking on her as a silly young girl fit only for marriage.

'I am going to join the Union,' she was announcing to her friends when suddenly they found themselves surrounded by a group of men who had been lying in wait. Morna was buffeted here and there, then a hand snatched the hat from her head, the pins pulling cruelly at the roots of her hair as they were wrenched free.

'Give it back!' She reached for her hat and the man who had taken it held it high above his head, laughing at her. 'Give it back, give it back,' he mocked. 'If ye think ye're good enough tae vote like a man ye should surely be ready tae fight like one. Come and get yer bunnet, hen!'

Just then someone fell violently against her back, sending her forwards into her tormentor's arms. He, too, was caught off balance, but grabbed at her outstretched arm and swung her round against a nearby wall. Pain burned through her cheek as it was scraped along the stonework and then she was grabbed again. This time her back thumped into the wall. Hair loosened by her struggles fell into her eyes but through its curtain she could see her captor's face and his triumphant grin, revealing several gaps where he had lost front teeth. His breath smelled of beer and his hands dug into her shoulders, pinning her helplessly against the wall.

Morna, aware that she was in real danger, kicked out at the man but felt the side of her booted heel slide harmlessly past his leg. His grin broadened and then gave way to an expression of astonishment as his body shuddered violently. Releasing Morna, he let out a bellow of rage and began to turn away from her; then she saw him toppling to one side, his arms windmilling in a futile effort to keep his balance. One of them flailed across her midriff, winding her, but as she doubled over, a hand caught her elbow and Ruth's voice said in her ear, 'Come on – quickly!'

Morna was dragged through the struggling crowd and then she and Ruth had broken free. Christina appeared from nowhere and took Morna's other arm. 'Straighten up,' she said with quiet urgency. 'Walk quickly, but as though there's nothing wrong.'

Whistles were shrilling behind them, and Morna could still hear the clamour of voices. 'My hat . . .'

'I have it here. We'll stop when we get to the railway station and make ourselves respectable,' Ruth said. 'But for now, we must hurry!'

Once the noise of battle faded behind them they withdrew up a dark close where they smoothed their hair as best they could and tidied their clothing. Morna made a valiant attempt to put her hat back on, but her hands were shaking so badly that Christina had to do it for her.

While the train rattled through the night and the other two discussed the meeting, declaring it to be a resounding success, Morna stared out of the window, though there was nothing to see now apart from her own pale smudge of a face reflected in the glass. Her mind, which had been filled with such feelings of excitement and exhilaration as she left the meeting, rang with the noise of feet scuffling, women gasping with pain and deep voices grunting filthy accusations. Her cheek, red and scraped, with a dark bruise beginning to form along the cheekbone, was throbbing and so was her head. She felt as though she were in the grip of a fever.

Even when she was back in Saltcoats Morna did not feel safe. She doubted that she would ever feel safe again.

'Why were those men so vicious?' she asked when they were back in Ruth's cluttered kitchen, drinking cocoa. 'Why did they attack us when we had done nothing to hurt them?'

'Some men only feel like men when they have someone to dominate,' Christina said calmly. 'They think we threaten their very existence because we ask for a right that has until now been theirs and not ours. The men you met tonight are frightened because they think we are invading their world.'

Morna felt that she was far more frightened than the men could ever be. 'I don't know what would have happened if you hadn't helped me, Ruth. How did you do it?'

'I jabbed him in the rump with a hatpin. Always have more pins in your hat than you need when you go to a meeting. When he turned to see what was happening I pulled on his arm while he was off-balance then put my foot against his ankle and down he went. It's a useful trick that my brother Tom taught me when we were children.'

'As you see, Morna,' Christina chimed in, 'we have in our midst a woman who can defeat a man with a mere hatpin.'

She and Ruth started to laugh and Morna joined in. It seemed like the most amusing thing she had ever heard, but when the others stopped laughing she went on and on until all at once her laughter turned into sobs, with tears pouring down her face and dripping off her chin.

'Brandy, I think,' she heard Ruth say crisply, and then someone thrust a handkerchief into her hand, while a mug held by Ruth clattered slightly against her teeth. 'Take a sip,' she was ordered, and while she was still grimacing over the fiery liquid's invasion, 'and another – go on, now.'

When the sobs had slowed to a series of hiccups Ruth said, 'And now, my dear Morna, you're going to your bed. You've had more than enough excitement for today.'

24

Morna fell asleep as soon as her head touched her pillow
and woke in the morning to hear Ruth and Christina
going down to the kitchen. She peered into the mirror
above her chest of drawers and saw that her hair was
tangled, her face bruised and her eyes still swollen from
the previous night's fit of weeping.

It all came back to her, more like a nightmare than a
real happening, as she rinsed her face again and again in
cold water, brushed her hair ruthlessly until she had
managed to straighten out all the knots, and dressed.

'I am so sorry,' she said as she joined the other two at
the table.

'About what?' Ruth wanted to know. She and Christina
looked as fresh as daisies.

'About the way I behaved last night. Why can't I be
more like you?' Morna wailed, tears beginning to well
up in her eyes again.

'Because you're not us and we're not you, and thank
the Lord for that. It would be a very drab world indeed
if we were all alike. Morna, my dear,' said Ruth gently,
'your heart is in the right place but the rough and tumble

of the movement is not for you. Not yet, at any rate. There are other ways in which you can help us if you so wish, and one of them is to eat your breakfast, for Anna and the children will be here soon.'

'But what will I tell the children when they ask about my face? You know how inquisitive they can be.'

'Tell them that you walked into a door,' Christina advised, and then, her voice suddenly flat, 'it is what women with bruised faces always say – and they are always believed, for there are times when nobody wants to know the truth.'

She got up to answer a knocking at the door.

'Did her husband. . . ?'

'We all have our private lives, and friends never intrude into each other's,' Ruth was saying when Christina came back into the kitchen.

'It was a wee ragamuffin of a lad with a letter for you, Morna.'

'For me?' Morna unfolded the sheet of paper and scanned the few lines; when she looked up at the other two the bruise stood out sharply against her paper-white skin.

'It's from my sister Belle. I must go at once to my aunt's house,' she said, and then, unable to believe what she was saying, even though she heard the words being uttered aloud, 'Aunt Beatrice is dead.'

'I can't imagine a world without Aunt Beatrice in it,' Morna said an hour later. She and her brother and sister were in Beatrice's parlour; Ena, red-eyed, had retired to her kitchen. 'I always thought she would go on for ever.'

'It's as if the life has gone out of the place,' Walter said uneasily, running a finger round the inside of his collar to ease the choking sensation he had had since arriving at his aunt's house.

'It has.' Belle's voice was bleak. 'Only yesterday morning she seemed to be getting better. Ena says that that often happens to folk. One last surge of energy before the . . . Morna,' Belle said sharply, as her sister leaned forwards to put her untasted tea down and what little light was allowed into the curtained room fell on her bruised cheek, 'what has happened to your face?'

'I walked into a door. Is that Juliet I can hear upstairs?' The faint keening was so desolate that it sent shivers down her spine.

'She's outside Aunt Beatrice's door and nothing we do will coax her to come away.'

'Was it . . . Was Aunt Beatrice. . . ?' Morna paused, and Belle said reassuringly, 'She just slipped away early this morning.'

'I'm glad of that.'

'Did she say anything about the house?' Walter wanted to know.

'Only that it was too warm, so we opened the window a little at the top. That was around two o'clock. We set a screen between the window and the bed, so the little bit of fresh air can't have harmed—'

'I meant, Belle, did she say anything about who was to get the house?'

'For goodness' sake, Walter, do you think that I sat by her sickbed chatting to her about her will?'

'She did make one, I suppose?'

'That,' Belle said coldly, 'is a matter for her lawyer, not for us.'

'As her nearest kin—'

'Surely the first thing to be done is to arrange the funeral and then put a notice in the newspapers.'

'I will see to that.' He got up and started to pace the floor, stopping now and again to examine an ornament or a painting. 'It will take me away from the shop, of course, and so I would be grateful, Belle, if you would look after it.'

'I have been doing that since your marriage, Walter,' she said dryly, but the faint sarcasm was lost on him.

'Who is looking after it now, with you and I both here?'

'Samuel Gilmartin. I sent a message to his lodgings first thing this morning to tell him what had happened, and to entrust the running of Forsyth's to him for the time being.'

'But Mr Stoddart is the senior shop assistant!'

'Mr Stoddart has not been at work for almost a week. He has a bad chill.'

'There are others – Gilmartin has only been with us for a matter of months.'

'Walter, he already knows more about the running of the place than . . .' Belle, grieving for the aunt she had come to care for and tired after a night spent watching over Beatrice, only just managed to bite back the words 'than you do' and said instead, '. . . than any of the others. He learns very quickly and never forgets anything. And he is entirely trustworthy, I can assure you.'

'I certainly hope so. Can't you do anything about that noise?' Walter asked as the keening from above rose to a long drawn-out howl of anguish. 'It's sending shivers down my spine.'

'I'll try to coax her out into the back garden.'

'And I,' Walter said briskly, anxious to get out of this house of death, 'will start seeing to my duties.'

'Aunt Beatrice had already attended to most of the arrangements.' Belle unlocked a drawer in the desk and handed him a sheaf of papers. 'Here is the notice she wants put into the local papers, and the order of service for her funeral, the list of people to be notified and the list of mourners to be invited back to the house, together with instructions as to the refreshments to be served. Ena and I will see to that – with your assistance, I hope, Morna? And she has also left instructions as to the disposal of her clothing and personal belongings.'

'Oh,' Walter said. Even in death, it seemed that Aunt Beatrice was still head of the Forsyth family.

'I shall miss Aunt Beatrice,' Morna said again when Walter had gone and the sisters were alone.

'So will I. Since Father left us she has become my family.'

'You still have me – and Walter.'

'Walter,' Belle pointed out, 'has got Sarah and their child.'

'Indeed, but he is still our brother, and we still have each other. Perhaps,' Morna said, 'it is time for us to become a family again.'

Beatrice McCallum had been a well-known Saltcoats resident and on the day of her funeral the North Parish Church was filled to capacity. The Forsyth shop had been closed so that the staff could pay their last respects, but only one of them – Samuel Gilmartin – had been included on Beatrice's list of mourners to be invited back to the house.

'What is he doing here?' Walter muttered to Belle as the parlour rapidly filled.

'He's been very attentive towards Aunt Beatrice in the past few months. She taught him to play cribbage and they played every week. Do you know how to play cribbage, Walter?'

'If he thinks that he can go ingratiating himself into my family he must be made to think again!'

'Mr Gilmartin has been of considerable assistance to me, particularly over the past week,' Belle retorted sharply.

Sarah, who had opted to help Ena rather than be left standing in a corner, was carrying a large tray of sandwiches into the parlour when Samuel appeared before her.

'Allow me, Mrs Forsyth.' If he had not taken the tray from her, she would almost certainly have dropped it.

'What are you doing here?'

'I'm here by invitation. Mrs McCallum was a charming lady who will be greatly missed.' He put the tray on the table and turned to smile down at her. 'If I may be permitted to say so, Mrs Forsyth, you look very elegant. Mourning becomes you, which is more than can be said for many of the ladies in our company.' His voice was low and intimate, but even so Sarah found herself glancing round guiltily to make sure that they were not overheard before she replied, her voice trembling, 'And you look very fine, Samuel.'

'The clothes maketh the man.' He raised an eyebrow at her. 'Who'd have thought, in the old days, that the two of us would end up like this?'

'Do you ever think of those days, Samuel?' she asked with sudden yearning. 'Do you ever think of what we meant to each other?'

'Now what sort of a question is that for a respectable married woman to be askin' of one of her husband's employees?' he enquired silkily. 'It would be improper of me to allow myself tae think of my employer's wife in such a way. And improper of you to give a thought to a man who's not your husband.'

'I *do* think of you, though, and I wish—'

'Samuel,' Belle Forsyth called at that moment, and he looked over at her before turning back to Sarah. 'The thing is,' he said, lowering his voice to a whisper, 'Miss Belle keeps me so busy that I scarce have time to think of any thing or any one else. Is that not a mercy for both of us?'

Then he had gone, and in the space left by his body Sarah saw her husband watching her. He beckoned her over with an imperceptible tilt of the head.

'What did Gilmartin want with you?' he asked as she reached his side.

'He was expressing his condolences to the family.'

'Hmmm. I don't know why Belle allowed his name to be added to the list of invited guests. She should never have let Aunt Beatrice make such a pet of the man,' he said, and then paused. She could tell what was happening by his sudden, slight wince and the small movements of his mouth.

'Is that tooth troubling you again?'

'Just a little. These biscuits Belle is serving are too sweet. The sugar is not good for anyone's teeth.'

'You should go to the dentist, Walter.'

'Nonsense, there's nothing wrong that a little oil of cloves can't . . .' he had begun when a slender, black-gloved hand landed on his arm and Clarissa Pinkerton said, 'Walter, my dear, I would have come to you as soon as I heard the sad news, but Mama felt that it was best to leave the family to themselves until the funeral.'

'You were always considerate, Clarissa. You know my wife, don't you?'

'Of course. How are you, Mrs Forsyth?' Clarissa asked sweetly, her grey eyes, which had been looking warmly into Walter's face, suddenly as cold as pebbles on the bed of a winter stream.

'I am very well, thank you, Miss Pinkerton. I trust that you are well yourself?'

'I am always well. Walter, I hope that you intend to take up tennis again this summer . . .' Clarissa turned towards him so that Sarah was excluded. Sarah hesitated for a moment, uncertain as to what to do; then Morna, who had been watching, came over.

'Sarah, come and tell me how my nephew is doing.' She linked her hand through the crook of Sarah's elbow and drew her to one side. 'My aunt told me when I last saw her that you have a new nursemaid. I hope that she is suitable.'

'Very suitable, thank you, Miss Morna.'

'I think you should call me Morna, since we are sisters now. I may not have behaved like a sister since your marriage,' Morna forged on as Sarah stared at her, open-mouthed, 'but I have changed, truly I have. You mustn't let Clarissa hurt you; she can be quite a cat when the mood takes her. To tell you the truth, I have come to believe that Walter is better off with you for his wife, since Clarissa's ambitions might have made his life quite miserable.'

'You must miss your aunt very much,' Ruth was saying to Belle.

'I had come to treasure her company, and now she has gone. Life will be quite lonely without Aunt Beatrice.'

'I hope that you will come to visit Morna and me whenever you feel lonely. My house is only a short distance away, and I know that she would be happy to see you. So would I — it's time we got to know each other.'

Belle looked doubtfully into Ruth's piercing blue eyes and decided that the woman was not just being courteous for Morna's sake. She was not the type to say what she did not mean.

'Thank you,' she said, 'I would like that very much.'

★   ★   ★

'This,' Beatrice McCallum's lawyer said as he settled himself at the dining-room table, 'is a particularly sad time.' He smoothed his black tie and then glanced down at the black band on his sleeve. 'First Mrs McCallum, a well-respected client for many years, and then this morning's tragic news of the death of our beloved king.'

'Yes indeed.' Walter, who also sported a black tie and band, bowed his head for a moment, then lifted it to glare at Morna when she remarked, 'The king is dead, long live the king.'

'Morna!'

'Isn't that what they say? Surely I am only wishing King George a long and healthy reign,' she protested.

The lawyer coughed behind his hand and then rustled the papers before him. 'Yes indeed, Miss Forsyth, a laudable comment. Now then, as to your aunt's will . . .'

Beatrice had left one thousand pounds each to Walter and Morna, five hundred pounds each to her housekeeper Ena, Sarah, her great-nephew Fraser Walter Forsyth and to an organisation for homeless animals. Her house and contents, together with the remainder of her estate, went to Belle, along with the request that she continue to provide a comfortable and loving home for Juliet.

'How much is the rest of the estate?' Walter wanted to know as the lawyer finished reading out the will and folded his podgy hands together on the table.

'Miss Forsyth?' the man asked Belle, and then, when she gave a dazed nod, 'Approximately four thousand and nine hundred pounds.'

Walter's mouth opened and shut, making him look like a fish cast up on a riverbank and gasping for air, then he managed to say, 'Almost five thousand pounds? All for Belle? Are you quite sure?'

'Mrs McCallum brought her will up to date two

months ago, Mr Forsyth, and she was most definite about every part of it.' The man smiled at Belle, who looked as stunned as her brother. 'I understand that she appreciated Miss Forsyth's companionship and was anxious that her niece would not be left homeless after her death.'

'Well,' Walter said when the lawyer had left them, 'you've landed on your feet, Belle.'

'I can assure you that I had no idea that Aunt Beatrice had left me anything.'

'She's been very generous towards you. I suppose that I should be grateful that she left me anything at all,' Walter's voice was sour. 'And at least she remembered my son – though why on earth she should include you, Sarah, I cannot imagine.'

'You have the business, Walter, and the family house,' Morna pointed out. 'It's true that Belle might have been left homeless if Aunt Beatrice had left her house to anyone else, or directed that it should be sold.'

'You have no home of your own either, but she didn't think of that, did she?'

'She left me a considerable sum of money, and I am grateful because I have done nothing to deserve it, while Belle has been a good companion and comfort to Aunt Beatrice for the past six months or more. And I know that Ruth will allow me to share her home for as long as I please. I am very happy there.'

Belle had supplied tea for herself and her sister and sister-in-law. Walter had opted for a glass of Beatrice's malt whisky – 'Though now, Belle, it is your whisky,' he had said with a cutting edge to his voice. He now drained the final drops from the glass, tilting his head in order to allow the spirits to bathe his bad tooth, which had begun to ache again, then set the empty glass down, saying, 'Come, Sarah, we must go home. Will you be in the shop tomorrow, Belle, or are you too grand to be involved in anything as mundane as trade now?'

'You know perfectly well that I will be there tomorrow morning as usual,' Belle said calmly, but once he and Sarah had left, she sank into a chair and pressed a handkerchief to her mouth.

'Oh, Morna,' she said in a muffled voice, 'it seems so unfair that Aunt Beatrice should leave me more than you and Walter!'

'Nonsense, you've been a great comfort to her since you moved here. You are more than entitled to your inheritance.'

'But Walter—'

'Bother Walter! You know what he's like – what he has always been like. Even when we were children Walter expected the lion's share of everything, and he usually got it, being the only boy. It's time he grew up.'

'I could always share out the money between the three of us.'

'And have Aunt Beatrice coming back to haunt you because you went against her express wishes? Certainly not,' Morna said briskly. 'I for one would not thank you for it – I don't know what I'll do with the thousand I have now. Consult Mr Pinkerton, I suppose, then put it into a bank account and forget it until such time as I might have need of it. Don't you realise, Belle, that this is the first time you have ever gained anything for yourself? Walter was given preference because he was the only son, while our parents made a lot of fuss over me just because I happen to be the baby of the family – and I'm not going to pretend that I didn't like it, for I did, but you were always expected to be sensible and undemanding because you were the oldest. You're the one who runs the shop – if it were dependent on Walter we

285

would have gone bankrupt by now. Aunt Beatrice has probably known the truth all along – and known that her money is safer in your hands than in Walter's, or mine.'

'You've changed so much since Papa left, Morna.'

'I have, haven't I?' Morna agreed, with a pleased smile. 'A year ago I would have rushed off to Glasgow and spent that thousand pounds on clothes and jewellery. Now these things don't seem to matter nearly as much as they once did. Let's ask Ena for a fresh pot of tea, shall we?'

As his sisters settled down to more tea, Walter was saying to his wife, 'I shall look after your inheritance, my dear, since you know nothing about money other than the house-keeping allowance. My aunt has been most generous towards you.'

'Most generous,' Sarah agreed, still unable to believe her inheritance. Suddenly, she was rich beyond her wildest dreams. If only, she thought as Walter held the gate open for her, and then followed her up the garden path, she had had that sum a year earlier. Samuel would have been happy to marry her and they could have afforded a nice place to stay. But on the other hand, she reminded herself as Nellie opened the door, she had only been left the money because she was Walter's wife. And she would far, far rather have Mrs McCallum, with her kindness and her words of reassurance and wisdom, than all the money in the kingdom.

25

That evening, while Morna listened to the spirited talk of the women gathered around Ruth's kitchen table and stitched at her section of the almost-completed suffragette quilt, and Walter sat at his desk in Argyle Road, chin on hand, trying to look as though he was lost in thought when in actual fact he was nursing his throbbing back tooth, Ena showed Samuel Gilmartin into the parlour where Belle Forsyth awaited him.

'You wanted to see me, Miss Forsyth?'

'Yes, Mr Gilmartin. Please sit down.' Belle indicated one of the two chairs drawn up before the fire. He moved towards it, but remained standing, one hand resting on the back of the chair. 'Ena is bringing tea, but perhaps you would prefer a glass of whisky?'

'Tea would be very pleasant, thank you.' Samuel waited until his hostess had seated herself before taking his own seat opposite her. 'How are you, Miss Forsyth?'

'Very well, thank you – considering the circumstances.'

His brown eyes, soft and warm, met and held hers, and she was soothed by their concern. 'It's a sad time for you – for all of us,' he said as Ena brought in the tea tray

287

and set it on a small table close to Belle's chair. Juliet had come in with the maid; she hurried over to Samuel, who made a fuss of her and her little body squirmed with pleasure.

'Behave yourself, Juliet,' Belle told her.

'She's missing her mistress.'

'I know she is, but even so – take her back into the kitchen, Ena, or we shall get no peace to take our tea.'

'I wonder,' Samuel said as Belle poured tea, 'if I might be permitted to wash my hands in the kitchen?'

'Use the bathroom upstairs. The first door at the top of the stairs.'

'The kitchen will do me fine, Miss Forsyth.'

'The bathroom,' Belle said sweetly but firmly, 'is for the use of guests, and you are a guest. The first door at the top of the stairs.'

'Thank you.' He went out and all at once Belle felt as though the room had changed. It lacked the warmth that had been there only a moment before. She shivered slightly, wondering if she had caught a chill, and wrapped both hands around her teacup for comfort.

Samuel took his time as he went up the flight of stairs so thickly carpeted that it was like walking on soft moss. The bathroom door stood half-open while the other doors around the landing were firmly closed. He knew what lay behind only one of them – Beatrice McCallum's bedroom, where he had visited the old lady in the final weeks of her life.

The water was hot and the soap smelled of flowers. He washed his hands several times, revelling in the un-accustomed comfort, before drying them on a thick, absorbent towel. Then he looked into the oval, wood-framed mirror on the wall to make sure that not a hair was out of place. On his way back downstairs he dared to touch the raised flock wallpaper with the back of one finger.

'Will you take a rock cake?' Belle asked as he sat down opposite her.

'Thank you.' The cake was home-made, crisp on the outside and soft inside, but Samuel scarcely tasted it. He was hungry for more than rock cakes; he was hungry for a life that included soft carpets and chairs, hot water and scented soap and flock wallpaper. He was hungry for a life far better than any he had ever known.

'I will miss your aunt,' he said. 'She was very good to me.'

'To all of us. How are things at the shop?'

'Going smoothly. You have a good, loyal staff.'

'I'll be in tomorrow.'

'Are you sure, Miss Forsyth?' Samuel stirred his tea carefully, so as not to spill any into the pretty saucer. 'Should you not take a wee while off to recover from your loss? I can keep an eye on things and visit regularly to report on how business is doing.'

'It's kind of you, but I would rather keep myself occupied.' She put her cup down and picked up an envelope from the small table by her chair. 'My aunt asked me to give this to you.'

'To me?' He took the envelope and turned it over, studying his name printed in strong, bold characters. 'What is it?'

'It's for you, not me. I know nothing about the contents.' Belle had placed a silver paperknife beside the envelope; now she held it out to him. 'You can open it now, if you wish.'

'Thank you.' He accepted the knife, beautifully made in the form of a tiny sword with an enamelled handle, and slit the envelope open neatly. Then he gave a soft exclamation as several notes slid out into his palm. 'It's — fifty pounds! Miss Forsyth, I can't accept this!'

'If my aunt meant it for you, then it's yours, Mr Gilmartin.' Belle was smiling now, flushed with pleasure at his almost childlike astonishment. 'Is there nothing else?'

Carefully laying the notes aside, he dipped a finger into the envelope and withdrew a folded sheet of paper. 'With your permission. . . ?'

'Of course.' Belle made a display of selecting a biscuit and taking another sip of tea, watching him over the rim of her cup as he read the letter. After a moment, he glanced up at her.

'It's — it is a very kind letter. Would you like to read it?' He held it out, and she recoiled as though he had offered her a poisonous snake.

'It's your letter, Mr Gilmartin. I would not dream of reading it.'

'Oh. Well, she says that she appreciated my visits and my company, and she asks . . .' he hesitated and bit his lip before carrying on almost shyly, '. . . and she asks that I continue to be your friend as I was hers, and to assist you if you ever need my help. As of course I will, with all my heart.'

Belle coloured slightly. 'I certainly hope that we will continue to be friends and that you will call on me again.'

'I would be honoured.' He gathered up the notes, folded them, and then paused. 'Are you quite sure that it's in order for me to accept this?'

'Of course. I know that my aunt would want you to gain some enjoyment from it,' Belle said, and was taken aback when his eyes grew moist.

'Mrs McCallum was an angel of a woman,' he said with a tremor in his voice, 'and I consider myself blessed among men for having known her.' Then, getting to his feet, 'If you'll forgive me, Miss Forsyth, I must be on my way now.'

She had hoped that he would stay a little longer, but she could not possibly say so. 'Of course.' She got to her feet and took his proffered hand; then was taken aback for the second time as he lifted her fingers to his lips. 'I hope you're not offended, Miss Forsyth,' he said when he had released her hand, 'but since I can no longer salute your aunt it gives me great comfort to be able to thank her niece, who has also shown me such trust and kindness.'

When he had gone Belle sat on in the parlour for some time, smiling at the curtains drawn across the windows and occasionally stroking the back of her hand, where the skin still tingled from the soft but firm touch of his lips.

Outside the house, Samuel put his bowler hat on his head at a jaunty angle, patted the pocket that held the envelope and all its contents, and set off towards his new lodgings in Melbourne Terrace at a fast pace.

Once in his snug little room he took Beatrice McCallum's envelope from his breast pocket and opened it. Inviting Belle Forsyth to read it had been a gamble that had paid off. The combination of luck and quick thinking that had stood him in good stead so far had not let him down; he had been right when he guessed that women of Belle's social standing would never read other people's letters. He smoothed the single page out lovingly, then read it aloud slowly, line by line.

Dear Mr Gilmartin,
I hope that you will accept the enclosed sum in appreciation
of our enjoyable meetings and our games of cribbage. You are
a swift learner, as I already knew from the way you have

settled in at the family shop. One of the reasons why I have enjoyed your company so much is that to my mind, Mr Gilmartin, you are a bit of a rogue and a rebel, and I have always had a soft spot for men like yourself. My own late husband was certainly a rebel, though never to my knowledge a rogue.

I trust that as well as showing my appreciation, the money enclosed will assist you to travel further afield than Saltcoats, so that you may begin to seek the fortune that you will surely find one day. But you should not seek it here, and not at the expense of my nephew or, especially, my niece Belle. She trusts too easily, and as she is content in her own quiet way I would not want to see her life disrupted. I am sure that you understand my meaning, and believe me when I say that my best wishes go on your travels with you.

Beatrice McCallum.

'You were a grand woman, Beatrice McCallum,' Samuel said aloud, 'and I'm grateful for the money. You're quite right when you say that it will take me to better things. But I've no need tae leave Saltcoats tae find my future. It's right here, and almost ripe for the takin'.'

He crumpled up the letter and held it to the gas fire until it caught alight, waiting until it was burned almost to the corner gripped between his thumb and forefinger before allowing the ashes to drop on to the hearth. Then he took the notes from the envelope and counted them slowly several times. Finally, he folded them over and clenched his fist around them.

Fifty pounds was a fortune, more money than he had ever dreamed of possessing in his lifetime. He could almost feel the notes glowing against his palm, clamouring to be spent. But Samuel Gilmartin was not going to give in to temptation. Everything he needed and wanted was now within his reach, and soon it would be grasped as closely as the money in his fist.

Morning classes were halfway through and the children were enjoying their milk and biscuits out in the sun-splashed back garden when the police came for Christina Baird.

'I'll go,' Morna said when a thunderous knocking was heard from the front of the house, but Ruth put a hand on her arm.

'Best if I go, Morna.' Her voice was quiet, and she and Christina exchanged glances. Christina nodded, and went quickly into the kitchen. Another volley of blows on the front door almost drowned out the sound of her footsteps going up the staircase.

'Ruth . . .' Morna stared at her friend, a chill beginning to trickle down her spine.

'It's all right, just leave it to me.' Ruth left the garden and Morna followed her as far as the kitchen door, where she hesitated, unwilling to go any further and yet not knowing what she feared.

The door opened to reveal two large policemen silhouetted against the brightness of the day. 'I believe that Mrs Christina Baird resides here, ma'am,' Morna heard one of them say.

'Yes, she's been unwell and I have been nursing her back to health.'

'I have a warrant here for her arrest. She must come with us to serve the rest of a sentence imposed on her by the Glasgow magistrates.'

'She is still not strong enough . . .' Ruth began, while Morna became aware of a soft murmuring and realised that small bodies were pressing against her legs. Some stared at the policemen in silence, grubby little fingers stuffed into their mouths, while others hid their faces in her skirt. One of the littlest children began to whimper, and Morna picked her up and held her close.

'The magistrates say that she *is* strong enough, ma'am. It is understood that Mrs Baird attended a meeting in Paisley recently.'

'Yes, she did, but that—'

'If you do not ask Mrs Baird to come to the door, ma'am, then we have been empowered under the terms of the warrant to enter these premises and—'

'That will not be necessary, Constable,' Christina said quietly from the foot of the stairs. She was dressed in her outdoor clothes and carried a bag that must have been packed earlier, in readiness. 'I am prepared to accompany you,' she said, then turned and smiled at Morna and the children. 'Be good, little ones,' she said, and then, to Morna more than the others, 'and be happy.'

She walked to the doorway where she and Ruth embraced briefly before Christina went out onto the top step. The police officers immediately moved to either side of her.

'Morna, take the children into your room, if you please,' Ruth ordered, 'and let them sing.'

'Come along, quickly.' Morna swept the little ones into the room and closed the door before hurrying to the bay window. A police van stood at the kerb, with yet another policeman waiting at the open back doors. A few passers-by had stopped to stare as Christina, as straight as a ramrod and tiny between the burly uniformed men, walked down the garden path.

'"Onward Christian Soldiers",' Morna said, setting down her tearful burden and opening one of the windows wide. 'We don't need the piano, do we? And we must sing it as loud as we can, so that Mrs Baird hears every word! One, two, three . . .'

She started singing, clapping time, and the children quickly joined in, their voices struggling at first and then gaining in power. They all stood by the window, watching as Christina reached the back of the van. She turned and smiled towards the front door, where Ruth must still be standing, and gave a little wave of the hand. Then she looked at the window, and this time her smile was broad and her wave a triumphant, farewell flourish. They all waved back, the song swelling, bursting out through the open window and pouring down the path to where, with fairly gentle assistance from the policemen, Christina Baird was clambering into the back of the van. As the doors closed one of the older children yelped, 'Sing louder, you lot, so's she can hear us!' and the children, abandoning their efforts to keep in tune, yelled the last verse at the top of their young lungs, some of them leaning out of the window to screech the final words as the van drove off.

Ruth clapped loudly from the back of the room as they finished. 'Well done, everyone,' she said, her mouth smiling and unshed tears sparkling like diamonds in her lovely dark blue eyes. 'The best singing I have ever heard. But now it's time to get back to our lessons.'

'Walter, you must have that tooth seen to.' Sarah picked up the current edition of the *Ardrossan & Saltcoats Herald*, which she had folded open at a prominent advertisement. 'Mr James Walker of Dockhead Street sounds very good. It says here, "It Don't Hurt a Bit." '

'It wouldn't hurt him, would it? He's the dentist, not the patient.'

'I doubt if he would claim not to hurt you if he

intended to hurt you,' Sarah said, thrusting the paper at Walter, who had no option but to take it and read the advertisement. 'I have decided that I will call on him this morning to make an appointment for you.'

'But it's just the occasional twinge. All it needs is oil of cloves now and again.'

'Walter, your face is swollen and you and I are both suffering from lack of sleep. And so is poor Nellie, after being dragged from her bed at all hours to make up hot poultices.' Sarah had never spoken so firmly to her husband before, but five nights of being wakened by Walter tossing and turning or pacing the floor and moaning quietly to himself had driven her to distraction. In any case, although she had no idea where he had invested her inheritance from Beatrice, and indeed, had never even seen the money, just knowing that she was now a woman of means had given her new strength and determination.

'I am not a child, Sarah. I will see the dentist when I need to see the dentist!'

'Since you mention the word "child",' she forged on, 'even poor little Fraser is being affected. Look at yesterday, when you were holding him and he threw his head up and accidentally hit your jaw. You shouted at him and reduced him to tears.'

'It was a moment's irritation, nothing more,' her husband mumbled, avoiding her gaze.

'It frightened him, Walter. If you remember, he was hesitant about being handed to you the next time Mrs Drummond brought him downstairs. He hid his little face in her shoulder. Do you want your own son to think of you as an ogre? Look at the advertisement again, Walter,' she pressed on as he began to weaken. 'You can have the tooth attended to under gas – you'll just go to sleep and you won't feel a thing.'

'Not gas! The last time I had that I thought I was suffocating. I won't take gas, Sarah!'

'Then try this cocaine he mentions. "Harmless, and with no side effects",' Sarah read out. 'And it only costs one shilling. I'll come with you, if you want.'

A few hours later she sat fidgeting in the dentist's waiting room, trying not to study the coloured pictures of damaged teeth and diseased gums that were hanging on the wall. Her ears strained for sounds of suffering from behind the closed door of Mr Walker's surgery, while at the same time she thanked her own good fortune in having strong teeth that rarely required medical attention.

When the door finally opened and the dentist ushered Walter out she sprang to her feet. 'How are you?'

'Absolutely very well,' her husband beamed. 'No trouble at all. It don't – didn't hurt a bit. This is a grand fellow,' he informed the entire waiting room, shaking the dentist's hand vigorously. A trickle of blood ran unnoticed down his chin and Sarah mopped at it with her handkerchief.

'Just rinse the cavity with warm water and salt, and get him to lie down for an hour or two,' Mr Walker advised. 'Bland food until tomorrow.'

'Fine man,' Walter called after him as he retreated back into his surgery. 'Salt of the earth. Wonderful stuff, cocaine,' he rambled on as Sarah, having paid the bill, escorted him out to the street. 'Everyone should try it. No pain at all.'

He pulled away from the hand she had slipped through the crook of his elbow and stepped out into the street, causing a butcher's van to halt abruptly and toot its horn. Walter waved benignly at the angry driver as he wove his way across the street and on to the opposite pavement.

'Where are you going?' Sarah asked when she caught up with him.

'To the shop, where else?'

'Mr Walker said you have to go home and rest, Walter. Your mouth is bleeding.'

He touched his mouth and then looked in surprise at the red smear on his fingers. 'So it is, by George. You go home, my dear, and attend to young Fraser. I must get to work. No knowing what they might be up to without my hand on the whatever-it-is.'

26

'Walter!' Sarah appealed, but her husband marched on, and there was nothing for it but to follow him to the shop, where the young female assistant rearranging shelves by the door dropped a swift curtsey when her employer entered and then reeled back, aghast, as he gave her a wide, bloody smile.

'Good morning, Walter – and Sarah too.' Belle came from her small cubbyhole. She also recoiled at sight of her brother's face. 'What on earth has happened? Did someone hit you?'

'Tooth out, no problem at all. Wonderful dentist, Walker. I may decide to get all my teeth out,' Walter said briskly. 'Save pain later. Now then, how is business?'

The door opened and a well-dressed gentleman came in. Walter tried to swing round to greet him, but halfway there he lost his balance and had to lean on Sarah's shoulder in order to steady himself. Her knees buckled under the sudden weight, and she threw a desperate, beseeching look at her sister-in-law.

'Mr Gilmartin . . .' Belle said, '. . . could you attend to Mr Harrison?' And then, to Walter, 'Business is doing very well, but I would like you to look at the books, since you are here.' Taking his arm she led him into the office while Sarah followed, keenly aware of the inquisitive stares from staff and customers alike.

'He should be at home,' Belle murmured once they had managed to get Walter into a chair.

'He insisted on coming here. What am I to do with him?' Sarah was almost in tears. Belle glanced at Walter, who was now doing his best to make sense of the neat rows of figures in the ledger before him.

'I'll ask Samuel to assist Walter home.'

'He's busy with a customer. Perhaps one of the others. . . ?'

'Samuel can be very discreet, and we don't want the whole of Saltcoats to know about this, do we? Wait here,' Belle said, and left the office.

When Samuel's customer had gone she drew him aside. 'My brother has had a tooth removed and he is not feeling very well. I would be grateful if you could fetch a cab and escort him and Mrs Forsyth home.'

'Of course, Miss Forsyth, it would be my pleasure.'

Ten minutes later Sarah was hurrying up the path while Samuel helped Walter from the cab. 'Nellie, the master has had his tooth removed and now he needs to rest,' she said as soon as the maid opened the door. 'Please go and turn the bed down.'

'Yes, ma'am.' The girl scurried upstairs, passing Leez Drummond on her way down, the baby in her arms.

'We're just off for our walk, Mrs Forsyth,' the woman said as she arrived in the hall. And then, as Samuel eased Walter in through the front door, 'Is Mr Forsyth unwell?'

'He's had a tooth removed and he . . .' Sarah was beginning when Walter, catching sight of the little boy, pulled free of Samuel.

'And here's my son! Come to Papa, Fraser.' He plucked the child from Leez's arms.

'Mr Forsyth . . .'

'Grand wee fellow, aren't you?' Walter beamed bloodily and before anyone could stop him he tossed the baby into the air. Sarah, Leez and Fraser all screamed, and Walter, turning to find out what the pandemonium was about, staggered off balance. For a terrible, heart-stopping moment Sarah thought that her precious little son was going to fall to the floor, or against the nearby banisters, then Fraser, eyes and mouth wide with terror, was caught by Samuel's outstretched hands.

'Good man,' Walter said heartily. 'Ever played cricket?'

Leez snatched her charge from Samuel and held him close while she fixed her employer with a gimlet eye. 'I think, Mr Forsyth, that you would be the better of a wee lie down,' she said in a firm voice.

The tone, and the look, caused Walter to deflate suddenly. 'You're right.' He ran the back of his hand over his mouth and then studied the red smear, surprised. 'Where did that come from?'

'Let me help you, sir,' Samuel said, and began to ease his employer upstairs.

'Get him to rinse his mouth with warm salty water, Mrs Forsyth,' Leez advised, then bore her precious charge out of the house and away from danger.

By the time Sarah took the water and some clean cloths up to the bedroom, Walter was in bed, his clothes neatly folded and laid on a chair. Between them Sarah and Samuel persuaded him to rinse his mouth out, and then settled him against the pillows. He fell asleep almost at once.

Samuel tucked one of the cloths between his cheek and the pillow. 'To catch any blood that might still be there,' he said. 'And now I'd best get back to the shop.'

301

'Would you like a cup of tea before you go?' Sarah offered when they were in the hall. 'Or something stronger, perhaps?'

'Miss Forsyth will be looking for me.'

She watched him walk down the path and along the pavement without a single backward glance, then hurried upstairs to the bedroom where she went straight to the window. She was too late; Samuel Gilmartin was already out of sight.

Behind her, Walter began to snore. She rested her forehead on the cool glass pane and thought longingly of what might have been.

'I was wondering,' Walter said a few days later, 'when you intend to sell Aunt Beatrice's house.'

'Why would I sell it?'

'Because it's too large for you.'

'I don't think so.'

'Of course it is. You should sell it and buy something smaller and more suited to your needs. Then you can invest the profits. I am more than willing to advise you.'

It was the end of the week and they were in the parlour of the house that had been Beatrice McCallum's, going over the shop orders and invoices. Now Belle laid down her pen and stared at her brother. 'Aunt Beatrice left it to me because she expected me to live here.'

'But Aunt Beatrice is no longer here. The house is yours, Belle, to sell as you wish.'

Belle looked around the comfortable parlour and realised that she had developed a great fondness for this house – more than she had ever known for the house where she had been raised. That had been her parents' home, and it was now Walter's, whereas this was her home.

'Aunt Beatrice didn't seem to find it too large.'

'That's because she came to it as a married woman. It is an ideal house for a married couple, but you, Belle, are a maiden lady.'

'I may yet marry, Walter.'

'My dear girl, there has been no sign of a suitor as yet, has there?'

'So you consider me too old for marriage – or too ugly, perhaps?' Belle asked icily.

'There is nothing wrong with your looks – though we both know that when it comes to beauty Morna was blessed with the looks while you have a good brain. And there is certainly no doubt that thanks to Aunt Beatrice's generosity towards you in her will you would be a good catch for any man. But even so . . .'

'Walter, I believe that I have a headache coming on.' Belle put a shaking hand to her forehead. 'I really must go and lie down in a darkened room at once.'

When her brother had gone, completely unaware of how close he had come to being physically assaulted, she paced the parlour floor, her hands doubled into fists. Then she did something that she would not have dreamed of doing a year earlier – she went to seek advice from Morna, who was working with Ruth on the next week's lessons. Belle sat down and poured out the whole story.

'Aunt Beatrice left the house to you,' her sister said at once, 'and you are the only person who can decide whether to keep it or move somewhere else.'

'Do you like the house?' Ruth asked. She put her pen down and concentrated her full attention on Belle.

'I like it very much.'

'Then you should keep it. Look at this place . . .' Ruth indicated the kitchen with a wave of ink-stained fingers.

'Your brother would no doubt say that it is too large for me, but I feel comfortable in it.'

'But you need the space for your little school. I've no wish to do anything like that.'

'Why should you? We all have different needs and interests. You're a woman of property now, and dependent on no one. You can do whatever you please.'

She gave the visitor a warm smile and an encouraging pat on the hand before returning to her work.

Belle, soothed by the atmosphere of the cluttered house, stayed for longer than she had intended. When she returned home she went upstairs at once. Juliet, who had accepted Belle as her new mistress, scurried at her heels, but to the little dog's disappointment she was shut out of the bedroom that had always been Belle's. After snuffling along the narrow space at the bottom of the closed door she settled down on the hall carpet, head on paws.

In the privacy of her room, Belle examined her face closely in the mirror above her dressing table. Walter had only spoken the truth when he'd pointed out that Morna was by far the prettier of his two sisters. Belle's jaw was a little too strong, her brown eyes heavy-lidded and her hair mousy brown, while Morna had a heart-shaped little face, soft fair hair and wide hazel eyes with thick, curving lashes.

Belle pulled out the pins skewering her hair to the top of her head in her usual style; after brushing it until it crackled she tied it back loosely at the nape of her neck. This look softened the lines of her serious face. She then moved to the standing mirror to study her figure. She had a reasonable bosom – not as noble as Clarissa Pinkerton's or as sweetly curvaceous as Morna's, but reasonable – and although her waist was not hourglass slender, it too was adequate.

She spent some time posturing and primping before the glass and by the time she let Juliet in, her mind was made up.

'How would you like to have a master as well as a mistress?' she asked, gathering the little dog into her arms. Juliet licked her chin enthusiastically as Belle went on, 'I think that we need a man about this house. That would stop Walter's interfering once and for all.'

She returned to the long mirror and decided that it now reflected a handsome woman in her prime, posing with her little pet dog.

As Morna had done months before, she had decided that it was time to marry. But unlike Morna, Belle was determined to succeed. As Ruth had said, she was a woman of property. She was a good catch for any man she set her heart on.

And she had already set her heart on one in particular.

Samuel Gilmartin took some time over his appearance on the evening he was invited to have supper with Belle Forsyth. His landlady, easily won over with a little Irish charm, pressed his one and only suit and ironed and starched his shirt. His fingernails were well scrubbed, and his normally curly hair oiled into place.

He inspected himself carefully in the flyblown mirror on his bedroom wall and nodded approval before going downstairs to snip a particularly handsome yellow rosebud from his landlady's back garden while she was chatting to someone at the front door.

'Froggy went a-wooing . . .' he whistled softly as he walked to Caledonia Road. Samuel Gilmartin was also going a-wooing and tonight, he had decided when Belle invited him to the house, would see the first step in his carefully thought-out plan.

But even carefully thought-out plans can go awry, and the one thing that Samuel had not anticipated was that the proposal would be that very night. Nor had he anticipated that it would come from Belle and not from him.

The supper, beautifully laid out in the small dining room, with snowy tablecloth, silver cutlery and delicate bone china hand-painted plates, had been delicious. After rising from the table they moved into the parlour, where Ena had left a tray by Belle's usual chair.

'I've discovered a fondness for coffee,' she said. 'Would you care for some? Or there's whisky if you would prefer it.'

'I'm not much of a drinker, Miss Forsyth.'

'It's a particularly good malt, my brother tells me.' She nodded to where the bottle stood on a side table, two crystal glasses by its side. 'In fact, I believe that I will try it myself.'

'You – drink whisky?'

'I believe that some ladies do.'

'I'm not sure,' Samuel said cautiously, 'if you would care for it.'

'How will I know if I never taste it?'

'Well – if you wish . . .'

'I do. Just a little for me,' she said as he opened the bottle. 'There's a box of cigars there as well; my father used to enjoy a good cigar after dinner. I like the smell of them.'

He handed her the glass and took his own. 'To your very good health, Miss Forsyth.'

'To the future, Mr Gilmartin,' Belle said, and took a sip of whisky. Samuel watched, amused, as her eyes widened and her nose wrinkled. She swallowed and then took a deep breath.

'Would you rather have coffee?' he asked gently, but she shook her head.

'I believe that this is an acquired taste,' she said, and took another sip.

Samuel tasted his own whisky, which was superb, then lit the cigar and sat back in the comfortable chair which felt like soft arms cradling his entire body. Belle Forsyth had freed her hair from its usual severe style and drawn it back to the nape of her neck, where it was twisted into a knot finished off with a pretty pale-blue bow that matched her blouse. The style made her look younger, he thought, just as she said, 'You're the first proper guest to be entertained in my very own house.'

'I'm honoured, but why me? You must have many friends just longing to spend time in your company.'

Belle flushed slightly. 'You really think that I still have friends after the way my father behaved, and after my brother married our servant? You know little about society, Mr Gilmartin.'

'No I don't, never having moved in social circles. Are you telling me that the sins of the brothers are visited on poor defenceless women?' he asked in mock horror, and then, when she laughed, 'If you'll forgive me for being forward, Miss Forsyth, you have a lovely smile.'

The flush became her as well; it warmed her normally sallow skin and brought a glow to her eyes. 'You think so?' Her pleasure was clear; this woman, he thought to himself, had not known many compliments.

'I do indeed. You should use it more often.'

'Perhaps I will – now.'

A companionable silence fell between them. The cigar was enjoyable and the malt slipped down Samuel's throat like silk. The room was peaceful and he could smell the delicate scent of the yellow rosebud, which had been received with delight and now rested in a tiny china vase on the mantelshelf. This, he thought dreamily, was the life he had always wanted, the life he was born to.

His mind flitted over the next few months; while giving Belle time to get over her aunt's death he would work at making himself indispensable, not only in the shop but as a friend and confidant. In three months' time, say September or October, he would begin to make her aware of his growing affection, testing the water carefully as he went . . .

'My brother,' Belle said, 'thinks that I should sell this house.'

'Sell it?' Samuel stared at her, dismayed. This house was part of his future. 'But why should you do that?'

She took another sip from her glass. 'He thinks that it's too large for a woman on her own.'

'That's nonsense – if you'll pardon me for saying so. It's a lovely house and it's just right for you.'

'That's what I thought.'

'And anyway, you might not be on your own for long.'

Once again a soft pink wash touched her cheekbones. 'I thought that too.'

'You have a suitor?'

'I plan to have one.' She drank again, her eyes sparkling at him over the rim of the crystal glass. 'That would annoy my brother,' she said gleefully.

'It would indeed.' Not only her idiot of a brother, Samuel thought. All at once the whisky lost its mellow tang and the cigar its fragrance. He shifted uneasily in the chair and then shot bolt upright as she went on, 'And the sooner the better.' She took another drink, a larger gulp this time, then said, 'So, Mr Gilmartin – will you marry me?'

'What?' He put the cigar on to its ashtray so abruptly

that his sleeve brushed the whisky glass and almost toppled it.

'I asked . . .' Belle put her empty glass aside and sat up in her chair, hands folded primly on her lap and her gaze fixed on his, '. . . if you would consent to become my husband?'

'But . . . how can you . . . how can we . . . ?'

'Quite easily. We are both free to marry, unless you already have a wife or a sweetheart I know nothing about? So . . .' she said when he shook his head, '. . . we are both free to marry, as I said. We get on together and I admire your abilities and your head for business. I believe that we could suit each other very well.'

Samuel felt as though someone had just punched him in the stomach. 'You're asking me to be your husband just so that you can defy your brother and keep this house?'

'That would not be a good reason for matrimony. I am twenty-three years of age, Mr Gilmartin, and you are . . . ?'

'A year younger,' he said huskily, still in shock.

'Oh. But no matter, our ages are close enough. You see, Mr Gilmartin, people such as my brother believe that a woman who reaches my age without receiving a single proposal of marriage is doomed to be a spinster for ever. I intend to prove him wrong. Thanks to my aunt I am now a woman of property and means; all I need to make my life complete is a husband.'

'There must be others of your own class . . .'

She inclined her head. 'Indeed, and some of them would no doubt be delighted to marry a woman of independent means. But I do not choose them, I choose you. Should you reject me,' Belle said calmly, although her heart was beginning to beat faster and faster, 'then

I will accept your decision and no more will be said of the matter. I promise you, by the way, that your position in the family business will not be taken from you. I am not a vindictive woman; in fact, I have decided that if you accept me, my wedding gift to you will be a junior partnership in the shop.'

'Your brother would never agree to that!'

'My brother,' Belle said, 'is fond of money. I believe that he will agree.'

'Could I . . . a turn in the garden . . .' Samuel said. 'Some fresh air . . .'

'Of course. Perhaps you would take Juliet out with you. I will go upstairs for five minutes,' Belle said, and stood up. Samuel immediately got to his feet and was further astonished when she stepped swiftly towards him, took his face in her two hands, and kissed him on the mouth. Her lips were soft, and tasted of whisky.

'Five minutes,' she said, and left the room.

27

Samuel swallowed the rest of his whisky in one gulp and took his cigar with him.

'Is she finished with the coffee?' Ena wanted to know as he went through the kitchen.

'I believe so.' He hurried past her into the neat garden, and while Juliet disappeared on some ploy of her own, he walked down to the wall at the end, where only months before he had endeared himself to Beatrice McCallum by burying the body of her other dog, Romeo. The thought of her reminded him of the letter she had left for him. It had made it clear enough that she had wanted him to use her gift of £50 to leave Saltcoats, and Belle. And now Belle herself had just made it possible for him to stay, and to live in comfort for the rest of his life. And if Belle made good her promise to buy him a junior partnership in Forsyth's, then he would be on the first step to easing Walter from the business altogether and taking it over.

On the other hand, he was shocked by Belle's bold proposal. Respectable women did not proposition men; they allowed themselves to be wooed and won, and Samuel had been prepared to do exactly that. He felt winded, and even used. Part of him wanted to prove himself a man – his own man and nobody else's – by refusing her, but standing there in the early summer dusk, looking across the garden towards the house where light glowed from the windows, he began to think of what he could lose by refusing her, and gain by accepting her.

She was not a pretty woman, or even a handsome one in his eyes, but tonight, her face flushed by whisky as she smiled at him nervously and the lamplight shone on the hair lying softly about her cheeks and temples, she had looked quite presentable. He thought of her kiss, still imprinted on his lips, and of the home she offered him, with its thick carpets and its flock wallpaper, its deep soft chairs, bone china dishes and crystal glasses. He thought of the days spent delivering groceries to the back doors of fine houses like hers and the hard, dirty, labouring job he had hated in Ardrossan dockyard – and the shop, where he could wear decent clothes and keep his hands clean and charm the money out of the pockets of wealthy women, many of whom had begun to ask for him personally when they came in.

'To hell with it,' he said softly, dropping the butt of the cigar on the ground and treading the glow from it with the toe of his polished shoe. 'Sure I was about to travel along that same road in any case. It's just as if she came along in her fine motor car and offered me a lift to where I was goin'. And where's the sense in sayin' no to a lift, when it helps a man to get where he's going sooner?' And whistling for Juliet, he returned to the house.

Belle had hurried up to the bathroom, where she dipped the corner of a towel in water and used it to cool her hot face. Her heart was beating fast and she was half-delighted, half-shocked by her boldness. How could she have come right out like that and asked him to marry her? The whisky had helped; bitter though it tasted, she could not have managed to be so forward without it.

She dabbed her face dry and smoothed her hair with trembling fingers. All at once she felt sick with fear. What if he refused her and told her that she disgusted him, and that he never wanted to see her again?

She would have given anything to retire to her room and stay there until he had left the house, but she couldn't do that. She had to return downstairs to face him.

She took a deep breath and went down to the parlour, to find it empty. The tray and the glasses had been removed and the fire made up.

When she heard the door at the back of the hall open, and Juliet's claws skittering over the polished wooden floor, Belle rushed to sit in her chair, snatching up a magazine as she went. She was idly flicking through the pages when the door opened and Samuel came in.

'Is the air cool outside?' she asked calmly as he made for the fire. He turned so that he stood with his back to the flames – just as Papa had done, and Walter did now. Why was it that men always wanted to warm their trousers, she wondered?

'A little, but pleasant. I must apologise, Miss Forsyth, if I seemed discourteous earlier,' he went on, and her heart sank. It was going to be a rejection then. 'I was – taken by surprise.'

'Of course you were. I am the one who should apologise for being so presumptuous.'

'Please don't do that,' he said swiftly, 'for if you do I shall have to believe that you regret everything that you said, and I would not be able to tell you how honoured I would be to accept your – proposition.'

'Accept?'

313

The magazine fell from her lap as he took her hands in his, still cold from the night air, and drew her to her feet.

'With all my heart,' he said, looking deep into her eyes. 'Believe me, I want nothing more than to be your husband and to cherish and care for you for the rest of my life.'

He bent to kiss her as a formal seal of their pact, and was taken aback when she pressed herself to him, holding him so tightly that he was keenly aware of the firm curve of her breasts against his chest. Her mouth opened beneath his and to his surprise he realised that he was becoming aroused.

It was Belle who finally drew away. 'How soon can we marry?' she wanted to know.

'Your aunt's death, and your mother's . . .'

'Soon,' she interrupted. 'As soon as we can. We can't be married in the church itself, of course, while I am officially in mourning, but in the vestry. You have no objection to being married in the vestry of my church?'

'None at all,' said Samuel, who had been born a Roman Catholic but had long since forsaken any form of religion.

'Then we shall visit the manse tomorrow evening to see the minister about having the banns called. You must invite your family, Samuel.' It was the first time she had used his Christian name.

'I will, of course, but I don't believe that any of them will be able to come over from Ireland. My grandmother's in very poor health and my mother can't leave her. As to my brothers and sisters, they're scattered all over, with families of their own to look after.'

'Write to them anyway, and tell them that if they can't manage to come to our wedding we shall certainly visit them as soon as we can. I've never been to Ireland,' Belle said. 'You can show it to me.'

'I will, I will. What will your brother and sister say about all this? And the others in the shop?'

'They may say whatever they choose,' Belle said blithely. 'I am my own woman and you are your own man. Let them chatter and disapprove if they wish, it need make no difference to us.'

She reached up to kiss him again, then took a small box from her pocket and held it out to him. 'This was my aunt's ring. She left it to me and I would like to wear it as a symbol of our betrothal.'

Diamonds and sapphires flashed as Samuel opened the box. He drew the ring out and slipped it on to the third finger of Belle's left hand. It fitted well.

'It's a beautiful ring.'

'Yes, it is. And now that's settled,' she said, then drew in a deep, shaky sigh, and smiled up at him, her face alight. 'What an evening it has been. I feel quite exhausted with excitement. Would you mind very much if we said goodnight now, Samuel?'

'Not at all . . .' He stopped short, then said, 'I don't even know your full name.'

'Isabelle, but nobody has ever called me that.'

'I will, and nothing else,' he said firmly. 'It's a name that suits you.'

'Isabelle.' She said the name slowly, with pleasure. 'Yes, I would like you to call me that.'

'Your brother . . .' Samuel said uneasily.

'I shall go to see him first thing tomorrow morning. That means that he and I will be late, so you must look after the shop until I get there.' She kissed him again, a quick, soft kiss this time. 'And now you must go. I have so much to think about.'

'You've lost your mind,' Walter said bluntly.

'On the contrary, I think I have just found it.'

'You? Marrying one of our employees? I won't have it!'

He and his sister were in the small dining room at Argyle Road, facing each other over a table still strewn with the remains of the breakfast that Belle had interrupted. As soon as she announced that she had something important to tell Walter, Sarah had excused herself and slid quietly from the room. Just as well, Belle thought now, looking at her brother's purpling face.

'Are you so determined to disgrace the Forsyth name by marrying beneath you?' he wanted to know now.

'Walter, have you forgotten that you married our servant?'

'So that's why you've come up with this preposterous suggestion? You just want to spite me for marrying Sarah. Stop that!' he raged as Belle burst out laughing.

'You really think that I would be so childish? My dear Walter, I can assure you that I have too much regard for myself, and for Samuel, to stoop to such a childish trick.'

'This has all come about because Aunt Beatrice made a pet of Gilmartin and invited him to visit her home. She filled his head with ideas above his station.'

'Samuel was very kind to Aunt Beatrice. He found the time to visit her more often than you did.'

'I am a family man. I have commitments. How far has this nonsense gone?'

Belle drew her glove off and held out her left hand to display the ring sparkling on her third finger.

'That's Aunt Beatrice's ring!'

'She left it to me and I choose to wear it as my engagement ring. Samuel was kind enough to fall in with my wishes.'

'This fanciful nonsense won't last, Belle. If I was a betting man I would wager that you'll have gone off the whole idea long before your time of mourning is over.'

'You would lose your wager, for we plan to marry quietly as soon as possible. We are going to call on the minister this evening.'

His eyes bulged. 'You're not even going to wait for a decent length of time before you commit yourself?'

'You didn't.'

'That was different,' he said again. 'You know full well that Sarah was – dear God, Belle, are you carrying that man's child? Because if so, I promise you that I will horsewhip Gilmartin to within an inch of his life!'

'I doubt if you would manage that, and in any case there's no need. Samuel and I, at least, know how to restrain our feelings for each other until after marriage.' Belle drew her glove on again and picked up her bag. 'I must go; one of us should be in the shop. And remember, Walter, that I will expect you to treat Samuel with respect. After all, he will soon be a member of the family.'

'You can't do this!' he bellowed at her in frustration as Sarah tapped on the door and then peered in.

'I brought some fresh tea,' she said timidly, easing herself and a laden tray through the half-opened door. And then, pausing uncertainly as she glanced from one to the other, 'Is something wrong?'

'Not at all, Sarah,' Belle said, but her voice was drowned out by Walter's furious, 'Yes, something is very wrong! My sister has just informed me that she is to marry Samuel Gilmartin!'

'Samuel. . . ?' Sarah whispered, and then the tray slipped from her hands and crashed to the floor, sending tea and broken china all over the place. Slowly, as though she was being neatly folded up joint by joint, Sarah collapsed to lie in a dead faint in the middle of the mess. Belle and Walter stared at her in astonishment, then at each other.

'Now look what you've done,' Walter fumed at his sister. 'You've upset her with your nonsense!'

There was a noticeable stir in church on the Sunday morning when the banns proclaiming a marriage between Isabelle Forsyth and Samuel Gilmartin were first called. Belle straightened her shoulders and lifted her head higher; by her side, Samuel stared straight ahead, a slight smile on his lips.

Walter, on her other side, also stared ahead, but stonily. Sarah was not in church that morning, pleading the need to stay at home with the baby, who was teething. Morna, next to Walter, was grateful for Ruth's company, both in the church and on the day when Belle had called to tell her sister about her engagement.

At first, the news had taken her breath away. Belle – and Samuel Gilmartin? The thought was almost as shocking as Walter's decision to marry Sarah – more so, since Morna had always thought of Belle as the most sensible person she knew. Walter marrying with their servant was one thing – she had never thought of Walter as sensible, but how could Belle also choose a life partner from a lower class?

'Samuel?' she said feebly when she was able to speak. 'You really want to marry Samuel Gilmartin?'

'Yes, I do want to marry him, very much. And I intend to marry him whether you like the idea or not.' Belle was on the defensive, her cheeks pink and her hands fumbling nervously with one of her gloves. 'I hope you can be happy for me, Morna?'

'Of course she is, and so am I,' Ruth said warmly. 'Isn't that right, Morna?'

Morna was recalling the day Samuel had kissed her in Meggie Chapman's kitchen – the day he had obtained a post at the shop. Even though she carried no romantic notions about the man, her heart still fluttered slightly at the memory of his lips, firm and warm on hers. Lucky Belle, she thought, to be marrying such a man, regardless of class. Then, looking at her sister, seeing how Belle's eyes were pleading for her understanding and support, she smiled and said, 'If it's what you really want, then I'm happy for you and for Samuel. Have you told Walter?'

'Yes, and he's not pleased.'

'Then he must get used to the idea, just as you and I had to get used to his marriage to Sarah,' Morna said firmly.

'Well done,' Ruth told her when Belle had left. 'I thought at first that you were going to let your sister down, but you managed to rally.'

'It's just that when I first met Samuel he was living in a rundown hostel and earning a pittance as a delivery man. And now . . .'

'And now he has pulled himself up by his bootstraps, with your help, and if he makes your sister happy, then surely that is all that matters.'

'It's strange to think of Belle marrying before me. All the time I was growing up,' Morna explained, 'I was expected to be the first to marry. I had no abilities, while Belle was clever. Father always meant her to go into the shop, but nobody ever planned a future like that for me.'

'We never know what life has planned for us. I will go with you to the church to hear the banns called,' Ruth said, 'for moral support. We women must show a united front.'

Morna nodded, while deep inside, a small voice clamoured, 'But what about me? When am I going to find someone who cares about me more than anyone else in the world?'

Clarissa and her parents were also in church, but after the

service they hurried away without speaking to any of the Forsyths. 'We are in disgrace,' Morna said as she watched the other members of the congregation avert their eyes.

'Again.' Walter's voice was grim, and his younger sister put a hand on his arm.

'Never mind, Walter, perhaps I'll marry well and save our reputation.'

'And perhaps not,' he said gloomily.

'You cannot seriously intend to go through with this marriage!' Clarissa flounced into Belle's parlour.

'You heard the banns being called in church this morning.'

'Belle, we have been closest friends for all of our lives – like sisters. That is why I urge you to stop this nonsense before it goes too far.'

'I don't see it as nonsense, Clarissa,' Belle said calmly. 'I look forward to becoming Samuel's wife.'

'But from what I hear in the town he was a common labourer, living in a lodging house down by the harbour!'

'And now he is a valued employee in our family business.'

'What do you know of his family?'

'I don't intend to marry his family.'

Clarissa glared, frustrated, and then tried another tack. 'Do you remember us promising to be bridesmaids to each other? I cannot agree to be your bridesmaid if you insist on going ahead with this marriage; nor can I ask you to stand by my side when it's my turn to marry, which may be quite soon. Arthur MacAdam is paying me a lot of attention these days.'

'Then I'm happy for you, Clarissa. Can you not be happy for me?'

'Not if you persist in going on as you are. Belle, Mama

has asked me not to see you again.' Clarissa made it sound like a threat.

'Perhaps you should tell your mama that you are an adult now, and free to choose your own friends – as I am. And I choose Samuel.'

'You know that he's only marrying you for your money, and for this house?'

'You don't believe that Samuel could want to marry me because he loves me?'

'Men of his class,' Clarissa declared passionately, 'know nothing about love!'

'They have feelings, Clarissa. They are flesh and blood and although it might surprise you to know this, they have brains too. Would you like some tea?' Belle asked calmly.

'It would choke me!' Clarissa said, and marched from the house. Belle watched her go without one pang of regret. Thanks to Aunt Beatrice, she was in a position to make her own decisions for the first time in her life, and she relished her newfound freedom.

It was one of those fairly frequent occasions when the west coast of Scotland forgot that June had arrived and presented its inhabitants with a grey, wet, windy day much more suited to November. Out in the Firth the waves threw up white spume as they rolled over hidden reefs; when they reached the shore they hurled themselves against the harbour walls in great spouts of spray that rose high into the air and then fell back to soak anyone foolhardy enough to be standing on the harbour walls. The pleasure steamers from Glasgow fought their way along as a few adventurous passengers clung to the railings to avoid being blown away entirely. Others had long since retired below to the comparative safety of the saloons, where they grasped the arms of their chairs and wished that they had stayed on dry land. From ashore it was difficult to make out the horizon, since the sea and the sky were of the same grey colour.

Morna had called in on Meggie Chapman in the afternoon, as she did every few weeks, and then done some shopping on the way back to the house. She was battling her way along Hamilton Street, the basket of groceries over one arm and her head bent against a wind that was doing its best to wrench her umbrella from her grasp, when an unexpected gust pounced from a narrow passageway between two buildings. It tore the umbrella from her fingers and then set about doing its best to pull her hat off.

'Oh!' Without thinking, she swung round to look for the umbrella while at the same time snatching with both hands at her felt hat, which was flapping like a bird about to launch itself into the air. The basket, looped over one arm, swung wildly against the underside of her raised arm. It was full, and the sudden jerk sent potatoes and onions spilling out of it.

A step or two took Morna beyond the passageway and out of reach of the gusting wind, which was one mercy. She set the basket down in the shelter of a wall, realising, as she straightened and turned to look for the fallen vegetables, that strands of damp hair had fallen over her eyes and her hat was now clinging to the side of her face, having managed to free itself from all but one of its hatpins.

As she hauled it off someone thrust her umbrella, now closed, into her free hand. 'Hold on to that for a moment while I pick your things up. Won't take a moment,' the man who had come to her rescue said cheerfully. Taking advantage of his assistance, Morna leaned against the wall and tried as best she could to pin her hat back into place while he scooped the vegetables up and returned them to the basket.

'I think that's the lot. May I?' He eased the umbrella from beneath her arm and opened it cautiously. 'It seems to be in good order,' he said, and then, surveying her sympathetically, 'your hat has suffered more harm than anything else.'

'Thank you, you've been very kind.' Morna rammed the final hatpin into place and reached for her umbrella.

'Let me help you.'

'Really, there's no need. I haven't far to go – just to Ardrossan Road.'

'I'm going there too,' he said, tipping the umbrella so that it protected her from the rain.

'You're going to get wet,' Morna protested.

'I can assure you that my hat is sturdier than yours, though not as pretty.' He stooped to pick up the basket and then said, 'Come along,' in a voice that dismissed any further attempt at protest.

She walked meekly by his side as he talked about the unseasonal weather and the train journey he had just made from Glasgow, where the sea had hurled spray right into the carriages as they approached Saltcoats.

'This is me,' she interrupted when they got to Ruth's gate. As he glanced beyond her shoulder to the house she saw raindrops dripping from his chin and running down his neck beneath the scarf that was drawn up around his throat. The poor man was soaking. She was just wondering if she should invite him in for some hot tea when he leaned past her, opened the gate, and urged her ahead of him up the path, still protecting her with the umbrella.

'You live here?' he asked with interest, waiting on the doorstep as she fumbled for her key.

'Yes. I wonder – would you like to come in for a moment?'

'I would indeed. Thank you.' He followed her into the hallway just as Ruth, hearing the front door close, came from the kitchen.

'My dear Morna, I've been worried about you. What dreadful weath— Tom!'

'Look what the storm's blown up,' Mona's rescuer put the basket down and opened his arms. Ruth ran into them.

'I didn't expect you until next week – oh, Tom, you devil, you're soaking me!'

'Why should you stay dry when we're both wet?' He indicated Morna, laughing. 'I rescued a damsel in distress and then found that she lives here.'

'Morna, this is my brother, Tom.' Ruth was flushed and glowing with pleasure.

'How do you do?' Tom Durie held out a large wet hand, then added as Morna put her own fingers, clothed in a sopping glove, into his, 'You should change into dry clothing before you catch a chill, Miss Morna. We both should,' he added, unfastening his coat and taking off his scarf to reveal the white collar of a minister of the Church of Scotland.

'Indeed you should, and the sooner the better. You're in your usual room, Tom.' Ruth picked up the basket, saying when her brother tried to take it from her, 'I can manage – I'm not helpless. Off you go, the pair of you, while I put these things away.'

28

Morna's bedroom mirror showed her that she looked like a scarecrow. Her hat, soaked and shapeless, sat askew on her head, while limp strands of hair drooped around a face wet with rain and red from the cold. Even her blouse was wet. She ended up stripping down to her petticoat before putting on a dry blouse and skirt. She unpinned her hair and towelled it vigorously before combing out the knots and pinning it up again, while outside the wind howled around the house and rain battered against the windows.

Below, someone began to play 'Claire de Lune' on the piano, and when Morna went downstairs Ruth called, 'We're in mother's parlour, Morna. Actually, Tom, it's Morna's parlour now,' she added as Morna went into the room. 'This is where she teaches music and drawing.'

Tom Durie stopped playing and swung round on the piano stool to smile at Morna. 'Ruth's told me all about your talents and the way you've helped her.'

'Don't embarrass the poor girl. Tell me what's happening in Glasgow,' Ruth ordered, dispensing tea. As brother and sister talked, Morna took the opportunity to study the newcomer. Tom Durie had his sister's black hair, now damp and tousled, and her thin face and piercing dark blue eyes. His straight nose was just a little too long, like Ruth's, and he also had a firm, well-shaped mouth. The features that seemed striking and slightly masculine in Ruth made him look interesting, though not handsome.

'Morna, I told you about the camp Tom works in each summer, didn't I?' Ruth belatedly remembered that there was a third person in the room. 'The one at Portencross?'

Morna nodded. There had been talk of some summer activity that would bring Ruth's brother to the area but she hadn't paid much heed at the time. 'What sort of camp is it?' she asked cautiously.

'It's for families from Glasgow and Greenock or Paisley who can't afford to pay for holiday lodgings in places like Saltcoats,' Tom explained. 'For a few shillings they can rent part of a big field at Portencross and bring their own tents. It gives them the chance to get some sea air and is a change from the streets and tenements.'

'Tom takes time off from his church every summer to work there – they hold open air services on Sundays and organise concerts, and games for the children.'

'We can always do with extra help, and from what Ruth has said in her letters, you're musical and very good with youngsters.' Tom raised a dark eyebrow at Morna. 'Why don't you go along with me this year?'

'Oh – I don't think I would be of much use to you,' she stammered, taken by surprise. He shrugged, then moved from the piano stool to a comfortable chair.

'Think about it,' he said.

At the end of June Belle Forsyth and Samuel Gilmartin became man and wife in a brief ceremony held in the vestry of the North Parish Church, with Morna and Walter as their witnesses.

'I would rather not have been part of this particular wedding party, but when Belle asked me I decided that it would be better than letting Gilmartin ask one of those rough fellows from the lodging house he lived in,' Walter said for the umpteenth time as he and Sarah walked to Belle's house on the day of the wedding.

'Yes indeed,' she said listlessly.

He tried to peer down at her face but was defeated by the large bunch of artificial cherries pinned to the wide brim of her straw hat. 'Are you well, my dear? You've been very quiet for the past three weeks or so. Not sickening for anything, are you?'

'No, Walter. I'm just a little tired.'

He patted the hand that lay in the crook of his elbow. 'Once this ridiculous wedding is over and Gilmartin established as shop manager I intend to spend more time with you and Fraser. That should cheer you up. You're not cold, are you?' he added as he felt a shiver run through the arm pressed against his.

'Just for a moment – but it has passed,' said Sarah.

'Good.' They walked on in silence, Sarah trying hard to prepare herself for the ordeal of seeing Samuel become Belle's husband, and Walter thinking about the shock he had had when Belle insisted on making Samuel Gilmartin shop manager.

'What do we need with a manager?' he had protested. 'You and I manage the place perfectly well between us.'

'But as a married woman I will probably want to spend more time at home. We need a manager and Samuel is the obvious choice.'

'George Stoddart has been in our employment for much longer.'

'Mr Stoddart's health is failing and I suspect that he will soon give up work altogether. Samuel is capable and

327

reliable, and since I am buying him a junior partnership as a wedding gift he must be given more responsibility. I would also like to train Miss Campbell to be promoted to the post of assistant cashier so that she can attend to the financial side of the business when I am away from the shop. She's good with figures and, like Samuel, she is trustworthy. I will still be in charge of the books, but I have decided that I shall keep them at home where I can work on them in the evenings. There will be a separate set of books in the shop from now on. I will be paying one thousand pounds into the business in Samuel's name,' Belle reminded her brother as he opened his mouth to argue further.

'Belle, I have to point out how foolish it is to squander your inheritance like that!'

'I don't see it as squandering; I firmly believe that with Samuel and Miss Campbell given more responsibility, Forsyth's will do very well. And in any case, Walter, let me remind you that I can do whatever I please with the money Aunt Beatrice left me.' Then, caressing her engagement ring with the fingers of her right hand, she added slyly, 'And I think that it would be fitting if you, as head of the family, announced Samuel's promotion at our wedding celebration.'

The suggestion flattered Walter's vanity, and he had come to realise, in the week since their conversation, that Belle's generous investment would be of benefit to the business. If his sister chose to make this foolish marriage and to throw her money away, then it was no concern of his.

Belle herself opened the door to them. She was dressed in her wedding finery: a high-necked, pale-grey silk dress with a bolero jacket. The bodice inset consisted of broad horizontal bands of embroidered flowers on a white background. The same floral motif was repeated around the hem of the slightly gathered skirt. Her brimless hat was also of grey silk, its severity softened by a great cluster of white feathers pinned at one side.

'You look – splendid,' Sarah said tremulously. 'So elegant!'

'Thank you, Sarah. Will I do, Walter?' Belle asked her brother, who cleared his throat before saying, 'Very apt, Belle. Just right for a small wedding.'

'I thought so,' Belle was saying calmly as Morna, in a brown jacket and skirt over a cream blouse, hurried from the kitchen.

'There you are, Walter. If we don't get to the church soon we'll be late!' She took a small feathered hat from the hatstand and used the mirror to settle it in place, tilted becomingly over her forehead. 'Ena's in the kitchen, Sarah,' she rattled on as she jabbed pins into the hat to anchor it, 'and Ruth and Tom Durie will meet us at the bottom of the brae after the ceremony and walk back here with us. Come along, then, let's not keep the bridegroom waiting.'

She ushered her brother and sister out, and Sarah, after taking a moment to steady her trembling lower lip, went to the kitchen to help Ena.

There were eight people at the wedding breakfast: the bride and groom, Walter and Sarah, Morna, Ruth and Tom Durie, and the minister who had performed the wedding service. When they had eaten, Walter officially, if somewhat stiffly, welcomed Samuel into the family and announced his new position as junior partner and shop manager in Forsyth and Son. He managed to make it sound as though it was all his own idea.

'I'm overcome by your generosity, but very happy to accept.' Samuel rose to his feet and held his hand out to his new brother-in-law. Walter, taken by surprise, clasped it briefly and then released it in order to lift his wineglass and propose a toast to the newly-weds.

'And may I propose my own toast,' Belle added, with a radiant smile. 'To Samuel, my husband.'

'And to Isabelle, my beautiful life companion,' Samuel said swiftly, raising his own glass. Catching his gaze, Sarah saw that his eyes sparkled triumphantly.

'I do declare, Belle, that you have never looked so beautiful,' Morna whispered to her sister as the guests prepared to leave. 'You're glowing as though a lamp had been switched on inside you.' Morna wondered, as she spoke, if any man would ever be able to make her eyes as brilliant as her sister's were at that moment 'You look so very happy.'

'I am,' Belle whispered, flushing like a young girl.

'It was your idea, wasn't it?' Samuel said as he and his new wife returned to the empty parlour. 'It was you who set me up as the manager.'

'You could scarcely continue as one of the shop assistants after today, and we need a manager we can trust.'

'So you trust me?'

'With my life,' Belle said simply, and he took her hand and kissed it. The warm pressure of his lips on her skin sent a tingle of excitement flaring through her entire body. 'My darling Isabelle,' he said huskily. 'I promise that you will never regret marrying me.'

'I already know that.' She gave a contented sigh as she unpinned her hat. 'It may have been a quiet wedding, but it was enjoyable. Though I thought that Sarah was very subdued.'

Samuel shrugged. 'She strikes me as a woman with nothing much to say. Just the right sort of wife for your brother.'

'I have to warn you that *I* don't intend to be a quiet, submissive wife.'

'I'd not want you to be,' he assured her as Ena came into the room.

'Is there anythin' else you're needin', Miss Belle?'

'I don't believe so, Ena. Where's Juliet?'

'Out in the back garden. Shall I fetch her in?'

'I'll see to her, my dear. I think I'd like a final cigar and a turn in the garden. You go upstairs and I'll join you soon,' Samuel said.

As he had done on the evening when Belle had proposed to him, he walked to the end of the garden and stood beneath the trees, savouring his cigar. There was one slight difference – this time, instead of studying the house before him with envy, he surveyed it with the satisfaction of an owner.

Juliet emerged from the shadows and sniffed at his shoes in her usual friendly fashion; she gave an astonished yelp as the toe of one shoe suddenly caught her in the ribs.

'Just to remind you that things are different now,' Samuel told her briskly before throwing his cigar away and scooping the bewildered little dog up under his arm. 'Bedtime, my lady, and from now on, I think – you sleep downstairs. No more pampering.'

Ena was still in the kitchen when he entered the house, locking the back door as he came in.

'Will there be anything else?'

Samuel set the dog down. 'I'll be looking for shaving water in the morning, Ena, but there's nothing else for tonight. You may go to bed.'

He crossed to the inner door, and then turned. 'Just one other thing, now I come to think of it. It's not Miss Belle any more,' he said with a pleasant smile. 'It's Mrs Gilmartin, or if you prefer it, ma'am – and sir. Good night, Ena.'

★   ★   ★

Ruth's bicycle looked as though it had been well used before being abandoned right at the back of the garden shed. Morna eyed it uneasily before announcing, 'I shall take a bus, or perhaps the train to West Kilbride, and walk the rest of the way.'

'Nonsense.' Tom Durie ran a big hand over the machine to dislodge dust, grit and spiders' webs. 'Fetch a cloth and I'll give it a good rub down and then oil it. It'll be as good as new.'

'I'm not sure that I can still ride a bicycle.'

'You never forget,' Tom said heartily. 'Now run along and find a clean rag, there's a good girl.'

Morna trailed miserably into the kitchen, where Ruth was busy writing at the table. 'I'm sure I won't be of any use at this camp, and there must be a lot of things I could be doing around the house.'

Ruth looked up over the top of the glasses she used for close work. 'Tom needs your help more than I do now that our little school is finished for the summer. You could do with some fresh air and exercise.' She sounded just like her brother, Morna thought resentfully as she found a clean cloth.

An hour later she wheeled the bicycle, its large basket loaded down with an assortment of items that Tom needed, to the pavement in front of the house. He was already waiting for her, one long leg slung over the crossbar of his own bicycle.

'Off we go,' he said encouragingly, 'and remember, it's all in the balance. In fact, don't even think about it, just push off and let the bicycle and your natural instincts do the rest.'

At first, the machine wobbled horribly all over the road, and at one point Morna narrowly missed running into the side of a delivery van parked by the kerb. A group of youngsters idling along the pavement stopped to watch, and to Morna's horror they actually began to run after her, whistling and jeering, as she swooped and swerved behind Tom, who tossed a grin at them over his shoulder.

It may have been the natural instinct that he claimed she would find again or it may simply have been a burning desire to get away from the children, who were drawing attention to her from everyone on the pavement, but all at once Morna felt the bicycle steady itself, and without knowing how it had happened, she caught up with Tom and then passed him, pedalling strongly.

'That's it!' she heard him whoop, and then the sound of the children's voices faded and they were off, the fresh sea wind in their faces and the bicycle wheels hissing pleasantly along the road surface.

With Tom now in the lead and Morna following, they cycled through the neighbouring town of Ardrossan and were soon on the coast road leading to the small community of Seamill, with its fine houses and its handsome Hydro. The sea sparkled and Arran was a soft purple outline so close to shore on that day that Morna felt as if she could almost reach out and touch it.

Beyond Seamill they came to the junction of three roads. The road ahead led to the large seaside town of Largs while the inland road headed for the village of West Kilbride. Tom took the third option, turning left towards the coast and the village of Portencross.

Portencross, Morna knew from infrequent visits in her childhood, consisted of a few houses, a shop and post office, as well as the dramatic ruins of a small watch-tower, known as Portencross Castle, that had been built on the shore. Portencross was a fishing village, but its picturesque harbour was so small that the fishermen had to anchor their boats at an island known as the Wee Cumbrae and row their catches ashore in dinghies.

She spun down the long tree-lined road after Tom, now sufficiently comfortable with the bicycle to enjoy the sense of freedom that she remembered from cycling trips with her brother and sister. Before they reached the village itself Tom slowed and stopped at a five-barred gate.

'Here we are,' he announced when Morna drew up by his side.

'Goodness!' The large field stretching from the road to the beach was dotted with tents of all shapes and sizes. There were vans and a lorry – even, she noticed, an old bus parked in one corner. Most of the tents were still in the process of being set up by people of all ages, and in others, clearly just erected, bags and boxes were being carried inside. Children raced around the place and a man clutching what looked like a large ledger seemed to be supervising operations from the middle of the field.

'Where do they all come from?'

'Greenock, Paisley, even from Glasgow, some of 'em. Most come back year after year,' Tom said with quiet satisfaction. 'I started to help out when I was studying for the ministry and now I come every summer. I wouldn't miss it for the world.'

'They stay here all summer?'

'Most of them do. The local farmers and tradesmen visit every day to supply them with everything they need . . .'

A horn sounded from the roadway behind them and they had to wheel their bicycles out of the way hurriedly to let a small open-bed lorry cluttered with bundles and cardboard boxes drive in through the gates. Several little faces peered out of the cab's nearside window, and as the lorry passed a hand shot out, index finger pointing, and a child yelled, 'Tom! It's Tom, Mam – Tom's here!'

Another four or five hands began to wave excitedly through the window and Tom waved back, grinning. 'See you in a minute,' he called, and then, as the lorry jolted past, bouncing over the grassy tussocks, 'That's the Kennaways from Paisley; they're here every year. Come and see where we'll be based.'

He set off at a brisk pace and Morna followed him with some difficulty. Not only were her legs weak from the unaccustomed pedalling, but the bicycle, as its wheels bounced from one grassy clump to the next, seemed to be doing its best to break away from her hold on the handlebars. She was relieved and breathless when they finally reached the old bus and were able to prop the cycles against it. The seats had been cleared from the interior and replaced by some rickety tables and chairs that looked as though they had already had a long and difficult life.

To Morna's surprise she recognised the young woman poring over a fistful of papers at one of the tables as a regular visitor to Ruth's house.

'Tom, good to see you again.'

'And you, Charlotte. You two probably know each other already.'

'We do,' Charlotte agreed, and then, to Morna, 'So he's roped you in to help us? We can always do with an extra pair of hands.'

'Talking of hands, the Kennaways have just come in. Come on, Morna,' Tom headed for the door, 'we'll go and help them to get their tent up.'

29

Morna, who would have sold her soul for a cup of tea after the long bicycle ride, followed Tom outside and back across the field on legs that were finally beginning to get used to walking again.

'Charlotte stays on site, together with Eddie and Frank,' Tom explained, moderating his long strides in order to give her the chance to keep up with him. 'The upper deck of the bus has been divided into compartments where they sleep. That way, there's always someone available in the event of an emergency.'

As they passed tents already erected, people sitting outside on wooden crates shouted greetings to Tom, who waved back. 'They're a friendly bunch; you'll get to know everyone quickly,' he assured Morna.

The lorry that had brought the Kennaways had been emptied of all its cargo and was bumping off across the field. Two teenage boys were putting together sections of wooden panels. 'This family has everything organised,' Tom said as he and Morna approached. 'The father's a joiner and a year or two back he made some flooring for their tent. He doesn't come with them – he prefers to stay in

Paisley. Let me do that, Jess,' he added, leaping forward to ease aside a woman struggling to unfasten ropes lashing together a large bundle of canvas. 'You sit down and have a rest.'

The woman straightened, her rounded belly pushing against her skirt as she put both hands on the small of her back. 'Thanks, Tom; it's nice tae see you again, lad.'

'You too – all of you.' He lifted a rickety kitchen chair from among the luggage, bedding and boxes piled on the ground and eased her on to it as though she were made of porcelain. 'Just rest here, now,' he instructed as two small children hurried over, one of them staggering beneath the weight of a shawl-wrapped baby.

'Mammy,' the first child whined, 'I'm hungry!'

'I know you are, hen.' Jess Kennaway took the baby. 'Stay here by me, both of you, until the older ones have got the tent up, then we'll have somethin' tae eat.' She smiled apologetically at Morna. 'Weans are aye hungry,' she said. 'It's been a long journey, and a while since they had much tae eat.' Then, glancing from Morna to Tom and back again, 'Are you Tom's sweetheart?'

'Not at all,' Morna felt herself redden, while Tom just laughed. 'He asked me to come here to help.'

'Oh.' The woman shifted the baby to her left arm and held out her right hand. 'Pleased tae meet you. I'm Jess Kennaway, and these . . .' a nod of her greying head included the baby and the two children sitting on the ground at her feet as well as the four children, two boys and two girls, busy unfolding yards of stiff canvas, '. . . are my weans.'

Morna took the work-roughened hand. 'How do you do, Mrs Kennaway. I'm Morna Forsyth.'

'Morna – that's a bonny name. Call me Jess, hen, everyone else does. Mrs Kennaway puts me in mind of *his* mother, and a right dragon of a woman she was!'

Tom was already helping the children and now he shouted, 'Lend a hand here, Morna. The more the merrier.'

Morna looked down at her skirt and jacket, which were plain, but clean, and then at the thick green canvas which looked as though it had been stored in a lean-to all winter. Then, realising that she was not going to get the tea that she craved for until she had earned it, she stepped forward and set to work.

As she, Tom and the children struggled with the stiff canvas, which seemed set on burying Morna beneath its folds, people arrived from other parts of the field to help. Within half an hour the large tent was in place and the mattresses, bedding and pieces of furniture had been stowed. Morna noted with surprise that there was even a cast iron stove.

'Oh, we know how tae turn this place intae a home from home.' Jess had lit the stove and set a kettle on it; now she was hewing thick slices from a loaf and scraping thin layers of margarine and jam over each one. 'We started with next tae nothin', me and him, but we've collected bits and pieces over the years. Collected the weans too,' she added with a wry smile, 'so now he stays behind in Paisley tae earn the money while we spend the summer down here. He'll mebbe come down for a day or two before we go back home.' She raised her voice, 'Come on, you weans, and get somethin' tae eat. You too, Tom, you've earned it.'

'And I'm ready for it.' Tom sank down on to the grass, running a hand across his brow and leaving a black smear, much to the amusement of the Kennaway children. 'There you are, Jess, a palace fit for a queen. You'll all sleep in comfort tonight.'

'You're a saint, Tom — and thank you too, Morna. This

is Morna,' Jess informed her children as they gathered, eyes fixed on the slices of bread and jam.

'Let me,' Tom interrupted, and then, pointing at each child in order of height, 'George, Joe, Kate, Mima, wee Jessie and wee Rena . . .'

'You remembered!' the thin girl called Mima crowed, dancing up and down with excitement. 'You remembered all our names!'

'Elephants and Tom Duries never forget,' he told her solemnly, and then, pointing to the baby, now on an elder sister's knee and sucking at a crust, 'but this one's new to me, Jess.'

'That's our Robbie.'

'And there's another on the way, I see,' Tom remarked, and Morna blushed.

'Not for another two months. We'll be back home by then.'

'I hope you're going to call it Tom.'

'What if it's a lassie?' one of the younger children – Rena or Jessie? Morna wondered, her brain reeling with names – asked cheekily.

'Thomasina – even better than Tom,' the young minister was saying when a woman came over from a neighbouring tent bearing a huge tin tray set with mugs.

'Yer stove'll no' be hot enough tae bring the kettle tae the boil,' she said, and Jess smiled at her. 'God bless ye, hen. Here,' she added sharply to her brood as they reached grubby fingers towards the great pile of bread and jam, 'mind yer manners. Tom's no' said grace yet.'

Obediently they bowed their heads, waiting until the brief blessing was over and their mother nodded permission before grabbing and devouring the bread. The tea was black and well stewed, and came with an open tin of condensed milk, but even so, Morna had never tasted anything better.

'Good afternoon, Sarah,' Samuel Gilmartin said amiably. 'May I come in?'

'Walter's out.'

'I know that. He's busy with a sales representative.'

Sarah hesitated, clutching the door as though ready to slam it if need be. 'Did he ask you to call? Did he forget something?'

'No; I was making a delivery to one of our customers who's too posh to carry her own purchases.' Samuel removed his hat. 'Keeping my hand in, you might say, having been a delivery boy at one time, as you'll remember. And since the lady lives near here, I thought it would be discourteous to pass the door without paying my respects to my sister-in-law. Are you not going to invite me in?'

'The maidservant's gone to the shops and the nursemaid's taken the wee one for a walk.'

'So you're on your own, then?' Samuel, who had hovered at the corner to watch the maid and the nurse leave the house before strolling in at the gate, hesitated, 'In that case it might not be right for you to invite me in. But on the other hand, we're both respectable married people, and we're related now. For all anyone knows I could be bringing a message from Walter.'

'But you're not.' Sarah didn't know what to do for the best. Beatrice McCallum had never told her whether it was proper for a lady to entertain her sister-in-law's husband in an otherwise empty house, and she could scarcely ask Samuel to wait on the doorstep while she consulted her book on household etiquette.

'If you wish, I could think of some message he might

have asked me to deliver to you,' Samuel said, and then, tiring of the game, 'or you could just invite me in, Sarah. It's been a while since you and me got the chance to speak to each other.' He moved forward and Sarah automatically stepped back to give him access.

'That's better.' He closed the door. 'Now then, do we go into your drawing room, or should we go to the kitchen, like the old days?'

'In here.' She led him into the drawing room and then asked uncertainly, 'Would you like some tea?'

Samuel dropped his hat on to a small table. 'Why must the Scots be so eager to offer tea to everyone? Do they have some obligation to support the producers in India and China all the year round? To tell the truth, Sarah, I'd prefer a wee glass of Walter's best whisky, but they'd smell it on my breath when I get back to the shop, so I'll settle for a few minutes of your company instead. Will you not take a seat?'

She perched on one of the fireside chairs and he took the other, leaning back and smiling at her. An onlooker might have thought that Sarah was the uncomfortable visitor and Samuel the host, at ease in his own drawing room.

'So – how is my young nephew today?'

'Fraser? He's very well, apart from trouble with teething.'

'And I know that Walter is well, since I saw him not half an hour ago. That only leaves you, Sarah. How are you?'

'I'm v-very well, thank you.'

'I'm glad to hear it. You look v-very well,' he imitated her nervous stammer, his eyes sparkling with amusement. 'Marriage suits you – or perhaps it's motherhood, or having proper meals and not having to rise at dawn and

341

be at everyone's beck and call all day. Tell me, do you enjoy being the mistress of the house?'

'I find it strange at times.'

'Do you?' He flicked an imaginary piece of thread from his trouser leg. 'For my part, I enjoy being master of a house. Who would have thought just a year ago, when I was a delivery lad and you a skivvy, that we would both do so well? And it's all been down to you.'

'To me?'

'Of course. If you hadn't allowed the son of the house to put you in the family way, you'd still be in the kitchen, and as for me – if Walter hadn't married you, Miss Morna wouldn't have left this house in a temper. She wouldn't have taken refuge in the Chapmans' lodging house, and then I would never have met her. She was the one who helped me to obtain a post in Forsyth's. And it was there that I met my dear wife.' He smiled at her. 'All down to you, Sarah. I'll never be able to thank you enough.' Then after a pause, during which she stared into the empty fireplace, aware of his eyes travelling over every inch of her, 'Tell me, Sarah – are you as happy as I am?'

'I – I don't know.'

'I'm sure you must be. Walter is a fine man. A fair employer, a devoted husband and a loving father to the child you gave him.'

Sarah could bear it no longer. 'Samuel . . .' she leaped to her feet, hands clenched by her sides, '. . . please go back to the shop. You shouldn't be here, alone in the house with me. What would Miss Belle think if she knew?'

'*Miss* Belle?' A sharp edge came into his voice. 'You must never call her that now that you're married to her brother. We're as good as any of the Forsyths now, you and me. Never forget that. Why should Belle think anything of me calling in to ask after your health? What other reason could I possibly have for being here?'

'No other reason, but you should go.' Sarah went to the door and waited, then as Samuel continued to lounge in the chair, 'Please go, Samuel.'

'Why are you so concerned about being alone with me?' He got to his feet slowly and went to her, standing so close that she was trapped between his body and the door frame. She stared down at her feet, silently willing him to walk past her and into the hall.

'Can it be,' Samuel's voice said softly above her bent head, 'that you still have feelings for me?'

She shook her head violently, more in denial to herself than to him.

'Are you sure of that? I believe that you still care for me, Sarah. D'you mind the times I came to the kitchen, when those that thought themselves better than you and me were sound asleep in their beds?' His voice lowered and softened and took on the Irish accent that had always sent delicious shivers down her spine. 'D'you mind the way we talked and talked in that nice warm kitchen, tellin' each other all about our past lives and our hopes for the future? You were my only friend then, Sarah, and God help me, I've not found another to match you.'

'You have a wife now.' Her voice was a mere whisper.

'Aye, I've got a wife and you've got a husband, but we both married a Forsyth, and they're cold, arrogant folk. Belle can never be you, Sarah, and it's my belief that Walter can never be me. Am I right?'

He lifted his hand and let the tips of his fingers rest against the curve of her cheek, smiling as he felt her entire body quiver beneath his touch.

'Tell me this, Sarah – do you and Walter ever laugh

together the way we laughed? D'you love with him the way you did with me?'

'We could have been together! That was always what I wanted, but you'd not agree to it!'

'Aye, we could.' He cupped his hand beneath her chin, forcing her to look up at him. 'We could have starved together in an attic, or died of the cold together in a ditch – us and the child that wasnae mine.'

'As God's my judge I thought he was yours, Samuel. With all my heart, I wanted him to be yours!'

The memory of her betrayal, and of the child with Walter Forsyth's features stamped for all to see on his small face still made Samuel seethe with anger, but he forced the censure from his voice. He had not come here to quarrel with Sarah. 'Even if it had been mine, how could I have looked after you both? Look what marriage to Walter Forsyth has given you, Sarah . . .' He took her by the shoulders and turned her to face the well-furnished room. 'You made a better marriage with him than you could ever have made with me.'

'You think that livin' in comfort matters to me?' Sarah turned back to face him, her eyes filling with tears. 'Oh, Samuel, I've missed you so much!' She laid her face against his jacket, feeling the steady beat of his heart against her cheek. 'I've never stopped wishing that things could have been different. But it's too late now.'

'Is it? Why d'you think I married Belle Forsyth if it wasn't to be nearer to you, with the chance to see you from time to time?'

She looked up at him with sudden hope. 'D'you mean that?'

'Do you think I could stop loving you just because you belong to another man?' he said, and took her into his arms. She came willingly, clinging to him and lifting her face to receive his kiss. As her mouth softened and parted beneath his, he felt the tremor run through her again and knew that he had achieved his purpose.

'Sarah . . .' he breathed into her hair when the kiss finally ended, '. . . I've hungered for you for such a long time!'

'We mustn't,' she said in sudden fright as he swept her off her feet and into his arms.

'We must!' He laid her down on the chaise longue and knelt beside her, kissing and caressing her, his mouth and hands swiftly growing bolder. 'We have so little time, my love; we must make the most of it,' he whispered into her throat.

Sarah, swept away on a great wave of longing and need, had just begun to give in completely to her hunger for him when the doorbell jangled and she sat up so swiftly that she almost knocked Samuel to the floor.

'Who can that be? Please God, don't make it Walter,' she whimpered, struggling to her feet. Her fingers flew to her bodice, fumbling with the two buttons that had become unfastened.

'Walter would surely have his own key.' Samuel was on his feet, smoothing his hair and snatching up his bowler hat. 'You have a headache and you were resting. Wait,' he ordered as she hurried to the door, 'give me time to get out by the kitchen.'

He dropped a swift kiss on her lips and then slid out of the parlour and along the hallway. As he closed the kitchen door noiselessly Sarah opened the front door to find Leez Drummond on the doorstep, Fraser clutched in her arms. The baby's hat was tipped over one eye and he was grizzling in a low monotone that emerged damply around the fingers he had crammed into his mouth.

'I'm sorry, Mrs Forsyth, if I had known that you'd open

the door, I would have gone round the back. I thought that Nellie would have been back by now.'

'It's all right,' Sarah said faintly, putting a hand to her dishevelled hair. 'I was sleeping in the parlour – a headache. Give him to me.' She took her son, and he swatted at her irritably as she tried to straighten his hat. 'You're home early, are you not?'

Leez began to pull the perambulator up the steps. 'He couldn't settle, poor wee lamb. It's another tooth coming through.' She left the perambulator in the hallway and reclaimed Fraser. 'Why don't you go upstairs and lie down, Mrs Forsyth? Once I've seen to this wee man I'll mix up something to help your headache.'

In her bedroom, Sarah sank down on to the bed, both hands pressed tightly against her heart, which was beating swiftly. What if Leez had brought the baby home a little later, and found – what she might have found did not bear thinking about. She should never have let Samuel into the house when she was on her own, and once he was in, she should have kept the conversation to everyday things instead of letting him break through her guard by reminding her of what had once been between the two of them.

She was a wicked, stupid woman, she told herself fiercely, but her heart continued to leap and her treacherous body to ache for him, while a voice in her head whispered that if only they had not been interrupted . . .

Samuel whistled cheerfully as he walked back to the shop. His plan had worked well enough, though it was a pity they had been interrupted. But there would surely be other chances, he thought with satisfaction, tipping his hat to a respected customer as he passed; other chances to repay Walter Forsyth for the day he had come home to find Samuel and Sarah together, and had thrown Samuel out of the house by the kitchen door – the tradesman's door. Cuckolding the man was the best thing Samuel could think of as a reprisal, and it would happen, he was sure of that.

Every man should have at least two wives, he thought as he strode down Hamilton Street: one with money and one, like Sarah, for enjoyment.

'You've been away for a good while,' Walter said when Samuel arrived.

Samuel beamed at him, 'Mrs McLennan was having a dress fitting so I had to wait until she was free so that she could make sure that the tea service was in perfect condition.'

'Was she satisfied?'

'Oh yes,' Samuel said breezily. 'Very satisfied indeed. The ladies always like personal attention.'

30

Morna enjoyed the camp more than she had ever enjoyed anything in her life. She never knew, as she and Tom cycled along the coast road to Portencross every morning, rain or sunshine, what the day would bring; she only knew that by the time they cycled back to Saltcoats that evening she would be exhausted, but exhilarated.

Each day became an adventure in a world she had never before inhabited. She looked after small children while their harassed mothers bought their daily groceries at the vans by the gate, held a sewing class for some of the older girls – and some of the mothers too – played rounders, organised games, helped Charlotte to bandage scraped knees and elbows and supervised anxiously as the older children scrambled over the rocks that formed that part of the shoreline. She also tucked up her skirts and waded in rock pools with the littlest children, finding unexpected pleasure in their excitement. When Tom held Sunday services in the large marquee she played hymns on the battered old piano that had arrived on the back of a small lorry while the congregation sang lustily, heedless of the fact that it, like them, was slightly out of tune.

The marquee was well filled for the Sunday services and also on Friday evenings, when the campers gathered for the weekly concert. Between them they could summon up a wide variety of talents – musicians played the accordion, the mouth organ, the spoons and the penny whistle, while others sang, danced or performed monologues. The closing event of every concert was a loud and lusty sing-song, with Morna thumping out all the popular tunes on the piano.

Her creamy skin reddened beneath the sun during those daily cycle rides, and within two weeks it had taken on a golden glow.

'You look like a farm worker,' Walter said disapprovingly when the family met round his table for Sunday dinner. Morna, arriving late after playing at a camp service, had just taken her seat. 'Anyone would think to look at you that you're a tinker woman who earned her food by working in the fields.'

'Tinkers are as brown and as tough as leather,' Belle protested, 'whereas Morna's skin has just taken on a little bit of sun.'

'I think it suits her,' Sarah ventured, and her sister-in-law took a moment from her meal to throw her a grateful smile.

'I don't,' Walter snapped. 'Don't you remember, Morna, how careful Mother was to shade her face from the heat of the sun? She always said that one could tell a lady by her pale, delicate skin.'

'I'm sure she was right, Walter, but it wouldn't be practical for me to go around the camp wearing wide-brimmed hats and trying to protect my face from the sunshine, even if I wanted to, which I don't. I like sunshine and I'm sure that it won't do me a bit of harm. I shall soon become pale again once the autumn arrives. Sarah, could I trouble you for another potato?'

'You'll put on weight,' Walter warned as his wife passed the bowl across the table.

'Better fat than hungry. In any case, I shall work it all off playing with the children during the week. Sometimes, Walter, you can sound like an old woman,' Morna said with exasperation, and her brother almost choked.

'Morna!' Belle remonstrated mildly.

'Speaking for myself, I think that a touch of sun makes the most of Morna's perfect skin. I am in complete agreement with you, Sarah.' Samuel smiled across the table at Sarah, who coloured and became busy passing the gravy boat. Since everyone else had finished the main course and Nellie was waiting to bring in the pudding, only Morna availed herself of the offer.

'I will never,' Belle had sworn fiercely to herself in the sweet dark hours of the night as she lay by her husband's side after he had made love to her, 'be a jealous wife.' She always, long after he had turned away from her and fallen asleep, lay awake listening to his even breathing and feeling happier than she had ever believed possible. Samuel was hers for evermore, and he deserved the best wife a man could have.

But gradually, in the cold light of day, suspicion and jealousy began to creep into her mind. Before they married she had approved of his easy, charming manner towards female customers in the shop, seeing it as good for business. Now that she wore his ring on her finger, his attentions seemed to her to be overdone, and she resented the way women of all ages glanced eagerly around the shop as soon as they entered, their faces lighting up when they spied her husband. She noted the pink flush that came to their cheeks as he made his way towards them, and the way that most of the women, if he was already busy with a customer, pretended to study the items on the shelves and display stands, waving away the other assistants and waiting until Samuel was free to attend to them.

During her entire life Belle had never known jealousy. As a child, she had been happy to share her toys with her brother and sister. When she was old enough to have a few pieces of jewellery Morna was always welcome to borrow a brooch or pendant necklace that might match whatever she was wearing, and any clothing Belle finished with was parcelled up and sent to those in need of such charity. But Samuel was different – he was her husband, and she resented every smile he bestowed on other women.

She tried hard to fight her feelings, telling herself that Samuel was as deeply in love with her as she was with him, and that he would never deceive her. But she could not help mentioning to him that at times, his attention towards some of the ladies who called in at the shop was a little too friendly.

'Isn't that what we're supposed to do?' he asked, eyebrows raised. 'I thought you approved of the way I deal with the customers.'

'Yes, I did in the past, but now that you're the manager and a member of the family a little more decorum may be in order.'

'So you'd like me to be more of a Walter now, would you? You'd like to see me going about the place like this . . .' He put his hands behind his back and stalked around the parlour, looking down his nose at the furniture and pausing at the elegant stand that held a pot plant to say stiffly, 'Good morning, Mrs McBain, the weather is damp for the time of year, is it not? How are you, apart from dripping rainwater all over my nice clean floor? And how are Mr McBain and all the little McBains? Mr Stoddart, kindly attend to Mrs McBain.' He snapped his fingers then asked his wife, 'Is that what you want me to do?'

His malicious impersonation of Walter was so accurate that Belle laughed until she almost cried. 'Of course not, you silly man,' she said when she was able to speak again. 'You've got a much better way with folk than Walter ever had; all I'm asking is that you be a little less – friendly – where the ladies are concerned.'

'You're never jealous, are you?'

Belle felt her face grow hot. 'Jealous? What a daft notion!'

'I do believe that you are, you silly little thing. You,' Samuel said, capturing her hand in both of his, 'are my adored wife, the woman who rescued me from a miserable existence and taught me the true meaning of love. You are the centre of my world.' He raised her hand to his lips and covered it with kisses before drawing her into his arms. 'You are my very own, adored Isabelle,' he said against her throat, 'and those other foolish women who come simpering into the shop are nothing more to me than profit for Forsyth's.'

Several minutes later, sprawled in an armchair and watching his wife tidy her dishevelled hair in front of the mirror, he said thoughtfully, 'Talking of the shop, what are we going to do with Walter?'

'What do you mean?' Belle peered at her reflection, noticing a red mark on her neck. It looked like an insect bite, but she had not been aware of it before, she thought, puzzled. Then her already flushed face went a deeper shade of red as she recalled Samuel's teeth nipping gently at her skin.

'He's rarely in the shop – he certainly never spends a full day there. All the work of running the place is left to you and me.'

'Walter has always been like that. It's a pity that he was the only son, and born to go into the shop whether he liked it or not.' The top three buttons of Belle's blouse had been unfastened; now she fastened them again, easing her collar up so that the red mark was hidden. 'Had he been left to make his own choice, he might have taken up some business that suited him better.'

'You think that any business would have suited him? It seems to me,' Samuel mused, 'that your brother has no great interest in work of any kind. It's odd that a man who could have married a wife wealthy enough to keep him in comfort should have chosen his penniless maidservant, while I, who had nothing, find myself married to a wealthy woman. I was merely making an observation, my dear,' he added swiftly as Belle swung round to stare at him.

'You have never taken advantage of my money and I will not allow anyone to say otherwise! You work very hard.'

'Which brings me to the point I was going to make. I think we should buy Walter out.'

'Buy him out of the shop? I couldn't do that!'

'Why not? You have a far better head for business than he has – even I have a better head for business than Walter. Between us, we could turn Forsyth's into even more of a success than it is already. We could open up branches in Stevenston and Ardrossan – perhaps further afield,' Samuel swept on, his eyes bright with enthusiasm.

'Buy him out?' Belle repeated, still stunned.

'You have enough in the bank to do it, thanks to your Aunt Beatrice.'

'But what would Walter do with himself then?'

'What he does best, my dear. He will lounge around at home all day, appreciating that little wife of his, and their son. We've both heard him express an interest in standing for the town council, and I'm sure he would enjoy that far more than pretending to run an iron-monger's business. But why should we care what he would do, my love? We'll be too busy pursuing our own dream – "Forsyth and Gilmartin".' The words rolled off his tongue and hung in the air between them, embossed in gold letters against a polished black background. 'It has a fine ring to it, d'you not think so?'

A faint scratching was heard from the other side of the closed door, 'That's poor Juliet,' Belle said. 'She wants some company.'

'Can she not do with Ena's company in the kitchen?'

'She's just a little dog looking for affection. Let her in, Samuel.'

'She should be taught not to damage the doors like that,' he grumbled, getting to his feet. Juliet was waiting out in the hall, head cocked to one side; as she saw Samuel standing at the opened door her ears flattened against her head and she backed away, a gentle rumbling starting up in her throat. Then she whined as Belle called her name from inside the room.

'Come along.' Samuel stood to one side, opening the door wider. 'Your mistress wants to see you and I'm not holding the door open for you all day.'

The little animal trotted by him, giving his polished shoes a wide berth. She had learned how the toes of those shoes could hurt when they connected with her ribs. Once inside the room she raced over to Belle, almost leaping into her arms.

'There's a good girl,' Belle crooned as Juliet licked her face.

'You shouldn't let her do that,' Samuel remonstrated, putting out a hand to restrain the dog. Then he pulled it back hastily as Juliet whirled round with a sudden snarl and lunged at his fingers.

'Juliet!' Belle sat down and settled the animal on her lap, stroking her ears. 'Naughty girl, you mustn't hurt Uncle Samuel.'

Juliet, the growl still rumbling in her chest and her top lip drawn back to reveal a glimpse of sharp white fangs, twisted her head round in order to keep watch on Samuel as he settled himself into his usual armchair. He smiled blandly into her bright black eyes before opening his newspaper and lifting it so that it formed a screen between him and the rest of the room.

That was at least one bitch who didn't find him in the least bit desirable.

Once, Sarah had done all she could to encourage Walter to go to the shop every day. When he stayed at home he tended to disrupt the daily household duties and annoy Leez Drummond by interrupting little Fraser's routine. But after the day that Samuel had found her at home on her own she did all she could to keep her husband close by.

On the days when Walter was out, Nellie was instructed to inform Mr Gilmartin, should he call, that the mistress was not at home.

'But why should I say you're out when I know you're in?' the girl protested, confused.

'Because I don't want to entertain Mr Gilmartin in this house.'

'Does Mr Forsyth know that Mr Gilmartin can't come into the house any more?'

'Of course he can visit when Mr Forsyth is at home, or if Mrs Gilmartin is with him,' Sarah tried to explain, then ended up with, 'Oh, for goodness' sake, girl, just do as I tell you!'

As it happened, Samuel only came to the house once when Walter was out, and on that occasion Sarah herself happened to see him striding along the pavement when she was taking down the net curtains in the nursery. She flew downstairs, almost missing the final step in her haste, and into the kitchen, where Nellie was sorting through the laundry.

'Nellie, Mr Gilmartin is on his way to the gate. Remember what I told you – I am out of the house and you don't know when I will return.'

'Are you sure, ma'am? It seems wrong to lie to such a pleasant gentleman, and Mr Forsy—'

'Yes, I'm sure! Just remember what I told you – I am out and you don't know when I will return.' Sarah sped back into the hall and had gained the upper landing by the time the doorknocker was lifted and dropped. She clutched at the banister, holding her breath and listening to Nellie plod through the hall.

'Good morning, Nellie, and isn't it a fine morning too? I've come to call on your mistress.'

'She's out, and so's the master and Leez Drummond and the bairn and I don't know when any of them's coming back, sir.' Nellie rattled the sentence off swiftly.

'Now that's a great pity, for I was hoping that Mrs Forsyth might offer me a refreshing cup of tea. So you're the only one at home, are you?' Sarah heard Samuel say, and all at once her blood ran cold. Surely he wouldn't stoop so low as to try to seduce her little maidservant?

'Only me, sir, and I'm busy sorting out the washing, since it's Monday. Mrs Forsyth—' Nellie stopped short, then said, 'Mrs Forsyth said that I had to have it all done by the time she got back, sir.'

'Are you going to manage it without help?'

'Mrs McCall should be here any time now, sir, to help me.'

'Ah. In that case, Nellie, I'll say goodbye. No need to mention that I called,' Sarah heard Samuel say, and then, to her relief, the door closed.

She hurried to the nursery window in time to see him walk along the path below, still carrying his bowler hat in his hand. Under the late July sun, his hair had a rich glow to it. He went through the gate, and as he turned to close it he glanced up at the house.

Sarah threw herself back from the window, coming up against the side of Fraser's cot. She clutched at it, closing her eyes tightly in a childish attempt to make herself completely invisible. He must have seen her, unless the sunlight on the glass had made it impossible for him to see anything. But he had guessed that she was at home, for why else would he have looked up at the windows? The thoughts flew around her head like fallen leaves scampering before autumn winds and she put a hand to her heart, which was racing. She had escaped this time, but what about the next visit? It was essential that she keep him outside the house, because if he came in again, and if she found herself alone with him, she knew that she would not be able to resist him. And if she gave in to him, what would become of—

'I sent him away, ma'am,' Nellie said from the doorway, and when Sarah, her nerves stretched to breaking point, screamed and whirled round, the servant also screamed and clutched at her flat chest. 'Oh ma'am, it's no' a mouse, is it?'

'It's just you, coming in without warning.' Sarah drew a deep, shaky breath. 'D'you think he believed you, Nellie?'

'I think so, ma'am. He wanted a cup of tea but I told

357

him a lie. I said that Annie McCall was coming to help with the washing.'

'That's all right, Nellie, it wasn't a wicked lie. Now then,' Sarah said as her heartbeat began to slow down, 'I think I could do with a cup of tea myself, and you deserve one for doing as you were told.'

31

'Miss, Miss, my mam's no' feelin' well. Could ye come and have a look at her?' Kate, the eldest of the Kennaway girls, tugged at Morna's skirt.

'What's wrong with her?'

'She's awful red in the face and she's breathin' heavy.' Kate's thin face was screwed up with worry. 'Could ye come now?'

Morna, who had been sorting through music for the concert at the end of the week, dumped the papers on top of the piano and followed the girl out of the marquee and across the busy field, winding their way around tents and wooden shacks.

The four youngest Kennaway children were huddled in a tight, frightened group outside their tent, the baby struggling and whimpering in Mima's arms.

'Give him to me.' Kate took him and propped him over one shoulder, her free hand patting his back. Robbie belched loudly and then settled down to study the camp from his new vantage point. 'Why aren't you lookin' after Mam like I told you?'

'Mrs Baxter came across and sent us outside,' Mima

was explaining when the young neighbour who had brought tea over on the day the Kennaways had arrived emerged from the tent.

'Yer mammy's doin' fine,' she assured the children, 'it's just a wee belly-ache, that's all.'

'It's the new bairn, isn't it?' Kate said rather than asked. 'It's comin' too early.'

'It might be the bairn,' the woman admitted, and then to Morna, lowering her voice, 'Can you come in for a minute?'

'Wait here, I'll not be long.' She followed Mrs Baxter into the tent and saw Jess Kennaway sprawled on the bed like a beached whale. Her face was flushed and her breathing heavy.

'I think it's the bairn comin', pet,' she whispered when Morna went to her side. 'Will you look after the weans for me, just till it's all over? They'll behave themselves for ye.'

'Of course I will.' Morna patted the woman's hand and allowed Mrs Baxter to draw her back towards the door. 'Could ye find Charlotte, hen? I don't think this one's goin' tae be easy. 'I'm comin', pet,' she added as Jess let out a deep groan and clutched at the metal frame of the bed. 'Get Charlotte quick,' she added over her shoulder as she hurried back to the bed.

When Morna went out into the daylight the children were grouped slightly apart from the women who had begun to gather as news of the imminent birth spread. 'Kate, could you run to the bus and fetch Charlotte?'

'She's not there,' Kate said, 'that's why I fetched you.'

'Charlotte's in the Kerrs' tent,' one of the women offered. 'Their wee one's got the bronchitis again.'

'Mima, run across there and tell Charlotte that Mam needs her,' Kate ordered, and then, as the little girl scampered off, 'I'm goin' in to see my mam.'

She thrust the baby into Morna's arms and disappeared inside the tent.

'She's too young to be in there!'

'She might be young, but she's got an old head on her shoulders, that one,' one of the women said. 'And she comes from the tenements; she's probably seen and heard things you've no knowledge of.' Another groan came from within the tent and wee Rena, the youngest Kennaway girl, started to cry. 'It's all right, pet,' the woman comforted her. 'Yer mammy'll be better soon.'

A few minutes later Charlotte arrived at a fast trot with Mima puffing along at her back. She hurried into the tent and a moment later Mrs Baxter ushered a protesting Kate out.

'I should stay with Mam! I know what to do, I was there when Robbie was born!'

'Mebbe so, hen, but Charlotte needs plenty of room, so the less folk in there the better. The wee ones need ye,' the neighbour coaxed.

'Where are the boys, Kate?' Morna asked.

'Down at the water.'

'Let's take the others there as well. We'll have a competition to see who can throw a stone furthest into the sea. Thruppence for the winner,' Morna suggested, wishing that Tom had not gone with Ruth to Glasgow for the day. Kate took the baby, casting several reluctant looks back at the tent as Morna ushered her and her sisters through the field and towards the shore.

'Look, miss – look!' Mima said as the others scattered to search for pebbles. 'Look at Arran – it's gone!'

Although the day was clear, there was no sun, and the island had indeed disappeared completely behind a bank of mist.

'It's a magic island, isn't it?' Mima's voice was a whisper, her grey eyes wide as she glanced up at Morna. 'I've been watching it, and sometimes it's there, sometimes it's not. Sometimes there's mist all round, so that it's floating, and sometimes it's got a white scarf wrapped round its neck.'

Morna, who had thought nothing before of Arran's mists and clouds or the days when it was not to be seen at all, was taken aback by the city child's vivid imagination.

'Where has it gone?' Mima wanted to know.

'Far away, to a place where the sea's blue and the sun shines all the time,' Morna improvised.

'Mebbe it'll like that place so much that it won't come back.' The child's voice was anxious.

'It always comes back – you'll see,' Morna promised. 'Now then, let's find some stones for you to throw into the water.'

The competition to see who could throw their pebbles farthest attracted several other children and grew into a complicated event with rules and handicaps. Finally, as the smell of food cooking began to waft from the field behind them, the children who had joined them on the beach began to disperse to their various tents and huts, until only Morna and the Kennaway children were left. Robbie was crying with hunger by now, so Morna took her charges to the bus, where a small store of tinned food was kept as emergency rations. With Kate's help, she managed to put together a meal, which the children fell on as though they hadn't eaten for days.

'Can we go and see Mam now?' Kate asked when they had finished.

'Best wait until Charlotte says it's all right.'

'But Robbie needs his afternoon sleep. He needs to go into his cot!'

Morna managed to borrow a well-worn perambulator from one of the tents, and Robbie was laid in it and covered with various coats and jackets, then trundled over the bumpy grass to the marquee, where Morna coaxed all the other children, including Kate, to start a game of musical chairs. Again, others straggled in to join them, and from musical chairs they moved to a game of Statues, then a sing-song. When it finally trickled to a close, Morna shut the piano lid, stretched her aching fingers and said with as much cheer as she could muster, 'What shall we do now?'

But Kate had had enough. 'We're goin' to see our mam,' she announced.

'But we should wait until Char—'

'It's been hours! We need tae see what's happenin',' Kate said. She burrowed into the pile of assorted jackets in the perambulator until she found Robbie, and gathered him, rosy and smiling despite being wakened from his sleep, into her arms. 'Come on,' she ordered the others.

'Wait – why don't you wait here and I'll go and see how your mother is?'

Kate's glare was suspicious. 'You'll come right back? Cross your heart and hope to die?'

'Cross my heart and hope to die.'

'You've got to do it, not just say it,' snapped Kate, and Morna obediently drew a cross across the area of her heart and chanted the oath once more.

'All right then, but mind and come right back.'

'I will,' Morna promised, and set off across the field, worn out by the day's events.

Several women were still by the Kennaway tent, talking in low voices. Their faces were sombre, and a cold hand clutched at Morna's heart as she approached. They watched silently as she lifted the canvas flap and went in.

The interior of the tent was oppressively hot and smelled of disinfectant with an undertone of something

363

she did not recognise; something eerily frightening. In the few hours since Morna had last seen her, Jess Kennaway had shrunk to a small, waxen image of her former self; she lay on the bed, her body motionless beneath the single blanket that had been thrown over her and her face as pale in the greenish light as a snowy water lily glimpsed just beneath the surface of a scummy pond. Her eyes were closed.

'Is she. . . ?' Morna whispered to Charlotte, who was unfolding a piece of towelling.

'She's fine, but she lost the baby and she's very tired. She needs her rest. Where are the other bairns?'

'I persuaded them to wait in the marquee while I came to see how their mother is.'

Charlotte picked up a bucket and covered it with the towelling, but not before Morna had glimpsed the water within, gleaming with a reddish shimmer. 'I'll tell them that she's sleeping and they can see her in a wee while. Mebbe you could give Mrs Baxter a hand.' She nodded to where the other woman was working in a corner, and then went outside.

Mrs Baxter was wrapping something carefully in a shawl. 'A wee laddie, it was,' she murmured as Morna joined her. 'Never even got tae draw his first breath, poor wee soul. We'll just . . .' A child started to howl outside, and her head lifted sharply. 'That's my Jimmy, he's hurt himself. Here . . .' She thrust the bundle into Morna's arms and ran from the tent.

A corner of the shawl had come loose and Morna lifted a hand to replace it, then stopped as she found herself looking at the dead child, its tiny face as white as a perfect rose petal. A tuft of dark hair stood out like a cockscomb along the top of the little head, and the eyelids, with their tiny stubby lashes, were closed as though in sleep. Moving carefully, unable to grasp that this child was incapable of being roused, she touched the little cheek with the back of a finger. It was as cold and hard as a china doll's.

She wasn't even aware that she was crying until a tear fell and splashed on to the baby's face. Carefully, Morna wiped it away with a corner of the shawl, then she jumped as Jess Kennaway said from the bed, 'Give him tae me.'

The woman was struggling upright, her arms reaching out for her child.

'Mrs Kennaway, he's . . .'

'I know that. Give him to me,' Jess ordered, and Morna placed the little bundle carefully into the arms waiting to receive it.

'Poor wee bairn,' Jess whispered, 'the road was too long and too hard for ye, wasn't it?' She eased the shawl back and bent to kiss the small face. 'It's a boy.'

'I know, and he's beautiful.'

'Just like all my other bairns. He has a look of my mother about him, God rest her. And something of his father too. My man's the handsomest in the whole street.' Jess smiled proudly, and in her smile Morna suddenly caught a glimpse of the beautiful girl lingering behind the older, careworn face – a girl still deeply in love. Then, with sudden concern, Jess asked, 'How have the other bairns managed without me?'

'I've been looking after them all day and they're fine, all of them. You've got a lovely family.'

'Did they get somethin' tae eat?'

'Oh, they've been well fed.'

'D'ye think ye could keep them busy for a wee bit longer? I just need tae spend some time with this one, then I'll get up and see tae the others.'

'But you need to stay in bed; you've just had a baby.

Someone else will look after the other children until you feel strong enough to get up.'

'I'm strong enough now,' Jess said impatiently. 'This isnae the first, ye know. Women like me don't have the time tae loll about in bed as if child-bearin' was an illness instead of somethin' that happens naturally. This one,' she turned her attention back to the bundle in her arms, 'was tae have been wee Thomas, after Tom.' She smoothed the black curl down, then gave a little laugh as it immediately sprang up again. 'And he would have been a right wee character if he'd had the strength tae draw breath; wouldn't ye, my wee mannie? Ye know, Morna, no matter how many bairns a woman births, every one of them brings its own love, even the ones that don't stay for long. Would ye mind, hen, givin' us a wee while on our own, me and my Thomas?'

'Of course not. I'll go and see to the others.'

'Thanks. Could ye keep an eye on them tomorrow, too?' Jess asked as Morna turned towards the entrance. 'I'll need tae take wee Thomas home and see that he gets a proper burial. I'll be back before night-time.'

While Morna watched Jess Kennaway hold her stillborn child and Belle, in the back office of the shop in Dockhead Street, frowned over the ledgers, trying to make sense of them and Ena, Belle's maidservant, sat in her sister's kitchen on her afternoon off, explaining that she was thinking of looking for another position, Samuel Gilmartin let himself into the house he shared with Belle.

He stood in the hall for a moment, looking around with a satisfied smile, then called 'Ena?' As he had hoped, there was no reply, other than yapping from the kitchen. As Samuel opened the door Juliet backed away from him, growling.

'That's enough! Out ye go,' he ordered, opening the back door, and then, as the dog retreated to a corner, glaring at him, 'Out, I said – now!'

Slowly, the growl rumbling in her throat, Juliet inched her way to the door, giving him a wide berth, but not wide enough. She had almost reached the door when Samuel, impatient to close it, helped her on her way with the toe of his shoe. Juliet gave a shrill yelp of pain, and then, as he bent down to push her through the door, she turned on him, sinking her sharp little teeth into her tormentor's hand.

It was Samuel's turn to yelp. He rushed to hold his bleeding hand beneath the cold-water tap while Juliet watched, half-triumphant at giving him a taste of his own medicine, but half-appalled at what she had done.

'Right, milady,' Samuel Gilmartin said as he turned the tap off and wrapped his hand in the towel again, 'you've done for yourself now, haven't you? Done for yourself good and proper!'

'How can she do that?' Morna asked Tom the following evening as they cycled back along the coast road to Saltcoats. 'How can she just get up and get on with her duties right after giving birth, then bury her baby and come straight back as if nothing had happened?'

They had arrived in the morning to find Jess Kennaway dressed in her hat and coat, her gloved hands clutching the shopping bag that contained the body of her stillborn child. Tom, who was going to Glasgow with her, had offered to find a carter to take them to West Kilbride railway station, but Jess had insisted on walking. 'It'll be good for me, after spending the best part of yesterday in my bed,' she had said, then instructed her subdued brood to behave themselves and not be a nuisance.

'Stop here a minute and enjoy the evening,' Tom suggested, and they cycled to the side of the road nearest the sea. Tom laid his bicycle down on the grass and when Morna had done the same, he reached out a hand to her and led her through the clumps of stiff grass towards the sandy beach. Jumping down on to the firm sand, he turned and put a hand on either side of her waist before lifting her down to stand before him.

'All right?' he asked, and when she nodded he released her. 'Look at that,' he said with satisfaction, indicating the vista before them with a sweep of one arm. It had been a day of high cloud and little sunshine, and now the slumbering sea reflected the soft pearl grey of the sky. Arran looked more like a fairy kingdom than a real island as it floated on the cushion of thick mist lying all along its shoreline.

Tom drew in a deep breath and stretched his arms out, lifting them over his head before he finally let them fall to his sides. 'I've been dreaming all day of standing on this beach, breathing in the salt air. I wish I was an artist, then I could paint that view in its every mood and hang it on the walls of my flat in Glasgow. But even if I were the best artist in the world, the paintings would never be able to compare with being here in the flesh.' Then, his eyes still on the sea and the island floating offshore, 'You were asking how Jess Kennaway could do what she did today, and the answer is, because it had to be done. She wanted to let her husband see his new son, and then the two of them wanted to make sure that their child had the decent burial he deserved. That was the only thing they could do for him, and it was all done properly.'

'Did you conduct the service?'

'The Kennaways are Roman Catholics while I am a minister of the Church of Scotland,' Tom reminded her.

'Their own priest officiated but I was there as a friend of the family.' He paused, then said, 'I saw Christina Baird while I was in Glasgow.'

'She's out of prison?'

'Aye, she's served her time, but it's near killed her. Ruth wanted her to come back to Saltcoats for a long holiday, but she's going to her cousin in Dumfries. He's a doctor and he'll be able to look after her properly. I doubt if she'd be able to stand another prison sentence.'

'It's not fair!' Morna said passionately. 'Women shouldn't be treated like that just because they want the right to vote. How can Parliament allow such terrible things to happen?'

'Men had to suffer and die in their fight for the vote,' Tom reminded her. 'It's a sad way for a country that prides itself on being modern to treat its own citizens, but sometimes protesting is the only way to make the stuffy old men in Parliament change their medieval way of thinking.'

'Don't you worry about Ruth getting thrown into prison and suffering the way Christina suffered?'

'Every minute of every day, but I can't do anything about it.'

'You could ask her to be careful, for your sake.'

'No, I couldn't, because God gave us the freedom to choose the paths we want to follow in life.'

'We don't all have the freedom to choose. I had to leave the home I was born and raised in because my father left home and my brother married our servant girl. They were able to do what they wanted because they're men. Neither of them had any thought for the way their selfishness might hurt me.'

'Did your brother order you to leave home?'

'No, but—'

'So it was your choice. And it was your choice to

accept Ruth's invitation to go and live with her and to teach the children in her little dame school. It was your choice,' Tom swept on as she opened her mouth to protest, 'to help with the summer camp. And I for one am very glad that you did.'

'I would hardly call those decisions freedom of choice.'

'Freedom comes in many disguises,' he said, amusement in his voice and eyes as he turned to look down at her. 'Sometimes it can be limited, but every single day of our lives we are all given a certain amount of freedom, even though we might not be aware of it. Look for it, Morna, and treasure it. As for now, let's go home. Ruth will have supper on the table and I am more than ready for it.'

They turned their backs on the sea, and on Arran, and headed towards the roadside and their bicycles. As they reached the grassy banking, Tom again took Morna by the waist and swung her up into the air, setting her down gently among the tufts of grass.

'Your turn now,' he said, and held out his hands. She took them in hers and he jumped nimbly up beside her, retaining her hands in his for a few seconds longer than necessary.

His firm, warm clasp and the intensity in his eyes as he looked down at her as though trying to fix a picture of her in his mind, suddenly caused an unfamiliar but pleasant fluttering throughout Morna.

32

August ended and the camp at Portencross resembled an ants' nest as the holidaymakers packed their belongings, took down their tents, unbolted the panels of their wooden huts and loaded everything on to the succession of lorries waiting to carry them off.

The final week was one of hard work and farewells. To Morna's surprise and pleasure, Jess Kennaway gave her a warm hug. 'Bless ye, pet, and thank ye for all ye did,' the woman said, while her children, faces rosy from sun and sea air, looked on, beaming.

'See ye next year,' they all yelled from the cab as their lorry jolted out of the field.

It seemed to Morna that an air of desolation began to blanket the field like a mist as the holidaymakers left, family by family. When Tom returned to his duties in Glasgow she was astonished to discover how much she missed him. She missed their cycle runs to and from Portencross, his stories about his work, their arguments and their laughter. She missed listening to his discussions with Ruth and she missed his cheerful whistling as he went about the house. Without him, it seemed a silent, echoing place, even when Ruth's friends gathered in the kitchen.

Noise returned to the place in September when classes resumed. The house was filled once more with the clatter of small booted feet and the chatter of childish voices, but busy though she was, Morna could not shake off a sense of loss, and a certain restlessness.

Guiltily aware that she had been neglecting her brother and sister, she first visited Argyle Road, where she found Sarah more confident and content than she had been since her marriage, thanks to Leez Drummond's calming presence. Wee Fraser, now seven months old, had begun to turn into a person in his own right. Watching him as he sat on his mother's lap, talking away to himself in some mysterious baby language and vigorously banging a rattle on the arm of Sarah's chair, Morna noticed that the poor little scrap still looked very like his father, but she had the tact to keep that thought to herself.

When she called on Belle the sisters spent a busy afternoon going through the possessions that had been stored for her. Most of the clothes were put aside to be sent to charity institutions, for Morna was now more in need of practical clothing than the pretty blouses, skirts and gowns she had once loved. 'It's like another world,' she marvelled. 'My life has changed so much since the days when I wore this sort of thing.' She spread a white lace evening gown over the bed in the back bedroom. 'I'll surely never wear that again.'

'Oh, you must keep it, Morna. You looked so pretty the last time you wore it, do you remember?' Belle fussed over the gown, smoothing out the tiered skirt and settling the cape-effect neckline and the tiered lace sleeves into place.

'The tennis club party last summer.'

'That's right. Mother had it specially made for you from

a picture in a magazine and Papa thought that the sleeves were far too short, even though you were wearing long gloves. I wonder where he is now?'

'Papa? Riding an elephant in India, or finding gold in California, or perhaps working in someone else's iron-monger's shop in England. Wherever he is, I hope he's happy,' Morna said, and then as Belle raised her eyebrows, 'Hating someone is much more tiring than just letting go.' She studied the dress, her head to one side. 'You really think I should keep this one?'

'Yes, because it's still very fashionable and you never know when you're going to need it.' Belle gathered the gown up and put it back in the wardrobe.

'My tennis clothes can definitely go to charity, for I won't need them again.'

'That reminds me – did you know that Clarissa Pinkerton and Arthur MacAdam are engaged to be married?'

'I saw the announcement in the *Herald*.' Only a year ago, Morna realised, she would have been distraught at the news; now she wondered why she had ever wanted to marry Arthur. 'Were you invited to the engagement party?'

'I think my invitation must have got lost in the post.'

'Mine too. Isn't that a pity?' Morna said with a grin.

'It's good to see you smiling again. You're in danger of developing frown lines and they don't suit you. What's the matter?' Belle asked, concerned.

'Nothing – I don't know. I feel as if I'm standing at a crossroads and someone's removed the signs, so I don't know which road to take.'

'I can answer that – we'll take the road down to the kitchen. Ena's out for the afternoon so we'll have to see to our own tea.'

'Where's that annoying yappy little dog? I haven't heard

her since I arrived,' Morna said as she set a tray with cups and saucers and plates. 'In fact, the house has been blessedly silent all afternoon, but I didn't notice it until now.'

'She – she's gone.'

'Gone where?' Morna asked, and then, realising that there had been a strange note in Belle's voice, she turned to see that her sister's eyes had suddenly filled with tears.

'Gone,' Belle said. 'She – she d-died.' Her voice broke and the tears spilled over.

'Oh, Belle, why didn't you tell me? Sit down here. Can I fetch you anything? Smelling salts, or a glass of water?'

'No, I'm just making a silly fuss.' Belle fumbled in her pocket for a handkerchief and wiped her eyes, then gave her sister a watery smile. 'Imagine missing a little dog – but I'd grown fond of her, Morna, and I think she was fond of me, if it's possible for dogs to care for people.' She began to get up. 'I'm being a dreadful hostess, you must be longing for your tea.'

'You just sit down again. I can see to the tray and make the tea. I know how to do these things now,' Morna said with a rueful smile. As she rinsed the teapot with hot water before measuring a spoonful of leaves from the tea caddy she said, 'I suppose she was quite old?'

'Elderly, perhaps, but still active. I always assumed that she would be with us for a while yet,' Belle's voice was still shaky. 'Samuel thinks she may have found something poisonous in the garden, and eaten it. He came home one afternoon two weeks ago and found her having a fit on the lawn. He was bitten on the hand when he tried to carry her into the house. She died shortly after he arrived and he buried her at once, to spare Ena and myself from seeing the poor wee thing.'

'Since you miss her so much, perhaps you should get another dog.'

'I couldn't. As you said, she was a yappy little thing, and so used to the company of womenfolk that she could never take to Samuel. When he was in the house she had to be kept in the kitchen or outside, and I know that she hated being denied the freedom of the house after having been used to it all her life. It's just that – Aunt Beatrice loved her so dearly that I feel as though I let them both down.' Belle got up to help carry the tea things through to the parlour. 'I can't think where she got hold of the poison.'

'Some ragamuffin might have thrown poisoned meat over the back wall – don't you remember that happening to Mrs Hepburn's prize Labrador years ago?' Then, as they went into the parlour, Morna stopped short so that Belle, carrying the teapot, almost bumped into her. 'You've moved all the furniture.'

'That was Samuel's idea. He thinks it looks better like this. Don't you think it does?'

Morna glanced around the altered room, frowning slightly. 'I'm not sure – it's not Aunt Beatrice's parlour any more.'

'I expect that that was what he intended. As he says, we must look forward to the future, not back at the past.'

'Are you happy in your marriage, Belle?'

'Of course I am. What a thing to ask!'

'Hearing about Arthur and Clarissa made me realise that you and Walter have both made marriages you would not have dreamed of when Mother and Papa were still here. Walter's very content – there's no doubt of that – and Sarah is beginning to look and sound like the mistress of our old home. And then there's you and Samuel – marrying out of one's usual social circle is probably quite a good thing. For myself, I'm convinced that I am very fortunate not to be marrying Arthur

MacAdam. Clarissa is more than welcome to him – and he to her!'

'There's a letter for you – from Tom,' Ruth said casually when Morna returned to the house. 'I recognise his handwriting.'

'Why would Tom want to write to me?'

'Read it and find out,' Ruth suggested.

'Later.' Morna stuffed the envelope into her skirt pocket, waiting until she was alone before opening it. His letter was like Tom himself – cheerful, funny and enthusiastic about everything that was happening in his life. As Morna's eyes skimmed over the pages, it was as though he was in the room, talking to her. 'Write to me,' the letter ended. 'Tell me all about life in Saltcoats.'

Apart from school, Morna had never in her life written anything other than invitations and polite thank you notes. She bought a notepad, pen and bottle of ink the very next day, but in the evening, when she sat down in the privacy of her room to write to him, she hadn't the faintest idea how to go about it. She read his letter again, smiling over the things he said, then drew a deep breath before dipping her pen into the ink bottle. 'Dear Tom,' she wrote, and then suddenly her pen started racing over the page as she began to tell him about visiting Sarah and Belle, and about poor little Juliet, and the engagement between Clarissa Pinkerton and Arthur MacAdam.

Belle was used to seeing the assistants spring to attention every time she walked into the shop. Like her father, she was of the firm opinion that employees should be seen to be earning every penny of their wages and that being obeyed was more important than being liked. If the truth were told, she enjoyed the way the half-dozen people who worked for Forsyth's looked at her with respect.

But respect and guilt were very different things, and when she entered the shop on a particularly pleasant October morning, opening the door briskly and setting the bell overhead jangling, she was suddenly struck by the scene facing her. The cash desk was directly opposite the door, and since there were no assistants or customers to block the view she found herself looking straight through the window at Miss Campbell, the assistant cashier. The young woman was seated at the desk and Samuel was leaning over her so closely as they studied some paperwork that his auburn hair almost mingled with her fair curls.

As the bell jangled both heads, auburn and pale gold, lifted swiftly, and the guilt in the two faces brought Belle to a halt on the matting placed just inside the door. Samuel immediately straightened up and without a word to the girl he turned and left the small booth. For her part, Miss Campbell ducked her head down in a futile attempt to hide the deep flush sweeping over her pretty face.

Belle moved into the shop, nodding to assistants and pausing for a quick word with one of the regular customers. When she reached the office she found Samuel seated at the desk, working industriously. He jumped to his feet. 'Isabelle, my dear, I thought that we had agreed that you should have some time to yourself today.'

'I was doing some shopping nearby so I thought I would look in.' She drew her gloves off, glancing at the papers spread out before him. 'You're seeing to the invoices?'

'I know that you like to pay the accounts on time.'

'Yes, I do, but I was going to work on them tomorrow.'

'I thought I would make a start. You work too hard, and it's high time you let me take on some of the responsibility.'

'You already do an excellent job in the shop itself. And we have Miss Campbell to deal with the customers' payments.' Belle seated herself at the desk. 'What do you think of her, Samuel?'

'Miss Campbell? She seems a capable young woman.'

'You have no concerns about her work?'

'None whatsoever,' he said easily, and began to ask her advice about one of the invoices.

Belle had a lot to think about on her way home. For over a month now, she had been aware of small but regular discrepancies in the shop's cashbooks. That, coupled with the scene that had greeted her on her arrival at the shop, was beginning to awaken the jealousy she had fought so hard to dispel. She tried to tell herself that Samuel had only been helping the girl with some problem, but a small, suspicious voice kept intruding, wanting to know why Samuel had hurried from the cash booth the moment his wife came into the shop, and why Miss Campbell had blushed so fiercely.

On the following morning she asked him to visit one of the Glasgow warehouses to decide whether a new brand of pots and pans they had in stock might suit the people of Saltcoats, and was in the shop just after it opened. It was busy, giving her good reason to ask her assistant cashier to go and serve customers while she herself took over the cash desk. In between dealing with customers she studied the large cash book, glancing up now and again to see Miss Campbell watching her anxiously.

As soon as there was a lull in the rush of customers she called the girl into the main office at the back.

'I think you know why I want to talk to you,' Belle said when the door was closed.

'I have no idea.' The girl's head was high, though her

hands were clenched into fists by her side, and there were two spots of bright colour on her cheekbones.

'Then I must tell you. I have noticed for some time now that the money being taken in does not agree with the stock going out. Figures have been altered in the cash book.'

'Are you accusing me of stealing?'

'Yes, I am.'

'How dare you!'

'I dare, my dear, because I have proof. You have been robbing me and my brother and I can't let it go on.'

Tears flooded into the girl's eyes. 'My mother's not been well – I needed money to buy things for her.'

'Then you should have come to me. We would have arranged something between us.'

'I won't ever do it again, I promise!'

A picture of the moment she had caught the girl with Samuel in the cash booth flashed into Belle's mind. 'No, you won't,' she agreed levelly, 'because you are leaving our employment here and now – and don't expect a reference.'

The girl drew herself up, dashing the tears from her eyes. 'I shall speak to Mr Gilmartin. He won't let you do this to me!'

'And what makes you think that?'

'Because . . . because . . .'

'Kindly leave the premises at once,' Belle interrupted as she swept towards the door and held it open, suddenly afraid of what she might be about to hear. Then as Miss Campbell, now weeping profusely, scurried past her she added, 'And leave by the back entrance, please. I don't want customers to see you in that state.'

When Samuel returned in the early afternoon, she beckoned him to where she sat at the cash desk and told him what had happened.

'You dismissed her? But she was a good worker!'

'She was robbing us, Samuel. I'm surprised that you didn't realise it, since you seemed to give her special attention.'

His head came up quickly at that. For a moment his eyes met Belle's and then as she held her gaze unblinkingly, his own slid away, much as it had done the day she saw him with Miss Campbell. 'No more than any other employee,' he muttered. 'I was only trying to help the girl. She was willing to learn and I think that she was an asset to the shop.'

'She was, until she took over as assistant cashier. But it seems that working with money was too much of a temptation.'

'Perhaps we should give her another chance,' Samuel suggested. 'I'm sure she's learned her lesson by now, and she has a sick father to support.'

'Is that what she told you?'

'Yes, and I have no reason to disbelieve her.'

'Nor had I,' Belle said, 'when she told me not three hours ago that she was only stealing from us in order to help her sick mother.' Then, as her husband stared at her in dismay, teeth nibbling at his lower lip, 'We must get back to work; we can talk about your visit to Glasgow tonight, at home.'

But that night Samuel went out after dinner, and when Belle asked where he was going he said curtly that he needed a walk to clear his head.

Left on her own, she tried to write some letters, but her mind was not on the task, and eventually she fetched her coat, told Ena that she too was going out for a walk, and went off to visit Morna and Ruth.

Life in the Gilmartin household was never the same after that day. Samuel lost some of his easy charm and began to spend time out of the house in the evenings. He refused to accompany Belle when she visited her brother and sister-in-law, telling her sulkily that he was tired of listening to Walter's self-important ramblings.

'When are you going to buy him out of the business?' he asked several times, but she found it hard to consider such a drastic step.

'The business has always been Forsyth and Son, even when my father was in charge of it.'

'Never mind what happened in the past – you know as well as I do that Walter's nothing more than a millstone around your neck. This is your chance to free yourself from him once and for all.'

'But it would take almost all that I – we – have in the bank.' Belle knew that Samuel hated to be reminded that the money, and the house that they lived in, belonged to his wife.

'We can make it up again once we own the business outright. I have plans for the place,' he said eagerly, 'plans that could make us both wealthy.'

These discussions invariably turned into arguments, ending with Samuel going for one of his long walks and Belle, who no longer took any pleasure from the house that had been a happy place when her aunt lived in it, usually putting her jacket on and going off to Ardrossan Road. She had discovered that sitting in Ruth Durie's kitchen listening to Ruth and whoever might have dropped in arguing about politics, education, or whatever else might come into their heads, soothed and refreshed her.

33

'I was wondering if you could recommend a trustworthy housekeeper.'

'Me?' Sarah gaped at her sister-in-law. Although Belle had become civil towards her once the shock of Walter's unsuitable marriage eased, Sarah was very much in awe of this capable woman who had the intelligence and ability to run a large shop as well as a home.

Belle, misunderstanding the younger woman's confusion, went quite red. 'I do apologise, Sarah – I didn't ask you to help me because you had been in service yourself, it's just that I'm so busy with the shop, and since you have managed to acquire such a good maidservant and nursemaid I thought that you might be willing to help me.'

It was Sarah's turn to blush. 'I didn't think . . .' she began to stammer, and then, pulling herself together, 'Why don't we have another cup of tea and start this conversation again?'

Their eyes met in mutual embarrassment, which swiftly turned to mutual amusement. 'What a sensible idea!' said Belle.

'It is so nice to see you here, Belle,' Sarah ventured as she busied herself with the teapot. 'You don't call very often.'

'The shop keeps me busy. Unfortunately, I had to dismiss our cashier, and that means that I have to be there most of the time at present. Once we get a new and trustworthy cashier I'll have more leisure time.' Belle sighed as she accepted her refilled cup, 'Ena could not have chosen a worse time to leave, just when I'm so busy. I'm going to miss her.'

'We can speak to Leez, the nursemaid, when we've finished our tea. She knows a lot of people, and if Leez speaks for them, you can be sure that they'll be reliable. If you wish,' Sarah offered tentatively, 'I could sit with you during the interview.'

'That would be kind,' Belle said gratefully. 'You probably have a better idea of my requirements. I've always left the running of the house to Ena, and the thought of starting all over again with someone new is not at all pleasant.'

'She was Mrs McCallum's housekeeper, wasn't she? I'm surprised to hear that she's leaving.'

'She feels that it's time to move elsewhere and there's nothing I can do about it.' Belle sipped at her tea, hoping that the sudden warmth sweeping over her face was caused by the hot drink rather than by embarrassment. She couldn't possibly tell Sarah, or anyone else, about the day Ena had handed in her notice, turning down Belle's panic-stricken offer of more money and more time off.

'I'm sorry, Mrs Gilmartin, but I won't reconsider. It has nothing to do with you, ma'am – I would be happy to stay on in your employment – but if I'm to be honest, I just can't get along with Mr Gilmartin. Nothing I do seems to be right with him, and so I think it would be best all round if I was to find work elsewhere.'

'Good riddance,' was Samuel's rejoinder when Belle told him that they were going to lose their treasured servant. 'She's a bad-tempered old bitch who thinks she rules the house.'

'Samuel!'

'I'm only telling the truth. She resents me being here and to tell the truth, I've had enough of her impertinence. It's just as well that she's decided to move on before she's dismissed.'

'I would never have dismissed Ena.'

'Tell the truth, my love.' Samuel came up behind her, put his arms around her, and nuzzled her neck. 'You insisted on keeping that noisy little dog because it had been your aunt's pet, you weren't happy when I rearranged your aunt's furniture . . .'

'I—'

'And you would never dismiss Ena, just because she had worked for your aunt,' he finished. 'When it comes to domestic considerations you're not as hard as you think.' Then, releasing her and turning away, 'It would have been better for poor Agnes Campbell if you had shown as much compassion for her as you're showing for our servant.'

'Miss Campbell stole from us!'

'And how do you know that that old harridan in the kitchen hasn't done the same thing? She could help herself to anything she wanted from the pantry and you'd be none the wiser.'

'She wouldn't do that,' Belle said hotly, and he shrugged.

'So no doubt you'll give her a good reference – which is more than you did for Agnes Campbell. D'you never wonder what became of her?'

'She's working in our coal merchant's office. I saw

her there when I went to pay the last account.' Belle bit her lip at the memory of the insolent stare the girl had given her. 'So she managed to find work after all, even without a reference.'

'Oh, she had a reference, all right,' Samuel said casually. 'From me.'

'You?'

They had just finished dinner and Samuel, helping himself to a glass of Beatrice McCallum's port, smiled at his wife from across the room. 'Yes, she asked me for one.'

'And you did as she asked without speaking to me first?'

'The poor lass wouldn't have found a decent job without one. She'd already been turned away from the shop with no mercy at all, and I thought she'd had enough punishment. Why don't you try some of this excellent port, my dear? It might soothe your hurt pride.'

'You know that I hate port, and this has nothing to do with hurt pride. You recommended that young woman to other employers when you know very well that she took money from us.'

'A sixpence here and a shilling there – you and Walter won't miss that, and Agnes needed the money more than you did.'

'You're on first name terms with her, are you?' The white-hot jealousy that Belle had learned to dread and despise began to glow deep in her heart.

'I know her first name, yes,' Samuel said easily, sinking into a comfortable armchair. He raised the glass to his lips, his eyes challenging her over the rim.

Pain stung Belle's palms and she realised that she had clenched her fists so tightly that her fingernails were threatening to pierce the skin. She stretched her hands out and fought to keep her voice level as she said, 'And what if she steals from her present employers? What will they think of you – of both of us – then?'

'She promised me that she'd behave. Even if she doesn't, we can always swear that she was honest while she was in our employment.'

'You can lie if you wish, but I certainly won't.'

'Ah, but you will, if it's to protect my good name. Isn't that what you promised when we were married? To honour and obey me?'

Now, sipping tea in Sarah's front room, Belle flinched over the memory of that conversation.

'Is the tea too hot?' Sarah asked at once.

'Not at all – just a slight twinge in a back tooth,' Belle improvised.

'If you need attention, Mr Walker of Dockhead Street was very good when Walter went to him with dreadful toothache.'

'Thank you, I'll bear him in mind,' Belle said.

When Sarah and Belle went into young Fraser's nursery, Leez Drummond was kneeling on the floor, helping Fraser to make a tower from his coloured building blocks. He watched, bright-eyed, and every time the tower began to take shape he knocked it down with a sweep of his arm, laughing uproariously.

Leez scrambled to her feet while Sarah stooped to lift her son into her arms. 'Say hello to your Aunt Belle,' she said, then wiped his mouth with her handkerchief as he blew some bubbles. 'Leez, Mrs Gil—' her voice faltered and she choked slightly, then shook her head as Leez tried to take the baby from her. 'I'm all right, it was just a sudden tickle in my throat,' she explained when she had recovered. 'My sister-in-law is in need of a good housekeeper and I wondered if you knew of anyone suitable.'

'Livin' in, ma'am?' Leez asked, and then as Belle nodded the woman pursed her lips. 'I can't think of anyone at this moment, but I'll make enquiries. If a daily woman would do in the meantime, I know of someone – a good plain cook with clean habits and a pleasant nature. I could ask her to call on you.'

When Sarah closed the front door behind her visitor she stood for a moment, her hands pressed tightly against her mouth. She had enjoyed Belle's visit right up until that moment in the nursery when the words 'Mrs Gilmartin' had suddenly turned into a hot, hard lump in her throat and the old, familiar sense of loss had pierced her heart. She liked Belle, but how could she ever bring herself to make a friend of the woman who had won Samuel as her husband?

She whispered his name into her palms and the pain shot through her again. It took several minutes before she could compose herself and go upstairs, yearning to hold her little son and cover his face with urgent kisses.

The unresolved problem of what to do about Walter nagged at Belle over the next week. The matter, she knew, was not done with, and sure enough, the evening came when Samuel again raised the issue.

'There are premises for sale in Ardrossan – I want you to come and have a look at them. It's time we branched out and we can't do that while Walter has any say in things.'

'But if we bought another shop he could run it.'

Samuel looked at her with barely concealed impatience. 'Do you really think that he would agree to that?

With the two of us keeping the Dockhead Street business going, he's able to laze about at home, enjoying the financial benefits. He's not fit to run a shop on his own. Be honest with yourself for once, Isabelle,' he surged on as she began to protest, 'you're much better at business than Walter is, and so am I, for all that I've come from nothing. I've got fire in here . . .' he thumped a fist against his own breast, '. . . and I've got the hunger a man needs to make something of himself. If Walter hadn't been born into comfort and security he'd be living down in the slums by the river right now, and probably working as a labourer in Ardrossan dockyard.' He gave a bark of laughter at the picture he had just conjured up. 'And by God, he'd be having a hard time of it. Ah, to hell with it, I'm going out.'

'Out where?' She followed him into the hall, where he was pulling on his coat.

'Just out for a change of air.' He picked up his hat and his stick. 'And while I'm gone, will you for goodness' sake make up your mind about how you're going to tell that brother of yours that he's out of the business?' He opened the front door, then turned back for a moment. 'Go to bed when you're tired, I have my key.'

'Samuel, wait . . .' But he had gone out into the darkening night, letting the door slam noisily behind him.

Tears stung Belle's eyes as she returned to the parlour. Her marriage was scarcely five months old and already things were changing. She longed for the early days, when Samuel had been gentle and loving and considerate. They were both tired, she thought as she listened to the soft, regular ticking of the clock, both in need of a holiday. She thought of Ireland, that land of blue skies and soft green hills where Samuel's family lived. None of them had been able to come to the wedding because, he had explained, his mother had her hands full caring for her own elderly mother and an aged aunt, and his brothers and sisters were working hard to feed their growing families. He had promised that one day he would take her to Ireland.

'You'll love it,' he had said, 'and you'll love my family. We'll have a grand time there.'

It was time she met his kin, but on the other hand, who would look after the shop? Certainly not Walter. Perhaps Samuel was right, she thought bleakly. Perhaps it was time to buy Walter out.

Leez Drummond had not as yet come up with a recommendation for the post of housekeeper, and although the woman who had taken Ena's place on a temporary basis was adequate, she returned home to her own family every evening. Belle was alone in the house, which seemed very empty. She would have given anything at that moment to hear the sound of claws scuttering along the hall floor and Juliet snuffling at the bottom of the door before noisily demanding entry. But there was no Juliet, no Ena, and no Samuel. She was alone.

She thought of visiting Morna and Ruth, but then she thought that Samuel might well repent swiftly of his angry outburst and decide to return home to make up the quarrel with her. And it was time that the ledgers she kept at home were brought up to date. She had brought the cash books from the shop for that purpose, and had been about to start work when Samuel raised the subject of Walter. The books were piled on the table, waiting for her.

Belle sat down and started work.

It was late when Samuel finally returned home to find his wife sitting at the table, the ledgers in front of her.

She knew by his flushed face and the way he swayed as he came to a standstill in the doorway, that he had spent the evening in one of the town's public houses.

'I thought you'd be in your bed by now, but here you are, still workin' away at this time of the night. My, my, Isabelle, but you're a conscientious woman right enough.'

'I've just finished.' She rubbed her sore eyes, smiling at him. 'I was thinking, Samuel, that we could both do with a holiday. Why don't we go over to Ireland to see your family?'

'Mebbe next year.' He went to the cupboard, straddling his feet wide in order to keep his balance as he bent down to get a tumbler and a bottle.

'Could we not go now?'

'Next year, I said.' He wrenched the cork from the bottle and poured himself a generous tot of whisky.

'Would you not rather have a cup of tea before you go to bed?'

'No, I would not,' he retorted, mimicking her precise voice. He took a gulp of whisky and reeled over to sit opposite her. 'So how is "Forsyth and Son",' he uttered the words with stinging contempt, 'doin', then?'

'Samuel, have you been working on these books?'

'Mebbe I have and mebbe I haven't.' He wagged a finger at her. 'That's for me to know and you to find out.'

'I think you have. I think,' Belle said steadily, 'that you've been altering some of the figures.'

'Oh God, here we go again! If it's not poor wee Agnes Campbell it's yer own husband. Ye always have tae suspect someone, don't ye, Isabelle?' he slurred. 'Mebbe it's all down tae you. Mebbe ye've just made mistakes. D'ye ever think of that? Or are ye too high and mighty tae make mistakes? Is that somethin' ye leave tae yer inferiors?'

'Have you been taking money from the till?' she asked, ignoring the drunken insults. He stared at her, working at focusing his gaze on her face. For a moment she thought that he was going to deny it – hoped that he would deny it, for she had already decided that she should have held her tongue. She would accept his word and that would be an end to it. Then Samuel laughed, loudly and open mouthed, leaning across the table towards her so that she was surrounded by the strong smell of whisky.

'Yes, my dear wife, I have been takin' money from the till. And what of it? Am I no' the manager? Am I no' a junior partner, thanks to your great generosity towards me when we married?' He grimaced with disgust. 'Dolin' out a manager's wage tae yer own husband while old man Pinkerton guards the money lyin' in the bank in your name. *Your* name, Isabelle, not mine. Is there any wonder if sometimes I take the bit extra that I deserve?' He flourished his glass in a toast and generous drops of whisky spattered the ledgers and Belle's hands. 'To you, Isabelle. You and yer oversh-overwhelming generosity!' He drained the glass in a few greedy gulps and then set it down, wiping the back of his hand across his mouth.

The room was warm, but all at once Belle felt chilled. 'And what about Miss Campbell? Did you stand by while I accused her of something she didn't do?'

'Poor wee Agnes. You can rest assured, my dear wife, that she wasnae entirely free of guilt. I let her have her share so's she'd keep quiet about the cash book being altered. By Christ, that upright woman that was your auntie fairly knew a good whisky from a bad one.' He refilled his glass with the last of the bottle of whisky he had brought to the table with him, and drank.

'Why didn't you tell me that you wanted more money? I would have given it to you.'

391

'Aye – given it. Doled it out, like the Lady Bountiful you are. Your house,' Samuel sneered, indicating the room with a wide sweep of one arm. The empty whisky bottle was knocked over and left to roll to and fro on the table, 'And *your* money – and *your* husband. Everythin' yours and nothin' mine! You Forsyths are always better than anyone else, aren't you?' he sneered at her. 'You get this place, Walter gets Sarah, and the rest of us can go to hell for all you care!'

Belle's head was beginning to ache. 'What has Sarah to do with it?' she asked, confused.

'She has everythin' tae do with it! Why d'you think I want Walter out of the business? It's what I've been waitin' for ever since he took Sarah from me.' He stopped to take another gulp or two of whisky.

'What do you mean?'

Samuel's chin was wet with whisky. 'I'm talkin' about when she worked in the Forsyth kitchen and I delivered the vegetables – d'ye not remember?' he asked irritably. 'She tried tae get me tae believe that that bairn was mine, but I wasnae goin' tae marry her – oh no. I wasnae goin' tae live in a ditch just because she'd a wean in her belly. But she didnae tell the whole truth, did she? Women never do!' His gestures became wilder as he plunged into his story. Belle listened, appalled and sickened.

'Lied, she did! Instead of gettin' rid of it like I wanted so's we could go on as we were, she had tae marry that useless brother o' yours. An' when he saw me darin' tae speak tae his new wee wife he put me out of the house and lost me my job. But that . . .' he sprawled across the table, his chin almost resting on its surface, grinning at her, '. . . that was his mistake, 'cos I made up my mind on that very day tae do him down one way or the other. And now ye know why I want him out of the shop and why I'll not have any more of your arguin'. You just take heed of what I'm tellin' ye! We'll throw him out tomorrow, the two of us together so's I can see the look on his face.'

Belle couldn't stand another moment of it. 'I think we should go to bed now,' she said as calmly as she could.

'Go to bed with *you*? Sure, where's the pleasure in that? If you were Sarah, now, it would be a different matter. She's soft an' warm and eager tae please, while you – I'd as soon go tae bed with the garden gate, so I would. Now don't start that,' he added as her eyes began to fill with tears. 'I'll not have that. My oul' bastard of a da knocked my ma clean across the room when she turned on the waterworks, and he'd the right way o' it.'

Belle blinked the tears back. 'How can you speak to me like this, Samuel?'

'You know what they say.' He took another mouthful of whisky. 'It's easier tae tell the truth when ye're in drink. An' I've wanted tae tell ye the truth time an' time again.'

'So you only asked me to marry you so that you could find a way to punish Walter?'

'No, no, no, Isabelle, I'll not have that. Now it's your turn tae tell the truth. I never asked you tae marry me – it was you that asked me tae marry you. In fact, you begged me. Ye were desperate for a man, weren't ye? Desperate.'

Sour bile rose into Belle's throat, and for a moment she thought that she was going to spew out her disgust and shame there and then, like a drunken man emptying his stomach into the gutter after an evening's consumption of cheap, raw whisky. She swallowed hard, and once the sensation had eased she said quietly, 'How dare you speak to me like that?'

He laughed in her face. 'I dare because I'm yer husband

and I can speak tae you any way I like. And because we both know that you're not goin' tae go running tae tell Walter or anyone else about this. D'ye really want folk tae know what a fool ye've made of yerself?'

'Buying Walter out won't punish him, it'll only punish us because we'll have to make up the money we pay him.'

Samuel shrugged. 'We'll make it up soon enough. But ye're right. The best way tae really hurt that brother of yours is tae take Sarah from him.'

'You wouldn't do that,' she said quickly, and then, as he closed one brown eye in an elaborate wink, 'You couldn't!'

'Could I no'? She's weakenin' already,' Samuel boasted. He picked up his glass and saw that it was empty. 'More whisky,' he mumbled, and levered himself up from the table. It took a few moments, and when he tried to walk to the cabinet his legs went sideways instead of forwards. Lurching like an ungainly crab, he reached the fireplace, and Belle jumped up, convinced that he was going to fall into the fire and burn himself. But he caught hold of the mantelshelf just in time, managing to swing himself round and into an armchair. 'Whisky,' he said petulantly.

'There's a fresh bottle in the kitchen press. I'll get it – and a blanket.' Clearly, he was in no fit state to climb the stairs to his bed. Belle picked his empty glass up from the hearthrug, where it had fallen when he almost fell into the fireplace, and went upstairs to fetch a blanket before going to the kitchen for a fresh bottle of whisky.

When she returned, Samuel, slumped like a sack of potatoes, legs sprawled across the rug, ordered, 'Fill the glass.' Once she had done so, he almost snatched the drink from her. 'Put the bottle on the wee table by my hand,' he slurred, 'an' make the fire up.'

By the time she had added fresh coals to the fire, which

had begun to burn low, the glass was half-empty. When she stooped to put the blanket over him he batted her hands aside irritably. 'Stop fussin', woman, and let me be!'

'Good night, Samuel – sleep well,' she said, and went out, closing the door softly.

In the bedroom, she took a small, brown glass medicine bottle from the dressing table and put it back into the shabby tin box. Locking the box, she returned it to the wardrobe, pushing it right to the back, out of sight.

After that she went to bed and fell asleep almost at once.

34

'A party,' Ruth Durie said, clapping her hands. 'We shall have a party for all our pupils on Christmas Eve. It might be the only celebration some of those poor little souls will have. We'll have lots of food and lemonade, and play games, and we'll buy a present for each child and put a tree up in the classroom, with sweets and gingerbread men on it.'

Belle and Morna looked at each other across the kitchen table. 'But Christmas Eve is only five days away,' Belle pointed out, while Morna chimed in with, 'How can we possibly do all that in such a short time?'

'I'll see to the tree tomorrow, as soon as school's over. And we'll call in reinforcements – Anna can make ginger-bread men, and I know that she'll be willing to help with the rest of the food. You'll help too, Belle, won't you?'

'I can't cook or bake, but I'm sure Ena would be will-ing.' On hearing that Belle had suddenly been widowed, Ena had given up all thought of a change of employer and returned to her former mistress's side.

'Do you think you could possibly choose suitable gifts for the wee ones as well? I'll give you a list of names and ages. We shall dip into the bank to buy them,' Ruth added to Morna. The bank was an old tea caddy where they kept money to buy food and pay their other expenses.

'There's very little in it at the moment,' Morna pointed out, and Ruth shrugged.

'Then you and I must save money by living on porridge and soup and bread for a few days. It will be just like being in prison, only much more fun.'

'I will pay for the children's presents,' Belle said, and Ruth beamed at her.

'You are a darling. Isn't it helpful, Morna, to know someone who has money? You'll come to the party as well, won't you, Belle? So that makes three of us helping with the children,' Ruth swept on when Belle nodded, 'and then there's Anna – and Tom, of course.'

Something in Morna's breast gave a sudden skip, like a child jumping for joy. 'Your brother will be here?' He had said nothing of it to her in his regular weekly letters.

'He always comes for Ne'erday, and sometimes he manages to be home for Christmas too. I shall write to him and insist that he attends our party.'

Ruth's enthusiasm for everything she tackled, no matter how uninteresting or unpleasant, warmed Belle. It was Ruth who had given her the strength to cope following Samuel's death – from a sudden and unexpected heart attack, the doctor said, while his manner, as his sharp eyes noted the empty whisky bottle still lying on the table, the half-full bottle on the floor by the fireside chair and the glass that had fallen from Samuel's hand to spill what remained of its contents over the rug, said clearly, without words, that excessive drinking must have played a part in the sudden death. It was later to come out that Samuel had been drinking heavily in one of the public houses down by the river on the previous evening. Belle had told everyone that she knew nothing of her husband's condition when he arrived home that night, because she had gone to bed early with a bad headache.

While those who had criticised and ostracised her after what they saw as her unsuitable marriage wondered whether they should call to express their condolences, Ruth Durie had not hesitated. Over the six weeks since the funeral she and Belle had become firm friends, and it was Ruth who had encouraged Belle to ignore the unwritten rules and return to the shop.

'You can't just sit behind drawn curtains for months with nothing to do,' she had said crisply. 'The boredom will drive you out of your wits and widowhood will do its best to make you old before your time. The family business needs you, and you must have something to do. Pay no heed to any old sweetie wives who might cluck and mutter about a sensible period of mourning – you can still mourn in your own way.'

Once the party had been decided on, Ruth was determined to find the ornaments for the tree she was going to buy. The three of them hurried upstairs, where they carried a small table from one of the bedrooms to the landing.

'Tom can reach the trapdoor from the table,' Ruth said thoughtfully, 'but I can't.'

'Then let your brother search the attic when he gets here,' Belle's voice was firm. 'Or I can send one of the shop assistants along tomorrow morning if you want. Mr Lombard is very tall.'

But Ruth, too impatient to wait, went back downstairs and reappeared carrying an upright wooden chair from the kitchen.

'I'm not climbing up there!' Morna said nervously as

the chair was settled on top of the table. 'It doesn't look safe.'

'It's perfectly safe, but you two must stay down here to hold the chair legs steady and pass the lamp up to me. If I happen to fall and break a limb, one of you can run for help while the other stays to comfort me,' Ruth said blithely, hitching up her skirts. She clambered on to the table and then got a firm grip on the back of the chair. 'Hold on, now,' she instructed, and in a moment she was balancing on the seat.

'I feel like a circus acrobat,' she crowed, and then, 'Oh dear, I can see a dreadful pile of dust above each of the bedroom doors! Remind me to do something about that before Ne'erday, Morna.' She reached up and managed to dislodge the trapdoor leading to the attic. 'Give me the lamp, please.'

Belle clung to the chair legs as Ruth stooped down to take the lamp from Morna. She set it on the floor of the attic and then with a flurry of skirts, petticoats, black-stockinged legs and a yell of 'Alley-oop!' she swung herself up into the attic and disappeared.

For several long and anxious minutes the sisters listened to bumping noises overhead. Finally Ruth reappeared, leaning over precariously in order to lower a box to the chair.

'Could someone take that out of the way?' she asked before disappearing again.

'You can do it,' Belle told her sister. Morna, her heart in her mouth, clambered on to the table and had just handed the box over to Belle when Ruth began to lower herself, feet first, from the trapdoor.

Once she was back on the landing and the dust and cobwebs had been brushed from her clothing, the three of them took the box down to the kitchen where they unpacked it, lifting piles of magazines, tracts and leaflets from the table in order to lay out a treasure trove of brightly painted wooden baubles, tiny dolls, nursery rhyme characters and an entire orchestra of miniature musical instruments. Ruth greeted each discovery with cries of delight, and it was quite late when Belle finally and reluctantly announced that she really must go home because Ena would be waiting up to make sure she got back safely.

'What about your sister-in-law?' Ruth asked as Belle was putting her coat on. 'Would she like to help us with the party? She could bring her little boy – and her nursemaid as well. The more the merrier.'

'Sarah? I don't know if she'd be able,' Morna was doubtful. 'She's not been well for weeks.'

'I'll call tomorrow to ask her,' Belle said. 'It's high time I visited her.'

What she meant was that it was high time she summoned up the strength to face Sarah, who had succumbed to whatever ailed her the day after Samuel Gilmartin's death. She had fainted, and then gone into a storm of weeping once she was brought round. After that, she had taken to her bed. Walter was deeply worried about her, but Belle had a very good idea as to what lay behind her sister-in-law's collapse. In the bleak days following Samuel's death she had been tormented by the memory of what he had told her during their final confrontation: then gradually she reached the realisation that Sarah, like herself, had been Samuel's victim. They were two helpless flies caught in his web, but now they were free, and the past must be laid to rest. Armed with a new sense of purpose, she walked round to Argyle Road directly after breakfast the next day.

Mrs Forsyth was out of her sickbed, the little maid told her in a hushed voice, but she was still weak, and resting at that moment on the sofa in the parlour.

'Bring tea,' Belle said, sweeping past the open-mouthed girl and into the parlour, where she opened the drawn curtains to let some light in.

'Who – Belle?' Sarah's voice was feeble, her face ashen and her eyes darkly shadowed.

'I've come to invite you to a party at Ruth Durie's, on Christmas Eve.' Belle drew her gloves off and unbuttoned her coat. 'It's a children's party for her pupils. She needs all the help she can get, so I'll be there, and Morna of course, and you must bring little Fraser. It will do him good to be with other children. His nursemaid would be useful too.'

'I couldn't . . . I'm not well enough . . .'

Belle drew a light chair close to the sofa and sat down. 'Sarah, I know that you're mourning for Samuel, and I know all about your – friendship – with him. Not that he was my husband then,' she added swiftly as Sarah's eyes widened and she cringed back against the cushions. 'It was while you were employed by my parents, and was over before you married Walter.' There was no sense in telling this terrified young woman the true extent of her knowledge.

'He told you?' Sarah whispered. 'Are you going to tell Walter?'

'It's none of his business, or mine. I just wanted you to know that I understand how you feel. His sudden death came as a dreadful shock to both of us,' Belle said, her voice steady, 'but I know that he would want us to think now of getting on with our own lives.'

Nellie tapped on the door and brought in the tea tray. When they were alone again Belle poured out two cups

401

of tea and then went to investigate the corner cupboard. 'Good – there's still some of Papa's brandy here.' She poured a little of the bottle's contents into each cup. 'Drink that up, Sarah, it will do you the world of good.'

The young woman took the cup in both hands and sipped cautiously. She grimaced, but sipped again. By the time the cup was half-empty, a little colour had returned to her face.

'You don't hate me, then?'

'Why should I? You knew Samuel at one stage of his life and I knew him at another.' The final stage, as it happened, but Belle had decided that she would not allow herself to dwell on that, ever. 'You must get better, Sarah, for Fraser's sake, and for Walter's. And you must bring wee Fraser to Ruth Durie's house on Christmas Eve. It will do you both good. Ruth has helped me so much through the past weeks.

'There's one thing I'd like to ask you – did Samuel ever tell you anything about his family in Ireland?'

'No, never. I don't think he had any family.'

'I see.' Before the funeral, Belle had searched in vain through Samuel's few possessions for letters that might have told her how to contact the mother and brothers and sisters he had promised that she would meet one day. There had been nothing at all – no family, no background. Samuel had rushed into her life like one of the stiff winds that so often blew from Ireland towards the Ayrshire coast, whipping the Firth into a frenzy of white foam, and now he was gone, leaving nothing behind. It was as though he had never been a part of her world, and perhaps, Belle decided, as she drained her cup and put it back on its saucer, that was for the best.

'You'll come to the party?' she pressed, and when Sarah nodded, said, 'Good. Now I must go to the shop.

'Goodness knows what Wal – I mean, I've left poor Walter to deal with everything.'

She buttoned her coat and picked up her gloves. She was drawing on the second glove when Sarah, her voice stronger already, said, 'Belle? I – I think I'm expecting another child.'

Belle's hands suddenly stopped bustling about each other. She froze for a moment, and then forced herself to turn and smile at her sister-in-law. 'But that's grand news. Does Walter know?'

'It's too soon to be certain. I thought that I would wait.'

'Very wise. He will be pleased, if your suspicions are correct.'

As Belle hurried to Dockhead Street she realised that Sarah's unexpected news meant that the wondering and the jealousy were not quite ready to be laid to rest. She had assumed, from Samuel's drunken ramblings on the night he died, that 'She's weakenin' already', meant that he had not actually seduced his brother-in-law's wife, although his intentions as to the future had been made very plain. But now she wondered . . .

For a moment the click of her boots on the pavement faltered, then they gathered momentum again. All she could hope, for the time being, was that if Sarah was right and another child was on the way, it would emerge from the womb looking even more like Walter than Fraser had.

As the children trooped into the house on the afternoon of the party their eyes rounded and their jaws dropped at the sight of the magnificent Christmas tree in all its glory, with brightly wrapped sweets, gingerbread men, coloured balls and miniatures hanging from its branches.

403

Parcels were piled beneath green branches that smelled of pine forests, and the room had been festooned with chains of coloured paper and wreaths of holly.

It was, as Ruth had predicted, the best party anyone had ever known. There were games in the back garden, an elaborate treasure hunt indoors, more food and drink than even the hungriest and thirstiest child could demolish, and then came the highlight – opening the presents.

Little Fraser Forsyth, who had until then been convinced that he was the only small person in a world of gentle, softly spoken adults, was quite terrified when he found himself confronted by a pack of noisy, excited children. Leez Drummond had to take him into the small parlour, where he sat on her lap and thumped vigorously at the keys of the piano, a pleasure that was not allowed in his own home. Once he had calmed down he was introduced in gentle stages to the party and began to enjoy himself. His mother, among a group of children playing the games she herself had once played and loved, was in her element, helping the smallest children to play Blind Man's Buff and Hunt the Thimble. For the first time in many weeks she was happy.

Morna, too, was enjoying herself, but all the time, even when she was playing the piano for the sing-song before the party ended, her ears strained for the sound of the doorknocker, and Tom's voice. She had memorised the times of trains from Glasgow, and kept glancing at the clock, but the afternoon came to an end without any sign of Tom.

At least, she told herself as she helped to button excited, wriggling children into coats and stuff small hands into knitted mittens, there was Ne'erday. Ruth had said that he always came to Saltcoats for Ne'erday.

When Anna had taken the children home and Sarah,

pink-cheeked, had departed with Leez and Fraser, who clutched a new velveteen ball that tinkled like a bell when rolled along the floor, Morna, Belle and Ruth started washing dishes and gathering up wrapping paper. Then Morna, longing for some fresh air, walked to Caledonia Road with her sister.

'Ruth,' Belle said thoughtfully as they crossed Ardrossan Road, 'is a most interesting person. I admire her passion for justice and the rights of women.'

'Does that mean that you're thinking of joining the suffragette movement?' Morna teased, and was taken aback when her sister said, 'I might.'

'Are you serious? You were horrified when you discovered that I was sharing a house with a suffragette!'

'That was before I got to know her and her friends,' Belle said calmly. 'Who knows what I might decide to do? We're approaching a new year – the perfect time to make changes in one's life. Come in and warm yourself by the fire before you walk back.'

It was dark, and it had started to rain. 'I'd better get home before this gets worse,' Morna said.

Glancing wistfully towards the town as she recrossed Ardrossan Road, her heartbeat speeded up as she saw a man hurrying along the pavement with long, familiar strides. She veered towards him, and as she approached he stopped beneath a street lamp to await her.

'I missed you,' she accused as they met.

'I tried to get away in time for the party, but I couldn't.'

'I'm not talking about the party,' Morna said impatiently, amazed by her own boldness. 'I mean – I've missed you.'

'And I missed you too. It's been a very long autumn.'

'Letters aren't enough.'

'I know. We must talk about this while I'm here,' he

said. 'We must find a solution.' The rain had begun to fall in earnest and he pulled off one glove and ran the ball of his thumb along the top of her cheekbone. She shivered beneath his touch.

'You're getting wet,' Tom said. 'I would shelter you beneath my umbrella, but I must have left it on the train.'

'It doesn't matter.'

'It does to me. I don't want anything to happen to you. I couldn't bear it if something happened to you. Come on,' he picked up the bag he had laid down on the pavement when they met, and put one arm around her shoulders, drawing her close, 'let's get indoors.'

He adapted his long strides to her pace and Morna leaned her body against his as they hurried along the pavement together, beneath rain that sparkled like threads of spun gold as it slanted past the gas lamps.

Bibliography

The *Ardrossan & Saltcoats Herald*, issues from 1909–1910

Burgh of Saltcoats – a Brief History, compiled and published by the Local History Department, Cunninghame District Libraries, Ayrshire, 1985

Burgh of Saltcoats – Quarter Centenary, 1528–1928, published by Arthur Guthrie & Sons Ltd., Ardrossan, Ayrshire, 1928

McSherry, R. & M., *Old Saltcoats*, published by Richard Stenlake, Ochiltree, Ayrshire, 1995

The *Paisley Daily Express*, 30 April 1910 – a report on Mrs Emmeline Pankhurst's visit to Paisley Town Hall

A Sparkle of Salt

Acknowledgements

My thanks to Isabel Harrison, David Mair, Bill Pirie and Jimmy Sinclair, and to the committee and members of the Buckie and District Fishing Heritage Museum for patiently answering my many questions about fishing and fisher-folk.

I also wish to thank Sheila Campbell, chief librarian at Elgin Library, and the staff of Buckie Library, and I am especially indebted to Lorna McAllister MA, who gave me access to her own research into the role of women in North-east Scotland's fishing communities from the 1850s to the 1930s.

I owe the people named above a great debt of gratitude, and I dedicate this book to them.

Lowrie Family Tree

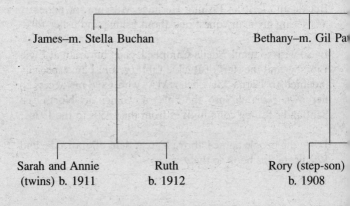

James–m. Stella Buchan

Bethany–m. Gil Pa

Sarah and Annie
(twins) b. 1911

Ruth
b. 1912

Rory (step-son)
b. 1908

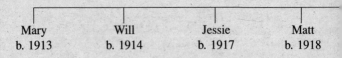

Mary
b. 1913

Will
b. 1914

Jessie
b. 1917

Matt
b. 1918

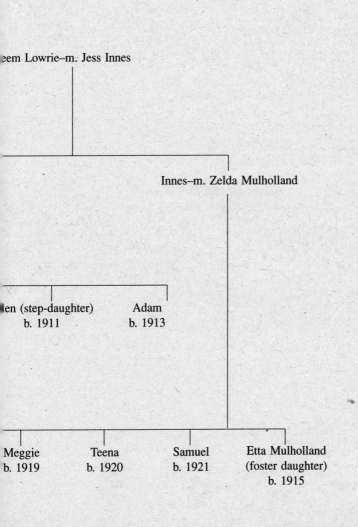

eem Lowrie–m. Jess Innes

Innes–m. Zelda Mulholland

en (step-daughter)   Adam
b. 1911   b. 1913

Meggie   Teena   Samuel   Etta Mulholland
b. 1919   b. 1920   b. 1921   (foster daughter)
                                                          b. 1915

Glossary

afore	before
an'	and
a pretty pass	a fine situation indeed [*sarcastic*]
arles	a binding financial agreement between curers and gutters
atween	between
aye	yes, always
ben the hoose	in the next room
bubblies	fish oil or paraffin lamps
ca'al	cold
cran	a basket used to measure the weight of herring
curer	the owner of a curing station where herring are gutted and packed
farlin	large wooden trough
fin	when
fit	what
gatherings	social events
greeting	welcoming, and also crying or complaining
know fine	know well
hoosie	house
ken	know
loon	boy or man
loupin'	jumping or throbbing

maskin'	letting a pot of tea stand, so that the liquid becomes stronger
Ne'erday	New Year's Day
quine	girl
shot	a fishing boat's catch
sneakit	sneaky, sly
staves	shaped wooden sections from which a barrel is constructed
thole	tolerate, bear
thrawn	difficult, stubborn

1

November 1918

The three Lowrie girls rushed along the street as though their lives depended on it, skirts tangling round their legs, faces red with exertion and arms swinging. Fetching up on the doorstep together, they became a clump of limbs and bodies thumping against the door, each determined to be the first in.

'I got here first!' Ruth shrieked as the twins, some eighteen months older and a full head taller than she was, tried to push her aside.

'No you didnae, it was me,' Annie panted, while Sarah claimed, 'I'm the oldest. I should tell her!' Then the latch gave way and they almost fell into the kitchen.

'Have you lassies got no sense at all?' Stella Lowrie scolded, pulling her daughters apart and setting them on their feet. 'Roarin' down the street like tinkies!'

'He's here, the boat's here,' Ruth gasped. 'He's back!'

'Who's here? What boat?'

'My faither,' Annie yelled.

'Don't be daft, of course he's not here!'

'He is, Mither,' Sarah insisted. 'We saw the *Fidelity* comin' in when we were playin' up the braes.'

'We ran down tae the harbour tae see it,' Ruth gabbled.

'And it's in a terrible mess,' Annie chimed in.

'Wait!' The one word came from their mother's lips like the crack of a whip and the three of them fell silent, the excitement fading as they saw that her brown eyes were huge

1

in a suddenly pale face. 'Wait,' she said again, and then took a deep breath. 'You're sayin' that the *Fidelity*'s comin' intae the harbour now?'

'She's already in,' Ruth told her. 'We went there.'

'You saw your father?'

'He came up the ladder tae the harbour wall and Mr McFarlane was waitin' for him.'

'Who else?' Stella Lowrie demanded to know.

'A whole lot of folk. I wanted tae talk tae my faither but Sarah made me come away.' Ruth glared at her sister, who glared back.

'I should think so too. What would he have thought if he'd seen the three of you lookin' like that? Off tae the wash house this minute and get cleaned up.'

The backyard was reached by a narrow passageway that ran down the side of the house. As the girls scrambled out of the street door Stella hurriedly checked the pots simmering on the stove. There was just enough meat for one more serving, and plenty of soup, but as for the potatoes . . . she started to peel more, tossing them into the pot as quickly as she could. James had written to say that the *Fidelity* – the steam drifter his father and Uncle Albert Lowrie had bought the year that she and James married – was to be decommissioned now that the war was drawing to a close, but he had not said that he would be home so soon.

She threw one final potato into the pot, now filled perilously close to the brim, and put the lid on before casting a quick look around the kitchen to make certain that all was ready for the man of the house. The newly blackleaded range shone, the blue and white patterned plates ranged along the dresser shelves were evenly spaced and the Stafford figurines that had belonged to her own mother were free of even a speck of dust.

She almost went to the mirror hanging on the wall, but stopped herself just in time. Once, knowing that James was on his way home would have been enough to send her rushing to study her reflection, pinching her cheeks to highlight them with colour, smoothing her brown hair, pulling the collar of her blouse straight. But not now. She had been a foolish young lassie in those days; now she was a wife, and a betrayed wife at that.

She could have done with one more winter of freedom, she thought as Ruth scampered back into the kitchen, her small face shining and her hair smoothed down by damp hands.

'Is he here yet?'

'D'ye see him?' her mother asked tartly, and when the child shook her head. 'Then he's not here, is he?'

'I'll go and look for him—' Ruth turned towards the door, almost colliding with her sisters on their way in.

'You'll stay here and mind your manners. Annie, set another place at the head of the table for your father. Sarah, see that there's a basin of water and a bar of soap ready in the wash house,' Stella ordered. 'He'll want a wash before he eats. And take a towel in with ye!' she added as her daughter made for the door again. 'D'ye expect the man tae dry his face on his shirt tail?'

Then she jumped as an ominous hissing rose from the stove, where the overfull pot of potatoes had started to boil over, and ran to tilt the lid and let some steam out.

Down at the harbour James Lowrie had lingered on board the *Fidelity* long after his cousin Jem and the rest of the crew had scaled the narrow iron ladder set into the harbour wall, to be met at the top by their families and friends and borne off to their homes.

They were all delighted to be home again, but James had mixed feelings. In one way, he never wanted to see Buckie again, and yet he knew that he was for ever tied to the place.

He looked about the silent drifter that had been his home for so long. The war and the part that the *Fidelity* had played in it as a minesweeper had kept him fully occupied day in

3

and day out over the past four and a half years. There had never been time to think of anything but the moment, and for James that had been a good thing. Heedless of whether or not he survived, he had taken chances; as a result, the *Fidelity* and her skipper had been mentioned in dispatches. But that meant nothing to him, for as far as he was concerned the real battle was here in Buckie, and always had been.

Time was passing, and he knew that although Stella had not been waiting on the harbour wall to welcome him along with the other wives, someone would have told her, by now, of the *Fidelity*'s arrival. It was time to go. He sighed, and hoisted up the shabby wooden box – his seaman's kist – that had travelled everywhere with him since his first trip at the age of fifteen, just as Jacob McFarlane, who had gone into partnership with him the year before the war started, came down the ladder, moving briskly despite his advancing years.

'Welcome home, lad.' He held out his hand. 'It's been a long time – and they've been hard years, eh?' Then, nodding at the strip of blue painted around the *Fidelity*'s funnel, the mark among fishermen of respect for a lost crewman, 'I see ye're honourin' Charlie.'

James set the kist down and shook Jacob's strong, hard-skinned hand. 'He deserved it. The boat's not been the same without him.' He had grown up alongside his cousins Charlie and Jem; they had gone to the fishing together as lads not long out of school, and Charlie had become the *Fidelity*'s mate when James took over the boat in 1913.

Charlie's love of life and everything in it had made him popular everywhere he went. While on minesweeping duties he had willingly volunteered to go out on another boat when one of its crew fell sick; the boat picked up a mine that exploded as it was being towed clear of the shipping channels, sending the vessel to the bottom immediately, with all hands.

'I'll have tae go and speak tae Uncle Albert about Charlie,' James said.

'He's no' the man he used tae be, I can tell ye that.' Jacob shook his head. 'For all that Albert has by-blows all around the Moray Firth, Charlie was his favourite. He's taken the lad's death hard. Ye think when ye're young that old folk can deal with death easy enough, bein' that bit closer tae it, but losin' folk ye've known all yer life seems tae get harder as ye get older. Look at me – I cannae tell ye how much I miss yer mither, James. I wish ye'd been here tae say goodbye tae her at the end.'

'It wasnae possible,' James said uncomfortably. He had been in Southampton when word of his mother's illness reached him and, had he wished it, he probably could have managed to snatch a few days' leave and travel home to Buckie. But he had decided otherwise.

'She went peaceful, with the rest of us here tae see her off on her final voyage. She's lyin' in the Rathven graveyard now, beside Weem.'

'The way she wanted it – safe in the ground by my faither.' Even after all these years James had to fight to keep the bitterness from his voice. Weem Lowrie, his father, had died at sea and James had wanted to return his body to the deep. Jess Lowrie's insistence on burying her man ashore, where she could tend his grave, had caused a bitter disagreement between mother and son that had never been completely resolved.

Jacob let the younger man's comment pass. 'The poor old *Fidelity*'s a sorry sight, is she no'?'

'She's been through a lot.' James rushed to the defence of his beloved drifter. 'We've scarce been on land these past few years. We did well tae keep her afloat at all, and we'd tae nurse her up along the coast tae here. That's why she was decommissioned early – she's worn out. But all she needs is cleanin' out and some repair work. New deckin', a good coat of paint, give the engine a good scour out and she'll be ready for the next fishin' season.'

'I was thinkin' o' puttin' Jem in as skipper of the *Homefarin*' next season,' Jacob said, naming the boat he had

5

bought to replace the *Fidelity* during the war years, and then, as James looked at him sharply, 'He's ready for it, is he no'?'

'Aye, well ready, but that means that I'd have tae train someone else up as mate.'

Jacob spat over the side into the harbour. 'I bought a bonny drifter from a man in Rosehearty a month or two back. I renamed her the *Jess Lowrie* for yer mother, and got up a crew tae take her tae Lowestoft so's she could start earnin' for us right away. She's younger than the *Fidelity*, and I thought you could take her over next year.'

'I've already got my boat.'

'The *Fidelity*'s gettin' older, though. Time for ye tae move tae somethin' better.'

James felt his hackles rise. 'This drifter's got years in her yet.'

'I'm no' arguin' with ye there, lad, but that's the very reason why we should sell her now. We'd still get a good price for her, and then we can put the money towards buyin' a third boat, or mebbe even have one built at Thomson's yard. This is a good time for consortiums like us,' Jacob said earnestly. 'A lot of men arenae comin' back from the war, God rest them, and some that have got home again are too sore wounded tae go back tae sea. Boats are goin' at good prices. This could be our chance tae start buildin' up a smart fleet, and I've got it in mind tae set the *Jess Lowrie* at the head of it. But this isnae the time for such talk,' he went on before James had the chance to argue further, 'for ye'll be wantin' tae see Stella and the bairns, after bein' away for all these years.'

James seethed as he walked home from the harbour. The *Fidelity* was the Lowrie family boat, and although he himself had not put a penny towards the cost of buying her, he had sacrificed far more than money. In the days of sail, a fisherman and his sons or his brothers could raise the price of a sailed herring boat between them, mortgaging their homes to borrow the initial outlay and repaying the bank from their labours, but the high cost of steam drifters had put them beyond the means of many men.

When the *Fidelity* came on the market Weem Lowrie and his brother Albert, hungry for one of the new, fast steam drifters, had raised as much money as they could, but even with a loan from the bank it had not been enough. Then Weem thought of a fellow Buckie fisherman, Mowser Buchan, who was no longer fit enough to run his sailed boat. Mowser, a widower with an unmarried daughter, Stella, was in search of a lusty son-in-law who could keep him in his old age and ensure Stella's future, while Weem had a son of marriageable age. Through marriage to Stella Buchan, James had fallen heir to Mowser's herring boat, and the proceeds from its sale had made up the rest of the money needed to buy the *Fidelity*.

He had paid a high price for the drifter, James thought as he reached the little fisherman's cottage that had once belonged to Mowser, and he was not going to see her sold on, not after all he and the boat had been through.

To his surprise, the cottage was quiet and still, with none of the sounds that passers-by would normally hear, such as children's voices from behind the small windows, or the clatter of pots as the next meal was prepared. Perplexed, James lowered his bag and his kist to the ground and rattled the latch. The door was locked, and when he rapped on it there was no reply. He stepped back in order to look up at the chimney; it was without the usual welcome wisp of smoke curling from the lit fire in the range below.

'Fit are ye daein' at this end o' the toon, James Lowrie?' a voice shrilled, and he turned to see their elderly neighbour peering from her own door.

'I'm back home, and home tae a closed door. D'ye know where Stella's off tae?'

The woman stared, and then gave a cackle of laughter. 'Surely ye ken that Stella and the quinies have moved intae yer mither's wee hoosie down in Buckpool? In the Main Street?'

'Oh aye, of course.' James felt his face redden. 'I forgot.'

'Bein' away frae this place has addled yer brain,' the woman said. 'Best get over there, lad. She'll be wearyin' for a sight o' ye.' Then, as he picked up his bag and kist and went past her, she laid a hand on his arm. 'I'm sorry, my loon, about yer mither. Jess was a fine woman.'

'Aye,' James agreed, and made his escape towards the old fishing village of Buckpool, now a part of Buckie.

As he walked along the shore road to the house where he had been born and raised, the house his wife now presided over in place of his mother, he felt his feet beginning to drag.

Stella's heart jumped into her dry mouth when the door latch rattled, but she stayed where she was, facing the stove and with her back to the kitchen. Only when her husband said awkwardly, 'Aye, Stella lass,' did she tap the wooden ladle on the edge of the big cast-iron pot, lay it aside carefully, and turn to face him, wiping her hands on her apron.

'So you're home.'

'We came intae harbour a wee while back.'

He was much the same as before, she saw in her first quick glance, still well built and broad-shouldered. Then as he pulled his cap off she saw that his hair had been cropped. The black curls that had once framed his square, tanned face had gone, and silver glittered about his temples.

'Ye'll be ready for some food.' Stella ran the back of one wrist over her face, which was flushed with the heat from the stove. 'It'll not be long. Sarah, Annie, Ruth!' she rounded on her daughters, who were clumped together in a corner, eyeing the newcomer. 'Where are your manners? Welcome your faither home.'

The twins murmured a shy greeting but Ruth went round the table to stand before him. 'I'd 've come tae the boat tae meet you but they wouldnae let me.' A backward jerk of her head towards her sisters sent a shock of light-brown curly hair swinging round a strong-featured face. This one had taken after him, James realised, while her sisters – glancing at the twins, he saw Stella in their round faces; Stella as she had been when they married, soft and pretty with serene eyes and a shy, hopeful smile. Now her cheeks were sunken and her brown eyes harder.

'Is this ye back from the war for good?' Ruth broke into his thoughts.

'Eh? Oh, aye, it is.'

'So it's over, then? Did ye beat the Kaiser?'

Stella turned to reprimand the child for her impertinence, but held her tongue when she saw that her husband's normally solemn face had been startled into a grin.

'Aye, nearly, though I had tae have some help.' James cleared his throat, searching for something to say to his three daughters, and finally ventured, 'Ye've all grown since I last saw ye.'

'That's what bairns do.'

'Ruth!' Stella snapped, while Sarah and Annie, clutching each other's hands, gasped at their sister's impertinence.

'I'm just sayin' the truth. I'm six,' Ruth informed her father. 'Not long since, but I'm tall for my age.'

'And cheeky for your age, too, ye wee lummock,' Stella said. 'There's soap and a towel ready for ye out in the wash house, James.'

'Aye. I'll just—' He nodded at the bag and the kist he had placed on the floor.

'Put them ben the house,' she said, adding as he went through to the room where his parents had once slept, 'There's space for your things in the wardrobe, and I kept the top two drawers of the cupboard empty for ye.'

'I went tae the old house first, and found it locked,' James said, when he was back in the kitchen. 'One of the neighbour-women told me ye were bidin' here now.'

'We've been here these six months past. I told ye about it

9

in a letter.' Stella didn't look at him, but he could hear the hurt in her voice.

'Aye, aye, of course ye did. I was so busy thinkin' of bein' back in Buckie that I let my feet take me tae the usual house.' It was a lame excuse, and he suspected that she knew it. He was not much of a reader or a writer, and her letters had been hurriedly scanned and then discarded, the memory of them leaving his mind as the paper fell from his fingers. His own letters consisted of brief reports that he and the rest of the crew were well and busy. Neither of them, throughout the past years, had written any words of affection, or even of comfort.

'I thought that since your mother had left the house to you as the oldest son, you'd want your family tae live here,' Stella said, then, 'The soup's ready. Ye'd best get washed.'

2

When James returned to the kitchen, his hair wet and his skin tingling from the cold water and the pummelling it had received from the rough towel, Ruth stabbed a small finger at the chair at one end of the table. 'That's where you sit. Mither says that's your chair and we never get tae climb on it, even though you havenae been bidin' here for a long time.'

They ate in silence, and when the meal was over James pushed his chair away and patted his stomach with both hands. 'That was good.'

'I'm glad ye enjoyed it,' Stella said formally, as though he was a guest. 'Lassies—'

'I'd best go and see my Uncle Albert,' James said as the three girls rose obediently to clear the table. 'He'll want tae know all about Charlie.'

'Don't stay away for long. Folk'll be comin' by tae see ye and hear about what's been happenin',' Stella said, and then, when he groaned, 'I know ye were never one tae enjoy a gatherin', James, but ye've been away for a long time and it's only natural for the neighbours tae want tae pay their respects.'

'Aye, I suppose so.' He pushed his chair back. 'I'll try not tae be too long.' There was no sense in antagonising the woman on his first day home, he thought as he went out into the street.

His father's brother, Albert Lowrie, was a confirmed bachelor who had fathered a large brood of children on a number of women up and down the coast of the Moray Firth, cheerfully acknowledging all of them. Charlie and Jem were both his sons, but Charlie, the older of the two by only a few months, had always been his favourite. When the *Fidelity* and her crew left Buckie just after the outbreak of war Albert had been a sturdy, active man; now he was a ghost of his former self, grey and silent, huddled in a big wing chair and looking as though he had somehow collapsed in on himself. Like a canvas bag that had been emptied and tossed into a corner, James thought, sitting opposite his uncle, trying desperately to think of words of comfort and knowing that none of them would help Albert.

'Jem's already been in tae see me.' The old man's voice was feeble, as though he spoke from a long way away.

'He's my mate now, in place of . . . he's a grand lad, Jem.'

'Aye, but Charlie was the one most like me. Can ye think of anythin' else tae tell me about Charlie?' Albert begged, hungry for memories to hold close in his heart.

James returned to Main Street, worn out by the old man's misery, to find the house full of neighbours with more filing in every few minutes, the womenfolk bearing plates and dishes and jugs to ensure a steady supply of food and drink for all the guests. The men were eager to hear about the *Fidelity*'s time down south on active war service, and James, never a great talker, was soon having to clear his throat again and again as his voice began to grow husky. It was a relief to him when the talk became more general.

Although there was an air of merriment about the gathering, there was sadness too. Hundreds of young men had, like James, gone from the Moray Firth to fight for their king and country, and many would never again return to their homeland. As the evening wore on their names were listed, names familiar to James – coopers and curers, fishermen and boatbuilders, carters and farm workers – all lost for ever.

As though the war was not bad enough, the Asiatic influenza that had begun to sweep across Europe as hostilities drew to an end had decimated those at home as well as those serving their country. Hundreds of the young servicemen who had miraculously survived the fighting succumbed instead to the insidious disease, while others returned home to find that parents, siblings, sweethearts or friends had sickened and died. Sometimes whole families were taken by the influenza, leaving empty, cold, dark and silent houses that had once been bustling warm homes. It was, the folk said, like the old Black Death they had learned about at the school.

When at last the well-wishers had all returned to their own homes and the girls were in bed in the upper room, James picked up a newspaper, flicking through its pages and glancing at Stella over the top of it as she put the kitchen to rights.

Her once comfortably rounded body was now slim, though still womanly, he noticed. The lamplight picked out grey strands amid the brown hair drawn loosely back into a knot at the nape of her neck, and at one point when she turned and lifted her head suddenly, as though listening for some noise from the attic bedroom above, he saw that her mouth, which had always been swift to tremble when she was upset, or quiver into a smile when she was happy, had firmed and there were new lines between her dark eyes. But then, the war had made a difference to them all.

Apparently satisfied that their daughters were asleep upstairs, and none of them needed her attention, she bent to pick something up from the floor, her breasts pushing against the front of her blouse. Recalling the feel of her soft body against his, James felt a sudden surge of desire and anticipation. He laid the paper down and cleared his throat.

'I'll just go out by and have a smoke before I go tae my bed.'

Outside, he leaned against the house wall, the smoke from his pipe twisting up from the bowl to lose itself in

13

the darkness, and thought about Stella. He had not been a good husband to her, he knew that. From the very beginning he had resented being tied down to a loveless marriage. It had never occurred to him to wonder how Stella felt about their union, and if she was content. All he knew, as time went on and their three daughters arrived, each birth dashing his hopes of a son, was that Stella – gentle, biddable, anxious-to-please Stella – was not enough for him and never would be. He needed more, and he had found it where he should never have looked. And Stella had found out.

He gave a soft groan at the memory of those dark days. In a way the Great War had been a blessing because it took him away from Buckie, away from sinful temptation and from Stella's silent condemnation. But now, five years on from those hot-headed, hot-blooded days, James Lowrie watched the smoke from his pipe swirl and drift and disappear into the night, and wondered if he and his wife could make another beginning.

Part of his irritation with her had lain in her failure to produce the sons he wanted; laddies to be taken to the fishing and taught the ways of the sea and of the silver darlings that came each year in their huge shoals, and to take over when James finally became too old to haul in a net heavy with the dancing, shimmering herring.

Stella had lost two children in the six years since Ruth's birth, one early in her pregnancy and the other stillborn in the week war was declared. The second child had been the boy that they both longed for. Stella, her eyes sunk in an ashen face, had scarcely risen from her bed when James took the *Fidelity* to war.

But they were both still young, and fit, James thought now. There was time yet for them to produce a laddie, or mebbe two.

Boots clattered on cobbles and a neighbour went by on his way home. 'Aye, James,' he said cheerily. 'It's a ca'al night. Winter's comin'.'

'Aye,' James agreed, and knocked his pipe out against the house wall.

Stella was already in bed when he went back into the house, lying on her side, her eyes closed and her hair in a long plait that lay along the curve of her back.

James was not entirely comfortable about undressing in the room his parents had shared. The big chest of drawers and the bed had been there for as long as he could remember, though Stella had brought two chairs, a plain wooden upright and a low nursing chair, from her father's house. He eyed the nursing chair, recalling her sitting in it, years back, head bent over the baby cradled in her arms. He remembered the easy, natural way she drew her blouse aside, baring a breast white as the milk that made it even heavier than normal, and the beautiful, delicate tracery of blue veins against her alabaster skin.

She did not stir when he blew out the lamp and slipped into bed beside her. For a moment he lay still, listening to her even breathing, then he laid a tentative hand on her shoulder. The muscles tensed beneath his fingers, and her breathing stopped and then began again, slow and steady and controlled.

James took his hand away and turned over so that they lay back to back. It was a long time before either of them slept.

James Lowrie strode down to the harbour on the following morning, his studded boots striking sparks from the cobblestones. He was his father's son – never happy unless he was free of the land and the people on it, and besides, he had been away from the fishing for too long. After years of searching the seas for man-made, death-dealing mines he yearned to get back to his own trade.

The older men who hung about the harbour, clinging to memories of their own fishing days, tried to draw him into their talk, but he finally managed to escape them and get along to where the *Fidelity* awaited him.

For a few minutes he stood on the stone wall above her, trying to see her through Jacob's eyes. In the watery morning sunlight the drifter was a sorry sight, but she could be put to rights. The first thing to be done was an inventory of all the work that was needed.

James skimmed down the ladder, his booted feet landing on the deck with a satisfying thud, and then made for the rope locker immediately below the forrard deck. Normally it was used to house the coiled messenger warp that carried the fishing nets, but over the war years it had become a glory hole, where all sorts of bits and pieces had been tossed out of the way.

As he opened the double doors, not much larger than window shutters, he heard a skittering sound from the dark, smelly interior. James swore roundly, snatching at a bucket lying close to the door; he'd have no rats on *his* boat!

'Get out of it,' he roared, banging the bucket against the decking by the door. 'Filthy stinking vermin!' Then, as there was no reaction, not even the scampering and panic-stricken squeaking he had expected, he threw the bucket into the darkness of the locker.

'Ow!'

'What the—? Come out of there!' When there was no reply, James, almost bent double in his attempt to peer into the thick darkness, dropped to his knees and reached with a long arm. His fingers encountered cloth; reaching further, they closed round the material and the flesh and bone it covered.

'Ow-ow-OW!' came the protests as his captive was pulled willy-nilly through the clutter of boxes, buckets, ropes and rubbish. Then he was out in the open, dishevelled and dirty, blinking up at James.

'What are you doin' on my boat?'

'Just lookin',' the small boy said defensively.

'Aye, an' just takin' too, I've no doubt. Turn yer pockets out!'

'I will not! I never took anythin' from yer smelly old boat!'

The lad's impertinence took James aback. His grip slackened, and the child, taking advantage of it, wriggled like an eel and would have been off if James hadn't managed to tighten his hold just in time. Enraged, the little boy kicked out and one of his sturdy boots delivered a painful crack on the man's shin. Without stopping to think, James hit back, an open-handed slap that rang through the air as it landed on the side of the boy's head.

'Ow!' he yelled again. His knees sagged, and James had to catch him with both hands to keep him upright. For a moment the boy drooped towards him, then he rallied and glared up at his captor, blinking back sudden tears of pain and shock.

'You hit me!'

'And I'll hit ye again if I get any more of yer insolence, so mind that, my loon! You need tae be taught a lesson and if yer faither doesnae see tae it, then I will. Where d'ye come from?'

'Buckie, the same as you.' Although one ear was scarlet from the blow, the child had not lost his bravado.

'I mean, where d'ye live?'

The boy hesitated, biting his lip, and then, as James shook him, he blurted out, 'Cliff Terrace.'

'Cliff Terrace? And what are ye creepin' around my boat for, if it's not for mischief?'

'I just wanted tae see it.'

'Ye'll not see much in there.' James jerked his head towards the black hole that was the rope locker. 'What's yer name? Yer name, lad,' he repeated with another shake as the boy remained silent, his grey eyes flickering from side to side as though in search of a suitable answer. 'And I want the truth, mind. I can find out easy enough if ye try tae lie tae me.'

The child gave a heavy sigh, and then said reluctantly, 'Adam Pate.'

'Pate?' All at once, James felt the blood drain out of him, from his skull pan to the soles of his feet. He would not have been surprised to find it puddling on the deck around his boots. 'Gil Pate's boy?'

'Aye. An' when my faither hears that you hit me he'll come after ye,' the child stormed. 'He's a big man, an' he'll—'

'How old are ye?' James asked hoarsely.

'Four years past.'

Aye, that would be about right, James thought, releasing the boy, who rubbed at his sore arm.

'You're my Uncle James home from the wars, are ye no'?' he asked. 'I just wanted tae see the boat. It's a sorry lookin' thing.'

'Aye, well, so are you right now, and the *Fidelity*'s been through a lot more than you have. Come on.' James made for the ladder leading to the harbour. 'Up you go. I'm takin' you home.'

'I can go home by mysel'. I came down here by mysel'.'

'I'm takin' you home,' James said again, and scaled the ladder, leaving the lad to scuffle up after him.

They walked up the hill to Cliff Terrace in silence, James easing back on his usual stride to allow the boy to keep up, and Adam too busy running alongside to find the breath to talk. As they reached the terrace James stopped, swung the child round, but with a gentler grip than before, and squatted so that they were eye to eye.

'Ye'd best get tidied up afore yer mother sees ye,' he said. By good fortune, Stella had tucked a clean handkerchief into his pocket before he left the house; he himself had no time for such fripperies, but now he was glad of the snowy square of material. He held it out to Adam, as he had seen Stella doing with his own children, and after the little boy automatically spat on it James carefully wiped the worst of the rope-locker grime off his face before running his fingers through the dark hair, then tugging at the lad's jacket. Adam squirmed, little knowing that the attention he was receiving had nothing to do with making him more presentable – it was done solely in order to allow James to study him and to touch him.

The grey eyes, he now realised, were just like his father's and his sister's – and his own, if it came to that. The child had a tumble of dark hair; again, the same colouring as James and his own father Weem before him. His face was square-chinned and pleasing to the eye, and his sturdy little body held itself well.

'Are ye done now?' Adam finally asked, a pleading note in his voice, and when James nodded and straightened, stuffing the handkerchief into his pocket, the lad grinned his relief and turned to point at the row of smart two-storey houses built not long before on the hill above the harbour, facing out to sea. 'It's that house over there,' he said, and set off at a trot.

James stayed where he was, watching him.

'What d'ye mean, lassie – gone?' Bethany Pate asked from the stove, where she was ladling porridge from a large pot.

'He's no' in his bed, and nowhere tae be seen in the house,' the maidservant said. 'That sort of gone.'

'Mind your impudence. He'll be in the back yard.'

'I've looked,' Leezie snapped back at her employer.

'Rory, was Adam still in his bed when you came down?' Bethany appealed to her stepson, waiting patiently at the table for his breakfast.

'He was up before me. I thought he was down here with you, or out in the back yard.' Rory wanted no part of the responsibility for his young brother. It was enough to have to share a bedroom with Adam, who never seemed to be at rest, even when he was sleeping.

'Are his clothes gone or is he still in his nightshirt?'

'I didnae see his clothes but they might have been in the room.'

'Leezie, go and see – and look round the rest of the house while you're at it,' Bethany ordered.

'I thought I heard the front door closing when I was getting dressed,' Ellen offered, taking two plates of porridge from the stove to the table, where she put one in front of her brother and sat down to eat the other.

'And you never thought to say?'

'Why would I?' seven-year-old Ellen asked. 'I thought it might be you goin' out early, or my faither home from Yarm'th.'

'He's not expected in as early as— The cooperage,' Bethany suddenly realised. 'That's where the wee imp of Satan's gone. Wait till I get my hands on him!' She stopped in the middle of ladling out her own porridge and hurried into the hall, while Rory and Ellen, used to their young half-brother setting off such alarms, rolled their eyes at each other and went on eating.

'Leezie!' Bethany shouted up the carpeted staircase. 'Is there any sign of him yet?'

The maid appeared at the top of the stairs. 'No there's not, but he's got himself dressed all right.'

'He'll have gone down to the cooperage.' Bethany began to unfasten her apron. 'See that Rory and Ellen get off to the school on time, lassie, and have your own breakfast. I'm away to the harbour to fetch Master Adam and give him the rough edge of my tongue!'

Snatching her jacket from the hallstand, she hurried out, pushing her arms into the jacket sleeves as she went. The first time Adam had found his way to the cooperage alone, when he was only three, he had not been noticed until one of the men caught him trying to peer over the edge of a vat of boiling water. There were so many dangers for a wee laddie in that place – the fires needed to bring the water to boiling point so that the steam could be used to soften the staves, the scalding water itself, the hammers – so many things to harm a small boy with an unquenchable curiosity and no fear at all.

She reached the gate and had gone through it to the road when she saw her son marching towards her.

'Adam? Adam Pate, ye wee imp!' She flew at him,

crouching down before him and taking his shoulders in her two hands so that she could study him and make sure that he was safe and unharmed. 'Where have you been?'

He shrugged himself free. 'I went tae see my uncle's boat.'

'Your uncle?' for a moment Bethany thought that he was talking of Gil's brother Nathan or her own brother, Innes, but neither man owned a boat.

Then, as Adam went on, 'He's come back with me,' and turned to point, she looked up to see her older brother standing several paces away, watching the two of them.

Worry and relief vanished, to be replaced by a strange sensation, as though time itself had stopped. Bethany got to her feet slowly, struggling to push her body upright through air that had become almost solid. She reached for Adam's shoulder, keeping him near to her, keeping him safe.

'James,' she said, and the word, dropping from her numbed lips, broke the spell.

'Ye look as if ye'd seen a ghost, Bethany.' He took a step or two towards her. 'Did ye not know I was back?'

'The bairns said they'd seen the *Fidelity* coming in yesterday,' she acknowledged, 'but . . .' She looked down at the child at her side and then back at James, who had pulled his cap off. Clutching it in one hand, he indicated Adam with the other.

'I – I found the wee lad down at the harbour.'

'I wanted to see what the boat looked like,' Adam prattled cheerfully. 'This is my Uncle James, home from the war.'

'I know who it is.' Bethany tore her attention away from her brother to her son. 'You're a bad laddie! I've a good mind to give you a whipping.'

'No,' James said swiftly, and then, as she glared at him he added lamely, 'He meant no harm. He was just curious tae see the *Fidelity*.'

'It's all right,' Adam assured him. 'She'd not really whip me. Anyway, my faither's comin' back today and he wouldnae let her.'

'Don't you be so sure of that, my loon,' Bethany spun him round to face the gate and then gave him a slight push. 'Go to the house at once and tell Leezie to get you cleaned up then give you your breakfast.'

'Come on in,' Adam invited James.

'He's too busy. Go on now before I change my mind about that whipping!'

3

'He only wanted tae see the boat,' James protested as the little boy went off.

'He knows that he's not supposed to go out of the house without permission.'

'Ach, he's a laddie, and laddies arenae good at keepin' tae the rules.'

'You're as soft as Gil is,' she said scathingly.

'It's been a long time, Bethany.' His eyes, grey like her own, and like Adam's, travelled over her face.

'Only four years.'

'But they've been long, long years.' He looked beyond her as he spoke, his eyes intent. Bethany turned to see Adam slapping the palms of both hands on the door panels. When Leezie answered the summons he pushed by her knees and disappeared into the house.

'That's a fine bairn ye've got there, Bethany,' James said, and she swung back to face him again.

'Gil's right proud of him.'

'Any man would be proud tae call that wee loon his son.'

Her hands clenched by her sides. 'Why have you come here, James?'

'I told ye, I found the boy on the boat and brought him back tae ye.' He studied the row of handsome houses. 'Ye've done well for yersel'.'

'Gil's a good provider.'

'Aye – good at packin' and sellin' the fish that other men catch,' James said quietly. 'Did A— Did the boy say that he's comin' home today?'

'Later, from Yarm'th.'

'I'll see him then.'

'What d'you want to see Gil for?' she asked sharply.

'Ye neednae concern yerself. I'm not out tae cause trouble.'

'If you mean that, you'll keep away from this house, and from Adam. He's none of your business.'

'Are ye certain o' that, Bethany?' He studied her, his head tilted to one side, his eyes searching hers.

'Of course I'm certain. I'm his mother.'

'When I saw him down there on my boat just now—'

'That's enough, James!'

'You weren't always so cold towards me, Bethany,' he said, and colour rose up beneath the smooth skin of her face.

'We all make mistakes we regret,' she said, and turned back to the house, her erect back daring him to follow. As he hesitated, the door burst open and two older children erupted down the path and out of the gate.

'Uncle James?' The boy came rushing towards James, grinning, with his sister just behind him. 'It's me, Rory.'

'We saw the boat comin' in yesterday when we were all playin' on the braes,' the girl chimed in. Her name was Ellen, James remembered, then realised guiltily that he had identified his sister's stepdaughter more easily than his own daughters.

'I knew right away that it was the *Fidelity*,' Rory said proudly.

'Did ye?'

'Off you go, the pair of you, or you'll be late for the school,' Bethany snapped, and as they hurried off with a final grin at their uncle, she added, 'And if you'll excuse me, James, I've got a house to see to.'

As Bethany went into the house Adam shot out of the kitchen like a cork from a bottle. 'Is my Uncle James not with you? I wanted tae talk tae him!'

'He's too busy to be bothered with wee loons like you,' Bethany retorted. 'Especially loons that run out of the house and give their mothers a fright. You deserve a good skelp!'

'But I came back. I always come back.'

For now you come back, Bethany thought, her very bones melting with love for her only child; but the day would come when her most precious possession would go out into the world to make his own way, and not return to her. She picked him up and carried him to the kitchen, where the maid was washing the dishes.

'Keep him close by you, Leezie,' she said, and went into the front parlour to peer out from behind the snowy lace curtains hung over the bay window to ensure privacy for the inmates of the house. At the other side of the road the ground dropped down to the harbour below, allowing a good view of the Moray Firth, stretching to the far horizon.

From the side window she could just see James disappearing down the road. Almost at once he went beyond her sight, and she gave a small, soundless sigh, then turned to face the room.

Until he and his brother Nathan, a fish curer, had gone into partnership with Jacob McFarlane, Gil had been content enough to live in a small house in the Catbow, a district of Buckie. But the fortune Jacob had amassed during years spent travelling the world meant that the Pate businesses were able to expand, and it was then that Gil became ambitious. The need for food production during the war had been lucrative for both brothers, and had enabled Gil to buy and furnish the fine house Bethany now stood in.

The drawing room, with its carpets and its large, comfortable chairs and gleaming furniture, reflected its owner's success admirably. Tall vases the height of four-year-old Adam flanked the fireplace with its polished fire irons, and carefully selected ornaments were displayed on the sideboard and on the mantelshelf, where they stood on either side of a handsome clock in the shape of a pillared temple.

It was a far cry from the cottage Bethany and her two brothers had been raised in, and although she had been mistress of the place for the past four years she had never felt at home there, for she was still a fisherman's daughter to the tips of her fingers.

She smiled slightly as she heard a faint peal of childish laughter from the kitchen, then bit her lip. She was more severe with Adam than she had ever been with Rory and Ellen, her stepchildren, and that troubled Gil at times. But Bethany knew that it was nothing more than a defence against the passionate, overprotective love she had felt for the child from the moment of his birth. She would kill, if need be, to keep him safe from harm. Often she lay awake at night, fearful of some harm coming to him.

And now, with the *Fidelity* lying down in the harbour, she was doubly afraid for her son, and uncertain of her own ability to safeguard him.

She turned back to the window and stared out over the white-flecked sea, wishing that James had never come back to Buckie.

James went straight from the confrontation with his sister to the harbour, where he dropped down on to the *Fidelity*'s deck and then walked up into the bows, staring down at the smooth dark harbour water below. It had been a difficult home-coming, and now there was the lad, Adam, to reckon with. Recalling the child's bonny wee face and his eagerness to see the drifter, James wished that he could have the chance to spend some time with him. But he knew that Bethany would never allow it.

'Welcome home, James.'

He spun round and stared at the tall, lanky man standing on the harbour wall above. 'Innes?' he asked uncertainly.

'Aye, it's me right enough. Can I come aboard?'

'Surely.' James watched as his younger brother descended the ladder from the harbour wall slowly and carefully, making sure of each handhold and feeling carefully for every rung with his foot before trusting his weight to it. Finally Innes put a foot on the gunwale, hesitated, then just as James started forward to help, he managed the final drop away from the ladder and down on to the deck.

'Welcome home,' he said again, holding out a hand. He had aged more than the four or five years since they had last seen each other. Silver streaks glittered in his thick black hair, and his dark eyes – their mother's eyes – were sunk into their sockets. Innes had always been thinner than James, but now he looked as if a strong gale might blow him away. Even so, his grip was firm.

'Are ye well? Stella told me in a letter that—' James stopped, unsure of how to put it.

'That I was invalided out because the mustard gas went for my lungs.' His brother completed the sentence for him. 'I'm fine.' He thumped his own chest lightly. 'I'll always be damaged, but it doesnae trouble me overmuch.'

'Ye're back workin' at Webster's garage, then?'

'I'm at Thomson's boatyard now. I earn more there, and with the bairns comin' along sae fast we needed more money.'

'How many bairns d'ye have?'

Pride shone from Innes's face. 'There's Mary and Will and Jessie, and wee Matthew's the youngest. And there's another arrivin' at the turn of the year.'

'Jessie. She'll have been named for our mother?'

'Aye, she was born just months afore Mither died. She was right proud tae have her name passed on tae the wee one. Will was named for our father – and Zelda's father too, though she'll not admit to that, with him bein' such a thrawn old bugger,' said Innes, who had been beaten black and blue by Zelda's enraged father when he discovered that she was pregnant with no wedding ring on her finger. 'We've got a wee hoosie in Gordon Street. Zelda would be pleased tae see ye there, James, and so would Aunt Meg.'

'Aunt Meg's bidin' with you and Zelda?'

'The old soul's not fit tae bide on her own now, and she's

good company for Zelda,' said Innes. Then, studying the faded paintwork and the decking, gouged and splintered in places, 'You've had a longer war than I had – you and the *Fidelity*.'

'It wasnae an easy time,' James acknowledged.

'The whole town misses Charlie. He was a friend tae everyone – specially the lassies.'

'Aye.' For a fleeting moment the brothers exchanged faint smiles, then James said, 'I keep expectin' tae see him everywhere I go on this boat.'

A brief silence fell between them before Innes asked, 'How's the engine?'

'As good as ever it was.'

'I'll just have a wee look at it since I'm here.' Innes made for the galley, where an inner companionway led to the engine room.

Years before, James recalled as he followed his brother down into the bowels of the drifter, Innes had had such a fear of the sea, and of anything to do with the sea, that it had been a struggle to get him to look at the engines. James had thought Innes a coward, but the long, hard war years had taught him that bravery was not always obvious. By forcing himself on to the boat in those days Innes had shown courage. He had demonstrated it again when he held to his determination to marry Zelda despite being half-killed by her father, and yet again on the day he had faced up to James on the *Fidelity*'s spray-soaked, heaving deck.

That confrontation was not a memory that James enjoyed, for Innes had been the victor, and the memory of the utter contempt in his look that day still made James wince.

'They'll do,' Innes finally pronounced.

'Of course they will. The drifter herself'll be finished afore the engines give out.'

Innes's teeth flashed white in the gloom as he grinned. 'Ye're right there,' he said, and then wiped a hand across his brow. 'Let's get out of here and catch a breath of air. This boat still has the stink of fish about it.'

'It's been years since she was at the fishin',' James argued as his brother pushed past him. 'There's no smell of fish tae her now.'

'There is,' Innes told him, and began to climb. His progress became slower as he went up, and once back on deck he leaned his shoulder against the engine cowling, gasping, hands on his knees, head hanging and his eyes closed.

'Are you all right?' James asked, alarmed, and his brother nodded, flapping a hand as though trying to wave the questions away.

'Leave me . . . for a minute . . .' His voice was a low, painful wheeze.

It hurt to watch him struggle to draw air into his damaged lungs and not to be able to help. James took him at his word and went into the wheelhouse, where he loitered until, to his relief, he finally saw Innes straighten up and wipe his mouth with a handkerchief.

'I just need time tae catch my breath when I've been too active,' he said in a matter-of-fact voice when James joined him. 'Ye'll get used tae it, the same as I've had tae.'

'It takes a wee bit of gettin' used tae.'

Innes made as if to wipe the worst of the oil and grime from his hands with the handkerchief, thought the better of it, put the handkerchief carefully into one pocket and took a rag from another. 'The mustard gas made a right mess of my lungs,' he explained as he cleaned oil from his fingers. 'For a while I'd not have given a penny for my chances, but Zelda told me straight that she wasnae goin' tae be a widow sae young. She's a grand lass, is Zelda. She and Mither nursed me back tae health atween them.' Then, straightening to his full height, 'So when are ye goin' tae start puttin' this boat tae rights?'

'Jacob wants tae sell her. He's got a new boat,' James said, 'and he wants me tae skipper her.'

Innes nodded. 'That would be the *Jess Lowrie*. She's a fine wee drifter, a good few years younger than this one. But you're surely not goin' tae let the *Fidelity* go, are ye? I may not be a fisherman,' Innes went on as James shot a startled glance at him, 'but I know what this drifter meant to our faither and what it means tae you.'

'That doesnae seem tae mean anythin' tae Jacob, though.'

'Why should it? This is the Lowrie boat, James, and Jacob McFarlane isnae a Lowrie, he's a businessman. Granted, he's made sure he got his feet well and truly below the Lowrie table,' Innes said, 'and he started that by buyin' a big share in the *Fidelity*.'

'I don't see what ye're gettin' at.'

'Jacob didnae come back tae Buckie tae set up in business with you and Gil and Nathan. He came back tae marry our mither. The man told me about it himsel', just after she died. He was in a terrible state, poor soul, he had tae talk tae someone,' Innes recollected, pity in his voice. 'He grew up next door tae her and he never wanted anyone else but her. Only she chose our faither and Jacob went away then, for he couldnae bear tae see the two of them together. When he heard that she was a widow woman he came back and tried tae get her tae take him as husband, but she'd no thought of marryin' again. So, since he couldnae wed intae the Lowrie family, he used the money he'd made in his travels tae buy his way in.'

'Jacob McFarlane told you all that?'

'Not word for word, ye understand, but enough so's I could work it out for mysel'. I don't think he realised just how much he did tell me. So there he was, with the biggest share in Weem Lowrie's boat, Weem's son tae catch the fish, Weem's son-in-law tae pickle them and Nathan Pate tae kipper them. A nice wee arrangement.'

'An' what about you?'

Innes grinned. 'Mind that bonny motorcar he bought when he first came back tae Buckie? I'd a grand time drivin' him about in it and lookin' after it for him. Oh, it was a bonny motor, James! I was still bidin' with Mither then, so Jacob was anxious tae make friends with me. He even offered tae buy a garage for me when I wed Zelda, but I refused him, for I wanted tae make my own way in life.'

'So I was the fool that let him dae what he wanted with me, is that it?'

'No fool, for Jacob was your only chance tae get command of the *Fidelity*. But now that he's built up a bonny business here he's got no need of her, can ye not see that? This was Weem Lowrie's boat, and to my way of thinkin', Jacob's happy tae replace it with a boat he bought himself – and renamed the *Jess Lowrie*.'

James stared at his younger brother, marvelling at the man's shrewd mind and wondering why he had never noticed the way of things himself. Then he turned and looked along the length of the drifter.

'You and Bethany have shares in her,' he said thoughtfully. 'Our mither had, too, though I don't know who has her shares now.'

'She left them tae me,' Innes said.

'You could help me tae talk Jacob round.'

Innes shook his head. 'For one thing, nob'dy can change Jacob's mind once it's set on somethin'. If you want tae keep the boat ye'll have tae find a way tae buy Jacob out.'

'Buy him out? But steam drifters cost more than £5,000. That's more than I can afford – more than I can borrow, even.'

'You could find yersel' a partner. Not me, for I can't afford it,' Innes said as his brother looked at him with sudden hope. 'And I doubt if Bethany would be interested – not that she'll have the money either.'

'Ye both hold shares in her.'

'Aye, but we've always looked on this as our faither's boat, James, and now it's yours – and Jacob's. It was never mine or Bethany's – or even Mither's.'

'Are ye sayin' that ye'll no' help me?'

'I'm sayin' that I can't. Ye'll have tae find yer own solution – or go along with Jacob's plans.'

4

It was peaceful, Stella thought that night, with her on one side of the hearth with her mending and James on the other, reading the newspaper. It was the way she wanted it, for Stella was the sort of woman who needed love and security. She knew that his father had pushed James, a carefree bachelor who had always had a string of sweethearts, into their marriage, but even so, she had agreed to the union because she loved him and had loved him for years.

Being timid and unsure of herself, she had kept her feelings for the good-looking young fisherman to herself, knowing that he would never freely choose the likes of her as a wife. Weem Lowrie's need for her father's sailed boat and the money it represented to him had made a dream come true, and it had been her fervent hope that in time, James would come to love her. But she had never been enough for him. He had looked elsewhere, and—

Stella's mind flinched away from the memory of those terrible, hurting weeks, and she made herself blank it out by concentrating hard on the needle busily dipping in and out of a tear in Ruth's underskirt. As the turmoil within began to ease, she wondered if she should after all have turned to him in bed the night before, instead of denying him. Perhaps it was time to forgive the past, even if it could never be forgotten. The thought of the two of them going through the rest of their lives like strangers was unbearable.

'I was thinkin' about yer faither's wee hoosie,' James said just then. 'It'll fetch a good price.'

'I've no notion tae sell it,' Stella said, keeping her head bent over her work.

'What else would we dae with it? We cannae live in two houses at the one time.'

'I was thinkin' of hirin' it out.'

'Ye what?'

'Now that the war's over, the summer visitors'll be comin' back tae the Firth, and I thought I could hire the house out tae them. And there's all the folk that come here for the fishin' season too.' She glanced up at him, anxious to get him to understand. 'I can use the house tae earn my own way.'

'There's no need for that now I'm back home.'

'Even so.' She looked back down at her work.

'But we need the money we could get for it. There's work tae be done on the boat, and new nets tae buy, and—'

'That's for you and Jacob McFarlane tae worry about, surely?' Stella asked, and then as James stayed silent she looked up to see him chewing on his lower lip. 'Is there somethin' wrong between you and him?'

'He doesnae think the *Fidelity*'s worth repairin'. He wants tae sell her, and he wants me tae take one he's not long bought.'

'Is it a good boat?'

'I'm sure it is, but I'm happy enough with the *Fidelity*.'

'Then get Mr McFarlane tae change his mind.'

'He'll not do that!' James tossed the paper down and got to his feet, pacing the small room. 'We might be a partnership, but it's Jacob that holds the purse strings. If I want tae keep the *Fidelity* I'll have tae buy him out, and then find the money tae do the repairs mysel'.'

Suddenly, Stella saw where the conversation was leading. 'And ye can only do that by sellin' my faither's house.'

'Aye, that's about the strength of it.'

Part of her mind told her that this was her chance to heal

33

the rift between them. If she did as James asked, sacrificing her own hopes in the process, then he would be beholden to her. But the thought had no sooner shaped itself than the clear and logical part of her mind reminded her that grateful though he might be, James Lowrie was not a man to feel beholden to anyone. He would repair his precious boat, the boat he loved far more than he could ever love his wife, and he would take her back to sea, leaving Stella alone again. And nothing would change.

She took a few final stitches in silence before biting off the thread and smoothing out the petticoat, now darned so neatly that the tear in the material had completely vanished. She folded it, and then, at last, she looked up at him.

'That cottage belonged tae my faither, James, and his faither afore him,' she said, her tongue feeling so heavy in her mouth that the words had to be forced out. 'Now it's mine, and I want tae keep it.'

He stared at her, perplexed, and then threw his hands out in a swift, impatient gesture. 'If ye're so set on havin' it then we'll move back there and I'll sell this place. I'm no' bothered.'

She shook her head. 'No, James. This is your house and it's only right that your family should live here. Rentin' the other hoosie out will give us extra money. Mebbe Mr McFarlane's right. Mebbe it's time ye took on a new boat.'

'I don't want a new boat! I want the *Fidelity*.'

'Ye sound like a wee laddie that's lost his toy,' Stella said, and saw his face flame beneath its tan.

'I've just told ye – I need the money we could get from the sale of that house. You're my wife. You should be puttin' my wishes first!'

Stella's careful serenity suddenly evaporated. 'Your wishes, is it?' She stood up, the neatly folded little petticoat falling unnoticed from her lap to the floor. 'Your wishes? And what about mine?'

'Eh?' He gaped at her, taken aback. 'Ye've got a home and bairns and a man tae keep ye. What more can ye want?'

'Dogs have homes, James, and cats are kept. That's not enough for me! Why should you get what you need when I never have, and never will? You married me tae get what you and your faither and your Uncle Albert wanted – the *Fidelity*. And you got her. But what did I get in return – tell me that?'

'You wanted a husband,' he blustered.

'Not just a husband. I wanted a man tae care for me and for the bairns I bore him. But you're like your father, James Lowrie – nothin' matters but gettin' your own way. Now ye're tellin' me that ye "need" the cottage I was raised in, the place my faither left tae me, so's ye can keep that damned drifter? Oh no,' Stella stormed, remembering even in her rage to keep her voice low so that the children sleeping above could not hear her anger. 'Why d'ye think I want the money from the rent of the place? It's because I've made up my mind that if I can't get what I've needed from you all these long, empty years, I'll at least become my own woman and earn my own way in life!'

'Stella—' He began to get up, one hand held out in an attempt to placate her, but she stepped back swiftly, shaking her head. A tendril of brown hair broke loose from its restraints and swung down to brush her cheek.

'Stay away from me, James. If it's money ye want, why don't ye ask yer precious sister for it? I'm sure she'd be only too glad tae help ye.'

'Bethany? Why should she help me?'

'Because you and me both know well enough that the only two things you've ever cared for are the *Fidelity* – and her!'

The blood drained from his face. He came out of his chair with such a rush that for a moment she thought he was intent on striking her. With an effort, she stood her ground, waiting for the blow and in a way almost welcoming the prospect. At least a blow would demonstrate some passion.

But instead, James swallowed hard before saying thickly, 'Ye're haverin'!'

'Am I? You didnae waste much time runnin' up tae her fine, fancy house, did ye?'

'Who said I was there?'

'Nothin' happens in this place without someone knowin' about it. Nothin', James,' Stella said, her voice heavy with meaning. 'Ye were seen speakin' together, you and Bethany.'

'I found the wee laddie hidin' in the boat and took him back, that was all.'

'Oh aye, Bethany's wee laddie. A fine bonny boy, is he no', James? A real Lowrie, that one.' Stella, her heart aching for the tiny boy she herself had birthed and then buried within days; the son that might have made all the difference to her marriage, almost spat the words at him.

They stood glaring at each other, both breathing heavily, both with fists clenched. 'I'm goin' to my bed,' Stella said at last, and he made no attempt to stop her as she went into the back room.

It was only then that she remembered she had not gone through her usual procedure of setting the table for the morning meal and steeping oatmeal in water to soften overnight. They would just have to break their fasts with bread and margarine, she decided, dragging her clothes off and tossing them haphazardly over the small nursing chair, for she was not going back into that kitchen tonight. She pulled the pins from her hair, letting it fall about her face, and got into bed without bothering to brush it out or plait it.

She had expected to lie awake half the night but the sudden flash of rage had exhausted her, and when James finally came to bed more than an hour later, Stella was asleep, her hair scattered over her pillow.

James was sitting in the *Fidelity*'s cabin, a bottle of whisky and a tin mug on the table before him, when heavy boots thumped on the decking overhead. He looked up, and then decided to stay where he was. Jacob would find him soon enough.

But it was Gil Pate who came down the ladder. 'James!'

He shook his brother-in-law's hand vigorously, a huge grin splitting his round, red face. 'By God, man, but you're a sight for sore eyes.'

'So are you, Gil. Ye'll have a drink with me?'

'Ye're at the whisky early in the day, are ye no'?'

'It helps me tae think. And I've a deal of thinkin' tae do.'

Gil rubbed his hands in pleasurable anticipation. 'In that case I'll keep ye company, for it's no' wise for a man tae drink on his own,' he said, squeezing his bulk into the bench seat at the table. The fringe of greying hair about his bald head was now pure silver, James noticed as he poured the whisky, and his face was even redder than before, thanks to a mixture of weather and whisky.

'I'm glad tae see ye home safe from the war, James. And I was vexed tae hear about Charlie.'

'Aye. Ye're back early from Yarm'th,' James said, anxious to change the subject. He splashed some whisky into Gil's mug and then more into his own before he sat down.

'There's a timber boat comin' in and I wanted tae be here for the unloadin'. Nathan's down south seein' tae things while I'm away.' Gil took a big swallow of his drink.

'Can ye trust him?' James asked, with a lift of one eyebrow. Normally the fish-curer, and not the cooper, hired the gutting crews and ran the business, but Nathan Pate was notoriously lazy, and so Gil had taken on those duties.

Now his brother-in-law grinned and then set the mug down, wiping his mouth with the back of one hand. 'I cannae trust him any more than I could afore ye went away, but the men and the lassies know what's tae be done, an' I'll be back with them the day after tomorrow. He surely cannae make much of a mess of things in two, mebbe three days.'

'How's business been?'

'Very good,' Gil said complacently, stretching his thick legs as best he could in the small cabin. 'Beth'ny was sayin' ye called in at Cliff Terrace. I've got myself a fine new house there, have I no'?'

'It looks grand. I went up there with the wee lad after I found him here on the boat. Bethany wasnae very pleased with him.'

'She cannae keep up with him. I thought Rory was a handful, but Adam's worse. He's intae everythin'. I've tae watch him like a hawk when he comes tae the cooperage in case he falls intae a brazier or gets himself built intae a barrel. But there's no harm in the lad. Beth'ny and me are forever arguin' over him, for I think she's over-hard on the boy. Ye'd think that bein' his mother, she'd be more likely tae spoil him, but not her. I'll never understand women.'

'Ye're not the only one,' James said with all his heart, thinking of the previous night, and his normally placid wife's spitting fury.

'He'll be goin' tae the University when he's old enough – Adam, I'm talkin' of,' Gil went on. 'I've set my heart on it.'

'University? Ach, away! That's no ploy for a Buckie loon!'

'You think he should be a cooper, or a fisherman?'

'Why not? He was takin' a right interest in this boat.'

'No, no, James, this one's for the University. I fancy a son o' mine doin' well in the world, and he's sharp as a knife, that wee loon. You see if I'm no' right, James,' Gil boasted. 'Rory'll come intae the cooperage with me when he's older, and Adam'll be a scholar and make his old faither proud of him. I just wish my mither had lived tae see him.'

'From what I mind of the woman – no harm tae her, Gil – she'd have wanted him tae be a minister.'

'Aye, ye're right. Mebbe it's as well she's no' with us now. Did Beth'ny show ye all round the house?'

'I saw it from the street outside, just. I'd business with Innes so I couldnae take the time tae go inside when she invited me,' James lied.

'Ye'll have tae come for yer dinner some night, you and Stella and the quinies. It's a far cry from the wee cottage I used to bide in at the Catbow, eh?'

'Ye've done well for yersel', Gil.' Trust Gil Pate to look

out for his own comfort, James thought, and prosper while other men were fighting and dying.

'So has Jacob, and so will you, now ye're back home. And now that the world's found peace at last we'll all dae well,' the other man rattled on.

'Is the English fishin' good this year?'

'We cannae make the barrels fast enough, James. Ye should be there.'

'The boat isnae up tae it, with all she's been through. But she'll be ready in time for the next herrin' season.'

'Jacob was in at the house last night,' Gil said casually, his eyes on his brother-in-law's face. 'From what he says, he wants you tae take on this new boat he's bought, the *Jess Lowrie*. She's a trim vessel, James, and she's bringin' in good catches down south. She'd do even better with you as skipper.'

'I'll stay with the *Fidelity*,' James said, and then, as Gil looked round the dingy cabin, eyebrows raised, 'All she needs is some deckin' planks and a good coat of paint and a set of nets. I'll not see her sold when she's still got years left in her. If Jacob won't put out the money for the work she needs, I've a mind tae buy her from him and bring her back intae the Lowrie family.'

'Buy her? Ye must have made yer fortune in the war, then?'

'No,' James said, the germ of an idea beginning to form itself in his brain, 'but I was thinkin' that you and me could mebbe manage tae raise the money between us.'

Gil sucked air in through his teeth, eyes narrowing. 'I don't know about that, James, not with what I'd tae pay for that new house of mine.'

'You've done well durin' the war.'

'A bit, mebbe,' Gil admitted, 'but I've got the weans tae think of, and Beth'ny. And I'm no' a young man, James, no' near as young as you.'

'Come and have a look around,' said James, 'and then we might have another drink.'

*

39

Half an hour later they were back in the cabin and the level in the whisky bottle had gone down noticeably.

'I ken what ye mean, James,' Gil was saying, his words tending to run into each other. 'She's a bonny, sturdy wee drifter still, and she's brought back a wheen o' herrin' in her time—'

'And made you a wealthy man,' James put in quickly, refilling his brother-in-law's glass.

'No' entirely by hersel', but you an' the *Fidelity* aye made a good team,' Gil acknowledged.

'So d'ye not think that you owe her a wee bittie o' help in her time o' need?'

Gil chewed his lower lip. 'I could speak tae Beth'ny—'

'Best leave Bethany out of it,' James said swiftly. 'What dae women ken about business?'

'Oh, she's got a good head on her shoulders, has my Beth'ny. Every year she's on at me tae let her take over the hirin' of the guttin' crews the way she used tae, but I'm no' so fond of the idea. She's got enough tae do with the hoosie and the bairns – and I've got her a servant tae do most of the work about the place,' Gil added smugly, 'so she's got that lassie tae manage as well. Servants need trainin', James, and watchin'.'

'That's just what I mean.' James topped up his brother-in-law's glass. 'Men are best seein' tae the money and women are best seein' tae the hoose and the bairns – and the servant lassies.'

'But I think Beth'ny'd want tae help you, James. You're her brother, and when all's said and done she's still got a part share in this boat.'

'Aye, but women don't see things the way we do. They like tae tuck money away in the bank. Tae them, it's like puttin' a bairn tae its bed where it's safe. They don't realise that ye should send it out intae the world tae make more siller for ye.'

'Just like the bairns when they're grown, eh?' Gil rumbled

with laughter at his own joke. 'By God, James, would life no' be much easier if we could faither sovereigns instead of children, eh?'

'It would that.'

Gil held his glass up and owlishly studied the effect of the light shining through the small window and on to the amber whisky before saying carefully, 'There's nothin' gone wrong atween you and Beth'ny, is there?'

'What could go wrong with blood kin?'

'There's somethin' about the look she gets when I mention yer name. It's as if she doesnae like tae hear it.'

James turned a wince into a shrug. 'Me and Bethany always fought like cat and dog. We're too alike. But I've noticed that she's not as friendly with Stella as she once was. They've probably fallen out for some daft reason.'

'Aye, that's likely it.' Gil took another swallow of whisky. 'And ye're right about the money. If I do manage tae help ye out with a wee loan it's probably best tae say nothin' tae her about it. She can be right nippy when she doesnae agree with the things I dae.'

'I can promise you,' James said eagerly, 'that anythin' you put towards the *Fidelity* will come back tae ye safe and sound, and bring more with it forbye. She'll not be ready for the English fishin', but give me till next year's season's over and ye'll get yer reward. What d'ye say?'

'I suppose I could spare somethin',' Gil began. 'As for Nathan – we'll leave him out of it, eh? He's a decent enough brither, but' – he winked, and tapped one blunt finger against his temple – 'he's no' got much of a business head on his shoulders.'

'Best tae keep this atween ourselves,' James agreed. 'That way, you get all the profit when I pay back the loan.'

Gil's eyes brightened as he reached for the bottle and poured the last of the whisky into his glass. 'That's true, I will.'

'Here.' James opened a drawer and produced a notebook,

a pen and an old inkwell. 'Best tae get it all put down in writin' now, before we forget the terms we've agreed on, eh?'

'Aye,' Gil nodded, and then, frowning, 'Whit terms were those? All this talkin's taken them from my mind.'

'Don't you fret yoursel' about that,' James said. 'They're still clear as crystal in mine.'

5

There was nothing new in finding an unknown child in Zelda Lowrie's kitchen, for her door was permanently open in welcome to all who cared to walk in. But this child, Stella discovered, was staying.

'Etta's come tae bide with us and help me tae see tae wee Matt, haven't ye, my pet?' Zelda said cheerfully to the little girl who was rocking baby Matthew's cradle with one hand while keeping the thumb of the other wedged firmly into her mouth. The child gave a barely perceptible nod. Her dark hair, brown eyes and almost olive skin showed that she was a member of the large family Zelda came from.

'She's worth her weight in gold,' Zelda went on in the same bright, firm voice. 'But now ye've got the wee one tae sleep, my lambie, why don't ye go out the back and play with Mary and Will and Jessie? Poor wee soul,' she went on, the cheerfulness vanishing from her voice as soon as the little girl was out of earshot. 'She's an orphan, but she doesnae know it yet for she's only three years old. How can I tell her that her mother's gone?' Her eyes filled with tears. 'D'ye mind my sister Elsie, Stella?'

'Aye, I do.' Zelda had so many brothers and sisters that it was hard to keep track of them, but Elsie stood out in Stella's memory. Like her older sister before her, poor Elsie had become pregnant to a young cooper who, by the time she realised that she was carrying his child, was serving in the army. Elsie's father had put her out of his house, and the young man's mother had taken her in. Sadly, the cooper had been killed before he could return home to marry his sweetheart, and Elsie herself had died in childbirth.

'That is Elsie's wee one?' Stella asked, and then, when Zelda nodded, 'I thought her grandmother was looking after her.'

'She fell poorly a year back and one of her daughters took her in. They didnae want Etta, so my mither got my faither tae agree tae take her. But he's that strict, and the bairn wasnae happy, Stella. So I said we'd take her and put an end once and for all tae her bein' passed from one pair of hands tae another.'

'Have you not got enough with your own four bairns?' Stella asked, and then, lowering her voice, 'Not tae mention—'

She nodded at the fireside chair where Meg Lowrie, aunt to Innes, James and Bethany, dozed. Widowed within months of marriage when her fisherman husband drowned at sea, Meg had earned her living with a variety of jobs: as a packer in a gutting crew, and either working in one of the local net factories or as a skivvy in domestic service between the herring seasons. In her prime she had been able to do as much work as any man, but years of hard physical toil had resulted in crippling rheumatism. Over the past few years Innes's mother Jess had cared for her, and when Jess died, Zelda and Innes had taken the old woman in.

'Ach, Auntie Meg's no bother at all, and neither's wee Etta.' Zelda's eyes filled with sudden tears. 'Elsie was only nineteen when she died, Stella, the same age as that poor lad of hers. And she didnae even live long enough tae hold her wee bairn in her arms. Anyway, what's two more mouths tae feed?'

'It'll soon be three more mouths.' Stella looked pointedly at her sister-in-law's swollen belly.

'But I couldnae leave her with my faither, Stella, not with her bein' a . . .' Zelda glanced at the old woman, who was snoring slightly, and lowered her voice, 'you know. Ye mind what he can be like – he would have it that Elsie's death was the Lord punishin' the poor lassie for her sins. When I went over there tae visit them last week he was talkin' about the wee soul's sins – as if it could be her fault that her mother and father got carried away with their feelin's for each other.' Zelda sniffed, and ran her arm across her face. 'She was that confused, Stella – ye could see that she didnae know what she'd done wrong. It fair broke my heart. How can anyone treat a wee orphaned lassie sae cruel?' Zelda seldom criticised anyone, but unmistakeable anger was creeping into her voice and her eyes.

Remembering the injuries Innes had suffered at his father-in-law's hands, Stella shivered at the thought of small, defenceless Etta living in his house and at his mercy.

'So I just took the few clothes she had, and I brought her home. I think my faither was pleased, and my mither too, because she felt as bad about the way Etta was bein' treated as I did – but she was never able tae stand up tae my faither.'

'How did Innes feel about you bringing the bairn back home?'

'He was fine about it. Why shouldn't he be?' Zelda poured tea from the pot that simmered on the range all day, ever ready for visitors.

'I can't think of Innes disagreeing with anything you wanted,' Stella said, and Zelda laughed.

'He's the finest husband any woman could have. Mother Lowrie used tae say that Innes was the best of the family; I suppose that that was because he was the youngest. You'd have thought that Bethany would have been the favourite, with her bein' the only lassie.'

At the very mention of her other sister-in-law's name, Stella felt her mouth puckering as though she had eaten something sour.

'Bethany was never easy tae like,' she said.

'Ye just have tae take Bethany as ye find her. I get on well enough with her, but I've noticed that the two of ye go awful quiet in each other's company.'

Stella sipped at her tea, strong and hot. 'We've nothin' in common. Bethany's a fine lady now, with her house on Cliff Terrace.'

'Och, I'm sure ye'd rather have James and yer wee cottage than Gil Pate and his big house. I know I'd choose my Innes over the king that lives in London.' Zelda's pretty face took on a sudden glow. 'We made our marriage vows taegether an' neither of us would ever think of breakin' them.'

A surge of bitter envy flooded through Stella. She stared down at her cup, thinking of the quarrel between herself and James the previous night. Zelda would be shocked if she knew the things they had said to each other. But then, Zelda and Innes had married for love.

'Auntie Meg . . .' Gently, Zelda shook the old woman awake. 'Here's a cup of tea for ye – and Stella's come tae see us.'

'How are ye, Auntie Meg?' Stella went over to the chair, and took one of the old woman's hands in hers. The bony fingers were twisted and the skin covered with raised scars from years of packing herring in layers of coarse salt, but Meg's grip was still strong.

'I cannae complain, lass. They've been awful good tae me, Zelda and Innes.' Her voice, too, was still strong, with not a trace of the querulous note often adopted by the very old. 'They've got hearts of gold, the both of them, takin' an old body like me in when they've got a houseful of bairns tae tend tae.'

'Tuts, Auntie, there's always room for one more,' said Zelda, mistress of a house only a fraction the size of Bethany's.

'Your James was here not long since, Stella,' the old woman said.

'James – here?'

'It seems that Innes told him Auntie Meg was bidin' with us,' Zelda explained. 'He'd some dinner with us and then he went off on some ploy of his own.'

'He looks even more like Weem than he did before. It was as though my own brither was standin' there in front of me, rest his soul.' Meg's eyes suddenly glistened. 'I was sayin' tae him how much I miss Weem, and Jess. She was awful good tae me when the rheumatics began tae trouble me. I wish she'd no' been taken afore me.' She released Stella's hand in order to scrub the tears away before they overflowed down her seamed face. 'Its hard when the folk ye ken best go afore ye, lass!'

'Now then, Auntie, ye've got years left in ye yet,' Zelda admonished her.

'I hope no'!' Meg shot back at her. 'If the good Lord doesnae send for me tae go home soon I'll have somethin' tae say tae Him when I do get there!'

'I'm sure ye will, and I'd no' like tae be in His shoes if He doesnae please ye. Here.' Zelda folded the stiff old fingers carefully round the cup. 'Have ye got a grip of it?'

'Aye, aye, my quine, I'm no' in my dotage yet. You see tae yer bairn,' Meg ordered as wee Matthew suddenly jumped awake with a startled cry.

'I'll take him.' Stella lifted the little boy from his cot and sat down by the table. The baby stared up at her, yawned, and then settled back to sleep. It felt good to be holding a baby close again.

'He's worn himself out, the wee lambie.' Zelda brushed her son's rounded cheek with the back of a finger. 'He's on his feet now – imagine, and him only just ten months old! He's quicker than Mary and Will and Jessie ever were. Ye're goin' tae be a handful, aren't ye, my wee mannie?' she crooned to the baby. 'As tae the next . . .' She patted her rounded belly and then eased herself down into a chair with a sigh of relief. 'We'll just have tae wait and see.' Then, after a pause, 'I thought with James home at last you'd be smilin' all over yer face, but ye're not. Is there somethin' wrong atween the two of ye?'

'It's just – there's times when I think that if I was his precious fishin' boat instead of just his wife James'd care more for me.'

'He's like his faither,' Meg Lowrie chimed in unexpectedly. 'The sea aye mattered more than anythin' else tae Weem. He was lucky that Jess understood that. I mind her sayin' tae me once that women cannae change men like that, and they can only destroy them if they try it. And destroy themselves at the same time. She was a wise woman, was Jess.'

'Aye,' Stella said. 'Aye, I think she was, Auntie Meg.'

Jacob McFarlane's comfortable house in West Cathcart Street was large enough to accommodate himself and his housekeeper, a widow of middle years. The soft carpeting and the thick curtains and the large chairs that all but swallowed a body up when she sat down on one impressed Stella, who had never been inside the place before.

She luxuriated for a moment in the armchair that Jacob had offered when she went into his study, then remembering that she had called on business, she struggled back to its edge and perched there, hands fisted on her knees.

'It's about James, Mr McFarlane, and the *Fidelity*. He wants tae buy out your share and own the boat himsel', since ye'll no' spend the money on repairin' her. And,' she hurried on as he opened his mouth to speak, 'I'd be grateful if ye'd agree.'

Jacob eyed her thoughtfully. 'Did he ask ye tae come here?'

'Ask me? He'd be in a right temper if he found out I was talkin' tae ye about his business. I'm here of my own accord.' Stella stopped speaking abruptly as the housekeeper brought in a tray.

'Thank you, Mrs Duthie.' Jacob waited until the woman had gone, closing the door noiselessly behind her, then said, 'Would you do me the favour of pouring the tea, my quine? It's no' often I've the pleasure of havin' a lady tae dae it for me.'

When the tea had been poured Stella asked, 'Will ye, Mr McFarlane? Will ye let him have the boat?'

'I'd not want tae lose James, for he's a good fisherman and a good partner.'

'You'd not lose him, not if ye handled him the right way. James knows every inch of the *Fidelity*,' Stella said earnestly. 'He's a good skipper, one of the best, but if he's made tae take over a drifter he doesnae care for, it'll spoil him. Ye cannae deny that the *Fidelity*'s more than paid her way over the years.' She cast a glance round the well-furnished room. 'You've done well out of her, Mr McFarlane.'

'I suppose I have.' He sipped his tea, watching her over the rim of the cup as though waiting for further argument. But Stella had already said what she had to say – more than she had meant to say; she was surprised at her own defence of James and the drifter that meant more to him than she and her daughters ever could.

Even though she had no notion for the tea, having drunk two cups with Zelda only an hour earlier, she sipped diligently, as though enjoying every mouthful.

Silence fell between them for a full four minutes before Jacob McFarlane laid his empty cup aside.

'Let me give the matter some thought. I'll not take long over it, I promise you.' He crossed to the fireplace and pulled at a bell rope; then, as they waited for the housekeeper to arrive, he added, 'I must say, my quine, that I envy your husband. I've never known the pleasure of a wife who cared enough tae go seekin' favours on my behalf.'

'Cared?' Stella felt her face colour at the very thought. 'Indeed, Mr McFarlane, it has nothin' tae do with carin',' she said sharply, hunting about for her gloves. 'It's just that the man can be like a bear with a sore head if anythin' comes between him and that precious drifter!'

It was late when James finally came home. As the clock ticked the seconds and then the minutes and then the hours away, Stella began to feel uneasy. Perhaps he wasn't coming back. Perhaps he had decided to stay on board the drifter rather than return to her and to their daughters.

She put the evening meal on the table, pushing her own food around her plate and snapping at Ruth when the little girl innocently asked where her daddy was.

The table was cleared, the dishes washed, the children sent to their beds, and still there was no sign of James. Stella put the kitchen to rights and then waited by the fire, her hands idle and her knitting neglected in her lap, ears straining for the sound of his return.

Several times, hearing studded boots clattering up the street outside, she picked up her knitting to give the illusion of being busy, but each time the feet went on past the door, the street fell quiet again, and the knitting was dropped back into her lap.

She was dozing by the time he finally returned, waking with a start when he knocked against a chair, scraping it over the floor.

'You're back.' She snatched up her knitting.

'I'd a lot tae see tae.' He shrugged out of his coat and hung it on the back of the door.

'I'll get your supper on the table while you get washed.'

By the time he returned from the wash house the meal was on the table and she was back in her chair, knitting busily.

'I hear ye were at Zelda's today.'

'Can a man not move in this place without everyone knowin'?' he asked, exasperated.

'Your Auntie Meg said. She was pleased tae see you.'

'Aye. She's no' as I mind her at all.'

'She's older. We all are. We've all changed,' Stella said. 'I saw Gil, too.'

'Is he back from England already?'

'So there's some things you don't know about?' James said, and she bit her lip, having the sense to keep quiet.

Jacob McFarlane arrived just as James finished his meal.

He pushed his plate aside and indicated the chair opposite. 'Sit down, man, I was just wonderin' if it was too late tae call on ye.'

'Never too late for business.' Jacob sat, and nodded his thanks as Stella put a mug of tea before him.

'Business, is it? Ye'd best hear what I've got tae say afore you tell me yer own business,' James said. 'I got Innes tae go over the boat with me this afternoon, plank by plank, and tell me what it might cost tae have her repaired. Then I went tae see the mannie at the bank and he's agreed tae take this house up as surety for a loan.'

'Ye've mortgaged the house?' The words were out of Stella's mouth before she could stop them. James gave her a cold smile.

'As ye said yersel', it's mine. Even if I cannae meet the loan – and I'll meet it – you and the lassies willnae be homeless if things go wrong, for ye've still got yer own cottage, have ye no'?' He turned back to Jacob McFarlane. 'So I'm offerin' tae buy your share of the *Fidelity*. Name yer price.'

'Well now, James, this is a right turn of events, for I'm here tae tell ye that I've thought things over, and I think we should keep the drifter. She's got years in her yet, as you said.'

James had been leaning so far back in his chair that, solid as it was, it had tipped back. Now he sat upright so suddenly that the front legs thudded to the floor. 'What made ye change yer mind?'

'I gave it a lot of thought,' Jacob told him smoothly, without so much as a flicker of a glance in Stella's direction, 'and decided that ye were right. We'll hold ontae her.'

Stella's pent-up breath had just started to go out in a long and silent sigh of relief when to her horror she heard her husband say, 'Ye'll not, for I want her for my own. I'm no' goin' tae give ye the chance tae do this again, Jacob. Name yer price.'

Jacob's thick, grey eyebrows immediately came together in a scowl. He was not used to being crossed like this. 'And if I refuse tae sell my share?'

'Then I'll keep on at you until ye change yer mind,' James said, his jaw set and his voice grim.

'James—'

'You keep out of it, Stella, this is men's business,' he ordered curtly without bothering to look at her.

'And if I ask for more money than ye can raise?' Jacob wanted to know.

'I'll find it, somehow.'

'Even if it means beggarin' yer own wife and bairns?'

James shrugged. 'I want the *Fidelity*, whatever the cost. I'll not have her and me held up tae ransom again.'

There was a silence, during which both men glared at each other, neither giving way, while Stella stood by helplessly. Then she jumped as Jacob slapped both hands palm down on the table with a sound like a gun being fired.

'By God, James, ye're a thrawn bugger,' he boomed. 'Aye, all right, ye've won.'

'Ye'll sell the boat tae me?'

'Aye, and for a fair price. We'll agree tae that in the mornin' for it's too late tae start hagglin' and bargainin'. Ye can pay half of it down now and I'll take the rest at the end of next season. I can't say fairer than that. There's two conditions, though,' Jacob said. 'The first is that I'll want ye tae go on sellin' yer catches tae Gil the same as afore.'

James grinned broadly. 'I can dae that all right. Better a contract than havin' tae hope for a good market every time. So what's yer second condition?'

'I still want Jem as skipper of the *Homefarin*', for tae my mind the mannie that's in charge of her at the moment would make a better mate nor a skipper.'

'But Jem's been my mate ever since Charlie was killed. We work well together, him and me.'

'I need him and I'll have him, or the agreement's off.'

Jacob's tone was inflexible, and Stella eyed her husband nervously, wondering if all the new plans were going to be for nothing.

James bit hard on the stem of his pipe, then said, 'Aye, I suppose it's time he'd his own boat. It's no' right tae stand in his way.'

'Good. That's that settled.' Jacob spat on the palm of his large, calloused hand then held it out to James, who shook it. 'And now I'm for home, and my bed. Come and see me tomorrow mornin', James, and we'll get the business finished. And I want you and Jem in Yarm'th as soon as ye can. You can take over the *Homefarin'* for what's left of the season, and it'll give Jem the chance tae get intae the way of her. Ye neednae fret about the *Fidelity*, for me and Innes can see that the work gets done.'

'It's a shame,' Zelda said as she watched Stella pack James's seaman's kist for his trip to Yarmouth, 'that your man's scarce arrived home and here ye are, losin' him again.'

'Aye.' Stella wondered if it was possible to lose someone she had never owned in the first place. But on the other hand, she had learned not to expect much else from her marriage to James Lowrie.

'Mind you, I'll mebbe be able tae get the chance tae talk tae Innes once James has gone,' her sister-in-law prattled on, pouncing on wee Matt as he toddled past and lifting him on to her knee. 'Your James has never been away from our house since Innes agreed tae see tae the repairs while he's down at Yar— Will ye get this bairn's hands off me afore he makes me bald?' Zelda winced as Matt reached out to tug hard at her black curls.

'Here, pet.' Stella cut a piece of hard crust from the loaf on the table, dipped it in her tea, and then into the sugar bowl before holding it out to the baby. Matt promptly let go of his mother in order to grab it. 'He's determined tae leave the boat in good hands afore he goes away.'

'It's in good hands, all right. It's funny how Innes cannae abide the boats when they're on the sea, yet he's as happy as a lintie workin' with them in the yard,' Zelda said. 'Not like me – I think a boat up on the stocks looks like a whale. It gives me the shivers. As far as I'm concerned, they belong in the water.'

Normally James Lowrie followed the fishing to the various ports by sea, but this time, since the *Homefaring* was already in Yarmouth, he and Jem had to go by rail. A carter passing through Buckie on his way to Aberdeen arranged to take him to the railway station, and he refused to let Stella walk to the meeting place with him.

'I cannae be doin' with goodbyes,' he said irritably, snatching up his kist and making for the door. 'I'll no' be away for long in any case, since there's only about four weeks left tae the English season.'

'You'll let me know how you're . . . how the new boat handles?' she said, and he nodded without looking directly at her. His relief at making his escape was so strong that it almost cut through the air.

'Aye,' he said, and was gone.

Alone in the kitchen, Stella bit her lip until it hurt, then went out to the wash house at the back, where water was heating in the big copper. Taking a pailful, she returned to the kitchen and began to scrub the floor.

They had finally lain together on the night before. There was nothing warm or loving about it – James had suddenly turned in the bed and reached for her, and this time she had not denied him. Minutes later they had been back to back again, with not a word said, but at least it was contact after all those years. As she scrubbed at the already spotless floor the following morning she wished with all her heart that there might be a result. A laddie this time, she begged the Fates from behind lips set in a thin tight line.

While his wife scrubbed and prayed, James waited for the

cart, his kist at his feet and joy in his heart. The war was all but over and at last he was free to escape to the sea where he belonged.

A week later Stella got her answer. There was to be no son to follow James to the fishing. Not yet, and possibly not ever.

6

If only, Bethany thought as she surveyed the bundle of scrap paper that Gil used to record his business transactions, he would give in to her pleas and demands and allow her to take charge of his paperwork. Instead, he insisted on seeing to it himself even though he knew that she was much better at figuring than he could ever be. Every time, he ended up having to turn to her for help when things got out of hand, and every time she had to spend hours putting the books to rights.

It was almost the end of November, and she had two weeks at the most before he returned from Yarmouth in which to transfer his scribbled records to the big ledger kept in the roll-top desk that dominated one corner of the parlour. Gil had tried to take the ledger down to the cooperage on several occasions but Bethany, knowing that it was not safe out of her keeping, had always managed to retrieve it. Now she thumped it on the desk, tutting as its arrival caused a waft of air that, in turn, floated several papers to the floor. She retrieved them and then settled to work. For once the house was silent, for the two older children were still at school and Leezie had taken Adam over to Zelda's for the afternoon.

An hour later she put the pen down and stretched her arms above her head and then rubbed her cold, stiff hands together, frowning over the neat lists of pounds, shillings and pence before her. The ledger was almost up to date but there was a discrepancy somewhere; a considerable amount of money unaccounted for.

Bethany picked the pen up again and chewed on it, her eyes flitting down page after page without finding the solution. She searched the floor around the desk, then began to pull the desk drawers right out. After emptying each drawer of its contents she reached into the cavities left in the desk to make sure that no papers had managed to get wedged out of sight.

Finding nothing, she went upstairs to the big front bedroom and took Gil's jackets and trousers from the wardrobe, laying them on the bed so that she could go through the pockets. At last, tucked into the small inner pocket of a waistcoat, she found what she was looking for – a piece of paper folded again and again until it was no more than a tiny square, little larger than her own thumbnail.

She unfolded it and ran her eyes swiftly over the contents. Then her jaw dropped and she sat down suddenly on the bed, heedless of crushing her husband's best suit. The handwriting wasn't Gil's, but the writer had signed his name in a clear, confident hand – James Lowrie.

Anger began to burn through Bethany as she took in the meaning of the paper, an IOU for money paid by Gil to James. A large sum of money, handed over without her knowledge or consent.

When Leezie brought Adam home a few moments later she found her mistress coming down the stairs, dressed to go out.

'Look after the house, Leezie, I've got business to see to.'

'I want to come with you,' Adam immediately clamoured.

'You'll stay where you are and do as Leezie tells you, for once.'

'When will you be back?' the maid asked.

'When I'm good and ready,' Bethany told her, and slammed the door on her way out.

*

'Never bother with tea for me, I'm not staying long,' she said half an hour later as Jacob McFarlane began to issue instructions to his housekeeper. 'I'm here on a matter of business.'

As soon as the door closed behind the woman she smoothed out the piece of paper she had found in Gil's waistcoat pocket and held it out to him. 'What d'you know about that?'

He studied the paper, then handed it back. 'Whatever it is, it's between James and Gil. It's not my concern, and surely,' he peered over the tops of the spectacles he now had to wear for close work, 'not yours, either.'

'I'm Gil's wife! He's got no right to be handing over that much money without speaking to me first!'

'Your brother's a man who'll honour his debts. And after all,' Jacob suggested carefully, 'it's Gil's money tae spend or lend as he thinks fit, and he'd never see you and the bairns goin' short.'

Bethany's temper boiled over. 'Gil's money, is it? He can only afford to save enough to hand out to other folk because I run his house for him, and I make sure there's never a penny wasted!'

'Sit down, lass, and we'll—'

'Time and time again,' Bethany fumed, pacing the room with a man's long steps, 'I've tried to get him to let me take over the books properly, and to let me hire the gutting crews the way I used to, but he just keeps insisting on doing it all himself. And now he's giving out money to anyone who asks for it, without a thought for me and his bairns!'

Jacob had been standing, as a gentleman should in the presence of a lady, but now his knees, plagued by rheumatism in cold weather, were beginning to protest. 'Sit down, Bethany,' he said again, 'and we'll talk about this.'

'Why would James be borrowing money from Gil?' she asked, ignoring the invitation.

Jacob gave up trying to be a gentleman and sat down behind his desk with a barely concealed sigh of relief. 'You know that James is buyin' my share of the *Fidelity*?'

Bethany stopped pacing. 'Buying her from you? Why?'

'Because I wanted tae sell her and put him intae the *Jess Lowrie* instead.'

At last he had her undivided attention. She came to the other side of the desk, planting her two hands on the polished wood. '*Fidelity*'s the Lowrie boat. Why would you want to sell her?'

With her wide grey eyes, dark brown hair slashed here and there with gold, and her comely figure, Bethany Pate was a strikingly attractive woman, Jacob thought. Even so, it was a pity that she had not been born a man, for her grasp of business matters and her strong temperament were to be envied.

Aloud, in answer to her question, he said, 'The boat's gettin' old.'

'Havers! She's got years in her yet!'

'That's what James thinks. That's why he wants tae buy her back from me.'

'But where would James get that kind of money?'

Jacob picked up the paper she had left on the desk. 'Some of it from Gil, as ye've just found out for yersel'. And he's mortgaged his house. He's already paid half my money and I'm tae get the rest at the end of next season.'

'Oh.' Bethany picked up the slip of paper, folded it and put it carefully into her pocket. Once again her eyes took on the cold, angry grey of a stormy sky. 'But even so, Gil had no right to lend this sort of money without consulting me first. I'll have something to say to the man when he gets back.'

'Poor soul, he doesnae know what he's comin' home tae.' A grin began to spread over Jacob's face.

'He does not,' Bethany agreed ominously. 'I'll bid you good day then, Jacob. No need to see me out or ring for the woman,' she added as he began to struggle up from his chair. 'I know how to turn a door handle.'

She opened the door and then paused, shut it again and

returned to the desk, a sudden light in her eyes. 'I hear that you're thinking of taking over that wee net factory in Buckpool, is that right?'

'I've already done it. My offer was accepted yesterday.'

'So you'll be looking for someone to run it for you.'

'I am.'

'I could do it,' Bethany said.

'You? Have ye ever worked in a net factory?'

'No, but I can mend nets – what fisher-lassie can't mend a torn net? I could learn about net-making fast enough, but what you need is an overseer, someone who can deal with folk. I can do that, and as for the bookwork, I've been doing Gil's books for years. You'll surely need someone you can trust to run it for you,' she added as he looked at her doubtfully.

'What would Gil say?'

A cold smile curled the corners of Bethany's mouth and she slipped a hand into her pocket and brought out her brother's IOU. 'I doubt if Gil can make a fuss about it,' she said. 'Not once he finds out that I know about this. Leave Gil to me. All you need to do is think about what's best for your new net factory.'

'I'm goin' tae have a look round the place tomorrow,' said Jacob. 'Why don't ye come along with me?'

'Are ye certain o' this?' he asked on the following day as he and Bethany emerged from the small factory.

'I am.' Bethany could scarcely keep her excitement under control.

'It'll be hard work for ye, lass.'

'Nothing like as hard as working at the farlins, and I could still do that if I had to. I want to earn my own keep again. I'll soon get to know the way of the business,' Bethany said earnestly, 'and then I'll see to it that the place makes enough to pay back the money you're putting out on it. I promise you, Jacob.'

'If ye're certain,' he began, then shrugged. 'Damn it, if ye're that eager, I'll away and see the lawyer this very minute. Will ye come with me?'

'Best you go alone, since it'll be your factory. Come to the house tomorrow and let me know when I start work. I'm off home to tell Leezie that she'll be in charge of the house from now on.'

The *Homefaring* was a fine wee boat, but she wasn't the *Fidelity* and never could be, as far as James was concerned. She handled well enough, though, and it was grand to be back at the fishing, but he had no sooner got the feel of the drifter and settled back into the routine of the Yarmouth fishing than the herring shoals moved on and it was time for the Scottish boats to turn towards home.

'At least it gave ye the chance tae try yer hand at it again,' Nathan Pate said, as the *Homefaring* butted her way through the choppy coastal seas.

'I didnae need tae try my hand at it. Fishin's like breathin' tae me; once I get back tae it, it's as if I've never been away,' James snapped. When Gil and Nathan had first arranged to return to Buckie with him it had suited him well enough, for the *Homefaring* was two crewmen short for her return trip. She had been one man short at the start of the fishing, and had taken on a Yarmouth deckhand who was staying in his hometown, while another of the crew had fallen for a local girl and opted to remain in England.

But Gil, who had been suffering from a bad cold when he first came aboard, had not been able to do his share of the work. As the drifter moved northwards his cold had become worse, and now he was tossing in his bunk, flushed with fever and with a chest that wheezed like a badly played squeezebox, as Jem had put it.

As for Nathan – James shot an irritated glance at the man now leaning against the galley wall and lighting his pipe – folk spoke the truth when they said that Nathan Pate was as lazy as the day was long. He had managed to get his pipe lit, and now he puffed out great clouds of smoke that were caught by the wind and blown back into James's face.

'Someone should go down below tae see how Gil is.'

'Ach, he'll be fine.' Nathan made no attempt to pull his shoulder away from the galley wall.

'I'll do it, then.' That pipe, James thought as he ducked into the galley, would finish Gil off completely and stink out the entire cabin into the bargain. All the men on board smoked, and James enjoyed the smell of pipe smoke, but for some reason Nathan's tobacco smelled vile.

His brother-in-law was asleep, his large body crammed into one of the shelf-like bunks and his lungs crunching and grinding as they sucked in air. When James put a hand to the man's forehead he found that it radiated as much heat as a coal fire. At his touch, Gil opened his eyes.

'Eh? Is it time tae get up a'ready?' He began to heave himself up from the bunk.

'No, no, man. I just came down tae see if ye wanted anythin'.'

Gil's furred tongue ran round his thick dry lips. 'I could dae with a wee sip o' water.'

The ship's boy had left a pan of water and a tin mug on the table. James filled the mug and helped Gil to sit up, then put the mug to his lips, refilling it when it was emptied. Halfway through the second mugful Gil sighed and pushed the mug away. 'That's enough.'

He was asleep by the time James had lowered him back on to the pillow. Realising that it was wet with sweat, he heaved Gil up again and managed to turn the pillow, cursing himself for agreeing to take the brothers home on the drifter. He was a fisherman, not a nurse!

Ellen erupted into the net factory and ran straight up the passageway between the looms and the net frames to where her stepmother sat at a small desk, writing out bills.

'My father's home.'

It was no surprise to Bethany, for the local boats had started arriving home from the English fishing several days ago.

'Leezie can surely see to him until I'm finished here,' she said calmly. 'Tell him that I'll not be long.' Let him wait on her, for a change. James's IOU, which she had been carrying about with her for safekeeping, seemed to glow in her pocket with eager anticipation. She was looking forward to having that little matter out with Gil. Not long to wait now.

'Leezie says to come now. He's not well,' Ellen said anxiously. 'He's got a terrible cough and his chest makes a funny noise when he tries to breathe. Leezie says you should come home and take a look at him.'

Gil was in his bed, with Nathan sitting on one side of the bed and James on the other, when Bethany and Ellen arrived back at the house. All three men held a glass of whisky, and the bottle was on the bedside table.

'I'm all right,' Gil wheezed peevishly as his wife went into the room. 'It's just a wee bittie chill, that's all.'

'He's had a bad cough for nigh on two weeks now,' James said, and Nathan nodded vigorously.

'That's the truth of it, Beth'ny. I tried tae get him tae come home early, but he'd have none of it.'

'D'ye think I was goin' tae leave when there was still herrin' comin' in and barrels tae be—' Gil started, before the words were overtaken by a fit of coughing that hauled him up and forward from the pillows to bend double, fighting for breath. James only just managed to save the glass of whisky from spilling over on to the quilt, while Nathan thumped at his brother's back.

'Easy there, man.'

'For goodness' sake, he's not a sack of chaff needing to be whacked into shape!' Bethany pushed Nathan aside and settled Gil back on the pillows.

'Where were ye?' he wanted to know when he finally got his breath back. 'It's no' seemly for a man's wife no' tae be waitin' at home tae greet him when he gets back after bein' weeks away.'

She put the back of her hand against his forehead and realised that this was no time for a confrontation. 'I was at the shops, just.'

'But Leezie said—' Nathan began, and she moved slightly so that her back was turned towards him, and she was blocking Gil's view of him.

'You're running a right fever, Gil Pate. This is what comes of working around those braziers then going out into the cold wind with no jacket on. How often have I told you about that?'

'For God's sake, woman, I've done it all my life and come tae no harm.' His voice sounded as though his throat was made of sandpaper.

'Mebbe not, but you're not getting any younger, are you?'

'Aye, that's true, and it was bitter down there,' Nathan put in. 'A right snell wind, and sleet as well. Terrible tae work in.'

James shot him a steely glance. 'You should try haulin' the nets at sea in that weather,' he advised. 'Then ye'd know what cold really feels like.'

'And you should try standin' at the farlins for hours on end in the winter winds and the snow, James,' Bethany snapped. 'Out of here, the two of you. This man needs rest, not talk.'

'Come back tomorrow,' Gil wheezed, and then, as his visitors got to their feet, 'Where's my whisky?'

Nathan blinked at the two empty glasses on the small table. 'I think I drank yours by mistake, Gil.'

'Mistake? Ye can just pour me another one.'

'Later,' Bethany said. 'You can have a hot toddy later, but first you're going to get a poultice on your chest, and a plate of broth. Outside,' she added to the other two, shooing them before her from the room.

As they left the house James said, low-voiced, 'Ye'll let me know if ye need any help?'

'I doubt if we will,' she said firmly, and when she had closed the door behind them she marched into the kitchen. 'Leezie, bring clean lint and linseed oil and some meal for a poultice while I warm up some broth and put the kettle to boil. The steam might help to clear the man's lungs.'

Gil was so hot and so restless that night that Bethany was forced to make up a bed for herself on two chairs pushed together in a corner of the large bedroom. Not that she got much rest, for she was up and down all night, sponging him with cold water, making a fresh poultice and fetching cool drinks. The house rang with his harsh, barking cough, and on the few occasions when she did slip into a light doze the sound of his laboured breathing was constantly in the background of her fragmented dreams.

She woke from one of her brief naps to hear Leezie, always the first to rise in the morning, moving about below. Opening the heavy curtains Bethany saw that dawn had finally arrived, turning the warm glow from the bedside lamp into a wan imitation of its former self.

Gil slept, sprawled in a tumble of sheets and blankets. His breathing was still laboured, and when she laid a hand on his forehead it was so hot that she could scarcely bear to leave her fingers there for more than a few seconds. When he opened his eyes and looked up at her it was with a blank stare, as though he could not think who she was.

Then his eyes cleared and he complained, 'I'm as dry as a bone. Fetch the whisky, Beth'ny.'

'Never mind whisky, it's water you'll have.' She took the jug that stood by the bed and hurried to the bathroom to rinse and then refill it. He drank half the contents of the jug, and once his thirst had been quenched he was more like his old self. When Bethany suggested sending for the doctor, he flatly refused to allow it.

'It's just a chill, woman! Keep on with those damned poultices and the hot toddies and I'll be fine.'

He managed to eat some porridge and drink a cup of tea, laced, at his insistence, with a little whisky. Then he slept throughout the day, rousing only to take some broth and a milk pudding Bethany made especially for him.

Once again, she spent the night on two chairs, rising frequently to attend to Gil as he tossed restlessly.

As she bathed his face in the morning, he opened his eyes and looked at her as though she was a stranger.

'Fetch yer mistress, quine,' he said, so hoarsely that it was scarcely much more than a groan, 'Tell Molly that I'm no' feelin' too well—'

His eyes slid up until only the whites showed, and the lids dropped, but only halfway. His strong, stubby fingers plucked at the edge of the linseed poultice on his chest, trying to pull it off. Bethany hurried from the room and downstairs to where the maidservant, her face still puffed with sleep, was raking out the kitchen range.

'Leezie, I don't care what Gil says, I'm bringing the doctor in to see him. Run and fetch the man now.'

'But I've got the dishes tae put out and the porridge tae make and—'

'Just do as you're told!'

'Is he worse, then?'

'A lot worse,' Bethany said. 'He doesn't know me, Leezie. When he woke up a minute since he thought I was his first wife's maidservant. Tell the doctor to be quick.'

7

Gil Pate's funeral was a handsome affair, with four black horses pulling the hearse up the hill to Rathven Cemetery, followed by a long procession of mourners on foot. Although women were not expected to go to the graveside Bethany insisted on leading the procession, with ten-year-old Rory walking by her side. Zelda had taken Ellen and Adam to stay in her already overcrowded cottage until the funeral was over.

On the way to the open grave the procession passed the Lowrie plot, where Bethany's parents, Weem and Jess, lay side by side. Jess had kept her husband's grave neat, but since her mother's death Bethany had only paid one or two visits. She cast a swift glance at their headstone as she went by and saw that someone had been tending the graves. Zelda, surely, or Innes – it was the sort of thing that they would do, and she could not imagine James or Stella taking on the task.

She would be expected to do the same for Gil, she realised, and decided there and then that she would pay for his grave to be kept decent. Unlike her mother, she had no intention of weeding and cleaning and tidying her husband's last resting place. She would be too busy earning her way and feeding and clothing the children.

Rory stood motionless by her side, shivering slightly in the chill December wind as the coffin was lowered into the fresh grave that had been dug in the cold earth. When Bethany threw a handful of soil in after it he followed suit, his fingers searching for hers even as the earth rattled on the polished lid of the coffin, and as they moved away from the grave-side after the short service he glanced back several times.

Jacob, unable because of his rheumatism to walk up the hill to Rathven, had come in his motorcar. It was waiting for him at the cemetery gates, with his driver behind the wheel. Jacob had never learned to drive; he used the motorcar infrequently, and when he did need it he hired a local man to drive it for him. He offered to take Bethany and Rory with him, but Rory opted to walk home.

'He'll be all right with me.' Nathan put a large hand on his nephew's shoulder. 'We're the men of the fam'ly now, eh, Rory? You and me are goin' tae have tae look after the womenfolk, are we no'?' His eyes were on Bethany as he spoke, and the gleam deep in their depths sent a shiver down her spine.

'This is a bad day,' Jacob said soberly as they drove down the hill. 'I never thought tae see Gil go so soon. He cannae have been much over forty years of age.'

'He was in his forty-first year, just.' Bethany spoke absently, unable to forget the look in Nathan's eyes, or the way his meaty hand had clutched Rory's shoulder, as though claiming the boy. She had never cared for her husband's brother; to her mind, Nathan was a sly, slippery creature, and more than once he had reminded her of the eels that were sometimes brought up in the fishing nets and writhed in the fisher-wives' creels, reaching out to catch and hold unwary folk.

'A fair bit older than yersel', then,' Jacob was saying.

'A good ten years.'

'Ye're young tae be widowed.'

'Not on this coast. There's many a lassie been widowed almost as soon as she wed. My own Aunt Meg, for one.'

'Aye, that's true.' He covered her gloved hand with his own for a brief moment. 'If I can ever help ye, ye know where I am.'

'You can help me,' Bethany said swiftly. In the dark nights between Gil's death and the funeral she had been laying plans. Now, she decided, was as good a time as any to speak in private to Jacob. 'Keep me on at the net factory,' she said, 'and pay me to keep the books for the curing and the coopering. You know that Nathan's no good at sums.'

'But surely ye'll have enough tae see tae—'

'I need to earn my way, Jacob!'

'But your man'll have made certain that you and the bairns are well provided for, surely.'

'Even so, I want to be my own woman, not Gil's dependant.' Bethany thought again of Nathan.

'If that's the way ye want it,' Jacob said, as the car drew to a halt before the house.

'It is.' Bethany had the door open and was out before the driver could assist her.

Four or five women were bustling about between the kitchen and the front parlour, where a long table held plates and glasses and trays of food. Zelda, usually the first to volunteer her services when help was needed, had stayed at home on this occasion to look after Ellen and Adam Pate as well as her own brood, but some of the neighbours had brought food for the funeral guests and stayed to help Leezie.

Stella was there, too, a black apron covering her black dress. When Bethany said, 'It's good of you to come, Stella,' her sister-in-law replied stiffly, 'It's my Christian duty tae offer help where it's needed.'

'Here, I'll take that in for you.' Bethany seized the tray of cold meats that Stella had been carrying from the kitchen. It was hard to believe, she thought as she went into the parlour, where a big table had been set up, that only five years ago, when the Pates lived in a cottage near the sea, Stella had almost driven her mad by calling in almost every day to chatter like a mindless sparrow about recipes and bairns and suchlike. Now the woman could scarcely bear to speak to her, and Bethany had no need to wonder why. A lot had happened in the past five years.

She put the tray down and stepped back to survey the table. Leezie had done her work well; the best cutlery and china and glassware had been set out, and there was enough food to satisfy even the largest appetite.

The guests began to straggle in, and soon she was too busy to think about anything other than the funeral tea. Nathan, she noticed, made a determined attempt to play the host and make sure that all the menfolk were kept supplied with drink, but Jacob had already appropriated that task for himself. Nathan finally resorted to sulking in a corner and trying to catch Bethany's eye. She ignored him studiously, though she was aware of his gaze following her as she moved around the room, making sure she spoke to each and every one of the people who had come to pay their respects to her late husband.

As always with funerals, the proceedings began in sombre silence, but as the meal progressed and the whisky bottles were passed around, tongues began to loosen, and what started as a low buzz of conversation steadily rose until they were all speaking at their normal level. Since many of them were outdoor workers – coopers, curers and fishermen – their normal level was loud enough to make the walls vibrate.

When they had eaten their fill, Jacob produced some bottles of port that he had brought with him, and Bethany judged it the right time to retreat to the kitchen, where the womenfolk were gathered about the table, drinking tea.

First, though, she made her way to where the coopers stood in a group, tongue-tied with shyness at finding themselves in their former employer's fine house.

'Thank you for coming, all of you,' she said warmly, shaking each and every one of them by the hand, 'and I hope that you'll stay on for a wee while and enjoy a glass of Mr McFarlane's port.' Then, turning to Wattie Noble, Gil's right-hand man, 'Wattie, could I have a wee word with you outside?'

In the hallway, with the parlour door firmly closed, she said, 'You make sure your men stay and have some port, Wattie, for I'm told that it's very good, though for now I'm more interested in having a cup of tea with the other women in the kitchen. I wanted to ask if you'd be willing to look out for the cooperage until Rory's of an age to serve his apprenticeship.'

'Me – take charge?' The big man stared down at her. 'I don't know about that, missus.'

'You can do it, can't you? You know as much about coopering as the master did – and he knew everything about it.'

'Aye, but . . . are you takin' it over, then?'

'I won't know that until the will's read tomorrow. It could be me and it could be Nathan Pate. All I'm saying,' Bethany said vigorously, 'is that I want to make sure that you're on my side.'

Understanding dawned on Wattie's face. 'It's like that, is it?'

'Aye, it is. And I'll be expecting you to consult me on everything, even if the place has been left to Nathan.'

The man looked uncertain. 'I'd not want tae get caught up in any quarrels, missus. I just want tae get on with my job.'

'There'll be a bit more money in your pocket from now on, besides your usual pay packet,' Bethany promised recklessly. 'I'll see to that.' And so she would, even if it took all the money she was being paid for her work in the net factory. She desperately needed to maintain control of the cooperage, for Rory's sake.

'In that case,' he said, 'I'll dae whatever ye ask, missus!'

'Good.' She gave him a push towards the parlour door. 'Now in you go and enjoy your drink. You've earned it.'

In the kitchen she hauled her hat off and flopped on to a vacant chair. 'Thank goodness that's over!'

'You mean you're glad tae see that poor man laid in his grave – at his age?' Stella asked, eyebrows raised.

'You know I didn't mean that, Stella. I meant having to

71

listen to the men talking and talking and never saying anything of interest or worth. Pour a cup for me, Leezie, I'm parched.' Bethany loosened the top button of her high-necked jacket and reached for a buttered girdle scone. 'Where's Rory?'

'He went upstairs a while back,' someone volunteered. 'He's missin' his faither, poor wee loon.'

'I'll look in on him later.'

A gust of laughter could be heard from the next room and a few of the women, Stella included, tutted and shook their heads. 'It's not seemly,' objected one of the neighbours.

'It's human nature, Mrs Marshall. What's done's done and Gil can't be brought back.' Bethany downed half a cup of tea thirstily and then bit into the scone. Suddenly she was weary to her very bones, and desperate to have the house to herself.

Eventually the guests in the parlour began to drift away and it was time for her to button up her jacket, put on her hat again and take up her position at the parlour door to shake hands and thank each of them for attending the funeral.

'D'ye want me tae take young Rory back tae the hoosie with me?' Innes asked.

'No, leave him here. I need to have a talk with him later. Besides, your house must be bursting at the seams.'

He grinned at her. 'It always is. I think the walls must be made of some stuff that stretches, for Zelda can aye manage tae find room for another body.' Then, serious again, he took both her hands in his. 'If ye need anythin', Bethany, ye know ye can come tae me and Zelda any time.'

'I do. Thank you, Innes.' She watched him go with a sense of wonder. She had never set much store by her younger brother, dismissing him as a weakling and a mother's boy, but Innes had grown to be a man with confidence in himself. He was a happy man too – it showed in his eyes and in his bearing. Innes was contented with his lot, which was more, she thought bitterly, than she and James had ever been.

'Bethany?' As if her thoughts had summoned him, James

stood before her, holding his hand out. She allowed her fingers to rest in his for only seconds before pulling them free. 'Stella's in the kit—' she began, and then stopped as James's wife appeared by his side. 'Thank you for your kindness, Stella.'

'It was only right, since we're kin by marriage,' the woman said sharply, and almost hustled James from the house.

Nathan was the last to go. 'I'm goin' tae miss Gil.' He took her proffered hand and held on to it. 'He was a fine, fine brither, Beth'ny, and a fine husb—'

'We'll all miss him.' She almost wrenched her fingers free of his grasp and moved swiftly along the hall to open the door. Today, at least, she was still mistress of the house, and could still decide who should be in it. 'I'll see you tomorrow at the reading of the will. Good day to you, Nathan.'

She closed the door behind him and stood staring at the stained-glass panel for a moment, biting her lower lip. She had searched high and low for a copy of the will, anxious to find out what it contained, but there was nothing, not even a scribbled note. It must have been left in the lawyer's keeping. She wondered, given Nathan's sly looks, if he already knew its contents.

Leezie and the neighbours had already begun to transfer the used dishes and glasses from the parlour to the kitchen, for all the world like a stream of ants, Bethany thought. She rubbed her hand down her skirt to rid it of Nathan's touch and then went upstairs to the bathroom, where she tore the hat from her head for the second time, heedless now of tousling her hair, and washed and rinsed her hands several times before drying them.

Turning back to hang the towel on its hook, she caught sight of herself in the mirror, clad in black from head to foot, her face flushed with the warmth of the house.

'The widow Pate,' she said aloud, and then again, tasting the words in her mouth. 'The widow Pate.'

Her hands, when she put them against the heat of her cheeks, felt pleasantly cool. She closed her eyes, inhaling the

73

smell of the coal tar soap she had used, and then went on to the landing and knocked on the door of the bedroom that Rory shared with Adam.

'Can I come in?'

His voice, when he said, 'Aye,' was surprised. Normally, only the adults were allowed privacy in that house; Gil had considered it his right, as head of the house, to barge into any room he pleased, other than Leezie's tiny bedroom close by the kitchen.

Rory was sitting on his bed, working away at a sketch-pad. Two or three open books were strewn about the bed and he looked up guiltily as his stepmother came into the room. 'I was getting tired of bein' down the stairs. Nob'dy was talkin' to me—'

'You were quite right to come up here. Are you doing your homework?'

'Just drawing.' He had been clutching the sketchpad to his chest, but relinquished it when she held her hand out.

She sat down on the bed and stared at the drawing. 'What is it?'

'A steam engine. It's not very good,' the boy said apologetically. 'That's why you didnae recognise it.'

'I didn't recognise it because I know nothing of engines. I didn't know you did, either.'

'It's easy enough when ye just think about it.' Rory knelt up beside her, pointing with his forefinger. 'It all makes sense. See, that's the cylinder, and that long bit's the rod, and there's the crank that moves the rod, and here's the main condenser—'

'I still can't make head nor tail of it. How d'you know all this?'

'Uncle Innes showed me. Those are the engines that make the fishing boats work. He took me down tae the *Fidelity*'s engine room and explained it all tae me,' Rory said proudly.

'Did he indeed? Now,' she picked up one of the open books, a book on birds that his father had given him at the boy's own request, 'this makes more sense to me.'

'They're bonny, aren't they?'

'They are that. Bonnier than engines, and they sound better too.' Bethany riffled through the pages, stopping at one. 'What's that?'

'A yellow bunting. And that,' the boy pointed to a picture on the opposite page, 'that's a greenfinch.' Then, as she turned the page, 'That's a merlin and that's a mountain linnet. Some folk call it a twite.'

'Was it Uncle Innes who told you about birds, too?'

'No, Peter taught me all about them – Peter Bain.'

'He must know a lot about the countryside.'

Before marrying Innes, Zelda had worked as a maid at the Bain farm in Rathven. Peter, the farmer's son, was two years older than Rory.

'And the shore, too,' Rory said. 'And I'm learnin' from him. I like learnin' things.'

'Rory, you were grand today.' Bethany closed the book and laid it on her lap. 'Your father would have been proud of you. You behaved like the man of the family,' she hurried on as tears began to sparkle in the boy's blue eyes, 'and that's what you are now, the man of the family.'

'Me?'

'Of course. I'm going to have to work hard to make enough money to keep us, and that means that I'll be away from the house during the day.'

'Are you goin' to look after the cooperage?'

'No, I can't do that because I'm not a cooper. One of the men will look after it until you're old enough to run it. That's what your father wanted for you. I'll be at the net factory, and when I have to be out of the house Leezie will be here to see to the three of you. But it would help me if you'd keep an eye on the wee ones and let me know if there's anything wrong with them, or with you.'

A tentative smile tugged at one corner of the boy's mouth. 'I could do that, all right.'

'I'm sure you could.' Bethany got to her feet. 'Mr

Morrison's coming in tomorrow morning to talk to me and your uncles and Mr McFarlane about some things, then you and me can go and fetch the wee ones home. The sooner we get back to our usual ways the better. For now, I'd best go downstairs and help Leezie. You stay here with your books and your drawings.'

The three of them – Rory, Leezie and Bethany – dined that night on the remains of the funeral tea before going to bed early, worn out from the day's business.

Alone in the big front bedroom she had shared with Gil, Bethany stripped off her widow's weeds and stretched before pouring water from the china jug into the basin. The bathroom, Gil's pride and joy, boasted a proper bath, but tonight she preferred to use the basin in the privacy of the room that had become hers. At least, she thought as she tossed the uncomfortable clothing aside, she was still slender enough to avoid having to wear corsets.

After putting on her nightdress, she gathered up the discarded clothing from the floor and hung it carefully in her half of the big wardrobe. She would have to put it on again tomorrow for the lawyer's visit, but after that she would return to skirts and blouses in suitably muted shades.

Unpinning her hair, she shook it out about her shoulders and started to brush it with long, slow strokes until it lay about her shoulders, soft and shining, the ends curling slightly. The electric light caught the fair streaks she had inherited from her mother, turning them to gold among the rich brown. Normally she put it into a single plait for the night, but now, too tired to be bothered, she fetched a ribbon and tied it at the nape of her neck, then turned the lamp out and drew the curtains back before climbing into the double bed.

The sash window was open at the top to allow fresh air into the room. Bethany stretched her limbs luxuriously across the bed and contemplated the task before her – to raise three children single-handed and at the same time earn her keep, and theirs, by working for Jacob McFarlane and, if possible, running the cooperage.

The prospect of taking on all those responsibilities did not frighten her at all. Ever since her marriage, and especially since Adam's birth, Gil had done all he could to turn her into a housekeeper, dependent on him for every penny. But now she was free to become her own woman again, answerable to no man.

Bethany Pate, widow, smiled to herself in the dark before drifting into a deep, dreamless sleep.

8

Gilbert Pate's will was brief and to the point – control of the cooperage was entrusted to his brother Nathan until such time as Rory had served his apprenticeship and was capable of taking charge. The house went to Bethany and any moneys Gil possessed at the time of his death, together with his share of future profits from the business that the Pate brothers and James had entered into with Jacob, would be held in trust for the three children by Nathan, who was also responsible for allotting a monthly housekeeping sum to Bethany. On reaching their twenty-first birthdays each of Gil's children would take control of a third of the money in trust. Nathan and Jacob McFarlane were named as trustees.

Bethany sat straight-backed during the reading, staring fixedly at the lawyer's shoulder. Her face was expressionless, though her hands were clenched within their black kid gloves, and behind her calm exterior she seethed at the thought of being beholden to Nathan for every penny, just as she had been beholden to Gil.

All these years of looking after his children, her brain clamoured so loudly that she felt the words ringing in her ears, caring for his home, submitting to his needs whether she felt like it or not – and what thanks had she got for it? The man had left her as good as destitute, dependent on the goodwill of his brother for every morsel of food she put into her mouth and every stitch of clothing that covered her body.

All she had was the house, and she could not sell that, for it was the children's home.

She could tell by the way Nathan's eyes kept flickering towards her that the terms of the will suited him very well. If she had only known the way the wind blew she would have done whatever was necessary to make Gil change it. But it was too late now, and she would either have to become an independent woman or spend the rest of her life under Nathan's thumb.

The very thought of it made her feel as though she was stifling. The room seemed very stuffy and she longed to get away, but as soon as the business was over Nathan was by her side.

'I want ye tae know, Beth'ny, that I'll look after you and the bairns as if ye were my own,' he said into her ear, standing so close that his tobacco-rich breath was hot on her cheek.

'We'll manage fine, Nathan.' She made as if to move away from him, and then turned when she was at a safe distance. 'You'll know that I'm running Jacob's net factory for him now?'

'I'd heard, but I don't approve. Ye deserve better than that. Gil left ye in my care and it's my duty tae take over his duties as a husband and faither until the bairns are grown.' He put a faint but definite emphasis on the word 'husband', and as his eyes slid over Bethany's body his tongue flicked out to moisten his lips. 'After all,' he went on, 'every woman needs someone tae support her, and who better than yer man's brother?'

'There's nothing wrong with a day's honest labour for a day's wages. I've no worries about supporting the children,' Bethany retorted, and then to her relief she heard James ask Jacob when the end-of-season reckoning was to be held.

'I'm sorry tae be bringin' business up at a time like this, Bethany,' James added uncomfortably as she joined them, 'but there's wages tae be paid out and bills tae be settled. Folk need tae know where they stand.'

'Bethany knows that well enough,' Jacob said briskly, 'as she's always been the one tae write out the final reckoning for Gil. That's why I wondered, Bethany, if ye'd continue with the task of calculatin' the money due tae each boat – for a reasonable payment, of course.'

'Beth'ny?' Nathan spluttered, while her knees went weak with relief. 'But I'm the curer! It's my job tae do the books!'

'Mebbe so, but it was always Gil who took charge of them, was it no'?' Jacob said easily.

'Aye, mebbe it was, but now he's gone it should be me.'

'It's just that Gil always relied on Bethany here tae do the final reckoning, with her bein' better at the writin' than he was. That why I thought it only right tae ask her tae go on with it.'

'I've no argument against that,' James cut in. 'Our Bethany always had a good head for figurin'.'

'The books should be my responsibility!'

'Nathan's right,' Bethany said, and as all three men stared at her, taken aback, 'What does a woman know of men's business? You should take over the books Nathan. In fact, I'd be glad to stop working on them. Here—'

She opened the roll-top writing desk and heaved a large, thick ledger over to the table, dropping it from a few inches away so that it arrived with a hefty thud. 'You'll easily learn from glancing over pages for the past years how to write it in. First, you need to get all the bills and receipts from James and the other skippers, then you take a different page for each boat, and you write down everything they got on tick down one page. Every single thing, mind. Then you write the number of crans taken during the season on the other page, and work out the payment for each cran. That's not many boats, so it should only take you a day at most. But it has to be done soon, for as James says, the skippers have to pay out the crews' wages as soon as they can. There are the gutting crews too – the way you work out their wages is this—'

'I've no' got the time tae do all that!' Nathan protested, and Bethany gave him a sweet smile.

'Neither had Gil. That's why he left it to me.'

'Aye, well, mebbe you should go on with it, just until I find the time tae take over.'

'If that's what you want,' Bethany said demurely. 'But what about these? You'll want to take them over yourself for certain.' She turned back to the desk and deposited another two ledgers on the table before his horrified gaze. 'These are to do with the cooperage – materials bought in and barrels made and the work each man did on each day. You have to work out their wages from the hours and the number of barrels, but it's quite easy once you get the idea of it. And you must balance the materials bought in against the barrels sent out. There are the stock records to keep as well; it's important to make sure that you don't run out of timber because then the men'll have nothing to do.. Gil was never over fond of paying his workers to be idle. And these,' a sheaf of papers landed on the table, 'are the bills still to be paid and the accounts waiting to be sent out. You have to balance them all in this ledger, and they'll have to be done soon, but even so—'

'Jings,' James said, grinning. 'I'm glad I'm just a fisherman, Nathan, and 'no' a businessman like yersel'.'

'You can keep on with the lot of them for the time bein', just until I get the time tae start doin' it mysel'.' Nathan flapped his hands at the books and paperwork on the table as though trying to make the untidy pile disappear, then added in an attempt to retain control over the situation, 'But I'll do the hirin' of the guttin' crews mysel'.'

'Now that's settled, if ye're willin', Bethany, I'll tell the skippers tae gather at my house a week from today for the reckonin',' Jacob suggested, and she nodded.

'I can have the books ready, if you'll make sure, James, that the skippers answerable to Gil and Nathan tell me what's owed and how many cran of herring they took. And now I'll go and tell Leezie to bring in some tea. I know I'm ready for it. Jacob, there's something stronger in the cupboard there, if anyone would care for a glass.'

Bethany watched from behind the parlour curtains as the three men walked along the road, Nathan and James flanking Jacob and walking slowly to accommodate him. Age was beginning to tell on Jacob, Bethany thought as she watched. He could do with an assistant – someone trustworthy and able.

She turned back into the room, a smile curving her lips as she glanced at the roll-top desk where the ledgers lay waiting for her attention. There was a lot of work to be done in the next week, but she could manage it easily enough.

She rubbed her hands together, and then went out into the hall. 'Rory?' she called from the bottom of the stairs. 'You can come down now. It's time for us to go and fetch Ellen and Adam!'

Passing the harbour on her way home from the factory on the following day, she saw that the *Fidelity* had been brought from the boatyard and was now moored in the innermost basin. She looked bonny in her new paintwork, with her name picked out in elaborately curling gold letters.

Bethany hesitated and then went to have a closer look at the drifter. Nobody else seemed to be around, but as she stood there, her mind seething with memories, James said from behind her, 'She's lookin' more like herself, eh?'

She spun round. 'I was just wondering how she was coming along.'

'Why not, since ye're a Lowrie, and this is the Lowrie boat?' The tide was in and the basin full, which meant that the drifter's deck was almost level with the harbour wall. James brushed past her and put a foot on the gunwale, then turned. 'Come aboard and have a proper look.'

'Leezie'll be expecting me home—'

'Bethany,' he interrupted with a touch of irritation, 'I'm

back in Buckie now whether you like it or not, and we cannae spend the rest of our lives tryin' tae avoid each other. Folk would notice, for one thing, and I'm sure you don't want tae arouse the gossips. So come and have a look at her.'

. He leapt lightly to the deck and she paused for only a second more before following him. As she put a foot on the gunwale, hesitating in order to adjust to the slight bounce of the boat, he held a hand out to assist her. Instead of taking it she jumped to the deck almost as easily as he had, then steadied herself and looked up to see him grinning at her.

'Ye've not lost yer skill with boats, then.'

'I never will.' She began to walk along the deck, past the galley. To her relief James stayed where he was, leaving her to enjoy the sensation of being back on the boat that she loved every bit as much as he did.

The drifter shifted slightly beneath her feet, and, drawing off her glove to put a hand on the smooth, solid wood of the mast, Bethany felt the years drop away from her. The *Fidelity* was part of her life, and being on board again for the first time in many years reminded her fleetingly, disturbingly, of what happiness had been like.

The smell of strong tobacco drifted towards her on the stiff breeze. James had lit his pipe and now he was standing, half turned away from her, studying the other boats in the harbour. Bethany climbed up to the wheelhouse and went in, resting her hands on the wheel's wooden spokes and looking unseeingly through the window before her as she thought of all the men the drifter had carried out to the fishing grounds and safely back to shore, low in the water on the return journey, her holds full of the silver darlings.

Her father, Weem Lowrie, the man who had edged rather than pushed her into becoming Gil's wife in order to further his own ambitions, had spent his last years in this wheelhouse; her Uncle Albert had taken over from him and now the boat belonged to James, her brother. She tightened her hold on the wooden spokes, thinking of his hands resting there, strong and confident in the ability of his boat. The *Fidelity* was the only part of James's life that was at all certain, she thought, and wished that it could have been otherwise for the older brother she had idolised, fought with and cared for deeply – too deeply.

Looking up, she saw that he was watching her from the deck below. For a moment their eyes met before Bethany turned away. When she rejoined him, he said, 'Are ye not goin' below? The whole boat's been painted and varnished.'

'Leezie's expecting me back,' she said again, then stared, startled, as James suddenly laughed out loud. It was a sound she had not heard from him in a long time.

'Ye fairly sorted Nathan out yesterday.'

'The man's a fool.' She leaned against the wall of the galley. 'Gil propped him up for years and he'd no right to leave Nathan in control of the cooperage. It should have come to me!'

'Aye, I agree with ye.' James took the pipe from his mouth and moved to spit over the boat's side before turning back to her, wiping the back of one hand across his mouth. The moment's amusement vanished as he went on coldly, 'I didnae care for the way he looked at you when the will was bein' read. He thinks tae take over from Gil in more ways than runnin' the cooperage and hirin' the fisher-lassies.'

'Nathan's all eyes and no wits and I don't give that for him.' She snapped her fingers. 'As to the cooperage, I've had a word with Wattie Noble, and he's agreed to tell me everything that goes on. I doubt if Nathan will be any better at managing it than he would have been at keeping the books. I think I'll be able to control things in my own way.'

'But can ye control Nathan himsel'?'

'Of course I can.'

'Ye're probably right, but if he starts tae cause ye grief just tell me and I'll soon put a stop tae it,' he said and then, nodding towards the wheelhouse, 'Ye looked just right up there. It's a pity that quinies cannae fish the deep.'

'I've always thought that myself.' Bethany said, and then, remembering, 'I found this in one of Gil's pockets.' She held the folded scrap of paper out to him and watched his face as he read it. 'I found it while he was away in Yarm'th,' she said when he looked back up at her. 'I was going to face him with it when he came home, but I never had the chance.'

'The loan was arranged fair and square—'

'I'm not saying that it wasn't, but I wish that one of you had had the decency to tell me about it.'

'We thought it best tae keep it between ourselves.'

'Because women know nothing of business, I suppose.' Bethany's voice was sharp, and colour rose under James's tan.

'Jacob wanted tae sell her.' He gestured to the drifter they stood on. 'The only way I could keep her was tae buy his share and find the money tae get her put tae rights. I mortgaged the house but it wasnae enough, so I turned tae Gil for help.' He held the paper out to her. 'We agreed that I'd pay him back at the end of the next fishin' season. Now I'll be payin' you.'

Bethany took the paper and stood for a moment, considering it. She had meant to use it to give her bargaining power over Gil, and now that he was gone, it could give her some power over James, not to mention some welcome income in a year's time. But even as those thoughts came to her she was tearing the note across once, twice – and then she opened her fingers to let the little scraps of paper flutter free. James watched in astonishment as the breeze wafted them over the gunwales and then released them, allowing them to fall into the dark water between the *Fidelity* and the neighbouring boat.

'What did ye dae that for?' he demanded to know as the last tiny white scrap disappeared.

'Your debt was to Gil, and now he's gone. And, as you said, this is the family boat. We couldn't let her be sold.'

'But . . . you've three bairns tae raise!'

'I've still got my own share in the *Fidelity*. And I'll manage fine on my lone,' said Bethany. 'No need to fret about me.'

*

A week later, Bethany sat behind the big desk in Jacob McFarlane's study, the ledgers open before her and a pen in her hand, as the skippers and mates of the drifters contracted to sell their fish to the consortium headed by Jacob filed in to collect their money.

If they were surprised to see her there, they were also happy to accept the money due to each boat. It had been a good season for herring, and there was enough money to last them and their crews through the winter.

'We'll be seein' a difference after this,' one of them prophesied gloomily, 'because the Germans are no' buyin' the way they used tae afore the war. And nob'dy kens yet about the Russians, after what's been happenin' in their country.'

'That's for me and Nathan tae fret over,' Jacob told him, and Nathan, standing by the desk, shifted uneasily. At the outbreak of the Great War considerable numbers of foreign buyers had been in Britain to bid for the herring catches as they always did. They had left abruptly, taking as much fish as they could; in almost every case their debts had not been honoured and, as a result, fish-curers up and down the coast had been made bankrupt and forced out of business. Nathan had been one of the lucky survivors.

'I dae a bit o' frettin' mysel', havin' a fam'ly tae feed,' the man protested. 'What's tae happen next year?'

'We'll engage you and your boat same as we've done before, and guarantee tae buy your first hundred cran of fish for an agreed price as usual, and mebbe more. With fewer curers around and the fishermen back from the war, we'll have another good season,' Jacob prophesied jauntily. 'Away through tae the other room with ye, now. There's a dram waitin' there, just desperate tae be swallowed.'

The man's eyes brightened, and as soon as he had pocketed his money he made for the door, followed by the other skippers.

'I'm no' so sure that it would be a good idea tae take on too many boats next year.' Nathan girned as he collected the money due to the women who gutted and packed the fish. 'If we promise the men a fixed price for the first hundred cran they take we'll be layin' out a lot of money.'

'You don't get money in if you don't put it out first,' Bethany said crisply, irritated by the man's fear. 'And if Jacob thinks it'll be a good season next year then it will be. He knows the fishing better than you and me.'

'Away and have a drink afore it's all gone, Nathan,' Jacob suggested, and when the man had gone off, still muttering uneasily, he remarked, ' I doubt if Nathan's comfortable with the notion of havin' tae put siller intae other men's pockets instead of his own.'

'He never was. He takes after his mother.' Bethany shivered at the memory of her late mother-in-law, a formidable woman who had never, until the day she died, released her grip on her two sons. It was only Bethany's strength and determination that had kept Phemie Pate from gaining control over Rory and Ellen and Adam as well. Nathan, a bachelor, had lived with his mother in her small cottage in Findochty, a nearby fishing village, and had continued to live there in the two years since the woman's death.

'There's nothin' wrong with a man takin' after his mither – I take after mine,' Jacob said complacently. 'But she was one of the finest women you could ever hope tae meet. Euphemia Pate, on the other hand . . .'

He chuckled, then said briskly, 'Only your James tae come. He'll be down at the harbour, no doubt, makin' certain that the *Fidelity*'s goin' tae be set up for the new season. Then I suppose I'll have tae find a crew for the *Jess Lowrie*, because James is determined tae get back tae his own drifter.'

'D'you really think it's going to be a good year next year?'

'Ye can depend on it. There'll be a few more good years at least, though I'm not sure as tae what'll happen after that. For the meantime, I'll be takin' on as many boats as I can.' He tapped the side of his nose with a gnarled finger. 'It'll be worth the outlay. The secret, Bethany, is—'

'Never pay out all your silver,' Bethany said as she counted James's share of the catch. 'Always keep back a wee bittie against the cold weather.' Then, glancing up at his surprised face, 'I've run a house for years, Jacob; I know how to handle money.'

He grinned. 'You take after the woman that bore ye, lassie. I wish Nathan had your way with money. Sometimes I feel that I'd be better without him.'

'Mebbe you would at that,' she said, and would have said more if Jacob had not started to hoist himself to his feet, clutching at the edge of the solid desk for support.

'I'm away in tae have a dram with the others. Can I bring one through for ye?'

'A cup of tea will do me fine.'

Bethany busied herself with the books, going over columns of figures that had already been added more than once. Jacob's comparison between her and her mother displeased her, for she liked to think that she was her own woman, owing nothing of her nature to either of her parents.

James came in, hauling his cap off and glancing around the room. 'Is Jacob not here?'

The skippers traditionally put on their Sunday best for the ceremony of dividing out the season's money, but he must have come straight from the harbour, for he was still wearing his work clothes.

'He's in the other room with the rest of them. I've your money here, and the list.' She held out the sheet of paper and he took it, his eyes skimming down the page as Bethany briskly accounted for every penny earned and every penny spent.

'D'you agree with it?'

'It seems right enough.'

'It is, you can be sure of that,' Bethany was saying when Jacob came in, glass in hand and followed by his housekeeper with a tea tray.

'There ye are, James,' he said affably as Bethany cleared

a space on the desk for the tray. 'Thank ye, Mrs Duthie.' He lifted his glass to his nose and inhaled the whisky's aroma, then drank some down, watching brother and sister over the rim of the glass as Bethany counted the notes and coins due to James into his outstretched hand.

There was something amiss between these two; he sensed it in the air each time he was with them. He wondered idly if he would ever know what it was, and then shrugged it out of the way. James and Bethany were thrawn, the pair of them, but they were strong and they were ambitious – and that suited him well.

The more he thought of it, the more he liked the idea of Bethany allying herself with him. She possessed more intelligence than her husband and his brother Nathan put together.

'Come on through to the other room and have a drink, James,' he said, and paused to drain his glass before following the younger man out.

'To Bethany Lowrie Pate,' he said to himself as he drank the whisky down. 'To the future.'

9

'Isa Thain's at the door,' Leezie said. 'She's askin' if she can have a word with ye.'

'What is it she's wanting?'

'Tae talk tae ye. I just said.'

'Leezie!' Bethany, in a hurry as she always was these days, glared at the maid. 'I've to get to the net factory as soon as I'm . . . Oh, you'd better send the woman in. Tell her I'll talk to her while I'm finishing my breakfast. See that the children get off to school in good time – and make sure that Adam has a warm jacket, for it's bitter outside.'

Isa's thin face was pinched with cold when she came into the kitchen, and Bethany immediately went to the big dresser to fetch another cup and saucer. 'Sit down, Isa, there's plenty tea in the pot.'

'I'm no' here for tea,' the woman said stiffly, standing just inside the kitchen door. 'I'm here tae ask for work.'

Bethany, pouring out the tea, gave a small, silent sigh. Isa Thain had always been a difficult creature. 'You can ask for work just as easy sitting down and drinking tea, surely? You might as well, for I'm in a hurry to get to the net factory and I want another cup before I go,' she said sharply, and after a moment's hesitation the other woman did as she was told.

'That's better, now I'll not have to twist my neck looking up at you all the time.' Bethany sat down and took a sip from her own cup before asking, 'Are you thinking to get work in the net factory for one of the quines?'

Isa, a widow, had three daughters, all in their teens, and she supported her mother as well. 'It's for mysel',' she said, warming her hands on the cup, 'an' the net factory's no use tae me, for I never worked there and I don't know the way of it. I'm lookin' for some skivvyin' work.'

'Skivvyin'? Here?' Bethany was unable to keep the surprise from her voice. Skivvying, kippering (smoking the herring) working in the net factory, baiting the lines for the white fishing, gutting and packing herring were all jobs open to women in the fishing community. Isa had worked for Gil as a packer for years and Bethany knew that the woman was highly skilled at the job. In a good year she could earn enough money during the herring season to keep her going for a month or two at least. But now, it was just two weeks into the New Year.

'What about your two eldest?' Bethany asked. 'Surely they're old enough to earn their way now?'

She could tell by the sudden colour in the other woman's face that the question had angered her. Isa Thain's worst fault was an inability to get on with other folk. Her sharp tongue often made her unpopular and in the days when she herself had been hiring the gutting crews for Gil, Bethany had had to act as mediator between Isa and the other women on many occasions.

When Isa finally managed to speak it was in a low voice, and she stared down at the table instead of meeting Bethany's gaze. 'Bella's already skivvyin' at one of the big houses out by Garmouth, but she's no' bringin' in enough tae keep us goin'. And Nanse hasnae been well enough tae work since she'd the bairn.'

'Your Nanse has a bairn? I didn't know that.'

'Aye, well, you've been too busy bein' a fine la—' Isa began with a flash of her usual self, then she stopped short and said, 'You've had things tae think of yersel', wi' Gil dyin'.'

'Aye, I suppose. What about Nanse, though?'

The story came out bit by bit. Isa's eldest daughter had fallen pregnant by one of the labourers who flocked to the coastline to make some money during the herring season. Who the man was nobody knew, for he was long gone before poor Nanse discovered that she was carrying his child. The girl had been at the Yarmouth fishing with her mother when the child was born prematurely.

'I should never have let her keep on at the packin', but she was scarce showin', so I thought it was all right tae let her follow the fishin',' Isa said. 'I kept an eye on her an' tried tae make sure she didnae have too much heavy work tae dae, but one day when I was at the mission havin' some right bad cuts dressed Nathan Pate made her an' some of the other young ones stack a whole lot of full barrels, an' that was enough tae bring her on.'

Bethany winced. The coopers usually handled full barrels, but when they were busy the women were expected to help. It was heavy work, too heavy for women, and many a fisher-lassie suffered later in life from medical problems brought on by the strain of heaving the packed barrels around.

'She'd the bairn that night and she lost an awful lot of blood. There was nothin' for it but tae bring her and the wee one back home, for he was a right peelly wally wee creature and he'd have died for sure if we'd kept him in the lodgin's with nob'dy tae look out for him while we were workin' at the farlins. Anyway, Nanse was awful ill. For a while,' Isa said, running her fingertip round and round the rim of her cup, 'I thought I'd lose the two of them. But the bairn's still with us, though whether he'll manage through the winter I don't know.'

'And Nanse?'

The birthing had been arduous and Nanse had never quite managed to struggle back to health. 'So, ye see, I've got tae bring in some money, with them tae look out for, and me and Nanse no' gettin' much money from the guttin'. That's why—'

'What d'you mean about the gutting money?' Bethany interrupted.

'With me havin' tae take her and the bairn home, it meant the two of us bein' away from the farlins,' Isa explained with a flash of irritation at Bethany's stupidity. 'It was a good fishin' too; there was that much herrin' that the quines were workin' from first light tae well after dark. But Nanse wasnae fit tae come back home on her own, let alone care for a wee bairn on the journey, so I'd tae bring the two of them back tae Buckie. The other lassies gave me somethin' from their own wages, but they couldnae spare much and it's all gone now.'

'Nathan only paid you for the time you worked?' Different curers had different rules, but Bethany had always seen to it that if a member of the gutting crew fell sick and was unable to work she got some sort of financial compensation, especially in a good season.

'Aye, snivellin' wee bastard that he is,' Isa snapped. 'I know he's kin tae ye, Bethany, but I've never liked the man.'

'Neither have I, and he was kin to my man, not to me.' Bethany thought hard, chewing at her lower lip, then said, 'If I took you on, Isa, you'd have to do as Leezie tells you, for she's the one that runs this place, with me being at the factory all day.'

'We'll get on fine,' Isa said, though Bethany doubted it.

'She'll put you to the dirty work – scrubbing the floors and suchlike.'

A faint smile touched the woman's thin lips. 'I'm used enough tae that.'

'Then you can start tomorrow. I have to go now,' Bethany said, and then, as they both got up, 'Will you and Nanse be going back to the fishing next season?'

'Of course we will, but it'll be for some other curer, for I'll never take arles from Nathan Pate again – nor will the other lassies if I have my way of it,' the woman said viciously. 'Not that he's likely tae ask me, for I told him a thing or two when I found out that he wasnae even goin' tae give my Nanse a decent pay for the hard work she put in afore she took ill.'

Isa's final words were still ringing in Bethany's mind when she reached the factory. The women, well used to the routine, were already at work when she arrived, and she eyed them thoughtfully. Most of them had started in this factory, and other local net factories, straight from school at the age of fourteen. Some stayed, but many left when they were fifteen or sixteen to follow the fishing, returning to the factory between the herring seasons. Now that Bethany came to think of it, some of the best gutters and packers in the business would be working for her during the next few months. And Isa would be in her own kitchen every day.

Her anger at the mean way in which Nathan had treated Isa and her daughter began to fade. She tapped the tip of a finger against pursed lips and then smiled broadly as she realised that long before the man even thought of going round the fisher-lassies offering them arles – a binding financial advance – to work for him during the coming season, she, Bethany Pate, could have made her own arrangements with each and every one of them. She knew those women far better than Nathan or Gil ever had, for she had worked alongside most of them.

It would give her great pleasure, she thought as she opened the order book waiting on her desk, to regain control of the Pate gutting crews while at the same time triumphing over Nathan.

'Isa Thain?' Leezie skirled. 'Isa Thain, in my own kitchen? I'll not have it, Mrs Pate!'

'Aye but you will. I'm the mistress of this house, and I've already told her she can start work tomorrow.' Bethany, caught up in the delight of knowing that she had found a way to take the gutting crews away from Nathan, had quite forgotten that she still had to face Leezie.

'She's a troublemaker! You know that as well as I do!'

'Isa's all right if you handle her properly.'

'The only way I'll handle that one's with the end of a broom. If she sets foot in my kitchen I'll sweep her out of it again!'

'Leezie, you need someone to help you now that I'm spending all my time at the net factory.'

'I'm managin'.'

'It's not right to expect you to see to the bairns and everything else into the bargain. I've told Isa that she'll be the skivvy and she'll have to do as you tell her. Just think, with her here you'll not just be the maidservant any more, you'll be the housekeeper. And,' Bethany added swiftly as the girl paused to think over what she had just said, 'there would be a wee bit more money for a housekeeper.'

'Aye, well,' Leezie said reluctantly, 'I suppose I could try her out. But if she causes trouble, Mrs Pate, she'll be out of that door – or I will!'

The herring shoals were congregating in northern waters as they did every June, and for weeks Buckie harbour had been buzzing with activity as the fleet was made ready for the start of the fishing season. There were nets to repair, boats to clean out, engines and sails to be inspected, stores to be laid in, drifters coaled in readiness for the new season and fresh chaff mattresses to be made for the crews and for the fisher-lassies who would follow them north.

Women were welcomed onto the boats only twice a year – in June, before the fishing season began in northern waters, and in October before the drifters went south to the English fishing. They streamed along the harbour wall, armed with mops and cloths and buckets, and stormed aboard drifter after drifter, a great invasion of skirted and head-scarfed pirates. Woe betide any man who had forgotten, before allowing his wife or mother or sisters or daughters on board, to remove the various pictures he and his crew had torn from magazines and pinned on the cabin walls to while away the lonely hours at sea.

In the Pate cooperage Wattie Noble and his men worked long hours in the heat from the braziers, rising at first light and arriving home late each night exhausted and soaked with sweat. Carts and lorries travelled back and forth between the cooperage and the harbour throughout the day, and the pile of new barrels waiting to be loaded on to the drifters grew daily. Herring barrels were never used twice, which meant that the coopers would be hard at work from now until the end of the season, six months away.

Men and women mended nets, either down by the harbour or at their doors or in their lofts, and as fast as the factories could produce new nets they were hurried off to have corks and ropes added, then to the barking yard, where they were seasoned and protected from the effects of sea water by immersion in a solution of boiling water and tannin. Once barked, they were hung out on every available piece of fencing to dry. This was only the first treatment – during the fishing season they would be barked every Saturday, as soon as the week's fishing was over.

Bethany's scheme, carefully hatched over the spring months, went smoothly. A word dropped into this ear and that as she moved about the net factory, the occasional visit to a fisher-lassie's house to deliver a parcel of Adam's old baby clothes here, a home-made cake there, and a solicitous interest in sick relatives soon brought the women she had once hired for Gil round to her way of thinking. When Nathan Pate finally stirred himself and began to make the rounds of the gutting crews to offer his usual arles in return for a commitment to work for him for the entire season, he found woman after woman, many of them with triumphant smirks about their mouths, turning him down.

'I've promised mysel' tae Bethany Pate,' was the refrain he heard again and again. And when he protested that they owed him some allegiance, having worked for him and his brother for years, they explained sweetly that Bethany Pate had offered more money – and besides, the more experienced women pointed out, they had dealt with Bethany long before Nathan took over the hiring.

When he stormed along to Bethany's house she received him with haughty courtesy, taking him into the parlour and offering him tea as if he was some stranger instead of her own brother-in-law and protector.

'I don't want tea, I want tae know what ye think ye're doin', hirin' my guttin' quines!'

'They're there for whoever speaks to them first,' Bethany pointed out coolly. 'And they're not very happy with you just now, Nathan, not since you treated Isa Thain and her daughter so badly in Yarm'th.'

'It was me that was let down – the pair of them came back here and left me tae find two new packers!'

'They had to come home with Nanse's bairn. He'd have died down there in the cold, with his mother too busy working to care for him. And from what Isa says, it was Nanse being made to lift filled barrels about that brought the wee one on sooner than he should have been.'

'I'm a curer, no' a nursemaid,' Nathan said sulkily.

'If you'd just asked me, I could have told you that you can't get these women to work for you if you treat them badly. They're not dumb animals – they've got brains in their heads, and tongues too.'

'Mebbe ye've got them this year, but ye'll no' do that to me again.'

'That depends on the women. They'll choose who they want to work for, Nathan, and if it's me I'm happy enough to hire them.'

Jacob, when Nathan appealed to him, was just as unhelpful. 'It was always your place as curer tae hire the crews,' he said. 'But you left it to Gil and he was content tae let Bethany see tae it. So am I, for she built up a good crew. If they won't work for you, Nathan, then they're best with someone they will work for.'

And so Bethany gained another foothold in her fight for independence and won another small battle over Nathan.

Zelda and Stella went, together with almost everyone else in Buckie, to see the boats go out. Zelda with a clutch of children about her skirt as always and the newest baby, Meggie, in her arms. Stella had a tight grip on Ruth's hand to stop the little girl from falling into the water in her excitement.

'Not too far away from me, mind,' she told the twins. 'I'll not have you fallin' in and gettin' yersel's drowned.'

'They'd be more likely to fall onto a deck,' Zelda said. 'You cannae see the water for the boats. Look, the *Fidelity*'s just about ready tae go. Wave tae her.'

James Lowrie felt the old familiar tingle of excitement as he curled his fingers about the spokes of the wheel. The tingle ran from the soles of his studded boots, clamped firmly to the deck timbers, up through every muscle and every vein to the top of his head. Freedom, that was what it was, he thought exultantly.

He leaned to one side, poking his head out of the side window in order to watch his new mate, Siddy, haul in the forrard rope. As the *Fidelity* began to peel away from the wall he glanced up and saw Ruth, still tethered to her mother but straining so far forward that she seemed to be in danger of dislocating her shoulder, waving vigorously with her free hand.

James, in a benevolent mood now that he was heading out to sea, took off his cap and flourished it in reply. Her bright little face was immediately split by a huge, proud grin. He had grown fond of the youngest of his three daughters over the past few months; she had a lot of courage and a good brain in her skull. If only she could have been a boy.

He glanced at Stella, still as a statue, her face so expressionless that she might have been a figurehead from some old boat. He nodded to her and she nodded back. In the eight months since his return from the war they had settled into a form of domesticity that suited them both well enough. He had his boat and Stella was busy with plans to let out her father's cottage to summer visitors. They were as content as they could ever be.

He waved to the twins, who gave shy, decorous little gestures in return, then the *Fidelity* was nosing into her position in the great procession of boats, a mixture of steam and sail and motor boats, easing out of the harbour to the sea beyond. The drifter moved smoothly and decorously beneath his feet, but even so, he could have sworn that he felt a slight tremor run through her as though, like him, she pulsed with excitement at the thought of escaping from the shackles of the land.

They were almost at the harbour entrance when he glanced up at the wall and saw Rory, Ellen and Adam, all waving energetically. He waved back, looking for and finding Bethany just behind them. Although she was still dressed, as protocol demanded of a woman in the first year of widowhood, in dark clothes, she was hatless, and the sunlight caught the gold tints as loose strands of hair whipped about her face in the breeze.

For a moment her eyes met his, but neither of them acknowledged the other. Then the drifter was through the harbour entrance and into the Moray Firth, plunging forward to meet the first of the big waves with skittish, almost flirtatious excitement.

Buckie fell swiftly astern, and fell as swiftly from James Lowrie's mind as he set his face and his mind and his boat towards the long anticipated meeting with the herring shoals.

'Some folk,' Zelda Lowrie said breathlessly, 'are right dirty tinks.'

'As long as their money's clean I'm no' complainin',' Stella told her from where she was blackleading the fireplace. 'When ye've done with the windows I'll bring in the curtains an' we can hang them again. They'll be dry by now.'

'Nearly finished. I wonder if they're as dirty at home as they are when they're here on their holidays?' Zelda wondered.

'Mebbe not. Mebbe they arenae bothered when it's no' their ain hoosie. It's been a grand summer for me, Zelda,' Stella said happily. 'I kenned it was the right thing tae keep this place on an' let it out tae summer visitors.'

Her old home had been let almost constantly since the boats had gone off to the northern fishing grounds in June, just over two months earlier. Now the women were putting the place to rights before the next batch of visitors moved in. 'And then there'll be folk comin' here for the fishin' soon,' Stella went on, 'so that'll keep me goin' till the herrin' move south. And over the winter I can get this place set tae rights for next summer's visitors. With the money I've made I can afford tae buy in some extra bits and pieces.' Then, glancing at the younger woman, she asked sharply, 'Are you all right, Zelda?'

'Aye, I'm fine.' The younger woman had suddenly stopped work and was holding on to the back of a chair.

'Ye're lookin' awful hot.'

'It's a warm day. D'ye think ye could fetch me a drink of water?' Zelda ran one rounded forearm over her forehead and lowered herself into the chair. By the time Stella had brought the water she was looking more like herself.

'Mebbe you should go home and leave me tae finish off the work.'

'I might as well stay, for all we've got left tae do. And Auntie Meg likes tae see tae the bairns; it makes her feel that she's needed, bless her. Anyway, your quines are there tae help her.'

'Better helpin' there than here.' Stella seated herself on another chair for a moment's rest. 'Every time I bring them here tae work they end up playin' or makin' more of a mess than there is already.' She peered at the younger woman. 'Are ye feelin' better?'

'I'm fine.' Zelda hesitated, then confided, 'Stella, there's another bairn on the way.'

'Another? But wee Meggie's no' five months old yet.'

'She'll be on her feet by the time this one comes, for it's no' due till next year.'

'Does Innes . . . ?'

Zelda gave her sister-in-law a radiant smile. She looked as if someone had promised her the best present she could ever want, Stella thought, amazed.

'I'm goin' tae tell him tonight. He'll be pleased, for he loves bairns as much as I dae myself.'

'It's another mouth tae feed, Zelda. And you've already got Etta tae raise intae the bargain.'

'We'll manage fine. Every bairn brings its own love and its own blessings,' Zelda said, then got to her feet. 'I've cooled down now. Let's get back tae work.'

'I'll finish the windows. You fetch the curtains in and I'll hang them.'

As she watched her sister-in-law go off to the small backyard, already adopting the leaning-back waddle of the pregnant woman, Stella was suddenly consumed by a sense of envy so strong that it hurt. Years ago, on the threshold of marriage to James, she had hoped for the sort of life Zelda now shared with Innes. In those days she had believed, in her naivety, that the children they made together would bind them together even though their marriage had begun with no love whatsoever on his part. She had been wrong.

She set her mouth into a hard thin line and started polishing the windows. At least she had something of her own now – the cottage, and the money it brought in. She'd show James, and Bethany too, that she was their equal.

'They're all dry,' Zelda sang out from the doorway, then buried her nose in the curtains. 'They smell of fresh air and sunshine. It's a grand day!'

10

It had been a good fishing. As Buckie came into view, James Lowrie settled his feet firmly on to the deck and knew a brief moment of contentment. The past few weeks had cleansed him of the bitter war memories; it was almost as if the *Fidelity* knew that she was back in familiar waters, for she had handled sweetly, even when the seas were mountainous and the wind blowing at gale force. He felt, as he and the others hauled in nets filled with leaping silver fish, that at last his world had come right again.

The engine throbbed with a strong steady beat as the drifter sped towards the harbour. There would be six to eight weeks of fishing from home, and then when the autumn began to turn to winter the boats would go south for the English fishing.

He stuck his pipe in his mouth and clambered up to the wheelhouse. 'I'll take her in, Siddy,' he said, and the mate relinquished the wheel.

It was a relief to Bethany when the official year of mourning for Gil ended and she was free to cast off her black clothing. Not that she intended to promenade along Buckie's streets dressed in all the colours of the rainbow, but it was pleasant to put on whatever she chose.

Today on her way to the factory she was wearing a warm grey jacket over her blue knitted blouse and grey skirt. The clothes felt free and light and comfortable after months of wearing only black and as she went along the street there was a new spring to her step.

Over the past year her life had settled into a pleasing pattern. All was going well at the net factory – Jacob was pleased with the way she ran it – and every day she made a point of calling in at the cooperage to have a word with Wattie Noble. Nathan's attempts to interfere in the running of his late brother's business had irritated the men, and this, like his treatment of the gutting crews, had played into Bethany's hands. She had made a wise decision when she had asked Wattie to supervise the cooperage, for the other coopers liked and trusted the man, and were happy to take orders from him. Now Nathan stayed away from the place, which suited everyone.

She had fared better in her handling of the cooperage than in her handling of her home. When Isa Thain first came in to help Leezie the two women had quarrelled and sparred like a pair of cats, but gradually, to Bethany's relief, a form of familiarity had crept into their rows, and now they got along well enough in their own fashion. When Isa went off to work at the Yarmouth farlins her place was taken over by her daughter Nanse, who had to bring her sickly, wailing baby with her since there was nobody to look after the child.

The baby's constant crying would have driven Bethany mad had she been at home during the day, but mercifully, Leezie had taken an interest in the little boy, and on more than one occasion Bethany had returned home to find Nanse working away while Leezie sat by the kitchen fire crooning to the puny wee thing cradled in her arms.

The first time her mistress came across her holding the baby instead of working, Leezie had glared at her, defying her to find fault, but Bethany had had the sense to hold her tongue. The arrangement between them had been that while she was at the factory Leezie was in sole charge of the house, and as long as the work was done, the meals made on time and her own three charges cared for, Bethany was content.

During the English fishing Buckie was almost emptied of fishing folk but now the streets were busy again, for the boats were back in harbour and the trains had brought the fisher-lassies home, bearing gifts for those who had been left behind. There were toys for the children, pipes and tobacco for the old men, scarves and gloves for the womenfolk, and hand-some hand-painted plates and figurines to be displayed on shelves and in corner cupboards for visitors to admire.

Christmas and New Year – the main Scottish celebrations – were approaching and for two months, until the line fishing for haddock and halibut, codling, skate and whiting started in February, the fishing community was freed from the usual routine.

But first there was the reckoning to be done. The fishing could have been better but the boats contracted to Jacob McFarlane had been among the most successful, and Bethany had almost finished the task of working out the payment for each of the boats contracted to Jacob McFarlane.

Her mind was filled with these figures, together with a mental assessment of the day's work ahead of her, as she gave a brisk 'Good morning!' to two neighbours already on their way back from the shops.

'Did ye see the colour she was wearin'?' one asked the other as Bethany continued on her way. 'Awfu' bright for a widow woman, was it no'?'

'It must be a year past since the poor man died,' the other calculated, adding, 'But even so, it was awfu' bright, ken.'

'There's surely nae need for her tae go out tae work at all, no' when she's still able tae go on livin' in a bonnie big hoosie like thon. He must have left her well off.'

'Aye, but she never was like other women, Bethany Pate,' the second woman opined. 'I mind when we were all wee quinies taegither – she was happier swimmin' in the harbour with the loons instead of playin' with the other lasses. Always walked her own road, that one.'

'Even so,' her friend said doubtfully, 'that colour's awfu' bright for a widow.'

James, with no knowledge of the sort of gifts lassies and women might like, had asked one of the Buckie fisher-lassies to choose something for his wife and daughters. Back home and watching the three girls' pleasure as they unwrapped their new dolls, he felt an unexpected and previously unknown moment of pleasure, especially when Ruth, always the most affectionate and the least timid of the three, hurled herself at him and gave him a hug and a smacking kiss on the cheek.

When they had gone off to show their new acquisitions to their friends, he dug his hand into a pocket and then held a small package out to Stella.

'For me?' There was genuine surprise in her voice and in her face. She was not used to such gestures.

'Just a wee thing,' he said gruffly. She opened the wrapping almost warily and then gasped at sight of the little china shepherdess in her delicate pink and green gown, her small pretty face peeping out from beneath a wide-brimmed bonnet.

'Och James, it's bonny!'

'It'll do, then?'

'It'll do,' Stella agreed, her voice shaking with shock and pleasure. For a long moment she cupped the little figurine in one hand, stroking it gently, almost reverently, with the tip of a finger, before reaching up to put it on a high shelf of the kitchen dresser.

'So that the lassies won't be tempted tae play with it, for they'd be sure tae break it,' she explained, as she stepped back and looked up at it. Watching her, James was surprised to see that in her sudden happiness she looked very like the young lassie he had married all those years before. It was as though the years had fallen from her. He marvelled at how easily pleased women were.

Then Stella opened a small drawer in the dresser, where she kept the household money and important papers such as their marriage certificate and the girls' birth certificates. She took out a small brown paper parcel and put it on the table before him. 'This is for you. I was goin' tae give it tae you at Ne'erday, but you might as well have it now.'

'For me?' He opened it and then stared down at the small wad of banknotes. 'What's this?'

'The money I made from lettin' the cottage.'

His jaw dropped. 'Ye got as much as that?'

More than that, if the truth be known. Stella, stunned by her own daring and sophistication, had gone on the bus to Elgin to open her very own bank account in a town where nobody knew her or her business. She had put some of her earnings into the account, and given the rest, the larger share, to James.

'Now the war's by, folks are wantin' tae take the sea air again,' she said proudly. 'And a cooper from England took the place for all the time the boats were fishin' in the Firth, so's he could bring his wife and his fam'ly with him. They'll probably come back next year.'

'But it's your money, Stella, you earned it. I can support us all now that the *Fidelity*'s back at the fishin'.' He folded the paper over the money and held the package out to her, but she shook her head and put her hands behind her back.

'No, I want ye tae put it towards that mortgage you took out,' she said, then couldn't help adding, 'I was right tae keep my faither's hoosie, was I no'? This way, we'll have a wee bit extra comin' in every summer. And,' she went on, triumph creeping into her voice and adding sparkle to her eyes, 'now ye can see for yersel' that I'm just as able tae earn my own way as Bethany Pate!'

Every year since her marriage Jess Lowrie had celebrated the New Year by preparing a Ne'erday dinner for her family. In the earlier years her parents and her in-laws had been the main guests; as the years marched by the older members of the family passed away, so then it was the turn of her own full-grown children and their families to fill the seats round the table.

There had been no thought of a New Year celebration for the Lowrie family the year before because of Gil Pate's death, but as 1919 gave way to 1920 Jacob McFarlane insisted on reviving the tradition. When Stella pointed out with some reluctance that she and James, now living in Jess and Weem's former home, should be the ones to follow the family tradition, Jacob shook his greying head.

'Na, na lassie, you've got enough tae do all the rest of the year. Mrs Duthie's more than willin' tae set up a grand meal for us and I've got plenty room for the wee ones as well as the adults. I'd like fine tae invite ye all tae my table, even if it's just the once.'

Large though Jacob's house was, Bethany thought as she sipped at a small glass of sherry, it was still overrun with children. As well as her own three, and Stella's daughters, there were Innes and Zelda's fast-growing family: six-year-old Mary; Will, her junior by one year; Jessie, almost three years of age; Matt, almost two; and nine-month-old Meggie, not to mention Zelda's niece Etta, now five years of age and as much a part of their family as the other children.

It was abundantly clear that Innes and Zelda loved being surrounded by children – nephews and nieces as well as their own. Innes thought nothing of sprawling about the floor with them while his wife, so heavily pregnant that she only just managed to hold wee Meggie on what was left of her lap, beamed on the writhing, giggling mass of arms and legs, heads and bodies at her feet.

Jacob's housekeeper, assisted by a woman brought in for the occasion, had worked hard to produce a fine table. The meal began with two large tureens of broth, rich and steaming hot, followed by the traditional steak pies as well as chicken and every kind of vegetable imaginable, and, finally, fruit-stuffed dumplings, custard and jelly. There was wine for the adults and fruit juice for the children, who, once the meal was over, were given the run of the house and told to seek out the gifts that Jacob had hidden away for them.

They scattered, shrieking with excitement, and the house-keeper followed with Meggie in her arms while Jacob sat back in his seat, looking down the length of the table at his guests.

Meg Lowrie was in a place of honour at the opposite end of the table, as befitted a woman of her mature age. She was wearing her best black dress with a handsome jade brooch, Jacob's Ne'erday gift to her, sparkling on her generous bosom. The excitement of the occasion had brought colour to her cheeks and straightened her shoulders, and she looked a good ten years younger than normal. Innes flanked her on one side and Zelda on the other.

Marriage and bairns suited these two, Jacob thought, but, strangely enough, widowhood seemed to suit Bethany just as well. For all that she was past the first bloom of youth there was a glow about her that warmed her grey eyes and empha-sised her natural beauty. A stranger might be forgiven for assum-ing that a new love had come into her life, but Jacob knew that her air of well-being and happiness was brought about by nothing other than the chance, at last, to be the independent woman she had always wanted to be, answerable to none.

Stella, too, had changed for the better; her tight mouth had loosened a little and there was less sadness in her eyes. She had also found a way to stand on her own two feet and it had brought a new confidence that showed itself in the way she took part in the various conversations floating around the table, instead of remaining silent as usual. She was even pleasant towards Bethany, and once or twice Jacob caught her giving James a warm look.

James was the silent one of the group, but that had always been the man's way. He was almost as lost on the land as the herring he caught in his nets.

'Are ye goin tae the line fishin', James?' Jacob asked, and the younger man shrugged.

'I might.'

'Then ye'll find someone else tae bait your lines, for I'm not for it,' Stella said, without rancour. 'I used tae hate havin' tae bait lines for my faither. It's awful sore on the hands, shellin' the mussels then puttin' them on the line.'

Each line held about fourteen hundred hooks, with each hook requiring two or three mussels, which had to be shelled before they could be attached.

'When I see the women workin' on the lines I'm just thankful that Innes doesnae go tae sea,' Zelda put in, while Meg's voice boomed along the length of the table: 'Mind workin' the lines with yer mither and me all those years ago, Bethany? You were there and all, Stella. We mended the nets, too, in Jess's loft. Mind those jellyfish they call scalders, that got caught in the nets?'

'I do that!' Stella made a face. 'When they died they dried tae a powder that stung yer hands somethin' cruel. And if ye got any of it on yer fingers and then touched yer eyes they were near stung out of yer face.'

As the others talked around him James stared down at the tablecloth, lost in his own thoughts. The sight of Innes's two healthy, lusty sons hurt him in a way he had not expected. 'The way those two are goin',' he had heard Stella say with disapproval of his brother and Zelda, 'they'll soon be able tae fill the schoolhouse on their own.'

Just then young Adam rushed into the room, his small face rosy with excitement and his eyes shining like stars, to show his mother the wind-up dancing bear he had found. James watched hungrily as Bethany lifted the solid little body on to her lap and ruffled Adam's dark hair; then, aware that Stella's sharp eyes were upon him, he wrenched his gaze from his sister and her son and reached for the wine decanter.

'After you, James,' Jacob said, and leaned forward to take the decanter once James had done with it. He filled his glass and then sat back and sipped at the rich red wine, well content with the way his life had gone. If Weem Lowrie had not charmed Jess away from him, Jacob might well have been father to those young folk. If Jess had not insisted on remaining true to her marriage vows, even beyond death, he would at least have been their stepfather.

But despite their mother's stubbornness, Jacob thought complacently, his wealth had enabled him to become closely involved with the family that had been Weem Lowrie's.

Just as close as if they had been his own blood kin.

11

June 1931

'Ye'll wish ye'd stayed home and kept on workin' in the net factory,' Adam Pate said with relish.

'No I won't.'

'Aye but ye will, once that steamer gets out intae the open sea an' starts its pitchin' an' rollin',' said Adam, who had been to the northern fishing grounds the previous year.

'I like the sea, and I've been in boats before this and never been up nor down.'

'Mebbe so, but this is different. This time ye'll wish ye'd paid heed tae me an' stayed home.'

'Will you stop your teasin'?' Etta Mulholland, kneeling by the fine new wooden chest she had recently acquired for her first trip to the Shetlands as a fisher-lassie, glared at Adam, and when he grinned at her, crossed his grey eyes, clutched at his stomach and made choking noises, she appealed, 'Aunt Zelda, can you no' make him stop his nonsense?'

'Leave the lassie alone, Adam,' Zelda ordered her nephew fondly. 'She's made up her mind tae go and she's lookin' forward tae it. Don't spoil it for her.'

'I'm only warnin' her,' Adam protested. 'Mary, you've been up north tae the fishin', you tell this lassie what the journey's like.'

'It's fine,' said Mary, who had her mother's kindly temperament; then, as Adam gave a derisive laugh, 'Sarah never has any bother with the journey.'

111

'Sarah's a good sailor, I'll give ye that, but last year you and the rest of the lassies were as green as grass when you got off the boat at Lerwick, with the tossin' and tumblin' you'd had.'

'I'm sure you were just as green when you were makin' the trip in the *Fidelity*.'

'Not me.' Adam shook his dark head. 'The sea never bothers me, even when the boat starts tae roll an' toss an' dip and lift an'—'

Mary caught at a handful of her cousin's hair in one hand while the other brandished the razor-sharp gutting knife she had been about to pack into her own kist. 'Another word from you, Adam Pate,' she said sweetly while Meg Lowrie cackled like a hen from her fireside chair, 'and I'll be usin' your hair tae stuff my mattress instead of chaff. I doubt if all the lassies would be so quick tae run after ye if ye didnae have those bonny black curls.' Her grip tightened, and Adam yelped.

'Let him be, Mary,' her mother ordered. 'And as for you, Adam,' she reached up to administer an affectionate swipe at his shoulder, 'ye'd best get away back home before yer mither sends Leezie out lookin' for you. Anger Bethany, and she'll pack you back tae Aberdeen tae do some extra studyin' instead of gettin' tae the fishin'.'

'She won't.' Adam, released, rubbed at his stinging scalp. 'I've told her it's bad enough havin' tae go tae the university without extra studyin' in the summer too.' Then, making for the door, 'See ye in Lerwick, lassies. You too, Auntie Meg. You and me'll have a wee turn on the dance floor when we get there, eh?'

'Right ye are, son,' said Meg, delighted, and then when he had gone, 'He's a fine laddie, that one.'

'The quines all know that, Auntie Meg,' Mary said dryly. 'And they make sure that he knows it too. He's gettin' bigheaded.'

'I'd be after him mysel' if I was a wee bit younger.' Meg slapped a wrinkled hand on her bony thigh.

'You behave yersel', Auntie Meg, before ye make yersel' ill with yer nonsense,' Zelda scolded, laughing. 'Anyway, Mary, there's no harm in a lad of his age enjoyin' the lassies' attentions.' Zelda, like many of the women in the town, had a soft spot for Adam, who possessed an abundance of charm and high spirits as well as good looks.

'I don't see Aunt Bethany settlin' for a Buckie lassie as wife to Adam,' Mary said. 'Rory can wed whoever he wants, but I'm sure she's hoping that when Adam marries it'll be to some well-born Aberdeen lassie he's met at the university.'

'Adam Pate'll go his own way. He's like a young horse that's awfu' hard tae tame.'

'You're right there, Aunt Meg.' Zelda began to fold the skirt she had been ironing, and then put it down as nine-year-old Samuel rushed in, clamouring for food.

'Ye've not long had yer breakfast!'

'Aye, but I'm hungry again,' Samuel said plaintively, eyeing the tray of scones, fresh-baked and still warm, on the table.

'Here, son.' Zelda lifted a scone, split it, and began to spread it with home-made jam. Samuel was her youngest, and doubly precious because his twin sister had been still-born and Samuel himself, a mewling, pitiful scrap of humanity the size of his father's hand, had not been expected to live.

Nor had Zelda, for several days; the only thing that kept her going was her determination to raise the child destined to be her last. Samuel had spent his first few weeks in the oven with the door propped open, baking, as Zelda put it, at an even temperature, and had survived, to become a healthy, active boy.

Now as he snatched the scone from her outstretched hand, gave her a broad grin, and then rushed out again, yelling to his friends as he went, she said indulgently, 'He's a wee tyke, that one.'

'Only because you spoil him,' Mary said.

'Ach, a wee bit of spoilin' never did anyone any harm,' her mother protested, and then, as she returned to folding the skirt, 'As for Adam, if Bethany tries tae make that laddie travel a road he doesnae want tae go she'll have a rare fight on her hands, for they're both thrawn. Bethany aye wants her own way and Adam's more her son than Gil's.'

'He puts me in mind o' my brither Weem,' Meg said from her usual place by the fire. 'Once our Weem set eyes on Jess nob'dy could have stopped him from takin' her tae wife. James is just like his faither, and so's Adam. The loon's a right Lowrie, no' a Pate at all.'

'Is it awful bad on the steamer?' Etta asked nervously. She had started learning the gutting trade the year before, during the late-summer fishing season on the Moray Firth. This would be her first time away from home.

'Sometimes – but ye'll like it once ye get there,' Mary assured her. Seventeen, and a year older than Etta, she had already been north to the Shetlands and south to Lowestoft. 'Ye'll meet folk from all over and the company's grand. Now then,' she cast her eye over the box Etta was packing, 'are ye managin' tae fit everythin' intae your kist?'

'Are you sure I need all this?' Etta sat back on her heels, looking at the great pile of items on the floor and then at the box. It had seemed quite large when she first got it, but now it seemed small beside all the items waiting to go into it.

'Every bit of it. Ye'll need good warm clothes for workin' in because the weather can be cruel up there, even in the summer. And ye'll want oilskins for when it rains, and scarves tae cover yer head.'

'And somethin' decent for the kirk on Sundays and when folk come tae wee gatherin's at your hut,' Zelda chimed in, 'and good sheets for yer bed.'

The items were all in a heap by the kist, together with towels and soap and a hairbrush, knitting wool to keep Etta's hands busy when she was waiting for the boats to come in, cups and saucers, cutlery and a tablecloth, her sturdy working boots, her knitting needles, the leather knitting belt with a section padded out with horsehair where the needles were kept when not in use, and her sharp gutting knife.

'Are ye certain about the wallpaper?' she asked doubtfully.

'The huts we've tae live in are awful dreary. A bit of wallpaper makes them bonny,' Mary told her, 'and we have tae take curtains tae hang over the windows, else everyone that's passin' can look in on us. And don't forget the cloths for yer fingers.'

'I have them here, all ready for you.' Zelda triumphantly produced a large bundle of soft, strong strips of flour sacking that had been washed and then boiled to make them flexible. They were needed to protect Etta's fingers from razor-sharp fish bones and from the worst of the coarse salt that was liberally scattered over the fish that the gutting crews worked on.

After a lot of effort and assistance Etta managed to get everything packed into her kist, which was then closed and locked. Each kist had been set on a large piece of canvas, which was now folded tightly over it and stitched into place with large needles and strong thread. The canvas provided extra protection for the kists during the journey to wherever the girls were to work.

'This is excitin',' Zelda said as she helped the two girls to heave the completed kists over to the doorway to await collection by the curer's lorry. 'It's an adventure!'

Etta smiled at her. To Aunt Zelda everything was an adventure and a joy to be explored and savoured. 'Were you never a fisher-lassie yourself?'

'Me? No, no, I'm from farmin' stock. I spent all my workin' days at Bain's farm in Rathven. And your Uncle Innes was never fond of the sea, for all that his folk were fishermen. Mind you, I'd've liked fine tae have been able tae go travellin' about, meetin' all those different folk. I'm pleased tae see you lassies gettin' the chance.' Zelda clapped her hands and beamed at her niece and her daughter. 'Ye'll have a grand time!'

*

Jacob McFarlane and Bethany were busy estimating the cost of coaling and equipping and victualling the drifters they had engaged for the season. This year, as Bethany pointed out with considerable satisfaction, even more skippers than before were under contract to them.

'Mebbe more than we can manage.' Jacob sucked at his pipe. 'We've undertaken tae buy fish from every one o' these boats, mind, and that's goin' tae cost us a pretty penny.'

'We'll be all right. We're not putting out more money than we have, and if the fishing's good this year, we'll do very nicely.'

Bethany Pate came to life when she was busy, Jacob thought, watching her as she bent over her work again, pen in hand. She had been running the net factory for eleven years now, and he knew, though she had not complained, that it had been a struggle at first. Many of the workers had resented her as an outsider, but she had won most of them over, gradually weeding out those who were determined to wear her down and replacing them with newcomers more willing to accept her regime. Jacob had given her a free hand with the place while he watched from the sidelines and said nothing. Now she had won the trust and respect of all the men and women employed at the factory.

As the years passed she had gradually taken over more and more of Jacob's paperwork; this was another great achievement, for Jacob McFarlane was a hard-headed businessman and there were very few people he would trust with details of his financial life.

She herself must have amassed a tidy fortune over the years, he thought now as he watched her; enough, mebbe, to keep her in relative comfort, and yet she kept on working.

'Are ye fond o' money, Bethany?' he asked now. She looked up, startled.

'What a thing to ask a lady!'

'Ye're right, I dinnae ken why I said it.'

'Since it's you, I'll give you an answer,' Bethany said, then pursed her lips, considering. 'No, I'd not say that I'm fond of the stuff,' she said at last. 'Though it's always nice to have enough. It's knowing that I'm doing something with my life instead of just frittering it away.'

'Ye've brought up three bairns on yer lone; is that no' doin' somethin' with yer life, woman?'

'Aye, and it's been hard work, but it's not enough,' Bethany said, 'I like to know that I've earned every penny I spend, and I'm not beholden to anyone else for it.' Then she added, with a sidelong glance at him, 'The one thing I've not done yet is to deal with the fish merchants. When are you going to let me try my hand at that?'

'It's no' a job for a woman,' Jacob said as he always did, and she scowled at him.

'Women are fine in their place, but there are some things that only the menfolk can do, is that it?'

'Ye've got the right way of it there, my quine.'

'But surely you need someone to take Nathan's place?'

'I don't need tae fill his place, for he was never much help tae me.'

'You're right there,' Bethany said complacently. Regaining control of the gutting crews had only been the first step in her campaign against Nathan. Over the years he had become increasingly lazy and when, after years of careful hoarding and investment, she was finally able to offer him a good price for his curing business, her brother-in-law had accepted and gone off to Fraserburgh, where he had married a spinster of comfortable means and settled into a life of ease.

'Let me go to Yarm'th with you this year,' Bethany coaxed now. 'Leezie can look after the house on her lone.'

'I'll think about it,' Jacob said evasively. He was in his sixties now, and rheumatism was slowing him down, especially in the colder weather, but he wasn't ready to hand over the reins of power just yet.

Bethany was still trying to work out a way of persuading him to take her to Yarmouth as she walked home, loitering at the harbour to soak up the busy atmosphere. Boats, most of them steam drifters, crammed the outer harbour and the four inner basins, and from where she stood Bethany looked over a great patchwork of colours, with black and white and yellow and green subordinate to the vibrant shades of blues and reds most popular with fishermen. The name of each boat was carefully painted in flowing script edged with gold leaf – *Handsome*, *Mary Cowie*, *Trophy*, *Homefaring*, *Furze*, *Olympus*, *Fidelity* . . .

Even as Bethany identified the drifter a familiar figure emerged from the galley and went across the deck, his cap set to the back of his dark head. As James stepped up on to the gunwale and then to the next boat as easily as if he was strolling along a street, she turned and hurried away.

'Tae think,' Etta moaned, 'that I've aye liked the sea! What have I ever done tae it that it should treat me like—'

The steamer began to climb the steep slope of another large wave and she clutched her stomach with both hands and closed her eyes tight, knowing what was about to come.

Up and up the *St Ninian* struggled until it reached the top of the wave, where it hesitated for a moment, as though unde-cided as to whether it should go down the other side or fall backwards into the trough it had just left. Then it opted for a forward plunge, with a corkscrew twist added in for good measure.

'. . . like this?' Etta finished the sentence as the ship dived, and then almost bit her tongue as the vessel hit the next trough with a bang, causing her jaw to snap shut.

'You've done nothin',' Sarah Lowrie said cheerfully. 'The sea just likes tae show us that it cannae be taken for granted. Think what it must be like for the fishermen – they have tae spend most of their lives tossin' like this, up and down an'—'

'If you don't shut your mouth it's you that'll be gettin' tossed – over the side of this boat,' Ruth snapped from where she sat on the deck, leaning against the funnel. Her face, like Etta's, had a greenish tinge. 'How is it that for all that you and me's sisters, Sarah, I'm the only one that gets sick when we go tae Lerwick?'

'Mebbe it's 'cos God likes me better,' Sarah suggested. 'It's the same with Annie – she gets sick and she's my twin.'

'I wish my mither had kept me at home tae help with the summer visitors instead of Annie,' Ruth mourned. 'Why didn't she pick me?'

'Because Annie's the better worker. You'd be too busy eyein' up the lads tae dae anythin' else,' Sarah pointed out.

Ruth glared and began to say something, then as the boat shuddered and plunged once more she shut her mouth hurriedly and pressed her fingers against it, eyes closed. The prettiest and the liveliest of the three sisters, she had no short- age of suitors, and the previous year she had become very friendly with the son of the people who had rented out her mother's cottage. As the young man was already engaged to be married his parents had cut their holiday short and whisked him home and out of danger. To Stella Lowrie's fury they had also cut short the full rent agreed by letter before their arrival.

'Look at these poor dumb beasts,' Sarah went on as the boat lurched and then settled again. 'They don't even know why they should be here, and they're no' complainin'.' Then she laughed as one of the cows penned in one corner of the deck, staggering to the ship's roll, bellowed its misery. 'That one must've heard me.'

It was true, Etta thought, glancing round the deck. The poor sheep and cows being taken from the mainland to the Shetlands must surely be suffering even more than the fisher-lassies who, like herself, were huddled on deck. But feeling sorry for the animals didn't make her feel any less sorry for herself.

'I wish I hadnae come!'

'You've been fair desperate tae get tae the Lerwick fishin',' Sarah pointed out.

'I thought it would be fun.'

'It will be, once we get there and your stomach catches up with you. I'll just go and see if Mary's all right.' And Sarah sauntered off to where Etta's cousin was nursing her own misery in the confined space of a cabin.

Ruth put a comforting arm about Etta's shoulders. 'Ye'll be fine, pet, an' I should know, for I'm sick with every crossin'. But ye'll enjoy yerself once we're ashore. The Shetland season's good.'

'When will we get there?'

'Tomorrow.'

'Tomorrow!' The prospect of another night on the steamer made Etta's stomach lurch. That was all that it could do, since it had long since emptied itself over the side.

'You'll be all right,' Sarah assured her. 'Most of us hate the gettin' there, but it's worth it. Think of the money you'll earn.'

'All I can think is that I'll have tae do all this again, only goin' the other way next time.'

'Goin' back's not near as bad as goin' out, because then we know we're on the way home.'

Home. The very word made Etta want to cry. She would have given a king's ransom, had she had such a thing, to be back home in the warm, crowded kitchen, listening to Samuel going over his multiplication tables or helping Teena, aged ten, with her sewing.

Although the sea was rough it was a pleasant early-June day. Etta looked up at the sun and guessed, from its position in the blue sky, that just about now her Uncle Innes would be getting home from his work at the boatyard, ducking as he came in through the door, which wasn't quite high enough for him. Her pale lips twisted into a faint smile at the thought. She always liked it when Uncle Innes was home because then the family was complete.

'Here.' Sarah was back, brandishing a green glass bottle. 'Try this.'

'What is it?'

'Whisky. One of the quinies from Aberdeen gave it tae me. She said that it—'

Ruth had taken the bottle from her sister and sniffed at the contents. Now she turned even more green and, thrusting the bottle into Etta's hand, scrambled up to make a bolt for the side of the steamer, reeling from side to side as the deck rolled beneath her feet.

'She said it would help tae settle your bellies,' Sarah called after her. 'It's helpin' the other quinies.'

Etta sniffed cautiously at the neck of the bottle and screwed her face up. 'I don't know, Sarah . . .'

'Go on, it cannae make you feel much worse than you feel now, can it?'

'I suppose not.' Throwing caution to the winds, Etta tipped the bottle up and took a good swallow, the whisky burning her throat as it went down. For a terrible moment she thought that it was going to hurl itself back up, bringing her entire stomach with it. The back of her tongue seemed to buck and writhe and she had to swallow hard to keep from losing control. Then as the whisky settled she became aware of a warm, soothing glow spreading through her sore, empty stomach.

Sarah was watching her anxiously. 'Has it helped?'

The glow spread, creating a sense of well-being. Etta drew a deep, shaky breath and would not have been surprised if, when she breathed out again, flames had spurted from her lips. She swallowed again, and smiled tentatively at Sarah.

'Aye,' she said. 'Aye, I believe it has.'

12

The fishing boats, with the curers and coopers on board, had gone off to Lerwick before the gutting crews, and by the time the women arrived the drifters were already out in search of the herring shoals. Tired, stiff and still queasy from the sea crossing, Etta and the others began to clamber aboard the lorries waiting to take them to the wooden huts that were to be their homes for the next two or three months.

Etta found a space beside Mary, who still looked far from well. 'Are you all right?' she asked anxiously, and her cousin managed to summon up the ghost of a smile.

'I'll be fine once we get tae the huts. I'm always like this,' she said, and then, as the lorry started up, 'Just leave me be for a wee while, for I'm not good company.'

The trip to the curing station was uncomfortable, with the women thrown about as the lorry jolted along. It did nothing to ease Etta's fragile stomach, and it came as a relief to her when at last they reached the huts. As they spilled out of the lorries the more experienced women hurried to find the best huts. Etta, wishing she were back home in Buckie, trailed after Sarah. She didn't care where they settled as long as there was a bed she could lie on.

'We'll have this one,' Sarah decided.

Each hut held two three-woman crews. Etta and an older woman, Jenny Logan, known as Andra's Jenny to differentiate her from other women called Jenny, were both gutters, and Sarah was their packer. The other crew consisted of Mary, Agnes – another older woman – and Ruth as their packer.

At first sight the huts were bleak; little more than sturdy wooden shelters with a cast-iron stove. There were two solid, wooden bed frames, each just large enough to hold three women, and a table and some shelving made up the rest of the furniture. Etta's heart quailed as she surveyed the grim place, but the others took it all in their stride.

'Etta and me and Ruth in that bed,' Sarah decreed, 'and the other three can have that one.' Then, glancing out of the window, 'and here's our kists already, so we can start cheerin' the place up a bit.'

'There's no chairs,' Etta said feebly, and was told, 'We sit on our kists once they're emptied. Besides, ye're not goin' tae dae much sittin' about, lassie.'

As the women went back outside to claim their luggage the coopers arrived to carry the sturdy wooden chests into the huts. 'Cheer up, Etta, it's not as bad as it looks,' Rory Pate said reassuringly at sight of her wan, worried face.

'Is it not?'

'Wishin' that ye'd stayed at home with Aunt Zelda?'

'I am that,' she admitted.

'Give it a day or two. You'll see,' Rory said. 'The lassies fairly know how tae turn a hut intae a wee palace. Which kist is yours?'

She eyed the growing pile. 'Er – that one.' A lump came into her throat as she identified the stitching – Zelda's hand-iwork – on the canvas cover. At that moment Aunt Zelda's warm, loving presence seemed very far away.

'And which hut?'

Etta pointed to the hut that Sarah had chosen.

'Right. Johnny, give me a hand here,' he yelled, and one of the other coopers came over. Even though the kist was full the two men handled it easily, and Etta followed them as they carried it into the hut.

Someone else was bringing in the mattresses and pillows

that had been brought to Lerwick on the boats. Etta eyed them hopefully as they were tossed onto the bed frames. After the shaking she had endured on the boat, it would be bliss to lie still and quiet for an hour or so.

But the others, even Mary, were already cutting the stitches and pulling off the canvas coverings so that they could open their kists and start hauling everything out. 'I'll take this bucket and start scrubbin' the floor,' Andra's Jenny was saying briskly, 'and you and Agnes can brush the walls down, Sarah. Ruth and Mary can get the stove goin' and the kettle on.'

'Could we not have a wee bit of a rest first?' Etta begged. 'A wee sit down and a cup of tea, even?'

'Lassie,' Andra's Jenny said as the others, all seasoned travellers, went about their various tasks, 'ye're surely no' goin' tae drink tea in this dirty place? Na, na, we'll have tae get everythin' decent first. Fetch that other bucket from the corner and give it a good clean out before ye fill it with water. There's a brush below the sink there. We can get the place scrubbed out twice as fast if we start at each end and work tae the middle.'

The prospect of all that work still lying ahead before she could rest sent Etta's heart plummeting to her sturdy boots, but there was no point in arguing, so she fetched the bucket and set to work, forcing her weary muscles and aching joints into action.

Little more than an hour later the hut had been scrubbed out and the walls brushed down and covered with wallpaper, tacked into place. The assorted curtains the women brought with them hung across the windows on lengths of string and the many nails already on the wooden walls were pressed into use as makeshift wardrobes. One or two of the nails held pictures and there was even a pretty paper fan pinned to one wall, adding a cheerful splash of colour.

Cups and plates and cutlery had been laid out on the table, the stove had been cleaned and lit and steam puffed from the big kettle. Someone was slicing a loaf coaxed from the cook-house, which catered mainly for the coopers and the fisher-men, and someone else was slathering the thick slices with jam. Although her back was aching and her knees sore from kneeling on the rough wooden floor Etta began to feel a bit more cheerful as she emptied her bucket out and rinsed it at the big stone sink standing below one window.

'Where do I put this?' she asked Andra's Jenny, who nodded at the long curtain someone had hung across the corner.

'Behind there,' she said, and then, smirking, 'That's the orra bucket you've got. It's our privy. The one Mary has holds the clean water.'

'Ye never had the lassie scrubbin' the floor from the orra bucket,' Sarah protested as Etta's stomach, which was improving but still fragile, gave a nasty lurch. 'That was a mean trick tae play on her, Jenny!'

'Ach, it did no harm. And she rinsed the bucket out first. Now it's got a clean start,' Andra's Jenny said airily.

Etta felt better once they were all round the table, using the wooden kists as seats, eating thick slabs of bread and jam and drinking strong, scalding tea.

'It's no' much of a meal, but it'll do for now,' Agnes said with satisfaction as she swilled down the last of her tea. 'And the place looks like a wee palace.' She gave the others a smug smile. 'If ye ask me, we've got the bonniest, clean-est hut of all now. We'll be fine here for the next few months.'

There was more work to do before they could go to their beds. During the fishing season, Etta was beginning to realise, there was always more work to be done as far as the fisher-lassies were concerned. While three of the women spread sheets and blankets over the beds she, Ruth and Mary set to work to peel a great pile of potatoes, which would be left in cold water and used over the next few days.

When all was done, Sarah stretched and yawned. 'I'm for

my bed. The boats'll start comin' in early in the mornin', and most of us have sleep tae catch up on.'

The mattresses, filled with chaff, and known to the lassies as 'caff mattresses' were not very comfortable when new, but even so, the other women in the hut were quick to fall asleep, judging by the low chorus of snores and groans and mumblings that floated through the hut. Etta envied them as she listened to their slumbers; tired though she was, she couldn't sleep for fancying that she was still at sea. The bed beneath her seemed to be lifting and falling and corkscrewing, and she had to dig her fingers into the mattress beneath her and concentrate on listening to the breathing, snoring and occasional mumbling as the other five sank into sleep.

Eventually the imagined movement of the bed began to slow, then settle, and her thoughts began to slow as well. She closed her eyes and floated into darkness.

'It doesnae seem fair on the lad, settin' him tae keep watch when he's got the cookin' tae do as well,' Siddy muttered to James as the crew prepared to turn in. Two miles of nets had been shot over the starboard side of the vessel, as tradition demanded, and lamps had been hoisted to show that the *Fidelity* was fishing. Now, as she drifted with the tide, the crew had a chance to snatch a few hours' rest.

'Ach, it'll do him no harm. He's the one that wanted tae learn what it's like tae be a real fisherman. Anyway, it's the way my faither taught me.' James only just managed to stop himself from putting the emphasis on 'my'.

'Aye, but that was different, for Weem was bringin' you intae the fishin',' said Siddy, an older man who had started his career as cabin boy for Weem Lowrie. 'Adam's only helpin' out till it's time for him tae go tae the university in Aberdeen.'

'All the more reason tae show him what real work's about,' James grunted, hauling off his left sea boot and letting it drop with a thud on the deck. 'If ye're so concerned for the loon ye're welcome tae stand his watch for him. It makes no difference tae me. Just mind that we've only got three hours afore we have tae get up an' haul the nets.'

His right boot thudded onto the deck.

'I'm no' that worried for him.' Siddy began to tug his own boots off. 'I like my bed.'

'Aye, I've noticed,' James said dryly, taking his jacket off and climbing into his own bunk. Fishermen always kept most of their clothes on, in case of emergencies during the night. There was no time to get dressed if the boat was going down. 'Now shut yer mouth and get tae sleep,' he advised his mate, dragging the blanket over his own shoulders.

To judge from the snores that echoed around the tiny cabin, Siddy and the others were asleep in no time, but James was restless. He soon tossed the blanket aside and turned on his back, hands behind his head, staring up at the bulging mattress only inches above his face and thinking of Adam, alone on the deck.

If, as Siddy said, he was hard on the boy, it was because Adam was a natural-born fisherman and James wanted to teach him as much as he could before Bethany whisked the lad off to resume his studies in Aberdeen. There was another reason, one that he could only admit to himself in the dark of the night, with nobody else around to read his mind. He had to be harder on Adam than on any of the other deckhands because it was the only way to prevent himself from being too lenient with the boy. Adam was the son Stella had never been able to give him, the lad who could, if Bethany would only allow it, keep the family traditions of fishing alive, just as James himself had been raised to follow in his own father's footsteps.

Instead, he was going to be sent away from Buckie and his heritage, and made to devote his time and his boundless energy to book learning. It was a terrible waste, James thought, tossing in his narrow bunk.

He remembered the day, in this very cabin, when Gil Pate

had first come up with the daft idea that Rory would go into the cooperage and Adam would become a scholar. James had thought that when Adam began to hang around the *Fidelity*, begging to be taken out on her whenever possible, Bethany would realise where her son's true interests lay, especially when it was what she herself had longed to do when she was a lassie.

He smiled slightly, remembering how angry she had been with Innes when after two disastrous trips on the drifter, he had refused to go to sea again. 'Why couldn't Innes have been the quine, and me the loon?' she had wailed. 'Then we'd both have been content!'

After Gil's death, Bethany could have dismissed the daft idea of university for her son, but for some reason known only to herself she had kept it on, even paying for a tutor to work with the lad during the school holidays. The smile broadened into a grin as James remembered all the times Adam had rebelled and gone to sea with him while his mother and the tutor hunted high and low for him. Many a scolding the boy had endured over these escapades, but that had never deterred him from doing it again.

Aye, James thought, turning over and settling himself down to sleep, Adam was a real Lowrie. His grandfather would have been proud of him. Mebbe Weem could have talked sense into Bethany, for she would not listen to James. The two of them had been close as children and close again for a while just before the war – too close, then. But now Bethany kept him at arm's length.

He slept at last, and woke while the others were still asleep and snoring. Gathering up his boots, jacket and cap he scaled the vertical ladder to the galley, where the huge teakettle, as always, was simmering on the stove. After putting on his boots and jacket and jamming his cap down over his head, he took the time to pour out two mugs of black tea, adding three heaped spoonfuls of sugar and a large dollop of condensed milk to each.

Sometimes the herring shoals were elusive and the drifters had to steam for miles in search of them; when that happened they could be away from the land for days at a time, and so their food rations had to be carefully hoarded. But tonight the boats were sitting over a large shoal, and once the nets were hauled they would head at full speed for the fishing station at Lerwick. James could afford to be generous with what was left of their stores.

He found Adam leaning against the wee boat kept in the stern, balancing himself comfortably against the drifter's continuous lift and drop.

'A fine mornin',' he said cheerfully as his uncle appeared. He took a long swallow of the sweet, piping-hot tea, and then lowered the mug. 'That's welcome!'

James grunted in reply and the two men drank their tea in silence, balancing their bodies easily to accommodate the boat's movements.

'I like the way she rides the waves,' Adam said after a long pause, 'as if she's just breathin' nice and natural. And ye get the sense that even when the sea's at its worst she can ride it out.'

'She can that, but ye've still tae taste a real storm at sea, lad.'

'Are ye ever frightened, Uncle James?'

James looked at the boy, his cap pushed to the back of his dark, curly head, his lithe body leaning back against the wee boat as comfortably as if he was at home in an armchair. 'Aye, often enough. When the seas are high and breakin' green over the bows and the wind's howlin' and the boat's bein' tossed about as if it was no more than a piece of grass I can be as scared as the next man. If I wasnae frightened I'd no' work hard enough at gettin' my boat and my crew back tae shore.'

'Are you ever scared for yourself?'

The question caught James by surprise. He took a while to think about it, and Adam was content to wait. 'I'm not

scared for mysel' as much as for my crew and the boat,'
James said at last. 'I suppose I'm like my faither – he lived
on the sea and he lived by the sea and he always said that
the sea owned him, and if it ever decided tae take him, it had
the right and he'd not deny it.'

'But he's buried in Rathven Cemetery, is he no'? So after
all his years at sea, he died on the land?'

'He died on this very boat, but it was a heart attack that
took him. I'd have put him over the side there and then, and
given him tae the sea like he'd always wanted, but my Uncle
Albert was the mate then, and he'd have none of it.' James
emptied his mug and put it aside, then began to fill his pipe
with tobacco. Adam waited, sensing that he would be more
likely to hear the end of the story if he kept silent. 'We took
my faither back tae Buckie, wrapped in a sail,' James said
when the pipe had been lit, 'and my mither had him buried
at Rathven so's she could lie by him when her own time
came.' Even now, long years after, bitterness thickened his
voice as he added, 'I still say it went against the man's own
wishes.'

Another long silence fell between them, while the boat
rocked like a cradle beneath the touch of a loving mother.
Finally Adam said, 'I think I'd have felt the same as you.
Would ye just look at that?'

The first promise of a summer dawn was just beginning
to draw a bright line across the horizon; here and there,
appearing and disappearing as the waves lifted and then
dropped them, they could see the lights of other boats spread
over the vast fishing grounds. The brisk wind fretted at the
tops of the waves, fraying them into white lace.

'There's nowhere else a man could want tae be, in life or
after it,' the boy's voice was hushed.

'I'm more interested in here and now,' James grunted,
suddenly embarrassed by the turn the conversation had taken.
'And what's happenin' down below us.'

'Ach, the nets'll be full. You said yourself that you could

smell the fish even before we saw the patches on the water. And you're usually right.'

'I wish I could be as certain as you. We need ten cran o' fish at least tae make this trip worth our while. Fishin' boats don't run on fresh air.'

'The old sailed boats did.'

'Aye.' Much as he loved his boat, James felt a moment's nostalgia for the great red sails that, with the wind to belly them out, had made grand engines.

'It'll be twelve cran,' Adam predicted cheerfully.

'Ten or twelve'll make no difference if we don't start haulin' soon.' James collected the mugs. 'Time we got started, or the other boats'll get tae Lerwick afore us.'

Five minutes later the rest of the crew had stumbled on deck, hauling their sou'westers on and knuckling sleep from their eyes. Murdoch, the boy, was despatched forward to the rope room, little more than a dark, cramped cupboard, to coil the lead rope as the steam capstan hauled it aboard, while the stoker and another crewman prepared to untie the buoys from the nets and toss them to one side. Siddy stood by to free the nets from the rope while three other men went into the hold to shake the fish loose from the meshes.

'Mind yersel', Adam,' James ordered as the lad leaned far out to watch for the first net.

'I'm fine.'

'I'll tell ye when ye're fine and when ye're no'!' James barked, then craned forward himself in time to see just what he had hoped for – a silvery glimmer a few feet below the plunging waves. The first net was full and with luck, this would turn out to be a good catch – a good shimmer.

The sun's first rays broke over the sea minutes later, just in time to turn the struggling fish to silver as the net broke the surface. The men waiting at the gunwales hung over the edge, arms at full stretch, hands straining to grasp the net and help to drag it over the side. As they hauled it towards the hold's gaping maw some of the fish dropped free, spilling onto the deck and flapping over its timbers, so that the men had to watch where they placed their feet for fear of slipping on the creatures and falling backwards into the hold, or forwards into the sea.

Hour followed hour and still the nets came in, each one carrying a handsome load of fish. The capstan rattled and roared and more steam was called for to help it to cope. In the rope room young Murdoch crawled frantically round and round the filthy, slippery floor, wrestling the great, thick soaking wet lead rope into coils. The men in the hold were thigh-deep in fish and those on deck were beginning to feel their muscles ache with tiredness. But it was a good catch, James thought exultantly, and to judge from the activity he could make out on the other boats in sight, they too were doing well.

The last few nets were on their way to the surface. Once they were aboard the *Fidelity* could make for the shore and the crew could snatch a hasty breakfast before turning to the job of clearing nets and buoys away, swabbing fish scales from the deck and putting the drifter to rights.

Then the next net broke the surface, and James's elation vanished at the sight of a sleek, dark back slithering among silver scales and torn, bloodied flesh. A wicked dorsal fin flashed as its owner managed to slide over the side of the net and disappeared into the depths.

James let out a howl of rage and despair as the net came up towards him, dead and maimed fish spilling back into the sea from the huge, jagged holes made by the marauding dogfish that had torn their way into the net in the dark of the night to eat their fill of the trapped herring.

13

It seemed to Etta that she had no longer closed her eyes than they flew open again to see early morning light streaming in through the drawn curtains. Someone was banging on the door and shouting, 'The boats is comin' in, lassies. Tie up yer fingers and get tae the farlins!'

The women scrambled out of bed, Agnes letting out a yelp as her bare feet landed on the rough floorboards. 'A splinter!' She sat back on the bed with a thump, hauling her foot up to examine it.

'Ye should have had the sense tae put down the canvas from yer kist at your side of the bed,' Andra's Jenny lectured her, hurrying to set the big tin teapot on the stove and rake through the ashes. 'It's still alight,' she reported, pushing kindling and coal into the stove.

'I was that tired that I forgot.' Agnes found the splinter and tugged at it. 'It's out,' she reported and began dressing.

There was just time for each of them to have a slice of bread and jam and a drink of stewed, reheated tea from the pot before they bound their fingers with the strips of cloth they had brought from home, securing them in place with strong thread. The cloths would stay in place until the day's work was done, even when they were eating.

Mary, mindful that her foster sister was still new to the work, insisted on checking Etta's bandages and making sure that there were no gaps to allow the tip of a gutting knife or a herring bone, sharp as a needle, to slide into unprotected flesh.

'They'll do,' she said at last. 'But mind now, if you get a cut you need tae tend tae it right away. Once the salt and the pickle get intae an open cut they'll eat the flesh off ye, right tae the bone.'

'Bread's the answer,' Agnes advised as they tied kerchiefs about their hair and strapped their leather knitting whiskers about their waists so that they had something to do should there be a lull at the farlins. 'A bit of bread well chewed an' then pushed right intae the cut keeps it safe and heals it too. It leaves its mark on ye for the rest of yer life, mind, but that's a sight better than havin' tae go tae the mission nurse and lose time away from yer work.'

A lorry tooted its horn outside and they hurriedly pulled on their work boots before scrambling out to climb aboard for the bumpy drive to the farlins.

It was a soft, cool morning with the air holding the promise of warmth to come. Some of the boats were already in, unloading their fish into wheeled carts known as bogies, while others could be seen hurrying shoreward across the serene waters. Sore though she still was from the journey, Etta felt her spirits rise as she and the other women jumped down from the lorries and went to the big wooden troughs, where the gutters immediately began the task of arranging the small tubs that would take the fish guts and the various sizes of herring, while the packers settled the first empty barrel into place and the coopers brought up the barrels of the salt that would be scattered over the fish on the farlins and between each layer packed in the barrels.

'Settled in?' Rory asked Etta as he and one of his men hoisted a salt barrel to its place. She smiled at him.

'Aye, I'm fine now.'

'Good.' He patted her shoulder and went on his way.

'That Rory's a nice lad,' Andra's Jenny said, watching him hurry back to the open shed where the coopers worked. 'We're lucky with him, for he's not like his faither and his Uncle Nathan.'

'Gil wasnae bad, just short-tempered and in a hurry all the time,' Agnes said, and Andra's Jenny nodded.

'Aye, I suppose you're right. Most of us kenned how tae deal with Gil. But his brother Nathan,' her lip curled contemptuously, 'that one thought he was better than us quines just because he stood on his hind legs tae piss. Most of us were pleased when Bethany began tae hire us again, the way she did when she and Gil were first married.'

'D'you like her, then?' Etta had always been in awe of her Aunt Bethany Pate, who had none of Zelda's warmth.

'I'd no' go so far as tae say I like the woman, but at least she was a guttin' quine hersel' afore she wed Gil, so she knows our ways. She's fair, I'll say that for her, and she's sly.' Andra's Jenny made it sound like a compliment. 'Mind that year she took the hirin' away from Nathan, Agnes?'

'I do that. Beth'ny came round early and engaged us for the guttin' sneakit like, before Nathan even began tae think about it. He aye left everythin' tae the last minute that one. By the time he came tae hire the crews we were all contracted tae Beth'ny. He near burst with rage, but there was nothin' he could do about it since we'd all taken arles from her.'

'He still found some crews of his own, though,' another woman further along the farlins put in, and she and Andra's Jenny roared with laughter.

'He did that, and my-oh,' Jenny said with relish, 'it was a right business! Beth'ny had made sure tae get all the best guttin' quines an' he was left wi' some that werenae so good. He was daft enough tae think that shoutin' an' bullyin' would make them work harder, but it went the other way. In the end, one of the lassies threw a fish at him, and then they all started at it. The man had tae run for his life, with everyone laughin' at him and fish fallin' like rain about his head. And then after a good while Beth'ny took over the curin' and the kipperin', just like she'd always wanted, if ye ask me. And

Nathan went off tae Fraserburgh with his tail atween his legs an' married some poor quine that's no doubt regrettin' the day she ever set eyes on him. Rory's nothin' like his faither nor his uncle – he's fair with the women, and the coopers forbye, as long as we all do the work we're paid tae do. Here we go,' Andra's Jenny finished as the first of the bogies arrived and the coopers took up their big wooden shovels and began to pile the fish into the trough.

Sunlight turned the salt being tossed lavishly over the fish into a sparkling shower of tiny diamonds and struck bright swords of light from the sharp gutting knives. The fish scales looked like silver mail and all at once it was easy, Etta thought, to see why the herring were known as the silver darlings.

She picked up her first herring and drew the knife's blade along the length of it.

The new season had begun.

The gutting crews always attracted bystanders fascinated by the speed the women worked at, and their dexterity with the gutting knives, but when a young man started setting up a strange contraption on three long, thin metal legs on the lassies' second day in Lerwick, Etta watched uneasily.

'What's that?' she asked the others.

'It's one of those fancy cameras. I've seen folk usin' them at Yarm'th,' Sarah said airily.

'He's going to take our photographs?' Etta suddenly felt very self-conscious. 'Why would he want tae do that?'

'Who cares why? It's nice tae be noticed,' Ruth said blithely. She smiled at the fair-haired young photographer and he grinned back at her before disappearing beneath a black cloth covering attached to the camera.

'Pay no heed tae him, pet,' Agnes advised. 'Folk can have all sorts of strange notions, 'specially those that don't have anythin' better do. Just go on with your work and pretend he's no' here.'

Etta tried to concentrate on what she was doing, but her gaze kept returning to the camera. To her, it was like a cold eye, recording her every move. Finally, in a desperate attempt to take her mind off the visitor, she asked the others, 'Are Yarm'th and Lowestoft as busy as this?'

'Busier, and with plenty folk gapin' round the farlins, so ye'll have tae get used tae bein' watched. Ye'll like the shops, though, and the music halls and the picture houses. My man doesnae like me goin' tae the farlins down south,' said Agnes, who was married to a fisherman. 'He thinks there's too much chance of me gettin' up tae mischief in a big place like that.'

'Why would he think that?'

Agnes grinned, the knife in her hand working at such speed that it was a blur. 'Because that's where him and me first met,' she said, 'so he well knows what I can be like when the mood takes me.'

In the time it took her to utter the sentence three fish had been split open and disembowelled, the guts tossed into a bin and the herring into one of the three tubs behind the gutters. Each tub held a different size of herring – full fish were large and with roe, matt was the name given to smaller fish with roe, and empty herring were known as spent fish. As the price of the fish depended on the different grades it was essential that the gutters selected the right tub every time.

Etta was becoming more skilled, and no longer needed the gauges used in the learners' farlins to help the girls to calculate the size of the fish, but she doubted that she would ever be able to work as fast as Agnes and the other experienced gutters. Even while they talked or sang a rousing hymn or a popular music-hall song their hands moved at speed, slitting, gutting and then flipping the finished fish into the correct tub without even having to glance round. Seagulls cheeky enough to touch down close to the gutters in the hope of finding fish that had landed on the ground instead of in the proper tub were seldom fortunate.

'Another catch comin' in, lassies,' Rory Pate said as he arrived at the farlins. 'An' this one's torn bellies.'

A groan ran up and down the rows of women. 'Torn bellies' was the name given to fish damaged by dogfish or conger eels that had got in among the nets in search of food. Those fish were difficult to work with, and brought in little money.

'Can we no' eat afore we start on them?' someone asked. 'It's intae the afternoon already an' my stomach's that empty I could take a bite out of a raw fish and enjoy it.'

Rory cast an eye over the farlins, now more than half empty. 'Aye, go on, the boat's no' started unloadin' yet. But ye'll have tae be quick.'

Several women, those detailed to do the cooking on that day for their huts, took to their heels and ran while the others went on with their work, heartened by the knowledge that they were soon going to eat. The coopers and fishermen had a cookhouse and a cook but the gutters and packers, being women, were expected to see to their own meals.

'I mind bein' here just afore the war,' one of the older women said as they worked. 'It was a bad year for the dogfish and we'd a lot o' torn bellies. But even so, the German buyers couldnae buy them up fast enough. We couldnae understand why, for they were usually particular about gettin' the best of the herrin'. Then they all loaded the barrels ontae their boats an' off they went, quick as winkin'. Next thing we knew we were at war wi' them. They'd already known it was comin' and they'd only been buyin' up all our fish, damaged or none, tae feed their own people durin' the war years. I hope it gave them the bellyache,' she added grimly.

As soon as the farlins were empty the women scattered to their huts to bolt down plates of herring and potatoes and slices of bread and jam, and drink as many cups of tea as they could manage before the lorries arrived to fetch them back to work.

Ruth loitered behind, arriving when the rest of the women were almost finished eating.

'Lost yer appetite?' Mary asked when the girl finally hurried in.

'I was talkin' tae that mannie with the camera. He's wantin' tae do a book,' Ruth said, glowing with excitement and self-importance, 'with pictures of women at work.'

'It's easier than doin' the work itself,' Sarah jeered, and her cousin glared at her.

'He says he could make a lot of money from it. His name's Jack Morrison,' Ruth announced importantly through a mouthful of bread and herring. 'He comes from Glasgow.'

'Ach, folk are always takin' pictures of the guttin' quine.' Andra's Jenny refilled her mug with strong black tea, and poured out a mug for Ruth. 'Ye'll have tae eat faster than that, my quine, for we'll be called back any minute now.'

The photographer was still there that afternoon, but as time passed Etta managed to get over her self-consciousness and soon she took as little notice of him as the others.

'How did ye like bein' at sea, Etta?' Adam Pate asked when he arrived at the farlins.

'It was fine,' she said jauntily, then as he raised his eyebrows at her she admitted, 'You were right, I didnae like it very much. I'm no' lookin' forward tae the journey back.'

'Ach, that'll no' bother ye so much because ye'll be goin' home,' Sarah assured her, while Agnes wanted to know, 'Should you not be at home, Adam Pate, and gettin' ready tae go back tae the university?'

The youth's handsome face twisted in a scowl. 'I'm not back there till September, and anyway, I'm tired of readin' books. All the time I was there last year I was hungerin' for Buckie.'

'And its bonny lassies,' Agnes gave him a near-toothless grin.

'Ye're right there, Agnes.'

'D'ye not want tae be a fine gentleman, then?' Ruth asked.

'Not if it means havin' to have my nose stuck in books all the time. It's all my mother's idea.' Adam nodded at the farlins. 'That's part of our catch. The dogfish got into the last of the nets. Ye should have heard my Uncle James cursin' when he saw the state the fish were in. And then when he saw the holes in the nets the air turned blue. We lost a lot of fish tae those damned creatures.'

'There'll no' be much money in your pockets, then,' Ruth said.

'That's where ye're wrong, for we're on wages. It's Uncle James an' Siddy and the engine driver that'll be out of pocket, no' me and the rest of the deckhands.' The skipper, mate and engineer were the only three crew members to be paid a share of the catch. 'There's one net that'll have tae go back tae Buckie for repair,' Adam went on, 'but we should be tae repair the others here. Uncle James sent me tae say that we could do with some help.'

'And when d'ye think we'll find the time tae mend yer nets for ye, my fine laddie?' Agnes indicated the farlins, still full of fish.

'Saturday, when the guttin's done?' Ruth suggested.

'We've got the hut tae put tae rights then, and clothes tae wash and food tae buy in, not tae mention gettin' a rest after the week's work,' someone else said peevishly.

'I'll help,' Ruth offered. 'And you will too, won't you, Etta?'

'I don't mind.'

One or two other women had volunteered their help before Rory brought a new barrel along, rolling it skilfully over the ground on its rim. 'Is this you keepin' my crews away frae their work?' he asked his half-brother.

'Ach, leave him be, he's no' gettin' in our way and we're enjoyin' the crack,' Andra's Jenny told the cooper amiably. 'We're women, we can work our tongues and our hands at the same time. It's men that have tae stop whatever they're doin' every time they open their mouths.'

'Well, since you're here anyway, Adam, you can just help Tod an' me tae take those full barrels away.'

'Have I no' done enough?' Adam complained. 'I was on watch all last night. I scarce got the chance to close my eyes.'

'You're young yet, ye can dae without sleep. Come on, give us a hand,' Rory ordered, and Adam shrugged and turned to wink at the women before taking hold of one of the barrels.

'It's lads like him that make me wish I was a bittie younger,' Agnes said, gutting so fast that the herring seemed to leap like salmon from her hand to their allotted tubs. 'He's grown intae a right fine man.'

'Ye'd need tae be more nor a bittie younger tae catch that one,' one of the other women scoffed, and Agnes wiggled her ample hips as she flipped another gutted fish into its tub.

'Ach, I'm sure a wee bittie would dae it, for the lad's more than ready for a taste o' fun with a comely lassie like mysel',' she said, and then, with a broad wink, 'an' if I was just young enough for him, I'd soon show ye why my man's no' happy about trustin' me in places like Yarm'th.'

Mending the *Fidelity*'s nets turned into a social event. Several of the younger women had volunteered, and since the weather was mild on Saturday afternoon they sat outside one of the huts, the nets spread around them, plying the bone needles filled with cotton yarn. The last net to be brought on board the *Fidelity* had been sent back to Buckie and would probably have to be remade, but the others, gashed in places, could be repaired.

Etta, too shy to join in the joshing that went on constantly between Adam and the younger lassies, flicked occasional glances at him as she worked. He was clever, and one of the best-looking men in Buckie with his dark, curly hair and his striking grey eyes and his smooth, brown skin. But to her mind he was too vain for her liking.

'Are ye comin' tae our hut the Sunday after next?' she heard Ruth asking the others. 'We're havin' a wee party for Etta here. It's her sixteenth birthday.'

'Ye don't need tae have a party just for me,' Etta protested, blushing as they all turned to look at her. 'It's just a birth-day!'

'It's a good excuse for a party, though. Will there be cakes?' Adam asked hopefully.

'Of course there'll be cakes, and jelly too. An' mebbe some dancin' if we can find the musicians tae play for it,' Ruth promised.

'I'd as soon not bother,' Etta said as the two of them walked back to the hut later. Ruth squeezed her arm.

'Listen, when folk work as hard as we do it's good tae have an excuse for a bit of a celebration. Anyway, this is your first time away from home, an' you deserve a wee treat.' Then, lowering her voice, 'Jack Morrison, that young man takin' our picture the other day, he's asked me if I'd like tae go dancin' in Lerwick with him on Monday night.'

'You'll be too tired for dancin'.' The fisher-lassies spent Mondays topping up the barrels of herring. It was heavy work, and on Monday nights they were usually too tired to do anything other than make their evening meal and then fall into bed to rest their aching muscles.

'I'm never too tired for dancin'.'

'But you don't know the man. You've not said you'll go with him, have you?'

'Of course I have.'

'What'll your mother say?'

'My mother isnae here,' Ruth said blithely. 'What she doesnae know won't hurt her, and Sarah knows better than tae try tae tell me what tae do. Goin' dancin's a sight better than staying in the hut with the rest of you. Etta, I've never met anyone like him before.' Her voice suddenly softened. 'He's really nice, and he's a right gentleman. How can I pass up the chance tae go out with the likes of him?'

14

Once she got into the way of the life at Lerwick Etta began to love every minute of it, even the long hours spent at the farlins. When the boats brought in good catches she and the other women worked from first light until nightfall and beyond, their hands stinging from the salt, backs aching and feeling as though they might snap in two at any minute; when the weather was bad they still worked on, their feet sinking into the mud and rain streaming down their faces and necks to trickle beneath their clothing and chill their bodies.

These trials were offset by so many pleasures – the screeching of the ever-present gulls and the smell, when the wind was blowing from the right direction, of the salt-laden sea and smoke from the drifters' chimneys. Her ears were filled with a mixture of accents – the soft, precise speech of the Highlanders, the Irish accents, sometimes gentle like the Highland way of talking and sometimes broad, depending on whether the speaker came from the north or the south; the broad vowels from the West of Scotland, and the differing English accents.

Although the heyday of the German, Russian and Dutch buyers was over there were still some visitors from those countries, putting their own stamp on the multicultural mix of folk drawn to the Shetlands by one common interest – the herring. As well as fishermen and coopers and curers and buyers there were salesmen and hawkers, lugging carpet bags filled with all sorts of treasure; ribbons and buttons and even hats and items of clothing as well as cheap jewellery. Etta had never seen so many things all together in the one place, and if Mary hadn't kept a close eye on her she would have spent every penny she had in the first week.

'It's easy tae part with the whole of yer wages,' her foster sister warned, 'for ye think at the time that ye've got a bargain. But ye'll soon find that there's always somethin' better in the next bag, so bide yer time and spend yer money wisely. God knows ye've had tae work hard enough tae get it!'

There were soft, fresh early mornings when the birds themselves had scarcely wakened and the world was still and at peace and it was a delight to be up and about. There were mornings when the fleet was in late and the womenfolk had time to walk to some pleasant spot where they could sit on rocks and grassy mounds, knitting as they watched for the first boats to appear.

There was the laughter and friendship and sing-songs and window-shopping in Lerwick when they could find the time, followed by the luxury of a cup of tea in one of the town's tearooms. There was Sunday worship in the Baptist Church in Lerwick, followed by gatherings in the lassies' huts or in the big hut where the coopers lived.

Sometimes a few of the lassies were invited onto one or other of the drifters for a sup of tea and a shop-bought cake, and occasionally they were entertained by local people who were then invited back to the huts or even the boats.

The other women in Etta's hut made a special effort on the Sunday she turned sixteen. They each presented her with a small gift – a little china brooch, a scarf, a ribbon, a wee doll dressed as a fisher-lassie – and set the table with plates of cakes and biscuits and plates of jelly with jugs of custard, all bought by Mary and Agnes, who had gone shopping in Lerwick after work on the Saturday. There were even home-made paper chains festooned from the dusty ceiling, and they all insisted on Etta getting first turn in the hip bath after work on Saturday when normally, as the youngest in the hut, she was the last to use it. It was a luxury to wallow in clean, warm water for once.

After she had washed her hair Andra's Jenny wound long strands of it around clean finger cloths, fastening each strand close to the scalp in a tight knot that brought tears to her eyes and made it almost impossible for her to lie comfortably in her bed that night. In the morning she brushed it out and tied it back with a piece of ribbon, and when they came back from church on Sunday, Andra's Jenny insisted on brushing it again before arranging it.

'It's fine just tied back,' Etta protested, but Jenny would have none of it.

'Na, na, lassie, ye've got bonny hair, and it needs somethin' different for yer birthday.' She sighed, running a glossy strand of black hair through her work-rough hands. 'I'd give a king's ransom tae have hair like yours. Make the most of it afore it starts tae turn grey, like mine,' she advised as she began to weave three strands into a thick plait.

When she had finished she fetched the hut's one and only mirror and held it before Etta. 'What d'ye think?' she asked as the others gathered again to study the new hairstyle. She had drawn Etta's long hair into two plaits and then wound them so that they cupped the girl's ears.

'It's bonny,' Mary said, and the others agreed.

Etta stared into the mirror, scarcely able to recognise the girl looking back at her. 'I look like one of those princesses in a fairy book, the sort that's doin' her sewin' while she's waitin' for her prince to come along.'

'That's all right then, because you're the princess for today,' Jenny said. 'And make the most of it, my lassie, because tomorrow ye'll just be another fishin' quine like the rest of us.'

It was a grand party. So many people crammed into the hut that there was scarcely room to move, let alone dance to music provided by an accordionist and a fiddler.

'I'm ready for my bed,' Agnes announced when the last of the guests finally departed. She gave a mighty yawn that showed the pink cavern of her mouth and the gaps where teeth had been pulled. 'There's the toppin' up tae do in the mornin'. We'll need all our strength for that.'

'We've got this place tae set tae rights afore then,' Andra's Jenny reminded her, and they all groaned. The bedding, which had been removed so that the beds could be used as seats, had to be replaced, and the table cleared and dishes washed before they could think of getting some rest.

'The sooner started, the sooner finished,' Mary said briskly. Then as Etta began to gather up the plates, 'Not you, it's still your birthday.'

'But that's not fair on the rest of you!'

'I know, but that's the way of it. Never fear, lassie, we'll make ye work twice as hard tomorrow tae make up for today,' Agnes promised. 'For now, just you sit down and play at bein' a fine lady while we put this place tae rights.' She grimaced and opened the hut door, wafting it to and fro on its hinges. 'The place is reekin' o' pipe smoke.'

A breath of cool, clean air from the door made Etta's mind up. 'Since I've not tae help I'd as soon go out for a walk than sit in here.' She reached for her jacket.

'Don't stay out too long,' Sarah called after her.

'Ach, the lassie's sixteen now, she can stay out as long as she wants,' Etta heard Andra's Jenny say as she went out into the night.

After the hut's stuffiness the night air was like a drink of clear, cold water. Etta drew it deep into her lungs as she made her way between the huts, each with lamplight glowing softly from behind drawn windows. Now and again she caught the sound of voices, a sudden eruption of laughter, a woman singing a snatch of song.

The moon was new, a crescent-shaped silver brooch pinned to the sky's black velvet cloak. Other than the lit windows and the stars scattered across the heavens there was little light, and she had to step carefully. As her eyes became accustomed to the darkness she began to make out the uneven shadows that told of grassy tussocks or bits of stone raised above the path she trod. The sea shushed softly against the shore, and as she moved towards it she began to make out glimmering lights where the moon's rays caught the wavetops.

Sixteen! She gloated over the thought, scarcely able to believe that she had finally made the step from childhood to womanhood. In another three birthdays she would be the same age as her own mother had been when she died.

She wished that she had known the girl who had birthed her and then died. She could remember very little of her father's grandmother other than a very old woman who moved slowly and painfully, but was kind in her own fashion. Her strongest memory of her early childhood belonged to the time she was with her mother's parents. Even at a very young age she was keenly aware of the tension that had settled over the farm cottage whenever her grandfather came home from his work, and the way her grandmother seemed to shrink into herself like a small creature trying to hide behind a stone whenever her husband was in the vicinity.

God ruled over her grandparents' home, a harsh and unforgiving God who used William Mulholland as His mouthpiece. Even though she had been little more than a toddler at the time, Etta knew that God was unforgiving because, for some reason she could never fathom, she was one of the people He could never forgive. She was expected to pray for absolution every night before she went to bed and every morning when she got up, and at the table her grandfather always begged the Lord to pardon Etta her sins before anyone was allowed to eat. Grandfather had also believed in cleansing the soul by punishing the body – she remembered the beatings clearly enough.

All the misery and bewilderment had vanished when Etta went to live with Aunt Zelda. In the Lowrie household God was a kindly personage who loved little children – and goodness knew that there were enough children to love in that house. As well as those who lived in the small cottage, there were always friends and cousins coming about the place. Aunt Zelda, like her God, loved children.

When she was twelve and old enough to demand an explanation from her aunt, Etta finally discovered that her unforgivable sin had come about because her mother Elsie, Zelda's favourite sister, had borne her out of wedlock.

'But that wasnae your fault, pet, nor hers,' Zelda hastened to explain. 'She was goin' tae marry your daddy, only it was wartime and he was away fightin' when she found out that you were on the way. And he was killed afore he could get back tae Buckie tae marry her, poor lad. He didnae even live tae see his bonny wee lass, or his twentieth birthday.'

Zelda, in the middle of baking when Etta marched into the kitchen and demanded to know more of her past, had scrubbed moisture from her eyes at this point with the cloth she held. When she took her hand away her round, normally happy face was smudged with white powder. Etta, on the verge of tears herself at the sad story about her poor young parents, had laughed instead, and Zelda, looking in the mirror, had joined in.

Etta smiled at the memory, but she was still wondering about her mother and her father as she started to walk back to the hut. She had nothing of theirs to keep their memories in her mind, not even a faded photograph.

'Good evenin' to ye, missie.' The voice, coming from the darkness around her, made her gasp, and the man immediately added, 'Did I startle ye? Sorry, missie, I'd no mind to do that. I was just after wishin' you all the benefits of this grand evenin'.'

She could see him now, a vague figure standing to one side of the path.

'G-good evening,' she said uncertainly.

'Are ye on yer own, then?'

'I just stepped out for some fresh air.'

'Allow me to walk ye back to yer lodgin', ma'am.' His arm swept up to pull a cap from his head as he sketched a clumsy bow.

'I've not far to go.'

'The Scotch huts, is it? I can tell by the way ye speak. They're along here.' He replaced his cap and began to lead the way, saying over his shoulder as she hesitated, 'I know this place like the back of my own hand, even in the night. This way.'

Realising that she had lost her own sense of direction, Etta followed him, her initial unease lulled by his steady flow of talk about the peacefulness of the night and the beauty of the area. His soft accent told her that he was one of the Irish labourers scattered about the yards, working wherever they were needed.

A hut loomed out of the darkness. The man walked confidently round a corner and Etta followed, blinking as they came on a small fire. Although it was little more than a glow with a few flickering flames it dazzled eyes that had become accustomed to darkness.

'Where are we?'

'This is where I sleep,' her guide said. 'The fire keeps me warm when the night gets cold. The fire, and this.' His silhouette was partly outlined against the red glow as he stooped and then straightened again, tilting his head back and lifting the bottle in his hand to his mouth. She heard him gulp the liquid down once and then twice before he lowered his arm again. 'It's good stuff, missie. Here, have a taste of it for yerself. It'll warm your bones, so it will.'

'I don't want it.' Etta took a step back as the bottle was thrust beneath her nose. The stuff within had a sharp, gut-churning smell. 'I have to go,' she said nervously. 'I'll find my own way back.'

'Indeed and you will not. What sort of gentleman would I be if I let a pretty lass like yerself wander off on her lone in the middle of the night? One wee drink for friendship's sake,' he coaxed, moving in on her, 'and then I'll take ye right to yer door and wish ye a good night's sleep.'

'I have to go n—' The words were choked off as a long thin arm suddenly snaked about her shoulders. His hand cupped her upper arm, tightening its grip so that she was drawn towards the man's body.

'In a minute, I said.' She was so close to him now that his mouth brushed her ear. 'It's only friendly to accept a drink when it's offered. Just one wee drink.'

As the glass bottle was pushed at her face Etta closed her mouth. The neck jammed into her lips, forcing them painfully against her teeth, and she thrashed her head from side to side, dislodging the bottle from his fingers.

'Will ye look at that!' he said breathlessly, his now empty hand closing about her waist. 'It'll have spilled out onto the ground. Ah well, there wasn't much left anyway, But surely ye owe me a wee kiss in its place, eh?'

His breath reeked of raw whisky and his mouth was still wet with the stuff as it found hers and latched on to it. Wild with fear, Etta kicked out with a booted foot and felt it connect with his leg. His body jerked and he took his mouth from hers to say, 'Ah now, what did ye have tae do that for?'

Etta wriggled frantically and managed to free one hand. She reached up to the shadowed face glimmering above hers and dug her nails in, feeling skin tear beneath them as she pulled down as hard as she could.

Her captor let out an animal-like cry and reeled away from her, his hands to his face. Seizing her chance she turned and fled, one shoulder hitting the corner of the hut and sending a jolt of pain down her arm as she went.

Etta still had no idea of where she was or where her hut stood, but at that moment all she wanted was to put as much distance between her and the Irishman as she could. She was bolting along, stumbling over tussocks of grass and sending loose stones rattling into the darkness, her breath sobbing in her throat, when someone caught at her arm, jerking her to a standstill and sending another wave of pain shooting right down to her fingertips.

Blind to everything but the need to protect herself she whirled, ducking at the same time so that the top of her head connected hard with the person who had accosted her. She heard an 'Oof!' from above her head and then, as she bounced back from the collision, a stone moved beneath her foot and she went down, landing on her backside with enough force to jolt her to the top of her skull and make her see stars.

In falling she had pulled herself free, but before she had time to scramble up and take to her heels again a door opened, sending out a beam of light.

'Who's there?' a woman called.

Etta opened her mouth to scream for help and then shut it as the man standing over her, both hands clasped to his midriff, straightened with an effort and said, 'It's all right, Anna, it's just me.'

'Is that Rory Pate?'

'Aye, it is.'

'Who's that with ye?'

'It's me,' Etta called, and heard the wobble in her own voice. 'Etta Mulholland.'

'What are ye doin' on the ground? Rory Pate, are you up tae mischief with that lassie?'

'I tripped on a stone, just,' Etta shouted. 'Rory's walkin' me back tae my hut.'

The woman standing at the hut door turned and said something to the other residents and Etta heard a burst of female laughter. 'A fine night for it,' the woman called, then the door closed and she and Rory were alone in the darkness.

'What did ye have tae grab hold of me like that for?' Etta asked angrily. 'You frightened the life out of me!'

'I wanted tae know what was amiss with ye.' His voice still had a breathless wheeze to it.

'Are you all right?'

'I've been better,' Rory said. 'Ye've got a right hard skull.'

'And you probably spoiled that nice hairdo Andra's Jenny gave me for my birthday.'

He gave a brief laugh, then said, 'What happened, lassie? Ye came out of the dark as if the devil himsel' was after ye.'

A shiver shook Etta from head to toe. 'It was a man. He tried tae—'

'Tae what?' All at once Rory's voice was grim.

'Ye know fine what! I gave him a good kick and he let me go. I was tryin' tae get away when I met up with you. I thought it was him catchin' hold of me again.'

'Whereabouts was this?' Rory turned towards the darkness as though set on finding the attacker. In a panic, she caught at his ankle.

'Leave him, Rory, he's probably run off the other way. I just want tae get home.' Her voice wobbled on the final word, and he peered down at her.

'Are ye hurt? D'ye want me tae get help, or carry ye?'

'I'm fine. Just help me up, will ye? I'm sittin' on the hem of my skirt and it'll no' let me get tae my feet,' she said, and then, when he had reached down to put his hands on her waist, and lifted her as easily as if she had been a doll, 'Now, can ye help me tae find my hut?'

'Here, hold on to my arm.' He drew her hand through the crook of his elbow then said as they started to walk, 'What were ye doin' out on yer lone at this time of night?'

'I just wanted some fresh air.'

'The rest of them should never have let ye go out like that. There's all sorts of folk come tae the fishin', from all over. Did ye know the man?'

'No.' She didn't say that he was Irish because she didn't want Rory to go looking for him. 'He'd been drinkin'.'

'Some of them do, that's why it's no' a good idea for quines tae go out on their lone. If ye ever want tae take a walk at night again, tell me and I'll go with ye.'

'What were you doin' out?' she asked.

'The same as you, no doubt – in search of some fresh air and a bit of peace and quiet.'

'I was thinkin' about my mother,' Etta confessed. 'She died when I was born. I don't even know what she looked like, or my faither. He died afore I was born.'

'My own mother died when I was just wee,' Rory said, 'but I knew my faither, at least. An' there's pictures of my mother in the house.'

'It must be nice to have pictures,' Etta said wistfully.

'Aunt Zelda and Uncle Innes are as good as parents to ye,' Rory pointed out. 'And the important thing is who you are, not who your parents are.'

A sudden wailing sound in the distance made Etta's flesh creep and she clutched Rory's arm tightly. 'What's that?'

'Just an owl, out huntin' for his dinner. An' there goes a bat.'

'Where?'

'It just flew by yer head. Look, there's another.'

She peered into the darkness. 'I can't see anythin'.'

'Can ye not? The night air's full of them. There – and there.'

But try as she might, Etta could not see a single bat in the night sky. She was still looking for them when Rory said, 'Here we are. This is your hut.'

'Are ye sure?' She looked doubtfully at the black bulk before them.

'Of course I'm sure.'

'One hut looks like another in the dark. I'd not want tae go wanderin' intae someone else's.'

'It's yours,' he said, amusement in his voice. 'I'm the one that can see the bats, ken? I know where all the huts are, even in the dark. Go on in now and get some sleep. There's hard work tae be done in the mornin'.'

'Aye.' She started to go, then turned back. 'Thank ye for yer kindness, Rory.'

'Och, it was nothin'.'

'Ye'll not say anythin' tae the rest of them? I feel a right fool.'

'It's not you that's tae blame, it's the creature that caught you. If ye see him in the daylight,' Rory's voice was suddenly hard, 'just you point him out tae me. And you neednae fret about me sayin' anythin' tae the rest of them. I know when tae hold my tongue. Just don't go out on yer own again.'

'I won't,' Etta promised fervently.

15

It was the right hut; Etta knew that as soon as she slipped inside the door and heard Agnes's distinctive snore, a guttural intake of breath followed by a long sigh that ended with three emphatic 'Humphs!' Surely nobody else in the whole of the island snored like that?

She stood just inside the door for a moment, bringing the hut's interior to mind and picturing just where her bed stood. Then she moved silently and cautiously across the floor, her hands stretched before her and each foot testing the ground before she put her weight on it.

She managed to reach the large bed without falling over anything, and undressed swiftly in the dark before slipping in beside Sarah and Ruth. It was just as well, she thought as she curled against the warm, solid curve of Sarah's back, that she slept on the outside, and had not had to crawl over any of her cousins to get to her rightful place.

Because the Scottish boats never went to sea on the Sabbath there was no fish for the farlins on Monday. Instead, the day was spent in topping up the barrels. The coopers bored holes in the side of each barrel, and tipped it to pour out the brine resulting from the coarse salt and the herring. The lid was then taken off and the women added another layer or perhaps two of fish and some fresh pickle. After the bunghole was sealed the barrels were covered and rolled off to the side, where they were stacked three tiers high to await the lorries.

It was heavy work, and although there were always labourers willing to earn a few shillings by helping out, the women were expected to take their full share of the backbreaking toil.

Much to Ruth's delight her young photographer friend, Jack Morrison, returned with his camera. She willingly posed for him, now clutching the rim of a barrel as though about to manhandle it on her own, now rolling an empty barrel or placing an extra layer of fish or pouring pickle in through a bunghole.

'That lassie's got a great conceit of hersel',' one of the older women sniffed.

'Ach, leave her be, there's no harm in that at her age,' someone else said, adding longingly, 'It just seems like yesterday that I was as young and bonny as she is. Who'd want tae take my picture now?'

Ruth did look particularly pretty that day, Etta thought, watching the girl talking and laughing with the photographer. Her lightly tanned skin and her hazel eyes glowed with health, and her teeth, when she laughed – which was often – were white and strong. She had wound a blue scarf about her head and strands of her light brown hair, escaping from beneath it, tossed in the breeze. Her plain skirt and blouse, with the sleeves rolled up to above her elbows and unbuttoned at the throat, showed off a body as comely as her face. It was clear that the young man was quite smitten by her.

Etta envied the two of them their pleasure in the day and in each other's company. Her arm ached and she had to steel herself against the pain each time she helped to lift a barrel. She was suffering from lack of sleep and although the cool, fresh wind helped to revive her it could never blow away memories of the groping, grasping hands she had run from the night before. As she struggled with the laden barrels the sheer terror of it kept returning to haunt her.

'Are you all right?' Rory asked at one point as he helped

her and Mary to lift a barrel that had to go up to the second tier.

'I'm fine. Why wouldn't I be?' Her voice was sharp, signalling a warning to him.

'I just wondered, after the party last night.'

'If ye ask me she ate too much,' Mary said robustly. 'She had tae go out and walk it off last night, and even so, she scarce ate a thing this mornin'.'

'Mebbe she slipped out tae meet with her lad,' someone called from further down the row.

'I did not!' Etta concentrated on lifting the barrel, keeping her head averted from the others in an effort to hide the sudden warmth flooding her face. Then as the barrel settled into its proper place and they turned back towards the farlins she felt the blood drain from her head to her toes.

Agnes and one of the coopers were lifting the next barrel into place, assisted by a labourer whose skinny body, not much more than flesh and bone, was buckling under the weight he was trying to lift. As he put his shoulder beneath the barrel and struggled to heave it upwards, trying at the same time to prevent the thin, patched shoes he wore from skidding in the mud, his head was twisted to one side and Etta saw that four raw strips of lacerated skin stretched down one cheek from below his eye to the line of his jaw.

Just as the barrel rocked into its place and the boy stepped back Mary said something to Rory. The two of them burst out laughing and the noise brought the lad's head round. As he glanced across at the three of them Etta flinched back, her hands fluttering up to draw the edge of her headscarf over her face in an attempt to hide from him. But his gaze swept over and past her without recognition.

She opened her mouth to call Rory, who was walking away from her, and then closed it again, realising that the ragged, bony youth would be no match for the broad-shouldered, well-nourished cooper, especially if Rory was as angry as he had been last night.

Safe now in the knowledge that he had no idea who she was, Etta watched the boy as the morning wore on and saw that he was having a desperate struggle to keep up with the other men. On one occasion, after helping to lift a barrel into place, he staggered slightly and had to lean against the stacked barrels for a moment. His chest heaved and she could see that his face was slick with sweat. When one of the coopers roared at him to stir himself and lend a hand, it was an effort for him to straighten up and return to work.

To think that she had run from this poor creature, she thought, astonished. She could surely have bested him in any struggle. Then as she recalled the tight grip of his hand on her waist and the way he had dragged her closer and forced his kisses on her, the panic came sweeping back. She had to turn away from the others and pretend to be adjusting the cloths about her fingers until the irrational fear subsided.

Again and again that morning she found her eyes drawn back to the young Irishman. His clothes, shabby and worn almost paper-thin, were little protection against the wind, and his hair was an untidy matted thatch. She remembered the small fire and his soft Irish voice saying, 'This is where I sleep.' He must be living out of doors, sleeping on the hard ground with no roof over his head and little to keep him going other than the raw whisky she had smelled on his breath. She had heard that some of the Irish labourers were in a desperate state, suffering from poverty unknown to the likes of her, but she had never encountered it until now.

The fisher-lassies often gave leftover food to the itinerant workers for, as Mary said, no matter how poor you were there were always folk worse off. She should know, for her soft-hearted mother frequently had whole families, down on their luck and with nowhere else to go, living in the little lean-to in her back yard.

At the midday meal Etta saved her bread, which was no hardship since she was still without any appetite, and stuck the two thick slices together with a scrape of butter and a generous spread of jam. She wrapped it in a bit of newspaper and put it into her pocket.

When she got back to the farlins the boy was sitting alone in the shelter of some barrels, hunched over and with his arms locked about his bony knees. Etta went over to him and held out the little parcel. 'Here you are.'

He lifted his head slowly, as though it took an effort, and looked at her, not understanding.

'This is for you.'

'For me?' he asked, astonished, and then as she pushed the parcel towards him, he took it and unfolded the paper with dirty, long-nailed hands. 'Bless ye, missie,' he said in his lilting Irish voice before cramming a huge bite of bread and jam into his mouth. As Etta backed away from him he added thickly round the food, 'May the angels watch over ye for yer kindness.'

She turned and walked away, not looking back until she had gained the safety of the farlins and the other gutters. He had finished eating by then, and he was licking his filthy fingers one by one, making sure that not a crumb or a drop of sweetness was lost.

That evening, while the other women rubbed embrocation on aching muscles and bathed sore feet, Ruth filled a bowl with water and washed from top to toe, including her hair, 'tae get the smell of the fish off me'. Then she put on the pretty blouse and skirt she had brought from home for special occasions and tied green and red ribbons in her hair before going off to meet her gentleman friend, looking, as Andra's Jenny remarked enviously, as fresh as a daisy, and as though she had never in her life had to do a hard day's work.

They were all asleep long before she returned to the hut, but the next day at the farlins they heard all about the grand time she'd had, and how she had danced all evening. Even though she had not had much rest, her eyes were clear and her skin glowed as she deftly arranged the fish in the required pattern, tossing generous handfuls of salt over each layer before starting on the next.

'I hope you're settin' these fish right,' Rory told her when he arrived to inspect the work. 'You're no' here just tae get yer picture taken.'

Ruth stuck her tongue out at him. 'I know what I'm doin'. Have a look,' she invited, standing back. 'Have ye ever seen a bonnier barrel o' herrin'?'

He grinned at her, ignoring the barrel. 'I know you're one of the best packers we have, so on ye go,' he said, and then to Etta, low-voiced, 'It looks like bein' a grand evenin'. D'ye fancy a wee walk round by the shore afore it gets dark?'

'That'd be nice – if we get away from here early enough.'

All that day she watched out for the Irish lad, at the same time dreading the sight of him. But he must have been put to work in some other area, for she never saw him again. Even so, it was a long time before he ceased to haunt her dreams.

'It's not fair!' Ellen Pate stormed.

'Nothing's fair in this life.' Bethany told her stepdaughter coldly. 'We all have to work for our living and it's time you started. I need you to help me with the net factory.'

'But I don't have to work! I have money; my father left it to me.'

'You don't get that money until your twenty-first birthday next year. In the meantime you're living under my roof and it's time you paid for your keep.'

'Paid?' Ellen said the word as though it belonged to a foreign language and was beyond her comprehension.

'I put money into my mother's house every week when I lived there. Your cousins do the same for their mothers. Why shouldn't you?'

'That's different.' Ellen stamped a neatly shod foot on the parlour carpet. 'They're all working folk and I'm a cooper's daughter. Coopers' daughters don't have to go out to work.'

'No doubt if your faither was still with us he would be happy to feed and clothe and house you out of his own pocket, Ellen, but he can hardly support you in idleness from the grave, can he?'

'Rory owns the cooperage now. It's his place to look after me!'

'Then you can speak to Rory when he comes back from Lerwick. If he wants to keep his sister in comfort that's his concern. I'm just saying that I can't do it any more.'

'You mean you won't. You've plenty money!'

'I do,' Bethany agreed, 'but none of it comes from your father. He left this house to me in his will, Ellen, but I couldn't sell it because it was your home, and Rory's and Adam's. And he arranged for your Uncle Nathan to pay me a sum of money every month to feed and clothe the three of you. But I'm not like you – I don't like to live off other folks' charity. So I've paid my own way by running the net factory and the smokehouse and the gutting crews, and keeping Jacob McFarlane's books. I work for my keep,' Bethany said coldly, 'the same as I always have.'

'My father kept you well enough when he was alive.'

'You think I didn't work for my food even then?' Bethany raised an eyebrow. 'All married women have to earn their keep, Ellen. Mebbe they don't have to go out to work but there are other ways, some of them mebbe not to our liking, though we can do nothing about it. No doubt you'll learn about that for yourself, one day.'

Ellen stared at her stepmother, chewing her full, artificially reddened lower lip. 'Uncle Nathan won't be pleased when he hears that you're making me work for my living. I can get him to give me my inheritance now.'

'You can try,' Bethany told her dryly. 'I know that you can twist Nathan round your little finger, and I know fine where the money for most of your bonny clothes comes from, but I doubt if he'll be willing to hand over your father's inheritance before it's due. And when it is, I'd not be surprised to hear that he's already deducted all the money you've wheedled from him in the past few years.'

Her stepdaughter's face suddenly paled. 'He wouldn't do that!'

'You'll not know the truth of it until your next birthday. And until then, you'll either work or you'll go hungry.'

'How dare you say such a thing to me!'

'If you don't want to go to the net factory I can always turn Leezie off and let you run the house.'

'Me? A skivvy?' The girl's voice was contemptuous.

'What's wrong with that? Most of the fisher quines work as skivvies between fishin' seasons. At least they'll turn their hands to anything to earn their keep. We can call you the housekeeper if it makes you feel any better about it.'

Ellen fiddled sulkily with her stylishly cropped brown hair, then asked, 'What would I do in the net factory?'

'Nothing that takes skill, that's certain. You don't know how to wind the skeins of cotton for the looms, or how to weave, and it takes a good year to learn how to be a beat-ster. It's a skilled job, mending nets. I should know, for I had to do it when I was your age.'

'It was different for you, you were only a fisherman's daughter!'

Bethany's clear eyes suddenly took on the deep, threatening grey of an approaching storm. Although the parlour was warm, Ellen felt chilled as those eyes surveyed her.

'It's the herring fishers that made your father rich enough to buy this fine house and turn you into a lady, Ellen Pate.' Bethany's voice was as icy as her stare. 'Never forget that. As to what you can do in the factory,' she went on as Ellen began to wilt, 'you can see to it that the materials the workers need are ordered in time, and that the men and women are content, and getting on with what they're paid to do. Contented workers work better. And you can make up their wages. You should surely be able to manage the writing and figuring.'

There was a moment's silence before Ellen heaved a martyred sigh. 'I suppose I'll have to do what you want – until Rory comes home from the fishing, at least.'

'Good.' Bethany sat down at her desk, a sign that the meeting was at an end. 'You can come to the factory with me tomorrow and I'll show you what has to be done,' she said, picking up a pen and dipping it into the inkwell. Then she laid it down again, sighing, when the girl had flounced out, closing the parlour door behind her with unnecessary vigour. Ellen had been a placid, biddable child, but for some reason that Bethany could not fathom she had grown into a self-centred young woman.

It was true that men who owned cooperages as successful as the Pate's were usually wealthy enough to support their families. Coopers' sons and daughters normally led easy lives and dressed in the height of fashion, and if Gil had lived, Ellen could no doubt have played the young lady to her heart's content. But it irked Bethany each time she came home from the factory after a day's work to find her stepdaughter loung-ing in the parlour, leafing through magazines.

It seemed to her that children were more trouble as they got older instead of less. When it came to doing her bidding, the only one of the three who had not given her any worry was Rory, who had calmly served his apprenticeship in the cooperage and then taken charge of it, as his father had planned. Even when he received his inheritance, a tidy sum of money, he had put it away in the bank where, as far as Bethany knew, it still lay.

Adam was every bit as difficult as his half-sister. Every time he went missing she had known where to find him – down at the harbour and as like as not on board the *Fidelity* if the drifter was there. Once he turned fifteen he was desper-ate to go out on the boat, pestering and badgering until Bethany was forced to agree. She had hoped that he would take after Innes and be a poor sailor, and that one voyage would be enough for him, but instead he had come home glowing with excitement, and determined to go out to the fishing whenever he got the chance.

'Let the loon have his way,' Jacob had advised her. 'The more ye go against him the more determined he'll be. James'll see tae it that he comes tae no harm.'

She had listened to him – and where had that got her? This summer Adam was off to the Shetlands with his uncle, and goodness only knew what sort of nonsense James would put into his head. When she was expecting her only child Bethany had longed for a son who would follow the fishing, thus fulfilling her own thwarted ambition, but when James returned from the war and she saw the hungry way he looked at the child she realised that, like her, he wanted Adam to follow in the family tradition. But that would mean that he and James would be in each other's company, and that she could not allow.

So she had adopted Gil's ambition for the boy, and now Adam, who had done well at the school, was attending Aberdeen University.

At least, Bethany thought as she went through to the kitchen, he would be well beyond James's reach there. He would meet new folk, follow new interests, and there would be no more talk of the fishing.

'What was all that about?' Leezie asked as her mistress walked in, and then, as Bethany raised her eyebrows, 'Ye neednae worry, I've not stooped as low as tae listen at doors. I didnae have tae, for I could hear the two of ye shoutin' at each other from here.'

'We weren't shouting, we were having a discussion.' Bethany took an apron from the hook on the door and tied it around her waist, noting with annoyance how far she had to reach to tie it at the back. She was into her forty-third year, and it seemed that every birthday brought with it a further slight thickening of her once slim waist. 'Ellen's going to be the new overseer in the net factory.'

'Ellen?' Surprise sent the maid's voice soaring. 'No wonder she was shoutin' at ye.'

'She wasn't shouting.' Bethany began to scrape carrots.

'That's as may be, but I'm certain sure she didnae come up with the idea on her own. That one's the laziest lassie in the town.'

'You mind your tongue. You're just a servant here.'

'I'm the hoosekeeper and I'm stayin' the hoosekeeper! Aye well, mebbe I did put my ear tae the door for a minute,' Leezie said as her mistress gave her a hard look. 'But I took it away again when I heard ye say that ye'd turn me off and give her my job.'

'You know as well as I do that she'd never have agreed to it.'

'Even so, it wasnae very nice tae hear ye offerin' tae put me out without a second thought.' Leezie underlined the words with a hefty sniff.

'I told you, it would never have happened so stop making such a fuss about it!' Bethany's knife bit into a carrot with such force that it pared off a large chunk of the red flesh. She swept it into the rubbish bucket before Leezie noticed. Leezie hated waste.

16

'It's about time that lassie was made tae do some work,' Stella Lowrie said when Annie came back from the shops with the news that Ellen was overseeing the net factory for her stepmother. 'It's not right, her walkin' about the town as if she owned it when she does nothin' for anyone. Did ye get that soap?'

'Aye.' Annie put the bar of yellow soap and the few coppers of change onto the table then returned to the task of black-leading the grate. The two of them were getting the holiday cottage ready for the next lot of summer visitors.

'After all,' her mother ranted on as she rubbed beeswax into the big dresser, 'she's no better than you and your sisters. You were born in this very cottage, and she was birthed in one just like it. What right has she tae put on airs and graces?'

'Uncle Gil did well for himsel',' Annie ventured. 'Ellen grew up in that fine, big house he bought, and he'd enough money tae keep her in comfort. She didnae have tae work for her livin' the way we did.'

'And what's come out of that? The lassie's got a right conceit of hersel'. The devil finds mischief for idle hands,' Stella snapped, and Annie took some comfort in thinking that if that was true, the devil would never be able to get close to her. 'She's spoiled, and so's that young brother of hers. University, indeed! What about that ash pan?'

Annie hauled the metal tray out from underneath the grate and held it out for inspection. 'It's been emptied.'

'Aye, but has it been cleaned?'

'Ye don't clean ash pans, mither!'

'Ye do in my house,' Stella said. 'Take it out the back and give it a good brushing, then ye can wipe it over with a bit of metal polish when ye've brought it in again.'

Annie opened her mouth to argue, then closed it again and did as she was told, wishing with all her heart that she was standing at the farlins with her sisters Sarah and Ruth and the other fisher-lassies. A fine drizzle of rain was falling, but even if it was the same in the Shetlands, with mud underfoot at the farlins, she would have welcomed it.

'Rory's the only one that's turned out right in that family.' Stella picked up the conversation again when her daughter brought the ash pan back into the kitchen. 'He's not afraid of a hard day's work, that lad.'

'Aunt Bethany works hard too,' Annie pointed out, and Stella sniffed.

'I wouldnae call overseein' the net factory and the smokehouse hard work. Not as hard as carin' for a house, but she's fly enough tae have someone in tae dae that for her.'

'She does Mr McFarlane's financial books too, Rory says. And it was Uncle Gil that brought Leezie in tae do the housework, surely.' Then, when her mother simply said 'Hmph!' Annie ventured, 'What did my Aunt Bethany do that was so wrong?'

'What did you say?' The words rattled out so quickly that Annie jumped. She turned away from the grate to see that Stella, too, had stopped her work and was staring at her, her eyes hard and her normally pale face looking almost yellow.

'I was just wonderin',' the younger woman faltered. 'She must have done somethin' tae make ye dislike her the way ye do.'

'Bethany Pate,' her mother said slowly and clearly, 'doesnae need tae *do* anythin' tae annoy folk. It's just her way of behavin' as if nob'dy's as good as she is – that's enough tae rile anyone.'

'Aunt Zelda gets on well with her.'

'Your Aunt Zelda would get on with anyone,' Stella snapped. 'How's that ash pan lookin'?' Then, when Annie held it out for inspection, 'It'll do. You can put it back.'

'It seems a shame tae fill it with ashes now,' Annie said as she obeyed.

'That's what it's for,' Stella was beginning when hurried footsteps rattled on the road outside, and the door was thrown open.

'Mind my clean oilcloth with your wet feet!' Stella skirled, but the order was ignored as Samuel Lowrie burst into the kitchen, heedlessly tracking prints from his muddy boots all over the scrubbed oilcloth.

'Mither says tae come at once,' he gabbled, his dark eyes wide with fear. 'It's Auntie Meg. She's sleepin' and when mither tried tae wake her she fell off her chair and we cannae get her up from the floor!'

Adam brought Stella's letter to James as he sat in the *Fidelity*'s cabin, enjoying a quiet smoke after a long night's fishing. 'One for you, and two for me,' the boy said, dropping the envelope with its familiar handwriting on the table and throwing himself onto the bench at the other side of the table. 'There's letters for some of the others, but Siddy took them.'

'And who's writin' tae you, then?'

Adam grinned. 'Ach, some lassies enjoy writin' letters,' he said, tearing open the first envelope. James watched him scan the single sheet of paper, remembering the days when he had been Adam's age and local lassies had written little notes to him while he was away at the fishing. Now, it seemed as if those carefree days had belonged to someone else entirely, he thought as he unfolded Stella's letter and began to read the contents.

He scanned the few lines once, and then went back and

read them again, unable to take in the news they contained. As he sat motionless, paralysed with the shock of it, Adam glanced up at him and then returned to his own letter; then, suddenly realising that something was wrong, he looked sharply back at his uncle.

'What is it?'

James tried to speak, but had to clear his throat and try again before he found his voice. 'It's your Auntie Meg. She's died.'

'Auntie Meg? But she wasnae ill when we left.'

'It was sudden, Stella says. She just went in her sleep. She'd reached a good age,' James said, his eyes still on his wife's letter. 'Longer than most. But even so, it's come as a bit of a shock.'

'Will we be goin' back tae Buckie for the funeral, then?'

James ran the back of his hand over his mouth and cleared his throat again. 'No, no. Stella says it's all in hand, and we'd not get back in time, anyway.'

'It'll seem strange, without Auntie Meg,' Adam said, and then, with the resilience of the very young, 'But she was a good age, as you said.'

'Aye.'

'D'ye want me to go and tell the others? Jem and Mary and the rest of them?'

'Aye, ye could. I've got things tae do here before I come ashore,' James said, and the youth departed, skimming up the ladder and whistling as he tramped across the deck overhead.

James put the letter down flat on the table, and sat stroking it with one finger, staring unseeingly at the opposite wall. For some strange reason Meg's death filled him with more emotion than he had known at the loss of either of his parents. He wondered if it was because of the resentment he had felt against his father for pushing him into a marriage he had not wanted, and with his mother because of the bitter quarrel they had had when she insisted on burying Weem Lowrie on land when James knew that his father's dearest wish was to be given back to the sea he loved.

Meg was different; Meg had always been different. A big woman with a big heart, she had only needed to walk into a house to set its very walls thrumming with her presence. And she had always met folk on their own level, James realised now, never judging, never criticising, always ready to accept them as they were.

For the past fourteen years she had been the head of the family, and with her dying she had handed that position over to James himself. Although he lived with death every time he took his boat out to sea he was suddenly reminded by Meg's passing of his own mortality. Who would follow him when his own days were over?

Adam had left his two letters, one envelope still sealed, on the table. James picked up the opened letter and glanced down at it, seeing only the beginning, 'Dear Adam,' and the girl's signature scrawled at the bottom of the page.

Dear Adam. He looked at the wall again, seeing with his mind's eye the young face beneath the shock of black curls that, like his own hair at that age, tended to tumble over the boy's forehead. And he railed against the knowledge that when he himself was gone there was no son to carry the bloodline forward.

No son, at least, that he could claim before the rest of the world.

Sarah had been right in saying that the sea journey home to the Moray Firth would be easier than the trip out to Lerwick. The sea was just as rough and the boat tossed as much as it had before but, buoyed up by the excitement of going home and memories of the good times she had had at the Lerwick fishing, Etta managed to get through the misery of seasickness without becoming too wretched.

They landed at Aberdeen, where Peter Bain, son of the farmer who had employed Zelda as kitchen maid before her marriage, was waiting to take the Buckie fisher-lassies home. Crowding onto the back of his lorry they roared out hymns and popular songs as they rattled and bounced along the coast to Buckie.

The local season lay ahead of them, and there was the English fishing to come after that, but at least, Etta knew, she would be able to sleep at home after a day spent slaving at the Buckie farlins. As for the move south, that journey would be made by lorry and train, with no more tossing about at the mercy of the sea.

Zelda was waiting down by the harbour with Annie, Sarah's twin, when the lorry arrived and began to spill its cargo.

'Where's Mary?' Zelda asked as the girls climbed to the ground.

'Milady decided to keep Peter company in the cab.' Ruth banged on the door, and Mary appeared, giggling as she was met by a chorus of cheers and jibes from the others.

'We've missed ye both!' Zelda ran to hug her daughter and then her niece. 'The house wasnae the same without ye!'

'Mither, how could you tell?' Mary wanted to know. 'There were still five bairns in the place – ye surely couldnae miss just two of us with all that noise goin' on.'

'I never feel right unless ye're all close by me,' Zelda said firmly. 'Peter, son, come and have a wee cup of tea before you go home.'

'I'd like that fine, but there's work tae be done, and my faither'll be waitin' for me. I said I'd get right back,' he said with genuine regret. Zelda had been his nursemaid when he was a child, and he still thought the world of her.

'Another time, then. Don't you forget, now.' She stood on tiptoe to give him a hug and a hefty kiss on the cheek, to another chorus of cheers from the fisher-lassies. 'Give my regards tae your mother and father, lad, and bless you for bringin' my lassies back tae me,' she said, and then as Peter climbed back into the cab and the lorry drove away, 'How did ye like the Lerwick fishin', Etta?'

'She liked it fine,' Sarah smirked. 'See that bonny wee shell necklace she's wearin'? Rory Pate gave it tae her.'

171

'Rory? Are the two of ye courtin', then?' Zelda asked eagerly. She loved a bit of romance.

'They've been walkin' out together,' Mary said.

'The necklace was for my birthday,' Etta protested, 'and Rory's just been showin' me round the place, and tellin' me the names of the birds.'

'Ruth's got an admirer too,' Sarah said, while Ruth giggled, well pleased with herself. 'He's a photographer mannie that photographed us at the farlins, and took her to the dancin'.'

'His name's Jack,' Ruth chimed in. 'Jack Morrison. He's takin' pictures for a book. I told him about Aunt Beth'ny's net factory and the smokehouse, and he's comin' tae Buckie tae take pictures of them.'

'You'll need tae bring him tae the house for his tea, Ruth. What about you, Mary? No boyfriend for you?' her mother asked wistfully. 'I'd fair like tae set up your weddin'.'

'I'm not in any hurry. It was terrible news about Auntie Meg,' Mary said, and tears sprang at once to Zelda's eyes.

'I miss her that much! But she went quick, and I suppose that's a blessin' for her, even though it's so hard on the rest of us,' she said, and then, scrubbing a hand across her eyes, 'Come on now, tell me all about Lerwick.'

She linked arms with her eldest daughter and they set off together along the street. As the other fisher-lassies followed in a ragtaggle group, Annie burst out, 'I'm that glad ye're back! I've made up my mind that I'm goin' back to the farlins, and if my mither wants any more help she can get it from you, Sarah, or from Ruth. We cleaned that cottage so much that it's a shame tae let folk live in it. It wasnae enough just tae wash the oilcloth on the floor – we'd tae take it up and put it outside so's we could get at the floorboards and give them a good scrub with bleach. Then the oilcloth had tae, be cleaned afore it could be put back down, and I'd tae black-lead the fireplace an' scrub up the fender wi' steel cloth – I even had tae clean the ash pan afore it went back below the grate.'

'My mither did that every springtime,' Agnes said, 'And she had this big black kettle that had tae be blackleaded every week. It was never used for anythin', mind, it was just for show. You young quinies don't know the meanin' of spring-cleanin' nowadays.'

'I do now,' Annie said from the bottom of her heart, while Etta asked, 'D'you clean your own hoosie like that, Agnes?'

'Me?' The woman boomed out a hearty laugh. 'Away tae damty, lassie, d'ye think I've got the time for all that palaver? Not at all!'

'Then when the whole thing was finished,' Annie went on, 'I'd tae scrub the floorbrush and clean the shovel. I kept waitin' for her tae tell me tae wash the coal in the back bunker. And once it was all done tae her satisfaction she hung up one of they samplers she'd found in a shop, with "Home Sweet Home" stitched on it. Home, indeed – I'm certain that even if the King and Queen themselves were tae take that cottage for their holidays they'd find it cleaner than their own home. I tell you, the thought of standin' at the farlins all day guttin' fish sounds like Paradise tae me, after what I've been through!'

Rory Pate was no sooner home from Lerwick than his sister pounced, bursting into his room before he had time to respond to the swift, impatient tap at the door.

'She's impossible!' she stormed, standing over him as he sat on the bed, leafing through the nature notebook he had been keeping during his walks in Lerwick.

'Who?' he asked, though he knew the answer well enough.

'I'm not talking about Leezie, am I?' Her arms were folded tightly across her chest and her eyes were angry. Rory gave an inward sigh and laid the book of sketches and notes aside.

'Mother.'

'She's not our mother, she's our stepmother! Our real

mother wouldn't have treated me the way *she's* treated me. Rory, she's got me working in the net factory!'

'You're makin' nets?' He looked in disbelief at her hands with their neat polished nails.

'How would I know how to make nets? She's got me writing out the invoices and doing the wages and keeping an eye on the place – the things she used to do herself. She's making me *work*,' Ellen said, her voice filled with self-pity, 'and she's making me pay money into this place every week.'

'I pay for my keep, and I suppose Adam will, from the money he's earnin' at the fishin'.'

'But it's different for you; you've got the cooperage to run. I shouldn't need to work!'

'You have to do somethin', Ellen.'

'Why should I? We don't need the money. People only work when they need to.'

'Sit down, Ellen, my neck's gettin' stiff with lookin' up at you. The thing tae do,' Rory said when she had thrown herself into the only chair in the room, 'is tae find somethin' you like better. Work in an office, or a shop, mebbe.'

'But that's still work!' Ellen's fingers drummed on the arms of the chair. 'And I don't want to work – I don't need to! I've written to Uncle Nathan to ask for my inheritance early, but he'll not agree.'

'I don't see that he can, since our father's will says that you have to wait until you're twenty-one.'

'I must have that money, so that I can get away from this place.'

'Where would you go?'

'Aberdeen – Edinburgh—'

'And what would you do when you got there? There won't be enough money tae keep you in comfort for the rest of your life.'

'I'll find something more suitable once I get there. Rory,' Ellen coaxed, 'you could lend me money, just until I reach my twenty-first birthday and get my inheritance.'

He gaped at her. This was something he had not expected.

'You haven't spent it, have you?' she asked sharply. 'What could you have spent it on? You never go anywhere or do anything but work.'

'I put it in the bank.'

'Well then, you can take it out, or some of it at least, and give it to me. I'll pay it back.'

'How will you do that?'

'I'll find a way. Please, Rory?'

He hesitated, and then shook his head. 'I cannae do it.'

'Why not?'

'Because it seems tae me that Mother's tryin' tae teach you that we all need tae pay our way. And she's right, because—'

Ellen dismissed the words with a melodramatic wave of her arms. 'You're saying no? You're denying me, your own sister? Your own flesh and blood?'

'If ye really can't bear tae work in the factory, I can pay money intae the house for you until you find somethin' more suited—' he said, but his sister was on her feet and glaring down at him, her face screwed into an ugly grimace.

'Go to hell, Rory Pate,' she said, and then went out, banging the door so hard that he was surprised to see it remain on its hinges.

The cleaning frenzy that had plunged Annie into gloom had been balm to Stella Lowrie's soul. For the first time in a life spent in ministering to others – first of all her mother, who had more or less become an invalid after the loss of her three sons at sea, then her father, and then her husband and daughters – she was a woman of property, an independent woman who earned her own money by renting out the cottage that had been her childhood home.

And for the first time, as she banked the rent money, Stella began to wonder if her self-willed, difficult sister-in-law had, like her, railed against having to be dependent on a husband.

But it didn't soften the dislike she felt towards Bethany. Too much had happened for that to be possible.

'I don't know why we don't just bring our caff mattresses down here an' save the walk home and back again,' Andra's Jenny grumbled as she gutted. The boats had been low in the water on their return to Buckie on the previous day, and the women, after an early start, had been kept at the farlins until close to midnight. After a few snatched hours' sleep they were back to start the new day's work. 'Andra made a right fuss last night when I got home,' Jenny went on. '"Where have ye been?" he wanted tae know – as if I'd been out enjoyin' mysel'! I told him "once you take the fish from the sea they cannae be left lyin' overnight. That's what keeps the guttin' quines standin' at the farlins, and if ye want yer wife at home, then ye have tae stop catchin' so much fish. Ye cannae have things a' ways," I said.'

'Men aye think they can have things a' ways. He'll be pleased enough when the money comes in at the end of the season,' Agnes grunted, and Jenny brightened up.

'He will that, and so will I. We'll be able tae give the bairns a right good Ne'erday when it comes.'

To Etta's surprise, Rory continued to seek her company on his beloved walks along the shoreline and over the farming country behind Buckie. 'It's peaceful here, is it not?' he said one Sunday afternoon as they sat on a hillside, looking down on Buckie's roofs and chimneys, the boats crammed into the four basins of the harbour, and the great stretch of glittering water beyond.

'I'd have thought you would have plenty of peace in that fine big house you live in. It's not like our place, with bairns near sittin' on top of each other and folk comin' in and out all the time.'

Rory picked a stalk of grass, drew the inner stalk from its sheath, and began to chew on its soft flesh. 'I like Aunt Zelda's house. It might be busy, but it's friendly, not like our place. Adam's moanin' about havin' tae go back tae the university come September and Ellen's in a right takin' because our mither's makin' her oversee the net factory. She goes off tae work with such a sour face on her that I feel sorry for the folk that have tae work for her.'

Etta knew all about the tensions in the net factory, for her cousin Jessie, now fourteen and working there, came home every night bursting with tales of the day's happenings. Bethany had an aloof way with her, but her employees had accepted that because she was a mature woman, and although she was strict she was fair. Ellen was different; for one thing, many of the younger women found it hard to treat her as their superior since they were of the same age and she had played with them in the old days when, like them, she had lived in a cottage. Ellen put on airs, Jessie said, and looked down her nose at folk, and the workers resented this.

Etta wondered if she should tell Rory what her foster sister had said, then she decided that it was none of her business, and settled for, 'Everyone has tae earn their way.'

'Aye, and she's not the only one who cannae do what she wants.'

A sudden bitterness in his voice caused Etta to look up at him from where she lay comfortably on the grass, her head pillowed on her jacket. 'You're all right, surely, runnin' your own cooperage?'

Rory picked another stalk and examined it closely, using his thumbnail to split it lengthways. 'Aye,' he said at last. 'I'm fine. I aye knew that I was meant for the cooperage. It was what my faither decided for me when I was born.'

Then he tossed the grass stalk away, and as it was caught by the slight breeze and carried down the hill he leaned over Etta and kissed her, his mouth soft and warm on hers. She liked his kisses, but to her mind, they were more safe than romantic, and she tended to look on him more as an older brother than a sweetheart.

Sometimes Mary Lowrie and Peter Bain went walking with

Etta and Rory. During the summer fishing Peter had taken time from farming to become a horseman, the name given to the carters who carried salt and baskets of fish from the boats – or from the auctioneers if the fish were sold on the open market instead of being contracted to a merchant such as Jacob McFarlane – to the farlins, and took the filled and topped barrels away.

More than one fisher-lassie had paused from her work to smile up at the young horseman as he rode past, controlling the horse with a twitch of the reins and the occasional swift command, and standing up on the cart as straight and as proud as a Roman charioteer. His shirtsleeves were rolled up to show tanned, muscular arms and the breeze tumbled his fair hair about his square, pleasant face.

But Peter only had eyes for Mary Lowrie. The friendship that had begun when Mary travelled in the cab of Peter's lorry as he drove the fisher-lassies back from Aberdeen had grown swiftly, and by the end of August, when the fish were once again on their way south, the two of them were officially walking out together, to Zelda's delight.

17

Jack Morrison, the young photographer, arrived in Buckie just before the summer fishing came to its end. He took lodgings with a widow woman who lived in a cottage in the Yardie, not far from James Lowrie's home, and he and his camera became a familiar sight in the town as he photographed the fishermen mending their nets and the old men sitting down by the harbour, smoking their pipes and exchanging stories of their time at sea. He rose early in the morning to photograph the boats coming into harbour after a night's fishing, and was back in the afternoon to record them coaling in preparation for the next trip.

'Ye'd have thought he'd have had enough pictures of us at our work,' Agnes said when he arrived at the farlins.

'It's no' us that's the attraction,' Andra's Jenny told her, grinning, while Ruth, beaming into the camera lens, posed with an empty barrel hoisted above her head. 'It's that lassie there, the one that gets all dressed up these days just tae gut the herrin'. I never thought she cared that much about fish.'

Jacob McFarlane, who had a keen interest in everything and everyone, invited the young photographer to his house on several occasions, and as often as not Ruth went with him. The two of them were made welcome, as everyone was, in Zelda's kitchen, and Ruth even managed to persuade her mother to invite Jack to their home, though when her youngest daughter first broached the subject Stella said nervously, 'I don't know, Ruth, I'm not used tae entertainin' gentry.'

'He's not gentry, Mither, he's just a man that makes his money by workin', the same as the rest of us.'

'Aye, but he comes from a city, and they do things differently there. What would he want tae eat?'

'The same as everyone else,' Ruth said, exasperated. 'Just give him what we'd be havin' ourselves. Auntie Zelda treated him like one of her own, and so can you.'

'Aye, but Zelda has a different way with her,' Stella argued, 'and I don't know what your faither'll say. He's not over fond of visitors.'

'Then it's time he changed,' Ruth said firmly, and marched down to the harbour to face James in his own cabin, where he spent a great deal of his time when the drifter was not at sea. She swept across the gangplank and into the galley, then clambered down the ladder to find him enjoying a glass of whisky with Adam Pate and Innes Lowrie.

'Are you old enough tae drink that?' Ruth asked her cousin.

'I'll be eighteen next month, and anyway, it's none of your business,' he shot back at her, but she was already studying some of the pictures torn from magazines and stuck up on the cabin walls.

'Who put these photographs of women up there?' she wanted to know, and her father almost bit the stem of his pipe in two, while Innes laughed.

'No' me, I'll tell ye that.' James reached up and tore down the nearest photograph, crumpling it in his hand. 'It's the younger lads, and there's no harm tae them. Anyway, you shouldnae be burstin' in here without askin' my permission first.'

'And I suppose you're one of the folk that put those pictures up, are you?' Ruth asked Adam.

'I might have. There's no harm in lookin'.'

'Move along.' She pushed him along the bench and sat down. 'You neednae fret about pictures, Faither, or the whisky bottle, for I'll say nothin'. I'm here tae ask a favour. I want tae ask Jack Morrison tae the house for his dinner, and my mither's in a fuss about it. Will ye tell her that it's all right?'

'Who the— Who's Jack Morrison?' James asked, confused. He never quite knew what to make of this quicksilver daughter of his, for she was quite unlike her mother and sisters.

Adam grinned. 'Ruth's sweetheart.'

'Sweetheart?' James took the pipe from his mouth. 'You're too young for that sort of nonsense!'

'Faither, I'll be nineteen years of age in another two weeks. I'm older than him,' Ruth exploded, giving Adam a hefty nudge in the ribs, 'and you're letting him sit there drinkin' whisky for all the world like a grown man.'

'Wait a minute – I've never heard of this Morrison loon. Is he from round here?'

'He's from Glasgow, and he takes pictures. Proper pictures, for a book,' Ruth added. 'Not the sort of thing you've got up on the walls there. You must have seen him about the harbour with his camera.'

'The camera with the long spindly legs? That man? You want tae ask him tae our house for his dinner?'

'Photographers need tae eat the same as the rest of us do. You and my mither should be pleased that someone's takin' an interest in me at last,' Ruth pointed out. 'You don't want me tae be an old maid, surely?'

'Damn the chance of that,' muttered Adam, rubbing his aching ribs.

'You're right,' his cousin agreed amiably. 'I'd ask the question myself before I'd die of waitin' for some man tae get round tae askin' it. So Faither, can I tell my mither that you said Jack can come for his dinner?'

'I suppose he can, if that's what ye want.'

'And you'll be there? Aye, you will,' Ruth said swiftly as her father began to argue. 'You'll want tae meet the young man I'm walkin' out with, surely?'

'Does he know that the two of you are walkin' out?' Adam enquired.

'If he doesnae know it now, he will when he gets invited tae meet my faither. How will ye find out, else, if he's suitable for me?' Ruth asked James. Then, before he could reply, 'And Adam, you could ask Aunt Beth'ny if she'll allow Jack tae take pictures in the smokehouse and the net factory for this book of his.'

'I don't think she'd object to that. I'll ask her tonight, and tell ye tomorrow,' said Adam, and she gave him a beaming smile and paused to ruffle his dark hair before hurrying back up the ladder to the galley.

'I'll never understand women,' James said when his daughter had gone, leaving little invisible whirls of energy in the air.

'Who'd want to?' said Adam.

'I've met this Jack Morrison that your Ruth's taken to,' Innes told his brother. 'He's been to our house, and he's a decent enough lad. You'll like him.'

James refilled his glass and held the bottle out to the other two, who both shook their heads. 'I never thought that fatherin' lassies was goin' tae be such a trouble.'

'Ach, it's no trouble, lassies are fine if ye just take them as ye find them,' Innes told him comfortably.

'It's a pity you never had sons, Uncle James, to follow you to the fishing,' Adam said, and then glanced uncertainly at the two older men, aware of a sudden tension in the cabin.

'You'd best be gettin' off home before yer mither starts lookin' for ye,' James told the lad abruptly, and Adam shrugged.

'Ach, she's got enough on her mind, with all the work she's taken on. It's Leezie who runs the house now, and she'll not be botherin' about me.'

'Ye'll soon be away tae Aberdeen and your studies, anyway,' Innes said, and the boy bit his lip.

'I wanted tae talk tae you about that, Uncle James.'

'Me? It's got damn all tae do with me!'

'Aye, but it has. I like goin' to the fishin', and I'm heartily sick of book learnin'. Will you talk to my mother?' Adam asked, leaning across the table. 'Will you explain to her that I come from fishing stock, just as she does? I've got the sea in my blood, and I don't want to go back to the university.'

'Indeed I will no'!'

'But you're the one that could get her tae understand that there's no sense in forcin' me in one direction when my mind and my heart's set on another way entirely,' the boy argued.

'What makes you think yer mither would listen tae me? Even if I tried, she'd be more set on the university than ever, just tae spite me for stickin' my neb intae her family business. No, no,' James said vehemently, 'I'll have nothin' tae do with it.'

'Uncle Innes—' Adam appealed, but Innes shook his head.

'Bethany's never listened tae me, laddie, and she'll not start now.'

'So you both want me to be miserable in Aberdeen, is that it?' Adam asked angrily, and when the two men glanced at each other uneasily, but kept silent, 'I'll do it anyway, in spite of the lot of you. If I have tae do the damned course I will, but as soon as I'm finished I'm comin' back to the *Fidelity* whether she likes it or not!'

'He will, you know,' Innes said when his nephew had stormed off the drifter.

'I hope he does, for by then he'll be too old tae be under Bethany's thumb.'

'He's damned near too old for that now, and his heart belongs to the sea just as much as yours does, James. Why won't you help the lad?'

James gave a short, angry laugh. 'Bethany's scarce looked my way for the past eighteen years. She'd throw me intae the harbour if I tried tae tell her how tae treat her precious son.'

'That's a pity, for the boy worships you. He does,' Innes persisted when his older brother looked up at him, startled. 'And he worships the sea, too.'

'He's a good enough seaman, I suppose.'

'From what I've heard from Siddy and the rest of them he's better than good. He's more flesh and blood to you and our faither than I ever was,' Innes said. Then, slowly and deliberately, 'There's little enough of Gil in his nature, would you not agree?'

James's fist, marked with old rope burns and the curved scars of dogfish bites, clenched the whisky tumbler so tightly that Innes expected to hear the sharp crack of broken glass. But the tumbler remained intact as he lifted and drained it. It even withstood being banged back down on the table.

'I've work tae do.' James lurched to his feet and made for the ladder. 'Go home, Innes,' he said over his shoulder as he began to climb. 'And mind your own business.'

Jack Morrison spent an entire day in Bethany Pate's smoke-house and arrived at Ruth's home that night with a parcel of kippers, which he presented to his startled hostess.

'I thought mince and tatties . . .' Stella said nervously.

'It sounds grand, Mrs Lowrie, but could I have a kipper as well?'

'Have you not tasted them afore this?' Annie asked in astonishment.

'I have, but this is the first time I've seen them being kippered. It would be grand to eat one right out of the smoke-house. Unless it's a bother to you?'

'No, no, it wouldnae be any bother.' Under his warm smile, Stella began to thaw. 'In fact, you're easy pleased. Would you like to come and stand by me and see how we cook them an' all?'

'You'll be goin' to the net factory next?' Ruth asked as the family sat down to their meal.

'I've to get back to Glasgow tomorrow, but I'll be in Buckie again to take pictures of the net making in a month or two.' Jack began to dissect his kipper carefully.

Ruth's face fell. 'You're goin' away tomorrow? I'll prob-ably be in Yarm'th by the time you get back here.'

'If you are, I'll go on down to Yarmouth when I'm finished here,' he promised, then went on to talk enthusiastically throughout the meal about the day spent photographing the women splitting the herring, washing and pickling them, then stringing them on poles to be hung up in the kilns and smoked.

The family, so well used to the kippering process that they thought nothing of it, listened in silence, stunned and bewil-dered by this stranger's enthusiasm for such an everyday event.

It was August, time for the herring to spawn. The Moray Firth fishing season began to draw to a close and Adam Pate reluctantly put away his high, iron-studded boots and sou'wester and the fisherman's gansey that his cousin Mary had knitted for him, and departed for Aberdeen, neatly suited and with his curly dark hair slicked down.

Etta saw very little of Rory over the next two months, for he and the other men in the Pate cooperage were working from early morning until late at night to make barrels for the big English fishing to come. She had work of her own to see to; once the gutting crews broke up, the women had to find other jobs such as working in hotels and big houses or, like Etta, in the net factory.

She had enjoyed her two years in the factory between leaving school and becoming old enough to take up the gutter's knife, but she soon found that Jessie was right when she said that things were different with Ellen Pate in charge, for the young woman made no secret of her resentment at having to earn her living.

Bethany had toured the factory several times a day to make sure that all was well, but Ellen preferred to stay shut up in her tiny office all day, and if she had to leave it to attend to a problem in any part of the factory, she did so with an abrupt, impatient air that irritated the men and the women who worked in the place. Although she wore a plain blouse and skirt to work the garments were clearly well made, and far superior to anything that the female employees could afford. It was as though she was constantly reminding them, as well as herself, of the social gap that yawned between them.

Since she had learned well during her first stint in the factory, Etta was put to work in the mending room. The menders were a privileged group of women, chosen because of their skill with the bone mending needles. They checked the new nets coming straight from the looms, repairing any small flaws; the nets they worked were still white and clean, whereas the employees repairing used nets had a dirty job.

'It's not as if Ellen Pate knows one end o' a net from the other,' one of Etta's colleagues complained one day when Ellen had just passed through the room looking, as someone muttered once she had gone, as if there was a bad smell under her nose. 'At least her mither could handle a needle. Many a time when we were extra busy she'd stand in this very room hersel', mendin' the nets along with the rest of us. But I doubt if milady there could even mend her own stockin's.'

'Not her,' said another girl. 'She'd buy new every time!'

'She's all right,' Etta said uncomfortably, remembering the far-off days when they had all played wee houses with each other on the shore, using shells for cups and sea water for tea. Ellen had been good company in those days.

The other girl snorted. 'She's a right madam, that's what she is, and the sooner she realises that she's no better than anyone else in this factory the better!'

A great rush of activity around the harbour soon followed the brief lull enjoyed by the drifter crews at the end of the midsummer fishing in September. Paintwork had to be freshened up and boilers scaled, bilges cleaned and bunkers trimmed. Nets had to be barked and the leader ropes that controlled the nets as they were paid out and hauled in again had to be tarred.

The entire harbour area carried the strong but pleasant smell from the freshly treated nets hanging the length of McLaren's Brae and on every other stretch of fencing available in the harbour area, while canvas buoys used as floats for the herring nets were repainted to keep them water-tight and prevent marine growth, then hung on poles to dry, giving the place a festive air.

New chaff mattresses and pillows had to be made, for after three months of use, those made in May had been thumped into place so often and so vigorously that all the chaff had been pushed to the sides and the men were more or less sleeping on the boards of their narrow bunk beds.

Barrels were stacked high along the length of the harbour wall, ready to be loaded into the holds and piled on the decks of the drifters when they followed the herring down the southeast coast. Coal boats arrived daily, and when the great bunkers on the harbour were full, two old hulks anchored close by were pressed into use to hold the coal that the fishing boats would require.

Once the men had finished work on the boats the womenfolk arrived to give the living quarters a good clean.

'As if I've not had enough cleanin' tae last me a lifetime,' Annie moaned as she and her mother and sisters tackled the *Fidelity*.

'You're a woman now,' Stella snapped. 'Old enough tae know that cleanin' never stops. And none of us is leavin' this boat until it's spotless. I'll not have fleas or vermin runnin' about on any boat that belongs tae this family. And once we're done here there's the bakin' tae see tae, so's your faither can be sure of havin' some good, hearty food inside him when he's on his way tae Yarm'th.'

While his wife and daughters toiled to make his boat the cleanest in the entire Scottish fleet, James Lowrie sat in the cabin of his cousin Jem's drifter, reading and rereading a single-page letter that had come from Aberdeen. It was addressed to James himself, but had been sent care of Jem.

'It's no' bad news, is it?' Jem asked, his eyes bright with curiosity.

'No, no, it's just a wee thing I'd half expected.' James scanned the letter one last time before folding it slowly and carefully and replacing it in its envelope.

'I wondered, with it bein' sent tae me instead of straight tae you,' Jem probed, watching every deliberate movement. 'Mebbe the person that wrote it didnae know your own address.'

'Mebbe.' James put the envelope into his pocket, pushing it well down to make certain that there was no danger of it falling out and getting lost.

'Or mebbe it's from someone that didnae want his business – or her business,' Jem suggested, 'known tae your Stella.'

'It could be that, I suppose,' James acknowledged, his face expressionless.

'Damn it, man, I'm yer own cousin and the letter was entrusted tae me.' Jem's curiosity boiled over. 'Surely I should be told what it's about? I'd not want tae be connivin' behind Stella's back, would I?'

'Not if you knew what was good for ye,' James agreed, getting to his feet. 'So it's best that ye don't know anythin' at all. That way, ye'll no' be goin' behind her back, will ye?'

'Is there an answer, mebbe?' Jem had one last try when the two men were back on deck. 'Somethin' ye'd like me tae post for ye?'

James considered the offer, pursing his lips and gazing across the boats strung between him and the harbour wall. 'It's a kind offer, Jem,' he said at last, setting foot on the *Homefaring*'s gunwale. 'But I think that I'm best no' tae send an answer of any sort. I'll just bide my time, and see what happens.'

As he leapt easily from the *Homefaring* to the neighbouring drifter and began to make his way, boat by boat, to the harbour wall, he could scarcely keep the smirk from his normally dour face.

*

The special train carrying coopers and fisher-lassies down to England was so full that Etta had to sleep as best as she could sitting bolt upright and with her arms jammed by her sides. Sleep was not easy, for there was constant noise – people talking or singing, and children who were accompanying their mothers because there was nobody at home to care for them crying with overexcitement and exhaustion or running up and down along the narrow corridors.

Some of the lucky people, those who had made the journey before and knew what to do, had managed to board the train early and hoist themselves on to the luggage racks, where they could lie down, even though the constant noise below kept them from sleeping.

But at least the rocking motion of the train was much easier to bear than the corkscrewing and plunging of the steamer that had taken the gutting crews to Lerwick, and there was a festive air among the passengers that kept them all cheerful and made the lack of sleep bearable.

'Ye'd never think we were goin' tae work,' Agnes said from her seat opposite. Despite the cramped conditions she had managed to fetch her knitting wires out, and Etta watched, fascinated, as the stocking the woman was knitting for her husband grew before her very eyes. 'Goin' down tae England's more like holidays for the likes of us.' She winked across at Etta. 'The rich folk travel round Europe for their holidays while the likes of us just get a change of farlins. But it's nice, all the same. You'll see.'

Great Yarmouth, being a popular holiday resort during the summer months, held a large number of lodging houses. In the winter, when the summer trade had gone and the herring season arrived, the landladies offered accommodation to the fisher-lassies and fishermen and coopers and curers who poured into the town and took it over for as long as the herring shoals swam off the English shores.

Bethany Pate, mindful of her own days as a fisher-lassie and of the struggle to cope with work and domestic duties, housed her gutting crews in decent accommodation. Etta and her crew, Andra's Jenny and Sarah, shared lodgings with Agnes, Kirsten Taylor and Ruth. They had a decent-sized bedroom with two double beds, one for each crew, and they also had the use of the front room.

'It's a far cry from Lerwick, is it no'?' Jenny bounced on the bed and looked about the small, clean room with satisfaction. 'Better than a hut, and we've a landlady here tae cook our food. Bein' in Yarmouth's the nearest the likes of us can get tae bein' treated like gentry!'

'You'll no' be so chirpy when ye're standin' at the farlins at eight o' clock at night, up tae yer hurdies in mud and with the rain bouncin' off ye,' Agnes reminded her.

'Nothin' comes easy,' Jenny shrugged. 'An' until then, we can enjoy ourselves. I'm for a walk round the town before the fishin' starts in the mornin'. Come on, Etta, it's you and me for the shops. We can choose what we're goin' tae buy tae take home when the time comes.'

They set out on what was one of the women's favourite pastimes, window-shopping and making up lists of all the things they would buy if they had enough money left over by the time the fishing season finished.

'Ye don't have tae be too serious about it,' Jenny explained as she and Etta and Ruth wandered down Glass Row. 'There's a difference between buyin' and just lookin'. Now, I think I'll have that' – she pointed at a smart woollen costume draped across a stand – 'an' that nice wee scarf, and I'd need a pair of gloves tae set it off.'

'Kid gloves,' Ruth chimed in.

'Oh aye, they'd have tae be kid. I'd no' want knitted gloves with thae sort of clothes. And I'd need tae get my hair permed, and mebbe buy a nice smart bag tae hang over my arm.'

'And shoes,' Etta joined in the game.

'An' silk stockin's. We'll decide on the shoes first,' Jenny said and the three of them set off, arm in arm, to find a shoe shop.

Reality set in the next morning when the lorries arrived to take them to the Denes, where the farlins awaited them. Dressed warmly against the chill dawn, they knitted busily, their cloth-covered fingers flying along the needles, while they watched and waited for the boats to come up river.

It wasn't long before the first dark shape came nosing through the grey mist that hung over the river. The women pushed their knitting into the leather whiskers hung from their belts, and hurried to take their places.

It was a long day. At nine o'clock the lorries took them back to their lodgings, where Mrs Rogers, the landlady, had made porridge and a great pot of strong tea, and a platter of toast.

'Are you sure it's all right?' she asked, nose wrinkling as she watched her six lodgers spooning up their porridge. 'I couldn't take it myself.'

'It's grand,' Mary assured her through a mouthful. She had insisted on steeping the oatmeal herself the night before, with a liberal handful of salt tossed into the pot. 'Ye've tae watch the English where porridge is concerned,' she had advised Etta, 'for they'll put sugar in it if they're left tae make it themselves, and never as much as a shake of salt. They make it far too sweet.'

They had to eat and drink swiftly, for in no time at all the lorries returned to take them to the farlins. They ran out, stuffing what was left of the toast into their pockets, for if the catches were good they would probably not have time for another break before six o'clock.

18

'It's your own fault.' Bethany said without sympathy. 'Everyone knows that scalders turn into an itching powder when they die in the nets.'

'I didn't know it. How could I know it?' Ellen sniffled. Her hands, normally white and smooth, were red and puffy from frenzied scratching and tears poured from her swollen eyes.

'Don't!' Bethany and Leezie yelped in unison, as the girl lifted a hand to mop the tears away. 'That's the way you managed to hurt your eyes in the first place,' Bethany went on as Leezie snatched Ellen's hand out of harm's way and muffled it in a clean towel.

'But my eyes are itching as if someone's thrown a handful of pepper into them,' Ellen whined.

'For goodness' sake, lassie, what does it take to teach you a lesson?' Exasperation sharpened the edge of Bethany's voice. 'Your eyes are sore because you touched a net and then rubbed the stuff over your face. You're lucky you didn't get it in your mouth, or you'd have right sore lips into the bargain. As to you not knowing about the scalders, you should make it your business to know that sort of thing now that you're overseeing the net factory.'

'I can't be expected to learn everything. I'm just there to keep an eye on the workers.'

'Exactly, so why were you handling nets that had come in

for repair?' Bethany swept on as Leezie sponged the girl's face with clear cool water in an attempt to ease the stinging pain. 'That's not your job.'

'I was showing that photographer man around the place and he wanted a picture of the nets being repaired.'

'And you pretended to be working at one, just to get yourself in the photograph?'

'It wasn't like that at all! The net was there, and the needle was lying beside it, and I just—'

'And you just happened to be dressed like the rest of the beatsters.' Bethany indicated the girl's smart, green, knitted costume, its low-waisted jumper chosen to disguise Ellen's tendency to plumpness.

'Should you not fetch the doctor?' Ellen whimpered as Leezie bathed her face gently with a soft damp cloth.

'No, you'll be fine – eventually. Clean water's all you need.'

'I might go blind!'

'You'll not go blind. You just need to keep bathing your eyes and your hands until the dust's washed away. Have you never thought to ask why the women repairing the nets always keep buckets of water close by? It's because of the scalders.'

'Give it to me!' Ellen snatched the cloth from Leezie and pressed it to her face.

'That photographer must have been right impressed when you started to skip about the place screaming and clawing at your eyes. And the lassies in the mending room must be having a good laugh, too,' Bethany said. Then, as the girl threw the wet flannel at her and fled from the kitchen, 'Leezie, take the basin and go after her. And tell her to have a nice cool bath and a lie down.'

'You're over hard on her,' Leezie disapproved as she gathered up the basin of water and the towels.

'No wonder. She's not got the sense she was born with. This'll mebbe teach her a bit of sense.'

When Leezie had gone upstairs Bethany went into the

parlour and began to open the day's post, still lying unopened on her writing desk. Using an ivory paperknife that Jacob had given her she slit the envelopes open, drawing out their contents and giving each a swift glance before dropping it on to one of several different piles – one for bills, one for orders, one for payments and one for personal letters.

She paused, frowning, as she came to a letter with the University of Aberdeen's name at the top of the page. She read it once, and then again, in disbelief and growing anger. Her first instinct, after the second reading, was to seek Jacob's advice, but he had gone to Yarmouth on the *Fidelity* with James. There was only one person she could ask about this business, she decided, and stormed from the parlour into the hall, shouting for Leezie.

'What is it now?' the maid wanted to know, appearing at the bend of the stairs. 'I'm bathin' the lassie's eyes.'

'I'm going out!'

'How long will you—' Leezie began, then stopped as the front door slammed shut so hard that the stained-glass upper half shook in its frame.

'One of those days ye'll crack it entirely,' she murmured, before turning back to answer a wailed summons from Ellen's room.

It had been many years since Stella Lowrie had opened her door to find her sister-in-law standing outside. Surprise swept across her face and was immediately replaced by a cold, blank look.

'What do you want?'

'I want my son.' Bethany's voice was as frosty as Stella's gaze.

'He's not here, and if he was he'd no' be welcome.'

'Not by you, mebbe, but James is another matter.'

Stella's thin lips tightened as though she was trying to hold back a sudden spasm of pain, then parted just wide enough to say, 'James is in Yarm'th.'

'I know that, but who else is there with him?' Bethany's head turned to the left and then to the right, her gaze sweeping along the street in both directions before returning to her sister-in-law. 'Am I to be allowed in, or would you prefer the whole street to hear my business?'

For a moment Stella looked as though she was going to refuse, and then she stepped back, opening the door wider. 'I suppose ye'd best come in.'

'Thank you.' For the first time since her mother's death, Bethany Pate, nee Lowrie, stepped over the threshold of the house where she had been born and raised. The kitchen, at least, had not changed much, she saw as Stella closed the door. The big dresser that had belonged to her parents was still in place, and she recognised some of the pretty china plates upon its shelves. She still recalled her mother's delight when her father brought them home from his fishing trips to other ports.

'Sit down,' Stella said, and then, after a slight hesitation, 'You'll have some tea?'

'Thank you, but I'm not stopping long. Ellen was trying her hand at repairin' a net in the factory,' Bethany explained, sitting in a straight-backed chair at the table, 'and it had scalders in it. She didn't know to look out for them.'

The ghost of a smile touched Stella's face as she seated herself at the other side of the table. 'I thought everyone knew about them. We came across them often enough when we were mendin' the nets at her age.'

'Aye, we did, but Ellen never had to do that.'

'More money than sense,' Stella observed, and Bethany had to rein in a sudden spurt of anger.

'Mebbe so, but I'm here about my Adam. Where is he?'

'How should I know?'

'I thought he was at the university, at his studying. I've just had a letter from the place,' Bethany took it from her pocket, 'and it says he's gone away. They don't know where.'

'Aye. I've heard that he's a loon that likes to have his own way.'

'Mebbe he is, but while he's under my roof he'll go my way!'

The smile flickered across Stella's mouth again as she nodded at the letter. 'From what you say it seems that he's decided tae keep tae his own road.'

'I blame James for this! He's the one that encouraged the lad to go to the summer fishing and now he's enticed him down to Yarm'th! I'm sure of it. Did he say anything of this to you before he left?'

Stella shrugged. 'He never tells me what he's thinkin'. There's another one that goes his own way. They're well matched, are they no'?'

'Adam's father had his heart set on him going to the university, and so have I, and that's an end of it!'

Stella, throwing caution to the winds, leaned across the table, her brown eyes venomous. 'Adam's father? You know as well as I do, Bethany Pate, that if your son's father had his way of it the loon would be at the fishin', not at any university. And you're right – the fishin's probably just where he is at this very minute, along with James.' Then, as Bethany stared at her, white faced and open-mouthed, she got to her feet. 'I know it's been a good while since you and me last spoke tae each other, Bethany, but for myself, I'd prefer to keep it that way.' She swept across the spotless kitchen and threw the street door open. 'Good day tae ye!'

There was never a minute's peace in this house, Leezie thought. If it wasn't one thing it was another. This was supposed to be her day for doing the ironing, and the basket still waited in the kitchen, piled high with crumpled clothing. First Ellen, half blinded and squawking like a bairn, had been brought home by two sniggering lassies from the net factory, then the mistress had gone rampaging out of the house, only to return half an hour later with a black mood on her, and announce that she was off to Yarmouth.

She had gone round her bedroom like a whirlwind,

throwing clothes into a bag, and finally departed, leaving a great list of instructions. No sooner had she gone than Ellen had taken over as mistress, reclining on her bed, a damp cloth over her sore eyes, issuing orders and keeping Leezie scampering up and down the stairs. And now, just as she had finally got down to the ironing, someone was ringing the doorbell.

Muttering under her breath she went into the hall, tidying her hair as she went. A smartly dressed young man stood on the step, a bunch of flowers in one hand.

'Is Miss Pate in?'

'She is, but she's no' well.'

'Mrs Pate, then?'

'She's gone away on business,' Leezie said flatly. His face was familiar but she couldn't put a name to it.

'Oh. Perhaps you could tell Miss Pate that I called, and give her this.' The man drew an envelope from his pocket and handed it over. 'And these, of course.'

'I'll tell her.' Leezie took the flowers. 'Good day tae ye.'

'Who is it?' Ellen wanted to know from the top of the stairs as the housekeeper closed the door.

'I don't know. He sent these to you, and this.' Leezie held out the envelope and flowers, and then as the girl beckoned impatiently she trudged up the stairs for the umpteenth time that day. Ellen snatched at the envelope, tore it open, then said breathlessly, 'It's Mr Morrison. Fetch him back!'

'But you're no' well. You're in your goonie and he'll be away down the road—'

'Fetch him back at once! And show him into the parlour. Then put these in water. I'm going to get dressed,' said Ellen, and fled into her room, calling over her shoulder, 'And make tea— or wait, perhaps he'd prefer whisky, or port. Get two trays ready, just in case. And for goodness' sake, get after him before he disappears!'

As soon as the mistress came back, whenever that was, Leezie swore to herself as she ran out of the gate and down the road after Mr Morrison, she was going to give in her notice and find another position somewhere else. Anywhere else.

When the gutting crews finished Monday's topping up, Mary and the others opted to go to the shops but Etta took the opportunity to stay behind in the lodgings to get some washing done. Since her boarders were free, for once, to see to their own evening meal, Mrs Rogers had gone out for the afternoon and evening and Etta was enjoying having the house to herself. Raised in her Aunt Zelda's busy household and, even at work, used to being surrounded by others, it was a joy to be all alone for once, with no sound but the ticking of clocks and the splash of water as she washed her clothes in the big kitchen sink.

She rinsed each item out, twisting it tightly between her strong young hands before running it through the big mangle, then hung it all up on the pulley to dry. When the pulley had been hauled up to the ceiling she tied the rope about the hook on the wall and stripped her clothes off before climbing nimbly from a chair to the counter and then stepping into the sink.

After a thorough wash she dried herself, dressed, and was mopping up the few splashes she had made when someone came hammering at the door.

Etta stood undecided, head tilted to one side. It couldn't be the postman, for the postman had already called and left letters for Mary and Ruth. They lay on the lobby table, Mary's envelope adorned with Peter Bain's square, firm handwriting and Ruth's from Jack Morrison, who wrote to her every two or three days.

While Etta was wondering if it was her place to open the door to folk when the mistress of the house was not at home the knocking came again, several pounding blows on the sturdy wooden panels. Such urgency couldn't be ignored, she decided, hurrying from the kitchen. If it was, the door might suffer permanent damage. It was just a blessing that whoever it was had at least waited until she was dressed.

The hammering began again, just as she went through the small lobby. 'I'm coming!' she shouted, drawing back the bolt and opening the door. As soon as it left the frame a firm hand from the other side swept it back, sending Etta staggering. As her shoulder bounced against the wall the door slammed shut again and the bolt was shot into place.

'About time – she near saw me!' Adam Pate said breathlessly, leaning back against the closed door.

'Adam? What are you doing here in Yarmouth?'

'Fishin', what else? Hello, Etta. Have ye got the kettle on?' he asked hopefully. 'I could fair do with a cup of tea.'

'You near broke the door down just to get a cup of tea?'

'No, no. Is Mary here? Or Sarah or Ruth?'

'They're all out but me.'

'What about your landlady?'

'She's out too.'

'Good.' Adam swept his cap off. 'You can make me that tea, then. Is the kitchen through here?'

'Why are you fishin' when you should be up in Aberdeen at the university?' she wanted to know as she followed his broad back through to the kitchen.

He picked up the kettle, shook it to make sure there was enough water in it, and then set it on the gas stove. 'Matches.'

'On that shelf. Adam!'

'I ran away.' He lit the gas ring before turning to face her, blowing out the match. 'I couldnae stand it there a minute longer, Etta. I was goin' mad stuck in those lecture rooms with no air tae breathe, thinkin' all the while of the rest of you gettin' ready to come to Yarm'th. So I sent a letter for Jem tae pass on tae my Uncle James, sayin' that I'd meet him here and work the season on the *Fidelity*.' He dropped the match onto the counter by the stove and hooked a chair out from under the table with one foot.

'Your mother's the one that'll go mad when she finds out

what you've done.' Etta picked up the spent match and put it into the rubbish pail Mrs Rogers kept by her back door.

'She did,' Adam said as he dropped into the chair. 'That's why I was in such a rush tae find somewhere tae hide. Uncle James told me tae stay out of sight when I wasnae on the drifter just in case she got old Jacob McFarlane tae bundle me back tae Aberdeen, but that meant bein' stuck in one room again, just like the university. So this afternoon I went out for a wee wander round the shops, and who should I see but my mither, chargin' along the street like a ship under sail.'

'Aunt Bethany's here in Yarm'th?'

'I got a shock, too,' Adam admitted, getting up as the kettle boiled. 'I'll make the tea.' He talked on as he scooped spoonful after spoonful of Mrs Rogers' tea leaves into the pot. 'She must have found out and come after me.'

'Did she see you?' Etta made a mental note to replenish the landlady's tea caddy.

'I didnae wait tae find out. I just about-turned and ran for my very life with the studs on my boots throwin' up sparks. I landed up in this street, and minded hearin' that Mary and the rest of them were lodgin' here.' He poured boiling water into the teapot and began to open drawers at random until he found a spoon. 'So I thought I could hide here for an hour or two, just until my mither gets tired of lookin' for me.'

'Adam,' Etta said nervously, half expecting to hear the door knocker being plied at any moment, 'she'll never get tired of lookin' for you.'

'Ye're right there.' For a moment his open, normally cheerful face clouded over, then it cleared and a grin broke through. 'But dammit,' he said, 'at least I'll give her a run for her money. Now then,' he whirled the chair about and straddled it, leaning his folded arms along the backrest, 'while the tea's makin', tell me what you think of Yarm'th.'

Bethany was certain that Adam had seen her, but he had melted into the crowds so swiftly that she had no hope of catching up with him. Instead, she made her way to Jacob's lodgings.

'You'll be lookin' for the lad,' he said as soon as his land-lady had shown Bethany into the comfortable parlour, then added, his eyes suddenly narrowing, 'or is there some problem back in Buckie?'

'None, apart from that daft quine Ellen making a fool of herself in the factory and near burning her eyes out with scalders.' Bethany sank down into a comfortable armchair. 'Of course I'm here after Adam. Why didn't you send him back to Aberdeen when you found out what he was up to?'

'It's not my business. And the laddie's stubborn, Bethany. If his heart's set on the fishin' I doubt you'll get him back tae his books.'

'But what sort of life's that for a clever young man?'

'I did well out of it – very well. And so has James,' the old man reminded her.

'I know, I know, but I'd wanted something more for Adam, and so did Gil. If he was here now he'd give the loon a good thrashing and drag him back to the university by his shirt collar.'

Jacob's eyes glinted with amusement. 'Is that what you're plannin' tae do?'

'I'll have a damned good try at it if I catch him,' Bethany promised. 'I saw him out in the street half an hour since, but he was off before I could get to him.'

Jacob's landlady brought tea in, and when she had gone out again Bethany said, 'I want to see James as well. I've got things to say to that man. Where's he lodging?'

'Not far from here. What about yersel', have ye got some-where tae stay?'

'Not yet. I've only just arrived. I left my things at the station.'

'Have your tea and then go to see James. There's a good hotel at the end of this street – I'll arrange accommodation for you there and have your luggage delivered,' said Jacob, a seasoned traveller as much at home in Yarmouth as he was in Buckie. He poured out the tea and brought a cup to her. 'Come round here for yer dinner tonight. I hope ye've brought a nice frock with ye?'

'I'd no' thought of dining out when I came here. I was just thinking of fetching Adam home.'

'I'm sure ye'll look bonny whatever ye wear, for ye always do,' Jacob said blandly. 'I've invited an Edinburgh merchant tae eat with me tonight, and now that you're here I want you tae join us. He's an important man and I'd like fine tae do business with him. You could help me.'

'You've changed your tune, have you not? It wasn't so long ago that you were telling me that business wasn't for women.'

'Aye, but ye're here now, aren't ye?'

'On my own business, not on yours.'

'Even so, ye might as well make use of your time and help me intae the bargain. I'm goin' tae leave it tae you tae tell the mannie why it would be worth his while buyin' his fish from Jacob McFarlane.'

'I don't need to wear a bonny frock to tell him that.' Bethany's voice was tart.

'Mebbe the frock's more for my benefit than his.' Jacob grinned at her. 'D'ye think ye can win the man over?'

'I've no doubt of it,' Bethany rapped back at him, doing her best to hide her rising elation. At last she was getting the chance to face a good challenge.

Jacob settled his heels into the rug before the fireplace, teacup in hand, and beamed down at her. 'Now you're here, my quine, I'm glad of it. Mebbe you were right in what you said back in Buckie; mebbe it's time for ye tae meet up with some of the folk I deal with.'

19

The lodgings that James Lowrie had found for himself and his crew were less comfortable than Jacob's, but suited them well enough. For once, James was taking his ease in shirt-sleeves and braces when his sister was ushered into the tiny parlour.

'I thought ye'd be down here after the laddie soon enough,' he said calmly, indicating a chair. 'Sit yoursel' down.'

Bethany stayed on her feet. 'Where is he?'

'I'm his skipper, Bethany, no' his prison warder.' James deliberately settled back into his comfortable chair. 'All I ask is that he's on the boat when I need him. The rest of his time is his own and that's the way we both like it.'

'I've come to take him back to Aberdeen.'

'No you've not, for I'll not allow it. He's contracted tae work out the season with me and I need him on the *Fidelity*.'

'You were a man short when you sailed from Buckie, because you knew he was going to meet you here,' she accused. 'You put him up to this!'

He rested his head against the back of the chair, looking up at her from beneath half-closed eyelids. 'Adam's a man now, Bethany, old enough tae go his own way. Nob'dy needs tae put him up tae anythin'.'

'He might be a man but he's still not got the sense to know what's best for him!'

'And you have?' James asked mildly.

'I'm his mother!'

'Aye, his mither, no' his keeper. How much heed did you pay to our mither when you were Adam's age? As I mind it ye never even paid heed tae her when you were a wee bairn. You always went yer own way and so does Adam.'

'I don't want him crewing on the *Fidelity*.'

'It's the family boat, and he's family. Dammit, you own part of it. It's where the laddie wants tae be; can ye not see that for yourself? He even spent the money he earned goin' out fishin' with me on lessons on navigation at the school in Buckie. And he never once missed a class, though he worked hard enough at hidin' from that damned tutor you insisted on hirin' tae get him ready for the university. Does that not show ye where his heart lies?'

'He's my son and I know what's best for him,' Bethany insisted, and then as her brother remained silent she rushed on, 'If that's the way you want it, I'll be waiting on the harbour for him when he tries to board the boat, and I'll take him back to Scotland with me. If you've any sense you'll tell him to pack his things and meet me at Jacob's lodgings before then.'

'You'll leave that lad be!' James came out of his chair, his face tight with anger. 'You've had yer time with him, Bethany,' he said. 'Eighteen years and more. Now it's a faither's guidance he needs, no' a mither's.'

'His father's dead.'

'That's what you've given him tae understand, but you know and I know that his father's very much alive!'

'How dare you! I know who fathered my own child!'

'Aye, ye should, and ye do, and it's time ye admitted the truth of it, tae me if tae no one else,' James said, and then as she flung herself round towards the door his hand caught her shoulder and turned her back to face him. 'There's just the two of us in this room, Bethany,' he said, 'so ye can stop yer pretence! Adam's not Gil's son and he never was.'

'Yes, he—'

'The sea's in that lad's blood, just as it's in mine and in yours. You can't deny that and it's time ye stopped tryin'. He's a fisherman tae the very marrow of his bones; he needs tae be with the sea, and I need him on my boat. It's my right and it's where he belongs.'

'I'll not have it!'

'Aye, ye will.' James's eyes blazed into hers. 'Stop tryin' tae make his decisions for him, Bethany. He's chosen his future and he's chosen my way, not yours. It had tae happen,' he went on, his fingers tightening as she tried to twist away. 'I've bided my time all these years, and I've held my tongue, because I was waitin' for the day when he'd make up his own mind as tae which road he wanted tae take. I knew that his choice would tell me who'd fathered him, and it has.'

'You're havering!' She wrenched herself free.

'And you're still lyin'. Face the truth, Bethany. Gil was never meant tae father a laddie on you, just as Stella was never meant tae bear one tae me. But you and me both wanted a son tae go tae the fishin' – and that's what's happened.'

Her face was as white as milk. 'You're talkin' of a mortal sin!'

'I know I am, but it happened all the same, and it happened because it was meant. We've both paid for it, me more than you,' James said. 'D'ye think it's been easy for me, watchin' the bairn grow up and hearin' Gil boastin' about him?'

'It's not been easy for me either. I wish to God,' Bethany said passionately, 'that you and me had never—' She stopped, unable to say it.

'If we'd both been more content with the folk we were wed tae it wouldn't have happened, but it did, and Adam's the result. Would you wish him out of the world?' James asked, then when she said nothing, 'Neither would I. He's here and now it's my turn with him. And I'll not let you deny me that!'

Fear leapt into her eyes and her voice. 'You'd not tell him? I'd sooner see us both dead than let Adam know.'

So would James, but, realising an empty threat was his only weapon, he hardened his heart and pressed on. 'I want him on the *Fidelity* with me, Bethany. I want a son tae take over from me when my time's done. If you agree tae let Adam go his own way he'll never know the truth from me, but if you keep crossin' him, and me,' he said, his voice as hard as iron, 'I'll tell the truth tae him and the whole of Buckie.'

'You'd turn him against the two of us!'

'Mebbe so, but I've got nothin' tae lose.' James released her and stepped back, his hands falling loose by his sides. 'Give Adam yer blessin', Bethany, or take the consequences. The choice is yours.'

'Oh, aye?' Andra's Jenny said when she and the others arrived back at the lodgings to find Adam sprawled at his ease in the parlour. 'I thought it was Rory that ye were sweet on, Etta, not his brother.'

'She's no' sweet on me, or me on her,' Adam grinned up at the girls standing round his chair. 'She took me in because I'm hidin' from my mither. Did ye see her when ye were out?'

'Aunt Bethany's here?' Mary asked in surprise. 'What's she doin' in Yarm'th?'

'Lookin' for this one, I'd say. Are you not supposed tae be at the university, learnin' how tae be a fine clever gentleman?' Agnes wanted to know.

'I'd as soon be here, goin' out with the *Fidelity* and havin' a grand crack with the lassies when I'm ashore. And if my mither manages to get hold of me, that's just what I'm goin' tae tell her – when her anger's cooled a bittie. Now ye're back, we'll just have a wee cup of tea. Did ye bring any cakes?' Adam asked hopefully.

It was as well that Mrs Rogers was not due back until night time, for the cup of tea swiftly turned into an impromptu party. Adam was good company, and his stories of university and the folk he met there had them all laughing till they cried.

'Ye're a right tonic, laddie,' Agnes said when he finally announced that he had to get down to the harbour. 'And ye're bonny tae look at an' all. Mebbe we should just let ye go on hidin' here for the rest of the season.' She swung her hips and winked at him. 'Jenny and Kirsten and me share a bed, but I'm sure we can make room for you.'

Adam grinned. 'I'd like that fine, but my Uncle James wouldnae, for the boats'll be goin' out soon and I have tae get tae the *Fidelity*.'

'What if your mither's waitin' for ye? That's the very place she'd expect tae find ye,' Kirsten pointed out.

'We could always dress you up as a woman,' Ruth suggested. 'And then we could all go out together arm in arm, as if we're takin' a nice walk in the fresh air before we go to our beds.'

'Agnes's clothes would fit ye fine, Adam,' Jenny agreed.

'Aye, and what d'ye think Uncle James and the rest of them would say if I went on board dressed as a lassie? You come with me, Etta,' Adam said, 'and we'll walk casual like, as if we're just out for a stroll. If my mither's at the harbour you can keep her talkin' while I get tae the drifter. Once I'm on board Uncle James'll no' let her haul me off again.'

It was dark outside, but the streets were still quite busy. Adam pulled his cap well down to hide his face and drew Etta's hand through his arm. 'Just pretend we're sweethearts out for a nice wee stroll tae the harbour.'

'You're enjoying this,' she accused, and he chuckled.

'Of course I am, it's an adventure, like ye see in the picture house. Have ye been tae the pictures yet, Etta? I'll take ye next week if ye like. What sort of picture would you like tae see?'

'All I can think about is what I'm goin' tae say if we meet Aunt Bethany.'

'Ach, we'll worry about that when it happens,' Adam said cheerfully.

As they neared the harbour they became part of a steady

stream of men, all on their way to their boats. To Etta's relief, there was not a sign of Adam's formidable mother.

'You'll be safe now,' she said, halting.

'Are ye not goin' tae see me right tae the boat?' he teased. 'I might get lost between here and the *Fidelity*.'

'Aye – and end up at my door again. On you go and let me get to my bed.'

'Thanks, Etta, you saved my life.' To her astonishment, he stooped swiftly and kissed the corner of her mouth. 'Ye're a grand lass,' he said, and then he was gone, mingling with the dark shapes moving along the harbour wall.

After Bethany left James she went for a long walk round Yarmouth in an effort to work off her anger. It had been a long and arduous fight, but now he had won. She had no doubt that if she pushed him far enough he would keep his threat to tell Adam the truth, and so she had no choice but to let her son turn his back on academic life and go to sea.

After all, she told herself as she travelled along street after street, it was what she had wanted for him, originally.

As her anger abated and resignation began to take over, she remembered Jacob's dinner invitation, and the merchant whose business he sought. She had packed for the journey in a fury with no thought to socialising while she was in Yarmouth, and had brought very little with her; so she went into the first shop she could find and bought the first blouse she tried – a square-necked garment in a pale green material with dark green embroidery at the neck and on the cuffs of the three-quarter-length sleeves. The blouse was pouched at the waist; it would do well enough, she thought, with the plain black skirt she had packed.

Jacob had indeed booked a room for her in the hotel near his own lodgings, and her luggage was already awaiting her. She laid the skirt and blouse out on the bed, decided that they would serve their purpose well enough, and freed her hair from its usual knot at the nape of her neck. It crackled as she brushed it out, venting the last of her anger with long steady strokes. Then she pinned it up, stripped, and saw with dismay that the marks of James's fingers stood out clearly in blue and black on the white, smooth skin of her upper arm. She put a hand up to touch the bruising, matching the outline of each of his fingers with her own. Even after she had washed, scrubbing hard at her skin as though it was possible to wipe the bruising away, and then put on the new blouse, she fancied that she could still see the outline of his fingers even through the sleeve.

Waiting with Jacob in his lodgings was a tall, well-built man, grey-haired and clean-shaven. He had an interesting face, Bethany decided as Jacob introduced her to Lorne Kerr. Her first impression was of shrewd green eyes, as clear as glass, set beneath well-shaped black brows. He might have been extremely handsome had his nose not been a little too large and his mouth a little too wide. As it was, the mismatched features added up to a face that, while almost ugly, had an attraction all of its own.

'I am very pleased to make your acquaintance, Mrs Pate.' The merchant took her hand in a firm grip. His voice was deep and pleasantly mellow, and his smile warm. 'Jacob tells me that you're an able business partner as well as a good friend.'

Bethany inclined her head and said something appropriate, and all the time she could feel the bruises left by James's fingers tingling on her arm.

Two days later Adam stopped by the farlins on his way back from a night's fishing on the *Fidelity* and drew Etta aside, leading her behind a great pile of barrels waiting to be taken to the railway station. It was a day of overcast skies and chill winds, and it was good to be in the shelter of the barrels for a few minutes. Even so, she protested, 'I've got my work tae do, even if you're finished.'

'It'll not take a minute,' he said. 'I just wanted tae thank you for helpin' me the other day.'

She glanced nervously over her shoulder. 'Your mither's still about the place.' Bethany Pate had visited the farlins on the previous day, in the company of Jacob McFarlane and a man that Etta had never seen before. After one horrified glance at the trio, especially her aunt, she had kept her eyes on her work, convinced that at any minute she would be pulled aside to receive a tongue-lashing for hiding Adam, and possibly be dismissed on the spot. But nothing had happened, and she had been left waiting and wondering.

'I know, she's stayin' on tae see tae some business for Jacob McFarlane. But it's all right, I've met with her.'

'She's lettin' you stay with the drifter?'

He grinned. 'She couldnae do anythin' about it. I want tae stay with the *Fidelity* and Uncle James needs me, and that's that. She's agreed tae leave me in peace from now on. No more university for me, Etta – I'm a fisherman at last! Are ye still willin' tae go tae the cinema with me on Saturday night?'

'Cinema? Me?' Etta vaguely remembered him making the offer the other night as they hurried together towards the harbour, watching all the while for his mother. 'Why me?' Every lassie in Buckie, and probably most of the lassies in Yarmouth, would be happy to go out with Adam Pate, and he had never shown any interest in Etta before, other than to tease her.

'As a way of thankin' you for what you did.'

'You don't need tae—'

'Stop fussin', lassie – will ye come out with me or will ye no'?'

'Aye, I'll come,' she said.

'Good. I'll meet ye outside the Red Lion at the end of King Street at seven o'clock.' And then, as a shaft of sunlight found its way through the cloud above and touched her face he said, 'Ye've got salt on your mouth.'

'It gets everywhere.' She put a hand up to rub at her lips, only to have it captured in his large fist.

'Leave it be. It's sparklin' like the diamond brooch my faither once gave tae my mither, and there's fish scales glitterin' in your hair as well. You look like a fine lady decked out in all her jewels.'

'Mebbe so, but the salt can give me blisters and I don't want that.'

'Then I'll take it away,' Adam said, and kissed her. His mouth was cold against hers, and yet the kiss seemed to burn its way from her lips to the very tips of her toes. When he raised his head – too soon! – he said, smiling down at her, 'There, it's gone.'

She watched, mesmerised, as the tip of his tongue slid out to run along his upper lip, then the lower.

'Sparklin' kisses that taste of salt,' he said. 'Saturday night, then?'

Rory was at the farlins when she scampered back. 'Where were you?'

'A call of nature,' Mary said quickly. 'Even guttin' quines have tae answer them.'

'We didnae want tae tell him that ye'd gone behind the barrels with young Adam,' Jenny said when Rory had gone. 'He might get jealous, with him bein' your sweetheart.'

'He's not my sweetheart, we just walk out together.'

'One tae walk out with and one tae kiss behind the barrels?' Ruth said with a grin.

'It wasn't a—' Etta began, and then, as a jeering chorus of disbelief began to rise, 'He just wanted tae thank me for helpin' him tae hide from his mither the other day.'

'I helped tae hide him an' all,' Agnes said, 'and he can thank me behind the barrels any time he likes!'

Etta lay in bed that night listening to the snores and groans and mumbles of the other women and thinking of Adam; the touch of his hand on hers as he drew her into the shelter of the barrels, and his voice telling her that the salt on her mouth made it sparkle like diamonds. And then – her bare toes curled against the lumpy mattress as she recalled his kiss.

She had only been kissed by one other man before – two, she suddenly remembered with a sense of disgust, but surely the desperate, greedy kisses of the Irish boy who had caught her alone on a dark night in Lerwick didn't count? The other man was Adam's own half-brother, Rory, but Rory had never ignited the sudden fire that blazed up when Adam kissed her. With Rory she felt no passion, no hunger, no yearning to be kissed again, and again, and for ever more.

Ruth suddenly sat bolt upright, said something so quickly that Etta, torn from her waking dream, could not make out the words, then flopped back down and turned over. Dreaming, no doubt, of her photographer sweetheart, Jack Morrison. Ruth was clearly in love with the man; since arriving in Yarmouth she had spurned the advances of more than one young fisherman, and she spent a large part of her free time writing long letters to Jack. She made no secret of her hope that once she got back to Buckie he would ask her to be his wife.

When she was certain that Ruth had settled down again Etta turned over carefully, so as not to fall off her side of the bed, and went back to thinking about the look in Adam's eyes as he spoke of the sparkle of salt on her mouth, and then . . . and then – his kiss.

20

The sooner the mistress was back home the better, in Leezie's opinion. With Mrs Pate and Rory both in Yarmouth Ellen had taken on the role of mistress of the house in Cliff Terrace, and Leezie was fair sick of being told to do this and do that and fetch the next thing as if she was new to her duties instead of a housekeeper with years of service.

True, Ellen was out at the net factory for most of the day, but with her stepmother away from home she tended to return earlier in the afternoons than usual. She had also taken to entertaining her friends to the evening meal, which now had to be served in the small dining room that had scarcely been used since Gil Pate's death. The big kitchen table had done well enough for Mrs Pate and her family, with the stove and sink conveniently close to hand, and a chair set in place for Leezie so that she could eat with the family.

Now she ate on her own in the kitchen while Ellen and her friends – a lot of silly, empty-headed idle folk, in Leezie's opinion, most of them the sons and daughters of well-to-do families in the area – chattered and giggled and played card games in the front parlour.

Scarcely an evening went by without Leezie being summoned time and again from her comfortable chair by the kitchen fire by the irritating tinkle of the little bell that Ellen had unearthed from the depths of some cupboard. The only time she got to herself in the evenings was when the young

213

folk all went off in their motorcars, and even then Leezie could not settle to sleep until she heard Ellen returning, sometimes in the small hours of the morning. After those evenings, she knew that she would have a struggle to get Ellen out of her bed in the morning in time to go to work.

Jack Morrison, the young photographer, was a frequent visitor to the house. On several occasions he had been the only visitor. He was a pleasant enough young man, Leezie thought, with more manners than some, and it was becoming more and more clear to her that Ellen was smitten with him. When he was the sole guest Ellen always took special care with her appearance and insisted Leezie light candles all round the room. Leezie, who had to clean the solidified wax up in the morning, and who had been raised in a cottage where the only lighting came from candles, could not understand the attraction of candlelight. Proper electric lighting was clean and quick, and it let folk see what they were eating.

She considered herself to be caretaker of both house and inhabitants when Mrs Pate was away from home, and so she fretted about what was going on. She tried to speak to Ellen, but the young woman immediately flared up at her and told her to mind her own business.

'It is my business. Mrs Pate expects me to take responsibility for this house when she's not at home.'

'That might be the case when we're all out,' said Ellen, who was sitting at her dressing table rubbing foundation cream into her face. 'But when I'm at home I'm the mistress of this house.'

'Indeed? Then perhaps you'd like tae give me some more housekeepin' money, for I've had to spend all that was left for me on the fancy food that you keep orderin'. Your mither didnae know when she went away that you were goin' tae feed half the young folk in the district. She'll no' be pleased when she sees the bills waitin' to be settled when she gets back.'

'My *step*mother,' Ellen said icily, emphasising the word,

'can well afford to pay the bills when she comes back from Yarmouth. It's not my fault if she didn't leave enough house-keeping money.'

She leaned forward to study herself in the mirror and then, satisfied with what she saw, she picked up a black pencil and began to thicken the line of one eyebrow.

'You've not told me what you want tae eat tonight,' Leezie reminded her, 'or how many visitors ye've invited. I might have tae go out to the shops again, if there's not enough in. And I'll have tae ask for tick again.'

Ellen wet a finger and ran it along the line of the completed eyebrow. 'Wealthy folk always pay their bill at the end of the month,' she said grandly. 'The shopkeepers are used to that. And don't bother about dinner, for Mr Morrison's taking me out. You can go now, Leezie.'

Oh, I can, can I? Leezie thought, and it was all she could do not to smack the little madam across the back of the head for her impertinence. Aloud, she said, 'Did I not hear that Mr Morrison was walkin' out with wee Ruth Lowrie?'

'What?' Ellen swung round, her eyebrows, one exaggerated by deft strokes of the pencil, the other as nature intended it, giving her face a lopsided look. 'That's nonsense!'

'I'm sure I've heard folk mention it. She's a nice wee lassie, Ruth. She'd be awful upset if she thought that someone else was makin' eyes at her laddie.'

'Jack Morrison's nobody's la— gentleman friend. He's free to choose his own company and so am I. And if you don't mind your tongue, Leezie, I'll have to turn you off!'

'Turn me off, is it? I came here when you were just a wee quinie, and a nice wee bairn you were in those days, so I don't know what's happened tae change ye. And as for turnin' me off, there's only one person can do that,' Leezie said, at the end of her tether, 'and that's Mrs Pate!'

'Then I shall write to her and complain about your behaviour—' Ellen began, and then broke off with a squeal of dismay as the front doorbell rang. 'He's here – and me not ready yet!' She turned back to the mirror and began to draw in the second eyebrow. 'Go downstairs at once, Leezie. Show him into the parlour and tell him I'll not be a minute. Go on!'

There was little Leezie could do but obey, but when she tried to usher Jack Morrison into the parlour he stayed where he was, in the hall, talking about the weather and about the photographs he had taken that day, and asking after Leezie's health. He was altogether too nice for Ellen, the way she had turned out, Leezie thought as she shifted from one foot to the other, trying to answer him and wishing that he would just go into the parlour and leave her to return to the familiar safety of her kitchen.

It was a relief when Ellen came hurrying down the stairs, wearing a smart frock that Leezie had never seen before, and with her bobbed hair sleek and her make-up immaculate.

'Jack, I'm so sorry, I was kept back. Such a nuisance,' she gushed.

'That's all right, Leezie kept me company,' he said pleasantly.

'That's good.' There was a brittle note to Ellen's voice, and the gaze she turned on Leezie was full of suspicion.

'We were discussing the weather. It always provides a grand topic of conversation in this country,' Jack Morrison said, taking Ellen's coat – also new, Leezie noted – and holding it out for her.

'Don't wait up, Leezie,' she said as she slid her arms into the sleeves. She made it sound more like an order than a request. 'I might be late.'

'But don't worry,' Jack added, 'I'll make sure that she gets back home safely.'

Ellen's scarlet Cupid's bow mouth curved into a warm smile. 'I know you will,' she said, and then they were gone, and Leezie was free at last to go into the kitchen and slump down in her usual fireside chair. At least she had the evening all to herself, for once.

As always happened when Ellen was out late, Leezie prepared everything for the night and then lay down fully clothed on her bed in the small back bedroom next to the kitchen, alert for the sound of the young woman's return. Ellen sometimes forgot to lock the front door, and so Leezie liked to make sure that the house was secured and, as often as not, pick up the shoes and coat and gloves and hat that Ellen shed carelessly on her way through the hall and up the stairs.

Tonight, possibly worn out by the confrontation she and Ellen had had earlier, she fell sound asleep, and woke with a start to find that the lamp still burned by her bedside and the house was quiet. A glance at the clock showed that it was after two in the morning. If Ellen had come home, then she had been quieter than usual, and if she had not—?

Leezie jumped up and hurried through to the hall, breathing a sigh of relief as she saw the smart new coat draped over the newel post at the foot of the stairs, and the hat Ellen had worn on the bottom step. Her shoes lay in the hall, where they had been kicked off, and the front door, though closed, was not locked. Leezie picked everything up, turned the key and went to bed.

Despite her broken sleep she was up bright and early the next morning. It was too early to rouse Ellen, so she set herself to putting the parlour to rights. She was on her knees, sweeping the hearth, when she heard a noise in the hall.

'Ellen?' There was no answer. It must have been the morning post falling onto the mat, Leezie thought, but when she went into the hall the mat was empty. It was also slightly askew, though she distinctly recalled setting it straight and locking the front door the night before.

The door, when she tried the handle, was unlocked. Surely, Leezie thought, puzzled, Ellen hadn't got up and gone out at this early hour? She opened it and went out onto the doorstep.

And was just in time to see Jack Morrison hurry off along Cliff Terrace, heading for the town.

*

It was Etta's very first visit to a cinema, and as she and Adam emerged her head was crowded with the images she had just seen of handsome men and beautiful women living in fine houses and leading lives that were so different from her own.

'They're only play actors,' Adam said, amused, when she wondered aloud at the splendour she had just witnessed. 'They were only pretendin'.'

'But surely their own lives must be grand.' She had skivvied for a brief time in one of the big houses in Buckie, and had marvelled then over the opulence and comfort of thick carpets and fine china and folk who could afford not only a bed just for themselves, but an entire bedroom each. But even these homes had not been as luxurious as those she had witnessed on the cinema screen. 'I don't suppose they live like ordinary folk – like us.'

'They live in America, so I suppose it's different there. Would you like tae live like the women in that film?'

'Aye,' she began, and then changed it to, 'mebbe. It would be nice, sometimes, tae have bonny things and nice clothes, and not have to work so hard.'

'I'd not want that at all,' Adam said firmly, and then, glancing up at the night sky. 'It's a grand evenin'; d'ye want tae go back tae your lodgings, or will we take a walk about the town?'

'A walk,' she said at once, and then, as they fell into step together, 'You could have all that – a nice house and a lot of money – if you went back tae the university like your mither wants you tae do.'

He gave a snort of disgust. 'Me? I've got the life I want right now, and I'd as soon sleep on a wooden bunk in the drifter than in a nice, soft bed. I want tae be like my Uncle James and my grandfather.'

As they walked, he talked about what it was like to be a fisherman, and Etta listened, enthralled, as he described the exhilaration of seeing the longed-for glint of silver beneath the tossing waves as they hauled the nets.

'There's no better thing tae hear than Uncle James shouting out that it's a good shimmer this time,' he said, 'and then when the nets are all inboard it's a race tae get tae the harbour and land the fish while they're still fresh.'

He proved to be a good listener, too, drawing out of her the story of the young father and mother she had never met and the harsh existence she had known in her grandfather's home – something that she would never entirely forget, not even if she lived to be very old – and being rescued and taken to live with Aunt Zelda and Uncle Innes.

'That was the best thing that happened tae me,' she finished.

'Aye, they're grand folk. It's a pity, though, that Uncle Innes could never thole the sea. He told me once,' Adam said, 'that my mither and Uncle James and my grandfather had little time for him because of that, and I can understand how they felt, for it's hard tae see how anyone can hate the sea. But even so, he's a fine man. He says that my mither never got over bein' born a quine instead of a loon, and that's why she took it hard when he turned against the fishin', when it was what she'd always wanted.' He paused, then went on thoughtfully, 'You'd wonder at her bein' so against me goin' out on the drifters, wouldn't you? You'd think she would have wanted me tae do what she'd have done herself if only she could.'

'But you're clever, and she's got the money tae send you tae the university,' Etta said. 'That means that you've got the choice. Not many folk have that.'

'I'm no cleverer than Rory, and university was never offered tae him.'

'That was because the cooperage was waiting for him, surely.'

'Aye, I suppose so. I'll tell ye this, Etta, if I have bairns, they'll damned well do as they please,' Adam said, and followed it up with, 'though I'd hope that the laddies would want tae go tae the fishin', like me.'

219

'And the quines?' Etta asked, and he laughed.

'I'd want them tae marry fishermen and breed more fishermen, of course. What more could a man ask of his daughters? Is that no' what you want for yoursel'?'

'I'd not mind it,' Etta said demurely. They had worked their way through all the main streets of the town, and now, as a church clock chimed ten times, she added, 'I'd best be gettin' back.'

'I'll walk ye to the door,' Adam offered. Then just as they turned into her street he suddenly caught her by the arm and whisked her into a darkened shop doorway and kissed her.

'Your mouth still tastes of salt,' he said when the kiss was over.

'So does yours, and no wonder, since we both work with the stuff.'

He laughed, and kissed her again, and this time she was ready for him and quick with her response. They clung tightly to each other, exchanging kiss for kiss, and Etta could feel his heart pounding against her breast. When Adam finally drew away from her he said, 'Ye're tremblin' like a wee bird I've caught in my hand. Are ye cold?'

'No,' she said, and drew him back into her embrace, unwilling to let him go.

The clock chimed the half hour and then the quarter before they finally stepped away from each other.

'D'ye kiss all the laddies like that?' Adam asked, his voice slightly unsteady.

'I've never kissed anyone like that. I didnae know I could.'

He laughed, then said, 'Are ye havin' a gatherin' in your lodgin's tomorrow?'

'Aye, after church, same as usual.'

'I'll see ye then,' he said.

As he went down the street, whistling, she ran the last few yards to the lodging house, where the other girls were either in bed or getting ready for bed.

'Has that Rory Pate been keeping you out late?' Annie asked with mock severity.

'No, and it wasnae Rory I was with anyway,' Etta said, and at once they all pounced, clamouring to know who her new sweetheart was.

'Is it one of our own laddies?' Mary pried when Etta refused to give them a name.

'I'm not sayin'.' She smirked at them, nursing her secret and enjoying the feeling of superiority it gave her.

'It's an English lad, or mebbe an Irishman,' Ruth guessed, while Jenny suggested, 'It could be a cooper, or mebbe even one of those folk that just come tae watch us workin' at the farlins.'

They were still guessing when they were all in bed, with the light out. But Etta kept her own counsel, knowing that part of the excitement that had turned her world into something as magical as the story she had seen unfolding on the cinema screen earlier was that only she knew the name of the man who had held her and kissed her so sweetly, and yet so passionately.

'I've not seen you for a while, Etta,' Rory said on the following afternoon. The weather was cold and wet, and the fisherlassies' parlour was filled with folk.

'You see me every day at the farlins.' Adam had arrived with his step-brother, but the place was so busy that they had not had a moment to speak to each other. She could see him at the other side of the room, talking to – flirting with, she thought to herself with a sudden pang – a pretty lassie from Fraserburgh.

'Aye, but we've scarce been on our own since we came tae Yarm'th. I've tae spend tomorrow evening with Jacob and my mother and some Edinburgh fish merchant that's interested in doin' business with us, but I'd like it fine if we could go for a wee walk on Tuesday night.'

'Aye,' she said, 'if we finish work in time.'

The afternoon dragged on and still she got no chance to speak to Adam, who finally left with only a casual nod in her direction. When the last of the callers went away the women had to set to and put the place to rights, and by the time they were done it was mid-evening.

'I'm away out for a breath of fresh air,' Kirsten announced, and Mary and Sarah decided to go with her. Jenny was out with her husband and Agnes was visiting local folk she had befriended on her first visit to Yarmouth years before. Ruth settled down with pen and paper to write to her sweetheart, Jack Morrison, and after mending a tear in her working skirt Etta decided that she could not stand being cooped up in the house for a moment longer.

She had walked a few yards down the street when a hand darted from a dark doorway and caught her elbow. She was whisked round and pulled into the shadows, while another hand was clapped across her mouth to stifle her squeak of surprise and outrage.

'Sshhh,' a voice whispered into her ear, 'd'you want the whole street tae start cryin' thief, or worse?'

Then there came a choked exclamation as she bit hard on one of the fingers that had been used to silence her, and the hand was withdrawn as swiftly as it had arrived.

'Damn it, Etta, d'ye have tae be such a vixen?'

'You think I'd be willin' tae be murdered without a fight? What d'you think you're doin', Adam Pate, hidin' in the dark and frightenin' folk that just want a breath of air?'

'I've been waitin' for you out here in the cold and the dark. Did you not see me noddin' at you when I was leavin'?'

'I thought you were just noddin' goodbye.'

'You've got a lot tae learn. I think ye drew blood,' Adam said, peering at his hand.

'Serves you right. You should be grateful I hadnae my guttin' knife with me. You couldn't even see me in the dark – you might have pulled anyone in here. Mary or Kirsten or Agnes. What would you have done then?'

'Thrown them back, the way we do when we catch the wrong fish in the nets.'

Etta giggled. 'I doubt if Agnes would have given you the chance tae throw her back. She's had her eye on you for a while.'

'There's only one lassie my eye's on and that's why I've been waitin' for her in the cold for the past hour and more.'

'I didnae know,' said Etta pertly, 'that that quine from Fraserburgh bided in this street.'

'What quine from Fraserburgh?'

'The one you were talkin' with half the afternoon.'

'Ach, I was only talkin' tae her because you were too busy seein' tae other folks' comfort tae spend time with me. Come for a walk with me next Saturday.'

'If you want.'

'I do want,' Adam said. And then, drawing her into his arms, 'And I want somethin' else as well.'

She returned to the lodgings an hour later, her mouth tingling from his kisses, and her feet scarcely touching the ground.

The fishing had been good but in the early hours of the morning the weather had turned cold and wet, and the incoming boats wallowing up the River Yare appeared suddenly through a grey curtain of rain. The gutting crews had started work at six o'clock in the morning and now, midway through the evening, they were still working by the light of paraffin lamps known to the women as 'bubblies'.

Rory and some of his coopers had managed to rig up a tarpaulin awning above the farlins but the women were only partly protected, for the slanting rain still drove its way in beneath the covering, and the ground was already waterlogged. The women were ankle-deep in sticky mud; each time they moved they had to haul first one booted foot and then the other from its grip.

'I don't know why they can't give us sheds tae work in,'

Ruth complained as she struggled to fill a barrel by the light of a lamp, rain streaming down the oilskin hood she wore and finding its way inside her waterproof jacket to trickle down her neck. 'It's no' much tae ask, surely?'

'It's probably no' worth their while for the time we're here, though if *they* were the ones tae do the guttin' they'd soon get shelter put up,' Mary said.

'Some places manage tae have their farlins in a sort of shed,' Ruth argued. 'Even if they'll not do it for us they should do it for their precious herrin'. The way the rain's teemin' down I'm packin' these fish in more water than salt. I'd not be surprised if they came back tae life and started loupin' out the barrel.'

'That's no' likely, with their guts taken out.' Annie peered through the downfall at her younger sister, 'How's that hand of yours?'

'It's all right.' Ruth had cut a finger a week before and despite being packed with well-chewed bread the wound had still not healed.

'We'll have a look at it tonight, and if it's not any better you're goin' tae the mission nurse in the mornin',' Annie said firmly.

'Ach, it'll be fine.' Ruth had other things on her mind, for there had been no letter from Jack Morrison that week. 'I'll steep it in hot water when I get back tae the lodgin's.'

'We'll not be long now,' Agnes assured her. 'The boats are all in and the farlins are emptyin'.'

Just then a chorus of squeals and curses broke out at the end of the long farlin as one of the posts holding the awning snapped under the weight of the water collecting on the tarpaulin, sending an icy deluge over the women working directly beneath it.

21

By the time the farlins were finally emptied and the coopers had rolled the last of the barrels away the rain had turned to sleet. Water cascaded from the women's oilskins as they trudged wearily over to where the lorries waited to take them back to their lodgings. The younger, more agile women were first on board, turning to offer a helping hand to the others as they climbed up, hampered by mud-slicked boots that skidded and slipped as they tried to gain a foothold.

For once they were too tired and too miserable to sing as they went jolting back to their lodgings.

'Take your boots off before you go in,' Mary, ever the housewife, instructed the others. 'We don't want tae muddy Mrs Rogers's lobby.'

'But my feet'll get soaked!' Kirsten protested.

'Don't be daft, lassie, they're already soaked.' Andra's Jenny settled her backside against the house wall and stuck one leg out. 'Here, pull that boot off.' When Kirsten had done as she was told, Jenny took it from her and ordered, 'hold yer hands out and I'll wash the mud off them.' She turned the boot upside down and a stream of water poured from it and over Kirsten's hands. 'Now help me off with the other one,' said Jenny, 'then I'll help you off with yours.'

When they finally got inside, the house was filled with the tantalising smell of a rich meat and vegetable stew, and Mrs Rogers was waiting to fuss over them. 'I've been stoking the boiler all day and there's a hip bath in your parlour with pots of hot water,' she said, and then, proudly, 'It's lucky I've got a bathroom of my own.'

'Four of us in the big bath,' Agnes said, 'Two at a time, and the other two can take turns with the hip bath. And the oldest gets tae be the first!'

It was too dark to see anything from the window of the small, private dining room, but Bethany Pate stood watching the sleety rain run sluggishly down the darkened pane for a while before letting the heavy curtain fall into place.

'Winter's coming in,' she said. 'It was a good catch today. The women might still be working at the farlins, poor souls.'

'Poor souls indeed, but I suppose they're used to it.' Lorne Kerr sat back in his seat at the table and held his glass up to the light to admire the rich glow of the port. 'Are you sure you'll not take a glass with me? It's particularly fine.'

'Perhaps half a glass. And you never get used to working at the farlins in all weathers and all hours,' she went on as he lifted the decanter.

He paused in the act of pouring her wine. 'Jacob told me that you had been a fisher-lassie, but I found it hard to believe.'

'Really?' Bethany held out a hand to him. 'You can tell a fisherman by the scars he carries on his hands, Mr Kerr, and the same goes for a guttin' quine. Working in all weathers with sharp knives and fish bones and brine pickle can be hard on the skin,' she went on as he set the decanter down and took her fingers in his, examining the fine white lines left by old scars. 'So you and Jacob McFarlane have been discussing me?'

'I was curious, and Jacob has a great admiration for you. So have I,' he said, and she withdrew her hand from his, suddenly aware that he had been holding it for a little too long. 'You're a remarkable woman, Mrs Pate.'

'I'm a Buckie woman, Mr Kerr. We're all remarkable.'

Bethany seated herself opposite him and accepted the glass of port. 'You should come to the Firth and see for yourself.'

'I intend to, now that we're in business together.'

It had been a very enjoyable evening, one that had been planned to celebrate their new business partnership and to mark the end of Bethany's stay in Yarmouth, but Jacob had bowed out at the last minute, pleading the need to visit an old friend who lived locally and had fallen ill.

Bethany and Lorne Kerr had enjoyed a very good dinner, during which she discovered that he was a childless widower who, like Jacob, had devoted himself to building up a successful business. She wondered idly why a man with his money and personable character had not found himself a second wife. Perhaps he valued his freedom and independence, just as she did.

'Tell me something about your life in Buckie,' he said now, and she started to talk about the net factory and the smokehouse.

'Who's in charge while you're in Yarmouth?'

'I've a good foreman in the smokehouse, and my stepdaughter's overseeing the net factory, though goodness knows what she's been up to in my absence. She's not been in charge of the place for long.'

'If she has half your ability, I'm sure that she will be looking after it admirably.'

'Ellen,' Bethany said, 'is not a business woman.' She launched into the story of the net that had been covered with powder from the stinging jellyfish, and felt absurdly pleased with her own storytelling skills when Lorne roared with laughter.

'I'm sure she learned her lesson well,' he said when she had finished.

'Perhaps – but I have a feeling that Ellen needs more than one reminder. It's just as well that I'm going back tomorrow.'

'Your company will be greatly missed,' he said.

'I've enjoyed my time in Yarm'th. But now I must get back to my hotel. I leave first thing in the morning.'

A sudden gust of wind buffeted against the windows and Kerr got to his feet. 'I'll arrange for a car to take you back.'

'No need for that. I'm used to bad weather, and I enjoy walking.'

'Then I'll accompany you,' he insisted.

The sleety downpour was being driven before a strong wind and the umbrella Lorne had borrowed from the hotel porter threatened to be more of a hindrance than help. After only a few steps he folded it and tucked it under one arm.

'Are you certain about the car?' He had to raise his voice above the sound of the wind, and when Bethany kept to her decision to walk, he drew his coat collar up and took her arm, drawing her close to his side. 'Then walk we shall, Mrs Pate.'

Even above the wind they could make out the deep boom of waves racing up river, and in the lamplight, as they passed close by the shore, they caught the occasional brief sight of white-flecked spray being tossed into the air. Bethany shivered, and was glad of the warm, strong body close to her own.

'It's a bad night for the boats,' Kerr said when they had reached the doorway of her hotel.

'Aye, it is.' She thought of Adam and James, and had to fight back a tremor of fear. 'But the boats are sturdy, and they've weathered worse,' she said firmly. 'Good night to you, Mr Kerr.'

'Good night, and safe journey home. We'll meet again,' he said, and disappeared into the rain-soaked darkness.

The hotel sign just outside Bethany's window squeaked monotonously as it swung in the wind, but even if it had been oiled into obedient silence she would not have been able to sleep for worrying about the *Fidelity*, out at the fishing grounds on this wild night with her son and her brother on board.

*

The wind had come up with unexpected speed, and by the time the *Fidelity*'s nets were ready to be hauled inboard a howling gale shrieked vindictively over the drifter. As she reared and then plunged, lacy white spume ripped from the crests of the racing waves flew from the darkness to spatter over the crew, blinding them and chilling faces and hands.

'As fast as ye like,' James yelled, his voice all but snatched from his lips by the wind and borne away into the night. 'Get the nets aboard and we'll turn her head tae wind and try dodgin' out the storm!'

It was a nightmare task. All about them as they worked the waters boiled and seethed in a massive tantrum; it seemed to Adam that the sea had suddenly become tired of the puny men who had the audacity to wrest their living from it and had decided to swallow them and their boats whole and draw them deep down below.

One by one the nets came inboard, and for each net – each fish, even – the men strung in a line along the gunwales had to fight the might of the raging waters. The steam winch roared and struggled and as they leaned overboard to haul the nets in with their bare hands the racing, tumbling waves were only inches below. They were using the rolling of the drifter to help in their task – when she dipped precariously close to the surface the men hauled desperately and as she lifted again they leaned back on their heels, still gripping the net, in a bid to drag a few more inches inboard. The deck was awash and, with the occasional herring slipping from the meshes to the deck before it reached the hold, there was the increased danger of stepping on a fish and skidding.

James, unable to keep away from the action, had sent Siddy to the wheelhouse, and he himself was among the crew dragging the nets up from the deep, yelling orders all the time.

A wave broke over the boat and while it covered them, seeking to pick them off one by one and carry them overboard, the men could only hang on to the net they were hauling, dig their feet in to the angle of the deck and the gunwale, hold their breath and wait until the water subsided. As he worked, Adam spared a brief thought for the boy creeping around and around on his knees in the tiny rope locker, coiling in the thick rope. He knew from personal experience that the claustrophobic little cupboard would be awash and that the boy would be soaked to the skin.

The next wave came in hard and fast from another direction, lifting the boat up and then dropping it so quickly that it fell away from beneath their feet. Sensing nothing but water beneath his sea boots, Adam knew a moment's panic. For several vulnerable seconds he was entirely at the mercy of the sea; this was the moment where the net could pull him over the gunwale, wherever that was, as easily as if he were a fish caught on a line.

Rain and spray blinded him – then at last the deck came up beneath his feet, connecting with a solid thump that vibrated all the way through his body and clashed his teeth together hard. He was aware of a stab of pain as he bit his own tongue, and the tang of cold salt water was replaced for an instant by the hot, brassy taste of blood. But at that moment the pain and the blood were the most beautiful sensations he had ever known, and he heard himself tossing a whoop of jubilant laughter into the wind.

After a struggle they won back the net, but as the winch began to haul up the next net a figure struggled out of the hold and clumped James on the shoulder.

'The hold's fillin' with water,' the man yelled. 'If we don't cover it she's in danger of goin' down!'

'Fetch the axe,' James shouted back, and then, to the others labouring alongside him, 'Let the net go, lads, we're cuttin' it free!'

The moon suddenly appeared through clouds as torn and demented as the waves below, its pale, cold light striking silver from the sharp blade of the axe as James lifted it and then slammed it down on the thick messenger rope straining over the gunwale. Two hard blows almost had the rope parted;

he lifted the axe high again just as another big wave swept in. James, intent on releasing the nets, was not paying enough attention to his own safety and the wave caught him and hurled him back. Still clutching the axe, he slipped and went down hard; even above the noise of the storm Adam, beside him, heard the dull thud as his uncle's head hit the raised wooden ridge about the open hold.

As the wave receded James's oilskin-clad body rolled sluggishly down the deck and thumped against Adam's legs, almost felling him. Even as someone pulled the axe from James's limp hand and chopped at the rope another wave, crosswise to the last, came racing in out of the darkness and reared its foam-flecked head above the deck. As it crashed down, almost swamping the drifter, Adam threw himself across James, curling one arm tightly about the man and reaching desperately for some sort of purchase with the other. If there was nothing to grip, he well knew, the two of them would almost certainly be swept over the side and perhaps become entangled in the net that, once released, would disappear swiftly into the depths. And it would be the two of them, of that he was certain, for no matter what happened he was not going to let go of the semi-conscious man.

The wave broke over their heads just as a deckhand, who had anchored himself securely on one of the mast stays, caught Adam's wrist in an iron grip. It seemed to Adam, as the receding wave fought for the right to claim him, that his arm was being wrenched from its socket, but even so he managed to wrap his frozen fingers round his saviour's wrist and held on until the wave was gone. Then he was hauled to his feet, while someone else dragged James back from the side of the drifter.

'Are ye all right, lad?'

'I'm fine, what about my uncle?' Adam yelled.

James had already come round and began to stagger to his feet just as the messenger rope parted. As the remaining nets and the fish in them sank swiftly below the turbulent water, the *Fidelity,* freed from the weight anchoring her to the seabed, bounced and then steadied, and the seasick, miserable boy in the rope locker was sent sprawling in several inches of dirty water.

'Cover the holds! Turn her head to wind, Siddy!' James roared, taking command again.

The storm began to ease towards dawn, and as they headed for Yarmouth Adam, climbing wearily down the ladder to the cabin for a short and much needed rest, found his uncle sitting at the table, both hands cupped round a steaming mug of tea.

'How's yer head?'

'Loupin' like a salmon goin' upstream, but I've a thick skull. It'll mend fast. Siddy tells me that I'd be fish-bait now if you'd not hung on tae me.'

'It wasnae just me; if Walter hadnae got a grip of me we'd both have been over.' Adam poured tea out for himself. 'It's a funny thing, but while we were sprawled there I minded what you'd said about my grandfaither Weem believin' that a fisherman belonged tae the sea.' He sat down opposite James. 'I mind wonderin' if I should just let it happen, for at least we'd have gone down together.'

'Here.' James reached into a locker and brought out a bottle of whisky. Opening it, he poured a good dram into Adam's tea. 'That'll do ye good.'

'Thanks. But then I thought – I've got a lot of livin' tae do yet, and I want tae get the chance tae enjoy it afore I go. And as for you,' Adam took a deep swallow of the hot, laced tea and then grinned at James over the rim of the mug, 'I need tae have you around, for who else can teach me how tae take over the *Fidelity* when my time comes?'

And then he wondered why, just before his uncle cleared his throat and looked away, the man's eyes suddenly took on a strange shine. It was for all the world as though they were damp.

*

Bethany did not even realise that she had gone to sleep until a gentle tapping at the door awakened her.

'Yes?' She struggled up in bed, realising that she could no longer hear the hotel sign creaking as it swung. The wind must have dropped.

The door opened and the chambermaid's head appeared round it. 'If you please, ma'am,' she said in the rich rolling local dialect. 'There's a gentleman below wants a word with you. A Mr McFarlane.'

Terror clutched at Bethany's heart. 'I'll be down in just a minute,' she said, and as the door closed she sprang out of bed. Something serious must have happened to bring Jacob to the hotel at such an early hour. As she dressed hurriedly she prayed all the while that he had not brought bad news of her son.

'What's happened? Is it Adam?' she asked as soon as she went in to the small parlour set aside for hotel guests. Jacob, heedless of the dark prints his wet, booted feet were making on the rugs, was pacing to and fro, his face ashen.

'Adam's fine,' he said swiftly, 'and so's James, apart from a lump on the back of his skull where he got bowled over by a wave. The *Fidelity*'s already come up the river and I've spoken tae the two of them. It's the *Jess Lowrie*.' His voice shook and the tears began to run down his face unchecked. 'She's gone down, and her crew with her. We've lost them all, Bethany.'

It was a sombre group that gathered at Jacob's lodgings an hour later. James was there, and Jem, who told his story in a dazed, halting voice.

'We were fishin' near tae each other, the *Homefarin*' and the *Jess Lowrie,* an' we'd tae cut the last net loose because of the weather gettin' worse. We were the first tae head back tae harbour when the storm began tae ease and I gave the *Jess Lowrie* a shout on the loud-hailer when we were near enough. Willie Gunner said he was goin' tae manage tae take in all their nets and that they'd be in afore us.'

He stopped and looked down at his hands, fisted together between his knees and moving continually, the knuckles grinding against each other. 'That's what he said, that they'd show us a good run. I wish tae God we'd stayed by her, but there was no reason for it. She seemed tae be fine. We were just past her when the rain started again. It came down in sheets an' we lost sight of her almost at once.' Jem paused, his broad face haunted by the memory of that last sighting, and the last contact with the missing drifter.

'Go on, Jem,' James prompted quietly. Glancing at him, Bethany saw that there was a grey tinge to his usual tan and he looked exhausted.

'There's nothin' else tae tell,' Jem said helplessly. 'We got back without a sight of the *Jess Lowrie* or any other boat until we were comin' up tae the shoreline. She wasnae in when we arrived and I waited for her, thinkin' she'd be up the river any minute. We all waited, James and his crew too, when the *Fidelity* got in. But she never came back and no other boats have seen her.'

'Is there a chance that she might have gone into another port because of the storm?' Bethany asked.

'Aye, mebbe,' James said, but there was little hope in his voice.

'Seven of a crew,' Jacob said huskily. 'Six men and the boy.' He had suddenly aged overnight.

'The boy's the son of one of the deckhands. They come from Findochty.' Bethany could not bring herself to speak of the missing crew in the past tense. 'And the skipper's Willie Gunner from the Yardie. The others are Highlanders down for the fishing. Two of them are brothers, and their cousin's aboard as well. Could the sea have got into her hold and swamped her?'

James nodded, then winced slightly and put a hand to the back of his head. 'Aye, it could, and if it did she could have gone down fast – too fast tae fire off a rocket.'

'I'll stay on in case there's more news. If it's bad I'll have to contact the families when I get back to Scotland.'

'D'ye want me tae travel back with ye?' Jacob offered.

'No, you stay here and see the season out.' She could tell that the loss of the drifter he had named after her mother meant almost as much to him as the loss of her crew. 'I can manage on my own.'

'It's a terrible thing tae happen,' the old man said. 'When ye depend on the sea for your livin' ye know that the price can be high. But even so, ye never come tae terms with it.'

He went upstairs just after Jem left. Bethany looked at James, still slumped in his chair. 'Jacob said you hurt your head.'

'Aye, I was cuttin' the last of the nets free because the hold was fillin' with the water pourin' inboard, an' a wave came over and knocked me off my feet. It damn' near tossed me right intae the hold. The edge of it caught me on the head, and then the wave tried tae take me back out with it. If it hadnae been for Adam I'd be down there with the nets we lost.'

'Adam?'

'He held me back till the wave was by, Siddy says. I don't mind much of it mysel'.'

'Let me see.' Bethany moved behind his chair and he bent his head submissively. The tips of her fingers found the large lump easily, and she parted his thick, dark hair, damp from the rain and the spray and sticky with salt, so that she could have a closer look.

'It's fair-sized but you've not broken the skin. Mebbe you should go to the hospital and let the nurses have a look at it.'

'No need for that. It'll go down in its own time.'

'You should at least go back to your lodgings and have a sleep. I doubt the boats'll be going out again today.' She glanced out of the window; the rain was still falling from a heavy grey sky, though no longer driven by heavy winds.

'We'll be out all right, if we can manage it.'

Because of the darkness of the morning, lamps had been lit in the room, and the artificial light caught the silver threads liberally woven through James's black hair. Against her will, Bethany remembered a time when his hair had been free of silver, and soft and thick to the touch.

'Be careful, James,' she said.

'I'll no' let anythin' happen tae Adam,' he promised. 'The lad saved my life, and I'd give it away without a second thought in order tae save his.'

'I didn't just mean Adam, I meant—' Bethany stopped speaking, then said, 'I meant the crew, and the boat. We've already lost one drifter.' She stepped away from the chair and picked up her coat. 'Is Adam at the lodgings?'

'I suppose so.'

'I'll walk back with you and have a word with him,' Bethany said, hungry to see her son and to reassure herself that he was safe and sound.

22

Ruth, and therefore Agnes and Kirsten, who shared a bed with her, had had a restless night because of the pain in her hand. 'It was loupin' all night,' she complained as Mary unwrapped the bandaging in the morning.

'I'm not surprised.' Mary took her cousin's wrist gingerly between her thumb and forefinger and held the affected hand up to let the others see it. 'Look at that.'

'No packin' for you today, my quine,' Agnes said after one glance at the hand, which was puffy, with an ugly bruised look to the skin around the wound. 'We've some toppin' up tae do while we're waiting for the first of the boats tae come in, and it's that cold that we'll have tae break the ice on the barrels afore we can start. You'll just make that sore hand ten times worse if ye try tae work today. Anyway, I doubt there'll be much fish in, given the storms last night. The nurses'll have tae see tae ye as soon as the mission's open.'

Protests were waved aside and Ruth watched wistfully from the window as the lorries carried the others away to the harbour. It was a gloomy place that day, for the *Jess Lowrie* was one of three boats that had succumbed to the storm. One crew had been saved by a fellow drifter close enough to see its rocket signals. Thanks to excellent work from the skipper and his crew they had managed, despite the heavy seas, to go alongside and take every man aboard before the stricken vessel slipped beneath the waves. The other, like the Buckie boat, had simply failed to return.

Ruth arrived at the farlins in the early afternoon, dressed for work and with her hand bandaged.

Annie and Sarah pounced on their younger sister as soon as she appeared. 'Let me see your hand,' Sarah ordered, and when she saw the neat bandage, 'You're no' workin' with that. Ye'll loosen it.'

'Or it'll be covered with salt,' Annie chimed in.

'I can manage,' Ruth was protesting when Rory arrived with another barrel for the packer who was standing in for her.

'What are you doin' here, Ruth Lowrie?'

'She thinks she's come tae work,' Sarah sniffed. 'Tell her, Rory!'

'What did the nurse say?'

'It's just a wee bit poisoned. But she punctured it and took all the poison out and bandaged it, and it's not sore at all now.'

Rory's blue eyes, normally cheerful, stabbed into hers. 'I didnae ask what she did, I asked what she said.'

Ruth bit her lip and finally admitted that the nurse had told her to stay away from the farlins, and get the hand looked at again in two days' time.

'That settles it, then, ye'll no' be back before Monday,' Rory announced.

'I could wrap it in a bit of tarpaulin. It wouldnae come tae any harm.'

'How can you pack barrels one-handed?'

'I can pack them one-handed and with a blindfold tied round my eyes,' Ruth snapped at him. 'You know I'm good at my job.'

'I know that I'd not forgive myself if that hand got worse. And Aunt Stella wouldnae forgive me either, so you're goin' tae stay away until the nurse says ye can come back tae work.'

'I need the wages, Rory!'

'You'll get yer wages.'

'For not workin'?'

'Aye, because you're right – you're a bonny packer and you're worth every penny I pay ye. It's not your fault ye've been hurt. Now do as ye're told and get away home and look after that hand,' he ordered.

'Any more news of the *Jess Lowrie* and the other boat?' Ruth asked when he had gone. 'They were speakin' of them at the hospital.'

'No. I don't doubt they're both lost, and all the poor souls aboard them,' Kirsten said, and a sudden silence fell over the women as they worked on the fish that all too often came ashore at dear cost to the men who harvested them.

Despite her brave words Ruth was still in pain, and that night her hand was throbbing so badly that they had to tie her wrist to the bedpost in an attempt to ease it, and to keep it from getting knocked during the night. She was pale and drawn in the morning, and content to stay in the lodgings with no further argument. When the others returned from the farlins for their midday meal she looked a little better.

'He's a good, kind soul, Rory Pate,' she said, and Andra's Jenny agreed, 'He's a right gem.'

When they left for the afternoon's work, Ruth was settling down at the table with her writing pad.

'No' another letter tae that photographer? You wrote tae him just the other day,' Agnes pointed out.

'Aye, but he's not answered it yet. It's a good thing it's my left hand that's bandaged,' Ruth said; and then, frowning, 'I'm wonderin' if Jack's mebbe ill. I'd have thought he'd have written before now.'

'Mebbe he's found better things tae do with his time,' Kirsten suggested, and Ruth glared at her.

'He hasn't!' she snapped.

Two days later the others returned from the farlins to find her in tears.

'Ruth, what is it?' Mary flew to her cousin's side. 'Did the nurse say your hand's got worse?'

239

'N-no, she's lettin' me g-go back tae work on M-onday!' Ruth looked up at them, her pretty face swollen with crying.

'Has there been a letter from home? Is someb'dy ill?'

Again, Ruth shook her head. 'It's Jack! I g-got a letter from J-Jack—'

'That's a good thing, surely?' Mary said, puzzled. 'You were worried because you hadnae heard from him, and now you have.'

'I didnae mean this kind of letter!' Ruth shrieked. 'He's gettin' wed! Gettin' wed – tae Ellen Pate!' She hurled a crumpled ball of paper across the room and then threw her arms about Mary, almost knocking her backwards, and burst into loud, noisy sobs.

'Ellen Pate and your Jack? Never! They scarce know each other!' Kirsten stooped to pick up the paper, which had landed almost at her feet.

'What does it say?' Etta and Agnes and Andra's Jenny crowded round as she smoothed it out.

'It's right enough, he's got himself engaged to Ellen Pate – of all people!'

'That cold lassie that runs the net factory? He's no' particular, is he?' Jenny said, and Ruth's wails redoubled.

'For pity's sake, someone, help me with the lassie,' Mary begged, her voice muffled as she tried to cope with the weight of the weeping girl.

It took all five of them, and a dram or two from a small bottle of brandy that Agnes kept by her for emergencies, before they could calm Ruth down.

'It's not the end of the world, hen,' Andra's Jenny said as she poured out a second dram.

'It is for me.' Ruth's face was swollen, and her voice thick with sobbing.

'Ruth, ye'd surely not want tae keep the mannie by your side against his will—' Mary began, and her cousin turned on her.

'You don't know what it's like tae lose someone ye care

for! Peter Bain would never do a thing like that tae you!'

'Lassie, we all know what it's like tae lose a lad,' Agnes told the distressed girl. 'If I'd a pound for every man that's slipped through my fingers I'd be a wealthy woman. But men's like herrin', there's always another shoal out there. Ye'll find that out for yersel' soon enough, for ye're a bonny lass. If ye've lost him it's because he wasnae meant for ye.'

'But he was!' Ruth hiccupped.

'What I want tae know is, what does he see in Ellen Pate?' Kirsten mused.

'She's made a play for him while I was down here in Yarm'th. She knew that him and me had an understandin', and she's deliberately taken him away from me, the nasty cat!'

'We'll have none of that talk, not about your own cousin.' Mary said sharply.

'She's not my cousin, she's my Aunt Bethany's step-daughter!'

'She's still family,' Mary insisted. 'I tell you what – we'll all go out tonight, and take a good look round the shops and decide what we're goin' tae buy tae take home.'

'I can't manage. I'm going somewhere else,' Etta said hurriedly.

'With Rory? Well, you can just tell him what I think about his sister when you're—'

'I'm not going out walking with Rory tonight.'

'There, ye see? Etta's discovered that there are plenty of men in the world,' Agnes cut in, and before Etta could protest, 'The rest of us'll go round the shops, then, and we'll mebbe go tae one of those music halls intae the bargain. What d'ye say, Ruth?'

'She says yes, and that's the matter decided,' Kirsten said, then sniffed the air. 'I can smell cookin'. I'm fair ready for my dinner!'

*

'Our Ellen, with that photographer fellow?' Adam asked in disbelief that night. 'Engaged to be married, did ye say?'

'So he told Ruth in his letter.'

'I can't imagine any man wantin' our Ellen.'

'She's a bonny enough lassie.'

'Mebbe so, but she's thrawn; the man'll find that out for himself, soon enough. And she likes tae have her own way.'

'Ruth's in a right state about it, the poor soul. She cared for him.' Recollecting the utter misery in the girl's face, Etta felt a shiver go through her. Adam's arm immediately tightened about her.

'Are ye feelin' the cold?'

'Just a wee bit.'

'Over here, then.' The storm had abated, but the sea was still rough and most of the skippers, the thought of the two lost drifters in their minds, had decided against putting out to sea. Adam and Etta were walking along the river's edge, the shingle crunching beneath their feet and the lights of Yarmouth falling away behind them. Now Adam veered away from the water, urging her towards the black hulk of an upturned dinghy. 'We'll sit here for a minute, out of the wind.'

'I'm wearin' my good skirt,' Etta objected, and he stripped his jacket off and spread it over the ground.

'There you are.'

'But you'll catch your death!'

'No I won't,' Adam said, urging her gently to the ground. 'I'll keep you warm – and you can keep me warm.'

He settled down beside her, leaning up on one elbow with his head propped on his hand. Thin clouds moved above them, parting now and again to show the pale moon and the frosty twinkle of far-away stars studding the black of the velvety sky. She could see the outline of his head against the stars and feel his eyes travelling over her face. The close examination, and his silence, began to unnerve her.

'What are you thinkin' about?' she asked, more to break the silence than anything.

'I was wonderin' why any man would want our Ellen when there's you instead,' he said.

'You're haverin'!'

'Shut up, woman.' Adam bent to stop her mouth with his own, then said, 'Your lips still taste of salt.' He kissed her again and then drew back, his fingers tracing a path from her forehead to her chin, down to her throat and then further down to the first button of the blouse she wore beneath her jacket. 'Salty lips,' he said, 'and sweet kisses.'

'Adam—' she said as the button was eased from its button-hole.

'What?' The second button was released.

'You know what.'

'Ye like me, don't ye?'

'Of course I like you, but—'

'And I like you, Etta. I like you an awful lot.' He kissed her again, with passion this time, and the heat from his lips sped like a fire out of control down the length of her body. His fingers, though deliciously cool against the skin of her breast, did nothing to quench the blaze.

'I've never—' she muttered against his shoulder as he shifted position, slipping an arm beneath her so that she was raised up against his body.

His soft laugh tickled her earlobe.

'Neither have I,' he whispered. 'I've been waitin' for you, my bonny lass.'

As the blouse fell open beneath his determined fingers and the blaze that had taken Etta over flared out of control, her last coherent thought before she gave in to his need and to her own was a vague realisation that she should have done as Mary urged and put on a warm jersey before going out that night. If she had, he might just have been deterred from leading them both into such terrible, delicious wrongdoing.

Things had been happening in the house during her visit to Yarmouth, Bethany realised as soon as she stepped inside the

243

front door. There was an uneasy atmosphere about the place and Leezie, lugging her mistress's bag up the stairs to the bedroom, almost radiated anger.

As well to get the air cleared from the start, Bethany thought. 'Right, then, what's been happening here?'

Leezie, who was as strong as a horse, heaved the bag on to the bed with a lot of huffing, as though it weighed more than a sack of coal. 'Nothin',' she said through a mouth as stiff as the slit on a post box. 'What could be happenin'? One day's much like another in this house.'

'Is it Ellen? Has she been difficult? Because if she has I'll have something to say to the lady.'

'She's been fine,' Leezie said, then added, 'I suppose.'

'What d'you mean, you suppose?'

'I mean,' Leezie snapped, 'I'm just the servant here, how should I know how she feels?'

'Don't be daft, woman, you know you're more than a servant. Has she been going to the net factory every day?'

'Aye. I'd expected you home long afore this.'

'I meant to be, but Mr McFarlane had business to do and he needed me with him. And we lost the *Jess Lowrie*.'

Leezie forgot her own grievances. 'Lost her? What about the crew? God rest their souls,' she whispered as Bethany said nothing. 'That's a terrible thing tae happen!'

'Aye. I've to go and see the families, and write to the folk up in the Highlands that had lads on the boat.'

'D'you want me tae hang your clothes up?'

'I've got two good hands, haven't I? I can see to my own unpacking. I could do with a cup of tea, though.'

When Leezie had gone downstairs Bethany went to the window, where she looked out towards the Moray Firth, a mass of surging white-topped water on this cold, grey day. Something had gone wrong during her absence; she knew it by Leezie's martyred air. Something that would have to be dealt with – once she had gone to the Yardie to see Mrs Gunner, widow of the skipper of the *Jess Lowrie,* and then visited the woman in Findochty who had lost a husband and a boy not long out of school.

A letter had to be written, too, to the relatives of the three young Highlanders who had come south for the fishing, and would not be returning home.

Leezie had taken the tea tray into the parlour and lit a fire in the grate. A pile of letters lay on the desk, and while she sipped at her tea Bethany began to open them. Soon she was involved in the business matters that had been gathering while she was away, while her second cup of tea cooled unnoticed close to her hand.

Ellen swept into the house as if she owned it, and was half way up the stairs before she heard Bethany call her name from the parlour. There was a brief silence and then the young woman came back down and into the front room, dropping her bag and gloves on to a chair and peeling her fur-collared coat off.

'You're back, then.'

'I'm back. That's a fancy coat to wear to the factory.'

'It's nice and warm on a day like this.' Ellen tossed the coat over a chair and then sat down, crossing slim, silk-clad legs and folding her hands around her upper knee. 'Did you find Adam?'

She was dressed soberly enough in a black skirt and long, warm cardigan over a white blouse but her hair, Bethany noticed, had been stylishly waved and she was wearing lipstick and eye shadow.

'I found him.'

'And is he back in Aberdeen, being a good laddie?' The sneer was subtle – too faint to cause open offence, but obvious enough to sting. The little madam knew the answer to that already, Bethany thought with a flash of annoyance, but she refused to be drawn.

'No, he's still at the fishing. It seems that Adam has no interest in getting a good education, so there's little I can do about it.'

'So my wee brother's won again.' Ellen moved her position slightly and a ring on one of her fingers flashed in the glow from the lamp by Bethany's chair.

'It wasn't a battle, Ellen, so nobody wins. Your brother's made a choice, and that's all there is to it.'

'Rory didn't get to make a choice.'

'Rory didn't have to; he always knew that the cooperage would be his as soon as he'd served his apprenticeship. That's what his father intended for him all along. Being the second son, Adam doesn't have a business to inherit and so it was only natural that I wanted him to do as well as he could.'

'And what about me? I didn't want to go into the net factory, but you made me.' Ellen's voice was sulky, and she shifted position again; it was irritating the way she could not keep still, Bethany thought. One minute her left hand was fidgeting with the buttons on her cardigan and the next it was smoothing her skirt over her knee. What was wrong with the lassie?

'You weren't doing anything at all with your life,' Bethany pointed out. 'It's not good for a healthy young woman to spend all her time trying to keep herself amused. I work, and so does Rory, and I am perfectly entitled to expect you to work as well. I thought I made that clear at the time. I hope you've been looking after the factory well while I've been away?'

'Of course.'

'Good,' Bethany said crisply. 'I'll take a look in there tomorrow.'

Ellen shifted in her chair yet again. Then as Bethany returned to the papers in her lap, she said, 'There is one thing I should tell you. You're going to have to find someone else to take my place as overseer in the factory.'

'Take your place? Have you found other employment?'

Ellen smirked. 'I suppose I have, and it's in Glasgow.'

'Glasgow? Ellen, what—' Bethany started to say, then stopped as the younger woman put her left hand up to her throat and the light again caught the ring she wore. A ring that Bethany had not seen before. 'Is that— have you got engaged?'

'I thought you'd never notice. It's nice, isn't it?' Ellen stretched out her hand to display the ring, three diamonds in a row.

'But— who is it?' It was not often that Bethany spluttered, but she was completely taken aback, and she could tell by the younger woman's eyes that Ellen was enjoying her discomfiture.

'Jack Morrison. You know,' she said as her stepmother gaped at her, 'the photographer who came to take pictures of the women working in the factory.'

'But Ellen, you've only just met the man! You scarcely know him! I've not been away much over a week – how could you possibly get engaged in that time?'

'I've been seeing him every day while you were away. We bought the ring in Elgin yesterday and I'm going to Glasgow over the New Year to meet his family,' Ellen crowed.

'You can't promise yourself to someone as fast as that! Not with me and Rory away!'

'Jack doesn't want to marry you, or Rory,' Ellen got to her feet. 'It's me he wants, not my family. We're getting married in the spring and living in Glasgow. It'll make a nice change – lots of places to go and people to meet. Are you not going to congratulate me?'

'I'm happy for you, of course, if you're certain that this is what you want.'

'I've never been more certain. Jack's just right for me.'

A thought struck Bethany. 'Was Jack Morrison not walking out with Ruth Lowrie?' she asked, and Ellen shot her a hard look.

'They met when he was taking pictures at the farlins in Lerwick, and Ruth showed him around when he first came here. But she never meant anything to him.' She threw the last few words over her shoulder as she sauntered to the door. 'I'm off to wash my hands before we eat.'

'Ellen!' Bethany called, and when the girl reappeared, one elegant eyebrow arched in a silent question, she indicated the hat, bag, gloves and coat spread over the chair. 'You haven't picked up your things.'

'That's what we pay Leezie for. She's the maid.'

'She's the housekeeper. I'm the one who pays Leezie her wages, and it's not for picking up after you or me,' Bethany said evenly. 'We're old enough to do that for ourselves. Once you're a married woman,' she added swiftly, seeing the threat of open rebellion in her stepdaughter's eyes, 'you can make your maid pick up after you all day if you wish. That is, if your intended husband can afford a maid.'

Ellen glared and then began to snatch up her belongings.

'You've not asked what's happening in Yarmouth.'

'Was there anything worth asking about?'

'There was a storm,' Bethany said quietly. 'The *Jess Lowrie* was lost, with all her crew.'

'Oh.' Taken aback, Ellen stared at her for a moment before saying awkwardly, 'I'm sorry.'

23

When Ellen had gone upstairs Bethany went into the kitchen, where Leezie was banging pots and dishes about.

'Why didn't you tell me that Ellen's to be married?'

'It's not my place tae talk about members of my employer's family. I'm just the maid.'

'You'd best watch your tongue, Leezie Watson, because I've nearly had enough for one day. It's been a quick courting, has it not?' Bethany probed.

'You know Ellen, once she makes up her mind to have somethin' she doesnae waste time. She's been like that from a bairn, as I mind.'

'So it's like that, is it? She saw the man and she wanted him, so she set out to get him?'

'I wouldnae know about that,' Leezie sniffed.

'D'you think she's making a mistake? I'd not want that to happen.'

'Since you ask, I think the lassie needs tae get out of here and intae a place of her own. And now she's got somewhere tae go. So if I was you,' said Leezie, 'I'd leave her tae it. And if you're lookin' for somethin' tae do, ye can drain these potatoes for me.'

'Etta,' Rory caught up with her as she left the farlins with the other women, and put a hand on her arm, drawing her aside. 'I've not seen ye for a while.'

'You see me every day.'

'Aye, along with all the rest of them. I was wonderin' if ye'd like tae take a wee walk round the town tonight.'

'I said I'd help Ruth with some mendin'. Her hand's still sore, and—'

'So it's true.' It was a flat statement rather than a question. 'You're walkin' out with our Adam, aren't you? I thought I saw the two of you comin' out of the picture house the other night.' Then as she said nothing, but just stared miserably at the top button of his jacket, 'Ye should have told me.'

'I know, and I tried, but I never found the right time.'

'One time's as good as another. Are you and him— d'ye care for him?'

'I like him – and I like you, Rory, it's just that—'

'The lorry's waitin',' Rory said, and turned away.

'It's awful bonny, is it no'?' Etta said wistfully.

'Are ye thinkin' of buyin' it?'

'I couldnae do that!'

'Ye've got the money for it,' Annie pointed out.

It was the middle of December and with the fishing season coming to an end the herring catches were small and dealt with in half a day. The fisher-lassies had been paid their wages, the reward for the long, hard hours they had put in at the farlins, working at times for up to fifteen hours in bitter weather, and now, in their free time, they were all buying gifts to take home.

'It wouldnae be right tae spend so much on myself,' Etta fretted.

'Ye've worked hard – ye deserve a wee treat.'

The afternoon was cold and dark, but the shop window the two of them peered into was brightly lit. Behind the glass, mannequins sitting and standing in elegant comfort, protected from the bitter wind, gazed aloofly out over the heads of the two girls on the pavement.

For the past month, ever since she first saw the dress, Etta had gone back regularly to look at it, convinced each time that someone would have bought it. But it was still there, and the wages she had just received from Rory seemed to burn in her pocket as she looked at the dress. It was cotton, with a V neck and long sleeves; fawn and trimmed with blue round the neck and cuffs. It had been cut in a wraparound style fastened on one hip, with the skirt falling in soft folds from fastening to hem.

'It might not fit me.'

'Ye'll not know until ye try it on. There's no harm in that.'

'Oh, I don't know—'

'I'm not freezin' out here a minute longer,' Annie said decisively. 'Come on.' And before Etta knew it the two of them were inside the shop and Annie was saying to the saleslady, 'We'd like tae see that light browny frock in the window. The one on the lassie that's sitting down.'

Etta's fingers trembled as she took her jersey and skirt off in the tiny changing room. Part of her wanted the dress to fit while the other part hoped that it would be too small or too large, because that would put an end to the matter. But it fitted as though it had been made for her, falling into place with a soft sound that was almost a sigh of relief.

When she stepped outside the cubicle to where Annie waited, the older girl said, 'You look bonny! Ye'll have tae buy it, Etta.'

'It's two whole pounds!' Etta hissed at her.

'Ye've got the money, haven't ye?'

'Aye, but—'

'And ye've bought wee gifts for the folk in Buckie.'

'Aye, but I should be savin' my wages, no' spendin' them on myself.'

'Ye've worked for the money, so ye're entitled tae spend some of it on somethin' ye want. Here.' Annie took her hand and led her to a bank of mirrors near the front of the shop. 'Look at yerself.'

The mirrors gave Etta views from the sides as well as from

the front. The dress fitted perfectly, there was no doubt of that, and it felt better than anything she had ever worn before. She felt taller, slimmer, and as glamorous as any of the actresses she had seen on the cinema screen. But she had never spent money on herself before, and it went against the grain.

'I don't think—' she was beginning when the shop door opened and Adam said, 'Etta? I thought it was you.' He advanced across the carpeted floor with not a trace of embarrassment, his eyes fixed on her. 'You look . ... you look like a princess.'

'That's what I think,' Annie said. 'She's had her eye on this frock for weeks and now we've got our wages I think she should buy it.'

'So do I.'

'No, it costs too much.' Etta made up her mind. 'I'll go and take it off—'

'How much?' Adam asked the saleslady.

'Two pounds.'

He dug a hand into his pocket. 'Here ye are – she'll take it.'

'I can't let you buy me a frock, Adam!'

'Why not? Ye look – ye're beautiful.' His eyes drank in the sight of her reflected again and again in the long mirrors. 'It's my Ne'erday gift tae you, come early.' He thrust the money at the saleswoman, commanding, 'Away and take it off and let the lassie wrap it up and then I'll take the two of you tae a tearoom.'

Annie rushed after Etta as she returned, dazed, to the cubicle.

'So it's you and Adam, is it?' she breathed, her eyes dancing. 'Ye sly wee cat. Wait till I tell the rest of them!'

The drifters carried the bulk of the fisher-lassies' purchases back to Scotland together with their kists, but every passenger on board the special train taking them back to Aberdeen had packed a good dozen sticks of sticky, striped Yarmouth rock in his or her luggage.

Most of them sang and joked and chattered non-stop on

the long journey, too excited to feel tired. They could sleep once they were back in their own beds.

'The bairns'll have grown since I last saw them,' Andra's Jenny said wistfully. 'The wee one'll mebbe not remember me.'

'Ach, it'll not take her long for her tae get tae know you again,' Kirsten comforted. 'It's amazin' how fast a sweetie can sharpen their wee memories.'

'And it's amazin' how soon ye get used tae bein' back with them,' Agnes reminisced. 'When my bairns were wee I spent the first half hour back home huggin' them and the second half hour scoldin' them.'

'One of the best things about bein' a herrin' quine,' Sarah said, 'is gettin' tae travel and see different places.'

'Different farlins, you mean,' Kirsten sniffed. 'An' different herrin'. It's true that the fish we gut in Lerwick's the largest, and in Yarmouth they're the smallest. There's nothin' like havin' a change.'

'Yarm'th's different, though, with the shops and the picture palaces and the music halls,' Sarah argued. 'And even though its grand tae be goin' home again, come the summer we'll be itchin' tae get away on our travels.'

'I'll not,' Mary put in from where she was crowded into a corner.

'Of course ye will, along with the rest of us.'

'I'll not, Sarah.' Mary blushed scarlet and then said, 'That last letter I got from Peter— He says he wants tae marry me.'

Suddenly she had the attention of the entire carriage. 'And ye never told us? You're a close-mouthed one,' Annie shouted from the far corner. 'Have ye written back tae the laddie?'

'Aye.'

'And what did ye say?'

'What d'ye expect her tae say?' Agnes boomed. 'He's a fine laddie. She said yes, didn't ye, my quine?'

'Aye,' Mary confessed, red as a poppy, and they clapped and cheered and began to chant, 'She's goin' tae be a farmer's wifie!'

In the midst of all the excitement Etta realised that Ruth, sitting beside her, was silent, her hands clasped tightly in her lap and her head bowed. She reached out and touched the girl's wrist.

'Are you all right? Is yer hand sore again?'

Ruth lifted her head. 'I'm fine,' she said, her eyes bright and hard, her voice razor-edged. 'It's grand news about Mary, is it no'?'

'Ruth, it'll happen to you one day.'

'I thought it *had* happened tae me,' her cousin said. 'I never thought anyone would be able tae take him from me.'

'I'm sure Ellen didn't mean to do it.'

Ruth's mouth twisted into a thin, hard smile. 'Didn't mean tae? She's deceitful, that one. She meant tae take him, all right, as soon as my back was turned. How else could it have happened so fast? But I'm not bothered,' she went on with a pitiful attempt at a shrug. 'Who'd want a man that turned away from her as easy as Jack Morrison turned from me? You be careful, Etta – never trust a man, especially Adam Pate. He could have any lassie he wanted, and there's always bound tae be plenty after him. You should hold on to Rory, for he's the better of the two.'

She lapsed into a moody silence. The girl on Etta's other side started to talk to her, but as she answered, smiled, and even laughed, Ruth's words burned deeper into her brain.

As it happened, Peter Bain was driving the lorry that collected the Buckie women. At sight of him the women let out a concerted roar and the young man took an involuntary step back, gaping in confusion. Then as Mary was pushed towards him his face went crimson.

'Ye told them?'

'Aye,' she confessed, and buried her own flushed face in his shoulder as the others crowded round them, fighting to kiss the future bridegroom and demanding invitations to the wedding.

'There'll be no weddin' if we don't get ourselves home afore we all freeze tae death,' Agnes shouted above the uproar. 'Peter, where's yer lorry?'

Once outside the station, they boosted Mary up into the cab alongside her intended.

'And straight home, mind,' Kirsten yelled up to Peter. 'No stoppin' tae have a wee cuddle on the way, for it's cold for the rest of us ridin' up behind ye.'

'Aye, ye can do whatever ye want with him once he gets us home, Mary,' Andra's Jenny chimed in, 'but until then we've more need of him than you have.'

It was a cold ride home, but they were all warmly dressed, with scarves about their heads, and there were so many of them that they generated their own warmth. Singing lustily, they endured the journey which, as Sarah pointed out, was better than the farlins, for at least they were sitting on their luggage instead of standing, and they weren't having to work with salt and brine pickle.

A great cheer went up as they drove into Buckie, waving regally at the folk walking along the pavements. It was almost dark and the light pouring from shop windows and doorways created a sense of warmth and cheer.

'Look,' Andra's Jenny pointed, 'is that not Ellen Pate comin' out of that shop?'

'Aye, I think it is. Here, Ellen,' Agnes shouted, cupping her hands to her mouth. 'Give us a wave, pet, and show us yer bonny ring.'

Ellen's head jerked up. She cast a swift glance at the lorry load of shouting, singing women and then turned away.

'Snooty bitch,' someone said, and a few of the women began to sing, 'Here Comes the Bride'. People on the pavement looked around, wondering who the women were shouting at, while Ellen began to walk faster, outrage in the set of her shoulders.

'Stop the lorry!' Ruth's voice shrilled above the shouting and singing. She struggled to the front and banged her fist on the cab and then, as it slowed, turning in towards the kerb, she began to fight her way back towards the tailboard, pushing the others roughly aside as she went.

As soon as the lorry had lurched to a standstill she jumped off, almost losing her balance but only just managing to stay on her feet. Then she began to run along the street, shrilling, 'Ellen! Ellen Pate!'

The women on the back of the lorry stared after her in astonishment. 'She's lost her wits!' Annie said. Ellen finally turned round and Ruth, now only feet away from her, launched herself forward. Because she had been running, the final leap had much the same effect as a battering ram. Ellen reeled back, taken by surprise, and if she had not come up against a house wall she would have been sent sprawling to the ground. Ruth recovered first, grabbing her cousin's shoulders and shaking her hard while she yelled accusations and abuse at the top of her voice.

'Stop her, someone! She's making a right exhibition of herself!' Annie struggled to get through the mass of women now standing up on the lorry to see the fun.

'She's managin' fine, leave her alone,' Agnes said as Ellen, recovering from the shock, started to fight back. In no time at all her neat little cloche hat was rolling in the gutter and the two young women, hands locked in each other's hair, were staggering up and down the pavement. A crowd gathered as swiftly as seagulls round a fishing boat, and people came hurrying out of shop doors and running across the street from the opposite pavement.

Both of the cab doors flew open and Mary tumbled out of one side while Peter jumped from the other. The young farmer raced back along the road and began to fight his way through the crowd, Mary in close pursuit. A disappointed groan went up from the fisher-lassies as Peter caught hold of Ruth and hauled her back, still kicking and shouting and clawing at the air.

Someone took hold of Ellen, but unlike Ruth, she had no

wish to pursue the fight. Instead she slumped against her captor, her hair standing on end, while Mary and Peter hurried Ruth back to the lorry.

'Help her up, will ye?' the young farmer appealed, and as several hands reached down to haul Ruth onto the back of the lorry he grabbed his betrothed's arm. 'Intae the cab with you, Mary, and let's get out of here afore someone brings the police out!'

The doors banged shut and the lorry jolted forward, leaving the crowd behind. As it picked up speed the women gathered round Ruth.

'Ye fairly showed her, pet,' someone said admiringly, and Ruth, her hair all over the place and a bruise already coming up on one cheekbone, beamed, looking happy for the first time since she had received Jack Morrison's final letter.

'Aye,' she said. 'I did that!'

It was the second time that Ellen Pate had been brought home weeping and bedraggled.

'Are you going to make a habit of this?' Bethany wanted to know as she surveyed her stepdaughter.

'It was Ruth Lowrie – she attacked me in the street,' Ellen sniffled. 'Jumped off the lorry bringing the women back and just threw herself on me. For no reason!'

'No reason? Was she not walking out with Jack Morrison before she went down to Yarm'th?' Bethany asked, and the girl glared at her.

'I told you already, they weren't walking out together!'

'Mebbe Ruth thought that they were. Here,' Bethany said as Leezie brought a basin of warm water and a soft cloth into Ellen's bedroom, 'give it to me.' She took the cloth, dipped it into the water, and dabbed gently at a split on Ellen's lower lip. The younger woman winced.

'You're hurting me!'

'Not as much as Ruth did, I'm thinking. Leezie, give me the iodine.' Bethany dabbed it on liberally and Ellen shrieked, tears springing to her eyes. Then she put a tentative hand to her head.

'Has she pulled out my hair? Are there any bald spots?'

'Not that I can see. You're just lucky she didn't have her gutting knife to hand.'

Ellen got up from the bed, pushing her stepmother out of the way, and went to inspect her scalp in the mirror.

'I've a good mind to get the police to her,' she said vindictively. 'That would teach her a lesson.'

'Are you sure you should?' Bethany wanted to know. 'You'd not want Jack to know you were brawling in the streets.'

'I wasn't brawling, it was her!'

'And you just stood there and never even tried to defend yourself? I'd let it be, if I was you.'

'I'm going to write to Jack and ask if I can go to Glasgow early. I won't stay in this place a minute longer!'

'If I was you I'd wait until that lip gets better,' Leezie advised. 'Ye don't want tae meet yer future in-laws with yer poor mouth all swelled up. They might think ye've been fightin'.'

'Get out!' Ellen shrieked, and the housekeeper shrugged and did as she was told. As she left the room, Bethany was sure that her shoulders were shaking.

'Ye should never have set yer sights on someone like that photographer mannie,' Stella told her youngest daughter. 'My mother aye used tae say, "Take cats of your own kind and your kittens won't scratch." That means that ye only face trouble if ye marry away from yer own kind.'

'Poor Jack Morrison's marryin' a cat, right enough,' Ruth said pertly, examining her bruised face in the mirror with a certain amount of pride. 'And they're welcome tae each other.'

'Quite right. There'll be someone else meant for you,' Annie consoled her younger sister. 'Someone better than Jack Morrison.'

Ruth's shoulders suddenly slumped and tears welled up in her brown eyes as she turned to face her mother and her sisters.

'But I didnae want anyone better,' she wailed. 'I wanted him!'

True to her word, Ellen Pate went off to Glasgow to meet her fiancé's family, and with her going, the atmosphere in the house on Cliff Terrace lightened. Bethany promoted one of the older beatsters in the net factory to the post of supervisor, and to her relief the woman was quick to learn the bookwork.

'And she's got more interest in the place than Ellen ever had,' she reported to Jacob. 'The other workers like her and they trust her. I think I've done the right thing this time, which is just as well since we've got a lot of nets in for mending, and orders for new sets to be ready for the summer season. There's plenty of work to do.'

'That's fine, lass.' He stood by the window, looking out, hands in his pockets.

'You might want to take a walk down there tomorrow and have a word with the woman herself, just to set your mind at rest,' she suggested. 'After all, it's your factory.'

'No, no, whatever you decide suits me.'

She frowned at his back, disturbed by his lack of interest in his own business. The settling up had just been completed and the skippers engaged by Jacob had gone home, satisfied with the money they had received for the season. All in all the local boats had done well, though some were saying that the herring shoals were smaller than before. But it seemed to Bethany that since the loss of the *Jess Lowrie* Jacob had lost his usual enthusiasm and drive.

24

With a wedding to organise, Zelda Lowrie was in her element. She flitted about the village persuading neighbours to help with the baking for the occasion, and insisted on going round every home in the fishing community with her daughter to issue invitations to the wedding early in January.

Once they had been round all the cottages, mother and daughter, dressed in their best clothes, walked up the hill to call on Bethany, spurning her invitation to walk into the parlour and opting instead for the kitchen.

'For I've got a favour tae ask of your Leezie,' Zelda said, her still-pretty face glowing with excitement and cold air, 'and anyway, tea tastes better in a kitchen than in a front parlour. Leezie, will you help us with the bakin' and the cookin'? Mary and Peter'll be livin' in the farmhouse with his parents, and the Bains have said that the weddin' party's tae be held in their big barn – they're gettin' it all set up for the occasion – but I want tae do my full share of the arrangements and not leave it all on Mrs Bain's shoulders. Ye'd not mind, would ye, Bethany, if Leezie helped me? Ye've got a fine big range in here.'

'I don't mind, if Leezie's willing; I'd not have time to do much baking myself.'

'It'll be no bother tae me.' Leezie poured out cups of tea all round.

'And ye'll come tae the weddin', of course, Leezie, for

ye're as near tae bein' a member of the family as anyone,'
Zelda said, and as the housekeeper glowed at the compliment
she hurried on, 'I've been lookin' forward tae settin' up
Mary's weddin' since the day she was born. Ye'll mind,
Bethany, how my faither was set against me and your Innes
gettin' wed because of me fallin' with Mary before we got a
church blessin'. It meant a quiet weddin' for us,' she explained
to Leezie, her face clouding at the memories, 'but now here's
my own daughter gettin' wed tae the very lad I'd have chosen
for her mysel'. So we're goin' tae make a right occasion of
it!'

'She's so set on a real traditional weddin' that she's got
me worried,' Mary confessed. 'She's even goin' tae have a
bed-makin'.'

'Are ye?' Leezie was fascinated. 'I mind some grand bed-
makin's in my young day.'

'Ye're more than welcome tae come tae this one if ye like,'
Zelda said. 'It'll no' be quite the same, with Mary and Peter
livin' in the farmhouse instead of havin' a wee place of their
own, but we can still go up there the night before the weddin'
an' set their bedroom tae rights for them.'

'I don't mind that part of it,' Mary said nervously, 'puttin'
the furniture in place and that. It's the other bits of a bed-
makin' that worry me, like fillin' the bed with feathers or
thistles, or grabbin' me and Peter and blackin' our hands and
our feet. I'd not want that sort of thing goin' on in front of
Mrs Bain.'

'As if I would! I used tae work for the woman, so I'm not
likely to misbehave myself under her own roof. All we're
goin' to do,' Zelda assured her daughter earnestly, 'is put your
room tae rights and make it all ready for the two of you. And
Mrs Bain's asked us all tae supper afterwards. It'll be a very
pleasant evenin'.'

Quite a crowd set out for the farm on the wedding eve. Mary's
two younger sisters, Jessie and Meggie, and some of Zelda's

own sisters were included, as were Leezie, Etta, Ruth, Annie and Sarah. They all carried an offering for the wedding – some had food while others were lending their good china. The night was clear and frosty, and although they shivered when they first stepped out of doors into the ice-cold air they were warm by the time they had climbed the hill to the farm, where Mrs Bain and her daughter Elizabeth were waiting to welcome them.

Peter had taken the lorry to Buckie earlier in the day to collect Mary's clothes and the few belongings she wanted to take with her to her new home, and in no time at all the womenfolk had put the place to rights. Mary hovered round her mother, eagle-eyed, but Zelda, as she had promised, was on her best behaviour.

Then they moved on to the barn that Mr Bain and Peter had cleared and cleaned out in readiness for the wedding party. The place had been decorated with great bunches of greenery and ribbons, trestle tables had been set up and a makeshift platform erected for the musicians. The women bustled around, decorating the kettles with bows of ribbon and setting out tablecloths and dishes and bowls and boxes of sugared almonds and the conversation lozenges that were a feature of every wedding. By the time they were done the barn was pleasantly festive, and the tables glittered with the beautiful china beloved of fisher-folk.

'It's all grand,' Zelda enthused when they finally sat down to supper in the large farm kitchen. 'It's goin' tae be a bonny, bonny weddin'.' She laid a hand on Mary's, her eyes suddenly bright with tears of emotion. 'This is what I've been lookin' forward tae since the day ye were born, my lass. I swore on that day that you'd have the sort of weddin' I'd have wanted for mysel' if only I'd not had such a dour father.'

'He was strict, I'll grant ye that,' Mrs Bain agreed. 'But he'd be right proud if he could see what a fine marriage you made, Zelda. And he was a grand shepherd, one of the best we ever had.'

'Mebbe he should have had sheep, then, instead of bairns,' Mary muttered.

'Who'd have thought, Zelda, when you worked in this very kitchen and looked after wee Peter for me, that one day he'd be marryin' with your daughter?' Mrs Bain said. 'It's a happy time for you and me both, so just you think on tomorrow an' forget about the past.'

'Aye, ye're right.' Zelda dashed a hand across her eyes, and beamed around the table. 'Now then, let's have a song.'

It was late, and they were beginning to think of going home, when the door opened and Peter came in. His mother promptly slammed the palms of both hands down on the table.

'At last,' she roared. 'Zelda, where's the boot polish?' And as Zelda triumphantly produced two large tins from her pocket, 'Come on, lassies, catch a hold of him – and Mary too!'

And the kitchen erupted into uproar as the bride and groom, protesting loudly, were pinned into chairs and their shoes, socks and stockings hauled off in readiness for the traditional foot blacking.

It was a fine wedding, fine enough to satisfy even Zelda. Mary, flushed and glowing with happiness, made a beautiful bride, and when the church service was over she and her new husband led their guests on the wedding procession to the Bains' farm.

Paraffin stoves lit first thing in the morning ensured that the barn was warm by the time the bridal party and their guests arrived. There was enough food to satisfy even the greediest guest, and at the tables set aside for the younger folk conversation lozenges were being passed around amid a lot of giggling and blushing.

Most chose their lozenge carefully, but when the dish was passed to Ruth she shut her eyes before dipping her hand into it, closing her fist about the sweet so that nobody else could see it. After reading it, she leaned across the table and presented it to Rory.

Startled, he glanced at the words, 'I Choose You,' and then stared at her. 'What's this for?'

'Because I want you to have it. And now,' she said cheekily as the musicians began to tune up, 'you can ask me up for the first dance, Rory Pate.'

Etta was wearing the dress Adam had bought for her in Yarmouth. 'You look bonny,' he murmured into her ear as he drew her onto the dance floor. 'I knew that that dress was just made for you. Here,' he slipped a conversation lozenge into her hand, 'I kept this one for you.'

'Be My Sweetheart,' the pink writing spelled out against the white background.

'D'you mean it?'

'Of course. Every man needs a sweetheart, and every lassie needs a beau. And I couldnae find one that said, "meet me outside in five minutes."'

'It's too cold to go outside.'

'There's a shed just a few steps from here, with some winter hay still in it. Would ye like tae see it?'

'Why would I want tae go and look at a shed?' Etta wanted to know, and he laughed down at her.

'Because it would keep us fine and warm if we were tae decide tae take a rest from the dancin'. I'm takin' a stroll outside after this dance, and if ye feel like takin' a bit of fresh air yoursel' in a minute or two, I'd be willin' tae show ye the shed.'

Once the dance ended he disappeared like a twist of smoke up a chimney, but it took some time for Etta to pluck up the courage to sidle towards the barn door. With every step she expected someone to call her back, or ask where she was going, but at last she reached it and slipped through it. A hand immediately came out of the darkness to grasp hers.

'Adam?'

'Who else were ye expectin'?' he said against her mouth. Then, when he had kissed her, 'No salt this time, just the sweetness. Come on—'

'I can't see,' she protested as he drew her away from the barn. 'I'm scared I'll trip over somethin' and fall.'

'You don't need tae see, and ye'll not trip. I'll look after ye,' Adam said, and stumbling over uneven ground, she followed where he led, trusting in him.

Bethany's faint hope that after Yarmouth, Adam might be content to return to his studies, was dashed when he announced his intention of going line fishing with Jem during the winter months.

She even approached Innes when the two of them met in the street a week after Mary's wedding, and suggested to him that Adam should be taken into Thomson's yard as an engineering apprentice.

His reply was a flat, uncompromising, 'No.'

'What d'you mean, no?' she asked, astonished. 'What's wrong with my Adam serving his engineering apprenticeship in the boatyard? Other laddies do it.'

'Other laddies *want* tae do it. Does Adam?'

'I'm sure he'd be pleased to get the chance.'

'The way you thought he'd be pleased tae get a university education?'

Bethany's temper began to rise. 'He's proved me wrong there, I'll admit that, and now I've accepted that his heart's set on going to sea. But an engineering apprenticeship would give him a better chance of being skipper of his own boat, or an engineer on a cargo boat or one of those big ocean liners. Is that not why your Will's serving his apprenticeship?'

'Aye, but Will cares more for the engines than the fishin'. He'd sooner be engineer on a drifter than a deckhand or even a skipper. He's like me.'

'How can he be like you when he's not afraid of the sea?' Bethany said waspishly, and regretted her quick tongue as soon as she saw the anger flash over her brother's normally placid features.

'I'm not afraid of the sea, Bethany.' There was a sharp edge to Innes's voice now. 'It makes me sick tae my stomach, just, and I see no sense in bein' sick day in and day out when I can be hale and hearty on land instead. And me and Zelda would never try tae force one of our bairns intae somethin' they didn't want for themsel's.'

He fell silent as someone brushed past them, then went on when they were alone again, with nobody in earshot, 'There's another thing – the townsfolk don't always take kindly tae loons from the fishin' community takin' more than their share of the engineerin' apprenticeships. Their own laddies are lookin' tae be engineers in land jobs, and sometimes they find it hard tae get in anywhere because of skippers takin' the apprenticeships for their own lads.'

'I just want what's best for my son!'

'What you're wantin', Bethany, is a way of takin' the laddie away from the *Fidelity* and away from James. I've always wondered,' Innes said, 'why you never sought an apprenticeship for Rory.'

'Rory had the cooperage, he didn't need anything else.'

'If he'd been allowed tae follow his heart, though, he might well have become an engineer, and a good one at that. He'd the right feel for it, just like Will. That lad used tae spend hours with me, gettin' me tae teach him about all the different kinds of engine. He could draw them well, too, and that's somethin' I never could do.'

Bethany suddenly found herself on the defensive. 'He never said that he wanted to be an apprentice.'

'I'd have thought you'd have noticed for yourself where his interests lay, but mebbe you were too taken up with what was tae become of Adam. Did you never think, Bethany,' Innes probed, 'that he could have taken on the cooperage instead of Rory? After all, he's Gil's son too – is he no'?' And then, as she stared at him, speechless, 'If Adam's still hungry for the sea our James is the best teacher he could have. And if you're so desperate tae come between them, why don't ye buy a drifter for the lad and be done with it? That way, once he's learned his trade he can go out on his own, instead of stayin' in the *Fidelity*. And now, if ye'll excuse me, I have tae get back tae work.'

He tipped his cap, and went loping off along the street, leaving Bethany in a state of confusion.

Innes's final words hung in her mind, gradually forming into the thread of an idea. After a week of deep thought, she called on Jacob.

'It's time we thought about another drifter.'

'Tae tell the truth, lass, I've no' got the heart tae think of replacin' the *Jess Lowrie*,' he said, the pain of his loss still raw in his voice.

'It's business, Jacob. We'll be a boat down come the summer fishing. We could have one built,' she suggested, eyeing him closely. 'The *Fidelity*'s a good age, and the *Homefarin*'s not far behind her.'

'They've still got years in them yet.'

'But mebbe this is the time for a new boat, built to our own specifications. If we commissioned it from Thomson's yard it would mean that Innes would be in charge of installing the engine, and there's few engineers better than he is. We could call her *Jess Lowrie II*,' Bethany coaxed.

'It would cost us.'

'I know, but I was thinking – if I could raise a third of the money, and you could raise another third, we could surely borrow a third from the bank.'

'How would you raise that sort of money?'

'I could take out a mortgage on the house. We'd be paying for the drifter as it was built, so we'd not have to find all the money at the one time.'

'Even so, if anythin' went wrong – if the next two seasons were tae be bad for us, say – you and your family could be homeless.'

Bethany shrugged. 'Ellen's already gone, and from the few

letters she's troubled to send she seems well settled in Glasgow and bent on staying there. No doubt Rory'll find himself a wife soon enough and want a place of his own, and I'd be just as happy in a cottage. After all, that's what I came from. As for Adam – he's old enough to see to himself. D'you think that you could persuade the bank to advance a third of the cost?'

'I think they can trust me.' A spark of interest began to glow in his eyes. 'After all, I've been dealin' with them for nigh on twenty years and I've never let them down yet.'

'You'll speak to them?'

'No harm in doin' that.'

'Then I'll find out how much I could raise on the house,' Bethany said. 'At least Gil had the good sense to leave it to me and not to his children.'

She raised the subject of the proposed new drifter one evening when Leezie was visiting cousins and she and Rory and Adam were alone at the kitchen table.

Adam reacted with enthusiasm, as she had hoped. 'It'd be grand, havin' a new drifter built to whatever specifications Mr McFarlane wants. Will Uncle James be skipper?'

'Mebbe. Jacob's not fully agreed to the idea yet, but I know now that I can raise my share of the cost, and I'm determined to coax him into it.'

'If he agrees, and if Uncle James takes her over, that means that I'd be crewin' on her.'

'Eventually,' Bethany said, 'you could take her over yourself – be her skipper.'

'Me?'

'The drifter's not even been commissioned yet. I was thinking – if you were to go to one of those nautical colleges for a year, you'd learn all you need to know faster than if you worked your way up from being a deckhand.'

His enthusiasm suddenly drained away. 'So that's what it's all about – more learnin'!'

'The sort of learning you want, though, that's the difference,' Bethany said swiftly. 'You'd learn about engines and navigation and the things that James has taken years to learn. And at the end of it you'd have all the knowledge you need to take over the new drifter.'

'Not the fishin' knowledge, though.'

'You're already getting that, aren't you? You've done a full season at the fishing now, and you'd still be able to go north in the summer, for the college year doesn't start till after that. You enjoyed those classes at night school, didn't you? This would just be more of the same. '

Adam chewed at his lower lip, then said, 'But this would be all the time, not just in the evenin's. It's still a lot of classroom learnin' and bookreadin'.'

'Will you just think about it?' Bethany urged, and he pushed his chair back with a swift gesture and got to his feet.

'Mebbe – but I'm not sayin' yes until I've had a chance tae think about it,' he said, and walked out of the kitchen. Almost at once, the front door opened and closed.

'Give him time tae himself,' Rory advised.

'Would you—?'

'If you're askin' me tae speak tae him about it, the answer's no. He'd give up the whole notion if we both started on at him.'

'But going on the way he is – it's such a waste of a good brain!'

'Waste? You call goin' tae the fishin' a waste? It was good enough for your faither and his faither afore him, and it's good enough for your brother. And it's the fishin' that keeps the net factory, and the cooperage and the boatyards goin'. It's the fishin' that made Jacob McFarlane the wealthy man he is!'

Bethany was startled by the sharp note in his voice. Rory never lost his temper, never even displayed irritation or impatience, but now he was looking at her with a mixture of both in his clear blue eyes.

'It's just that – Adam has choices,' she found herself trying to explain.

'Choices, no' obligations. There's a difference.'

'Are you thinking about the cooperage? That's what you wanted to do, isn't it?' Bethany asked, recalling what Innes had said about Rory showing an interest in engineering.

'It was what I was always meant tae do.'

'What choice would you have made if the cooperage hadn't been waiting for you?'

'I don't know why you're talkin' of me havin' choices when you won't accept Adam's right tae have one,' Rory said, and the accusation so stunned Bethany that she did not even notice that he had avoided answering her question. 'Anyway,' he went on, 'ordinary workin' folk like us are never asked what we want tae do with our own lives. We have tae make the most of what we're faced with and we have tae earn our food and the roof over our heads and the clothes on our backs, and that's all that's tae it. Look at you – I doubt if you married my faither of yer own free choice.'

Bethany gasped, floundered, and finally managed to choke out, 'Of course I did!'

'I never thought that, even as a wee laddie. It's my guess that you were expected tae marry with the first man who asked ye, and there was my faither, a well set up widower lookin' for a second wife tae care for his house and his bairns and see tae his own comforts. I mind once when I was on the farm with Peter,' Rory went on while she stared at him, completely taken aback, 'we found a wee bird that had got trapped under a bit of nettin' in his mother's kitchen garden. Peter took it out and gave it tae me tae hold in my hand. It didnae struggle, because it knew that there was no use in that, but I could feel its wee heart just burstin' tae be set free, and I could see the misery in its eyes. It minded me of the way you looked at times.' He spoke as if it made all the sense in the world. 'It wasnae fair on you, havin' tae take on two wee bairns you'd not birthed yoursel'. I'm no' complainin', mind,' a smile tugged at the corners of his wide, strong mouth, 'for you did a grand job and we'd some good times together, you and me and Ellen, when we were wee. But the best times were always when my faither was away from home.'

He was right, and there was no sense in denying it. Bethany could still remember the sense of freedom she experienced each time Gil was out of the house, and the feeling of being trapped the moment he stepped back over the threshold.

'I didn't realise that you saw so much and understood so much.'

He shrugged, and then said, 'You changed when Adam was born, though. You were more settled after that. Mebbe you just needed tae have a bairn of your own.'

'Do you ever feel trapped, Rory? Innes told me the other day that you could have served your apprenticeship as an engineer.'

He stared down at the table, then said, 'It's like I said – I was born tae be a cooper, like my father. And I like workin' with wood, for it's a livin' thing.'

The doorbell rang, and she put out a hand to stop him as he began to get up.

'I'll see to it.'

As she opened the front door Jacob stepped from the dark of the night into the light and warmth of the hall, ever confident of his welcome in this house.

'There you are, my quine. I'm glad you're at home, for I've brought you a visitor – a man willin' tae put up a third of the cost of havin' that new drifter built,' he said, and stepped aside to let Lorne Kerr enter.

25

Bethany burst into the kitchen, where Rory was cutting another slice of cake for himself. 'Jacob's here, and he's brought a fish merchant from Edinburgh,' she hissed.

'What's a mannie from Edinburgh doin' in Buckie at this time on a January night?'

'Jacob says he wants to put money into this new drifter – and look at me in my working clothes and my pinny!'

'Ye look fine.'

'I do not! Rory, I've put them into the front parlour; could you go in and see if they want whisky or port or mebbe tea, and talk to them for a minute or two – just until I get time to sort myself out?' Bethany begged, and fled up to her bedroom, where she tore off the apron and blouse and skirt and splashed water over her flushed face before pulling a suitable dress from the depths of the huge wooden wardrobe. Once dressed, she unpinned her hair and gave it a swift brushing before pinning it up again.

Her unexpected guests, glasses in hand, were seated on each side of the fire, which Rory had poked into a good blaze, and Lorne was questioning him about the cooperage.

'Ye're welcome tae come and see round it,' Rory was saying as Bethany came into the room. 'This is a busy time for us, ken, with all the new barrels tae be made for the summer fishin', but even so, you'd be welcome.'

'The busiest time is the best time to see how a place

operates,' Lorne said, and then as Bethany entered he scrambled to his feet and offered her his chair. 'I insist,' he said when she shook her head. 'I'll be very comfortable over there. Would tomorrow do for the cooperage?'

'Aye, of course. Ye're only here for a day or two?' Rory asked.

'I'm here for as long as I care to stay. I want to see everything that Jacob and your stepmother are involved with, and I'd like to go out on one of the drifters if I can.'

'Jem's line fishin' in the *Homefarin*',' Jacob said. 'I'm sure he'd no' mind takin' you out with him.'

'Why would you want to put money into a drifter?' Bethany asked when Rory had excused himself and gone up to his room.

Lorne fixed her with his clear green gaze. 'Speaking to you and to Jacob in Great Yarmouth made me realise that fish doesn't just appear in boxes at the markets,' he said. 'I've become interested in the people involved in the fishing process – those who make the nets, catch the fish, smoke and pickle them, the coopers who make the barrels – and when Jacob mentioned in a telephone conversation that you had persuaded him to commission a new drifter I realised that this was the perfect opportunity for me to become more closely involved.'

'So you've decided, Jacob?'

'Aye, I have. Ye've got a good head on yer shoulders, my quine, better than a lot of men, and if you think a new drifter's a good idea then so do I.'

'I would say that it's an excellent idea,' Lorne said, and then, raising his glass to Bethany, 'and I would also like to say that it will be a pleasure doing business with someone who has beauty as well as brains.'

Adam walked from Cliff Terrace along East Church Street to the town centre, where he took the road leading down towards the sea and then along the shore. He passed the rows of fishermen's cottages known as the Yardie and walked on to Buckpool where, in the Main Street, he knocked at a door.

It was opened by his Aunt Stella, her face darkening when she recognised the caller.

'Yes?' Her voice was flat and uncompromising.

'Is my Uncle James at home?'

'Aye, he is.'

'Could I speak tae him?' Adam gave her his warmest smile, and then thought to himself that he might as well have grinned at a rock for all the reaction he got.

'Wait here and I'll get him,' she said, and closed the door in his face.

There was no understanding his Aunt Stella, Adam thought as he paced up and down the street, hands thrust into his pockets. In any other instance he would have been invited inside, especially on a cold January night like this. When he visited his Uncle Innes's cottage he just lifted the latch, like everyone else, and walked in, sure of a warm welcome, but not here – never here. He got on fine with his uncle and his cousins, but for some reason Aunt Stella had never taken to him.

The latch lifted and James Lowrie came out onto the pavement, closing the door after him. 'Adam? Is there somethin' wrong?'

'No. Well, mebbe . . . I just need tae speak tae ye.'

James glanced over his shoulder at the closed door, and then jerked his head towards the narrow passage that led round the side of the house to the back yard. 'We can stand in here, out of the cold,' he said, and led the way. Once in the passage he said awkwardly, 'Your aunt's givin' the kitchen a bit of a clean and she doesnae like folk tae see the place in a mess. What's troublin' ye?'

'It's this drifter that Jacob McFarlane's havin' built tae replace the *Jess Lowrie*. You'll have heard all about it?'

'He told me. Tae my mind he could have bought a boat just as easy, and had it in time for the new herrin' season,'

James grunted, 'but if he feels he can afford tae build a new drifter, then that's his business.'

'It's not just him that's payin' for it; my mither's puttin' up some of the money, so they'll own it between them.'

'Bethany? Where did she find the money for that?'

'I don't know, but she has. She told me and Rory all about it just this evenin'. She's not certain that Mr McFarlane's goin' along with the idea, but—'

'Wait a minute,' James interrupted, 'are you sayin' that this is all Bethany's idea?'

'It seems so. The thing is,' Adam hurried on, 'now she wants me tae go tae one of the nautical colleges in the autumn. She says that if I do that I'll learn enough tae be able tae take over the new boat when I'm done.'

'Does she now?'

'I don't care for the idea of more studyin', but my mither might be right. What d'you think I should do?'

'Don't bring me intae it. It's between you and your mother.'

'But she doesnae understand how I feel, and you do,' Adam argued.

'I think,' his uncle said after a long silence, 'that you should take yer time over yer answer. And if ye want, we'll talk about it again, later. For now, it's too cold tae stand here.'

Even so, he stayed where he was for a while after Adam left, turning the boy's news over in his mind. Since Bethany was behind the plan to build a new drifter, then it seemed clear to James that she hoped to use it as a way of getting Adam away from the *Fidelity* – and from him. He could easily talk the younger man into turning down the offer of a college place, but if he played Bethany at her own game then Adam, the person who mattered most to both of them, would become little more than a pawn, and James didn't want that.

'What was he after?' Stella asked as soon as he stepped inside the door.

'Nothin' important,' he said, and she bit off the end of her sewing thread with a vicious snap of the teeth.

Lorne Kerr became a familiar sight about Buckie in the next two weeks. He toured the net factory and the smokehouse and the cooperage, and he went line fishing on the *Homefaring* with Jem and Adam.

'I'll say this for him – even when the boat took a bit of a tossin' the man did his fair share of the work, though he looked a bit green about the mouth,' Adam reported in the Pate kitchen as he downed a large plate of meat and potatoes.

The day after his fishing trip Lorne asked Bethany to drive around the area with him. 'I've hired a car for the day, but it's not the same without a companion. It would be helpful to be with someone who knows the place. You can tell me something of the villages along the coast.'

'Jacob can do that, and he's got more time than me,' she pointed out, and he grinned down at her. When she first met him in Yarmouth, and when he first arrived in Buckie, he had been immaculately dressed, but during his stay on the Moray Firth he had reverted to more casual wear, and now he was clad in a thick gansey of the type the fishermen wore. He had allowed the wind to ruffle his normally immaculate hair; the result gave him a slightly piratical air.

'Are you scared to be alone with me, Bethany Pate? I could always hire a chauffeur if you want a chaperone.'

'Of course I'm not scared!' She felt herself reddening, and hated herself for it.

'Good. I'll collect you from the house at two o'clock this afternoon,' he said.

Lorne Kerr was a pleasant companion, though it took Bethany, unused to dealing with a man on a social footing and unused to being driven in a car, some time to relax as he drove along the coast, weaving in and out of the fishing villages –

Findochty, Portknockie, Cullen and Portsoy – strung along the coastline.

'You must be ready for a cup of tea,' he said some time after they had started out.

'I'm fine, and anyway, there's nowhere around here that serves tea. We're not in Edinburgh,' she pointed out. 'We don't have hotels waiting to cater for folk.'

'We brought it with us. Jacob's housekeeper very kindly made up a basket for me.' Lorne drew the car into the side of the road at a spot high above the Firth. 'It's in the back.'

As well as tea in a thermos flask the basket held neatly cut sandwiches, biscuits, scones and a sponge cake, together with milk, sugar, napkins, cups and all the necessary cutlery.

'I think Mrs Duthie enjoyed making it up,' Lorne said as he unpacked it. 'She used to be a housekeeper to some titled people, and I think she misses the little niceties that the lady of the house demanded.'

'I didn't know that. How did you find out?'

'I'm interested in people; I always have been. I take after my mother in that way, though my sister says I'm just inquisitive. Sugar?'

As they had their tea he told her about his sister and her family, and about his late wife, who had been fond of music and had encouraged him to learn to dance.

'It's a pleasant pastime and I miss it now that I no longer have a partner. Do you dance, Bethany?'

'We never had much time for such things,' Bethany said dryly. 'There was always more important work to be done.' And then, with a sidelong glance, 'Speaking of work, I would have thought you'd be needed back in Edinburgh by now.'

'I have well-trained employees. There's no sense in building up a business only to become its slave. I always made sure along the way that I taught others to work well for me. And why should I hurry back to the bustle of the city when I can enjoy a good long holiday in a bonny place like this?' He paused to indicate the Firth stretching to the horizon, glittering in the sharp January sunlight. 'Very bonny,' he added, turning to survey Bethany. 'Though now that I've done all I came to Buckie to do, I suppose I must think of returning.'

'Your sister and her family will be glad to see you back home.'

'I'm sure that it will do them good to be rid of me for once,' Lorne said easily. 'Sometimes folk feel obliged to keep offering hospitality to a man on his own. The one thing I regret in my life is that Margaret and I never had children. I would have liked to have had a daughter to spoil, or a son to follow me in the business. I enjoyed my fishing trip with Jem and I enjoyed working alongside your Adam. He's a competent fisherman.'

'Fishing's not what his father wanted for him, but he's set on going to sea.'

'We work hardest at the employment we want most.'

'He says you did well on the drifter,' Bethany said, and Lorne laughed.

'I don't know about that. Look.' He held his hands out, palms up, and she saw the fresh calluses where he had been handling the ropes. 'I'm too used to soft living. And I had to swallow hard a few times, I can tell you, when the waves grew and the boat began to toss. I'd a sudden notion to say that I'd just get off now, but there was nowhere to go. So I had to persevere, and it worked out well in the end. Though I was glad to see the shoreline appearing as we made our way back. I'm trusting you not to repeat anything of this to Adam, mind.'

Two days before Lorne Kerr returned to Edinburgh the entire Lowrie family was invited to dinner at Jacob's house to celebrate the commission of the new drifter.

An extra table had to be squeezed into the dining room in order to accommodate the twenty-one people, including Lorne Kerr, Mary's husband Peter Bain and Jacob himself, and extra staff was hired to help Mrs Duthie in the kitchen. The older members of the family, including the newly-weds, sat at one table with Jacob and Lorne, while the younger members were at the other table.

'Have you any news of Ellen?' Zelda asked Bethany, who cast a swift look over her shoulder at the other table before answering. Seeing that Ruth was too busy tormenting Adam to listen to their talk, she said, 'She seems to be well-settled in Glasgow, and the Morrison family have taken to her.'

'She'll be comin' back tae Buckie for the weddin', though?'

'From what she says, I think she'd prefer to marry in Glasgow.'

'She'd be well advised tae do that,' Stella said stiffly.

At the other table, Etta had been seated opposite Adam. Every now and again he smiled across at her, and once she thought that his foot had pressed hers beneath the table, though she could not be certain. For the most part she sat silent while the others chattered and laughed all about her, toying with her food.

'Etta, are ye all right?' asked Jessie, sitting beside her. 'You're not sickenin' for somethin', are ye?'

'No, I'm fine. Just not hungry,' Etta assured her, and looked across at Adam again. He looked, she thought enviously, as though he hadn't a care in the world.

'That man's taken a right shine tae Bethany,' Stella said as she and her husband walked home at the end of the evening.

'Lorne Kerr? Away, woman!'

'I'm surprised you didnae see it for yoursel'. He'd be a grand catch for a widow woman; I've heard that he's got as much money as Jacob McFarlane, and a fine big hoosie in Edinburgh. Your sister could do very well for hersel'.'

'Bethany has more sense than tae get tied down tae another marriage,' James said roughly. 'Would ye listen tae the noise these lassies are makin'?' He nodded at their daughters, walking ahead of them. 'They've no consideration for the folk that's tryin' tae sleep!'

He pulled up his coat collar and quickened his pace, and Stella hurried after him, well pleased with the thought she had planted in his mind.

'I've been watchin' our Mary,' Zelda said. 'It's been more than a month since she and Peter wed, but I've not seen any signs of a bairn on the way.'

'It's surely too early for that.'

'Oh, it just takes the once. And I can tell the signs early – sometimes before the lassie herself knows it. For instance,' Zelda said with a sidelong look at Etta, 'I might not see them in our Mary yet, but I can see them in you clear enough.'

'What?' They were working in the little wash house built on to the rear of the cottage. Etta had been hauling the dripping clothes out of the boiler and lowering them into a tub of cold water so that her aunt could plunge them and then wring them out by hand before putting them through the mangle. Now she dropped the tongs, which hit the edge of the boiler before bouncing off and disappearing into the steaming hot water.

Sweat had been running down her face; now it turned to ice, and a chill went down her spine as she stared at her aunt. 'What are you talkin' about?'

'About you carryin' a bairn. I'm not blind, lassie,' Zelda said as Etta began to shake her head vehemently. 'And I'm not angry either. I've been waitin' for ye tae tell me. You surely knew it yourself?'

'I wondered,' Etta whispered through numbed lips. 'But I thought mebbe I was wrong.'

'Ye're not wrong, and hopin' won't do a bit of good. Come on,' Zelda said gently, 'the washin' can wait while we have a nice cup of tea and a bit of a talk.'

She took Etta's hand and led her to the kitchen, which was empty, for once, and poured two cups of tea from the pot on the hob, adding a dollop of condensed milk to both. She also put several spoonfuls of sugar into Etta's cup. 'Tae help tae settle yer nerves,' she said comfortably, sitting down at the table. Then, carefully, 'Are ye willin' tae tell me who the faither is? I'll not force ye if ye'd rather keep silent.'

Now that Etta's secret fears were confirmed there was no sense in keeping anything back. She needed help, and Aunt Zelda was the only person she could turn to. 'It's Adam,' she said huskily.

'Oh, pet!' Zelda covered one of Etta's hands with her own. 'I thought it might be, but I was hopin' I'd the wrong way of it.'

'Why?' Etta looked up sharply. 'What's wrong with him?'

'Nothin' at all – I'm as fond of the lad as I am of you and all my bairns. It's Bethany; Adam's the apple of that woman's eye, and I'm sure she'd her heart set on him marryin' with some rich man's daughter.'

'He loves me!'

'Has he said?'

'No, but I'd not have—' Etta hesitated, then rushed on, 'not if I thought he didnae love me.'

'Does he know about the bairn?' Zelda asked, and then, when Etta shook her head, 'He has tae know, pet. Why haven't ye told him?'

'I – I wasnae certain myself, and I wanted tae wait until . . .' Etta's voice trailed away, then the tears began to flow. 'Aunt Zelda, what'll I do if he refuses tae marry me?'

'You'll stay here with me and your Uncle Innes, and you'll have the bairn and we'll help ye tae raise it, that's what you'll do.'

'Does Uncle Innes know?'

'Of course not. I'd never say a word tae him without speakin' tae you first. But he'll not be angry, and he'll agree with everythin' I've said. We both know what it's like tae be in your situation, my quine. But the first thing tae do,' Zelda finished, leaning forward and stroking Etta's hair back from her forehead, 'is tae tell the laddie about the wee one.'

'Aunt Bethany—'

'We'll worry about her when the time comes. No need tae go seekin' trouble before then.'

At almost the same moment, Bethany was staring in disbelief at Lorne Kerr, who stood in the middle of her front parlour, hat in hand.

'Come with me,' he had said as soon as the door closed behind Leezie. 'Come to Edinburgh.'

'Why should I do that?'

'Because I want you to meet my family and my friends.'

'I can't.'

'Can't, or won't?'

'I can't,' Bethany said again. 'I've too much to do. The house, for one—'

'You have a very capable housekeeper.'

'There's the net factory, I need to keep an eye on that.'

'You have an overseer, and Jacob will be here to watch over it. After all, it is his factory.'

'And there are the financial ledgers as well.'

'Again, I'm sure that they could be left to Jacob. In fact, I know that he would be quite willing to take over all your duties for a week or two.'

'You've spoken to him about this idea of yours, even before you spoke to me?'

'Last night, when all his guests had gone home. I knew exactly what you would say when I asked you,' Lorne said, putting his hat down on a table, 'and I wanted to make sure that every argument could be defeated. So yes, I did speak to Jacob.'

'I'm not a possession!' Bethany sought refuge in anger. 'I can make my own decisions.'

'Then decide to come to Edinburgh with me. I want you to see my home, which I hope will be to your liking, and to meet my sister and my friends. I want you to realise that you could be just as content – perhaps even more so – in Edinburgh as in Buckie.'

'You make it sound like a proposal of marriage.' Bethany suddenly realised that her fist was still gripping the pen she had been working with when Lorne arrived, and that it was beginning to hurt her fingers. She put it down, glad of the excuse to turn away from him.

'We haven't reached that stage yet,' he was saying now, 'though I'd not mind if we did, for we're very well suited, you and me. For the moment, though, I'm just asking you to visit Edinburgh. I know that my sister would be happy to have you as her house guest; the two of you would take tea with her friends and visit the theatre together and spend hours in the shops. You would love the shops in Princes Street, Bethany. Edinburgh would suit you, I'm sure of it.'

'I'm very content with what I have now.'

'Are you? Your children are grown. You had to work to support them and yourself when you were widowed,' Lorne said, 'but they no longer have need of you. I know what a good business partner you've been to Jacob McFarlane; you could help me to build my business, and' – his eyes travelled over her in a swift, all-encompassing glance – 'you would be an asset in my home. My first marriage gave me a taste for the companionship and the pleasures of sharing my life with a woman. We've both been alone for too long, Bethany. A woman of your beauty and your temperament should not be on her own.'

'As it happens, my temperament is well suited to the single life.' Bethany rose from her chair. 'My marriage was more of a business arrangement than a love match, as Jacob has no doubt told you, and I've no wish to repeat the experience.' She held out her hand. 'I wish you a good journey, Lorne.'

'I've offended you. That was never my intention.'

'I'm not offended.' She drew her fingers from his as soon as was decent, clasping them tightly in her other hand.

'If you change your mind you only need to let me know.' He picked up his hat. 'Now I must go and spend a little time with Jacob. He has been a very good host.'

'Why don't you invite *him* to Edinburgh, then?'

'Perhaps, one day,' Lorne said, with just a glimmer of a smile. '*Au revoir*, Bethany Pate. No need to trouble the house-keeper, I can let myself out.'

As the front door closed behind him Bethany relaxed her hands and held them out before her. As she had suspected, they were shaking; whether from shock or from anger she could not tell.

26

A cold wind swept in from the sea, and Etta, huddled behind a pile of coiled ropes and lobster pots, had long since begun to shiver. She had watched from the shadows as the crew of the *Homefaring* came ashore, but there had been no sign of Adam, and if he didn't come soon, she thought, she would have to go back home.

She was on the verge of leaving when at last two men came along the harbour wall. One was unmistakeably Adam, his voice and laughter giving him away, and when the other spoke she realised that it was Jem.

She shrank back, dismayed and unwilling to let anyone witness her meeting with Adam. Then, as they began to draw level with the lobster pots, her fidgeting uncertainty caused one of the pots to rock and topple. The two men stopped, peering through the darkness.

'Who's that skulkin' about?' Jem barked. 'Come on out of it and show yersel'!'

'It's only me.'

'Etta? What're you doin' out here?' Adam wanted to know.

'I was waitin' tae have a wee word with ye.'

'It must be an important word tae keep ye waitin' about here in the cold and the dark. I'll see ye in the mornin', lad,' Jem said. 'Good night tae ye, lass,' and he walked on as Adam took Etta's hands in his.

'You're frozen. How long have ye been waitin' here?'

'Long enough. I'm fine,' she added hastily as he began to take his thick jacket off.

'Your hands are like ice. And your face too,' he said, the back of his hand warm as it brushed across the tip of her nose. 'Here.' He put the jacket about her shoulders and she clutched at it gratefully, burying her face in it to inhale the smell of him.

'Is somethin' the matter?' he asked as his arm crept round her, 'or is it just that we've not seen much of each other lately? You know what it's like in this place; when I'm not on the boat, my mother keeps—'

'I'm expectin', Adam.'

'Expectin' what?'

She had been fretting over her condition for weeks, and she had been trying all day to summon up the courage to tell him about it. Now that the news was out, his total lack of awareness infuriated her. 'A bairn, ye daft loon,' she said sharply. 'What else would I be expectin'?'

'A bairn?' His arms fell away from her and he took a step back. 'A bairn?' he said again, and then, 'Are ye sure?'

'Of course I'm sure. And if I'd any doubts, they're gone for good now, since my Aunt Zelda's noticed it for herself.'

'Are you sayin' that it's mine?' Adam asked, and then yelped as the toe of her boot cracked against his shin.

'Ye devil!' she screeched, too angry to keep her voice low. 'Sayin' such a thing tae me! No, get away from me!' She pushed him away as he tried to take her into his arms again. He staggered back and almost tripped over the lobster pot she had earlier dislodged, and as he danced about in an effort to keep his balance Etta started walking quickly away, so blinded by tears that she could easily have gone over the edge and into the water below.

'Wait – Etta, wait!' Adam caught up with her and grabbed her arm, turning her towards him. She fought him off, knotting her fists and lashing out at him, her blows catching his face, shoulders and chest.

'Etta!' he protested as he tried to ward off the assault, but she was too far gone to listen, or to care. By the time he finally managed to capture both her hands in his the two of them were breathless, and the tears were dripping from Etta's chin.

'I'm sorry – I'm sorry, I shouldnae have said that. It was just the shock of hearing you say— Etta!' he said as she kicked out at him. 'Cripplin' me isnae goin' tae make things different.'

He was right; Etta stopped fighting him and stood submissively in his grip, sobbing out loud now, like a child in abject misery.

'Oh, lass!' Adam said, and began to kiss her forehead, her wet cheeks, her nose, and her mouth. 'Ye taste of salt again,' he said, wiping the tears away with the heel of one hand.

'But this time there's no sparkle tae it,' she meant it to be a witty remark, but the half sob, half hiccup that followed spoiled the effect.

'Aye but there is, for yer eyes are glitterin' up at me. Here.' The jacket had slipped from her shoulders; now Adam lifted it from the ground and settled it snugly round her shoulders again. 'Come to the *Homefarin'*,' he said. 'There's nob'dy aboard her, an' at least we'd be out of this wind.'

There was another boat between the harbour and the *Homefaring*. Adam went down the iron ladder first, and Etta followed slowly, her feet settling cautiously on each rung while he guided her with a hand on one ankle. As she put her foot on the gunwale he lifted her as though she was no heavier than a baby and carried her across the deck.

'Adam, let me down! You'll have both of us in the water if you try tae carry me across between the two boats!'

'I'm not goin' intae any water on a cold night like this, with nob'dy about tae fish me out, and I'll not let you fall in either. Hold on!' he ordered, and she wrapped her arms about his neck and buried her face in his thick knitted gansey, pressing her cheek so tightly against his chest that the special pattern, which told the initiated of his family history, dug into her skin. She could feel the steady thump of his heart, hear the rumble of his breathing, and sense the sudden lift as he stepped onto the gunwale. He leapt the gap, and she was jolted in his arms as one foot thudded onto the *Homefaring*'s gunwale and then the other landed firmly on the deck.

She held on, wanting to stay safe in his arms for as long as she could, until he said into her hair, 'We're here now, and I'll have tae put ye down if I'm tae open the galley door.'

The galley stove was out, but the iron casing still held some heat and Etta was grateful for the warmth as she followed Adam into the blackness.

'Over here,' he said, and his hand sought and found hers. 'We'll go down tae the cabin.' And then, when she hung back, 'I cannae light the lamp up here, someone might see it. We'd be able tae have a light down below.'

'We don't need a light, we're fine here.'

'If ye're sure,' he said, and guided her over to where a wooden bench was fastened to the wall. They sat close together, his hands holding hers. 'Now then,' he said, 'about this bairn—'

'It's yours, Adam Pate.' The anger returned, sharpening her voice. 'Mebbe you don't know about how bairns start, but there was that time in Yarm'th in October, when we went walkin' on the beach, only we didn't walk all that far. And then there were another two times on that same bit of beach. And there was the hay shed at the Bains' farm the night of Mary's weddin', though by that time I was beginnin' to know what had happened.'

'Why didn't ye tell me then?'

'I wasnae certain, not until Aunt Zelda faced me with it. She knows about these things, but don't ask me how.' Etta said, and then, her voice trembling, 'And anyway, I didnae know how you'd be about it.'

'I don't rightly know mysel',' Adam admitted. 'I never thought of it.'

'Mebbe you got away with it when you were with other lassies,' Etta said, and was startled by the jealousy that stabbed through her when he didn't deny what she was saying. He had told her, that first time at Yarmouth, when he had loved her in the shelter of an upturned dinghy, that it had been the first time for him, too, but she had not believed him. She knew that Adam went with plenty girls before her, and he had known just what he was about. 'I suppose I never thought of the consequences myself,' she said dismally. 'I wish now that I had.'

'D'ye – d'ye want me tae marry ye?'

Her heart and her body all shrieked at her to say yes, yes, and yes again, but her mind was in control, for all that day she had been imagining the different ways in which he might react to the news she had to tell him, and she had carefully worked out an answer to every eventuality. So while her heart raced she forced herself to say calmly, 'I'd not want you tae marry me just out of pity. Aunt Zelda says that the bairn and me can live with them if I want it that way. So ye don't need tae provide a home for us, or tie yerself down. We're both young yet, Adam, and mebbe there's more ahead of us than marriage tae each other.'

'You're awful cold about it!' He sounded quite shocked.

'I've had more time than you tae think about it. I have tae be practical,' Etta said, while her heart quailed within her at the thought of being left to bear and raise a child without his love to sustain her.

'D'ye want the bairn?'

'I've no' got much choice, have I?'

'I've heard that there's ways—'

'Not for me, and now that she knows, Aunt Zelda would never hear of such a thing. I'm – I'm willin' tae birth it and rear it, for what's happened isnae the poor wee mite's fault.'

'No, I suppose not.' He released his hold on her hands and drew away slightly. They sat for so long in silence that Etta's heartbeat began to slow and her blood to cool. She became aware that the galley was not as warm as she had first thought, though the chill that gradually crept over her as Adam remained silent was not entirely due to the cooling of the big iron stove.

'You neednae worry,' she said at last, resigned to her fate. 'Nob'dy will know who the faither is. I'd not want tae do that tae you.'

Adam stirred. 'What?' he said, sounding as though his mind was returning from somewhere far away.

'I said I'd never tell folk the faither's name, so you've no need tae worry about—'

'Are ye willin' tae marry me, Etta?' he asked. 'D'ye want tae marry me?'

Etta had been so sure that he was going to leave her to face the town alone, with only her aunt and uncle for support, that her carefully nurtured serenity and self-reliance deserted her there and then. 'Yes,' she said, 'oh yes, Adam, it's what I want most in the whole world!'

'That's it settled, then,' he said, and reached for her.

'What about your mother?' she asked when he finally gave her the chance to speak. 'She'll not be pleased.'

'What makes you think that?'

'Aunt Zelda said – she said that Aunt Bethany would want you tae marry with some rich lassie.'

He laughed, his breath warm on her cheek. 'That would never have happened! I'll tell her tomorrow, but it doesnae matter what she thinks. You're all that matters now, Etta. You, and the bairn.' One hand reached beneath the jacket still about her shoulders, to stroke her belly. 'It's more comfortable down in the cabin,' he suggested.

'We'd better not—'

'What can happen that hasnae happened already? Besides, we're goin' tae wed, aren't we? As soon as we find a wee cottage and the banns are called in the kirk. Come on, Etta.'

Adam drew her to her feet and over to where the vertical ladder led down to the drifter's cabin, and she followed her man.

'It's true what they say,' Bethany said tartly. 'Men *do* turn into gossiping women when they get older.'

'What makes ye think that, my quine?'

'You've been talking to Lorne Kerr about me and my business.'

'He was talkin' tae me about you,' Jacob corrected her mildly. 'Wantin' tae ken all about ye, he was.'

'He invited me to visit his sister in Edinburgh.'

'And why not? You work too hard, Bethany, you deserve a wee holiday.'

'I had one when I was in Yarm'th. Anyway, it wasn't just a visit he was thinking of.'

'Did he say that?' Jacob asked, delighted.

'In a roundabout way. He thinks that we're suited.'

'And you sent him away with a flea in his ear?'

'I told him that I preferred to be single, if that's what you mean.'

'That would explain why he downed such a lot of my whisky on his last night. He went away with a right sore head – and a sore heart too, mebbe.'

'His heart had nothing to do with it,' Bethany sniffed. 'He made it sound more like a business proposition than a marriage. All the man wants is someone who can look after his fine house and warm his bed.'

'There's a lot to be said for . . .' Jacob took one look at her face and finished the sentence with 'companionship.'

'I've no wish to marry again, Jacob! In any case, I'm too old and set in my ways.'

'Nob'dy's ever too old tae want a bit of happiness. Tell me this, Bethany – have you ever known real passion for a man?' Jacob asked, and she stared at him, taken aback.

'What a question to ask a body!'

'You're a passionate woman; I can see that, and mebbe Lorne Kerr saw it as well.'

'I doubt that, for he didn't seem to be interested in passion – and neither am I,' Bethany said hotly. 'That's one thing we're agreed on.'

'If ye don't need that sort of warmth in yer life, lass, then all the more reason tae consider Kerr, for he could make ye very comfortable for the rest of yer days.'

'I've no wish to leave Buckie. It's my birthplace and my home. And there's Adam. I'm not easy in my mind about him,' she confessed. 'I still feel that he could do better in his life than being a deckhand.'

'Ye'll need tae think up a very good ploy tae get that laddie tae dance tae your tune instead of his own, for he's as stubborn as you are yourself.'

'I know that.' Now that Lorne Kerr had disappeared from the conversation and they were on safer ground, Bethany felt more comfortable. 'I've suggested to him that he should go to one of the naval colleges. By the time he comes out the new drifter'll be on the water.'

'You're never suggestin' that the lad should come straight from college tae skipper the new boat?'

'No, but he'd have all the knowledge, and according to James and Jem he's a good fisherman. He could go on the new drifter as mate until he's proved himself, and then take her over.'

Jacob rubbed his jawline, considering the suggestion. 'Aye, I suppose it might work out,' he said at last, and Bethany, having sowed the seed in his mind, was content.

'So what are ye goin' tae do about it?' James asked.

'I've said I'll marry her, as soon as it can be arranged.'

'Is that what ye want?'

'Tae tell the truth, when she told me last night it came as such a shock that for a while I just wanted tae run away from Buckie and away from her, as far as I could go,' Adam admitted, staring at his hands, fisted loosely together on the *Fidelity*'s scarred cabin table.

'That's the way most of us feel at the beginnin'. Men never seem tae be ready for fatherhood and domestic responsibilities.'

'Then when I thought about it, I realised that it could work out tae my advantage,' Adam went on enthusiastically. 'If

'I've tae marry Etta Mulholland soon tae give the bairn a name, then I cannae go away tae college, can I? I'll have tae find somewhere for us tae live and stay on at the fishin' tae support the lass. And that'll put an end once and for all tae my mother's nonsense about me gettin' some learnin' instead of stayin' here in Buckie.'

'You'll be a deckhand, on a deckhand's wages. Her plan would see ye bringin' in more money eventually,' James pointed out. Opposed as he was to Bethany's college scheme he wanted to make sure that the lad made his own decisions.

'We'll manage. Besides, I've already said that I'll marry Etta. I cannae go back on my word now – Aunt Zelda would have the scalp off me, and once she was done, Uncle Innes would no doubt start on me.'

'That's mebbe nothin' tae what yer mother'll do when ye tell her ye're marryin' a fisher-lassie that works in the net factory, instead of some fine Aberdeen lassie with a father that has his own shop.'

'She cannae stay angry with me for ever,' Adam said confidently. 'And even if she does I'll be out of the house and well settled with Etta, so it'll not matter.'

James stayed silent for a moment, then lifted his head and looked the younger man in the eye. 'I tell ye what I'll do,' he said. 'Siddy's gettin' too old for the fishin', he's said that himself. When the summer fishin' starts you'll come back tae the *Fidelity* as deckhand, and I'll train ye up so's ye can take over from Siddy as soon as we can manage it.'

Adam's face glowed. 'D'ye mean it? I'd as soon be mate on board this old drifter than any fine new boat.' Then, hopefully, 'I don't suppose—?'

'Oh no,' James said emphatically. 'You've admitted that you're faither tae this lassie's bairn, and that makes you a man now. Bein' a man carries responsibilities, and the first of them is facin' up tae yer mother and tellin' her about yer change of plan.'

*

Zelda could scarcely wait for Innes to get home from work. As soon as he and Will set foot in the door she ordered Teena, only weeks away from her twelfth birthday, to keep stirring the broth and make sure the potatoes didn't burn, and then dragged her husband into their bedroom, the only room in the tiny house where they could find some measure of privacy.

'What's amiss?' he asked in alarm as she closed the door behind him.

'Nothin's amiss – it's the other way.' Her eyes were dancing and her still-pretty face wreathed in smiles. 'Innes, there's tae be another weddin' from this house!'

'But Jessie's no' fifteen yet – or is it Will? The laddie never said a word tae me down at the boatyard.'

'No, ye daft loon – it's our Etta!'

'Etta's gettin' wed?' Innes said in wonder, taking his cap off and scratching his head. 'I never even knew she was courtin'.'

'Neither did I, but she's been courtin' for the past three months. Since she was in Yarm'th, I'd say. Imagine, Innes, two weddin's from this house in the space of a few months,' Zelda said excitedly. 'The first thing tae do's tae find somewhere for them tae live—'

'Is she stayin' on in Buckie, then?'

'Where else would they live?'

'When you said she met him in Yarm'th I thought mebbe it was a laddie from those parts.'

'No, no, it's Adam!'

Innes gaped at his wife, lost for words. 'Adam Pate?' he said at last. 'Bethany's lad?'

'Of course, and I didnae say they met in Yarm'th. I said they probably started courtin' there, for there was no sign of it before then. Unless it began during the Lerwick fishin',' Zelda began, and was interrupted.

'Does Bethany know?'

'If she doesn't then she soon will, for the weddin's tae be held as soon as they can find a place tae live and get the banns called.'

'She'll never agree tae it.'

'I don't see why not, for the lad could do a lot worse than our Etta. She'll be a grand wee wife and he's lucky tae have found her.'

'She'll not have it, I'm tellin' ye. Bethany's got her sights set higher than our Etta for her son.'

Smirking, Zelda played her trump card. 'The choice isnae Bethany's, though, for there's a bairn on the way.'

'A bairn? Etta's carryin' Adam Pate's bairn? Are ye sure of this?'

'I knew about it even before she did. I could see the signs. I couldnae tell ye till I got the chance tae speak tae the lassie. And Adam's agreed that he's the father.'

'A bairn!'

'Ye neednae sound so shocked about it, Innes Lowrie. They're two young folk with all the hot blood that runs in young veins. Ye've surely not forgotten that you gave me a bairn before ye gave me yer name and yer gold ring. You and me arenae in a position tae judge others.'

'No, of course not, and I never would. But Bethany won't like it,' Innes repeated.

His wife put her two hands on his shoulders and went up on tiptoe to dab a kiss on his lips.

'Bethany,' she said smugly, 'will just have tae like it, because for once she's not goin' tae get things all her own way.'

27

Despite his brave words to Etta, Adam was finding it hard to tell his mother about his new plans. Once or twice on the following morning he went into the front room where she worked at her desk but she looked so busy and so businesslike that his courage failed him and he retreated without saying anything.

Finally, not knowing what else to do, he went down to the cooperage. It was mid-morning, and within the rough shed the air was hot and stuffy, for the braziers were still burning, providing hot water to soften the barrel staves. Coopers and their apprentices were busy all about the three-sided shed, each group or duo working on a different barrel at a different stage. No sooner had Adam gone in than his ears began to ring with the non-stop noise.

Rory was working on his own, circling a barrel rapidly and continuously, forcing the final hoop into place with hard, evenly spaced hammer blows. The barrel, open at both ends, stood over a small brazier filled with burning chips of wood; the heat was needed to keep the well-soaked staves of wood pliant enough to be drawn together to make the traditional shape. Rory's free hand, supporting the barrel, was precariously near to the flames, and sweat ran freely down his face and dripped from his hair as he worked.

When Adam approached his brother a brusque nod signalled him to stand out of the way. Watching from near the open end of the shed he marvelled at the way the coopers could work in such heat and noise. Give him the fishing life any day, with the fresh wind in his hair and on his face, and the open waters all about him. He was glad that he had been born the younger son, and not his father's direct heir.

He had not long to wait before the barrel was finished, its hoops in place and the staves bent to the cooper's will. Rory deftly twisted it away from the flames without damaging it or toppling the fierce fire, then came to Adam, buffing sweat from his hair and face with a rag. His eyes, irritated by the smoke from the burning wood chips, were red-rimmed and streaming with tears.

'What is it that can't wait till later?'

'I've got a favour tae ask ye.'

'And I've got more barrels tae finish before the day's end, so out with it.'

'I want ye tae stand by me at my weddin',' Adam said, and Rory stared at him in disbelief through eyes that were still watering.

'You? Marryin'?'

'Aye, as soon as it can be arranged, and I'd like ye tae be my best man.'

'Who's the lass?'

'It's Etta, Etta Mulholland. We've been walkin' out together for a month or two now.'

'Ever since Yarm'th.' Rory's voice was suddenly flat.

'Aye,' Adam said, 'that's right. Ye knew about it?'

'I knew somethin' of it, but I didnae know it was serious. She's not the first lassie ye've courted, not by a long way.'

Adam grinned. 'She's the first tae catch me, though.'

'I thought you were goin' tae naval college. How can ye do that and get wed as well?'

'That's the good thing about it,' Adam started to explain. 'I wasnae sure at all about this new idea of Mother's because tae tell the truth, I'd rather just stay in Buckie and keep on with the fishin'. But now that Etta's expectin' a bairn—'

'Etta's carryin' your bairn?'

'Aye, that's what I'm tryin' tae tell ye,' Adam said, impatient with the interruption. 'Don't ye see? My mother surely can't blame me for doin' the right thing by the lass, and if I'm havin' tae get married, then I can't go tae the college, can I? Mother'll just have tae go along with it whether she likes it or not. Etta's solved my problem for me. It couldnae have happened at a better time for—'

The world suddenly exploded in a great burst of stars against a crimson background, and pain shot through his jaw as he went staggering backwards, arms flapping in a bid to keep himself upright.

'The fire – for God's sake mind the fire!' he heard a voice yell from far away. Adam felt his heel catch on something and as he fell heavily his left hand hit against something hard. Then the back of his head bounced on the ground, sending another great rush of stars flashing before his eyes. They passed in an instant, and then everything went black.

He came round within seconds to find himself being rolled roughly about the ground and slapped at by what seemed to be a host of hands. For a moment he lashed out feebly against his tormentors, under the impression that he had become embroiled in some sort of a fight, then he gasped as a panful of cold water was dashed into his face.

'What the—?' He came to, choking and spitting, to find himself lying on the ground in the cooperage. Several men were gathered around, looking down at him.

'Ye were burnin', man,' one of them said. 'Ye went right back and fell against one of the wee fires an' knocked it all tae damty.' He indicated a spot not far away, and Adam, cranking his head around carefully, saw that the ground was littered with smoking wood chips. 'Some of them caught yer jacket and if we'd not slapped the flames out ye'd have been a torch. Christ,' the cooper went on as Adam began to struggle to his feet, 'Rory fairly hit ye a right crack, man. I've seen him lose his temper once or twice, but I've never known him lift a hand tae a livin' soul afore this. Here.' He reached down and caught Adam's arm, jerking him to his feet with one swift, hefty pull. When Adam was upright, he added softly, so that nobody else heard, 'I don't know why he hit ye, but if I was you I'd not let him get away with it.'

'Get back tae yer work,' Rory roared, storming through the group and sending them scattering. 'I don't pay ye tae stand about gossipin'!'

He glowered at them as they slunk back to work, then turned on his brother: 'As for you, get out of here before I throw ye out!'

Adam put a hand to his jaw, which throbbed and felt as though it had swollen to twice its normal size.

'I'll go when ye've told me what the hell ye mean by this.' It hurt to speak.

'Ye'll go now,' Rory said, his hands loose by his sides and his face, despite the sweat that still dripped down it, as hard as if it was hewn from stone.

Adam's head was not yet completely clear, and his jaw hurt abominably, but aware that the men were watching from the corners of their eyes while appearing to get on with their work as their employer had ordered, he took a swift step towards Rory, knotting his right fist. Rory fended the blow off easily, then caught Adam's gansey in his two hands, bunching it tightly and dragging Adam towards him so that they were almost nose to nose.

'Don't be a fool,' he said, his voice thick with loathing. 'I'm just as strong as you are, mebbe stronger, and if you try tae start a fight with me I'll kill ye, I swear tae God I will.'

'What's wrong with ye?' Adam asked, bewildered. 'All I asked was—'

'That's what's wrong with me!' Rory released him, taking his arm instead and hustling him to the wide doorway. 'I'm heart sorry for Etta and I'm damned if I'll stand by yer side and watch you makin' use of her for yer own ends. Find

299

someone else – and for the meantime,' he added roughly, pushing Adam outside, 'get out of my sight!'

Adam, reluctant to face his mother's fussing, spent the rest of the day on a secluded part of the shore, bathing his face and head in sea water in a vain attempt to rid himself of the bruising and swelling on his jaw as well as the throbbing knot on the back of his skull, where his head had hit against the ground. His left hand had been burned when it hit against the small iron pot holding the wood chips, and although the salt water stung at first it eventually helped to ease the pain and prevent a blister from forming.

Between times he sat on the shingle, huddled against a rock large enough to provide some shelter and privacy, his knees drawn to his chin and his arms wrapped tightly about them as he puzzled over his half-brother's uncharacteristic behaviour.

As a boy he had always run to his Aunt Zelda when he was involved in a fight or had hurt himself through some daredevil prank. Aunt Zelda was good at soothing scratches and bruises and helping to disguise them, too. And in her house there was always room at the table for hungry visitors. But Etta lived with Aunt Zelda, and no doubt she would start to fuss over him and to ask questions, the way women did when they owned a man – or thought they owned him – through motherhood or betrothal.

His intention was to sneak back home when everyone had gone to bed, but darkness, cold and hunger forced him back to Cliff Terrace long before that, stiff-limbed and chilled to the bone.

As ill luck had it, his mother was coming downstairs just as he let himself into the house.

'Where have you been?' she asked at once, and then as he looked up at her and the light shone on his bruised and swollen face her voice rose. 'And what in the name of God's happened to you?'

'Nothin'.' Dinner was almost ready, and the smell from

the kitchen made Adam's mouth water. He tried to escape to his bedroom, where he could at least wash his face and brush his hair and change out of his scorched gansey, but Bethany blocked his way, shooing him before her to the kitchen.

'Sit down there. Leezie, fetch the vinegar and a cloth, and make up a hot compress.'

'I would, if I'd more than just the one pair of hands,' the housekeeper said from the stove. 'But as I've no', ye'll just have tae follow yer own orders.'

'I'm fine,' Adam said irritably, going to the sink to wash his hands.

'Fine? Look at you! Have you been fighting?' She caught his sleeve and pulled his arm away from the sink so that she could examine the angry red patch on the back of his hand. 'Is that a burn? How did you get that?'

'It was just a wee mishap,' he said, and then yelped as Bethany caught his bruised chin and pulled his face round towards the light. 'That hurts!'

'I'm not surprised, for someone's hit you a right hard blow. Who was it?'

'Nob'dy. It's my own business.'

'It must have been somebody, and I want to know who?'

'It was me,' Rory said from where he leaned against the frame of the kitchen door.

'You?' Bethany and Leezie said in unison. 'You hit your own brother?' Bethany asked.

'My half-brother.'

'What in the world did you do that for?'

'That's for him tae tell ye – if he's got the courage,' Rory said with cool contempt. 'I'm goin' out. Keep my dinner hot, Leezie, I'll have it when I get back.'

'Rory!' Bethany shouted after him, but the front door was already closing behind him. 'What's going on between you two?' she asked in despair. 'Why did he hit you? Rory's never hit anyone in his life before. What did you do to him or say to him to make this happen?'

For hours Adam had been trying to think of the right way to break the news to his mother; now, thanks to Rory, it had all gone wrong and there was no longer any need for a careful approach.

'I just asked him to be my best man. That's all I did, as God's my witness.'

'Best man?' Bethany's voice was faint with shock. 'You're getting wed?'

'I was goin' tae tell you tonight.'

'Who is she?'

'Etta Mulholland.'

For a moment the only sound in the kitchen was the clash of pots from the stove, where Leezie worked with her back turned but her ears flapping. Then Bethany said, 'Leezie, keep the dinner warm for a wee while. Adam, come into the front room.'

'She'll hear all about it anyway,' Adam protested as he followed his mother's straight back and squared shoulders. 'We could have talked about it while we were eating. I'm starving.'

'Even if Leezie does hear it all later it starts in here, between you and me. Close the door,' Bethany ordered. 'As for food, you can just starve a bit longer.' Then, as he came further into the room, 'Etta Mulholland? Zelda's niece? A guttin' quine? You're marryin' with a guttin' quine?'

'You know fine who Etta is, and a guttin' quine was good enough for my father,' Adam pointed out coldly. 'I don't see why you should take against the lassie like this.'

'I've nothing against her, but she's not for you, Adam.'

'I think she is.'

'But you could do better for yourself! Why else d'you think I wanted you to go to the university, or the naval college? You'll still be going to the college, won't you?' Bethany said swiftly. 'The two of you can get married after that, if you still want to. It'll give you a wee while to think things over and make sure of your feelings.'

'We'll be gettin' wed as soon as we can, Mither. We have tae, for Etta's havin' a bairn.'

One of Bethany's hands groped about as though the room was in darkness, then found the back of a chair. Her ability to seat herself slowly and gracefully, her body folding itself while her back remained ramrod straight, had always fascinated Adam, but tonight she dropped into the chair as though her knees had given way and could no longer keep her upright.

'Your bairn?'

'Aye.'

'Are you certain, Adam? It could be anyone's.'

'Etta says its mine and I think she's tellin' the truth,' he said sharply. 'I've said I'll marry her and I will.'

'But if you marry now, how are you going to get to college?'

'I'm not, I'm stayin' here in Buckie. Uncle James is goin' tae arrange for me tae crew on the *Fidelity* and he's said that when Siddy leaves the boat I'll be mate.'

'You told James about this before you told me?'

'He was easier tae tell,' Adam said bluntly, 'and I wanted tae get the future right in my mind before I spoke tae you.'

'You can't do this.' Bethany's voice was suddenly strong again, as cold and as hard as iron. 'I'll not let this happen to you. I can help the girl – I'll give her enough money to take care of herself and her child, rent a wee place for them to live in if that's what she wants. You can still go to college and then you can take over the new drifter—'

'It's all decided, Mother. I'm marryin' Etta and I'm crewin' on the *Fidelity*. I'm old enough tae make my own decisions.'

'Old enough?' Her eyes blazed up at him. 'You're a fool, that's what you are! Where are you going to live, you and this future wife of yours?'

'We'll find somewhere to rent.'

'You needn't come asking me for the money to pay for it!' Bethany raged.

'You've just offered tae find a place for Etta and the bairn.'

'That was for her, while you were at the college. But if you're so set on marrying her now then you can support her. I'll not pay good money to see you ruin your life before it's properly begun!'

'Then I'll borrow the money, or I'll find work on one of the farms until the new fishin' season starts. And there's the line fishin' with Jem. I'll pay my way somehow. I'm nineteen, Mother, and in less than two years I'll get my inheritance from my faither. We'll manage until then, me and Etta and the bairn.'

'D'you love her?' It was a challenge rather than a question.

'Aye, I do,' Adam lied, looking his mother straight in the eye. He had always been able to lie convincingly; not even Bethany could tell his lies from his truths.

'Very well,' she said now, rising to her full height, a good six inches short of his. 'Ruin your life if you must. But I tell you here and now that you'll live to regret it – bitterly. Tell Leezie I don't want any dinner. I'm going to my bed.'

When he was alone Adam let his breath out in a long sigh of relief. It was done – not in the way he had intended, but at least she knew now.

Despite the throbbing in his jaw and at the back of his head he was cheerful as he went into the kitchen.

'My mither's gone tae her bed, Leezie, and she doesnae want any food. So that means more for you and me. I'm right famished. Serve it out now and I'll tell ye what's been happenin'.'

'Rory?' Etta asked in disbelief. 'Rory hit you?'

'Aye, he did that. Near knocked me into one of the fires in the cooperage, too.' Adam displayed the red weal across the back of his hand. 'My gansey got the worst of it, though, for the wood chips landed all over it.'

'I'll knit ye a new one,' she promised at once. 'I'll start on it tonight. But what was Rory thinkin' of?'

'You, seemingly. He doesnae think I'm good enough for ye, Etta. Now I'll have tae find another best man. Mebbe Will would stand with me,' Adam said, brightening. 'I'll ask him.'

'Aunt Zelda'll be pleased about that. She's fair delighted to have another weddin' tae arrange.'

'Tell her no' tae make it a grand event like Mary's, because we can't afford it.'

'Have you told Aunt Bethany yet?' He had waited outside the net factory for her at the end of the working day, and now they were walking slowly back to Innes's cottage, hand in hand.

'I was goin' tae tell her carefully, but when I went home lookin' like this' – he gestured to his face, still swollen and now, as the bruise matured and spread, looking very colourful – 'she started tae fuss the way women do. I was tryin' tae make little of it when that fool Rory came in and said that it was him that hit me, and I'd tell her why. Tell her? I still don't know the reason for it mysel',' Adam said. 'So that was that.'

'How did she take it?'

'She was a bit upset,' he admitted, and she bit her lip.

'I told you she doesn't think I'm good enough!'

'No, no, it's not that.' Adam slid into another lie. 'She was a guttin' quine hersel', so how could she think ye werenae good enough? It's me stayin' in Buckie instead of goin' tae the university or the naval college that's botherin' her.'

'I've spoiled everythin' for you, Adam.' Etta felt tears prickling the backs of her eyes. 'I've wasted your chances!'

'Ye've not! I'd far rather stay here with you than go away from here.'

'You're not just sayin' that tae make me feel better?'

'No!' It was only a half-lie this time, for unwittingly, she had saved him from another year or so of classroom learning. He drew her into the shelter of a house end, taking her into his arms. 'I'd a million times rather stay here with you.'

305

'Oh, Adam!' She planted a passionate kiss on his lips, and then recoiled as he let out a yelp of pain. 'I'm sorry, I forgot you were hurtin'!' She reached up and touched the bruise gently, the tips of her fingers feeling the nasty swelling along the jawline.

'It's all right, ye just took me by surprise.' He kissed the corner of her mouth, a delicate butterfly kiss that, sedate as it was, sent an unexpected tremor through her. 'Now then – we'll have tae find somewhere to live, for there's certainly no room at Aunt Zelda's. Have ye any savin's, Etta?'

'No, have you?'

'No,' he admitted.

'Aunt Bethany?'

'She says not – because of me not goin' to the college,' Adam added hastily.

'We'll find somewhere. One room would do at first, just as long as we're together.'

'Mebbe my mother'll calm down soon. My room at home's big enough for two, and a bairn.'

'No!' Etta said sharply. The thought of living in that grand house in Cliff Terrace, under Aunt Bethany's roof and, worse still, under her disapproving eye, filled her with terror. Nor could she bear to be in the same house as Rory. She knew, even if Adam didn't, why the young cooper had reacted so badly to the news of their hurried marriage. 'No,' she said, 'I'd as soon live in the old shed in our back yard than in your house. At least I'd be welcome in the shed.'

'I'm not livin' in any shed!'

'Other folk have, when they've had no other way of putting a roof over their heads. Come on, Aunt Zelda'll be wonderin' where I am. You can stay for your dinner if you like.'

'I will – but don't tell them how I got this.' Adam indicated his bruises. 'I'll tell them I fell in the dark and hit my face against a wall.'

The family were already eating when they arrived, and there was an immediate banging of spoons on the wooden table and a disjointed rendering of 'Here Comes the Bride', while Zelda jumped up at once and came to Adam, her arms outstretched.

'I'm the happiest woman alive! Tae think that you and my wee— for goodness' sake, laddie, what's happened tae ye?'

'Have ye started bossin' the man around already, Etta?' Will shouted.

'She has not, and she never will. I'd a bit of an accident in the dark last night.'

'Celebratin' yer engagement? Why didn't ye invite me along?'

'It wasnae that – I just turned clumsy-like and fell over against the corner of some house.'

'Aye,' Innes said, 'I heard about that already today, from one of the coopers.' Then, as the young couple looked at him in horror, he added to his noisy brood, 'and a hurt face is nothin' tae laugh about, so we'll have no more of it. Though there's just one thing – I hope tae God nob'dy thinks that I did that to ye because ye've got this lassie—' he glanced at the younger members of his family, then said, 'because of you and Etta gettin' wed.'

Zelda was already busy at the stove. 'Sit in, the two of ye,' she instructed. 'Matt, Meggie – move along and make room.'

'I was wonderin',' Adam said as he and Etta settled themselves at the table, 'if you'd be my best man, Will.'

'Our Will? But what about Rory?' Zelda leaned over their shoulders so that she could set plates of food in front of them. 'Surely your own brother's the one tae stand by you on your weddin' day?'

'He's— he'd be happier for me tae find someone else,' Adam mumbled. 'You know Rory, he's a bit shy about things like that.'

'Then you'll do it, won't you, Will?'

'Would I have tae wear a suit?'

'Aye ye would, and have your hair brushed, and cut your

fingernails, since it's the only way tae get rid of the oil that's always caught beneath them.'

'I'm no' sure it would be worth the bother,' Will began, and his mother cuffed the side of his head.

'He'll do it, Adam, and he'll do it right – I'll see tae that.'

'Where are ye goin' tae live?' Teena wanted to know, while Jess asked, 'And what about your bridesmaid, Etta? Can I do it?'

Meggie and Teena immediately began to claim the honour, and the noise only abated when Innes thumped on the table and announced that if a man could not enjoy a peaceful meal in his own house at the end of a day's work, things had come to a pretty pass.

'Yer father's right.' Zelda settled back into her own seat. 'No more weddin' talk – me and Etta'll sort it all out in our own time. Samuel, pass the bread.'

'Now then, where are the two of ye goin' tae live?' Zelda asked later that night. Innes had stepped out to the back yard, as he always did, to enjoy a final pipe of tobacco in peace, and the others had gone to their beds.

'I don't know.' Etta felt her lower lip begin to tremble. 'Adam says that Aunt Bethany won't help him, seein' as he's disappointed her over not goin' tae the college,' she said, her voice little more than a whisper, 'but I think it's because she's angry that it's me he's marryin' and not someone she can be proud of.'

'Don't be daft, lassie.' Zelda put her arms about her niece and hugged her close. 'Any woman that has you for a daughter-in-law's blessed. We'll find somewhere for you and Adam tae live. Now, about your bridesmaid – I was thinkin' that if you choose one of my lassies it's only goin' tae cause trouble with the other two, and in any case, they'll all end up standin' as bridesmaid tae each other in time – if I'm fortunate enough tae get the lot of them married off. What about Ruth? You like her, don't you?'

'I do, but d'you think she'd agree tae it, with the disappointment she's had?'

'I think it would be the very thing tae help her tae get over her own hurt. You ask her,' Zelda advised. 'And let me sort out the weddin' arrangements.' She dropped a kiss on the top of Etta's head before releasing her. 'I'm good at that!'

28

Ruth almost burst with excitement and pride at the prospect of being Etta's bridesmaid. 'It'll be the best day of my life,' she declared, her eyes alight for the first time since she heard that Jack Morrison was to marry Ellen Pate. 'We'll have such a good time, you and me and Adam and Rory!'

'Will's to be the best man. Rory's too shy for it, Adam says.'

'What? Not standing by his own brother at his marriage? We'll see about that,' Ruth said, and the very next day she marched into the cooperage and tapped Rory on the shoulder.

'I want a word with you. Outside, so's we can hear each other.'

He followed her out. 'What's amiss?'

'What's amiss is you not standin' by Adam on his weddin' day. Etta says you're too shy tae take on the job, and it's tae be Will instead. And I only agreed tae be her bridesmaid because I thought you'd be best man.'

'I didnae care for the job,' he said shortly. 'Will's welcome tae it.'

'Please yerself, but I'll still want a dance from you at the celebrations after.'

Rory bit his lip, shuffled his feet and looked over her head at the grey sea beyond the harbour. 'I'm no' sure I'll be there,' he muttered at last.

'Not be at your own brother's weddin'?'

'He's my half-brother, no' my brother.'

'Don't be so daft, Rory Pate – Etta's cousin tae Will and Mary and the rest of them, and that's further apart than you and Adam, but they all call her their sister. And why wouldn't you go to his—' She stopped, understanding dawning in the hazel eyes that were a mixture of her father's grey eyes and her mother's brown eyes, then said, 'It's because you still care for Etta, isn't it?'

'That's none of your business, Ruth Lowrie!'

'It is my business, for we're all related, even if it's only by marriage. I knew the two of ye were walkin' together, but Etta said it was just in friendship – though from the look on your face,' Ruth said shrewdly, 'it was more than that tae you.'

'I have tae get back tae work.' Rory made to walk away, but she danced quickly to one side, putting herself between him and the cooperage.

'No ye don't, not until we get this business sorted. Rory, it's Adam she's marryin' because it's Adam she cares for, and the sooner you accept that the better.'

'You don't know what ye're talkin' about!'

'You say that tae me that had tae stand by and see your own sister steal away the man I cared for? There's nothin' you can teach me about the pain of losin' someone ye wanted tae spend the rest of yer life with.' Ruth's voice was suddenly fierce, her eyes bright with loss as well as anger. 'But as I see it, what's done's done, and mebbe Jack was never meant for me after all. Mebbe I'm supposed tae get someone a hundred times better than Jack Morrison. That's what I tell myself, and that's what you have tae think too. And never mind how you feel about Adam – I'll not let you spoil our Etta's weddin', Rory Pate, and it *will* be spoiled for her if you're not there, for she counts you as one of her dearest friends. And I'm still goin' tae have that dance with ye, even if I have tae come out of the hall and along tae your house and drag ye intae the street and make ye dance with me there, in front of all your fine Cliff Terrace neighbours. And wouldn't that just upset yer mither!'

There was a short, angry pause, during which Rory glared down at the small, bristling figure before him, and Ruth glared back.

'So ye'll be at the weddin', then?' she asked at last.

'Aye.'

'Good. And mind that dance you owe me. Forget it and I'll make ye sorry for the rest of yer life.' She stepped aside and said graciously, 'Ye can go back in now.'

'And you'd best get back home. Your nose is red with the cold.'

'It's not the only bit of me red with the cold, but we'll not discuss that any further,' Ruth said pertly. As he went into the cooperage she called after him, 'Mind that conversation lozenge I gave ye at Mary's weddin'?'

'Aye.'

'Have ye still got it?'

'Aye,' Rory said without thinking. Then he blushed.

'Good,' Ruth said. 'It'll be your turn tae choose one for me when Etta gets wed. Make sure it says the right thing, for I'm awful particular.'

Bethany's anger with James was so great that she had to wait for two whole days before she could allow herself to confront him. She sent a note, asking him to call at the factory to have a look at the set of new nets he had ordered for the *Fidelity*, and when he arrived she took him to where the first of the nets had been hung for his inspection.

'They're fine. A grand job. Ye'll have them ready in good time for the new season?'

'Of course.' Bethany led the way back to the tiny office, a route that took them through the mending room where Etta Mulholland worked among the other menders. James nodded affably to her, while Bethany offered the girl no more than a dip of the head.

'Ye're no' very friendly tae the lassie that's tae be yer new daughter,' James said as she closed the door, shutting the two of them away from the eyes and ears of her employees. She had already arranged for the woman who had taken over from Ellen as overseer to be busy elsewhere for the morning.

'The lassie that's to be Adam's wife,' she corrected. 'She's one of my employees. It wouldn't be seemly if I was seen to be favouring her.'

'I doubt there's any danger of that; just as I doubt that you only wanted me here tae look at a few nets.'

'You're right. Adam tells me that you've promised him the mate's job on the *Fidelity* when Siddy leaves.'

'I think he'll be ready for it.'

'You'd do anything to get him to turn against my wishes and go along with yours, wouldn't you?'

'I just want the laddie tae follow his own inclinations, Bethany. Not mine, and not yours.'

'You probably approve of him marrying Etta Mulholland.'

'He's acceptin' his responsibilities,' James said levelly, 'the same as the two of us had tae do all those years back.'

'Can you not see that he's making a mistake? He's going to regret this, but by then it'll be too late!'

'We all have tae put up with the consequences of our own mistakes.'

Bethany looked at her brother for a long moment and he met her gaze without flinching. She was the first to look away, turning to the desk to fidget with the papers lying there.

'I just want him to be happy.'

'Etta's a decent enough quine, and if she cannae hold on to the lad, that'll be her worry, not ours,' James said, and when she did not reply, he got up and went to the door, turning for one last comment.

'My greatest regret is that you refused all those years ago to come away with me to some place nobody knew us, and start again. But you'd not have it – and now you have tae deal with the result, Bethany.'

*

'There's a wee cottage for rent in the Catbow,' Bethany said that night to Adam. 'Two rooms and a sail loft, just, but I think it might do you and your— and Etta, if the two of you would care to have a look at it.'

'What rent are they lookin' for?'

'That needn't concern you. If you want it I'll pay the rent for two years. That'll see you through till you inherit the money your father left in trust.'

He gaped at her, and then asked cautiously, 'What're the conditions?'

'There are no conditions. It's my wedding present to you. You'd best go and tell the lassie. Now's as good as any other time,' Bethany added sharply as he started to speak. 'Best to see it before someone else takes it.'

Now that Bethany had found them somewhere to live and Ruth, by some piece of cunning she would not divulge, had managed to get Rory to come to the wedding, Etta felt that life could not be more perfect.

She and Zelda and her foster-sisters threw themselves into wedding plans; the banns were called, the church hall booked for the reception, the local fishing community invited, and every night the kitchen table was taken over with patterns, stretches of cloth, ribbons and buttons and lace. Mary spent more time at her parents' cottage than she did at the farm, while Meggie and Teena and Samuel, still at school, were banished from the big kitchen table and had to do their homework as best they could in the two small bedrooms upstairs.

'It's not fair,' Samuel raged. 'We always have the kitchen table for our books – why can't Etta use a bedroom? Why does it have to be us?'

'Because we need the big table tae cut out the cloth,' his mother pointed out.

'We need it too. There's more beds than floor in the bedrooms,' Samuel argued. 'Why did ye have tae have so many bairns?'

'Because your father and me like bairns – though there's times when I wonder if we did the right thing,' Zelda said, and then, suddenly repentant, she drew her youngest, and most dearly loved for it, against her and kissed his mop of unruly curls. 'It'll not be for long, just till the weddin's over.'

'And then it'll be Jessie's weddin', then Meggie's, then Teena's!'

'I hope so, but by the time Teena gets wed you'll be a workin' man, mebbe with a wife and a house and bairns of your own, so you'll not be bothered about my kitchen table.'

'Not me,' Samuel said, disgusted by the very thought. 'I'm never goin' tae get married. Can I have a scone with raspberry jam on it tae help me tae do my homework?'

Thanks to the generosity of the local folk, the little cottage that Bethany had rented for her son and Etta acquired enough furniture to suit their basic needs. Jacob McFarlane gave them a brand new bed, and the girls in the net factory contributed bedding. Zelda and Innes gave them dishes and cutlery and someone donated an unwanted table, complete with four chairs. Two comfortable, if well-worn, armchairs came from someone clearing out her dead parents' home, together with some rugs for the floor.

Ruth, Annie and Sarah helped Zelda and Etta to scrub out the house and get it ready for the furniture, which would be moved in on the day before the wedding, and put in place that night as tradition demanded. There would be no feet-blackening however, for Adam, warned by Mary and Peter, had decided to stay well away from the cottage that night.

'I'm goin' over tae Elgin with Will and Peter and Uncle James and Uncle Innes – and Rory, if he'll come,' Adam said when he and Etta were working in the cottage. 'We'll have a wee drink tae set us up for the weddin'.'

'Not too much,' Etta said, worried. 'I don't want you too drunk tae say ye'll marry me when the minister asks ye.'

315

'I doubt my uncles'll allow that.'

'Uncle Innes surely wouldn't, but I'd not be so sure of Uncle James. It's bonny, isn't it?' Etta looked round the empty kitchen, eyes shining. 'Our very own home!'

'It's no' much, is it?'

'It'll do to start with,' she said, stung by the criticism in his voice. 'We can't manage anythin' near as grand as what you're used to at Cliff Terrace. But once the new fishin' season starts and you're bringin' in more money we can get things we need – a cradle for one.' She looked away, suddenly too shy to meet his gaze, then went on with mounting enthusiasm. 'And I'll get wee bits of material tae make baby clothes. Aunt Zelda says she can let me have a bonny shawl, and a few other wee things.' She put a hand on his arm. 'We'll be all right, won't we, Adam?'

'Aye, of course we will. It's a fine, sturdy place, with thick walls and a good roof. We'll be snug in here whatever the weather.'

'I meant you and me – and the bairn when it comes. We'll be happy, won't we?'

'I don't see why not,' Adam said. 'Other folk seem tae make marriage work, so I expect we will, too.'

On the day before her wedding Etta came face to face with Stella Lowrie in the street. For a moment the older woman hesitated, as though she wished she had had time to cross the street or disappear into a shop, and then she stopped, hefting her shopping basket from one arm to the other.

'Etta.'

'Is Ruth all ready for the weddin'?'

'As ready as she'll ever be.'

Etta smiled tentatively into the grim face. 'We're goin' tae get the house ready tonight. Would ye like tae come with us?' she asked.

'I've got enough tae do without that.'

According to Zelda's reminiscences, the younger Stella

Lowrie had been a gentle girl, happy with her lot as a wife and mother. Etta could see no sign of that girl in the woman confronting her. Sometimes she wondered what had happened to change Aunt Stella so much. Since Stella showed no signs of walking on, she persevered.

'Are you lookin' forward tae the weddin', Aunt Stella?'

'A weddin's a weddin' and if ye ask me, the only folk that look forward to it's the couple gettin' wed,' the woman said bleakly. 'I hear ye're expectin'.'

Etta's hand flew to her stomach, which had only just begun to fill out.

'Aye,' she said, and the older woman sniffed.

'It's one way tae catch a man, I suppose,' she said, and then, with a thin smile, 'and the other's tae have a father with property that the groom's family needs.'

'Adam's marryin' me because he cares for me,' Etta said, stung.

'Ye think so? Ye're goin' tae rue the day, lassie. Like father like son – and that lad you're promisin' yersel' tae is a right copy of his father. The only two things he loves are the sea and himsel', an' ye'd be a fool tae trust a word he says. Go ahead with this weddin' and the day'll come when ye find yersel' lyin' in a lonely bed and wishin' ye'd never walked up the aisle tae meet him.'

'But Adam's not— Uncle Gil surely didn't—' Etta said, bewildered, then she was brushed aside as Stella continued on her way.

The cottage that would be Etta's home from tomorrow night had been set to rights. Innes was still out with the groom's party, and the others had gone to bed. Zelda watched as Etta tried on her wedding outfit – a crêpe de Chine petticoat beneath a pale blue blouse and an oatmeal coloured woollen skirt with box pleats down the front.

'It is all right?'

'Aye, it looks grand,' Zelda said, head to one side. Then,

317

as Etta stood mutely before her, 'Lassie, what's wrong with ye? Ye've not been yersel' all evenin'. Are ye ill?'

'I'm fine.' Etta had made up her mind to say nothing about the ugly confrontation with Stella Lowrie. It had been a long and difficult evening, trying to smile while everyone else enjoyed the fun of putting her new home to rights, and the supper that followed – herring and potatoes served from the cooking pots onto newspaper spread on the kitchen table, and eaten with the fingers since the dishes would not be unpacked until the bride and groom were living in the house.

'You're not fine at all. I don't know what's wrong with you, but if ye're beginnin' tae have doubts about this weddin', ye don't have tae go through with it.'

'But everythin's been arranged!'

'It's still not too late. You know we'd be happy for ye tae stay here, and the bairn too. It'd be grand tae have a baby in the house again, and if that's what you want, ye just have tae say the word.'

The love in her aunt's voice took Etta to the verge of tears; she swallowed hard, then said, 'I love Adam and I want tae be his wife more than anythin' in the world.'

'That's all right then. The drape of the blouse and the skirt pleats are perfect,' Zelda went on briskly. 'Nob'dy would know you were expectin'. Now try on the jacket and the hat.'

'Everyone knows I'm expectin' anyway,' Etta said as her aunt helped her on with her straight, hip-length jacket. 'Aunt Stella mentioned it when I met her in the street on the way home.'

'Stella!' Zelda, who had picked up the blue felt cloche hat trimmed with a small bunch of artificial cream and blue flowers, put it down again. 'I might have known. What's she said tae upset ye?'

'She didn't say—' Etta began, and then the treacherous tears filled her eyes and overflowed before she could stop them. 'Oh, Auntie Zelda!'

'It's all right.' Zelda opened her arms, then just as Etta

was moving into them she said, 'Wait a minute!' and seized a clean towel that lay, folded, on top of the pile of newly ironed clothes. Shaking it out, she tucked it carefully about her foster-daughter's shoulders. 'Tae stop the bonny jacket gettin' marked,' she said apologetically, and then, sweeping Etta into her embrace, 'Now tell me!'

The story came pouring out along with the tears. 'I don't know what she meant,' Etta wept.

'Who knows what's in Stella's mind?' Zelda said helplessly, stroking the girl's back. 'She's changed. There's been a bitterness eatin' away at her for years now, and I can't for the life of me think what's brought it on her.'

The door opened and Will burst in, his cap and the shoulders of his jacket damp. 'It's rainin',' he said, taking the cap off and shaking it over the hearth. The hot iron range sizzled as the cold drops hit it. Then, turning and seeing the two women, he asked, 'What's amiss?'

'Nothin'.' His mother moved forward, putting herself between him and Etta.

'But our Etta's been cryin'.'

'That's what women do when they're happy.'

'Are ye certain that that's—'

'Will, get tae yer bed,' his father said from the doorway. 'Go on now,' Innes added sharply as the boy opened his mouth to argue. Will closed his mouth again, shrugged, and went up to his bedroom in what had once been the sail loft.

'It's somethin' Stella said tae the lassie today,' Zelda said, low-voiced, when her son was out of earshot. 'It's upset the lass.'

'On the eve of her weddin'? That's no' right.' Innes stripped off his damp cap and jacket and handed them to his wife. 'Come here, my quine.' He settled himself in his fireside chair and drew his foster-daughter down onto his knee, just as he had done in the past when any of the children in his care were upset. Zelda moved to stand behind him, with one hand on the back of his chair. 'Now then, tell me what Stella said tae ye.'

His face stilled, and then darkened as Etta, still clutching the towel about her shoulders, stammered out the story.

'We cannae make head nor tail of it,' Zelda said when it was told. 'Like faither, like son? Gil Pate was a decent, civil soul. A bit sharp with his coopers, mebbe, and with the guttin' quines working at the farlins from what I've heard, but there was never any badness in the man.'

'It's somethin' of nothin',' Innes said firmly. 'Take my advice, lass, and don't give it another thought.'

'I know James married her because him and his faither wanted her family's fishing boat,' Zelda said, 'and I can understand her feelin' bitter, since we all know that James isnae exactly a perfect husband, but—'

'Somethin' of nothin',' Innes said again, patting Etta's shoulder. 'We'll say no more about it, none of us. Not tae Adam or anybody else. Now stand up, lassie, and let me have a look at ye. By God but ye're goin' tae be a bonny wee bride,' he went on as she stood obediently before him. 'I'm not so sure of the wee cape, though.'

'It's a towel, ye daft loon.' Zelda snatched it from Etta's shoulders. 'It was tae keep her from cryin' on her fine jacket.'

'There's no need of it now, for the tears are all gone, aren't they, Etta?'

She smiled at him, comforted by his presence and his gentleness. 'Aye, they are. Is Adam—?'

'I took him right tae his door and saw him inside. And he had just enough drink in him tae be merry, and tae make him sleep like a bairn so's he'll be fresh for tomorrow,' he said, and then, with a wink, 'Mind you, it was a lot of work, for Will and James were determined tae get him as drunk as a lord.'

'Was Rory there?' Etta wanted to know.

'No. There's another one that's actin' strange. Ach well, it's not our concern,' Innes said, and began to pull his boots off. 'Time we were in our beds. It's goin' tae be a busy day tomorrow.'

*

'Ye don't think,' Zelda said in the darkness of the bedroom half an hour later, 'that Stella was hintin' that Adam's not Gil's son?'

'Eh? Stop haverin', woman, how could that be?'

'I don't know, but if I'm right, then Stella is in on it. Do you know anythin', Innes?'

'Aye, I do. I know that if you don't stop your tongue and let me get some sleep I'm goin' tae carry ye intae the kitchen and make ye spend the night on top of the table. Get tae sleep!'

Long after his wife had done as she was told Innes Lowrie lay against her warm, soft back, his eyes wide open and his mind full of secrets that he wished he had never discovered.

29

Bethany was disconcerted when Lorne Kerr returned to Buckie in the middle of June.

'I wanted to see how the new drifter's coming along,' he told her over dinner at Jacob's, where he was staying. 'And I'd a notion to see the start of the herring fishing. Jacob and I took a stroll down to the harbour just after I arrived – the place is buzzing like a beehive.'

'Aye, there's a lot of work tae gettin' the boats ready. I mind in my own young days,' Jacob reminisced, 'what an excitement it was after bein' on shore for a few months – unless ye were at the white fishin', but that's no' got the same feel about it if ye're a drifter man tae trade. Man, it was grand – like bein' let out o' the school after a long hard day spent wi' yer books!'

'I was speaking to your brother down at the harbour,' Lorne said. 'Your brother James. He says your Adam's sailing on the *Fidelity* with him.'

'Yes.' Bethany crumbled a bread roll with restless fingers, wishing that she had never accepted Jacob's invitation. Lorne seemed to be completely at ease, but every time she looked at him or heard his voice she recalled their last meeting and his almost businesslike suggestion that she should visit Edinburgh to find out if the two of them were suited.

'Adam's wed now, tae a right nice wee quine,' Jacob

boomed. 'Ye've met Etta, Lorne – she's foster-daughter tae Innes and Zelda. She'll be havin' a bairn just about the end of the summer fishin'.'

'You'll be looking forward to that event, Bethany.'

'Yes, indeed,' she said flatly, and was saved from having to say more by Jacob, who chattered on, 'And Ellen – Bethany's stepdaughter – has got married in Glasgow since ye were last here.'

Bethany felt her mouth tighten at the girl's name. Ellen had married Jack Morrison in a quiet, very private ceremony, and now sent her stepmother brief but triumphant letters every other week, bragging about her new flat and her maid. Her overworked maid, Bethany thought, feeling pity for the servant that had to put up with Ellen as a mistress.

She dragged her mind back to her surroundings and her companions, and asked Lorne, 'Have you seen the new drifter? She's nearly ready.'

'Not yet. We're going to have a look at her tomorrow.'

'I just wish James would agree tae be her skipper,' Jacob said, 'but he's determined tae stay with the *Fidelity*. I suppose, since she's his own boat, I cannae argue about it.'

'What about Jem?' Bethany suggested.

'He's no' as sharp a skipper as James. I cannae think of any man as good at handlin' a boat an' findin' a good shimmer o' herrin' as James. But if he'll no' do it, then it should by rights be Jem, for he's competent enough and I'd sooner find someone else tae take the *Homefarin'* than put a man I don't know on the new boat.'

'Ye'll never make me believe that that mannie's only back in tae see how the *Jess Lowrie II*'s comin' along,' Zelda said sagely.

'What other reason could there be?'

'Tuts, Etta, the man's fair daft about Bethany.'

'Aunt Bethany?' Etta still could not bring herself to refer to her mother-in-law by any other title, and Bethany herself

323

seemed to be quite content to leave things as they had always been. 'You can't be right!'

'If ye're thinkin' of their age, then let me tell you that gettin' older doesnae mean losin' interest in livin' altogether,' Zelda said with a twinkle in her eye. The two of them were sitting in the back yard of the little cottage Bethany had rented for her son and his new wife. Etta was knitting a new gansey for Adam and Zelda had the basket of mending that never seemed to be empty.

'If ye'd looked close enough when the mannie was last here and we were all invited tae Jacob McFarlane's for our dinner,' Zelda went on, 'ye'd have seen that he couldnae keep his eyes from Bethany. Not that you'd have noticed,' she added, the twinkle broadening into a grin, 'since you were only interested in Adam.'

Etta laughed. 'I was.' The sun was warm and the little flagged yard, newly swept that morning, was neat and clean. Snowy washing hung on the line strung across the tiny drying green and a pot of flowers she had lovingly grown from seed stood by the house wall, glowing all the colours of the rainbow. The baby kicked in her belly, and at that moment she would not have changed places with anyone in the world.

'You're shinin' like a star in the sky,' Zelda said just then. 'Marriage suits you.'

'I just wish Adam wasnae goin' away. I'll not see him for six weeks.'

'That's what bein' wed tae a fisherman means, my quine. Will ye miss goin' tae the farlins this year?'

'Aye, but gettin' things ready for the bairn'll keep me busy enough. Aunt Zelda, what if it comes while Adam's gone?'

'There's little fear of that,' Zelda said comfortably, 'since ye've still got six weeks tae go and a first bairn's usually late. Mary was two weeks past her time and I was near demented by the time she arrived. You wait and see – the last month's the longest. Anyway, we'll look after you, ye know that, and you can come and stay with us any time ye're worried about bein' on yer lone.' She reached out and patted Etta's hand. 'Imagine, I'm goin' tae have two wee ones tae nurse now that Mary's expectin' as well. I'm well blessed, Etta!'

'And I'm thirsty.' Etta rolled her knitting up and got to her feet slowly and clumsily.

'I'll make the tea.'

'No you won't, you just sit there. I want tae see that the stew for tonight's dinner's doin' well while I'm in the house,' Etta said, and then gave a startled cry as her toe caught on a raised flagstone. Burdened by her swollen belly, she stumbled in an attempt to stay upright, but lost her balance completely and fell forward, desperately reaching out with her two hands to break her fall and ending up on hands and knees.

'Etta?' Zelda threw down the sock she had been mending and rushed to her aid. 'Etta?'

'I'm fine, I'm fine,' Etta wheezed. 'Just – leave me for a minute till I – catch my breath.'

It was a minute or two before she felt strong enough to start lumbering to her feet. Once she had managed it Zelda helped her up and into the kitchen, where she sank down on to the comfortable armchair that had become Adam's.

'Are ye sure ye're all right?'

'Aye. I just got a bit of a fright.' Etta looked up into her aunt's worried face and managed a shaky laugh. 'I must have looked a right sight, down on the ground like that. It's lucky you were here tae help me up again or I might have had tae wait there till Adam came home for his dinner.' She made to stand, but Zelda pushed her back into the chair.

'You just sit there and rest, my lassie, and I'll see tae the tea.'

'Have a look at the stew first.'

Zelda opened the oven door and a fragrant smell drifted out. 'It's fine,' she reported, shutting the door and reaching for the tea caddy.

'I've made a right mess of my stockin's,' Etta mourned, examining the damage the fall had done. 'They're well torn, and my knees'll be black and blue in the mornin'. And my hands—' she held them out to show the grazes to her aunt.

'Just let me get the tea goin' and then I'll take a wet cloth tae them, and mebbe some iodine if ye have it.'

'In that wee cupboard. I'll get it,' Etta said, and began to get up. Then she stopped, gasping, as a sharp pain lanced through her back, gripping her in crab-like pincers for a long moment before vanishing.

She fell back into the chair, clutching at her belly, her face suddenly drained of colour. 'Aunt Zelda,' she said feebly, 'I think . . . mebbe ye'd better send someone tae find Adam.'

Adam paced the back yard until dark, when Zelda sent him off to his mother's for the night.

'It's goin' tae take a while, and with me and the midwife stayin' with Etta there's no room in the place for you.'

'Ye'll let me know as soon as anythin' happens?'

'Aye, but I doubt if it'll be before mornin'. Go on now, I've work tae do,' his aunt said, shooing him out. 'Yours is already done.'

The baby arrived the following afternoon, a tiny dark-haired scrap of humanity, loudly expressing his fury at being launched into the world before he was ready for the big journey. Exhausted though she was, Etta only needed one look at him to know that her life had changed for ever, and for the better.

'At least he's greetin',' the midwife said as she put him into his mother's arms. 'That's a good sign for an early bairn.'

'He's – he's awful wee, is he no'?' Adam asked when he arrived an hour later. He peered at his son and heir, well wrapped up and lying in the crook of Etta's arm. 'And awful red intae the bargain.'

'Just think where he's been these last months.' Zelda stroked the baby's face gently with the back of one finger.

'Red or not, he's bonny, and he'll grow intae a right lusty loon, just you wait and see, Adam. We'll need tae look after him well for a while, though, with him bein' so early. And it'll be a week or two before Etta's strong enough tae look after him and the house,' she added later when she got Adam on his own. 'She's had a difficult time of it and she's worn out.'

They named the baby Daniel, after the father Etta had never met. Weak and emotional after childbirth, easily moved to tears, she wept when Adam suggested the name.

'I thought you'd want him tae be called Gilbert after your own faither.'

'I wondered, but when I said tae my mother she didnae seem taken with the idea. Anyway, it's mebbe better tae let Rory have that name for his own firstborn son, seein' that he's the oldest. And when Aunt Zelda said that your own father that was killed in the war was named Daniel, I thought it went well enough with Pate,' Adam explained, adding, 'But I'd like him tae have Lowrie as his middle name.'

'Daniel Lowrie Pate.' Etta spoke the name aloud. 'It sounds grand.'

'Mebbe a bit much for such a wee thing,' Adam said doubtfully.

'He'll grow.' Etta wiped the tears away and gave him a shaky smile. 'One day he'll be as big and strong as you are, and then the name'll suit him handsomely.'

'I suppose ye're right.' As yet Adam had refused to hold his new son, terrified that he might drop him or damage him in some way. 'When he's older,' he kept saying, but in truth, he didn't feel in the least like a father. Etta seemed to have taken to parenthood but he himself had not changed at all. He had asked his Uncle James, the only person he could safely confide in, about it, and James had sucked thoughtfully at the stem of his pipe and then said, 'There's some born tae be fathers, like Innes, and some who never seem tae take tae it, like me. Though I have a right likin' for our Ruth.

She's a bright wee quine, and if only she'd been born a laddie I think her and me would have got on fine together.'

'I think I must be like you,' Adam said, and stopped worrying about his lack of feeling for the mewling little scrap, no larger than a kitten, that had taken over his home and all his young wife's attention. Being like his Uncle James had always been the main ambition of his life, and now, with the two of them sitting in companionable silence in the *Fidelity*'s cabin, he was glad that within the next week they would be off to the Shetlands for the fishing, leaving their domestic concerns behind them.

Daniel Lowrie Pate was christened a few days before the fishing fleet left Buckie, and on the day they sailed Etta was strong enough to manage the walk down to the harbour to see them off. Zelda was with her, pushing the baby in the brand new pram Bethany had given them.

Etta clung to Adam on the morning of his departure to the fishing ground, and wept. She was always weeping, he thought in despair. Aloud he said, 'Etta, quine, you know I have tae go. Uncle James has kept the *Fidelity* back for as long as he could tae give you time tae get yer strength back, but he can't wait any longer and he's dependin' on me. And we need the money, with the wee one tae see tae now.'

'I know, but I'll miss you,' Etta wept, her arms as tight around him as possible.

'You'll have Aunt Zelda for company, and my mother.' Not that his mother had been of much help. She had called in at the cottage to inspect the baby, and said how bonny he was. She had sent Leezie with nourishing food to tempt Etta's appetite back, and had given them baby clothes and the pram. But there had been no warmth – not that he had expected that from his mother. She was quite unlike Aunt Zelda.

'I know they'll still be here, but it's you that we want – me and wee Daniel,' Etta wailed.

Adam sought further words of comfort, and found them.

'Siddy's talkin' of stayin' ashore when the boat goes tae the English fishin' in November. I could be mate of the *Fidelity* within the year. And when that happens I'll get more money.'

'You'll be careful, won't you?' Etta pleaded. 'All the time?' Since Daniel's early birth she had suddenly become aware of the fragility of life. Less than a year ago she had had nobody to think of but herself, but now . . . if anything happened to her man or to her bairn, she thought, she would not be able to bear it.

'I'm always careful.' Adam disentangled himself and picked up his seaman's kist and his bag. 'I have tae go, Etta.'

'Aunt Zelda's comin' for me. We'll walk down to the harbour together, with the wee one. Mind and wave tae me – and mind and write,' she added.

'Of course I will.' He cast a glance into the crib and then put a finger into the palm of the tiny hand lying on the pillow. To his astonishment the baby's fragile fingers closed on it, and held on. 'Look at that!' Adam said, delighted. 'He's got a hold of me!'

'He's gettin' stronger already.' Pride dried Etta's tears, which could vanish as swiftly as they arrived. 'And he wants his daddy tae stay with him, don't you, my wee mannie?' she added to the baby.

'He's got a strong grip for such a wee thing, right enough.' Adam began to feel affection stirring deep within him for the little creature that had disrupted his life. 'But can ye get him tae let go now, Etta? I'm feared tae try in case I hurt him.'

As the *Fidelity* surged through the harbour entrance, one of a long line of boats moving gracefully towards the open sea, he remembered to look up at Etta. She was crying, as he knew she would be, holding a handkerchief to her face with one hand and waving the other so hard that it was a blur. Adam waved back. Over the past few months he had at times had his doubts about the wisdom of marrying so young. Who would have thought that a kiss and a cuddle with a pretty quine could lead to a man being tied down to such responsibility? But now, looking up at Etta and remembering his son's tiny, fragile fingers gripping his, he felt that marriage could suit him after all.

His Aunt Stella and her three daughters stood further along the harbour, well away from Etta and Zelda. Ruth and her sisters waved to their father and to Adam, while their mother simply stood motionless. As the *Fidelity* passed by them Adam saw his uncle, leaning out through the wheelhouse window, doffing his cap and nodding slightly to his wife, who nodded in return.

As James Lowrie took the drifter that was his very life through the harbour entrance Adam was surprised to see his mother, who rarely came to see the boats go out, standing there with Lorne Kerr. She was smiling down at him, and when he gave a tentative wave she waved back. It looked as though she had begun to forgive him for refusing to dance to her tune. Glancing at the wheelhouse he saw James salute them both, then the drifter was through the entrance and prancing slightly as she met the larger waves. To Adam it was almost as though she was giving a shiver of excitement and anticipation at leaving the confines of the stone harbour walls. He knew just how she felt, he thought as she settled down, her forefoot biting into the sea as she turned towards the horizon and the herring shoals.

It was ironic, Bethany thought as Adam beamed up at her from the deck of the *Fidelity*, that at one time all she had wanted was to see her son, her flesh and blood, going to the fishing just as she would have done had she had the chance. There was no denying that he belonged to the sea. But she had lost him to it, and to James, and there was nothing she could do about it.

'I must go back to Edinburgh,' Lorne said as the two of them turned to walk from the harbour. Boats were still sailing out; it would take some time for the harbour basins to empty, but already the first of the fishing fleet, the *Fidelity* included, was scattering across the face of the Moray Firth, and becoming smaller to the eye every minute.

'When?'

'Tomorrow morning.'

'Do you always arrive unexpectedly and leave unexpectedly?'

'I like to cultivate a certain air of mystery; it keeps me in folk's minds. Dine with me tonight. I've not seen much of you during my stay.' Lorne had spent most of his time with Jacob, visiting the yards where the nets were barked before being dried and then carried down to the harbour and put aboard the boats, and talking to the fishermen and the coopers and the carters and the old men, former fishermen, who congregated down at the harbour. He had watched the boats being painted and cleaned and coaled in readiness for the journey to northern waters.

'Come to the house for your dinner,' Bethany said on an impulse. Rory had already gone south, and the house Gil had bought for her and his children suddenly seemed too large, and too empty.

Leezie, pleased to have someone new to cook for, excelled herself, and after an excellent meal Bethany and her guest settled in the front parlour. A tea tray stood by Bethany's chair while Lorne enjoyed a glass of port.

'Bethany, I owe you an apology,' he suddenly said. 'The things I said to you just before I left for Edinburgh that last time – the words I used – it was clumsy of me, and wrong of me.' He held up a hand to stop her when she tried to speak. 'Give me time to say what I have to say, please. I realised after I got home that I had gone about things entirely the wrong way. You're a businesswoman and so I thought, foolishly, that it would make more sense if I spoke in a business-like way. But I ruined everything, and I offended you. I can't apologise deeply enough.'

331

'You invited me to see Edinburgh for myself, and I declined. That was all.'

'It was not all, and you know it. I was so intent on sounding practical that I ignored the fact that you're a woman – a very beautiful and passionate woman. I should have spoken to that woman. I should have said, Bethany Pate, I believe – no, I know that I love you, and I hope that you love me, or that you can bring yourself in time to love me. Because I think that we could be very happy together, and I want nothing more in life than to make you happy.'

Then, as she stared at him, he stood up, set his glass down on the mantelshelf, knelt before her and took her hands in his.

'Bethany,' he said, his voice gentle now, his eyes pleading, 'will you marry me? Will you please marry me and be with me for as long as we both shall live, and with me wherever we may go after that, for all eternity?'

'I – but—'

'I hope you're not going to say that this is so sudden,' Lorne said with a faint smile. 'Because I'm sure you knew what I meant that last time, even though I put it so badly. You don't have to give me your answer now. You should visit Edinburgh and meet my sister and my friends. I want you to see my home and I hope that you will feel that you could live there, with me. If you don't care for it then we can find somewhere more suited.'

She moistened her lips, drawing her hands free of his. 'Lorne, this is most flattering, but I've been married once and I've no great notion to take on another husband.'

'Then you must have married the wrong man,' Lorne said, rising from his knees and moving to stand by the mantelshelf. 'In my case marriage gave me a taste for the companionship and the pleasures of sharing my life with a woman, especially if she is the right woman. Let me introduce you to those pleasures, and that companionship. You've been on your own for too long, Bethany. You need – you deserve – so much more than you have now. I know that you would hate to do nothing else but look after a house, and so I'm offering you a partnership in every way. I want you to share my business interests as well as my bed.'

She fumbled through her mind for a defence but could only come up with, 'I'm needed here.'

'No, you're not. Your children have lives of their own, and Jacob can find someone else to work for him. You're using these folk to hide behind, Bethany, and the person you want to hide from is you. How long have you been widowed now? A dozen years or more, isn't it? Far too long for a woman of your temperament.'

His eyes caressed her face and then moved down over her body, and she felt the heat of his gaze on her skin.

'What you're suggesting,' she said, her voice uneven, 'might prove to be a mistake for one or other of us.'

'My dear, is that not what life's all about – taking risks and finding out if they have succeeded? And if such a move does turn out to be wrong for either or both of us, I promise that you will be free to seek happiness back here or somewhere else. I would never hold you against your will.' He drained his glass and set it back on the mantelshelf. 'Take time to think over what I've said. In the meantime I hope that you'll come to Edinburgh on a visit, at least. Now, I must go.'

Bethany got up to lead the way to the door, and was taken entirely by surprise when he caught hold of her arm and deftly spun her round and into his embrace.

His kiss was demanding, probing, and not to be denied. Almost against her will Bethany found her lips parting beneath his, while her arms lifted of their own volition to hold him. When he finally released her she was breathless and dizzy with shock at the strength of her emotions.

'As I thought,' he said huskily. 'How can such a passionate woman deny herself for so long?'

If he had bent his head towards hers again she would not

have been able to stop herself from responding, but instead, he released her and stepped back.

'I'll let myself out,' he said, and then he was gone.

For several long minutes Bethany stood where he had left her. When she finally moved, it was to put a hand to her lips; they felt soft and swollen, and when she looked in the mirror above the fireplace she saw that they had a new fullness, ripeness, to them. Her entire body felt different. She moved about the room, unable now to stand still, or to sit down.

With one kiss, Lorne Kerr had awakened something that had been dormant for years, something that she had thought was dead. He was right, she did have passion; only one man had awakened it before, and that man was not her husband. She had managed after a terrible struggle to subdue it, but now . . .

'Is Mr Kerr gone, then?' Leezie asked from the doorway, and Bethany jumped guiltily.

'D'you never think to knock?' she snapped.

'I've never had tae do it before. Why, have ye got somethin' tae hide all at once?'

'Don't be daft, and don't be impertinent!'

'I'm too old tae be impertinent. He's gone, then?' Leezie asked again, and when her employer nodded, she came into the room. 'I can take the tea things away, can I? Or would that be imposin' on ye?'

'Take them, and then you can get to your bed.'

When the housekeeper had gone Bethany noticed that the glass Lorne had used still stood on the mantelshelf, overlooked. She picked it up to take it to the kitchen and then, on an irrational impulse, she ran the tip of a finger round the rim then put it in her mouth. It tasted of brandy, and it tasted of Lorne Kerr.

'Daft quine!' she muttered, and put the glass down so sharply that it almost broke. Then she put the lights out and went upstairs to bed.

30

Bethany spent a lot of time on her own over the next few weeks, walking all around Buckie, visiting the net factory and the smokehouse and the cooperage, which was quiet now that Rory and most of his men were in Lerwick.

She went down to the harbour every day and stood gazing down into the dark waters where once, a lifetime ago, she had swum with the laddies. Then she looked up and over the Firth to the horizon where the *Fidelity* and the other boats had vanished on their way to the northern fishing. She climbed the hill to Rathven and visited the cemetery where her parents and Gil Pate had been laid to rest.

Once or twice she visited the little cottage in the Catbow, to Etta's surprise and alarm, and sat nursing little Daniel, who was beginning to thrive.

'I'm not a motherly woman,' she found herself confessing one day. 'Though I always loved Adam dearly.'

Etta, who now understood what it was to be a mother, nodded and said, 'I know. It's different when ye've birthed the bairn yerself.' And then the two women smiled at each other over the baby's dark head, and formed an understanding that, although not close, was as close as they could ever reach.

Finally, Bethany spent two weeks visiting Lorne Kerr's sister in Edinburgh. True to his word, Lorne left her in peace to get to know his family and his city and his handsome home and never once asked her, even when he was saying goodbye to her at the station, if she had come to any decision.

'I'll write to you,' she said from the train window. 'Whatever happens, I'll write.'

'I look forward to your letter. And, if you decide to stay as you are, I hope that I can look forward to your friendship, at least,' he replied, and when she leaned from the window to look back as the train left on its journey, he was still standing there, his eyes holding hers even as he dwindled and disappeared.

'Lorne has asked me to marry him and live with him in Edinburgh,' she said to Jacob two days later.

'I thought he might, eventually. The man never stopped talkin' about ye the times he was here.' He put down his pen, folded his hands on his desk, and said, 'I hope ye said yes.'

'I've not said anything yet. It's a big step, Jacob. I've never lived anywhere else but Buckie.'

'I thought I'd spend all my days on this Firth,' he mused. 'But marriage took me away, too – only for me, it was yer mither's marriage tae Weem Lowrie that did it. I never thought I'd survive bein' away from here, but I did.'

'And now you're back, and a wealthier man for being away.'

'Money can bring its own comforts,' he said placidly.

'The thing is, how would you manage if I went away?'

'Tuts, lassie, ye mustn't put my well-being before yer own happiness. Ye've put good overseers intae the smokehouse and the net factory, and I'll surely find someone tae see tae the books for me. James has a good head on his shoulders; I've been wonderin' about askin' him if he'd take on more of the business, so's he can take over from me when the time comes. He deserves it.'

'I think the two of you would work well together. As to the gutting crews – if I'm not here to hire them next year, Sarah Lowrie could do the job just as well. Mebbe even better.'

'What would ye do about the house?'

'Rory's the only one living there now, apart from Leezie and myself. His father bought it, and it should pass on to him.'

Jacob reached for his pipe and his tobacco pouch. 'Mrs Duthie wants tae settle down in a wee place of her own. She says she's got enough money tae live in comfort, so as ye can see, I've been payin' the woman far too much. If your Leezie should be lookin' for another position I'd like fine tae have her as my new housekeeper – if Rory doesnae have need of her, and if she's willin'.'

'I've not gone yet, or said I would go, Jacob McFarlane! Would ye take my grave that fast?' Bethany wanted to know, and then when he grinned at her, 'If it comes to it, I could speak to her for you. But only if it comes to it.'

'Aye, aye. Let me know when you've made yer decision.' Jacob finished filling the pipe and put the stem into his mouth, striking a match. His hands, lumpy now with rheumatism and scarred from his days as a fisherman, fumbled slightly and the first match dropped to the desk.

'Here.' Bethany found the match and struck it, then put it into his hand.

'Speakin' for mysel',' Jacob said when the pipe was lit to his satisfaction, 'I think ye should tell the man yes. Ye deserve a bit of happiness, my quine.'

Bethany kept her own council until the fishing fleet returned to Buckie in August, and then Rory was the first to hear that she was going to marry Lorne Kerr and move to Edinburgh.

His reaction was swift. 'Good. I thought that the man liked you and I'm glad he's had the sense tae do somethin' about it.'

'You needn't worry about having nowhere to stay, for I'm giving the house to you. Ellen won't come back here, and Adam and Etta seem happy enough in their wee cottage.'

'I don't want the house. You're not the only one gettin' wed,' Rory said proudly, though his face went brick red.

337

'Ruth?'

'How did ye know?'

'Leezie's always saying how well suited you two are. If you're certain that you don't want the house—'

'Can you see Ruth Lowrie livin' in a place like this? We'd be happier in somethin' smaller.'

'Then I'll sell it and give the three of you equal shares of the price I get.'

'Even Ellen?'

'She deserves to be treated the same as you and Adam. And I'm sure,' Bethany said, a gleam in her eye, 'that she'll find something to do with the money. I'll write to Lorne tomorrow, and tell him that I'll join him in Edinburgh next week.'

During the next few days she quietly told her news to Adam, Zelda, Innes, and everyone who needed to know. She missed out just one person, for she could not bring herself to tell him of her forthcoming marriage face to face.

She knew that word would travel swiftly round the community and that he would soon come to hear of her departure from Buckie, but she hoped that he would do nothing about it. It was a foolish hope.

On the day before she left, she was working at her desk when Leezie came into the front parlour.

'It's yer brither James. He wants tae see ye.'

'Tell him that I'm not at home.'

'Tell me that yourself,' James said from the doorway, and she spun round, and then got to her feet. He brushed past Leezie and then bundled the astonished woman out to the hall and shut the door.

'And tell me tae my face,' he said. 'Don't let me hear it from other folk, the way I heard that you're goin' tae Edinburgh tae marry Lorne Kerr.'

'I thought I'd leave it to Stella to tell you. I knew she'd enjoy doin' that.'

'Is it true?'

'Yes, it is.'

'Why?'

'Because I've come to the end of my time here. Because Lorne's a good man and I'm tired of being on my own.'

'Does he love ye?' he asked, his face expressionless, his hands hanging by his sides, the fingers slightly curved. 'D'you love him?'

'Folk our age don't talk about love. Lorne . . . cares for me,' Bethany said, choosing the words carefully. 'He'll look after me, and mebbe that's what I want now.'

'I cannae bear the thought of not seein' ye.'

'We scarcely see each other anyway,' she said. 'Most of the year you're at the fishing grounds, or in Lerwick or Yarm'th and even when you're here, we don't spend time together.'

'But at least I know ye're here. Even when I'm far away I know ye're here.'

'James, I have to make my own life. I have to go away,' Bethany said wildly, unable to bear any more. 'And I have a lot to do before I go.'

If he stayed for much longer she knew that she would change her mind about Lorne, and Edinburgh. She would stay, as he wanted, as she herself wanted, but nothing would change. The torment would just go on, as it had done for the past nineteen years and more.

She walked quickly past him to the door, opening it, waiting, with her back to him, for him to walk past her and leave.

'Don't go,' James said from behind her, his whole heart in his voice.

And it was then Bethany knew that she must.

Etta Pate stood on the shingle, looking out on the Moray Firth. It had been a bright November day, a good day for the fleet to start their long journey south to the English fishing, but now that the sun was setting it had lost what little heat it had, and there was a sharp chill in the air.

The *Fidelity* had left the harbour in the company of the new drifter, the *Jess Lowrie II*, and Adam had been so excited at making his first journey as mate to his Uncle James Lowrie that he had almost forgotten to wave to her as she stood on the harbour wall, drinking in the last sight she would have of him for weeks, trying to burn the image of him into her memory. He had finally seen her, and waved, and then he was gone.

Daniel, possibly sensing his mother's misery, had been difficult all that day, grizzling when she tried to put him down in his crib to sleep, and so she had dressed him in the coat and pantaloons and hat and mitts she had knitted, and wrapped a shawl about him for greater protection against the cold before carrying him, so well wrapped that he felt like a bolster in her arms, out along the shore road to a spot where there were no houses and they could be alone.

He had fallen asleep as soon as she started walking, but now she heard a soft murmur of sound, and saw that the change in motion as she left the road and began to walk carefully over the shingle had woken him. Just then the fiery early-winter sun broke through thin cloud and suddenly a broad crimson carpet, glittering as though embroidered with rubies, spilled across the sea, reaching from the horizon almost to where Etta stood. The horizon itself was suffused with rich pink, shading to a pale rose colour and then rising into soft grey.

'Look, Daniel.' She angled her arm to lift him up slightly, turning so that he too was looking out to sea. His eyes, as dark as her own when he was first born, but now showing signs of turning grey like his father's, widened beneath the knitted cap pulled down over his forehead.

'Yes, it's pretty – and it's all for you.' She made for a conveniently placed rock and sat down, glad of the chance to rest. Daniel had made good progress since his premature birth, and now, at five months of age, he was sturdy – and heavy.

He gave a little cooing sound of approval and pleasure, and then blew a few bubbles. 'That's where your daddy is,' she told him, pointing to the horizon. 'He's gone away, but he'll come back to us. He'll always come back to us.'

She knew that Adam would always prefer being at sea to being at home with her. It was something she must accept, for if she tried to change him she would lose him. And she was never, ever going to let that happen.

A small, mittened fist punched her gently on the chin. Daniel had managed to free one arm and now he waved it at the jewelled sea, talking earnestly in a tongue that only he and his mother understood.

'Aye, I know,' she said. 'You're as anxious tae get out there as yer faither is. You want tae go away from me too, don't ye, and follow the silver fishes? Your turn'll come, my wee mannie, but not yet, not for a while. For now, you're my own wee bairn.'

Then the winter sun went down with startling suddenness, and all at once the world was grey. She shivered, tucking her baby's arm back into the shawl, then got up, anxious to return to the warmth and safety of the cottage.

Back on the road, she turned and took a last look at the sea. It was Daniel's inheritance, she thought as she started the walk home, just as it was his father's.

For there would always be fish in the sea, and there would always be need of men with the courage to seek them out, and harvest them.

Bibliography

Following the Fishing by David Butcher. Published 1987 by Tops'l Books (an imprint of David & Charles). Newton Abbot, London, North Pomfret.

The Herring Fishing by W. M. Gibson. Published 1984 by BPP, 27 Broughton Place, Edinburgh. Printed by Dunedin Press Ltd, Telford Road, Edinburgh.

Dear Gremista: The Story of Nairn Fisher Girls at the Gutting by Margaret Bochel. Produced 1979 by the Design Section, National Museum of Antiquities of Scotland, Edinburgh, for Nairn Fishertown Museum.

A Stranger on the Bars: The Memoirs of Christian Watt Marshall. Edited by Gavin Sutherland. Published 1994 by Banff and Buchan District Council Department of Leisure and Recreation, with kind permission of the Trustees of the late Christian Watt Marshall.

Steam Drifters Recalled: Portgordon to Portsoy. Compiled by Alexander S. Buchan, David Mair, Joseph Reid, James Campbell Smith and David E. Williamson. Published 2000 by Joseph Reid, Enzie, and David E. Williamson, Cullen.

Living the Fishing by Paul Thomson with Tony Wailey and Trevor Luminis. History Workshop Series. Published 1983 by Routledge & Keegan Paul, London, Boston, Melbourne and Henley.